Advance Praise for A Fool's Paradise

"At a time when most of what contemporary romantic suspense seems to offer readers is overwhelmingly stagnant, Robyn Williams, author of the well-received novel, *Preconceived Notions*, and the critically-acclaimed follow-up, *A Twist of Fate*, fittingly returns with a triumph that is her crowning work to date.

Forgive the cliché, but talk about a book that pulls you in! *A Fool's Paradise* easily, thankfully delivers the goods but very confidently defies categorization. *A Fool's Paradise* quite notably is one high caliber page-turner that grabs you from the very first word.

Ms. Williams' prose is colorful without overdoing it, and sets scenarios quite nicely. Its characters' stories of growing up poor, becoming self-aware survivors, trusting in mentors along the way and then strangely falling for them are relatable, without being preachy. From the innocent naiveté of youth, to the wisdom that only comes with love, loss, heartbreak and, in the end, hard-earned success, one becomes an unwitting passenger on the tumultuous journey borne between this book's two covers.

The author deftly navigates what are sometimes familiar waters for avid fans of the genre, without succumbing to the base mentality, shallow mindset and lazy conclusions that typically comprise gimmicky, so called "Urban Romance" titles of late. *A Fool's Paradise* is smart, intelligently crafted, very attentively detailed and flows perfectly.

Hollywood insiders take note: There's a really good film on the horizon here."

~ Ronald E. Childs, Black Entertainment

Praise for A Twist of Fate

"Cleverly written and arranged and peppered with just the right dose of edginess, *A Twist of Fate* is a top literary choice that should be digested and internalized by anyone whose insatiable desire for a dramatic, fluid story outside of their own lives has yet to be quenched. I recommend it for adults with a vivid imagination and a predisposition for works that challenge the mind, warm the heart, and flame the fire for passion and romance."

~ Derrick K. Baker, Editor & Columnist, N'DIGO

Other Books by Robyn Williams

A Fool's Paradise

A Twist of Fate

Preconceived Notions

A Fool's Paradise

by

Robyn Williams

Lushena Books, Inc.
607 Country Club Drive, Unit E
Bensenville, IL 60106
Tel: 630-238-8708
Fax: 630-238-8824
E-mail: Lushena_books@yahoo.com
www.lushenabks.com

Printed in the United States of America.

ISBN: 1-930097-95-6

Library of Congress Catalog Card Number: 2008907205

First Printing: 2008

Dedication

This book is lovingly dedicated to the people who have stood with me and dared to believe that dreams do come true.

Special heartfelt thanks is extended to Chanette Beasley, my lifelong best friend (since kindergarten!) for never failing to believe; to Michelle Partee, a wonderful woman whom God uses in the oddest of ways. Her insight into the spirit world is sometimes frightening; to Sheila Downer, for her unfailing entrepreneurial spirit; and to my beloved blood sister, Valerie Jeffries-McClodden, always so soft spoken. And yet, God uses her mightily in the area of prophesy.

Lastly, a tremendous note of gratitude to Pastor John F. Hannah and Bishop Noel Jones, two very special and true Men of God.

Acknowledgment

It is with exceeding joy that I acknowledge my Lord and Savior, Jesus Christ, without Whom none of this would be possible. It is truly Him who gives us the faith as well as the ability to triumph over every adversity in life.

A Fool's Paradise

Prologue

ilence reigned along each row of the Kodak Theatre, as if a hair breath's escape could upset the fragile balance between victory and obscurity.

"And the Academy Award for Best Actor in a Leading Role goes to..."

A surge of adrenaline quickened his already tightened muscles. The small half smile on his face belied the nervousness behind his heightened senses. Outwardly, he bore the look of calm repose—as if tonight's outcome would have no effect on him. Inside, his raging emotions rushed in quick succession from anticipation to fear.

A lifetime passed in the seconds the infamous host deliberately took to open the coveted Oscars envelope. "...Jayson Denali for *Hyperion Fields*!"

As the opulent mass surrounded him with applause, Jayson stood to his feet, accepting the laudatory claps on his back from those seated nearby. On his way to the stage he clasped outstretched hands of well wishers. Some of his peers fawned for the fleeting gaze of the cameras. Some bore platitudinous smiles that hid the bitter taste of defeat, and a few were genuinely pleased at his capturing the coveted award.

As Jayson climbed the stairs leading to the podium, his one emotion that dominated all others was relief. He had yet to hold the golden statuette in his hands. Nevertheless, he was glad the waiting was over. Tonight's victory was sweet, but he vowed to never again allow himself to want something so desperately, that he seemed to lose his grip on reality. In the weeks leading up to the Oscars, he hadn't slept, eaten or concentrated very well. All his energy seemed poised towards coveting the once-in-a-lifetime achievement. Jayson hoisted the 13½-inch award in the air. As the people quieted, he cradled the gold-plated statue in his arm to begin his congratulatory remarks.

Part I

"So you know the beginning from the end, hmmm?
Then tell me what the future holds for me."

~ The Author

Chapter One

Jayson Denali didn't remember his father, having lost him at an early age. His mother explained that when he was two years old, his dad—a good, hard working man—had been the victim of a fatal robbery one evening on his way home from work. Shortly thereafter, his mother moved him and his sister, Carmin, from Chicago's Cabrini Green Housing Project to escape the inner-city's drug and gang-infested environment. Hence, it was in a tiny house on North 27th Street in Milwaukee, Wisconsin, that Jayson grew up.

His grandparents were deceased and because his mother was an only child, she and Carmin, who was five years older than him, were the only family Jayson had. His mother struggled to raise them by working nights cleaning office buildings. Though they were poor, she always managed to keep a roof over their heads.

Carmin, who was just seven years old, was expected to watch Jayson when his mother left for work. Each time she left, Jayson stood at the window watching her disappear down the street, gripped by an innate fear that she might not return. Sometimes he slept fitfully during the night, his childish dreams rocked by inexplicable images of abandonment. But each morning when his mother slipped the key into the lock, Jayson would awaken and tumble out of bed to greet her at the door, his world once again in rightful order.

He learned early how to unlock the key to his mother's heart. A simple hug and kiss would bring a smile to her often weary face. Jayson was the apple of her eye and she favored and doted on him. Unlike Carmin, he was never a problem child. He realized he could get away with things that would never be tolerated from his sister, whose rebellious nature created a rocky relationship with their mother. Jayson adored his sister and tried to be the mediator between Carmin and their mother, who always seemed at odds.

When he was five, his mother began taking them to a local Kingdom Hall and soon his family converted to Jehovah's Witnesses. It was a confusing time for him because of all the restrictions the religion imposed upon their lives. They were no longer allowed to celebrate each other's birthday, nor could they acknowledge Christmas or other holidays any longer. There could be no more parties and no more gift giving.

Several months later, during bible study at another member's home, Carmin asked to use the bathroom. A minister offered to show her where it was and led Carmin away. After a minute or two, wanting to be with his sister, Jayson followed them. At first he couldn't find them, but then he heard faint voices nearby so he ran toward the sounds and came to a stop at a closed door. Jayson heard the man's voice but couldn't make out what he was saying. When he heard Carmin's voice, it was small and pleading. He tried opening the door but found it locked.

Panicked without knowing why, Jayson started banging on the door. He called out Carmin's name and heard a click before the door swung open. Seeing Carmin squeezed into a corner near the tub, Jayson ran to her. He didn't understand what was happening. All he knew was that his sister was frightened and as he hugged her, he became scared as well.

Bolstered by each other's presence, together sister and brother stood looking at the man. Suddenly, he snickered loudly before turning to walk away. Carmin quickly closed the bathroom door and locked it before again grabbing hold of Jayson. He could feel her trembling and though he still didn't quite understand what had transpired, he held onto her tightly. They stood that way a while before Carmin released him and made him face the wall while she peed.

Later that evening when she told their mother about how the minister touched her privates and tried to pull down her panties, Sylvia didn't believe her and forbade her to tell anyone else about it, fearing it would get them disfellowshipped from the congregation. But Jayson knew Carmin was telling the truth. And although their mother embraced the religion wholeheartedly, for the two of them, the incident left an indelible pall on their lives. It drew them closer as siblings and made them wary of the very people they were encouraged to trust. That incident was the first in a series of strikes that would drive them away from religion as they grew older. However, as children they were required to faithfully attend service every Sunday.

Notwithstanding, Jayson's childhood was filled with fun. Girls were drawn to him from the very start. He was cute, he was popular and fun to be around. Jayson loved school because he treasured being around so many other children.

In Milwaukee at the time, there were no gangs to contend with. Though the city had its seedy underbelly, Jayson never caught wind of it. There were lots of children his age in his neighborhood and they found many creative means to occupy their time. They listened to great music from the 60's and 70's, skateboarded, played red-light/green-light, softball, tag football, marbles, Uno and whenever they could sneak it in, an occasional game of dice. Many times, they made up their games as they went along.

By the third grade, Jayson was dubbed the class clown because of his Dennis-the-Menace-like antics. But because they detected no malice in him, his teachers often chided him but never sent him to the principal's office. His affable personality enamored him to many, for it seemed that everybody loved Jayson.

While Jayson was average in his studies, every classroom had that student who excelled and whose grades surpassed everyone else's. In Jayson's class, Desmond Lloyd was the star pupil.

But as smart as Desmond was, he was a social pariah. Behind his back, kids called him "Stinky." And he stood out for yet another reason: Desmond was huge. Though average in height, he tipped the scales at nearly 200 pounds. Whereas none of the other kids would give Desmond the time of day, there was Jayson inviting him to participate in all the games. Though Desmond couldn't run as fast or as far as the others, he did the best he could. There began for Desmond a case of hero worship toward Jayson that would last the rest of his life.

For his part, Jayson was able to get Desmond to do something no amount of derisive cajoling from either of his parents could accomplish. He got Desmond to be active and less of an introvert.

He and Desmond (whom he soon nicknamed "Dez") lived only two blocks apart and the two became inseparable. But out of their friendship came something even more precious to Jayson. In Mr. James Lloyd, Dez' father, he found the father figure and male role model that he was desperately missing.

Jayson adored Mr. Lloyd, who owned his own mechanic shop on North 31st Street. Dez never liked going to his dad's shop nor tinkering with his tools. He'd much rather read a comic book. But ever since Jayson came into his world, if they weren't playing or studying, they were at his dad's shop.

Mr. Lloyd took to Jayson right away and when he learned that he didn't have a father, he treated him like his own son. Within a week's time, if Mr. Lloyd needed a particular tool, he'd ask for it and Jayson would scamper like lightning to get it as Dez sat nearby reading a Spider-Man, Batman or Captain America comic book. It was an arrangement that worked all around.

Dez loved coming to Jayson's house, especially around dinner time because there was always a hot, scrumptious meal on the stove. Plus, Mrs. Denali enjoyed feeding Dez and always had a kind word for him. Jayson, however, never hung out at Dez's place because he was afraid of Mrs. Lloyd. She was mean, never smiled and reminded him of the skinny predatory buzzard birds he often saw on Mutual of Omaha's Wild Kingdom, a TV show about African wildlife. She always had a cigarette dangling from her lips and it seemed to him that all she did was look through catalogs or play solitaire with her cards.

When Jayson was out playing, no matter where he was when the city's street lights came on, they served as his curfew guide, a reminder that it was time to hightail it home. One day, just as he was about to head home, Mr. Lloyd surprised him with a brand new bicycle similar to the one Dez owned. Initially, Jayson squealed with excitement. And then just as quickly, his joy turned to tears because he knew his mother would never let him keep it. He knew she would say, "They couldn't accept gifts from strangers."

Even when Mr. Lloyd volunteered to come speak to his mom, Jayson knew it was a lost cause. But when they arrived at his home, something amazing happened.

He quickly introduced Mr. Lloyd and with one long breath, rapidly told his mom about the "cool" bike Dez's dad had bought for him and why he should be allowed to keep it. After all, she knew how much he wanted and needed a bike. Without pausing for breath, he promised to never ask for anything else as long as he lived. He even promised to sweep the floors and wash the dishes, which for him the latter was the worst chore in the world.

As Jayson rambled on, he didn't notice how Mr. Lloyd and his mom were staring at one another. He thought nothing of how his mom patted her hair self-consciously and retied the apron around her shapely hips. But suddenly, in the midst of Jayson's free-for-all speech, as if he weren't even in the room, his mother asked Mr. Lloyd if he would like a slice of homemade pie and a cup of coffee.

Realizing he was no longer the center of attention, Jayson watched bemusedly as Mr. Lloyd smiled and wordlessly moved toward the kitchen sink to wash his hands before being handed a towel by Mrs. Denali.

At his tender age, Jayson had no way of knowing that for his mom, the dark hulking giant of a man who'd just stepped through her kitchen door made her knees weak and her toes curl. Meanwhile, all Mr. Lloyd saw was a gorgeous, curvaceous, caramel-colored goddess. He was a workaholic, not a skirt-chaser, but at that moment his wife was the furthest thing from his mind. The woman standing before him could have offered him flies on a donut and he would have gladly acquiesced.

As the two of them sat down at the table, seeing Jayson's confused stare, his mother told him he could have the bicycle and to go find his sister since dinner was ready: fried pork chops, okra, lima beans with rice and gravy. The apple pie, which Mr. Lloyd was so obviously enjoying, was dessert.

Jayson shot out the back door in search of his sister, unaware of the budding, illicit romantic liaison developing between his mother and his hero. For years to come, theirs would be a covert affair to which Jayson would remain blind as the only subsequent times Mr. Lloyd visited their home was when something was in need of repair. It was not until his late teens that Jayson discovered the true nature of their relationship.

In the interim, Jayson's hero worship grew as Mr. Lloyd often took him and Dez to County Stadium to see the Brewers baseball games. And despite Mr. Lloyd's disappointment in the Milwaukee Bucks for trading Kareem Abdul-Jabbar to the Los Angeles Lakers, he still took the boys to The Mecca to see several basketball games. Once, Mr. Lloyd even took them to Lambeau Field to see the Greenbay Packers play.

By the time Jayson entered high school at the Milwaukee Technical School on South Fourth Street (which would later become Bradley Technology & Trade) his gentlemanly manners quickly had those teachers eating out of his hand as well.

Because of Mr. Lloyd's earlier influence, Jayson loved working with cars, so he took up auto mechanics in high school and worked parttime in Mr. Lloyd's garage. Unlike Dez, who was a whiz with numbers, Jayson didn't have collegiate aspirations. The Kingdom Hall his family attended taught strongly against higher education. They preached that after high school everyone should strive to become ministers. But becoming a minister of a gospel in which he didn't believe, never figured into Jayson's plans. Since his family couldn't afford college anyway, Jayson assumed he would just stay on and work with Mr. Lloyd after graduating high school.

That goal went up in smoke during his senior year of high school when Jayson found out about the affair between his mother and Mr. Lloyd. It was his sister who broke the news.

At 22, Carmin had been gone from home for four years. She left when the bickering and between her and their mother became too incendiary. When Sylvia slapped her senseless during an argument, Carmin figured it was time to leave. What she didn't know was that Sylvia was trapped in her own repetitive cycle. Unbeknownst to Carmin, Sylvia and her own mother had played out the same dance ritual with similar disastrous results. Sylvia, too, had been at odds with her mother and when she was just 18, her mom kicked her out of the only house that she had grown up in. However, lost in the current battle of wills with Carmin, Sylvia was blind to the recurring pattern with her own daughter.

Instead of pulling herself up by her coattails and making it by any means necessary, Carmin floundered. With no educational aspirations, she found herself hanging out with the wrong crowd. She drifted from an occasional job into the arms of one man after another. It seemed her beauty was the only thing she had going for herself. Before long she fell into the forbidden world of drugs.

Though she started out smoking marijuana, her appetite turned to stronger, more lethal substances as she began experimenting with cocaine and heroin. What initiated as a recreational and divertive thrill soon led to an overwhelmingly destructive addiction as her use of heroin increased.

At first, Carmin lied and stole to support her habit. But shortly thereafter, she began selling her body to gain the drugs she desperately needed. Given her looks and youthfulness, she had no problem attracting men three to four times her age.

Carmin's wasn't the only life that was turned helter-skelter by her drug use. Her addiction took a devastating toll on the entire family. Jayson would never forget discovering the needle tracks on her arms and legs. He confronted her and remembered all her subsequent denials and empty promises to reform. And he remembered the thefts. The many times he and Sylvia came home to the evidence of Carmin's visitations in gaping but plain view: a missing television, a missing radio, a missing stereo, missing LPs and always the crumbs from hastily eaten food scattered all over the kitchen floor. Carmin's thievery became so pervasive that they were forced to change the locks on both doors.

Now when she visited, Carmin was forced to ring the doorbell to be let in. Though it broke their hearts to see her in her predicament, there was nothing they could do—except continue to love her. After stealing Sylvia's jewelry, Sylvia made Jayson promise that whenever Carmin came to the house, he would not let her roam through it unattended. It seemed that Carmin timed her visits and came only when she knew Sylvia would not be around.

One evening Carmin rang the bell shortly after 8 PM. Happy to see her, Jayson let her in and playfully grabbed her in a bear hug. If no one else in the world loved her, Carmin knew Jayson did because he never judged her. Laughing, she broke away to raid the refrigerator.

Jayson noticed how thin she was, almost gaunt, and that her appearance was severely unkempt as if she hadn't bathed in a long while. Yet, he was simply happy to see her since she was so secretive about wherever it was she was living. It was as if Carmin didn't want them to know how to find her.

"You just missed Mama," he told her.

"I timed it because I knew she'd be gone by 8 o'clock. If nothing else, Ms. Sylvia is dependable. She always talked about me, but then she's no better herself." Carmin had long since stopped referring to their mother as "Mama."

Jayson was compelled to come to their mother's defense. "Her shift sometimes starts at 9 PM instead of 11. That's why she leaves early."

Scarfing down a leftover chicken drumstick, Carmin looked at Jayson pityingly. "Jay, you just don't get it, do you? If only I could find a man as blind to my faults as you are to Sylvia's, I'd marry him and have a quick bunch of babies." Pulling a chocolate cake their mother had baked from scratch out of the fridge, she kicked the door closed with her foot.

"After all these years, you never caught on. See, unlike you, Jay, I couldn't be fooled. And she's fooled you right up to this very minute."

At every pause in her words, Carmin wolfed down another mouthful of food. The ferocious way she ate reminded Jayson of a starving dog who feared someone might come and snatch it away. He found himself watching her eat with fascination mingled with disgust.

Knowing she had his captive attention, Carmin took a swig of milk before biting into another chunk of cake.

"You know Jay, that's always been the difference between you and me. I could never be bought off with a hug and a few well-timed kisses. Not that I ever got any.

Because I've seen through Ms. Sylvia ever since I was seven years old and was forced to play the role of an adult."

Not liking the turn of conversation, Jayson watched with a sense of unease as Carmin gobbled down her food and licked her fingers with feral abandon.

"But," she wiped her mouth with the back of her hand, "that's what happens when you make a child grow up before her time. We see and begin to understand things we're not supposed to. I stopped believing in fairy tales a long time ago, Jay. It's time for you to stop too. Your mother, who you think is a saint, ain't no saint at all. She may pretend to be a Holy Roller, but she's a sinner like all the rest of us."

Disliking the look of malice on Carmin's face, Jayson shook his head as his stomach muscles clenched.

"And your precious Mr. Lloyd, he's definitely no angel either. He's certainly not the hero you've made him out to be. But then again, let's hope he's a hero to Sylvia when he's humping her every night."

Jayson recoiled as if she'd slapped him. "Stop it, Carm. That's a bunch of crap and you know it. You're just saying these things cause Mama put you out of the house."

Carmin laughed cruelly. "Poor Jayson. Ever the sucker, aren't you? You wouldn't know the truth if it bit you in the balls. Those two have been carrying on like back-alley dogs ever since we were little kids. I caught them doing it in her bedroom one day when I was supposed to be in school. That was ten years ago when I was just 12 years old, Jay. By now, you'd think he'd have the decency to leave his wife and make an honest woman out of Sylvia." Carmin drained her glass of milk and stared glumly into the empty container. "I guess it's true what they say: 'Why buy the cow when you can get the milk for free?' Don't believe me, Jay? Go see for yourself." She glanced at the clock on the wall. "Right about now, they should be buck naked at the Diamond Inn, right up there on West Fond Du Lac Avenue."

Seeing the hurt expression on Jayson's face, Carmin shook her head as the venom she felt toward their mother subsided. It wasn't Jay's fault. Her kid brother may have been naïve, but one thing about him, Jayson always saw the good in everybody, even her. After all that she'd been through and had put them through, he still loved her and treated her with the same adoration he had when they were kids growing up. That's why Jayson was the only person in the world she could say she honestly loved. And she did. Carmin loved Jayson unconditionally.

Suddenly, Carmin felt liked an embittered ogre forced to deliver the dreaded news that there was no Santa Claus. Her shoulders slumped. "Jay, we're not kids anymore. And in real life, there are no fairy tales with happy endings. I'm not going to feel bad about telling you the truth. Not when old Syl doesn't care about anybody but herself. Well, that's not quite true. At least she's always cared about you."

Feeling tears begin to well up, Carmin turned away to angrily chop off another slice of cake to take with her for the road. She would not allow herself to become maudlin about the stormy nature of her relationship with their mother. Still, she couldn't refrain from thinking that if Sylvia loved her a tenth as much as she loved Jay, she, Carmin, wouldn't be stuck in the horrible situation she found herself in: addicted to men and drugs (and not necessarily in that order) with no end in sight.

"Can I use the bathroom, Jay? I promise I'll just be one minute. I promise, Jay."

Jayson nodded, his heart heavy with grief. Things weren't like Carmin said. They couldn't be. He didn't think of their mother as a saint. He was just deeply disappointed. If, that is, Carmin was telling the truth. It was just that Mr. Lloyd was a married man and their mother, well, she went to Kingdom Hall every Sunday. Besides, she was always preaching to him about the devastating effects of sex outside of marriage. Not that Jayson was innocent. He'd tested the forbidden waters, though not as much as some others he knew. How could he be expected to remain a virgin when girls, much more experienced than he was, were constantly throwing themselves at him? Most he'd turned down out of conflicting feelings of guilt. But there were one or two that he hadn't. Even though he didn't like attending the religious meetings, he was obligated to attend them because he still resided under his mother's roof.

Realizing Carmin had been gone too long, Jayson got up to go see after her. He passed the bathroom and saw the door ajar. Carmin was not in it. He heard rumblings coming from his mother's room, which was across from the bedroom he'd shared with Carmin when they were little.

Jayson spoke from the doorway. "I can't let you take those things, Carm. Put them back. Put all of them back."

Startled, Carmin swung around quickly. She started pleading. "I just need a little something to get me over, Jay. You know I'll pay it back."

Crushed as he was, Jayson just wanted her to leave. He reached into his wallet and pulled out a $20 dollar bill. But just as she moved to grab it, he pulled it back and said to her, "Put Mama's things back, Carm."

Carmin tossed the jewelry she was about to steal onto the bed and Jayson led her out of the house. He went into the livingroom and sat on the sofa, not bothering to turn on the lights. Thoughts about the things Carmin had said ran rampant through his mind. Twenty minutes later, Jayson grabbed his keys and headed out the door.

He had to catch two buses to get to the Diamond Inn. It was 9:20 PM by the time he exited the Number 23 bus on West Fond Du Lac Avenue and walked to the motel at the end of the block. Just as he was nearing, Jayson's footsteps slowed ominously. He asked himself if he really wanted to know. But it was too late to turn back. He walked onto the motel's parking lot noting that there were only a few cars present, probably because it was a week night. On the weekends it was always packed. This he knew from experience.

He scanned the lot and his heart froze when he saw Mr. Lloyd's Caddy. There it was standing out from the other cars, diamond in the back, sun-roof top, whitewalls and all the rest.

There were two levels to the motel. A couple was coming down the stairs above him so Jayson quickly darted into one of the doorways, his body hidden in the shadows. He stood there for what seemed an eternity, but thirty minutes later a door on the first level flew open and out came Mr. Lloyd with Sylvia in tow. He opened the passenger door of his car and she slid into the seat. After Mr. Lloyd settled into the driver's seat he leaned over and they kissed lingeringly before he started the car.

As the car reversed, Jayson remained riveted in his spot, hidden deep in the shadows of the doorway. But as Mr. Lloyd backed out of the parking lot, the car's headlights shined briefly on the doorway where Jayson stood, illuminating his face and body. Jayson stared directly into Mr. Lloyd's eyes. Momentarily, Mr. Lloyd seemed to freeze, but then he recovered and drove away. Sylvia was refreshing her lipstick and never noticed Mr. Lloyd's startled look.

For the next several days, Jayson avoided his mother. When she came home from work he was already gone from the house and he didn't return home until after she'd left for work. He also avoided Mr. Lloyd and his garage. It wasn't until that weekend that he could face either of them.

Jayson went to the shop to gather up his tools and to tell Mr. Lloyd that he could no longer work for him.

Mr. Lloyd accepted his resignation saying, "Son, it would break your mother's heart to know you'd found out about us. If you have to blame someone, then blame me. I'm the one who wore your mother down and coaxed her into the relationship. If there's anything you should know about me, it's that I love Sylvia and I've never before cheated on my wife. I married my wife only because she was pregnant with Desmond." Mr. Lloyd approached Jayson and tried to put his hand on his shoulder.

Jayson jerked away from him. He remembered was how passionately his mother had kissed Mr. Lloyd outside the motel. "You must not have needed to do much coaxing," Jayson said bitterly. "How could you do it? I trusted you. I respected you."

Jayson shook his head. With betrayal weighing heavily in his gut, he brushed past Mr. Lloyd to gather up his things and walked out of the shop. He found another job the same day at an auto shop across town.

Jayson never confronted his mother. But when it came time for them to go together to the Kingdom Hall, he told her adamantly that he was never going back.

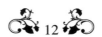

Sylvia expressed her outrage and disappointment but for the first time in Jayson's life, she did not challenge him. It was as if he'd thrown down a gauntlet which she deliberately chose to ignore.

One evening Jayson was home watching a rerun of Miami Vice. Just as undercover agents Don Johnson and Philip Michael Thomas raced their Ferrari Testarossa down Miami's Ocean Drive preparing to apprehend the next immoral drug dealer, the doorbell rang. The clock on the wall indicated it was shortly after 8 PM. He knew it was Carmin at the door, only this time Jayson didn't get up to let her in. Moments later the doorbell sounded again but still, he made no move to answer the door. The lights were on in the front of the house so Carmin knew he was home. Angrily, she pressed the bell repeatedly until Jayson finally came to the door.

His eyes were cold as he stood in the doorway staring at her without offering to let her inside. The screen door separated them. "What do you want, Carm? Did you come to gloat?"

His callus abruptness threw Carmin for a loop until she quickly understood that he was referring to the revelations she'd told him about their mother. Nearly a week had passed and Carmin hadn't given it another thought. In her world, a week was a lifetime and surviving until the next hit was all that mattered. "I…I wanted to come in and get something to eat…" Carmin stuttered as her voice trailed away. Never had Jayson treated her so harshly. It was unfamiliar and unpleasant territory.

Jayson reached into his wallet and pulled out a ten dollar bill. But instead of opening the screen door to hand it to her, he slid the money through the door's mail slot. Stepping backward, he closed the front door and returned to the livingroom to finish watching Miami Vice.

Carmin stood outside staring at the closed door with her mouth hanging open. Jayson had treated her with such cold indifference! Flabbergasted, it took her a moment to reach into the mail slot to pull out the ten dollar bill. As she turned to walk dejectedly down the porch stairs, anger rose within her to battle the hunger in her belly. She never thought she'd see the day when the one person in the world she loved most would turn against her. By the time Carmin reached the end of the block, rage had set in leaving her convinced that Sylvia had somehow turned Jayson against her.

Carmin's hands balled into fists and a vein swelled along her temple. Revenge was the word swimming through her brain—the overwhelming need to get even with Sylvia for delivering another painful dagger to her heart. It wasn't enough that Syl had never loved her and had ruined her life. Now she'd managed to cause Jay to hate her as well.

Instantly, Carmin knew what she had to do. The ramifications of her actions would be severe but that's just the way she wanted it.

It was a thirty-minute walk to her destination—the Kingdom Hall where she'd attended growing up and where her mother still fellowshipped. When Carmin stepped inside the Hall, all conversations came to a screeching halt. Every person in the corridor stared at her as though she was some alien monster who happened into their midst.

Taking advantage of their appalled surprise, Carmin demanded, "Where is Elder Taylor?" In the years she'd attended the Hall, she remembered him as the elder who carried the most influence. When no one moved, Carmin screamed, "Y'all can call the police if you want to but I'm not leaving until I've spoken to Elder Taylor."

Despite her lack of hygiene and her sorely disheveled appearance, everyone recognized her as Sylvia Denali's daughter. They also knew that Sylvia worked nights and was not in attendance that evening. The ministers were unsure if they should forcibly remove her from the building. But someone must have signaled Elder Taylor because in he walked.

"Sister Carmin, how can I help you?"

Elder Taylor sat listening to Carmin's tale of her mother's longstanding salacious affair with a married man in stunned disbelief. Since the elders decided matters as a group (only the men could become elders as women weren't allowed to carry any titles), Elder Taylor called two fellow ministers into the room and had Carmin repeat her tale. She began by detailing how she'd stumbled upon her mother and Mr. Lloyd doing it doggie-style when she was but a child. Using shock and awe as the denominator for her story, Carmin spiced things up for her captive audience, leaving nothing to the imagination.

The elders listened with bated breath, glued to her every word that depicted the graphic nature of her mother's wicked, clandestine affair—even listing times, dates and places. So erotically vivid was the verbal picture she painted, the elders appeared swept away by her narration. It was only when one of the elders started shifting uncomfortably and pulling at the knot of his old-fashioned tie did Elder Taylor rouse himself to thank Carmin for coming in to tell them her story. They understood completely that she came to them only because she feared her mother losing her soul to the devil. But as admirable as it was of her, they told Carmin that she should also be concerned about her own soul.

After shoving her outside the Kingdom Hall doors, the elders reconvened and decided they would interview Sylvia. If what her daughter said was true, the only recourse would be to disfellowship Sylvia from the congregation. On the other hand, if her affair was a one-time event, then she would merely be silenced and no one among the congregant would be allowed to talk to or fellowship with her for a span of time. But first things first. They would interview Sylvia and get her side of the story.

Sylvia Denali lay prostrate across her own bed.

Her eyes were swollen shut from all the crying she'd been doing. Mingling with the tears that continued to seep from her eyes was deep shame, hurt and embarrassment. When the elders of the judicial committee had ambushed her and told her of all the dastardly things she stood accused of, she could only hang her head in abject humiliation. The elders spared no detail of Carmin's story. When finished, Sylvia just stared at the floor in disgrace. But she did not deny the accusations. Whatever else she was (a flamboyant, despicable harlot in their eyes), she was not a liar. In the elders view, she'd dishonored their faith. Her punishment would fit the crime. She would immediately be disfellowshipped from the Kingdom Hall congregation and cast into the regions of outer darkness.

As Sylvia had slunk home from the Hall, her heart was heavy from the verbal indignities she'd suffered at the hands of the elders. But her anger was directed only toward Carmin. Instead of acknowledging the error of her sinful ways and determining to give up her illicit relationship—something she had absolutely no intentions of doing—Sylvia wished she owned a gun. At that moment in time, she would surely have retaliated by blowing her daughter's head off.

Jayson didn't see Mr. Lloyd again until the day of his and Dez' graduation. Ironically, Dez, who was preparing to go away to Morehouse College in Atlanta, insisted that both families stand together for a last minute photo. The situation was so awkward for everyone except Dez that it was comical.

Mrs. Lloyd stared daggers at Sylvia, who would not return her gaze, while Mr. Lloyd made sure he stood between Jayson and Dez. They all squeezed together for what surely was the most unpleasant photo op of their lives.

Dez was scheduled to depart in a few short weeks, and for the first time, Jayson felt lonely and adrift. He didn't have any college aspirations (Dez was the smart one in their duo) but suddenly he wished that he, too, could leave town for other adventures.

After graduation, Jayson registered for his Automotive Service Excellence certification and was able to get on with Milwaukee's Loomis, Fargo & Company as a fleet mechanic. Nearly every dime he earned he socked away into a savings account. He gave money willingly to his mother, but she insisted he put it away in a separate checking account. Jayson suspected that Mr. Lloyd was giving his mother quite a bit of money on the side. Before, Jayson had never thought to question where the extra money came from for all the home renovations, the new furnishings and his mother's new clothes. Now, he knew.

By the time Jayson turned 18 years old, he'd purchased an old reliable 240 Volvo and he insisted on driving his mother to work each evening. He was earning

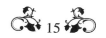

$13 dollars an hour and the money in his savings account was beginning to add up. Jayson figured he would save enough to one day open his own auto shop. He wasn't cynical enough to think his mother was with Mr. Lloyd just for the money, but he dreamed of earning enough money so Sylvia wouldn't be beholden to anybody. He also wanted to get Carmin into some kind of treatment center for her drug addiction. But all that required money that he didn't yet have so Jayson continued to squirrel away his savings.

❖

Unfortunately, tragedy struck later that same year. Carmin, who was just 23 years old, died of a heroin overdose.

He and Sylvia went through so much with her. They saw her go through stages where she would steal anything that wasn't nailed down. And sometimes even that hadn't prevented her from taking and pawning their valuables. Out of love and compassion, many times they had urged her to get help. Though she'd tried to kick her seditious drug habit, like an old friend who merely had to whisper her name, she would go right back to the drugs and their debilitating effects. When she was no longer welcome at their home, she'd bunk with friends who were also addicted to drugs in abandoned buildings or cars.

Carmin was a beautiful girl—too beautiful for her own good—but despite severe weight loss, she could always find a man willing to support her habit for a while and for a price.

Every time she showed up at their home, having worn the same filthy clothes for weeks at a time, their hearts would harden and break at the same time.

Even in death, Carmin wreaked havoc on their lives. Subconsciously, both he and Sylvia had thought that with time, she would come to her senses and kick her drug habit. Her death left them devastated and wracked by guilt. Both of them felt like they had given up on her too soon and had somehow let her down. By not doing more to save her, each felt like they had ultimately contributed to her death.

Coming up with the necessary thousands of dollars to bury Carmin presented a problem as well. But thankfully, a group of Sylvia's co-workers took up a collection on her job and one senior executive at the company where she cleaned donated $5,000. These funds, combined with his and Sylvia's, enabled them to prepare Carmin an elaborate send off.

If a silver lining could be found in the situation, it came for Jayson on the same day of Carmin's funeral. The executive who gave his mother the five thousand dollar donation came to the wake to pay her respects.

Porsha Carrey-Bertini was a well seasoned woman. She took one look at Jayson and knew immediately that despite his youth, he had that certain charisma that money couldn't buy. There was more to his facial features than mere beauty. He had

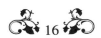

looks that bespoke character, strength, intelligence and passion. Porsha knew that as he matured, he would become even more handsome. Her intention had been to leave immediately after she bid the family well. Her home was in New York and she visited the Milwaukee office about once every other month. But whenever she came, she would arrive to work at the crack of dawn and that was how she'd come to know and develop a fondness for Sylvia.

Instead of leaving like she'd originally planned, she found herself squeezing onto the front row right alongside Sylvia. She rode with them to the cemetery inside the limousine designated for the family. By the time they arrived at the Denali residence for the repast, people assumed Porsha was a distant relative given the way she took charge of the proceedings.

Porsha was 47 years old and married with twin daughters who were older than Jayson. But the thoughts she had toward him could not be categorized as pure. Porsha was a heavy weight in the modeling industry and she knew raw talent when she saw it. Jayson, in her estimation, was a diamond in the rough. His strong, classical facial features coupled with his muscular 6′3″ frame made him stand out in any setting. Tall, broad shouldered, lean and hard, he was downright, drop-dead gorgeous. But because he was unaware of his effect on others, he had even more of a turn-on effect. And he was so sweet natured! Every time he spoke to her, he addressed her as Mrs. Bertini in that deferential manner of his. Porsha had to restrain herself from dragging him off into one of the back bedrooms.

Seducing him in current surroundings was absolutely out of the question. Not with all the sharp-eyed harridans occupying every seat in the house. *Good God,* Porsha thought. She hadn't seen so many women wearing so much gothic black garb since her field trip to the nunnery as a child. And with the way they watched her every move, they reminded her of giant black birds perched in a tree. Dressed in a short orange Ralph Lauren blazer with a matching thigh-high mini skirt and her Amano 3½-inch, clear acrylic, open-toe, sling-back sandals with rhinestones on the gold leather straps, Porsha definitely stood out from everyone else. The old birds stared at her icily as if she were some kind of weird, brazen hussy fresh off Prostitute's Row.

Hours later, after the last of them had finally departed, Porsha was prepared to help with the dreaded clean up. But thankfully, Sylvia insisted Porsha had already done enough and that she would never be able to repay her for all her many kindnesses.

Porsha, ever the gracious benefactress (especially when she wanted something) reassured Sylvia that it was the least she could do under present circumstances. Secretly, Porsha was glad to finally be rid of all the religious sad-sacks who'd been lingering and moping around. She'd noticed she wasn't the only woman eyeing Jayson with a leering eye. Most of the church women, both young and old had been casting their gazes upon him (the sanctimonious cows!). Whether for themselves or their daughters, she would never know.

But if nothing else was required of her, could they possibly call her a taxi since her car was back at the funeral home's parking lot? When Jayson quickly volunteered to give her a ride to her car, Porsha knew there was a God.

And later, when he escorted Porsha up to her hotel room at her request, Porsha's seduction of him ensured that the ride to her car was the first of many rides he would offer her before the night was over.

Chapter Two

If a certain mystique surrounds the modeling industry, Porsha Carrey-Bertini's impact on Jayson's newfound career was inestimable.

Her obligation stemmed in part from a promise to his mother. Having recently lost one child, Porsha understood how devastated Sylvia would be if she also lost Jayson. Still, Porsha was able to persuade Sylvia that because of his height and rugged looks, her son had more than a good shot at becoming a successful model. According to Porsha, New York City was the heart of the fashion industry, making it the number one city for models. She felt it would be in Jayson's best interest to move there and Porsha assured Sylvia that she would take him under her protective wing. He would only be a phone call away.

After listening to Porsha's persuasive discourse, some of Sylvia's reservations were overcome. She'd done her best raising Jayson and he was quickly becoming a man. Her biggest fear, however, was that the seductive vices of New York would be too much for a small-town boy to handle on his own. Though Sylvia had never viewed their situation in the dire context which Porsha painted, Porsha convinced her that allowing her son, who had so much potential, to languish away in Milwaukee with no further goals other than repairing cars for the rest of his life, was all but criminal. Jayson's eagerness to travel to New York sealed the deal.

As quiet as she wanted it kept, Porsha's urgent desire to aid Jayson's career was also nefarious. Her body temperature rose whenever she allowed her mind to reminisce about the night they had spent together in her hotel room. Although an obvious tyro in the art of lovemaking, Jayson was a quick study. And what he brought to the table by way of size, tenderness, initiative and stamina, caused her heart to palpitate and caused moisture to develop in certain unmentionable parts of her body.

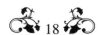

At nearly three times Jayson's age, Porsha was no greenhorn. Neither was she new to the game. If her Italian husband of 25 years could undergo a mid-life crisis at 53 years of age, who was she to deny a mid-life crisis of her own? That is, assuming an extra-marital affair could be linked to a mid-life crisis. It wasn't as if she was unhappy at home. Neither did she want a change in life partners. However, a temporary switch in dance partners would suffice quite nicely. She was, after all, just fulfilling her promise to the boy's mother to shelter and nurture him. It wasn't as if she was robbing the cradle for keeps! Besides, wouldn't it be far better and safer for him to submit to her tutelage than to be taken advantage of by someone who didn't have his highest good at heart?

Porsha was a level-headed business woman. She didn't need to validate her own beauty via empty flings or meaningless one-night stands. However, there was something about Jayson Denali that drew her to him like a moth to a flame. With the promise of lush, sensual abandon easily within reach, having a side affair with Jayson was irresistible and all too easy for Porsha to justify. But her failure to factor in the residual effects of a pleasurable, clandestine relationship would lead to future jealousy, misery and heartache.

With nearly thirty industry years under her belt, Porsha had fought hard to achieve the status she currently enjoyed within the ranks of the fashion glitterati. A distant relative to Lena Horne, Porsha shared the same rich, striking genes and was a diva in her own right. She knew that successful models were made, not born. And even when success was found, one had to work even harder to sustain it. In addition to possessing great looks, having good business sense was also a must. Similar to any other industry, potential talent needed to be properly financed and positioned in order to compete. While she would do everything within her means to aid and champion Jayson, at the end of the day he alone would bear the responsibility for paving his own path to success—through his willingness to work hard. Porsha knew that if he developed an ambitious and hearty work ethic, there would be no limit to the rewards he could acquire. Oh yes, she would show him the way, but only Jayson would be accountable for his own success.

With little thought for the future, Sylvia taught Jayson the ins and outs of the fashion arena, steered him clear of scam artists who preyed upon newcomers and introduced him to people who could open the right doors. Jayson was her protégé in every sense of the word.

New York modeling agencies compete to fill demand with the finest talent in the world. When an agency finds someone who satisfies the demand, they invest in that individual to get them ready for the market. They aren't dispensing charity—they invest in a model's formation in order to make a profit—a loan, if you will, against future earnings. These top modeling firms work with big-budget ad agencies and fashion designers so they can well afford to develop new talent. If a person proves unmarketable, they are quickly scrapped and all losses are cut.

At the Elite Model Management Corporation (EMMC) on East 22nd Street in New York, Jayson was one of numerous new kids on the fashion block. One of the things he was constantly being told was that a model's career lasted only as long as they were wanted or needed—one day someone's hot, the next they're not. So he should never allow himself to become complacent. Turnover was such that scouts, art directors, photographers and just about anyone else who worked for a modeling agency were always in search of fresh new faces.

EMMC had a solid reputation for launching many successful modeling careers. Jayson thought of his employment with them as on-the-job training because they coached and prepped him, got him test shoots and laid out his portfolio. They booked his jobs, negotiated his contracts, handled the billing and eventually cut him a check (less their 35% commission) for any work he performed. Operating quietly in the background, from ensuring he received choice assignments to giving final sign-off approval to each of his contracts, was Porsha who acted as his agent.

Although Jayson started out modeling for men's catalogs, with his Adonis-like beauty and tawny skin, he tended to get people's attention with or without clothes. But it was his infamous underwear debut for a Calvin Klein Body campaign that caused his career to skyrocket overnight. The two-page layout sizzled with sensuality and became the masculine image of Calvin Klein, fast tracking Jayson's career and making him the hottest buzz in the fashion industry.

At the same time, a new mode was developing for the African American male model. With the dawning of the hip hop era, Madison Avenue wanted to capitalize on the lucrative and expanding crossover market. Clients were seeking a specific look: High fashion meets urban America. They just weren't sure who or what it should look like—until Jayson Denali came along. His face helped define a new and innovative marketing approach for ready-to-wear couture causing him to emerge as the one to capture the hearts and minds of a cutthroat fashion industry.

With so much effort being poured into his marketability, the hardest part for Jayson was adjusting to his new surroundings. Far from his preconceived notions of leisurely days spent sprawled on sandy beach fronts, being a model required hard work and patience. And it wasn't nearly as glamorous as he'd envisioned. The long hours were rigorous and every assignment required that he reveal something more of himself other than what was presently on display, be it through a stride, pose or facial expression. During a particularly grueling photo shoot with Ansel Wolfe, a brilliant photographer known industry-wide for being difficult to work with, Jayson grew irritable after sixteen hours of non-stop shooting. With no end in sight, his irritation began to show. He glared fiercely at Wolfe who kept snapping photos as if deliberately trying to provoke him. When the session finally ended, everyone involved from makeup artist to fashion designer was exhausted. But Wolfe knew he'd captured beauty and magic on film. Despite his eccentricity, it was this genius that made him one of the most sought-after photographers in the business. And Wolfe didn't disappoint. The black and white images of Jayson Denali were a phenomenal hit. Dressed in a Karl Lagerfield ensemble, Jayson's stance and fierce glare made him the model of the moment and landed him even more coveted campaigns.

The sturdy work ethic he developed served him well because 12- and 14-hour days became the norm. When the Calvin Klein Body campaign netted him a larger paycheck than what he would have earned in three entire years back in Milwaukee, Jayson became obsessed with earning more money. He wired funds to his mother's Maritime Savings Bank account twice a month and dreamed of buying her a big, elegant new home. Since he didn't know how long his modeling ride would last, he was motivated to work even harder. As his assignments increased, he welcomed the long hours and earned a reputation as someone whom photographers were eager to work with.

Seeing himself in magazine spreads was surreal and took some getting used to. Jayson also had to adjust to being an instant celebrity. He was always surprised whenever someone stopped him on the street because they recognized him from a magazine. He was nonplussed when people were extra nice to him. Strangers smiled at him and said hello as he passed. Women did double takes and lowered their sunglasses. Men stared deep into his eyes. It seemed everybody wanted him. When he walked down Fifth Avenue on his way to the next appointment, sometimes Jayson would look behind himself to check out whether people were really looking or pointing at him.

But when he wasn't modeling, socially Jayson felt like a fish out of water. Listening to music became his favorite pastime when he was to himself. Despite his newfound status, inside he was still a young man who in many ways was unprepared for his sudden fame and fortune. He'd always made friends easily, but this crowd was altogether different. He wasn't a drinker. He didn't smoke. And he wasn't interested in experimenting with drugs. Compared to his modeling peers, he was an obvious square. He worried about his mother, grieved for his sister, and more than anything, he wondered where his relationship (if he could call it that) with Porsha was headed.

Jayson's studio apartment was in Greenwich Village, a neighborhood of beautiful brownstones and tree-lined streets where starving artists lived and created. It had lively bars and cafes and some of the best jazz clubs in the city. It was also the core of New York's gay scene, a whole other subculture that he never would have believed existed. Jayson had never been around people from different cultures and ethnicities, let alone people who were openly gay. He remembered a man from back in Milwaukee who everybody had whispered about. They had ostracized him and called him "queer." But in New York, with so many diverse races and types of people, life was simplified by a cosmopolitan approach: *live and let live.*

He remembered when he'd first arrived in NYC. His studio apartment was bare except for a mattress on the floor. He had the impression that it had quickly been vacated by some unclean person who'd left dirty dishes piled high in the sink and garbage strewn throughout the apartment. Still, it was like a palace to him because it was his alone. Having a place all to himself excited him and symbolized his freedom. Mere hours after he arrived in New York, Porsha and another woman whom she introduced as her assistant came to whisk him away. Porsha had looked around the place with disgust and promised to have it cleaned. She was true to her word because when Jayson returned late that evening, the studio was freshly painted and outfitted with new furniture.

Porsha's assistant had given him his schedule for the remainder of the week. However, the following day was free of appointments so he figured he'd get to know the city. When someone rang his bell the next morning at 7 AM, Jayson was pleasantly surprised to find Porsha standing there with a breakfast bag in one hand and her briefcase in the other. Once inside, breakfast was long forgotten as the two eagerly engaged in a slow libidinous, hedonistic mating marathon.

Hours later, drenched in the aftermath of passion spent, they lay sprawled on his sofa, limbs entwined. She in her scantily clad red silk underwear, him in his briefs. Both were comfortably enveloped by feelings of warm inertia brought on by deep satiation.

She told him of her marriage, her two girls and how she'd never before cheated on her husband. She and Armondo were complete opposites and came from different cultural backgrounds. She grew up a poor little black girl in Baton Rouge, Louisiana, while her husband's familial roots were in Naples, Italy. She'd met and fallen in love with Armondo while in Milan when she was 22 years old and still a highly sought-after runway model. He was a wealthy financier who treated her like a queen and swept her off her feet. Now, all these years later, she suspected he was seeing someone else. But she still loved him in her own way. She had her girls, she had her career and she also had her husband's wealth. She was happy with the status quo and would never dream of leaving him.

She told Jayson about all the potential she saw in him and how the world yet lay before him. He was to her like an oyster with a beautiful, rare pearl tucked safely inside. She loved his mannerisms, his gentleness, his willingness and desire to please, his thoughtfulness, his handsomeness and his latent sensuality.

To Jayson, her experiences were so vast and his so incomplete that he felt inadequate. He had little to offer by way of comparison. "Teach me how to please you," he whispered in her ear as he cupped the back of her neck to draw her closer.

Porsha knew well how to school him in the artful ways of pleasing a woman. And it was her pleasure to do so. But what she couldn't teach him was how to be a man. That, Jayson would have to learn on his own.

And learn he did.

On January 3rd, three years into his career, Jayson celebrated his twenty-first birthday. Financially, he was much doing better than he'd ever dreamt. EMMC had raised his rates from $3,000 to as much as $20,000 per day, which made him more selective about the jobs he took. He could now do three or four campaigns instead of the usual number but still earn more money. A year before, he'd built his mother a lovely new English Tudor-style home in South Milwaukee. The two-storied home was a charming manor with three bedrooms and two baths. Most of all, it had a huge, fenced front and backyard, something Sylvia had always wished for so that she could indulge her gardening skills. She no longer worked as a cleaning woman, but instead volunteered several days a week for different organizations.

Ever since Jayson was plucked from the obscurity of Milwaukee and vaulted to the top tier of male supermodels by the band of his Calvin Klein underwear, he had to contend with being viewed as a sex object. Instead of being treated as a minor background prop or as an anonymous walk-on, he was celebrated as one of the sexiest male models in the world.

The erosion of his privacy finally forced him to move from his humble abode in Greenwich Village. Jayson began receiving huge bundles of mail at his home address from fans, the majority of whom were male. Emboldened women—and men—began to ring his doorbell at all hours surprising him with illicit sexual offers. The last straw that pushed him to buy an apartment on the Upper East Side of Manhattan was when a photographer snapped a picture of a male prostitute appearing to leave Jayson's studio apartment in the wee hours of the morning. All the gossip magazines' headlines screamed that Jayson had been caught with his gay lover. The rumors were only partially squashed when it was proven that he'd been in Milan for a week-long campaign at the time the photo was taken.

Modeling menswear collections had taken him around the world to Milan, Paris, Madrid, Sydney and London. Paris was Jayson's favorite city because it was the most intimate, vibrant and romantic place he'd ever visited. He loved everything about the city—its nightlife, its beauty and elegance, the architecture and cuisine, the haute couture shops and grand museums. After studying the language for two years, he became fluent in French.

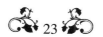

As much as he loved Paris, Porsha preferred Italy. A mecca for lovers, it was one of the most enchantingly seductive cities on earth. Exploring Venice and seeing its beauty through Porsha's eyes was an incredibly fascinating experience that made Jayson fall head over heels in love with her. Porsha knew the city's history thoroughly and she delighted in demonstrating her knowledge. She spoke Italian and every time she whispered something in Jayson's ear he had the urge to carry her off and secret her away for a quick dalliance. Very often, he did just that, slaking their lust, leaving her breathless and him hungrier for even more of her.

In bed, Porsha matched his every move. She was insatiable—a skillful, sexy tigress who demanded everything he had to give—and more. Jayson knew how to please her only too well. He knew how to caress, hold and stroke her body for maximum pleasure. By pleasing her, he pleased himself. But it was more than just the sex between them that made him realize he loved her. He adored and admired her.

She'd taught him so much about life. She'd been places, seen things, and had a sophistication and wisdom about her that he soaked up like a sponge. She knew who she was and what she wanted in the world. She was comfortable with herself and was comforting to be around. She laughed at herself and at him for making her laugh. She never looked down on him nor denigrated him for his lack of knowledge or inexperience about any subject. She encouraged him to read, to know his history and to not just accept someone's word for everything without verifying on his own whether the facts supported their claims.

He was even attending New York University's Tisch School of the Arts pursing an acting career at her insistence. Jayson loved Porsha because she inspired him and being with her was magical and fun. Spending time with her broadened his perspective on life. Through her, he came to realize that being a desirable woman didn't mean being a woman younger than what she was. Increasing his knowledge and understanding of finances, wine, traveling and the human condition were as important as all the sexual tutorials she'd ever given him.

Not only did Jayson love Porsha, he wanted to be with her permanently. He no longer wanted to avoid certain provinces of Italy because her husband's family resided there. Her age was not a barrier for him. In fact, their age difference was of no consequence to him. He was growing tired of having to sneak around with her. Part of the joy of traveling so much was that they could be together more openly. He wanted to hold hands with her in public wherever they went. He wanted to feel her body molded to his whenever he rode his motorcycle.

But Porsha grew melancholy whenever he broached the subject of their future or when he whispered, "*Ma chérie, je t'aime*," in French or, "*Cara mia, ti voglio bene*" in Italian. My *darling, I love you.* Jayson would drop the subject because he couldn't bear to see her unhappy, nor could he stand the thought of being without

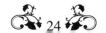

her. He felt that sharing her, having a small part of her was better than having no part of her at all. But his discontent was growing. He'd not been with anyone other than Porsha since the night she'd seduced him in her Milwaukee hotel room because he was convinced that she was the only woman for him. It angered him when she scolded him with words of how he was too young to understand. They would argue. She would attempt to leave. And he would drag her away from the door and show her why she needed him and why he hungered for her.

But people were beginning to talk. Industry insiders knew the two of them were an item. Now others outside the world of fashion were talking about them as well. It was fine for Jayson, but the things they were whispering about Porsha, angered her. Even her own husband commented on her lack of sexual enthusiasm. *If he only knew*, Porsha thought. The fact was that after being with Jayson, she had nothing else to give—physically or emotionally. Jayson drained her. But he also built her up. The problem for her was that her husband *did* know. He understood what time it was far better than Porsha imagined and his comments to her were his way of telling her to end this madness.

Not only was her affair affecting her home life, it was beginning to seep into her professional life. Porsha found herself becoming extremely jealous and possessive of Jayson. For the first time in her life, she envied younger women their youth. She hated it when women fawned and draped themselves all over him. She hated that other women viewed him as an object of desire. Whenever he traveled overseas, Porsha was right by his side. But while Jayson saw it as their chance to be together, it was much more than that. Porsha couldn't bear the thought of him being with another woman. The fear of him sharing all of his passion and excitement with someone other than herself woke her up in the midnight hour.

Porsha knew she was losing her objectivity, but felt powerless to stop it. Her husband, Armondo, loved her beyond a shadow of a doubt. But Porsha had never been obsessed with a man as she was with Jayson. And she was starting to feel like a fool. Was it love that she felt for him? Or was it the way he loved *her* that was causing her to lose all reason? She knew Jayson thought she'd taught him everything he knew about lovemaking. Privately, Porsha was not so sure. What he had was already in him and had just been waiting for the right person to bring it out. Perhaps his passionate nature was the result of having been religiously brainwashed to believe that sex was something dirty and to be done quickly in secrecy. But once those idiotic notions were wiped away, Jayson and everything he had inside of him was more than a notion. He had become for her a drug and she needed him constantly like a junkie needed a fix.

Physically, he was extremely well endowed. But he was also gentle and kind and loving and tender…Jayson's size, ardor and eagerness left her exhausted but already hungry for their next passionate coupling. Matching his passion was his desire to love her unconditionally. He loved buying and sending her flowers and expensive trinkets, holding her hand, trailing his fingers along her body, talking with her, listening to her, sharing himself, his fears, what he thought of as his inadequacies. He was transparent with her about everything and he trusted her emphatically.

Porsha knew it was time for her to end their affair. But whenever she thought she'd developed the courage to tell him it was over, she found herself instead on her knees before him embracing him with an oral grip. The whole affair was sheer madness! What had begun so innocently had enveloped her and was tearing her mental seams apart. She'd started the relationship as a woman in control, but now found herself resorting to all manner of acts far beneath a woman of her stature.

Eunice Wallace was Porsha's closest friend in all the world. One day she came to whisk Porsha away from work, refusing to take no for an answer. Eunice drove them to her home in East Hampton on Long Island, New York. Unbeknownst to Porsha, Armondo had called Eunice and had told her everything that was happening. He asked her to talk to her life-long friend, as nothing he said seemed to be getting through to her. Armondo was an indulgent husband. He loved Porsha but his patience was growing thin. She worked late, neglected him and the girls and traveled all the time—even more than him. At first Armondo had thought her affair was in retaliation for his outside indulgences. But as time passed, he knew this not to be the case.

The final straw was when Porsha had forgotten their anniversary. For the past twenty years, it was their custom to travel to Naples, Italy and spend two weeks with his family. It was also customary for her office to handle all the arrangements. This year as the time grew closer, Porsha had not even mentioned it. And when he finally brought it to her attention two weeks from the time of their usual departure, she grew agitated and distant. The week of their departure, Armondo was shocked when she waltzed into their bedroom to tell him that she would not be going and that he and the girls would have to travel without her. She'd sailed out the door of their multimillion dollar Fifth Avenue super-luxury co-op, leaving him sitting on the bed dumbfounded with a puzzled look on his face. Short of asking for a divorce, he'd picked up the phone and called Eunice.

If anyone could break through the blanket of misjudgment which Porsha had wrapped herself in, it was Eunice, who after sitting her down with a double shot of straight bourbon, pummeled Porsha with a verbal assault that left the adulteress bent over wracked by sobs. Mercilessly, Eunice had walked from the room and returned with a manila envelope from which she pulled nine, 8x10 glossy black and white photos and threw them harshly at her best friend. Some landed on the sofa where Porsha sat, some fell to the floor. When Porsha saw the glaring evidence of herself in Jayson Denali's arms, she could only close her eyes in shame and horror.

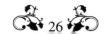

In a flat voice bereft of compassion, Eunice proceeded to tell Porsha that she hadn't wanted to believe Armondo when he called her. After all, Porsha had told Eunice about Jayson three years ago but had lead Eunice to believe it was a fling that was never repeated. Not only had Porsha betrayed Armondo, but she'd betrayed their long standing friendship of more than forty years. The two of them had known hard and rough times growing up in Baton Rouge, Louisiana. The fact that they had risen to their current heights was remarkable. What was even more remarkable was that both had raised families and remained married to the same men during the whole time.

In a world where people change marriage partners as often as they change underwear, being married to the same person for more than twenty years was no small feat. Eunice was no prude. Neither was she a punk. She was a strong black woman who had helped heal her husband's wounds every time his back had taken a verbal lashing from corporate America. Her husband of thirty years was now one of only three existing African American CEOs of a Fortune 500 company. Together, they had raised four children, all of whom were being educated at Harvard University. They had come a long way since their meager days in Baton Rouge. Eunice loved Porsha and she was not about to let her throw it all away on a fly-by-night fling that was unfortunately more than three years in the making.

Eunice had hired the private detective because she hadn't wanted to believe Porsha would be so stupid to throw away her marriage and all that went with it.

As Porsha's sobs quieted, she sat bent over at the waist with a glass of Distiller's Masterpiece cradled in her hands. Masterpiece was an ultra-premium 20-year old Bourbon costing $300 a bottle. *On this occasion, the entire bottle might be needed,* Eunice thought as she stared at all the photographs surrounding Porsha. The photos showed two people obviously in love and oblivious to the world around them.

Each shot was taken in a different setting. The couple strolling through Central Park, she smiling at him whimsically as she reluctantly pulled her hand from his grip. Them laughing and enjoying a meal at Alain Ducasse, a stylish and highly expensive French restaurant at the Essex House on 58th Street in Manhattan. Them, embraced in a deep kiss on a bridge overlooking the Seine River in Paris, France. Them again in Paris, bonding with nature and with each other as they strolled through the beautiful gardens of the breathtaking Luxembourg Castle. Them, walking arm in arm to the Ile Saint Louis, a tiny island within the Seine near Notre Dame. Them, snuggled up sipping wine as they listened to the jazzy sounds of gay Paris inside a smoky hole-in-the-wall jazz club. Them, amongst Italy's high-fashion, high-style ski scene, nestled within the pink craggy peaks of the Dolomites in the Italian Alps of Cortina D'Ampezzo. Them, in Milan enjoying themselves at the La Scala Opera House.

The last photograph, the investigator had thrown in for free. It was a photo of them coupling erotically on the top balcony of the opulent Eremo Dell Giubiliana Inn located in the wealthy region of Val di Noto, Sicily. He was nude as Porsha straddled his lap wearing only his shirt, her head was tilted back and her expression held the stark look of naked, timeless passion.

In each photo, the boy was breathtakingly beautiful. A magnificent work of art, he was eye candy for the soul. About that, there was no equivocation. He possessed an intelligent face and had that elegant, square jawed GQ look, an athletic body complete with iron pectorals and chiseled abdominals. Staring at his golden bronzed body and the way his long, thick fingers gently but firmly encircled Porsha's neck, it was difficult to think of him as a boy. But Eunice took a swift drink of the bourbon, consciously hardening her heart as she refused to call him anything but a boy because of the age difference between him and Porsha. Eunice knew her words would have even more of a devastating impact if she kept referring to him as a "boy" instead of calling him by his name. As Eunice stared at the photos, flashes of her own youthful passions stirred within her remembrance. But those days were replaced by something more deeply fulfilling and trying to resurrect the past as her friend was doing only led to destruction.

Porsha glowed in each of the photographs as well. So much so that Eunice momentarily envied her her happiness. The boy was so possessive of her and so obviously in love with her, how could she not glow? Eunice had studied each picture in detail and had come to the conclusion that there was so much passion and tenderness in the way the boy held Porsha as he gazed at her adoringly, she had no doubt that he loved her. What Porsha's state of mine was, one could only wonder. In the end, what Eunice knew was that at the cost Porsha was about to pay, her liaison with the boy was not worth all that she stood to lose.

Porsha had discarded the very sensibleness that had catapulted her to the top of the fashion industry. Her recklessness was insane. Physically, Porsha glowed but mentally, she was a wreck. And it was time for her to choose before she wrecked other's lives as well. For some reason, Eunice sympathized with Armondo in this instance. She recalled the time of her own husband's affair with his secretary and how she'd wanted to kill him when she found out about it. As hurtful as the experience was, she'd pulled herself together (with Porsha's help) and rallied to save her marriage. Even now, years later and despite their financial success, the memory still hurt.

After her verbal assault, there was only one more thing Eunice could think to say to Porsha. Her next words would stay with Porsha for the rest of her life and inspired within her the courage to take the necessary parting steps.

Eunice told her, "Porsha, you bought and paid for that boy's time—not his soul. *Loose him and let him go.*"

When Porsha lifted her head to stare at Eunice, her eyes appeared...dead. As if some light inside of her had literally died. And when Eunice drove her back to Manhattan, she knew that Porsha would finally do what needed to be done.

With his heart and his world in tatters, Jayson sat in the dark listening to Gloria Estefan's "Here We Are." *The time we spend together's gonna fly...And everything you do to me is gonna feel so right...Baby, when you're loving me, I feel like I could cry...Cause there's nothing I can do...to keep from loving you...*

Jayson had never before known the kind of pain that gripped him at that moment. The only thing that came close to the level of pain he felt was when his sister, Carmin, had died. He remembered Carmin's ominous words to him from what now seemed like eons ago. *"Jay, you just don't get it. If only I could find a man as blind as you are. After all these years, you never caught on...In real life, there are no fairy tales with happy endings...You're a fool, Jay. You've always been a fool..."* If those were not Carmin's exact words, they were very close and that was how Jayson remembered them.

He vowed that he would never again compromise himself to where he was blinded by love or passion. He hoped that in time his heart would heal from the deep wounds that had been inflicted. Going forward, he would keep both his heart and his head where they belonged—separate from his emotions.

Two days later, Jayson received a telephone call that propelled him into his next profession. Barry Blaustein, screen writer and film producer extraordinaire, called with an offer for Jayson to star in his upcoming film. Jayson flew to Hollywood the very next day and never looked back.

To erect walls that barricaded him from emotional pain and heartache, Jayson selectively gave himself to many women so that he would never be beholden to one. Unfortunately, his heart hardened in the process causing his spirit to fracture into a million little pieces.

As he struggled to heal and to put the heartache of his past behind him, it never occurred to Jayson that he would generate intense Hollywood heat and soon become one of the most successful male models turned actors ever to grace the silver screen. All he'd sought to do was put the past behind him.

Chapter Three

Enroute to the east wing of the medical center where she worked, Aaryn Jamison paused in front of tinted windows to take in the dramatic view outside. The dawning sunrise captured the sky's brilliant colors as clouds parted to give way to an amber sun. Each slow moving cloud formation seemed to take on a shape and life all its own, illuminating the morning sky with fiery reddish glows. From her location on the eighth floor, soaring pine trees highlighted the dazzling hues and grand majesty of the Wasatch Mountains looming in the distance. Though she'd lived there all her life, the incredible beauty of Utah's landscapes still had the ability to render Aaryn breathless, leaving her in awe.

Lost in a reverent gaze, minutes passed before she tore herself away to continue on to the Healing Gardens, the section of the facility where highly sought-after healing massages were performed. Shriners was a licensed Naturopathic Medical Center, world renowned for the successful treatment of diseases and health restoration using natural therapies. People came to Shriners from all over the world having been diagnosed with rare, incurable diseases. Those with debilitating bone diseases, those with life-threatening illnesses and many who were given a limited number of days to survive arrived in hopes of receiving a miracle or cure. Rare was the individual whose health could not be vastly improved by using the therapeutic remedies Shriners dispensed.

Shriners Naturopathic Medical Center was the only accredited institution of its kind in the nation to have received awards from many independent agencies in recognition of the quality of their services. Nestled in a secluded and heavily wooded remote area of Salt Lake City, Utah, the beautiful private facility was eight stories tall and boasted a state-of-the-art research unit that pioneered clinical research in many areas, most notably women's health, pediatrics, and health services. Theirs was the kind of prestigious facility that attracted its patrons more from word of mouth than from any form of direct advertising. And their funding came from wealthy corporations and ultra high-networth private citizens, some of whom donated entire wings to the facility.

With around-the-clock patient care, staff manned the Medical Center seven days a week. Early mornings were Aaryn's favorite part of the day. Like clockwork, but without the use of an alarm, she awoke early and on most days arrived at Shriners just as the sun was rising. She loved her work. For Aaryn, satisfaction came with an inner knowing that right here, right now, she was in her rightful place doing what she loved and what she felt called to do. Whenever the lure of lucrative offers from other hospitals in far away cities were put before her, or the enticement of owning her own private practice was offered, Aaryn was comforted by the belief that, for now, her world was as it should be.

The Healing Gardens took up nearly half the eighth floor. The pristine whiteness of Italian marble was offset by natural sunlight and by the greenery of tall trees and exotic healing plants strategically placed throughout the unit. The unit itself was sectioned into ten large healing centers—each one uniquely named including, the Rophe Room, the Yahweh Room, the Yeshua Room, the Yakushi Room, the Kabbalah Room and the Kundalini Room.

The first part of Aaryn's day was spent inside the various rooms where she would administer two or three ninety-minute healing massages. More than just an ordinary massage, Aaryn's touch massages were distinctive healing treatments. While Shriners specialized in all types of massages of both eastern and western variety, of all the therapists working in the unit, Aaryn's healing treatments had the highest overall recovery success rate. *Healing dwelled within her hands.*

She didn't focus on any one type of massage technique. Aaryn just knew that, through her hands, healing was allowed to flow into the bodies of the patients she worked with. Like anyone uniquely gifted in an area of their life, Aaryn learned not to question the gift, but to respect it. Akin to a seasoned artist open to the mysteries of creativity's flow, Aaryn's massages were an adventure in healing—an unspoken language exchanged between patient and healer. While exploring her patient's body, she never knew what direction her hands would take until she was deep into the rhythmic flow of a therapeutic massage. Similar to the harmony of a humming bird's wings flapping in rapid succession while its beak pulls the sweet nectar from a flower's essence, so too did Aaryn's hands flutter in painted strokes over a person's body.

A journey in touch sensation, every stroke and feel revealed a cell's cryptic biographical and biological message. As she firmly or tenderly kneaded flesh, tendons and muscles, a person's body talked to her, emitting elements of that individual's journeys taken in life. She received impartations of painful memories, loving memories, or memories long since forgotten. Aaryn couldn't explain how people's lives were revealed through touch stimulation. She just knew that when she ran her hands over flesh, bodies spoke to her telepathically through senses and vivid pictures transferred to her mind's eyes. Where often there was paralysis on one side, she kneaded flesh where patients could feel no sensation. Even so, the paralyzed tissue itself recognized it was being touched, searched and offered healing. If receptive, over time, the body responded by consciously yielding to her insistent healing touch.

Why have you shut down? her hands would inquire of nonresponsive cells. Reticent at first, sometimes Aaryn would receive no response at all, the flesh beneath her seeking fingers not responding or wanting to respond, preferring to remain silent beneath immobile paralysis. And suddenly as if not wanting to pry, her hands would float to another area. Another area willing to yield its story. With a change in direction, her hands would return to the body's silent area, entreating it to give up its secrets.

Sometimes, the responses would be slow in forthcoming—some people's bodies took weeks or months to emit their truth. At other times, without hesitation, an organism's story would come gushing forth in untenable waves of emotion: *I shut down because I was being ignored, abused, underfed or overfed; our voices were never acknowledged; though we gave signs often, our input was never valued.* Thus, Aaryn learned the body's "truth" of why sickness was allowed to dwell therein.

Almost everyone Aaryn ministered to suffered some form of paralysis. Some were unable to walk, others had limited used of their extremities. Regardless of their state of health, touching their bodies was like mining their life's history. Without them uttering a spoken word, Aaryn received details about a person through touch therapy. Long forgotten childhood incidents, some never retold, would surface through to her fingers. She often found that the more enjoyable episodes, those moments that evoked smiles and loving memories, were retained in the parts of the body which still functioned properly, while dark remembrances lay hidden deep in the membranes of unworkable flesh. Concealed beneath immobility were stories of abiding horror or tragedies that the patient's mind was unwilling to confront.

Whenever Aaryn hit pockets of flesh that evoked sorrowful memories, almost always the patient would experience physical pain. Sometimes there would be an outpouring of tears as years of masked anguish released itself from the body's cells. Some described the return of sensation to once paralyzed flesh as a rash of quick-silver needle pricks to the skin; others felt a gentle outpouring of warmth flowing slowly throughout the body. During these moments, Aaryn's hands would become the perfect curative instruments, her fingers intuitively knew the level of tender determination required to effect a person's healing. But there were also times that demanded she be merciless. During such sessions, *Aaryn had no mercy toward ailing spirits lingering unchecked in a person's body.*

The ironic part for her was that as healing took place, she too, relived the painful journeys of each of her patients. A part of her sustained the same joy or sorrow or deep sense of loss that they did. If she couldn't read a person's thoughts, Aaryn could literally *feel* their senses talking and responding to her. Thus, it was imperative that she disconnect emotionally in order not to be affected by the patient's life experience.

Nearly all the patients Aaryn took on regained some, if not all, use of their limbs. On the rare occasion resulting in no improvement, it was generally because the patient had committed him or herself to the idea of bringing an end to their life's journey. Consequently, a person's recovery depended not so much on the severity of their paralysis but on how willing and ready they were to walk in renewed healing.

As rewarding as each assignment was for Aaryn, it was also completely draining. For this reason, she saw no more than three patients a day, working with them three times a week. Her early afternoons were spent detailing and documenting notes about each of her sessions. If she so chose, by midafternoon she was free to be on her way. Unless, of course, she had scheduled afternoon consultations or was asked by another doctor for her professional opinion.

Aaryn's office was on the seventh floor of the facility. It was spacious and was dominated by a tall potted Ginkgo Tree with yellowing leaves. The walls were a glazed yellowish-gold color that gave the space an energetic, comfortable feel. Two huge paintings hung on the walls: one an abstract that exploded with an array of exciting colors, and the second, a huge framed topical photo of Bryce Canyon National Park with its mountainous, spiraling tiers ablaze with orangeish hues. A heavy Cyber-flora plant with buds that resembled white tulips was in one corner while a huge flowering Aloe Vera plant sat in another. Her favorite was the fragrant Lemon Balm plant which rested on the corner of her desk, its lemony scent filling the entire room.

Even the sleek natural ash wood office furniture with its contemporary sweeping lines provided an inviting and light atmosphere to work in. Above her desk hung framed degrees and medical certificates including a Doctorate in Naturopathic Medicine (ND) from the Southwest College of Naturopathic Medicine & Health Sciences; and from the University of Utah, both a Master of Science in Occupational Therapy and a Bachelor of Science in Organic Chemistry.

There were four photos on her desk. A stunning and dramatic mountain vista shot showed Aaryn in deep concentration as she reached upward to rock climb The Prophesy Wall, a 500-foot high vertical cliff in St. George, Utah; there was a picture of her posed in hiking gear underneath the majestic Delicate Arch in Arches National Park; another one with her twin sister, Erika, each with an arm around the waist of their mother, Dorothy, whom they affectionately called "Dot"; and the fourth photo was of Erika with her husband and their three children, ages nine, six and two. Erika had married and moved to Indianapolis, Indiana, many years ago. The time since she'd left Utah had gone by in a blur. They'd been exceptionally close when they were younger, but as they matured there had developed a need to find their own uniqueness.

Aaryn was typing notes on her laptop when her phone rang.

"Hello Aaryn. Can you spare a few minutes?" Dr. Kyle Baldwin was the head Naturopathic Physician at Shriners. Having overcome his own life-threatening illness, Kyle understood what it was like to be critically ill. Aaryn admired him for the integrity with which he ran Shriners. Although heavily focused on the hospital's financial outlook, Kyle was a trustworthy man and he was committed to constantly improving the staff's skills and therapies in order to help patients attain the best levels of optimal health.

"Sure, Kyle. I'll stop by momentarily."

For all the medically proven research Shriners had pioneered, many still considered Naturopathy to be a field of medicine practiced only by quacks and witch doctors. But such perceptions were slowly beginning to change because of all the undeniably good things Naturopathy was accomplishing. Still, most Naturopathic services were not covered by Medicare or most insurance policies. Because Shriners was privately owned and operated by a network of Naturopathic Physicians, of which Aaryn was one, most of their patients were people who could well afford to pay out of pocket for their medical services.

It came as no surprise that the majority of their clients were wealthy. And Shriners had no shortage of clients. They also provided services on a case-by-case basis to those who could not afford treatment. Kyle and several other physicians determined who would receive the Medical Center's largess. Aaryn suspected that there was an indigent patient Kyle needed her to treat. Knowing her present work load, he may have decided to approach her directly. It wouldn't be the first time.

Or quite possibly, he wanted to discuss Darius Grey. A patient of hers who had previously resigned himself to never walking again, his startling recuperation was nothing short of miraculous. Even Aaryn was surprised by the rapidness of his recovery.

Eighteen months earlier, Darius Grey had been the star running back for the New England Patriots. With five years as an NFL player under his belt, Darius had rushed for over 8,000 yards and had three Super Bowl Championship rings to show for it. He was on the fast track to toppling Barry Sanders and Walter Payton's yardage records before his career-ending injury. In his last season, Darius suffered a broken neck and was completely paralyzed. Even after intense surgery, because of the fractured vertebra, he remained paralyzed from the neck down. Every one of his doctors counseled him that it was unlikely he would ever walk again.

By the time Aaryn had come into Darius's life, he was wheelchair bound and as distant and unreachable as any patient she'd ever encountered. It was his wife, Gayle, who had talked him into coming to Shriners. Darius had seen a number of doctors in a short period of time until he finally had met with one who promised him he would walk again. When that assurance proved unfounded, it caused Darius to lose all faith. The pain of having his hopes dashed yet again was more than he was willing to bear so Darius became rigidly resigned. Outwardly, he appeared to be taking his newfound status in stride.

Inwardly, he'd cloaked himself behind a mountain of anger, selfpity and regret. When it appeared former teammates and fans had forgotten him, his wife Gayle was the only one left to fight for Darius's emotional and physical survival. Against the advice of his doctors, she told him about the astonishing, groundbreaking work that she'd heard was being done at Shriners. How men and women with similar prognoses as his were walking again after undergoing treatment. She even showed him several articles that were written about one physician in particular, Dr. Aaryn Jamison.

Incredibly, only three months had passed since Gayle had contacted Aaryn in hopes that she could convince Darius to undergo treatment at Shriners. That initial call had left Gayle devastated on two fronts. First, Darius refused to participate in the conversation and secondly, Aaryn explained that she didn't influence anyone toward treatment because there were so many people who *wanted* to walk in healing that she didn't have time for anyone who didn't. Aaryn had not been callus in her explanation, just straightforward about the plentiful pool of people from which there was to draw. Besides, the Center already had a waiting list.

But Gayle was stalwart in her efforts to get Darius into treatment. She even lobbied the NFL to make a sizeable donation to Shriners on Darius's behalf. Three weeks later, Gayle and Darius were on a chartered plane from Potomac, Maryland, bound for Salt Lake City.

As the three of them sat in consultation, Aaryn understood the dynamics at play. She truly admired Gayle's strength and tenacity because it was obvious she was fighting for the survival of her family. Gayle just needed Darius to fight as well. But that fight was becoming increasingly harder to conduct on her own as Darius withdrew deeper into himself. Aaryn could only imagine the strain the couple was undergoing. Thirty minutes into their conversation, with Gayle doing most of the talking, Aaryn noticed neither of them had broached the issue of conjugality—or the lack thereof, which surely was a contention between them. But a marriage counselor Aaryn was not. Her only aim was to uncover whether Darius was serious about healing. If he wasn't, it did not mean he would not receive treatment, it just meant that Aaryn would not be the one treating him.

Having established a foundation of trust, Aaryn asked, "Gayle, may I spend a few minutes alone with Darius?" A nervous Gayle stepped outside the office.

Aaryn pulled her chair close to Darius until their knees nearly touched. She laid her outstretched hands on his lap, her palms facing upward as she took his hands in hers.

"Darius, all I want is for you to take several deep breaths and relax."

What transpired was an experience Darius would later describe to his wife as one he'd never before encountered.

He and Aaryn had stared at each other unblinking for several minutes. Uncomfortable at first, Darius looked away to study objects in the room. But the intense way Aaryn stared at him willed him to return his gaze to hers. His eyes scrutinized her face and he found himself examining her in a detached and non-judgmental manner.

Darius saw a woman with beautiful, flawless dark chocolate skin whose age was indecipherable. Her face was devoid of makeup, except for the clear coat of gloss on lips that were full. She had a wide nose and thick bushy eyebrows that most women he knew would have plucked long ago. Her hair was thick, course, wavy and long. Tendrils escaped the knot she wore at the back of her head. As his eyes drifted back to hers, the word that came to Darius to describe her was "natural." She wasn't beautiful in the model-like way that his wife, Gayle, was. However, she struck him as an unusual woman who didn't need the adornment of facial makeup because her beauty lay inward.

Darius recalled the two articles he'd read about her and wondered what had led her to become a doctor and to work in Salt Lake City. Hers was the only African American face he'd seen since his and Gayle's arrival. He found that significant in light of the photo on her desk that showed her concentrating intently as she scaled a mountaintop peak. Darius was a sophisticated, well-traveled man. But in all his life, he'd never met an African American person who climbed mountains. Hiking, he could understand. But climbing a mountain? That was beyond him. And people thought that football was dangerous!

He wondered if she was married. Though she wore a loose-fitting white overcoat, he could tell she was an extremely shapely woman. Darius was at once curious about who she was. For some reason, he had the sense that she was an intensely strong and private woman—one who was nurturing, guileless, different. As she held his hand, Darius began to sense something strange, a foreignness he couldn't quite identify. Brief flashes of something inexplicable confused him momentarily before giving way to...certainty—a knowing that everything was going to be alright. Suddenly, it felt like he was transported through a dark vortex where everything around him traveled faster than the speed of light. And yet, Darius felt safe and knew he had nothing to fear. From out of nowhere, he had a strong sensation of aloneness. Not loneliness, but a state of austere solitude until he realized intuitively that it wasn't him who felt this way...*it was Aaryn!*

Feeling like he was prying on her thoughts and not understanding how he was able to sense these things, fearfully Darius wanted to pry his hands from hers but he couldn't because of his paralysis. As if sensing his desire to withdraw from her, Aaryn merely gripped him tighter until he relaxed again.

When she didn't release him, a calm stillness came over Darius. The moment he stopped mentally fidgeting, childhood memories and images of his mother came to mind. Until the age of seven, he'd been raised in a small town called Alligator, Mississippi. Though his mother had called them "hard times" Darius hadn't known it. All he remembered was the warm feeling of being loved. After his mother had died, he was sent to live with relatives in a neighboring town. For the first time in his life, Darius knew what it meant to be lonely. But it wasn't the loneliness he remembered as he stared into Aaryn's eyes. It was the warm sensation of love. Inexplicably, Darius felt the same rush of emotion he'd felt as a young boy whenever his mother would pick him up and plant kisses all over his face. He remembered how she would laugh uproariously as he made a show of wiping away her kisses, both of them knowing he loved receiving them as much as she loved giving them. The feeling was so strong Darius could almost feel his mother's arms around him.

And then he remembered how she was abruptly snatched away, out of reach, like one of the butterflies that had often evaded his youthful grasp. At that precise moment, Darius realized that like Charles Foster Kane in the classic film *Citizen Kane*, he had lived his entire life trying to recapture that same feeling of unselfish, unconditional love that his mother had planted in him as a child. With his emotions raw, Darius suddenly felt the magnitude of frustration Gayle was suffering from as she tried to be strong for the both of them. Unexpectedly, Darius began to weep.

Five minutes after his wife had closed the door on her way out, as Aaryn's hands gripped Darius's, sobs overtook him. For once, Darius forgot about the age-old stereotype that said men do not and should not cry. It certainly wasn't planned, but he found himself shedding tears for his mother, to whom he'd never had the opportunity to properly say goodbye or to even tell how much she'd meant to him. He grieved for his wife, whom he secretly feared would someday leave him for another man—one who was worthy of her. And he grieved for the manhood he now felt stripped of, knowing he would never enjoy the thrill of having children of his own.

Quietly, Aaryn got up and opened her door to beckon his wife back inside. Gayle immediately went and knelt in front of her husband throwing her comforting arms around him. Aaryn left to give them privacy. Fifteen minutes later, she stepped back inside and pulled up another chair so that the three of them were sitting in a small circle. Aaryn sensed the room's atmosphere was "clear" because in that moment anything could be created with and between the couple. What Aaryn wanted to know was if Darius was *willing* to believe he could walk in his healing.

The next week, a determined Darius returned to Shriners. After two months of furious therapy, what some of the finest surgeons in the world had said would never happen, happened. Darius began walking, albeit with the use of two canes. Two weeks later, he was walking unassisted. Because of his enormous progress, Darius was released from the Medical Center the following week.

His recovery generated headlines around the country. A press conference took place the day of his release. Former fans returned in droves to support him, and even people who weren't fans were happy to know the man who once rushed over 8,000 yards for the NFL, whom many doctors proclaimed would never walk again, was well after all. His story was carried in every major newspaper and press footage of him leaving the hospital unassisted was replayed on all the major television and cable networks.

The news coverage was huge for Shriners as well. It was also free publicity. The only drawback was that Aaryn didn't want any part of the media blitz. She'd already spoken to Darius and Gayle about her wishes to remain behind the scene. Kyle was then designated to speak for the Center.

As miraculous as Darius's case was, to Aaryn his story was no more exhilarating than the many others she'd had the good fortune to witness. The only difference was that Darius was a beloved and celebrated sports hero who commanded media attention. Of all the people she'd treated, whether wealthy or poor, their healing was no less amazing. To witness firsthand someone's spinal column reconnecting or to feel bones move back into proper alignment with just a light touch, left Aaryn so humbled that it mattered not what race the person was—it only mattered *who* the healing originated from.

She had her own philosophy about avoiding the limelight. Aaryn knew God was the Supreme Healer—she was merely the vessel. In her estimation, the general public tended to make gods out of ordinary people instead of acknowledging the extraordinary one who ultimately gave the increase. Aaryn had said as much in the statement Kyle read on her behalf. While it had its benefits, in the end, news coverage always served to attract unwanted spirits as it caused doubters and curiosity-seekers to come out in droves. *New levels bring new devils* was a phrase Aaryn was intimately familiar with.

She got up to go find out what Kyle wanted.

Aaryn flipped to the last page of the report Kyle had given her. They were seated across from each other at the cherry-oak conference table in his office. She closed the thick manila folder and looked up to find Kyle watching her expectantly. Her expression was noncommittal as she leaned back into the high-backed leather chair and crossed her legs.

In all the years Kyle had worked with Aaryn, he still found it difficult to read her. He knew she would sit staring at him without saying a word until he was blue in the face. Thinking she would make an excellent poker player, he got right to the point.

"Sylvia Denali is a WL. She's being transferred here next week. I was hoping you would take her on."

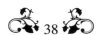

The Center had a backlog of Wait-Listed clients. While most were put on a two to six-month waiting list, exceptions to the rule were not uncommon, as in the case of Darius Grey.

"Her chart indicates she's assigned to Dr. Naoto. Why are you reassigning her?"

"Taku is taking a six-month leave of absence to return to Tokyo, Japan. He's agreed to manage his current caseload but he's not taking on anyone new. Seven of his patients are WLs needing reassignments. I thought you might be interested in Mrs. Denali's case because of the nature of her paralysis."

This was the first Aaryn was hearing of Dr. Naoto's leave of absence. He would be missed as his departure would leave them shorthanded since only a handful of the Naturopathic Physicians on staff specialized in healing touch therapy. Their need for additional licensed Naturopaths was great but recruitment was problematic as very few were able to pass the rigorous standards established by Shriners.

"What of his other WLs? Are you reassigning them by natural selection?" Aaryn knew where Kyle was headed with his request and she wasn't sure she wanted to buy into it. If everyone else was hand picking patients from Taku Naoto's wait-listed pool, Aaryn wondered why Kyle was selectively placing someone with her.

"Yes. The goal is to place each of them so none will be Wait-Listed again. I thought Mrs. Denali would be a good fit for you."

"Kyle, I've not met with her so I can't speak to that. But isn't this just semantics? This is really about the possibility of Mrs. Denali's case turning into a high profile one. Or would you have me believe that who her son is has no bearing on why you'd like to reassign her to me?"

The cynical expression she cast him caused Kyle to grin at her. "Yes, you're correct. There is potential for prominent recognition. However, Aaryn, that's only part of it. You know you're the best ND we have. Therefore, it's only natural that I steer certain people your way." Still smiling, Kyle said, "Besides, what would make you think I had ulterior motives?"

"I don't know, Kyle. Possibly because it's written inside Mrs. Denali's medical folder in big, bold block letters that her son is Jayson Denali, *the* three-time Oscar nominee slash megastar? The only thing missing from her chart is his 8x10 glossy. What does any of that have to do with her treatment? Kyle, I'm beginning to suspect you're becoming starstruck." Aaryn leaned forward to rest her arms on the table. "And stop looking at me with that puppy dog expression. I'm not buying it. Really, Kyle, it would be different if I were seeking acclaim. You know that I'm not. We both know that any of our NDs can take her on. Plus, there's no assurance that I can treat her anymore successfully than the next physician. After the success we've had with Darius Grey, every ND here would snap up Mrs. Denali's case in a heartbeat."

Kyle noted her use of the term "we" relative to Darius Grey. His recovery was her success alone, but she continued to deflect any and all praise. He got up to take a seat next to her on her side of the table. "Everyone would except you, Aaryn. You're not a media hound and that's exactly why I'm asking you to take her on. Your unselfish commitment to health and well being is why you're so successful. With you, it's not about the challenge of healing someone so Aaryn Jamison gets all the glory and notoriety. With you, it's about helping someone to heal from the inside out. See Aaryn, I *know* you." Kyle swiveled his chair to face her, his tone suddenly intense.

Though subtle, Aaryn detected a slight inflection in Kyle's voice. She turned away from him to stare straight ahead, not wanting to think about what message his body language was signaling or what look might or might not be in his eyes. She was well aware that some thought Kyle displayed favoritism toward her because of all the high profile cases he steered her way. Though there had never been anything untoward between them, Aaryn took great pains to avoid the appearance of impropriety. They both did. Still, there were times when she sensed a yearning in Kyle.

"Stop patronizing me, Kyle. Let me first meet with the Denalis and we'll see if I'm the best fit. But," Aaryn looked at him sternly. "If I sense another ND would be better suited to treat her, you'll have to honor that."

"Fair enough." Kyle rose to return to the opposite side of the table to put proximity between them. Whatever moment existed passed and they were back on familiar ground. Kyle moved to his desk to rifle through files until he found the one he wanted. "While you're here, let's discuss the NFL's recent proposal. You know that Darius Grey's case has driven individual teams to want their own private Naturopathic Consultant onboard."

Aaryn nodded. "The exposure is great for Shriners but we need to ensure that our NDs remain consultants and not any of the teams' fulltime staff physicians."

In the advent of Darius Grey's recovery, NFL sports teams wanted to work with Shriners' physicians to facilitate healing of their players' sports injuries. It was a very worthwhile endeavor that would earn Shriners many millions of dollars. Kyle needed Aaryn's input as to how Shriners' NDs could be assigned to the various NFL teams. It would also require recruiting and training additional staff. Not an easy task.

With over ten year's experience, Aaryn's work with touch therapy was groundbreaking. She was the one physician each of the NFL teams wanted to immediately work with. Aaryn was willing to oversee the program, however, she preferred to work independently with individuals of her choosing on a case-by-case basis. Inclination led her to work with those whose injuries were uncalculated. Not that sports injuries were any less serious. But to Aaryn, the NFL was synonymous with danger. If a player played long enough, eventually they were destined to taste the bitter fruit of being injured. And for the injury-prone player, NFL meant "not for long."

Still, Aaryn wasn't naïve. It was an extremely lucrative offer. The demand was strong. The need was great. And NFL teams were offering an open check book. All that remained to be decided was how to fit the new program into an already compact schedule.

❖

The sketch began to take form between bold, meaningful strokes. A valley surrounded by mountainous peaks, its basin a dry bank littered with crumbling rocks. In its midst was a bone weary traveler in search of a resting place that offered sanctuary—a respite from the turmoil and strife that plagued every life's step. It was a journey whose markings looked decidedly familiar to the traveler until dawning recognition proved that the path chosen was the one of least resistance. A path which at first glance had appeared smooth but had deceptively led to entrapment and bondage. An insight hinted that just beyond the horizon was rest from struggles that sought to overtake. And once reached, the realization dawned that this gateway of freedom had always been there, an escape route hidden in plain view. Though the weary traveler was faceless, the dreamer recognized herself and knew that the way out had been there all along. Nevertheless, taking the final steps to reach the edge where freedom waited left her motionless with fear. Better the devil that you know. *She found herself rooted to the spot unable to take the final steps required to bring tranquility to her journey. She kept hearing the words "fear not, be of good courage" and yet, courage was the one thing she lacked—that and the strength to bring an end to her own internal nightmare...*

Chapter Four

Aaryn and Erika grew up in Kenilworth, Utah, a small coal mining town about 117 miles outside of Salt Lake City. The town was a melting pot with people from all walks of life. It had one major street with a restaurant, a grocery store, a movie house, a saloon and one general-purpose store. Kenilworth was an out of the way spot and was not merely passed through. No one wound up in the town of Kenilworth unless a conscious decision was made to go there.

Their parents, Ben and Dot, were already married when they migrated to Utah from Alabama in '55. Times were tough for the couple in rural 'Bama so when word reached them that good-paying jobs could be found in Utah regardless of skin color, they packed their meager belongings and headed west.

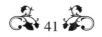

Ben found a job within days of their arrival. The Carbon Coal Mine was a traditional mine shaft that used a series of elevators to bring its excavated coal to the surface. The twelve-hour shifts Ben worked deep inside the mine were hard, dirty, and very often dangerous. Yet, despite the roughness and ruggedness of the job, there was a sense of worth and dignity about the labor. There existed a unique relationship between man and mine that defined the parameters of mining life. Each day of work, miners tempted death and knew that survival depended upon the skill of their fellow workers. Ben never complained about the risky, arduous nature of the work. It was simply what he had to do to provide for his wife and the children they were hoping to one day have.

The property they purchased had a simple cabin-like home on nearly an acre of land. Ben, a strong, stocky man, could build anything he set his mind to. He enlarged their home and built Dot a huge enclosed garden house that enabled her to grow root crops and many other herbs, spices, fruits and vegetables. Dot loved harvesting the garden with her bare hands. She possessed an innate knowledge of plant life and always seemed to know which herbal combination would heal or soothe someone's illness. When word of her healing gift spread throughout the small town, although she didn't think of herself as such, residents began to view her as the local midwife since her healing poultice creations were better and cheaper than seeing the town doctor.

Dot had yet another talent, one that she sought to downplay. She had a strong gift of prophesy. Her knack for peering into another person's future was definitely not something she advertised. In fact, she avoided it except when she felt a fervent need to deliver a message for someone's good. But her accuracy was always dead on and caused people to whisper about her. How could she know the hidden things about people? Some whispered out of fear, calling Dot a witch. But others talked about her with reverence because she always spoke of God's healing and curative powers.

When a visitor commented on how the Jamison's property had become so green and rich with trees and wild flowers compared to the surrounding land, Dot explained that God had reversed the curse on their land and had healed it, leaving the land ripe for growth. Dot told only one person but within hours of the visitor's departure, word had spread throughout the town. It had to be true, some said. The Jamison's land was barren when they first purchased it, but after only a few short years, it was lush and fertile and was surrounded by dense trees. How else could Dot grow certain fruits and vegetables that could not be grown anywhere else in Northeastern Utah? Some called the rumors simple tomfoolery, but others weren't so quick to dismiss them.

When the twins were born years later, Dot knew both her girls were special. The moment she first held Aaryn and Erika in her arms, she had a vision of two warriors riding powerful horses. Each wielded a sword and a shield in their hands. In Dot's vision, a huge cloud of smoke rose from the ground symbolizing a battle far off. The horses reared and the two riders strove to gain control of their mounts. With sword and shield raised, one rider charged in the direction of the ensuing battle. The second rider brought her steed to a halt. Turning her horse in the opposite direction, she threw her sword and shield to the ground. When the vision ended Dot knew that one of her children would embrace the call on her life, and the other would reject it. What Dot couldn't see was which of her daughters would go in the appointed direction.

As they began to grow, the differences between the fraternal twins were notable. Erika, the oldest by three minutes, favored Dot. She was a fair-skinned beauty who was trusting and affectionate. She loved being held and cuddled and enjoyed being the center of attention. Aaryn, on the other hand, had smooth, dark chocolate skin and favored her father. She was reticent around strangers and didn't like to be touched by anyone other than her parents. Erika was a Daddy's girl while Aaryn was closest to Dot.

When the time came for them to attend elementary school, the nearest school was eight miles away in Helper, Utah. Kenilworth children were bussed to school and their parents were expected to deliver them to and pick them up from one centralized location.

For Erika, school was wonderful given all the indoor games. Her favorite game was "tea and crumpets" because without fail she was always the queen and the other children her royal subjects. She loved wearing the frilly dresses and matching ribbons her mother handmade for them. She loved playing "house" with her dolls as much as she did entertaining and making them her captive audience. Erika idolized all things girlish and was the exception to the rule that said one couldn't grow up in Utah without loving the outdoors.

If Erika was like Shirley Temple in her mannerisms, her sister, Aaryn, was just the opposite. She was more like Darla Hood, the ragamuffin girl from *Our Gang: The Little Rascals*. Aaryn hated dolls as much as she hated wearing frills and lace. Neither did she easily adapt to school. When she finally assimilated, she was more comfortable climbing trees with the boys than playing with the girls. Aaryn loved pretending to be a pirate and would deftly wield her plastic sword while playfully cutting her enemies to shreds. Unfortunately, the drawback occurred that Aaryn was also a fighter even when she wasn't playing pretend games.

If one of the children made the mistake of making fun of her sister or calling their mother a witch in Aaryn's earshot, a fight ensued. Regardless of size or gender, Aaryn never backed down from a fight—much to her mother's despair. Even the teachers were at a loss to explain how someone so tiny and quiet could intimidate children twice her size. Secretly, many of the children considered Aaryn an oddity, especially when she would loudly call them evil demons from the pit of hell. They might not have known exactly what an evil demon was, but from the way Aaryn said it, they knew it couldn't be anything good. Most of the kids just avoided her altogether.

Though she never needed to scuffle with anyone, it bothered Erika that the other children ostracized Aaryn and called their mother names. She heard the things they whispered when Dot picked them up each day. As they grew older, Erika recognized that people could be such vipers. The main gossipers amongst her peers were the offspring of the ones who were always at the Jamison doorstep begging for a handout or asking Dot for a "Word from God." It irked her that her mother never turned any of them away. Erika wished Dot wouldn't be so forgiving and quick to help those who scandalized their name. She began to resent what her mother called the "anointing" that rested on their lives. If having the gift of knowledge, prophesy and discernment brought scorn from others, Erika wanted no part of it. She resisted her mother's talks whenever Dot would tell her and Aaryn that they also possessed these same gifts. Erika didn't want to read, interpret or discern spirits as Dot promised they someday would. More than anything, Erika just wanted to be normal like everyone else.

Years later, a horrific accident would shatter their lives. It came to pass two weeks to the day that Erika saw it in a dream. One night, she awoke crying because she'd dreamt that there was an explosion down at the mine. She ran to her parent's room in tears and as her father held her tightly, he soothed her, assuring her it had only been a nightmare. But as Erika retold the dream in chilling detail, Dot began to silently pray in tongues. Erika hadn't wanted her father to go to work the next morning but when he returned safely that day and the days thereafter, her fears were allayed. After a week's time, Erika was able to put the unsettling dream behind her.

On the morning of April 1, 1970, the Carbon County mine disaster would become the worst mining catastrophe of that time. Ben, like hundreds of other miners, left home to begin another typical day of work, unaware of the impending horrifying event that would culminate in the deaths of 187 miners.

Shortly after 8 AM, the Carbon Coal Mine exploded. So loud was the sound of the blast that the noise reverberated throughout the nearby towns. When news of the explosion spread, a rescue team was quickly organized to calculate the damage and assess whether there might be any survivors.

What the rescuers saw as they approached the mine was gruesome. Ben Jamison was standing at the opening of the mine at the time of the blast and was thrown 850 feet. Parts of his mangled body were never recovered. It took the men nearly forty-five minutes to clear away debris blocking the entrance to the mine. Each second lost proved deadly because in the end, it was too late to save those trapped inside. When the rescue crew finally entered the mine, they found that many of the men were blown to pieces. Others had suffocated from the deadly, toxic gas fumes left by the explosion.

All of Kenilworth and the nearby towns mourned as they began the sad process of caring for the dead and severely wounded. Once dragged from the mining shaft, lifeless bodies were taken to a nearby boardinghouse where they were cleansed and dressed for burial and where grieving wives and mothers anxiously waited to claim them.

For Dot and the girls, losing Ben was devastating. Months after the mass burial, the tens of thousands of dollars the mining company shelled out in settlement to each victim's family may have shut the door on a tragic event and paved the way for *them* to continue conducting business as usual, but for the Jamisons and others who lost a loved one to the mining tragedy, life was irrevocably altered.

For the first time since her days in Alabama where lynching had been commonplace, Dot knew real fear. At night, she and the girls slept huddled together in the big bed she'd shared with Ben. As the night winds whipped throughout the town and the surrounding mountainous valleys, its sound carried an ominous portent: the mournful cries of souls snatched violently from the earth realm.

By nightfall, strong winds surrounded their home causing them and the house's contents to tremble. Shadowy, distorted, dark-shaped figures slithered underneath doors and entered their bedroom. With both her children on either side of her and her arms wrapped around them, Dot lead them into spiritual warfare through speaking in tongues. At first, they watched in fear as the dark silhouettes lurched around the room coming dangerously close to their bed. But as Dot and the girls' spiritual warfare strengthened, the demonic forms retreated. By morning, the house was back to normal and all that remained of the spirits' visitation were shattered jars of dried fruit on the pantry and kitchen floors.

Night after night, the apparitions appeared. During that harrowing time, Dot kept the girls home from school because she wanted them close by. Recognizing only to a degree what she was up against, she began to teach them about the nature of spirits.

"The good ones," Dot said, "need no introduction." So she taught them how to identify and name the daemonic. Little did she suspect that her daughters would also teach her.

One morning as they were seated at the breakfast table, Aaryn asked, "Why do the spirits come to *our* house each night? Why don't they find somewhere else to go?" Though she addressed her questions to Dot, it was Erika who surprised them all by answering.

Erika said, "The spirits *do* visit other houses. But the people in them don't recognize them without their fleshly bodies. These spirits are haunting our home because *we* are the only ones in this town who look past the natural to see into the *super*natural. Others have the same abilities, but their unbelief prevents them from seeing beyond what the natural eye can see."

With an advanced wisdom, Erika described what had been revealed to her through dreams. She explained, "The spirits who inhabit our home each night come for different reasons. Some of them are the miners who are sorrowfully distressed that their lives have ended so abruptly and unexpectedly. Some just want the familiar contact with those of us still among the living. They can't grasp reality—that their earthly bodies have suddenly been transformed into an ethereal form. Some of the spirits have hopelessly rejected the knowledge that they now exist outside the human plane and will forever be without body mass."

Erika started rubbing her arms as if to ward off a sudden chill. "Others among the spirits are trying to communicate with us. They want us to deliver messages to their loved ones since the spirits can no longer do so in their non-fleshly selves."

"But," Erika cautioned as she stared directly at her mother, "we are not to engage these spirits, nor to entertain them. *We are not* to pass on their messages to the people of this town. If we do, the people's hearts will harden against us even more and they will bring harm to us. If the people of this town would but still themselves and listen, the spirits' messages would be revealed."

Dot nodded her head all while Erika was speaking. She explained to the girls, "What you've said is true. But you need to understand that pre-existing spirits, wicked spirits which have walked these lands for many years, are also mingling with the newcomers to the spirit world. These territorial spirits are called principalities and they have joined themselves with the newer ones simply because they are accustomed to inhabiting and ruling the surrounding Utah valleys. This Northeastern province is the only resting place some of these principalities know. These kinds of spirits are the ones who roam to and fro seeking a resting place but finding none."

Dot laid both her hands flat on the table. "Many of the spirits are timeless trespassers in the earth realm and are seeking to delay the revocation of their souls. They have become retaliatory spirits who encourage weakened and armorless humans to do wrong and to harm others."

"But Mama, there are also godly spirits who inhabit the lands too, right?" Aaryn asked.

When Dot nodded with a sad but comforting smile, Erika said jubilantly, "There are good ones here in our house at this very moment, even as we're eating our breakfast. These kinds of spirits watch over us, protecting us from harm's danger. These spirits are sent straight from the throne of God to carry out His will and to make sure that God's people are not cut off from the fold."

When Erika finished speaking, the three of them lapsed into thoughtful silence. After some time, she said, "I believe I know these things because they've been shown to me in my dreams. When Daddy died, I didn't want to live anymore. I felt guilty, like I was responsible for his death. If only I'd been able to convince him that my dream was real, he never would have gone back to the mine. But then one night when I was in my bed crying, a Spirit came and comforted me. This same Spirit sat with me for a long while. It showed me that a famine is coming, Mama. It said that we must prepare immediately while the time is at hand—the season for us to live here in Kenilworth has ended. The Spirit said we should sell our land and move because danger is about to befall this place." Erika stretched out her arms and the three of them just sat there holding hands.

Finally, Aaryn said, "I've also seen Daddy in my dreams. He's one of the angel spirits now. He said that we're to remember that he loves us. That he's watching over us and has petitioned the throne of grace on our behalf so that no unclean spirits will touch us so long as we are doing the will of God. Daddy told me that no matter what shape or form the demons take, we're to know that they have no power over us. He said to remember that God has not given us a spirit of fear, but one of power and love and of a sound mind."

Squeezing their hands, Aaryn continued speaking, but with greater confidence. "I think the demons will continue to come here until we bless the house with Holy oil. Erika is right about the destruction that's coming to Kenilworth. I've seen it as well. There will be deaths and slayings to come. But in my dream, I also saw a town called Halle. Or, it might have been Holiday? We must find it because that's where our new home is. I saw a widow woman who's been waiting impatiently for us to come and buy her property. She doesn't know why she can't sell her home to any of the people who've come to purchase it. All she knows is that she's waiting for the right people to come along. She just doesn't realize she's waiting for us. We must hurry though because her patience is wearing thin."

She stared into her mother's eyes and said, "And Mama, Daddy told me that he loves you. That he's always loved you. He was so happy when you graduated from high school. He said he knew even then that although he only had a fourth grade education, he would do whatever it took to care for you and provide for you and love you to the ends of this earth. He said you were the best thing that ever happened to him. But the very last thing he said to me before the dream ended was that whenever any of us see a rainbow, to know that he's thinking of us and that he'll ever be watching over us all."

Dot released their hands to swipe at the tears cascading down her face. Every word her girls had spoken was confirmation of what God had already said to her. When they came and knelt on their knees to embrace her, Dot crumpled as she gave way to huge sobs. The months following Ben's death was sheer hell and the pain of losing him was hardly bearable. She'd known Ben since early childhood and had been married to him for more than thirty years. Just thinking about living the rest of her life without her friend and life partner was daunting. The only thing that kept her strong was the knowledge that she still had her daughters to care for.

Up until the morning of the breakfast revelations, Dot was going through the motions. Her mental strategy was solely to survive each day. She'd literally been unable to look to the next—only the present day mattered. When God had spoken to her spirit about the things to come, Dot had closed the spiritual door upon His voice. Silently, she was angry at her Heavenly Father for taking away the main entity that added richness, warmth and breath to her life. In the aftermath of Ben's death, she had few words for her God, and those few words were laced with bitterness. The God whom previously she had celebrated as the Prince of Peace, the Keeper and Lover of her soul—the One whom she knew as Alpha and Omega—the same God who had spared her husband's life many years ago when wicked men had sought to hang him from a tree, the same God who woke her up each day and poured out His love upon her in worship—was the One whom her heart had now hardened against.

Gone were the days when she would awaken before the rest of the household and meet Him down by the Japanese Cherry tree in their yard. People marveled at the tree's beautiful blossoms because the Weeping Japanese Cherry was unique to Tokyo, Japan. But God had enabled it to grow upon her land and so Dot had pledged the tree back to Him as a symbol of her love and affection. But since Ben's death, she hadn't gone anywhere near it. It hurt too much to think that her Heavenly Father loved her so little that He would take away her husband. Had all her prayers for her family been for naught? Had all her sacrifices meant nothing? Had everything been in vain? Didn't He know that everything she had *already* belonged to Him? As Dot released her pain and anguish through the honest marrow of her tears, something unexpected happened—her brokenness began to heal. Through her shed tears, she gave voice to her inner rage and sorrow. And as she did so, something within her spirit quietly shifted and the breach between her and her God began to be repaired.

When Dot dried her eyes some time later, she looked up to find herself kneeling at the base of the Japanese Cherry. How she'd gotten there or how long she'd been there, she could not say. She didn't remember rising or leaving the house to kneel at the tree. Exhausted, she stood and walked back toward the house. Resolve strengthened her with each step. Healing was the overriding word she heard within her spirit.

Her girls had only spoken words that she, herself, had heard but refused to heed. She could hear the Spirit of the Lord saying to her that the time to act was now. The time had come to put away her grief and to look to the hills from which would come her help. Ben was gone forever, but she still had his seed to tend to. She still had a piece of him with her in the form of her girls. And she would ever carry his memory in her heart. Though Erika and Aaryn were only 14 years of age, she drew strength and courage from both of them. God had used them to get her to see that the time for her to dry her eyes and allow the healing process to begin was at hand.

Dot realized that her life would not end just because her husband's had. God still had need of her. She saw and heard in the spirit that if she followed God's leading, the remainder of her life would be full and rich and that her end would be far better than her beginning. With that promise buried deep in her heart, Dot felt safe and reassured like never before.

Their remaining time in Kenilworth passed swiftly as a sense of normalcy returned to their home. The girls went back to school and Dot put their property on the market. There was so much to do in preparation for their relocation. She felt as if a new chapter was unfolding in each of their lives, hers especially. At 50, Dot was making decisions on her own that previously would have been made solely by her husband. Confidence and strength flourished within her. Though intelligent and articulate, Dot's reassurance lay not in her own abilities, but in the belief that her God was with her every step of the way.

Dot researched and found the town of Holladay, Utah, 115 miles away. In order to locate their new home, she planned a week-long trip to Salt Lake City. She and the girls would drive there, check into a hotel, do a little sightseeing, and visit the for-sale properties listed in the local papers. They never doubted that they would find the house they saw in their dreams. And they didn't doubt that they were leaving the town in advance of terrible tidings to come.

Ben's 1974 Buick Electra 225 was five years old and very well-maintained. The four-door vehicle was built to last; it was spacious and could take them hundreds of miles in quiet airconditioned cruising comfort. Excitement and anticipation loomed. As the three of them packed their things into the trunk of the car, they were like merry little children bound for Disney Land. The girls had never traveled beyond the surrounding Kenilworth area and could not contain their enthusiasm. Seeing them smiling and so happy, Dot vowed that things would be different going forward. She would ensure that her girls were educated and properly equipped to survive and thrive in a world that had quickly evolved beyond what she'd known when she was their age. More than anything, Dot wanted her girls to accomplish things that she, herself, had not ever dreamed possible. She wanted them prepared to stand alone, if the need arose, selfconfident and assured that they could make it on their own.

Even as they drove down US-6 to Interstate 15, the quiet, sleepy town of Kenilworth was rapidly changing. As a few of the residents moved away to begin afresh elsewhere, a new influx of people drifted to the town in search of available mining jobs. These newcomers, however, were cut from a different cloth than previous generations. They brought with them advanced technology, but they also brought more unsavory characteristics that were intensified above the norm. If anger, lust and avarice already existed to a very small degree within the people of Kenilworth, the newcomers brought an abundance of it in open display. Within months, one tavern soon morphed into many, prostitution thrived, and the days when people could leave their homes unlocked and unattended ended as a general lawlessness began to pervade the land.

When the promise of a booming coal economy failed to materialize, a huge setback struck the Utah coal industry. The newcomers who came in search of a rosy outlook were suddenly faced with a depressed economy as the overall demand for coal sharply declined. It would be years before the trend reversed itself. Where in past times, families had banded together to share their rations so that everyone in the town survived until the economy revived, people now hoarded their provisions. As was prophesied in the twin's dream, a famine-like hunger descended upon the town and a wave of violence surfaced amidst the destitution. Some began to steal to meet their needs. But others began to kill. An evil and murderous spirit infiltrated Kenilworth, Utah. In time, it would manifest itself in the committal of even more heinous crimes.

Chapter Five

The Jamisons fell in love with their new home the moment they laid eyes on it. Located in Salt Lake County, the custom handcrafted Aspen log home was one of the most beautiful homes they had ever seen in their lives. Looking like a fabulous home fresh from the pages of a magazine, it sat nestled under a huge beautiful oak tree on three acres of land. They drove up the driveway and sat inside the Buick in open-mouthed amazement. Not wanting to give voice to the unbelief stirring inside her, Dot realized she didn't have the courage to get out of the car. The simple truth was that she didn't have the faith to believe they could own such a wonder.

They sat in the car so long that the owner, Mrs. Seymour Hirsch, wondered if they were lost. She opened the front door and stood impatiently just inside the entrance with her hands on her hips. Mrs. Hirsch was a third-generation Utahan. She was of Russian Jewish ancestry and her ancestors had immigrated to Utah in the late 1800's. The Hirsches had invested in banking, railroads, mines and merchandising. Though they still maintained their business holdings, the bulk of the Hirsch clan had moved east to New York. At 82, Mrs. Hirsch intended to spend her remaining years in Israel. Selling her home was part of the moving process, but there was one caveat required that meant more to her than the money she could garner for her home.

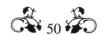

At her beckoning, Dot and the girls got out of the car and walked the distance to the home's entrance.

The log home had a stunning stone, wood and glass entrance that was designed to make an impression. As Dot and the girls entered the home, there was a reverential awe to their demeanor. They had the certainty that whoever built the home had done so with tender loving care. They stared upward at the 25' cathedral ceiling with its dynamic log rafters and handcarved diagonal support beams which boasted sweeping design lines with angled planes. The livingroom was open and spacious with extra-wide Eastern Pine plank floors. The exquisite mountain-theme decor and furnishings gave the home an elegant and regal appearance. There were even log stair railings and trim.

Every room seemed to have its own exceptional view of the surrounding mountains. There were six huge bedrooms and three modernized baths. The extra-wide doorways featured arched custom-carved Mahogany doors that brightened the living spaces. The large open kitchen had granite counter tops, custom cherry cabinets, a huge walk-in pantry. There was luxury in every detail of the beautiful furnishings and fixtures, the high ceilings, the massive wooden beams and the large picture windows.

After oohing and aahing over every room, they gravitated in unison to stand before the enclosed hearthstone fireplace. The wall of warm, multicolored ageless stones stretched from floor to ceiling. Each stone varied in size and texture but lent stature and conveyed an image of quality. When Dot reached out to touch the mosaic stone pattern, a rush of emotion overwhelmed her. As she lovingly ran her palm along the surface of the smooth stones, she closed her eyes and imagined the expression of awe that would have donned Ben's face had he been alive to see it. She envisioned the home as the perfect place for her family and saw them spending time near the fireplace, enjoying the peacefulness of solitude.

Mrs. Hirsch took a seat in one of the sofa chairs to watch as the two girls stood on either side of their mother and wrapped an arm around her waist. She could tell they were a closeknit family. She didn't know what their financial background was and at that moment, didn't much care. What struck her about them was how they honored her home. Mrs. Hirsch couldn't define why, but she knew they were different from all the other buyers who had viewed her home. Others had spoken only of how they couldn't wait to tear this section down, or rebuild that section. It wasn't her business what anyone did to remodel the home after she'd sold it. It was just a nostalgic idiosyncrasy within her that demanded she sell only to someone who would cherish what she and her family had built it for. Mrs. Hirsch stood abruptly and asked if they would like to see the "grounds."

Wiping the tears from her eyes before she turned to face the homeowner, Dot composed herself and they followed her out of the door. Dot didn't know what Mrs.

Hirsch was thinking, all she could tell was that something was afoot that she couldn't put her finger on. The only thing Dot knew for certain was that they could not afford the house. Nevertheless, she would finish the tour and thank Mrs. Hirsch for her time and graciousness.

As they stood on the deck of the home, just above the two-car brick garage, they stared far into the distance at the land's boundaries. Without turning to look at her, Dot told Mrs. Hirsh, "The only thing missing from your property's landscape is an abundance of trees. A botanical garden would compliment the lush greenery of the land. The garden should be a tribute that includes a spectacular assortment of trees strategically placed to take one's breath away."

Dot raised her arm and pointed far off. "In that part of the field, I would plant huge shade trees. Trees like the Cottonless Cottonwood, the Western Catalpa, the Silver Dollar Gum, the Arizona Ash, and the mammoth Weeping Willow. There should also be medium-sized pines and oaks like the Stone Pine, the Pine Oak and the Red Rock Oak Tree.

"I would grow flowering trees to give vibrant color to the landscape such as the Purple Smoke Tree, the Purple Robe Locust and of course Flowering Plums for their rich, varying shades of purple blooms. I'd include the Chaste Tree for its lavender blue flowers and I'd plant Wisteria and Crape Myrtle Trees for their pink, white, and red blooms. I'd round out this scenic landscape with fruit and nut trees. Peaches, apricots, pomegranates and figs. The fruit would be so sweet and succulent, it would melt instantly in your mouth. And quite naturally, I'd have to plant a pecan tree. Every flower, every tree, every pond and all the grasses, would be loved and well tended and would compliment the surrounding land."

When Dot finished verbally creating her dream garden, every one of them envisioned the Garden of Eden. They could see the raw beauty and extraordinary vividness of colors spawned by abundant plant life. So descriptive was Dot's vision that with her eyes closed, Mrs. Hirsch swore she could smell fresh peaches and that she could see and hear the white flowering Wisteria trees fluttering in the wind. She opened her eyes and was disappointed that the trees had not magically appeared. Feeling the ache in her knees, she sat in one of the cushioned deck chairs.

Mrs. Hirsh had only one question for the Jamison family. "Perhaps you could sell some of the land and use the money to build your garden," she suggested.

With her back still turned to Mrs. Hirsh, Dot peered out over the land. "I would not sell one inch of land on this property." With her arms wrapped around herself, Dot spun around to face Mrs. Hirsch. "In fact, that was your husband's dying wish, wasn't it? He passed away in the very chair in which you sit. He didn't want the land sold piecemeal as some of your children do. He, like you, wanted to ensure that it remained intact."

Mrs. Hirsh stared at Dot in silent wonder. She was quiet for so long that, not knowing how she would respond, Erika reached out to grasp Aaryn's hand. When Mrs. Hirsch finally spoke, she said, "Have a seat, Mrs. Jamison. Tell me about your family."

Hours later, they settled on a price, one that made Dot insist that Mrs. Hirsch's attorneys draw up the paperwork as she wanted no one to think she was taking advantage of an elderly person. Mrs. Hirsh had slashed her asking price by more than half solely because she wanted the Jamisons to own her property. How Dot Jamison knew so many intimate details of Mrs. Hirsch's personal and family life, the Jewish woman could not say. Judaism was her faith, but she understood that God worked through people in mysterious ways. In advance of the Jamison's visit, Mrs. Hirsh's heart had already been prepared for a family of three that would come to purchase her home. Quite frankly, she hadn't expected the family to be African American. Not that their race mattered. Mrs. Hirsh knew what it was like to be persecuted and typecast. She just hadn't seen it in all the dreams she had recently begun having.

Before she and the girls left, Dot promised to make Mrs. Hirsch several blended herbal tea bags of Alfalfa, Black Cohosh, Ginger and Rosemary for her arthritis.

By the time the property changed hands weeks later, Mrs. Hirsch had indeed used the tea bags and all the other herbs Dot had sent her. Not only did her arthritis recede, but for the first time in many, many years, Mrs. Hirsch was medication free and at 82 years of age, her joints felt as good as new.

The Jamisons settled easily into life in Holladay, Utah. The girls were entering the ninth grade at Olympus High School. Though both of them were highly adept at mathematics, it was at once clear that they were behind academically. Dot quickly hired a tutor for private after-school sessions. It was unacceptable that her girls not be in the top tier of their class. She expected A's from them. Certainly, nothing less than a B. One of the many things Dot instilled in them was that they had an *obligation* to succeed in life. The girls understood what it was like for their parents to grow up in Alabama, so Dot made sure they studied hard and knew the value of an education. She taught them to hold their heads high and should they ever encounter it, to know that one way to overcome racism was to channel its negative energy into becoming an even better person.

Studying was a breeze for Aaryn. She was more comfortable with written words but was less socially adept. Whereas with Erika, Dot had to push her harder because she was more easily distracted. Perhaps because of Erika's strikingly good looks, it was paramount to Dot, that her child be not just another pretty face.

By midyear their grades were on track and Dot eased up on her restrictions. Erika soon blossomed into a social butterfly while Aaryn began to run track and discovered a love for rock climbing.

When she wasn't spending time with her girls, Dot was planning and planting her botanical garden. She and Mrs. Hirsch kept in touch through written correspondence because Dot had promised to send pictures of the garden as it developed. One of the parting gifts Mrs. Hirsch dropped in Dot's spirit before her departure to Israel was that she should seriously consider branding and selling her teas. The more Dot thought about it, the more she liked the concept until finally she sat down and mapped out a strategy. She would name her teas "Nature's Brew" and market them as an upscale brand. Cherry Blossom, Orchard Peach, Peppermint Spice and Honey Dew Vanilla were a few of her original creations. All she needed to finance her dream was the necessary funding. She would not touch the money from Ben's life insurance policy because those funds were set aside for the girls' college education. Still, Dot believed a way would be made.

Just as everything seemed to take off for Dot and the girls, the second half of the prophesy Erika and Aaryn had spoken about Kenilworth unfolded. An increasing number of deaths were being reported in the town, but some of the killings were bizarre. When the decomposed bodies of two missing children were discovered, the town demanded the killers be found and brought to justice. A week later, a pair of seven and eight year old sisters were reported missing. Their plight made national headlines. Kenilworth was portrayed in the news as a heathenish bastion of crime—a modern day Sodom and Gomorrah.

One night, Dot's dreams were interrupted. She saw a small hand reaching out from a grave, groping as it tried to claw its way from beneath the surface. She awoke distraught and could not return to sleep. Grieved in her spirit, Dot got up and went outside on her bedroom balcony to quietly pray in tongues. An image of spilt blood crying out from the ground came through to her as she prayed. The smell that assaulted her nose made her flesh crawl. She sought her bible and turned to the Twenty-third Psalms.

After the girls left for school that morning, Dot walked the grounds of her property and began to talk to God. She inquired of His wisdom, direction and guidance. But above all, she asked Him to remove from her the darkness which her dream had left within her soul. Dot knew from what was revealed to her, that something horrible had happened to one of the missing Kenilworth girls. Now, she desperately feared for the life of the other child. But if she called local authorities to tell of what she knew, would they believe her? Her ties to Kenilworth were severed.

Why should she become involved with something so removed, especially when her present circumstances were going so well?

What spurred Dot to action was asking herself the simple question, *"What if it were her daughters?"*

Realizing there would be no reprieve until she acted upon what was revealed to her, Dot went inside to make the call.

The Carbon County Sheriff's Office was located in Price, Utah, about nine miles from Kenilworth. The four-man crew policed the surrounding areas which were made up of about twelve tiny towns. Accustomed to bare minimum crime levels, Sheriff Owens and his deputies were overwhelmed by the surge of Kenilworth crimes as well as the current child crisis at hand. When Salt Lake City law enforcement volunteered their services and staff, the Sheriff gladly accepted their assistance.

A hotline was established for callers with information about the missing Kenilworth children. Most of the resident's "hot tips" were useless and unverifiable. Manpower was too precious to waste tracking dubious claims. Some callers swore aliens from another planet were responsible for the recent rash of violence. Others professed that ghosts and demons were the sole perpetrators.

One drunken caller, David Swyder, demanded to be immediately arrested. Mr. Swyder confessed to committing all the crimes which had recently taken place in town. In a whispered voice, he also confessed to killing his own wife and chopping her body into a million little pieces—a crime the Sheriff would have taken seriously had he not suddenly heard the physically abusive Mrs. Swyder screaming in the background for Dave to get off the bleeping phone before she busted his head. Just before the phone line went dead, the Sheriff heard a loud thwack that resounded through the receiver.

The Sheriff was on duty the morning of Dot Jamison's call. As he listened to her describe the whereabouts and condition of one of the missing children, a chill went through his body. Gut instinct told him that her details were too specific to dismiss. Her descriptions too graphic. He knew well the area she named. It was an abandoned farmhouse off US-6. When he hung up the phone, the Sheriff quickly radioed one of his deputies to check out her story. Twenty minutes later, one of the missing children's shoes was found at the specified location. Search units were hurriedly assembled to scour the property. One of the Blood Hounds picked up the scent and led his handler to a freshly dug grave near the base of an old Oak tree.

When the shallow pit was partially uncovered, a nearby officer lost the contents of his stomach. Others turned away from the sight of the young girl's mutilated body.

Less than an hour had passed from the time Sheriff Owens had taken the hotline call. He contacted the Salt Lake City Police Department and asked the Chief to send a car to pick up Dot Jamison.

When the enemy comes in like a flood, the Spirit of the Lord shall lift up a standard against him. Dot knew she would need the comfort of those scriptural words in the days ahead. As the police vehicle drove up her driveway, she'd known intuitively that they were coming. She closed the pages of her bible and rose from her seat on her balcony to prepare for the two officers who would knock at her door.

Driving at speeds of 100 miles an hour, they arrived in Kenilworth in record time. At their destination, police cars with flashing lights were parked along the road leading to the house. Police officers had formed a line to keep reporters and the gathering curiosity seekers at a distance. The immediate area surrounding the house was cordoned off with yellow crime scene tape. They parked and one of the officers opened the door to extend his hand to Dot as she stepped from the back seat of the vehicle. She was lead the distance to the rear of the house.

When Sheriff Owens saw Dot Jamison and the Salt Lake City officers approaching, he broke away from his conversation to go meet them. There were nearly ten thousand residents combined in all the nearby towns and it was impossible to know them all. But he did remember Dot Jamison. She was a woman regal in posture and mannerisms. A no-nonsense kind of person who didn't suffer fools gladly. Yet, whenever someone was in need, she was the first to lend a helping hand.

"Thank you for coming," Sheriff Owens said as he clasped her hand.

"I won't tell you that I'm pleased to be here, Sheriff. Nevertheless, here am I."

The Sheriff nodded his understanding. He, too, wished the circumstances were different. He thanked the Salt Lake City officers and led Dot toward the sight of the grave. He felt her hesitation as they approached the mounds of unearthed dirt. Thankfully, the young girl's body was covered with a black tarp. The grounds were photographed and forensic samples taken. The area was now considered part of the crime scene and was not to be disturbed.

When the Sheriff had spoken to Dot over the phone, she'd told him she needed to visit the scene in order to know more about the other missing child. She'd told him it wasn't something she could give voice to over the phone, it was an inner leading that she was following.

Sheriff Owens had only spoken to one other officer about Dot Jamison. He had told all others the tip came from a hotline caller. While his statement was true, what the Sheriff couldn't explain to anyone was what Dot told him of how she knew where the child's body lay buried. No one would believe that she'd seen it in a dream. The Sheriff hardly believed it himself. He was a God-fearing man. But he was also an empirical man who needed tangible evidence in order to believe most things. Though she was a civilian, Dot Jamison was batting a thousand and Sheriff Owens wanted to hear more of what she had to say about the missing children.

They had almost reached the grave when Dot leaned toward him and whispered for him to have the officers standing around it to depart. Her need for privacy didn't make sense to Sheriff Owens but he honored her request. As the men departed throwing puzzled looks over their shoulders, the Sheriff watched Dot approach the tree, which stood about four feet from where the child lay buried. She squatted before it and patted the ground beneath her. Dot scooped up a handful of the earth's soil and shifted it around in her palm. Some of the dirt drifted back to the ground as it slipped between her fingers. As Dot's hand slowly closed around the remaining soil, she lurched forward onto her hands and knees as if someone had punched her in the stomach. When the Sheriff hurried to her side, she waved him away and crawled to the tree's base before running her palm along its bark in jerking motions. The Sheriff didn't know if she were *feeling* the tree or if she was trying to regain her balance. She just kept patting the tree and whispering unintelligible words.

It was eerie watching her. But as he stood to the side, Sheriff Owens' surroundings seemed to fade away. He was no longer aware of all the background chatter but was suddenly conscious of the gentle sway of the tree's branches and the rustling of its leaves. He saw the tears streaming down Dot's face. Although her stream of words became slightly louder, he still couldn't understand what she was saying. Unconsciously, Sheriff Owens edged forward and knelt beside her prostrate body. It was when he touched her softly on her back that he felt it. Something shot through his body like a jolt. It was the kind of strong feeling one might get from a small electrical shock. As the sensation traveled his body, an expression of awe mingled with horror dawned on his face.

When Sheriff Owens raised his eyes upward, he *swore* he could hear the trees whispering. The strange language Dot was uttering was made as clear to him as it already was to the trees surrounding them. *He understood!* Suddenly, he saw what she saw! Blood crying out from the ground! Like a film rapidly rewinding, he saw the series of events as they unfolded. The brutal, sickening and revolting images twisted his gut. Sheriff Owens staggered to his feet and ran toward the house as fast as his aging legs could take him.

He reached the broken down stairs and hurried up the porch. "She's inside!" he shouted to the officers who were standing nearby staring at him with perplexed expressions.

"Sheriff, we've already searched the house. No one's in there," one of the officers said.

"I'm telling you, she's here! And we've got to find her quickly!" The Sheriff beckoned his deputies and shouted at them to tear the already decaying farmhouse apart. No one was leaving until the little girl was found.

This time Dot sat in the front seat of an unmarked squad car. Sheriff Owens wanted to drive her to the hospital, but despite her soreness and exhaustion, Dot wanted only to go back to her home in Holladay.

Little Shelby McKoye was found gagged, beaten and bound in a hidden cellar deep beneath the abandoned house. She was alive, but barely. She'd been rushed to the closest hospital and would require years of psychological therapy just to overcome the terrible ordeal she'd suffered at the hands of one twisted and demented child molester. The man was a drifter who had come, like many others, in search of a mining job. He was arrested outside a tavern in Kenilworth. The police could barely restrain the mob of people who sought to exact their own brand of justice.

Sheriff Owens and Dot were silent during the drive to Holladay. Dot was simply grateful that he drove within the speed limit.

There was so much the Sheriff wanted to say, but every time he tried to speak, no words would come forth. He'd been a law officer for over forty years, yet he couldn't explain to anyone what had happened back on that property. The soft, muted language of the trees. The tiny voices from the blood crying from the ground. The bright flashes of light that accompanied the ghastly images of what had been done to the little girls. The precognitive glimpse he had of the bound child that assured him, despite what everyone else said, that she lay hidden somewhere on the grounds of the property. The images of the other children who had also been murdered. The face of the man who had committed the deeds. How in God's name could he explain any of it?

So many times did he try unsuccessfully to speak that Sheriff Owens gave up. Sensing his inner turmoil, Dot reached out her hand and he immediately grasped her palm with no questions asked. He, a man of an ultra-conservative background, held fast to Dot Jamison's reassuring hand as it rested on the car seat. There was nothing romantic in their touch. But somehow the firm clasp of her hand yielded all the communication he needed. When she finally released him, words were unnecessary. A peacefulness about the entire situation had crept over him. A gentle knowledge that, despite the evilness of what had taken place, goodness still remained within the world.

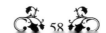

Sheriff Owens remembered that Dot had asked that he keep her identity private. But he didn't see how that was going to happen. Not after the events of the day. It would certainly be impossible given that reporters had snapped photos of her left and right as she was carefully assisted into the police vehicle. He also remembered seeing a photographer take a photo as Dot was helped off the grass where she'd fallen near the tree. Unfortunately, it was beyond his control.

As he continued driving with both hands on the steering wheel, Sheriff Owens knew he might not ever be able to verbally explain all that had transpired—not even to his wife. But his spirit knew what had happened. Though other children had died, at least one child's life was spared. That's what he would focus on when he completed his written report. That, and bringing the perpetrator to justice, was enough for him.

Dinner was ready and waiting for the girls when they arrived home from school around 4PM. But the house was unnaturally quiet and Dot was not around to greet them when they walked through the door. Normally, she was there waiting for them so they could all share about their day. But on this occasion, she lay upstairs in her bed and when they knocked on her bedroom door, she told them she just needed a few hours of rest.

Erika and Aaryn washed up, ate and were sitting in the livingroom laughing at Gary Coleman's antics on Diff'rent Strokes while they completed their homework. The television volume was set low so they had no problem hearing the first of several television crews on their drive way. Alarmed and unaware of the day's events, they were clueless as to why a rush of reporters would be standing outside the entrance of their home, ringing their doorbell.

Instead of answering the door, they ran upstairs to Dot. But it wasn't the news reporters at their door that frightened them as much as the sight of their mother shivering and lying on her side with her knees pulled to her chest. The only time they had seen their mother looking so fragile was after their father had died. Somehow, they thought that whole experience was behind them.

When told of the reporters outside, Dot was able to tell them only in part what had happened. When she finished speaking, the girls sprang into action. Aaryn hurried to mix together an herbal brew for Dot while Erika ran to shutter all the windows. They came back to the bed and stayed by Dot's side hovering and praying over her for hours.

The herbal mixture Aaryn had made consisted of flax seed and coconut oils. But it also contained a hefty dose of cascara sagrada, a natural laxative. When several hours passed and Dot didn't get up to go to the bathroom, Aaryn wanted to give her an enema. But Erika was completely against the idea. She couldn't see them spreading their mother's butt cheeks and sticking a douche bag tube up her behind, no matter how desperately Aaryn claimed it was needed.

The nature of what her daughters were discussing as they quarreled outside her bedroom, brought a small smile to Dot's face. She had to admit that as unpalatable as the tea was, it did ease the queasiness she felt in her system. However, at that moment, the tea's powerful laxative force was making itself known. Dot struggled to rise from the bed and made it to her bathroom in the nick of time.

Outside in the hall, Erika and Aaryn fell silent the moment they heard motion coming from inside Dot's bedroom. They peered inside just as she slammed her bathroom door. Relief spread through them as they sensed that their mother was going to be okay.

But turmoil rumbled throughout their house over the next weeks. The flurry of media attention in the wake of Shelby McKoye's rescue was overwhelming and unwanted. Dot was forced to put a "no trespassing" sign on her front lawn to keep the reporters at bay. She couldn't stop them from taking pictures from beyond her property's borders, but they had to respect her curtilege, the area of privacy around her property. It prohibited them from camping out at her door.

All of it wouldn't have been so bad had the media not fabricated and stretched the details of the story out of proportion. Sensational headlines nicknaming Dot "The Kenilworth Witch" and dubbing her "The Crime-Busting Psychic of Holladay, Utah," were splashed across the papers. Dot didn't condone the use of psychics. The very title offended her. But since she'd chosen not to speak to the media, in the absence of her personal story, they created their own. The newspapers gathered gossip and tidbits about Dot from the many Kenilworth residents who professed to know her personally.

Most of their claims were downright ridiculous. Craving the media's spotlight, people stepped up to the microphones and blatantly lied. One man, whom Dot had never seen before in life, told the Salt Lake reporters that she'd sold him a rabbit's foot that had healed his hemorrhoids and helped him to win the lottery. Not to be outdone, a woman standing nearby claimed it was true because with every full moon, she and Dot Jamison personally went on witch hunts to find rabbits and cut off their feet.

Outrageous as the stories were, they made salacious headlines and sold newspapers to a voracious public that was immediately curious about the "wealthy" and "secretive" people who had purchased old man Seymour Hirsch's property.

Ironically, Dot also acquired a fan club. She began to receive all kinds of phone calls and mail. People wrote to find out where their lost pets were. Wives called in the middle of night demanding to know where their husbands had disappeared to and who they had run off with. But the saddest cases were the letters and checks she

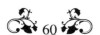

received from parents desperately wanting to know where their missing children were. Most of the mail Dot didn't respond to. But the checks she always returned, sometimes with a note that included several verses of scripture.

If there was one bright side to the whole sad affair, aside from the child's life that was saved, it was the $50,000 reward check that Dot received. She hadn't even known there was a reward. She accepted it because she knew she could use the money to form her Nature's Brew tea business.

Although Dot was able to brush the rumors aside with ease, it was her daughters that concerned her. Aaryn was less troubled by all the gossip and attention. Years of ribbing from Kenilworth children about their mother and about her own skin color had thickened her hide and inoculated her from needing the approval of others. She was that rare individual who was not overly concerned about what others thought of her.

Erika, on the other hand, had grown sullen, withdrawn and resentful over the unwarranted media speculation. She felt she was reliving the Kenilworth nightmare and was embarrassed by her peers at school. She went through a period where she was clearly unhappy and she spoke often of wanting to transfer to another school. Unfortunately for her, Holladay had but one high school and an excellent one it was. Erika was angry and felt that Dot should have let the local authorities handle the Kenilworth crisis and should not have gotten involved.

For the first time, there was a wide rift in their familial bonding. At night when they prayed, when it was Erika's turn, instead of praying in complete sentences, she would simply say "Amen."

Dot understood the reasons behind her child's rebellion. All she could do was talk to her and continue to keep their lines of communication open. She made clear to both her girls that she was not a perfect person, neither was she a perfect parent. Though she couldn't pinpoint them, Dot figured she'd made mistakes as she raised them. She could only ask for their understanding and their forgiveness. She'd done her best, given them her all. She made it plain that in the end, they were both responsible for how they lived out the rest of their lives.

Erika and Aaryn had previously decided they both wanted to study Biomedical Engineering and attend the same college. But after the Kenilworth incident, that changed for Erika. She was determined to put space between her and her sibling, and at every cost to be different from their mother. Whatever college Aaryn picked, Erika would go in the opposite direction.

All she knew was that it galled her to be thought of by others as "lesser than." Right or wrong, people's opinions did matter to her and she did not see the wisdom of attracting unnecessary attention. Which was why, in her opinion, the so called "gift of prophesy" was no "gift" at all.

Chapter Six

Erika Slaughter knew her marriage was in trouble. She and her husband, Michael, were a far cry from divorce proceedings, but something had certainly shifted in their union. Married for seventeen years, they had three children. Joshua was nine and deeply analytical. He loved baseball and building things with his hands. Mia at six, was an unusual child. She was tenacious and not above throwing a punch to settle things in her favor. Marcus, the baby boy, was two.

They had met while Erika was a junior studying Chemical Engineering at Tennessee State University. Michael, a Nashvillian, was a first year law student down the road at Vanderbilt University. His four-year M.B.A./J.D. program had examined business law and produced top tier lawyers who understood the complexities of corporate finance.

Erika had received a full scholarship from TSU. Unlike her twin sister, Aaryn, she couldn't wait to leave the State of Utah. Of the three full scholarships awarded her, she'd chosen TSU because, not only was it a Historically Black College, but it had an excellent Engineering program and was over sixteen hundred miles from Utah. The distance was important. Having been raised all her life around most races other than her own, Erika wanted to experience being around other African Americans.

By the end of her third year of college, despite all her extracurricular activities and her academic success, Erika remained a virgin. It bothered her that this was the case. Every time she and her friends got together, the conversation inevitably turned to men—how many they had and what they were doing with them. Though Erika laughed along, she was too embarrassed to admit to being an untried maiden. If one believed all the stories her peers told, apparently she was the only one on campus who wasn't having multiple orgasms and swinging from the chandeliers every weekend.

She desperately wanted to experience being with a man and now that she was out from underneath her mother's rule, she couldn't guarantee she would wait until marriage before that happened. What she could guarantee was that her first encounter would be more than just a one-night stand. However, finding that special someone was looking increasingly impossible.

Until she met Michael. They met at a Shoney's Restaurant over an all-you-can-eat breakfast buffet. She was scooping up the last bit of grits when someone spoke from behind her saying, "You could save some for the rest of us."

When Erika looked up and saw the tall, dark, handsome hunk smiling down at her, it was all she could do to keep her plate from slipping from her fingers. As captivated as she was, recovery was none the less essential. Cool as a cucumber, she

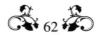

smiled and said, "I wouldn't mind sharing if there was more. But since you look like a steak and eggs kind of man, please allow me." Reaching for the tongs, she picked up three slices of bacon to add to the strips he already had on his plate. "Have some bacon instead."

They stood smiling at one another until one of Michael's friends called from the back of the line, "Can you two move along so the rest of us can eat?"

Michael was clearly beguiled. He'd noticed her from his table and had deliberately left his pals (and his uneaten portions) to grab another plate and had edged his way behind her. When she smiled at him and teasingly put bacon on his plate, his heart was hers to claim. Michael thought there must be truth to the adage that *"a way to a man's heart is through his stomach."*

He ditched his buddies and followed her back to her table where he cajoled her friends into making a spot for him. With a silver tongue, he charmed them all. Humoring and encouraging them to talk about themselves, all the while trying to elicit information about Erika.

For her part, Erika was completely enamored. She loved his smile, his tone of voice and his mannerisms. She loved staring at him. Just watching him eat captivated her attention. Had he asked for it, she would have laid the entire breakfast bar at his feet. On the way back to their campus she gladly endured the ribbing of her friends.

Theirs became a stormy romance. Michael's curriculum didn't leave much room for many social activities. But every spare moment he had, he spent with Erika. Within months of knowing him, she was the one who wanted to take their relationship to the next level. The heated kisses and fiery embraces were fine, but she wanted more. Michael, however, knew she was a virgin and was very respectful of that. He wasn't compelled to bed her just to strip her of her virginity. He simply enjoyed being with her, being in her company, and making her laugh. He loved that she challenged him intellectually. He loved her attentiveness. And because she was gorgeous, he loved having her on his arm. It was a paradoxical role reversal that Erika was the one pressuring him for sex and he was the one holding out. Finally, Michael told her he wanted her to meet his parents. But first, he invited her to church.

When he extended the church invitation, Erika really didn't want to go. She accepted only because she could tell it meant a lot to him. Though she'd led her mother to believe otherwise, Erika hadn't been inside a church since she'd left Utah. And the truth was, she hadn't missed it. That Sunday as she walked down the aisle of Michael's Pentecostal church, heads swung in her direction. She became aware of the furtive looks and knew she was being sized up only because of who she was with. Erika found herself being as judgmental about the people around her as they were of her.

When the service was over, Michael introduced her to his parents and Erika knew right away that his mother didn't like her. Neither did his sisters. That following week, Michael didn't call her like he normally would have and Erika knew it was because his family had said some negative things about her. When she confronted him, he denied it. But clearly he was avoiding her. Crushed and devastated as she was, Erika was also angry.

Weeks went by before she finally accepted the fact that Michael no longer wanted to be with her. When one of his friends invited her out on a date, she accepted out of spite and loneliness. There were no sparks, but he was sweet and she felt comfortable in his presence. One night, they were entering a movie theatre as Michael and the girl from his church were leaving. When he did a double take, Erika pretended not to notice him. She kept walking and pulled her date right along with her.

When Michael phoned that very night, Erika had her roommate tell him she hadn't yet returned to the room. He continued to call over the next several weeks and she kept avoiding him. Maliciously, she hoped he felt the same pain she'd felt when the shoe was on the other foot.

One afternoon Erika was thrown for a loop when she came back from class to find him waiting in her dormitory room. How he'd managed to sneak past the security guard and bribe her roommate into letting him in, she had no clue. But because he'd gone through all the trouble to do so, Erika knew she held the upper hand.

Michael was angry at being rejected, but one look told Erika he was also hurting and jealous. She had him sit in one of the wooden chairs and she shocked him by straddling him with ease. His anger evaporated as she assaulted him with passionate kisses. She was in the driver's seat and knew how far she would allow the petting to go. What she had once offered him freely could now only be obtained at a price. She would find out if the asking price was one he was willing to pay.

At Michael's request, she dated no one but him. She started attending church with him on a regular basis. She didn't go because she enjoyed it. She went because her attendance was a means to an end. It was obvious to her that his family had not warmed up to her. His exgirlfriend sat with his parents in one section of the church and she and Michael sat in another.

Erika was due to graduate at the end of the following semester. So, a few weeks later, it was with excitement that she told Michael about the job offer she'd received from an engineering firm in Boston. Erika doubted she would take the job, but she didn't let Michael know that. Ignoring his sullenness, all she spoke of was her future in Boston. Instead of expressing happiness for her, two weeks after dropping her bombshell, Michael proposed.

He wanted a big church wedding. But because she didn't want to contend with his family, Erika convinced him that they didn't need an elaborate ceremony. She reasoned that if they waited until she graduated, she could find a good job in Nashville while he continued pursuing his law degree at Vanderbilt. They could get their own apartment and once he graduated, they could use the money saved from not having a huge wedding as a down payment on a home—especially if that home just so happened to be in another city, state, and town. Erika had it all mapped out. She spoon fed her strategy to Michael by talking dollars and sense. And of course, he loved every one of her ideas.

One evening during a particularly heated petting session, they nearly went all the way. And because he burned hot for her, Michael was the one who suggested they slip away to Las Vegas where they were married that same weekend.

Erika's machinations may have conjured up a husband, but there was no guarantee she would keep him. In her haste to outmaneuver, outwit and out-strategize Michael's family, whom she viewed as her opponents, it never occurred to her that she and Michael had never said "I love you" to one another. Illogically, Erika put her God on the backburner and promised to someday return to all things spiritual. By confining Him to the distant recesses of her memory, Erika had, indeed, managed to put her past behind her and craft a new life for herself. But, in the process of this reinvention, Erika treated her God like a toy—something to be used only when and if He suited her purposes. She didn't know it then, but she would pay dearly for her spiritual betrayal.

Part II

"Maybe all one can do is hope to end up with the right regrets."
~ Arthur Miller

"Sometimes the heart sees what is invisible to the eye."
~ H. Jackson Brown, Jr.

Chapter Seven

Timing was everything, the difference between life and death. Odds were against him saving them both, but he would not leave without her. Forty seconds remained before the next explosion ripped throughout the building, decimating the entire southeast section along with him and the girl. The air above him was thick with smoke from rapidly approaching flames. Mindful of the electric wires that dangled menacingly around him, he ignored the pain in his body as he crawled through glass and rubble to reach her. *"Thirty seconds!"* announced the voice recorder on the bomb. Struggling to his knees, he wrapped his arm around her waist to pull her up. *Trapped!* Her dress was crushed beneath a huge chunk of fallen concrete. Forced to improvise, he ripped it from her body, hauling her to her feet. *"Ten seconds!"* Lunging through the broken glass doors, he thrust his weight against hers, propelling them both over the iron railing. Milliseconds after their feet left the tenth floor balcony, the thermal explosion rocked the building. Huge balls of fire erupted from the eviscerated structure. Shattered glass and concrete fragments cascaded through the air. He and the girl plunged ten floors below crashing into the ocean. Moments later, he resurfaced amidst wreckage holding her body above water. Clasping her close, he spotted the shoreline and led them to safety.

Jayson lay sprawled in the sand gasping for breath. The female stunt double quickly departed to be replaced by Rita Danza, his leading lady. The actress positioned herself atop him, clad in a skimpy bra and thong bikini. Water droplets streamed down her lush body giving her the appearance of someone freshly hauled from the ocean. Her wet jet black hair fanned dramatically around their faces as she clung to him desperately. The cameras and lighting were angled to maximize her sex appeal. Though she was positioned to look helpless, Jayson knew the Salma Hayek look-alike was anything but.

"Cut!" yelled Kurt Wyler, the movie's director.

The sharp feel of teeth piercing the side of his jaw caused Jayson to wince and pull away.

"That's for standing me up last night, you jerk." The beautiful Latin bombshell jumped to her feet and kicked sand in Jayson's face before turning to stalk back to her trailer. Staring after her, Jayson stood to wipe sand particles from his face and neck. His and every other male eye on the movie set followed, in appreciation, the curvaceous starlet's angry departure.

"Don't remember that scene in the script. What was that about?" Kurt asked as he approached.

Jayson's jaw clenched as he stared at the blood on his fingers. Without displaying his mounting ire at the temperamental star, he replied, "I guess she felt the need to embellish the script."

Kurt Wyler was directing the action film Jayson was presently starring in. He was as world famous for his films as Steven Spielberg or James Cameron. Jayson had starred in several of Kurt's films. Each one was a box office hit. Their current film, *Pendulum II,* was expected to generate even greater ticket sales because of the sequel's daring special effects. The movie was a guaranteed draw for millions of viewers because of its dazzling death-defying stunts, action-packed thrills and chilling edge-of-the-seat suspense. Critics were already abuzz with pre-movie hype though the movie's release date was more than six months away.

Mikyra, Kurt's Executive Producer, came and stood alongside them. She worked with Kurt on most of his films. Interrupting their ogling, she said to Jayson, "If she bit you, you should let the set medic look you over to make sure she didn't give you rabies."

Kurt laughed at Jayson's expense as they walked towards the front of the film set. "You asked for her, Jay, you got her. I told you from the beginning we should have waited for Angelina Jolie. But you had to have Rita. After eight weeks of putting up with her histrionics, thank Christ that was the last film shot."

Jayson wasn't about to permit Kurt the luxury of selective memory. "Need I remind you that we *both* agreed to go ahead with filming so the release date wouldn't be delayed by nine months while we sat around waiting for AJ? Besides, Rita has her own box office appeal. Every red-blooded male able to breath on his own accord will pay to see the film just because of the junk in her trunk."

Mikyra said, "At least we've got good footage of the dustups between you two. We should release some of the photos to the rag mags to ensure we put our own spin on what's written. Otherwise, someone else on the set will sell the story and the gossip mags will have a field day. I can see the headlines now. 'Fireworks on *Pendulum II* Movie Set.' Or, 'Jayson Denali Attacked by Scorned Actress.'"

Jayson nodded reluctantly. He'd known better than to become entangled with his highly strung leading lady. He was more irritated with himself than anything. Since he'd ignored the warning signs, he was forced to deal with the consequences. The good news was, now that the production phase was complete, they could both move on to greener pastures—something Jayson was willing to do after only two weeks into the affair.

Jayson said, "Can you have PR work with my publicist? Tell them to neither deny nor confirm there's anything between Rita and I. If they must add to the rumor mill, I want them to say she dumped me and not the other way around. I've got enough negative publicity and paparazzi hounding me as it is without sparking a war of words between her camp and my own."

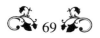

The action scene Jayson had just completed was the last sequence needed to usher the movie into post production, the phase where the director, editor, sound engineer, composers and musicians worked their magic to transform raw footage into the actual movie. It was not unusual for a film to be shot out of sequence. Most movies were. In the final scene they'd just completed, the moment he and Rita's stunt double had leapt from the tenth floor balcony, they had landed on a cushiony air bed that broke their fall and were then driven by boat to the spot of water from where he would swim, with Rita's double in tow, back to shore. In real time, if someone jumped from the tenth floor of a building and landed in water, it would pretty much be like hitting the ground. So the scene was filmed using weighted, life-like dummies that hit the water with a huge splash.

All around them was chaos as production assistants barked orders to an army of men and women who rushed to break down the set's cables, wires and blazing lights. This was the anonymous mass that worked away from the spotlight but who labored as hard as anyone. Since the final scenes of the film were shot in warm and spicy Miami, the wrap party's location was set at The Crobar, one of the most popular night clubs in South Beach. The entire crew was invited to the celebration that evening. As tired as Jayson was, it was his intention to attend for a few hours before flying to Los Angeles to his home in Beverly Hills for a weekend of rest. Come Monday, he was set to fly to Salt Lake City to take his mother to Shriners Medical Center.

Jayson welcomed the upcoming weekend of rest. The 12- to16-hour work days he could handle. It was performing many of his own stunts in back-to-back feature films that had tired him out. The demands of dangerous fight, fall, and explosion-packed action scenes were causing him to go the extra mile to execute increasingly difficult stunts. At 36, each fall somehow seemed harder than it had when he'd first started acting. Over the past fourteen years, he'd had his fair share of bruises and hospital visits: an injured shoulder, a torn Achilles tendon, a broken rib after falling three stories while filming a fight scene. As exciting as his action films were to his fans, they were becoming downright perilous for him. And yet, he loved every moment of it.

During the span of his Hollywood career, Jayson had become known as the "man's man" actor because of his gritty action roles. He relished portraying intelligent characters with sheer determination under the most extreme circumstances. Avoiding roles where he was cast as the romantic lead, he preferred the comfort of gunfire and the naked female form. Men related to his onscreen presence because of his cool virility. To them, he came across as the type of person they would want to hang out with.

Jayson's career trajectory saw him play everything from a crafty spymaster and unflappable undercover CIA agent, to edgier roles like the brilliant detective who cracks the unsolvable case, to the mastermind criminal and the misunderstood rogue cop. In each role, he was always the hero who saved the day and ultimately won the girl. Jayson was among the few elite actors whom moviegoers watched in anything he starred in and whose photo moved people to buy magazines in grocery stores. He was the versatile actor whom people wanted to dine with and the elusive one whom many women wanted to marry.

Constantly tracked by bellicose paparazzi, experience had taught him to avoid being overexposed by the media. Whenever he granted interviews he evaded questions about his personal life. Since he was very often photographed with a new and different bombshell beauty, the question on most people's minds was when would he pick one and settle down. He was after all, the sculpted, ruggedly handsome, charismatic superstar whom Hollywood viewed as one of its most sought-after eligible bachelors. Hollywood insiders knew him as suave, witty, and capable of oozing persuasive charm at the press of a button. Yet, Jayson was also known as much for his heavy partying as he was for his venerable acting skills.

He was that rare actor who viewed it as his personal obligation to pour his all into each of the roles he portrayed. Jayson realized that people hungered for the escapism that his films provided. They were the vehicle that thrust people from their daily lives and catapulted them into a whirlwind of fantasy and drama. There was truth behind the old adage that said people would forget what was said and that they often forgot what was done, but they never forgot how someone else made them feel. That was the impact he wanted his movies to have on people, transporting them through an emotional wind tunnel before safely delivering them back to reality.

Because of his struggles in the early part of his acting career when he was on a steep learning curve and forced to quickly grasp the complexities of the trade, he took his roles seriously and was intensely disciplined, which kept him in demand as an actor. One successful movie led to the next. He took absurd cinematic risks, became ungodly hot at the right time and simply rode a wave of star-like momentum. Jayson became a young gun who developed into a superstar, one fantastic film at time.

Directors loved working with him because he was the consummate pro—dependable, always prepared and he was never late. Jayson would forever be grateful to Al Pacino, Morgan Freeman and Clint Eastwood for their coaching and expert advice to him in the early days of his acting career. Over the years, he'd co-starred with the best of Hollywood's elite. He had teamed with icons such as Russell Crowe, Denzel Washington, Robert DeNiro, Sam Jackson, Angela Bassett and Jodie Foster. And every Mother's Day, for the past thirteen years, he sent bouquets of roses to Ruby Dee and Eartha Kitt out of gratitude for the way they had taken him under their wings and showed him so much love and affection.

Jayson's intensity as an actor had earned him the reputation of being aggressive and driven. Unlike many of his star-studded peers who fought to outdo one another, his goal was not to be better or greater than the next actor. Three times he'd been nominated for an Academy Award. Two of those times, he'd known outright he hadn't stood a snowball's chance in hell of collecting the award. The third time, he'd thought differently because that same year he'd walked away with the Golden Globe for Best Performance by an Actor in a Motion Picture. The subsequent whispers of him taking home the Oscar were strong. Everyone knew the Golden Globe Awards was the precursor to the Oscars. Normally, success in a category at the Golden Globes translated to success in the same category at the Oscars. Only, in his case, it didn't happen. Now, Jayson just wanted to be the best actor that he could be, regardless of whether he ever had the hardware to prove it. The total gross earnings of all his films combined was more than three billion dollars, something only a handful of stars could lay claim to. In spite of his box office superiority, Jayson still felt his best work was ahead of him.

He found, too, that acting could also be a lonely endeavor. The more isolated the film's set location, the less of a social life he had. Whenever he worked in heavily remote places, such as the time he spent eight weeks in Antarctica filming an action sci-fi thriller, Jayson would see very few people while shooting his movies. The close confines and proximity between actors, actresses, cast and crew was why many ill advised romantic liaisons sprang up between them. Curiosity and boredom was an iniquitous combination. It was for this reason that many times he traveled with his own personal crew when he was filming.

Jayson had known all four members of his entourage for more than ten years. Each of them worked for him and loved to travel. Years ago, he'd established The Bestow Foundation, a not-for-profit company that specialized in steering inner city children in the Milwaukee and New York City areas away from drugs and gangs by focusing on education, sports and the arts. Each member of his crew worked to run, fund and manage the charitable organization. The set up ensured that they could travel with him at a moment's notice to many of his film locations.

Three males and one female comprised his personal phalanx. Unlike a typical star's posse of hellbent, substance addicted losers who constantly blazed a path of troubled commotion, Jayson considered his friends a well-read affable bunch whose humor and wit melded nicely as a group. Their presence also kept him grounded and down to earth in a world filled with late-night parties, prowlers, revelers and rabid fans.

Despite being a workaholic and always on the go, more often than not, Jayson managed to surround himself with people. He occasionally stole away for solitude, particularly during the times he traveled by himself to Paris where he owned one of his three homes. But people everywhere flocked to him because of his fame and he learned long ago how to cope with a lifestyle where everyone wanted something from him, whether it was his money, his time or his person. Lack of companionship was never a problem. His challenge lay in carefully selecting the people he allowed into his circle. Especially the women, who were plentiful and came at him from every direction in all shapes, colors and sizes.

Jayson had kept his word over the years, by not becoming heavily involved with any one woman. His relationships were habitually brief, lasting anywhere from a few weeks to a few months. However, the passionate burnout cycle of meet, greet and delete was growing old even for him. Not since his modeling days had he felt the persistent gnawing urge for something more. The feeling was subtle but present nonetheless and he threw himself into his acting roles to subvert it. A new Bugatti Veyron, a short, curvy two-seater car with massive power that could hit 62 mph in 2.5 seconds, cost him more than a million dollars and diverted his attention for while. A spacious, custom-made luxurious Sun-Reef yacht of unsurpassed quality temporarily indulged his senses. And owning a private Gulfstream G650 jetliner with designer VIP interior intended to reflect his distinct personality and taste, certainly satisfied him a long while.

Still, all the expensive toys and fancy trinkets in the world couldn't fill his need for inner solvency. The next femme fatale, the next piece of eye candy, the next challenge conquered, none of it filled the void he identified but would not bring himself to give voice to. In his private reflections, Jayson wondered why he hadn't met that certain woman who could make him want to give up his freedom. The few times he'd thought he'd found "the one," blissfulness invariably fizzled after a while. Perhaps he was a victim of the very fantasies he portrayed on screen. He'd seen enough movies and read enough books to know that happy endings abounded everywhere. Everywhere, he felt, except in real life. A part of him had become jaded and hardened over the years. What once was hard for him to do, sleep with more than one woman at a time, was now improbable for him *not* to do. He'd noticed a certain callous streak within him that was unbecoming given that he'd not always been that way. Softening his stance or changing his outlook was unlikely. He couldn't turn back the clock, nor did he want to. He could only move forward and hope that at some point in his life, the relationship gods would smile down upon him.

He had returned to his trailer to escape the humidity of Miami's 98-degree weather as well as the lurking, ever present crowd of female onlookers and autograph seekers. He was seated on a stool as the set medic cleaned the nasty wound on his ear and applied a small Neosporin patch. Even though he'd been bitten hard, Jayson would have simply swabbed some alcohol on the bite mark had Mikyra not shown up at his door with the nurse at her side. He was signing one of his photographs for the woman when his cell phone rang.

"Denali."

"Jay, it's Dez. What's this I hear about you heading back to the coast tomorrow morning? You're supposed to come to New York. Did you forget about the gettogether I lined up for this weekend?"

"Aaagh! I forgot all about that. Hold on." Jayson put the phone down to thank the medic and give her the autographed picture. As he was showing them to the door of his trailer, Mikyra quipped, "Stay away from women who bite, Jayson. There are plenty of us who don't."

Jayson sighed at her and shook his head. "Get out," he told her, though not unkindly, as he steered her to the door in exasperation. Every time he worked with Mikyra, she needled him for dating women outside of his race. Happily married to the hip hop rap star, Lewdakris, Mikyra was one of many matchmakers who felt they knew just the right person to rock Jayson's world and sweep him off his feet. He was not about to debate with her the fact that he felt all women were essentially the same, regardless of race, with only slight variations.

"Dez," Jayson said as he grabbed his cell phone. "Is there any way we can postpone the spread for a week or two?"

"Can't do that, Jay. Man, how could you forget? I've been planning this thing for weeks. Studio execs from Paramount and Universal will be here. I've got the CEO of J.P. Morgan Chase coming with several other deep-pocketed moneymen. There will be about three top models attending, plus as a personal favor, Ashela Jordan has agreed to give a private musical performance. You can't blow this meeting off, Jay. The funding of your next two films is at stake. My own credibility would take a hit if you failed to show up. What's going on with you?"

Dez had found his own brand of success. A numbers fanatic since childhood, he'd obtained his MBA in Finance from Harvard Business School. He'd been with J.P. Morgan Chase, one of the premier investment banks in the world, for ten years and was an Investment Manager. Ever since Jayson had brought him a hundred million of his dollars to manage and invest, new financial frontiers were opened to Dez. The clientele he now provided expert financial solutions to was wide and varied. He was a hard working, polished professional and savvy at navigating the fine prism between street professionals and corporate board room execs. He didn't judge or discriminate when he used innovative wealth management concepts to enhance the financial portfolios of people from all walks of life. When persons with questionable backgrounds approached him with millions of dollars that they needed to invest, he directed them to investment bankers who could legitimately set up corporate structures for them to invest their funds. Dez didn't do what he did just to earn a living. He worked solely because he loved the challenge and intensity of the financial arena. He had what was for him, the ideal career and harbored not the barest hint of jealousy for anything Jayson had accomplished.

Not only did he successfully oversee a portion of Jayson's wealth, but Dez was part of a new avant-garde financial group on Wall Street responsible for raising funds from institutions that had not previously invested in films. These new investors were flush with fat cash and were changing the way films were being made in Hollywood. With the availability of bundles of cash, the film industry was focused on making big budget movies that could provide vast returns along with profitable merchandising deals.

A prime example was the film Jayson had made the previous year called, *The Evil Within*. Produced by Barry Blaustein, it was a screen adaptation of Walter Mosley's novel, *The Man in My Basement*. The thriller cast Bruce Willis as the psychopathic villain who offered Jayson's character $50,000 in cash to rent out his basement for the summer. However, once the money changed hands, he was quickly caught up in a terrifying and bizarre series of murders. The movie had cost $75 million to make but had generated a worldwide box office total of over $360 million. And then there were the Jayson Denali and Bruce Willis action figures along with the teen-rated video game offshoot of the movie.

Amid huge profits margins from that particular film, Dez brought in the CEO of J.P. Morgan Chase to put together an enterprise that could help finance films costing over seventy-five million to make. Even with studios culling their profits before anyone else saw a dime, he figured private investors could still realize significant yields. Dez knew that if he could create buy-in with his CEO, their company stood poised to rake in millions from movie financing.

With the success of independently financed films such as *The Evil Within*, a new wave of outsiders were salivating at the prospect of investing in a movie's potential profits and they were pouring in to finance movies. Dez just wanted to ensure that he, Jayson and J.P. Morgan Chase were well ahead of the curve. Additionally, Jayson was hot property right now. It seemed everyone was clamoring to cast him in their films. Directors Martin Scorsese and Quentin Tarantino had written roles specifically for him and Jayson's agent was sifting through scripts that were pouring in by the truckload.

Dez repeated his question. "What's going on, Jay?"

Jayson thumbed the covered wound on his ear as he paced the length of the decked-out trailer. "Wendy, my assistant, left me a message on my cell reminding me about the party tomorrow night, but I thought she was referring to tonight's wrap party at The Crobar. Here's the deal, Dez. I was supposed to fly out tonight and head to LA to spend Saturday and Sunday with Syl. I'm taking her to Shriners in Utah on Monday morning. You know she hates to fly so we're giving her a sedative so she'll be knocked out during the flight." Jayson sighed. He hated disappointing his mother, but it looked as though there was no way around it. "But I'll come to

New York tonight after the wrap party and head back to LA after your spread is done. That way, at least I'll be able to spend all of Sunday with her."

"How's she doing, Jay?" Dez's voice was filled with quiet concern.

Jayson took a seat on his leather sofa. "Honestly, I don't know, Dez. Sometimes, she just sits staring into nothingness. I've tried everything just to get her to smile like she used to. And every blue moon, it seems I'm able to break through. But for the most part, there's just nothing. It's the most frustrating thing I've ever encountered in my life. She's not experiencing dementia. Her therapist says she's suffering from something called Dysthymia, which is nothing but a fancy term for clinical depression. I could be wrong, Dez, but I think she's stuck in the past, filled with all kinds of regrets. From what she's said, she regrets how she treated Carmin. And I know she certainly misses your dad. Man, after he died, that's when it seemed like she started going downhill. After she had the stroke, she just seemed like a shell of her former self."

"What are they going to do for her at this place you're taking her to?" On the other end of the line, Dez got up to stare out of his Wall Street office window. High on the thirty-third floor of New York's Financial District, his view from the Emporis Building was crowded with elaborate concrete structures.

"Shriners comes highly recommended. There's much more information available about the hospital than about their individual doctors. But there is one doctor in particular who's renown for working with paralyzed people. They say she's a miracle worker. You remember Darius Grey, the football star who was paralyzed from the neck down after he went in for the game winning touchdown? He wrote a book where he talked about his healing experience. I didn't read the entire book, but the little I did read was fascinating. I don't know if she can do anything for Syl's paralysis, but I need to give it a try. She's all I've got, Dez. Her and you, you're the only family I've got."

Despite finding out about what transpired between his dad and Jayson's mom, Dez harbored no ill will toward Mrs. Denali. She'd simply been too kind to him when he was growing up. While his own mother was emotionally unavailable, Mrs. Denali had treated him with nothing but fond affection. She'd welcomed him nightly at her dinner table as part of her family. As much as his dad had treated Jayson like his own son, Mrs. Denali had showed him no less love. Dez found out while in college about his dad's affair because his mother had told him about it. By that time, his mom was drinking so heavily that she was sober only fifty percent of the time.

Shortly before Dez graduated from college, both his parents were killed in an automobile accident. His mother had been behind the wheel when the car crashed head on into a brick wall. Though the Dept. of Motor Vehicles had categorized the wreck as an accident, it bothered Dez that no tire treads were found at the scene. It indicated that no effort was made to stop the car from crashing at the speed of 85 miles per hour. He didn't want to believe that his mother may have deliberately crashed the car. But the conversation he'd had with his father weeks before the tragedy during spring break of his senior year of college, made him wonder.

His friend was entrenched in his modeling career at the time when Dez had asked his dad if he was seeing Mrs. Denali. Mr. Lloyd admitted it and told Dez that he'd asked his wife for a divorce. Of course, Dez's mother wanted everything, the house, their savings, his business assets, anything that was worth value. It only served to enrage her further when his father failed to put up a fight. She was infuriated that he was willing to sign away everything merely to gain his freedom. He had made it clear that he intended to marry Sylvia Denali and was more than willing to start over with nothing but his good name.

Dez would never forget how saddened his father had been at having to tell him he was leaving. But he'd brightened instantly the moment he spoke of Sylvia Denali. He said he'd never loved or been loved as unselfishly and unconditionally as when he'd met her. His shotgun marriage to Dez's mother had occurred only because she was pregnant. They hadn't ever loved one another, but they had both been determined to make the best of a bad situation. He worked long hours at his business. She smoked, drank and made a career out of ordering unnecessary things from every catalog known to man. Every time his dad mentioned Sylvia Denali by name, this goofy grin would spread across his face. And Dez, who couldn't remember ever seeing his dad so contented, couldn't begrudge him his newfound happiness. When his dad had asked for his forgiveness, Dez was only too willing to give it. Three weeks after he returned to Morehouse College, Dez received the tragic news that his parents were killed in a car accident.

With both his parents gone and no other siblings to speak of, Jayson was the closest thing to family that Dez had. In his mind, they weren't just best friends, they were also brothers. There was nothing he wouldn't do for Jayson. Though they rarely talked about it, he knew Jayson felt the same way about him. Distance often separated them but they remained closer than ever. There was very little, if anything that they didn't share between them. At one point, the sharing had even included women.

They were in their midtwenties when he and Jayson became embroiled in a paternity suit after a three-way, one-night stand. The entire sordid affair had taught them a valuable lesson about keeping their sexual liaisons separate from one another. They met the woman at a party at the home of another influential actor. After several drinks and establishing a quasi-bond, the three had agreed to a night of consensual sex. Except, what appeared to be a brief enjoyable bout of forbidden pleasure turned into a nightmare when many months later, Jayson was served a summons notifying him that he was named in a paternity suit.

At the time, Dez's name had not been mentioned in conjunction with the lawsuit. Jayson, however, had questioned its merits because both he and Dez had used condoms that evening. Initially, the woman denied that Dez was present at the time of consummation. Things turned nasty when DNA testing proved that Jayson was not the bi-racial child's father. Up until the DNA submission, Jayson had nearly settled out of court because of all the negative publicity surrounding the case. But he'd balked at the $35,000 a month payment the plaintiff's lawyers were demanding.

During the course of the court proceedings, an anonymous tipster revealed that the woman had slipped his used condom into her purse and had later harvested what she thought was Jayson's sperm to become pregnant. Jayson's attorneys hired investigators who found several witnesses who testified that the 36-year old woman, who had three children from three prior relationships, bragged to friends about how she'd deliberately secreted Jayson's condom into a ziplock bag and then wrapped it in a hand towel filled with ice.

Court reporters cleared the courtroom in their haste to report the shocking news. The media dubbed the case the "Million Dollar Stolen Sperm Spree." After new developments exploded onto the media's front pages, the woman's attorneys fought unsuccessfully for closed-court proceedings and a gag order preventing both sides from discussing the case with the media. But it was like closing the barn door after all the animals had escaped. The complainant was branded as one of a new type of predatory women who targeted men, mostly stars and athletes, exclusively for their sperm. The entire affair was sordid to begin with and Jayson was completely embarrassed and ashamed of his actions. Nevertheless, to say that he felt violated was putting it mildly. The woman's credibility was shattered. Under intense cross examination by Jayson's female attorneys, the woman admitted to having sex with the two men and confessed to taking the condom. Dez had already submitted a DNA sample, but surprisingly even he wasn't the child's father.

With public empathy on Jayson's side, the case wound up being dismissed. But both of them learned a mighty lesson from the entire incident. Though he was under no obligation to do so, but more likely out of guilt, Jayson had his attorneys create a trust fund for the child so that her educational costs would be covered. A third party would administer the small fund so it would not be connected to Jayson in anyway. The child was, in his opinion, the only victim of the entire mishap. The flip side for Dez was the moral lesson they both got schooled on. They learned to flush their prophylactics and to be more discerning about the women they slept with.

Dez's reverie was broken when another call came through to Jayson and he was asked to hold. He knew that Mrs. Denali's health was a dark cloud looming over his friend. He also knew from experience how devastating it was to lose a parent. It was even more traumatic to lose both of them at the same time as he had. What bothered Dez was that lately his friend was not his normal "happy-go-lucky-never-had-a-bad-

day" self. When Jayson came back to the line, Dez said to him, "You know, Jay, I should fly to LA with you to visit Syl."

Jayson jumped at the offer. "Man, that would be great. She'll be glad to see you, too. We could leave right after your spread and be in LA within six hours."

As he zipped through the calendar on his palm pilot, Dez said, "Yes, I can do it. I'll line up some meetings in LA for Monday while you're in Utah and be back here in New York by Tuesday evening." Dez added, "J-Man, we could even get in a couple of rounds of golf Tuesday afternoon. You up for it, or what?"

As competitive as he was, compared to Dez, Jayson sucked at golf. The only way he could get geared up for the game was if they bet money on each hole. Dez was an above average golfer with relatively low scores. Jayson on the other hand had only recently improved his game because he was tired of getting creamed by the competition. When he stepped on the greens, to him, it was just a game. But to each of his fellow players, it was an opportunity to beat a larger-than-life hero who was known for saving the world—even if it was only in the movies. Jayson's biggest problem lay in correcting a wicked golf slice in order to shave strokes off his game. Dez didn't know about the private lessons and was in for a surprise.

"You're on, chump. Don't forget to bring your checkbook," Jayson said. He could hear Dez laughing even as he hung up.

Over twenty five hundred miles away, Aaryn was engaged in a different kind of challenge. She stood at the base of Burning Sun, a towering sandstone that snaked 1,500 feet above the floor of Kolob Canyon in Zion National Park. The sandstone crag she was preparing to climb was steep and overhanging, its ruddy, salmon-like color giving its walls a smooth, almost varnished look. Perhaps only the top ten percent of climbers in the world could handle the route Aaryn was about to navigate. Few, if any, would attempt climbing it without a rope. Indeed, Burning Sun, like most rock routes with a grade above 5.11, was not for the faint of heart.

Aaryn dipped her fingers inside her chalk bag to dry the sweat on her fingertips. Nature's soothing sounds comforted her, romancing her adventurous sense of freedom, while deep, relaxing breaths focused her on the task ahead. Dusting excess chalk from her fingers, she stared upwards planning and assessing her route. She'd climbed Burning Sun years before. But she'd had a partner then, a belayer to prevent her from falling as she climbed. Back then she'd scaled the full length of the canyon within nine hours. Today she was alone, free soloing without the benefit of a rope. She was out to push her limits this time around so her goal was to improve her time by climbing halfway to its top in less than four hours. Though the route was well defined, the challenge for her in ascending the long and difficult finger and hand cracks lay in balancing precise, fluid maneuvers with skillful patience. That, and not being overly cocky as the simplest mistake or smallest broken rock hold could send her tumbling to her death. Countless experienced climbers had suffered fatal injuries due to a casual attitude. Just because she'd climbed routes much harder than Burning Sun didn't mean she could fly.

With her descent rope strapped securely to her back, Aaryn began her ascent. Using excellent footwork, she ambled up the first 100 feet with ease. At this level, the rock holds were large and allowed her plenty of options as she moved up the face of the cliff. Since climbing was mostly in the legs and feet, she didn't need brute strength as much as she did a finely honed sense of balance. Three hundred feet above ground, the route steepened and handholds were located further apart, making each vertical foot she had left to conquer that much more difficult.

At four hundred fifty feet, the route was now about nuance, finesse and the skillful presence of mind needed to get her out of the tight spots she was about to encounter. She knew the climb was beginning to test her comfort level because the natural fear of falling attempted to assert itself into the back of her mind. She forced herself to breathe deeply and to push aside the niggling fear threatening to creep over her. Contrary to popular belief, climbers knew fear. But it was their ability to push beyond the barrier that enabled them to scale the highest mountains while others remained grounded. She knew, too, that the greatest challenge facing any rock climber was not allowing their fear to control their movements. Aaryn needed to channel hers into concentrating on the rock and each successive move. Her face was a picture of intense deliberation as she brought her thoughts back into focus. With fingers gripped tightly inside a small two-finger pocket, she pulled herself into a handsized crack that would lead her up the rest of the way.

Even as she scaled higher, it became a lethal dance of balancing herself into precarious positions on the rock without falling. Five hundred feet above ground, Aaryn reached the crux, the most difficult part of her climb. The crack had long since narrowed to accommodate only her fingers and the tips of her toes. Her muscles glistened with sweat as she quickly dipped her fingers in her chalk bag to dry the moisture accumulating on her fingers and palms. The visual Aaryn had of herself at the top of the route enabled her to ignore the growing ache in her fingers and toes each time she jammed them into a tiny crack. Fifty feet higher, she reached a jutting overhang that required enormous strength to pull through.

To complete the climb, Aaryn knew she'd need every ounce of her energy to connect with the desperate finger jams and tiny pockets spread throughout the crack above her. Taking several deep breaths, she steeled herself before relinquishing her last good hold to tackle the daunting overhang. One move, two moves. "Breathe. Focus," she told herself almost harshly, the rock feeling unnervingly slick beneath her fingers. She looked down at her feet, willing them to find purchase inside the tiny cracks and the featureless surrounding walls. Three moves, four moves. Everything around Aaryn faded into a blur of hand, foot, hand, foot combination moves. The ledge above beckoned, her finishing point looming like an impatient lover waiting to embrace her. With her end goal before her, Aaryn moved upward with machine-like determination—doing as opposed to just thinking.

She blew past another hundred-plus feet of rock before pausing to visually lock in the large ledge that marked the end of her route. Though only a scant thirty feet away, to Aaryn's tired muscles, the distance appeared more like a mile. Admitting the climb was more difficult than she'd presumed, Aaryn consoled herself that it was almost over. Just thirty feet to go. But in that brief moment of inattentive mind wandering, she felt her tenuous foothold vanish. Without warning she found herself dangling more than 600 feet above ground. Fighting a desperate surge of panic, Aaryn's feet skidded wildly over the smooth rock below her as she struggled to find footing. Her jaw clenched as she forced stillness throughout her members. She could not afford to swing wildly in the wind. Tentatively, yet with the skill of a ballet dancer, her toes searched the rock below her like a blind man reading braille. As she searched for a hold to prevent herself from plummeting to the ground, time slowed to a crawl while she clung to the rock by fingers and hands only. Aaryn could feel her fingers sweating, their traction loosening as her hold in the crack slackened. With imminent death looming, just before her fingers popped free of the crack, Aaryn's toes latched onto the smallest of holds. Instantly, before gravity cast its decisive vote, she quickly propelled herself up to a large hold above.

She clung to it, her muscles quivering and her breath coming in short gasps. Forcing her muscles to return to normal from their jelly-like state, Aaryn climbed the remaining distance to the ledge. With fingers on both hands splayed, she stretched and reached for its edge. Wrapping her fingers around it, she pulled herself up onto the ledge and dropped rag-like into a lotus position praying and thanking God that she'd made it.

Minutes passed before glancing at her watch, she noted her timing was precisely at the four-hour mark. "Not bad, girl. But you can definitely do better," she told herself smiling. Cheating death left her with a sense of euphoric satisfaction. Wiping the sweat from her face, she took a moment to survey the landscape around her. Everything looked different from such a great height.

It was a mental workout as much as a physical one. Yet reaching the top of the rock was not the only goal for Aaryn. It was the journey along the way that was equally as important. As physically strenuous as the climb was, Aaryn had made good use of her kinesthetic skills, her ability to use her body and sense of touch to learn about her environment. There were many reasons why she climbed. For the challenge, for the thrill, and the acute sense of personal accomplishment that followed each of her successful ascents. As she leaned against a large boulder, she stared far into the distance before closing her eyes to concentrate. Potentially distracting stimuli which she'd blocked out during the climb, she focused in on now. The sweet sounds of nature, the rustling of the wind, the warm breeze blowing over her, the rock's changing array of colors caused by the sunlight and the screeching from the redtailed hawks soaring far above.

As she closed her eyes again and brought her attention inward, mere moments passed before Aaryn sensed the nearby presence. It never failed that whenever she reached the peak of one of her climbs, she would feel the presence of an angelic force. Aaryn had come to identify the specter as her father. In the aftermath of every climb, she could sense his closeness in the stillness that hovered around her. Maybe that was the other reason why she climbed, so she would be reminded of rainbows and that she wasn't alone on a journey that at times felt completely isolated.

Minutes later, the spirit departed and her reverie was broken. Aaryn grabbed some chalk and located the bolts that she would need to safely scale downward. She checked her anchor and brake system, secured the knots in her rappel sling and started her descent toward ground level.

"...he *knows* how much I love him. How could he treat me like this after I've declared my love?" The stylish pair was strolling through New York's East Village engrossed in conversation. As the man poured out his heart over his troubled affair, his female companion listened compassionately. Apparently, martyrdom had its benefits.

Clasping one hand to her chest, the blond woman elbowed her friend, "Oh, my God!" Interrupting her friend's unceasing stream of babble, she said, "Tell me that's not Jayson Denali?"

Conversation came to a fast halt as they stopped dead in their tracks. "Well, pluck my brows! Honey, that *is* him. Hurry, so we can get his autograph."

Jayson was exiting his chauffeur-driven Mercedes S600 in front of Dez's Carriage House on 2nd Street. He had just reached the curb when he spotted the man and woman quickly bearing down upon him. There were times when he traveled with a body guard and then there were short trips such as this occasion when he did not. Though the couple appeared harmless, looks were often deceiving in today's world of gawker-stalker fans so he was forced to make a snap judgment about the two people rushing toward him. The effete-looking man wildly waved a piece of paper overhead while his other hand swung limp from the wrist. Jayson knew such feminine sashaying in a man indicated only one thing. Trailing just behind him in her miniskirt and four-inch pumps, the man's companion was every inch a woman. Within seconds they were in front of him.

"Mr. Denali, can we pleeeeease have your autograph? We've seen all your movies and we're such huge fans!" A pen was wielded in Jayson's direction as the excited man proceeded to run down a list of Jayson's films.

By comparison, his friend appeared speechless. Awestruck, she stared at Jayson in complete fascination. Her mouth formed a paralyzed "O."

Used to fans accosting him even in the unlikeliest of places, Jayson scribbled his signature on the piece of paper before handing it back to the man. Noticing the woman's muteness, Jayson reached out to shake hands with her. "Nice meeting both of you," he said and slipped inside the door suddenly held open by Dez's doorman.

"Honey, can you believe it? Jayson Denali just shook your hand! If I were you, I wouldn't wash it for a week! At least *I* got his autograph. Ohmagawd, he's so gorgeous! Those eyes, those lips…And did you notice how his big hand dwarfed yours?" The man's eyes rolled as he shivered delicately. "They say Denali's better endowed than most stars. After meeting him tonight, I believe it. He's definitely got that "it" factor that lets him connect with his audience. Namely me."

Recognizing his friend was still in a trance-like state, he said, "Honey, snap out of it! I think I just fell in love." As he slipped his arm around his friend's waist to pull her forward, his relationship troubles were put on pause. "What a man…" he continued as he led his mute, starry-eyed companion down the street.

As soon as Jayson stepped inside his friend's home, he was embraced by several of the models and quickly introduced to the rest of the guests who swarmed around him.

Two days later, Aaryn was inside the Rophe Room at Shriners having a one-on-one/heart-to-heart with Betty Billenjer. Betty was a wealthy Bostonian whose family heritage was *WASP* and steeped in old money. Unlike the rest of her socialite clan, she cared little about the fact that her family lineage descended from one of America's earliest presidents. She cared even less about their influential financial, cultural, and political spheres. Social registers and society pages were anathema to Betty. In fact, all she cared about were her cats. At 50, Betty was the black sheep of her family. She was a no-nonsense recluse of a woman weighing in at a formidable 347 pounds. Betty was a big girl. She nearly tripled Aaryn's weight and because of it Aaryn required help with positioning her onto the healing station for her first therapeutic massage. No ordinary massage tables these, the bottom of the healing stations were made from titanium steel while the upper portion that people stretched onto was five feet wide and seven feet long. The stations were equipped with a gas spring to automatically raise and lower at the press of a button to various positioning heights minimizing the risk of injury to patients who might have difficulty moving onto and off of it. The stations were also a blessing to the backs of physicians and staff alike. Built for the patient's security, the table top was a heavily foam-padded luxurious bed of comfort. Each station could hold a maximum of six hundred pounds.

At issue were the male nurses who would assist Betty onto the Rophe Room's healing station. While Aaryn had lowered it to an eighteen-inch height, because Betty was paralyzed on her left side, she still required assistance to help her onto the table. However, when Betty saw the assisting nurses were male, she was overcome by a sudden wave of selfconsciousness and insisted that only female nurses be allowed to aide her. After she threw a royal fit at the sight of the three male nurses, Aaryn had asked everyone to leave the room so that they could discuss the matter in private.

From previous consultations, Aaryn suspected some form of physical abuse at play in Betty's medical histogram. Even though she denied it, Aaryn knew in time Betty's body would reveal whatever truths her mind decried. Because Betty was eager to get well so she could continue to care for her cats, Aaryn was committed to helping her in her healing process. As for calling in additional female nurses to help haul her onto the table, Aaryn was adamantly opposed. She would not endanger herself or any of the other nurses just to accommodate Betty.

"Betty, I know this is an anxious, insecure moment for you, but the nurses are only here to help. Once they assist you onto the table, their work will be done and they'll leave immediately. Only you, Kyoko and I will remain in this room."

Aaryn wasn't the only one holding firm, so was Betty. "Out of the question," she harrumphed. "Why, they would see me naked and I simply cannot allow that. I wouldn't be surprised if all they wanted was to get a good gander at the girls. Why can't you and Kyoko help me onto that contraption?"

Kyoko was Aaryn's resident-in-training. With her petite frame, the Japanese girl barely tipped the scale at a buck-o-five while Aaryn weighed 125. Together, Betty still had them outgunned, outmatched and overpowered. And "the girls" that Betty so affectionately referred to were a pair of awesome 60HH beachballs that appeared surgically affixed to her chest. Only Betty's boobs were The Real McCoy upon which gravity had taken its toll. When Betty Bellinjer was introduced to people, most didn't look her in the eye. Men and women alike (although for different reasons) instead stared at her colossal-sized bosom. Rather than be embarrassed by the massive size of her chest or suffer the pain of a breast reduction, her breasts became a source of pride for her. Betty embraced the hefty pair and lovingly knick-named them "the girls." She often remarked to the nurses attending her, "Be careful with 'the girls'." And during her breast examination, extreme care was taken to heave "the girls" onto an exam table of their own. Even now, in order for Betty to lie flat on her stomach on the healing station, Aaryn was going to have to separate "the girls" by placing them on either side of her.

"No one is going to see you naked, Betty. I promise. As the nurses lift you onto the station, Kyoko and I will hold your gown together. You have my word that 'the girls' will be kept safely under wraps the whole time. So what do you say?"

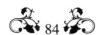

Betty sniffed haughtily, only slightly swayed. "I say it's poppycock!"

Finally, Aaryn said, "Kyoko and I cannot do this by ourselves, Betty. Neither can you. I thought you wanted to get well for the sake of your cats? How can that happen if we can't get beyond point A?"

Reminding her of her cats appeared to be Betty's undoing, the magical open-sesame. Gradually she relented and so began Aaryn's day.

Dr. Kyle Baldwin knew his 11:00 appointment had arrived because of all the commotion in the hallway outside his office. He was used to occasional voices of camaraderie between doctors and staff passing by. The din he heard now was louder and sounded like it came from more than just five or six people. He and his staff were used to accommodating well known and well-to-do individuals. Shriners had tended to a former United States President, an Israeli Prime Minister, stars and rock stars just the same. The buzz emanating from the corridor was the kind that resulted from someone who possessed a mixture of both star and rockstar quality. Just as Dr. Baldwin stood to investigate, there was a knock at his door.

"The Denali's have arrived, Dr. Baldwin." The receptionist's voice was tinged with excitement. The smile on her face was wide and her natural color was heightened.

Smiling, Dr. Baldwin said, "Show them in, Ambi."

The door opened wide and Jayson Denali strolled through it pushing his mother, Sylvia Denali, in a wheelchair.

He certainly makes an imposing impression, Kyle thought to himself. This man has the kind of charisma that only a handful of people possess. An analytical, mano a mano assessment of Jayson left Kyle with little doubt of why women flocked to him. The guy definitely had that "it" factor that drew women by the droves. Whether "it" was a blessing or a curse, Kyle was glad he, himself, would never know.

"Welcome to Shriners Medical Center. I'm Dr. Kyle Baldwin. And you must be the lovely Sylvia." He shook hands with Jayson before reaching down to clasp Sylvia's left hand as he knew she was paralyzed on her right side.

"I appreciate you seeing us. We've heard so much about your center."

"Thank you. We aim to heal. How was your flight and may I offer you something to drink?" Kyle directed Jayson to a seat.

"Our flight was good. My mother didn't complain too much. Although the sedative probably had something to do with that. She hates to fly, don't you Ma?"

Though the sedative Jayson spoke of had worn off, Sylvia remained quiet and subdued. As the hospital staff and nurses had fawned over her, she was aware that it was her son who really captivated their attention. She'd managed a half smile because Jayson was always a source of pride for her, with or without his fame, regardless of the circumstance. She nodded in response to her son's question and afterwards seemed to become lost in her own thoughts. Internally, Sylvia wasn't sure that she wanted to be shipped off to another hospital, irrespective of how highly recommended it came. She would have been content to be left alone with her past memories.

"That's understandable. I'm not too fond of flying myself," Kyle said, trying to break the ice. "Tell me, Mrs. Denali, would you like to see our facility?" When no response was forthcoming, Kyle spoke to Jayson. "I've arranged a short tour for you. I want you to know the place where your mother is going to spend the next six months rehabilitating. When we return we'll be joined by Dr. Aaryn Jamison. Shall we?" Kyle rose to lead them out of his office. He could easily have had one of his staff members conduct the tour, but he wanted to do it himself. He wanted a feel for the mother and son's interaction with one another. Thus far, the son was the picture of thoughtful benevolence as he sat close to his mother attending to her needs. Kyle would also use the opportunity to draw them out and form his own opinion in the event that Aaryn decided to shift Mrs. Denali to another physician.

Thirty minutes later, they were once again seated inside Kyle's office. Jayson Denali was overwhelmingly impressed by Shriners' state-of-the-art facility. Despite Mrs. Denali's silence, which he attributed in part to the mild sedative she'd been given, Kyle was confident that Shriners was a good fit for her. He liked Jayson Denali. In spite of his fame, the man appeared to be a down to earth person who genuinely cared about the well being of his mother. He was solicitous to the staff, speaking to everyone. Because Kyle believed in respecting an individual's privacy, Shriners had a strict no-autograph policy prohibiting staff from asking patients or their family members for autographs.

"Kyle, talk to me about Dr. Jamison. I've heard about her and I've read Darius Grey's autobiography so naturally I'm intrigued. But there's only a brief bio of her on your website. I guess in an era where most people want all their intimate details available for the world to see, I'm just surprised there's not more information available about her. Even a Google search didn't turn up much except for the two bestselling books she's written on the subject of Quantum-Touch healing. I couldn't even find a photo of her on your website. What more can you tell me?"

Kyle smiled. Aaryn's photo was removed at her own request. He was used to people and even the media wanting to know more about Aaryn.

"Dr. Jamison is one of the top doctors we have on staff. She's also the leading authority and force behind the breakthrough healing methodology known as Quantum Touch. The books you were directed to on Google have sold millions of copies. She's very much in demand and we're simply lucky to have her." Kyle was interrupted by a knock at his office door. "And speaking of her, this must be her now." Kyle got up to open his office door.

Jayson watched a woman walk into the room. There was something about her that he couldn't quite define and he found himself staring. Admittedly, he was also frozen in his seat because he wasn't sure if she was Dr. Jamison or another of the army of staff members he'd greeted earlier.

"Jayson, this is Dr. Aaryn Jamison. Aaryn, please meet Sylvia Denali and her son, Jayson Denali." As he made the introductions, Kyle felt discomfited and couldn't say why. He was used to people's reactions when they learned that Aaryn was an African American woman. Not always, but occasionally he was met with shocked expressions, such as the one Jayson was now caught wearing.

Near embarrassment because of his gaffe, Jayson quickly stood to his feet. He stretched out his hand to Aaryn, wondering if she knew he'd been expecting a Caucasian woman.

Wordlessly, Aaryn studied Jayson, her eyes narrowing imperceptibly. She stared at him so long that his hand fell awkwardly back to his side. When he returned her gaze questioningly, her penetrating gaze became almost rude. Finally, with her head tilted to the side, she seemed about to say something but changed her mind. Instead, Aaryn turned to Mrs. Denali and said, "Hello Sylvia."

Syl watched curiously the interaction between her son and the doctor. It was impossible for her to keep the half smile from alighting her face. Without saying a word, this woman had issued a subtle putdown of her son, but rather than be offended by how she'd dressed him down, Syl found she liked the doctor right away. Something about her informed the world that she was a woman who stood her ground. Besides, any woman who didn't fawn over Jayson at the drop of a hat deserved a second look in Syl's opinion. She was used to people greeting her with special attention because of her son's notoriety. Some people were jealous of Jayson and others wanted his attention, men and women alike. But there was definitely something about this doctor. Syl could hear it in the subtle authority in which the woman had spoken her name. Without giving it a second thought, Sylvia extended her hand in greeting.

Aaryn took her hand and held it in hers for a few moments. It was highly unlike her to be rude to a patient or to any of their family members. But her reaction to Jayson was intensely strong—and unexpectedly negative. His beauty at close range was unnerving and she'd forced herself to peer through his seductive gaze. All she knew was that in no way had she wanted to touch him. He was causing her sensory antennae to go haywire. Needing to block his energy from invading hers, she focused her attention on his mother.

Nonplussed by her reaction, Jayson sat down. The puzzled expression on his face was replaced by one that was deliberately void to mask his irritation. He couldn't remember ever being left hanging the way this woman had deliberately hung him out to dry with a simple handshake denial. He guessed it had something to do with his shock at discovering she was a black woman. Though he was guilty of the misjudgment, he'd meant no disrespect. He'd just been taken by surprise. He felt bad about it but it was too late to correct his faux pas. His couldn't have been the first time she received such a reaction. In fact, she probably got it all the time. If that was why she wouldn't shake his hand, his advice to her would be to toughen up. *Welcome to the real world,* he thought. But there was no accounting for the way she looked at him. It was an uncomfortable look, *as though she had stared right through him* and found him wanting. To be honest, Jayson was more disturbed by the way she stared at him than by her refusal to shake his hand. He was used to different reactions from women he first met. Some immediately assessed him physically as carnal thoughts ran across their mind, some were awestruck by his star symbol quality, and others were genuinely pleased to be in his presence. But none of that from this woman. The good doctor had assessed him and clearly formed an impression from which she'd written him off. In spite of her apparent rudeness to him, at least she had the good sense to be kind to Sylvia.

And speaking of his mother, there she was smiling at the doctor. Extending her hand to the enemy. *The enemy?* Jayson thought. Where did that come from? This woman wasn't his enemy. He didn't even know her. At least he didn't think he did. Just because she'd obviously made a bad snap decision about him didn't mean he had to make one about her. All that really mattered was whether or not she could heal his mother. But as he watched her embrace Sylvia's hand with both of hers, suddenly Jayson didn't want her touching his mother. Before he could say so, Kyle interrupted his thoughts.

In a conciliatory tone, Kyle said, "Aaryn, right before you came in I was telling the Denalis about your breakthrough work with Quantum Touch. Based on Mrs. Denali's medical history I think she would be an excellent candidate for Shriners' services." Kyle didn't quite understand the dynamics at play between Aaryn and Jayson, but he knew Aaryn. And knowing her as he did, he could see half a million dollars or more walking right out of his door and potentially out of his grasp. "Perhaps you could explain more to them about your work." Kyle threw a warning look her way, which Aaryn promptly ignored.

Without bothering to look at Jayson, Aaryn said, "I'm sure Mr. Denali didn't travel all this way to discuss my credentials. I'm more interested in you, Sylvia. Where would you say you are in your healing process? Are you prepared to heal or are you content to wallow in this sorry state that you're in right now?" Aaryn's tone was harsh as she gripped Sylvia's hand.

"Wait a minute. Don't talk to my mother like that. Just who do you think you are?" Jayson's anger at this woman's gall had boiled over. He could overlook her

blatant disregard of himself, but he would not tolerate her rudeness toward his mother.

Without addressing Jayson, Aaryn leaned forward and spoke directly to Sylvia. She said, "Sylvia, it appears the ball is in your court. If you've come all this way expecting me to heal you, you're going to be disappointed. I don't heal anybody. Whether or not you do heal is between you and your God. I'm only the facilitator. So again, I ask: are you prepared to heal or will you continue to welter in the past and forfeit your future? Only you can truthfully answer that question."

Suddenly Sylvia started crying. Without warning, a sob wracked her body. Aaryn released her hand and stood. So did Jayson. He looked menacing, as if he could bust a cap in Aaryn's behind.

Kyle was appalled as he sat looking from one to the other as though he was watching a movie at the picture show. When Jayson stood, Kyle rose and said, "Umm, why don't we all take a step back?"

"Who the hell do you people think you are? I thought this was a healing place." Jayson spoke to Kyle but stared dead at Aaryn. He had never hit a woman, but at this particular moment, he could have throttled Aaryn. "Dr. Baldwin, I suggest that you teach this doctor of yours some people skills. Apparently she's lacking in both social manners and sensitivity. Lady, I don't care how many stupid books you've written, I wouldn't leave a dog in your care." Jayson pulled Sylvia's wheelchair away from Aaryn's proximity and swiped several tissues from the Kleenex box on Kyle's desk. Still angry, he bent to console and tenderly wipe his mother's face.

Aaryn looked at the scene in front of her and said, "Kyle, you can relax. I'm not here to wipe Mr. Denali's nose. Nor that of his mother's. If Sylvia really wants to get well, I recommend one of the other doctors treat her." With that, Aaryn turned and walked out the room, softly closing the door behind her.

Kyle was totally at a loss for words. What had just transpired was unbelievable even to him. Aaryn's unprofessionalism was unprecedented and uncalled for. Instead of seeing dollar signs exiting his facility, Kyle simply wanted to avoid a lawsuit and the negative publicity that was sure to ensue if the Denalis left without a resolution to this situation.

Jayson and Kyle stared at one another. An apology on Kyle's lips and a string of curse words on Jayson's.

Surprisingly, it was Sylvia Denali who brought tempers into proper perspective. Sniffling, she took a deep breath and finally said, "She's right." Both Jayson's and Kyle's eyes swiveled in her direction as if she were a mad woman who suddenly discovered she could speak. Sylvia took the tissue from Jayson's hand and dabbed at her own eyes. After blowing her nose, which sounded like a horn, she said. "I needed that cry. Believe it or not, I feel cleansed and relieved. Like a heavy weight has been lifted. What Dr. Jamison said was true."

Ignoring everything his mother had just said, Jayson spoke out of anger. "Ma, that woman had no right to talk to you the way she did. It's unacceptable and I demand an apology." Jayson's anger was now directed toward Kyle since the original object had fled the scene. *Women,* Jayson thought.

"Jayson, be quiet, please. I can't explain how she knew these things, but she's right. I *have* been wallowing in self pity. I know I've been a burden to you."

"No, you haven't…"

Sylvia interrupted him, "Hear me out, please. When Dr. Jamison said the things she did, I realized I've been trapped in my own grief and remorse. The truth is, Jayson, I've merely been waiting to die." When Jayson shook his head, adamantly refusing to hear or believe a word she said, Sylvia reached out for his hand. When he took it, she said, "Son, it's true. Death was more appealing to me than the future. But, I'm telling you when that young woman spoke her words, something in me sprang to life. I realize now, *I do want to live.* I want to live to see you married and have my grandbabies, Jayson. I want to get better so I can care for them. But not just you, Jayson. I want Desmond to settle down as well. The two of you cannot continue to live as though you have no responsibility to anyone but yourselves. James would want me to look after Desmond. I know he would. He's as much my son and your brother as he was James'." Sylvia sighed deeply. "I can only do that if I get better. I want to stay here at Shriners and I don't want anybody but that good doctor, Aaryn Jamison, to care for me. No one else will do. Whatever it takes I want it to be her." Seeing the stubborn look on her son's face, she added, "Even if I have to pay for it myself."

Jayson looked mortally wounded. "Ma, you know you don't have to worry about money. Why would you even say that?"

"I say it because you've hurt her feelings, Jayson. And unless you go find her and apologize, she will want nothing to do with me."

Irritated beyond explanation, Jayson said, "Ma, there are plenty of other facilities we could go to. They would offer us the best of service for what our money could buy. Besides, even Kyle knows that woman's actions were unprofessional. Don't you agree, Doctor Baldwin?"

Kyle looked like a deer in headlights. Fortunately, he didn't have to respond.

"Shut up, Jayson. I mean it. Do you know, that's your problem? You think you can throw money at every situation and that's all it takes to solve it. I'm telling you I'm not leaving this hospital. So why don't you just get on your airplane and go back to wherever it is you'd really rather be. I'll pay for the treatment myself."

Stunned, Jayson couldn't believe his mother was arguing with him when this was all that silly doctor's fault. His mother hadn't spoken to him in this manner since childhood. Hell, not ever. At least not that he could remember.

Kyle cleared his throat. "Well, it seems that we've reached an impasse. Mrs. Denali, Shriners would be honored if you decided to stay. By all means, we would have it no other way." Relieved, Kyle was glad the situation was under control, though it was far from resolved.

"And what of Dr. Jamison? Can you speak for her as well? Would she be delighted to have me? Or will I be passed on to someone else like an old hand-me-down sock?" When he failed to respond, she said, "Just as I thought. Speak up Dr. Baldwin. Can you guarantee that I'll be treated by Dr. Jamison?"

Sighing, Kyle turned to Jayson and said, "I'm afraid, Jayson, your mother is correct. I cannot stress how much this facility would love to have her. But no, I cannot guarantee that Dr. Jamison would be the physician treating your mother. Unfortunately, or fortunately however one wishes to view it, Aaryn chooses her own patients. I cannot command her to attend anyone. It's specified in her contract. However, perhaps if you spoke to her, she'd reconsider. It's my professional opinion that your mother would receive the best medical treatment no matter who attended her, but Aaryn is our best. You and I may not agree with her methodology, or how she conducted herself in this meeting, but you only have to look at your mother and judge for yourself her effectiveness. Since Mrs. Denali was first wheeled through that door, she hadn't uttered a word. Now all of a sudden, she's speaking with renewed life, expressing a passion to get well. I don't know how or even why Aaryn does the things she does. I just know that she's effective. And what neither of you know from this first meeting with her is that she has a heart of gold. If I had to choose a person to have in my corner, believe me, it would be Dr. Jamison. Now, if you want Aaryn to relent, my suggestion to you is that you talk to her. Her office is down the hall, last door on the left."

Jayson sat staring from Kyle to his mother. He couldn't believe what was happening. And he was still mad as hell. On top of his anger, he'd been made to feel like a little boy who had just been chided in the school principal's office. As if *he* was the culprit. And for what? Just moments earlier he'd been fawned over like the megasuperstar he was with everyone around him pleased to be basking in his orbit. Minutes later, here he was sitting before his mother feeling chewed out over something that wasn't even his fault. He'd be damned if he searched out this doctor and grovel before her. Besides, he didn't even like the woman! Yes, his mother was acting like her old self again, but damn it all to hell, who wouldn't be changed after someone ripped your ass off and handed it back to you with a smile. If that was all it took for Syl to come to her frigging senses, had he known it, hell, he could have hollered at her himself and saved everybody the hassle.

With his mother and Kyle watching him as though he were a repulsive-looking martian, Jayson got to his feet and slammed the door behind him.

As he walked down the hallway towards the doctor's office, Jayson's brow was furrowed in anger. He still refused to believe the turn of events. This was all so childish to him. Here he was a grown ass man having to deal with kid stuff. A *rich* grown ass man! And he was expected to grovel before some woman he didn't even know. Obviously, she had something against him even before she met him. If he'd had his way, he'd tell her to go to hell. Right after she kissed his "a" double "s" that is. Jayson reached her office door and instead of knocking began to pace back and forth outside it. Noticing he was beginning to attract attention from onlookers, he finally knocked.

Even when he heard her say "come in," it took Jayson another moment before he turned the knob and entered.

Aaryn was on her knees sifting the soil of her plants and watering those that needed it when Jayson walked in.

The moment he entered, he was struck by the lemony scent and the sunlight that filtered throughout the room. It wasn't overpowering, it just had the surprising effect of stripping him of his anger, righteous though it was. As he stared around her office, he noticed it spoke volumes about her. Things he couldn't find on the website were revealed in the color, smell and décor of her office. It was richly decorated, but not ostentatious. Warm, comfortable, solitary were the words that came to him. She stood to her feet in the corner of the room staring at him. Jayson turned to her, prepared to just apologize and be done with it. His lips parted to offer apologetic words but they closed immediately. She'd removed her doctor's smock and was dressed in a pair of fitting grey slacks with a matching sleeveless grey turtleneck. There was nothing revealing about her attire and yet, Jayson was immediately physically attracted to her. He didn't mean to ogle her, but unattached red-blooded male that he was, his eyes drifted over her figure in obvious approving appraisal. Well muscled arms that told him she lifted weights, full breasts that were round and supple, a waist narrow and small, hips that flared and a well-rounded butt that begged personal attention.

Aaryn placed the jug she used to water her plants on the floor. Dusting her hands of excess soil, she reached for her smock and buttoned it all the way down. She was used to men eyeing her appraisingly as this one just had. "Did you need something, Mr. Denali?" Aaryn's tone was brusque, one hundred percent business-like.

Caught staring at her like a hungry dog, Jayson turned to stare out her window as she buttoned her doctor's smock. He continued staring at the mountains looming in the distance until she cleared her throat, reminding him of his purpose for being there. "Yes, actually I do need something." Jayson reached behind him and closed her office door before stepping further into the room. He approached her desk and stared down at the photos on it. He dared not touch anything in her office. Except, when his eyes fell on the picture of her climbing a 500-foot rock called The Prophesy Wall, Jayson couldn't help but pick it up to stare at it closely. It took balls to climb mountains. Jayson scaled mountains in his movies. But those were props that were flat on the ground while special effects did the rest to make it look like he was scaling the tallest mountains in the world. This, what he held in his hand, was the real thing. It explained the strong muscle tone of her arms. Man that he was, he ogled her butt, thighs and legs all on full display in the photo. Jayson's opinion of the good doctor was quickly changing. It could be they had simply gotten off to a bad start after all.

He was startled when she plucked the photo from his hands. Seeing that he'd just rekindled her anger, Jayson wanted to quickly ward off her vituperative onslaught. He offered her a smile that had never failed to soften a woman's heart and said, "Dr. Jamison, I'm sorry."

She, however, never batted an eye but continued to stare at him with those piercing eyes of hers, not saying a word.

"Look, for what it's worth, I apologize. You were right back there. If I flew off the handle, it's because I was only protecting my mother. You have to admit you were a little rough on her. When she broke down crying, all I could do was lash out in anger. I came to your office because my mother wants to stay here. And she wants you to treat her. Both she and Dr. Baldwin seem to think that won't happen unless I apologize. So here I am. I'll even get down on my knees if you want. We might have just gotten off on a bad foot. If that's the case, again, all I can say is, I'm sorry." Jayson quieted because in the face of her stonewall silence he was beginning to feel as though he was babbling. Jesus, what was it about this lady that he found so intimidating? And there she was staring at him with those impenetrable eyes of hers. His smile usually worked on most women, but he had yet to see her crack one. What was it about her anyway?

"What I'm asking, Dr. Jamison, is for you to attend to my mother. I'm asking you not to let my behavior or your opinion of me get in the way of my mother's care." Jayson stared at her, waiting for a response.

Aaryn had stepped away from him after she took her photo from his hands. She crossed her hands over her chest. "Your mother will be just fine, Mr. Denali. Shriners, as you know, is an excellent facility. There are any number of physicians here who can and are qualified to treat her. She'll do well and that will be my recommendation to Dr. Baldwin, that someone else other than myself treat your mother. As for you, Mr. Denali, you, I do not like. Period. You waltz in here and think you can throw a blinding, megawatt smile my way and all will be forgiven? It's not even about the words you spoke to me back there. Don't kid yourself by thinking I was offended. I don't give a rotten apple about what you said or what you think about me. It's you I don't like. I find that I'm offended by your very person. I don't like your cavalier, disdainful attitude toward people and I definitely don't like your chauvinistic, dismissive attitude toward women. Your mother's a lovely woman, but you, Mr. Denali, are an asshole. End of story."

Jayson looked as though he'd just been harpooned. All apologies forgotten, Jayson said, "Damn! Who died and left you judge and executioner of the free world? To think I came here to apologize?" Jayson's lips curled in derision. "Lady, you are one *serious* piece of work. I don't know who put a bug up your ass, but you most definitely take the prize for 'Unprofessional Doctor of the Year'. No wonder I couldn't find anything about you on the hospital's website or even on the internet. People don't have anything nice to say about you so they don't say anything at all. I don't have a clue of what gives you the right to judge me given that I don't know you and have never ever laid eyes on you before this day, but you have got major issues. And you don't know a damn thing about me, Lady, because you've got your facts all wrong."

"I may not know you personally, Mr. Denali, but your history is written all over you. You've got more broken hearts trailing after you than a cemetery has dead bodies. You've traded on your good looks to get by all your life. You use women like paper plates at a picnic. You're selfish and you think only about yourself. There are women who have slit their wrists and ended their lives because they were foolish enough to think you would love them while in reality you couldn't be bothered to give them a second thought after you left their beds. They may have lain down with you and given you their hearts, but when they got up, you took a piece of their soul. These same women, and countless others, would have settled for a piece of you, but you couldn't even give them that. Their deaths will follow you forever, Jayson Denali. I pity any poor soul foolish enough to become involved with you— especially the one whose bed you left last night. Her stench is still all over you. And you really want to know the kicker? The kicker is, you're not capable of loving someone unselfishly. You walk around punishing every woman you meet simply because of one woman who broke your heart more years ago than you can remember. Oh, yes. I may not know you personally, Jayson Denali, but I can read your spirit and root out your serial dishonesty toward women. The little that I do see, I. Do. Not. Like." Aaryn walked to her door and held it open for him to leave. "Now, if you'll excuse me, I have other patients that I need to see about."

Jayson stood in the middle of her office for a long while feeling completely denuded. He didn't stand there because he wanted to, but because he was rooted to the spot. Too many jumbled thoughts were clamoring through his mind at once to focus on any one of them. Maybe this lady was a tabloid reader and believed everything she read in the gossip mags. That was all Jayson could come up with. It was the only way she could know so much about him. Or it could be she was best friends with one of the many women he'd slept with and later dumped. Or perhaps she was related to a friend of a friend of a friend. The scenarios were too many to consider. On top of that, her words had a stinging effect deep inside him, leaving him bereft of speech. Finally, as Jayson walked out of her office she swung the door shut behind him. She may as well have added, *"Don't let the doorknob hit cha where the dog shoulda bit cha."* He walked down the hall, zombie-like, and went straight past Dr. Baldwin's office heading for the men's room. He needed a moment to get *himself* together.

Twenty minutes later, Jayson was still sitting on the bench in the men's room. The spaciousness and beauty of the marbled men's room was lost on him as he was deep in his own thoughts. The room he sat in was separate from the one that housed the stalls and urinals. Given any other occasion, Jayson might have appreciated the deep green Italian marble and gold designer inlays. Instead, he sat with his elbows on his knees, his hands folded, staring at his feet. He'd loosened the silk tie of his Armani pinstripe suit. On the other side of the wall, voices came and went but no one ventured into the area where he sat in solitude.

Jayson looked up when a voice from the opposite end said, "Only the charming Dr. Aaryn Jamison can cause someone to look so dejected and out of sorts." Kyle leaned against the wall, his arms folded over his chest. He studied his nails and said, "Experienced one of her heart-to-hearts, did you?"

"Is that what you'd call it? A heart-to-heart? Felt more like an ambush to me." Jayson's fingers stroked his chin. "As for charming, I'd say she's more pitbull or barracuda than anything else. What is she, a private investigator in her spare time?" How the hell could she know he'd been with someone the night before? Did he reek? Of course not. He'd showered and was even wearing a tinge of Clive Christian No. 1, a men's cologne that cost more than $650 an ounce because of its fine, rare, and exotic ingredients.

"Ahhh. Read you your last rites, did she?" Kyle smiled. He knew the feeling all too well as he, too, had been subjected to one of Aaryn's verbal assaults. Years ago, he'd cheated on his wife, God rest her soul. At the time, he'd made the unfortunate mistake of using Aaryn as his alibi. His wife knew and trusted Aaryn, so any time Kyle said he was working late with her, no questions were asked. Everything was going along swimmingly until Aaryn confronted him about his deception. According to her, his affair was his own business but he'd abused their professional friendship by bringing her into it. Aaryn told him that his wife was about to come to her and inquire about their alleged late night assignments and that she, Aaryn, had no intention of lying or covering for him. The divorce that was guaranteed to ensue in light of his philandering would be devastatingly costly and emotionally scarring. Unless, that is, he changed his adulterous ways. Scared straight, Kyle had ended his affair. He didn't even question how Aaryn knew of his cheating or how she knew his wife was growing curious. In the thirteen years he'd worked with her, he'd witnessed too many strange occurrences with Aaryn. Although that had transpired years ago, he still remembered the sting of her confronting him and he sympathized with Jayson now.

"Perhaps if your mother met with some of our other doctors we could sway her towards treatment with someone else."

"Funny you should mention that. I was thinking the same thing." Jayson stood and they left the men's room together.

"I've had our staff show your mother to her room. I can have someone take you to her now. You know, you could try pleading your case. Perhaps Dr. Jamison would change her mind."

"Forget it. I have no intentions of ever going near that lady again."

"Yes, well…remember, even the best laid plans of mice and men…"

"*…can blow up in your friggin' face*," Jayson wanted to add. But he didn't bother to respond.

Chapter Eight

Inside the door to his mother's room, Jayson paused at the sight of her sitting at a huge mahogany desk with pen and paper at hand. Like him, Syl was a southpaw and was fortunate that her paralysis did not extend to the left side of her body. She looked up and saw her son watching her from the doorway. "Come, sweetness, have a seat."

As he sat in a nearby chair, Sylvia stared out her window admiring the colorful mountain vista. "I never realized how beautifully serene the mountains could be, Jayson."

Sure, if you're a caveman, Jayson thought to himself. He didn't say anything aloud because he recognized he was in a funk and didn't want his sour mood affecting his mother's newfound happiness. Instead, he looked around her room. It resembled a luxurious hotel suite more than it did a hospital room. It was certainly large and spacious enough to accommodate three or four people.

Sylvia brought her gaze back to Jayson. "Did you speak with Dr. Jamison?" Her voice was soft and held none of the irritation with which she'd spoken to him earlier.

Now it was Jayson's turn to stare at the mountains. Only he wasn't admiring their beauty. He shook his head. "I tried Ma. I even apologized but she wouldn't

have any part of it." Jayson looked at his mother hopefully. "She said you were a wonderful person and that any of the doctors here could treat you."

Sylvia nodded as if she'd expected as much. "What else did she have to say?" She watched her son closely.

Jayson didn't answer right away, but finally he said, "Nothing that I'd care to repeat."

"Hmmm." Sylvia said, suddenly turning reflective as she gazed once again at the view outside her window. "I remember when I was a little girl…"

Jayson stared at her and listened avidly. He loved hearing his mother talk about how things were for her back in the day. It wasn't something she spoke of very often and he knew she'd not had a happy childhood.

"Momma and her friends would sit around and talk. Things weren't like they are today. Children knew their places back then. There were certain times when we weren't allowed to hear the things grownups discussed. But one afternoon, I snuck by the front door to hear what the ladies on the front porch were saying. They were speaking about a friend of theirs who had "the gift." As a child, I didn't know that "the gift" was considered second sight. I thought the gift was a birthday present or a toy you received at Christmas time. My mother started telling the ladies about how she'd whipped the daylights out of me for telling her the biggest lie.

"You see, I had told my mother that I saw my grandmother sitting in a rocking chair on the front porch one afternoon when I came home from school. I didn't lie. I described her mother to the tee, even down to what she was wearing as she sat rocking in the chair. I never knew my grandmother but I had seen a picture of her. A very old black and white picture that you really couldn't tell what color she was wearing. But that afternoon when I came home from school, I saw her just as clear as day. I swear, I sat on the porch right beside her and she proceeded to tell me all about her life and then she held my hand and told me to run along and be a good little girl. So I went inside to get my mother to bring her out on the front porch to see her. But of course she wasn't there when I returned and my mother said I made it all up.

"No matter how long and hard my mother beat me that day, I wouldn't change my story. My mother wanted me to say that I was lying but I wouldn't do it. Instead, I kept repeating everything my grandmother had told me. As Momma described the incident to the ladies on the porch, they kept telling her that I had "the gift." But again, back then I thought they were telling Momma that I had stolen someone's present. Over the years, I forgot all about that day. I haven't thought about it since I was a little girl growing up in Chicago. Not until today did I even remember it. When Dr. Jamison held my hand, Jayson, I saw the event just as vividly as though it had happened yesterday. I think that doctor has what my mother's friends called the gift."

She's got the gift alright, Jayson thought sarcastically. The gift of using her razor-sharp tongue like a rapier. But of course, Jayson didn't say that aloud either. Instead, he humored his mother. "It sounds like an old wives tale to me, Ma. But stranger things have happened, I guess."

"Hmph," said Sylvia, bringing him back to today's current event. "Just because she said no doesn't mean you can't change her mind, Jayson. Did you barge into her office and demand that she do your bidding or did you apologize and ask nicely? You weren't always this arrogant, you know."

"Ma, I'm not arrogant. You of all people know that. You read and hear all the time about how other stars are rude to their fans or look down on people who don't have as much money or fame as they do. I'm never like that. I always try to be considerate of other people's feelings." Jayson closed his eyes and unconsciously ran his hand over his head. He would do anything for his mother. And she knew it.

"Contrary to what you're thinking, Ma, I did not barge into her office and demand that she do anything. I tried to apologize to her but she wouldn't accept it. I've never met the lady before in life and she seems to think I'm some kind of deranged serial killer."

"I'm afraid she wasn't attracted to you, was she?" Sylvia stared at her son sympathetically.

Jayson made a sucking noise with his tongue and teeth. "That has nothing to do with it. Trust me, Ma, I'm no more her type than she is mine."

"Then you should have no qualms about asking her once more then, should you? Jayson, I'd like for you to go now. I want to take a nap, so please get my nurse, will you? If you're still here when I wake up, you and I can have dinner. If the Doctor says no again, then I'll accept that. I'll just return to Milwaukee and we'll work things out from there."

Hiding his mounting frustration, Jayson went to get a nurse. At the nurses' station he asked for someone to assist his mother. As three of the nurses gathered around him complimenting him on the great movies he'd made, Jayson smiled at them listening only halfheartedly. He stared down the hallway which lead to the suite of offices, particularly the one belonging to the infamous Dr. Jamison. Thinking there was no time like the present, Jayson decided to try to reason with her one more time. He thanked the nurses for their kindness and just as he was about to walk away, a little boy about five years old tugged at his suit sleeve.

"Hi, Mr. Incredible." With a timid smile on his face, the little boy thrust an action doll toward him that bore a startling resemblance to Jayson. The toy figure was a product of a movie he'd starred in with Schwarzenegger. Staring down at the redhaired little boy, Jayson felt his heartstrings tug. Without thinking about it, he

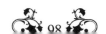

bent down and swooped the little rascal up into his arms and swung him around. It was a move he'd done in the film and the little boy yelped with laughter.

"Tommy, there you are! Didn't I tell you not to wander off? I've been looking everywhere for you. Are you bothering that man?" Guessing by the woman's age, Jayson figured she may have been the little boy's grandmother. She appeared too mature to be his mother.

When he set him on the ground, Tommy ran to the woman screaming, "Look Grandma, it's Mr. Incredible!" Little Tommy may have been impressed, but clearly his grandmother was still angry at him over giving her the slip. She grabbed his arm and marched him back in the direction from which she came. He kept waving to Jayson as he was dragged away.

"That was such a sweet thing to do. Tommy carries that doll everywhere. His mother will be so happy to know he met his hero. She's paralyzed from the waist down, you know." Jayson's stock just rose even higher with those at the nurses' station.

Staring after Tommy, Jayson smiled and said, "It was nothing anybody else would not have done." As he turned to walk down the hallway toward the Doctor's office, he remembered a clip he'd seen on the animal channel one day when he was at home channel surfing. A cougar had dived out of nowhere to attack a large bird who, by a stroke of great fortune, managed to escape. Minutes later, not having sufficiently learned his lesson the first time, or because he was too stupid to remember, the scatterbrained bird returned to the same spot. Sure enough, the big cat rushed in to rip his prey apart. Jayson felt pretty much like that big dumb bird who hadn't learned his lesson the first time around. As he neared her office, his steps slowed curiously like that of a prisoner headed to his own execution. He came to Aaryn's door and hesitated before finally knocking.

A minute or two later, he was about to knock again when a nurse passing by said, "If you're looking for Dr. Jamison, you just missed her. She left for the day."

Jayson thanked the young woman and was prepared to return to his mother's room to check in on her once more. However, when he reached the nurses' station he spotted Dr. Jamison getting onto the elevator. He hurried to reach her but the elevator doors closed shut. Jayson quickly pressed the down button and got on the next elevator. By the time he reached the ground floor, when he got off, he spotted her walking through the parking lot. She stopped at a navy blue Range Rover, climbed inside and fastened her seatbelt. As she pulled out of the parking lot, Jayson quickly walked to his limo and knocked on the window. He startled the chauffeur who was about to get out of the vehicle but Jayson beckoned him to unlock the passenger door.

Instead of climbing into the back of the limo, Jayson hopped into the front seat with the driver. "I want you to follow that dark blue Range Rover that just left the lot. But stay a distance back because I don't want her spooked."

"Whatever you say, Sir." The driver was being handsomely compensated for his time and had nothing to complain about. If a wealthy Hollywood actor wanted to ride up front and follow another car around, who was he to complain?

They followed her to Interstate 15 and drove for about thirty minutes before exiting at 1300 South. Trailing her by about three cars, they turned south onto 500 West and went three blocks to the corner of Whitney & 400 West.

"Pull over here for a moment." The place was called The Front Climbing Club. The huge sign on the building said it was an indoor bouldering and rock climbing facility. From a safe distance, Jayson watched as Aaryn exited her vehicle and pulled a gym bag from the back seat. He wanted to follow her inside the club but he didn't dare risk running into her. If he'd managed to piss her off having done nothing at all, he couldn't even imagine how angry she would be at having been followed. Also, if he went inside someone might recognize him. Even in Utah, his movies played to strong audiences. He had spotted a billboard of his latest film release on the way from the hospital.

Jayson turned to the driver. "We've never been formally introduced. I'm Jayson." He extended his hand.

"George Mason, at your service, Sir."

"Pleased to meet you, George. I know this will sound strange, but can I borrow your cap and your jacket?"

The driver looked at Jayson curiously before finally handing over his cap and shrugging out of his jacket. With obvious hesitation, he handed them over.

"We're about the same height and your frame is only slightly larger than mine. I think I'll borrow your pants too."

The chauffeur laughed. He had a good fifty pounds on the young man he was driving. The uniform was going to sag on him. "Well, okay Fella. But as long as I git everything back." He peered out the window and said, "Let's step to the rear of the limo. In case folks wander by."

"Good idea, George. Let's do it." Jayson hopped out and held the rear door of the limo open so George could climb in. Anybody passing by would have wondered what the two of them were up to.

"Never had nothin' like this to happen," George said as he proceeded to shuck his pants. Left wearing only his underwear, he felt very much like an ill at ease peacock without any plumes.

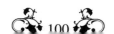

Jayson grinned at the man's apparent discomfort. He would tip him well for his troubles and his patience. "I promise to return them without a speck of dirt. Scouts honor." Quickly donning the man's uniform, Jayson got out of the vehicle pulling the cap down over his face and slipping on his sunglasses.

He entered the facility and approached the front desk. The man behind the counter was built like a bodybuilder who ate steroids for breakfast, lunch and dinner. He bore a nametag with the name "Cliff." As Jayson drew closer, the man said, "Welcome to The Front. Can I help you?"

"Cliff, how are you?" Jayson offered his hand. "Do you think I could have someone show me around the club? I've heard a lot about this place and I'm thinking about joining."

"Sure, Dude. No prob. We've got three different types of memberships that we offer. How advanced a climber are you?" Cliff studied Jayson thoroughly. *Too thoroughly,* Jayson thought.

"I guess I'd say intermediate. I'm not a beginner, but neither am I top of the line." He didn't know any of the climbing lingo either and he was trying to wing it as safely as possible.

"No prob. That's Candice, our manager, who's waving at you from over there by the door. I can have her show you around if you like. Or if you prefer, I can give you a tour myself."

"I think I'd like you to show me the ropes, Cliff. Nothing personal to Candice, just a man to man kinda thing, you know?"

"No prob. I'd love to show you around, Dude. Let's go." Flexing his muscles for show, Cliff grabbed a clipboard and started leading Jayson around the club. He was already counting the commission from the sale.

Something told Jayson that despite all of Cliffs oversized muscles, he had a little sugar in his tank. At the moment, Jayson just needed him for cover. He didn't want to be distracted by a female escort who might possess a sharper eye or be more discerning than Cliff.

The facility was huge and may have been primarily for rock climbers but it was upscale chic. Jayson imagined membership costs were a pretty penny.

They toured a large room that was crowded with the latest weight machines and cardio equipment which only a handful of patrons were taking advantage of. Men were on stairmasters climbing to eternity and a few women were on treadmills running nowhere fast. Despite his baggy clothes, several of the women looked him up and down, eyeing him curiously. Jayson prodded Cliff to lead on to the rock climbing area.

"You know, has anyone ever told you that you look like that actor who plays in the new movie, *Mania*?" Cliff looked at Jayson closely. Even with the oversized clothes, the sunglasses and the cap low on his brow, Cliff could tell the man was good-looking. Tall, broad shoulders, jutting chin with a John Travolta cleft. No wonder the women passing by were throwing second glances at the tall, thick, handsome hunk. *If he wasn't a star, he looked like one,* Cliff thought.

"Nah. But I sure love his movies though."

"Yep, that dude is ice cold snap! I can't wait for *Pendulum II*. I hear it's gonna be the bomb."

Jayson didn't know why he was surprised to hear Cliff use what he considered urban slang. He guessed he figured the good folks of Utah didn't get out much. They were approaching the rock climbing area when Jayson spotted Aaryn. She looked very appealing in her short sports top and nylon Capri pants. Versatile clothing Jayson guessed to allow her greater flexibility. The mint color highlighted her creamy, deep dark chocolate skin and her hair was loosed from its bun and hung wildly in a pony tail down her back. And yes, her womanly curves were on full display. He saw men and women alike glance at her appreciatively. Aaryn definitely stood out from everyone else.

He gestured to Cliff. "Cliff, let me hang out in this spot for a bit. I want to check out the action."

"Sure dude. Just meet me back at the front desk. I'll be waiting for you."

Jayson stayed hidden behind a tall Ficus tree. There was a glass window separating him from the rock wall area. He guessed it was so others like him could watch the climbers do their thing. He saw Aaryn stroll casually toward the rock wall. There were about twelve people already climbing. The brochure he had in hand said the area was 150 feet high and stretched 10,000 square feet. Aaryn surprised him by embracing a man already standing at the wall with his hands on his hips. She wrapped her arms around the man's waist and rested her cheek against his chest. The man was much taller and embraced her in a bear hug. But it looked like a fatherly embrace. He had reddish blond hair, was about six feet tall and ruggedly built. As Jayson studied the man's face, he guessed he might be in his late 50's, early 60's.

They were laughing about something when two other men joined their circle. Jayson was too far away to hear what they were saying but it looked as though one of the men was challenging Aaryn. He kept smiling and pointing to some spot high on the rock wall. Finally, he turned to Aaryn and extended his hand. "Here we go," Jayson murmured to himself, thinking the guy was about to get stiffed. Instead of shaking his hand, she did something strange. She reached out and clasped her hand around the guy's forearm. *Weird,* Jayson thought. *Maybe shaking hands with people was against her religion or something.*

They seemed to have reached an agreement of sorts because the man stopped shaking his head and they approached the wall while staring upward. Jayson watched as they strapped on all the bells and whistles needed for the climb. Again, Jayson was no punk and he was no stranger to crazy stunt moves as he performed many of his own. He just couldn't get into rock climbing and was curious about it because Aaryn did.

The man stood a good five or even six inches taller that Aaryn, who Jayson guessed was about 5'6". Her opponent certainly had her beat in the muscle department because he probably weighed a good 220 lbs. But there didn't appear to be an ounce of fat on his lean, muscular body. If they were about to race, Jayson relished seeing Aaryn get her comeuppance. Surely a burly guy like her opponent wouldn't be beat by a slip of a girl. The redhaired man whom Aaryn had embraced so affectionately pulled a whistle out of his pocket and he and the other guy's partner stood back to watch. Lifting the piece to his lips, he blew it and the two climbers were off.

Wanting to see clearly, Jayson came from behind the Ficus tree to get an even better view. Already, the guy was several feet ahead of Aaryn. Jayson smiled because she was obviously about to get her butt mopped with the floor. Whereas her opponent seemed to climb with brute force strength, she seemed to be choosing her moves with care, as though she was pacing herself. About halfway up the rock, seventy-five feet or so, her speed started increasing. Movements that before seemed deliberate became almost spider like as she quickly gained speed to nearly catch up with her opponent. As Jayson watched her scramble the wall, he found himself switching loyalties and suddenly started rooting for her. The man kept looking down to see where Aaryn was but she never took her gaze off of the top of the wall. Her feet were swift and sure as she sped upward like lightning. She scrambled past her challenger to reach the top leaving him a good distance behind. She touched the ceiling and instead of pausing to celebrate, started rappelling down the rope toward the ground passing the man on her descent.

"I'll be damned," Jayson thought. "She smoked him." Here's a bet he would have blown good money on.

When Aaryn reached the ground, the old man picked her up in a bear hug and swung her around like a toy. For the first time, Jayson realized she could smile. In retrospect, he believed she'd known all along she could beat the man to the top of the wall, but she'd lulled him into a false sense of security. Her rival hit the ground and dusted himself off. His friend, none too happy at the loss, looked at him like, "Dork, how could let a girl beat you climbing?" The opponent's friend reached into his back pocket and pulled out a wallet from which he removed several bills and handed them to Aaryn. Jayson saw her shake her head and raise her palms in the air, refusing to take the money. But the old man obviously had no such qualms because he reached for the bucks and stuffed them into his front pocket. Aaryn grabbed his hand in hers and they started walking toward the exit doors.

Feeling like a voyeur, Jayson roused himself from the glass and quickly headed to the front of the club. He definitely wanted to beat her out of the facility.

"Hey Dude, there you are. I was starting to think you got lost."

"Sorry, I got caught up watching the other climbers."

"So, can I sign you up?" Cliff's question seemed to innocently include a double entendre.

"You know, I don't think I'm prepared to join today. But I definitely thank you for showing me around the club." Jayson reached into his wallet and palmed a bill. He reached out and cupped Cliff's hand pressing the money into his palm.

"Thanks, Dude. Hope I'll see you around then." It was an open-ended question.

Jayson doubted it as he quickly headed for the exit.

Cliff looked down at the Benjamin Franklin in his hand. The hundred dollars was great, but he would have preferred the man's phone number. Just then, Cliff realized with disappointment that he'd forgotten to even ask him his name.

Jayson jogged to the end of the block and climbed into the limo. "That's some club back there, George. You ever climb?" Jayson pulled the cap off his head and started stripping, handing the clothes back to the chauffeur.

"No, but lotsa folk round these parts do. It's a popular pastime. Where to now?" George asked as he quickly redressed himself. He was glad to have his clothes back and grateful no one had knocked on the limo's window.

"The lady will be exiting the building shortly. We need to follow her. Wherever she goes, stay on her tail." George opened the door to get back into the front seat as Jayson pulled out his cell phone. He couldn't believe it, but he was actually enjoying himself. Behind schedule as he was, it didn't appear likely that he would be leaving Salt Lake that day. Not unless he got an opportunity to talk to the good doctor and somehow changed her mind.

A voice answered on the end of Jayson's cell. "Scott, I've got some bad news. We can't leave by 5:00 as originally scheduled." Scott was Jayson's pilot. "No. We may not be able to pull out until sometime tomorrow afternoon. I hate doing this to you, Buddy. Can you square away things and hang out till then? Hold on a sec." Jayson rolled back the glass again that separated his compartment from the chauffeur's. "George, what do people do for entertainment in Salt Lake?"

"Well, guess that right depends on what you have in mind, Fella." George seemed to think about it. "There is a game tonight at the Delta Center. The Miami Heat is in town." Natives loved and faithfully followed their Utah Jazz team. The

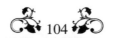

glory days of Karl Malone and John Stockton were long gone, but the fans remained loyal and hopeful that the NBA gods would soon bless them again.

"Hey Scott, the defending NBA champs are at the Delta Center tonight. If I can get tickets, do you want to go with me? At least let me make it up to you for raining on your parade. Great. Hang tight, Scott. I'll call you right back." Jayson dialed another number.

"D. It looks like I might be stuck here in Salt Lake for another day."

"Awww, man. How did that happen?"

Jayson lounged back on the leather seat. "Man, have I had a day. You wouldn't believe it."

"Try me," Dez said.

Jayson gave him a quick rundown of the day's events.

"Wow. And you're sure you've never met the broad before?" Dez asked.

"I'm certain of it." Jayson could have said more, but he was suddenly reluctant to trash Aaryn's name.

"Well, that's red state territory. Republican Senators Hatch and Bennett, if I'm not mistaken. I could reach out and see who knows them on this end. I could have one of my people ask them to make a call and put in a good word to the folks at Shriners."

Jayson laughed. Smiling, he said, "That's more firepower than I think I need. It would probably piss her off even more. I'll think I'll just try the old fashioned way."

"Ahhh, option number one, huh? It might not work if she's the tough ballbuster you indicated. But let me know how it turns out. In the meantime, I'm going to book a return flight back to New York. Syl's doing better though?"

Jayson pursed his lips. "Yeah, she said she wants to get well because it's high time you and I settled down and had a bunch of babies."

"Yeah, well, I wouldn't hold my breath if I were her."

"Try telling her that," Jayson replied.

"No thanks. You know, J-man, if you wanted to get out of our game on the nines, all you had to do was say so."

"Whatever, Chump. I can burn you anytime. Golf is the furthest thing from my mind right now."

"Alright, son, we'll see about that. Look, I've got to get back to my meeting. I'll holla." Dez disconnected.

Next, Jayson called his assistant Wendy. Before he finished dialing the number, George knocked on the panel and the partition parted again. "The Rover's on the move, Sir."

"Thanks, George. Don't lose her."

"Who's George?" Wendy asked on the other end.

"Someone who follows instructions and directions a lot better than you do."

Wendy was nowhere near cowed. She understood Jayson sometimes better than he did himself. She was a happily married battle ax and she and Jayson had a great professional relationship. To outsiders, she was his first and main wall of defense. She was dedicated, reliable, and most important of all discreetly loyal. Jayson could trust her with sensitive details and not find his business plastered all over the National Enquirer the next day. He'd stolen her from the Elite Model Management Corporation about ten years ago and she'd been keeping him straight ever since. "Let's see *you* try to juggle the comings and goings of one extremely demanding, temperamental star and then attempt to have a normal life after the day is finally done. Where are you anyway? You've got a ton of messages here. You must have had your phone turned off. Everybody who couldn't reach you has called here. Even your crew called a while ago to find out when you're coming back to New York."

"Can't say right now," Jayson said. "I'll call them later though. I had my phone off because I was inside Shriners. You have to turn your cell phone off once you're inside the hospital. What I need you to do is get me a couple of Utah Jazz tickets for tonight. See if you can work your magic and get me front row seats. It never hurts to get some face time on the tube."

"Let me see what I can arrange. I'll call you back. In the mean time, why don't you check the messages on your cell so these people can stop bugging the heck out of me?"

"I'm on it." Just before Jayson hung up he said to her, "Wait a minute. When did I become extremely demanding and temperamental?"

Jayson's question momentarily surprised Wendy. Figuring he had to be humoring her, she quipped, "Uh, probably the day you were born. It's hard to say though because it might have even started before then. At any rate, let me run. I've got a ton of things to do here and you've just added to that list. I'll get back to you about the tickets."

As Wendy hung up it occurred to Jayson that regardless of what some people thought, women were running *his* life instead of the other way around. He was listening to his messages, writing down numbers and notes to give to Wendy when George said, "This is a residential area we're entering. I think the Rover may be turnin' in for the evening."

Jayson stared out the limousine window. The area homes were on acres of land and were spaced far apart. The black-tarred asphalt road was winding and lead along a stretch that was lined with trees. There were only three estates, each one sitting on a surplus of land.

Up ahead, the Range Rover slowed and pulled over to the side of the road. "Uh oh," George said. "I think we've been spotted."

Thinking quick, Jayson said, "Turn into this driveway, George. Pull all the way up to the house."

When the limo turned into the driveway, the Range Rover started moving again. As Aaryn pulled off, Jayson watched her drive into the entrance of the third and last estate. From his vantage point, he couldn't see further into the property because of the ten-foot pine hedges that lined the estate blocking his view. Jayson had George back out and drive halfway up to the estate where Aaryn had entered. His curiosity was peaked and he had to see the place. It could belong to someone else for all he knew, but he wanted to see the lay of the land. As he got out of the limo to walk the rest of the way to the entrance, it didn't occur to him that he was doing the very thing he'd chided others for doing who attempted to invade his privacy by gaining access to his home.

Jayson stood at the entrance of the estate. The red brick driveway lead to a breathtaking log home beautifully nestled under a panoply of exotic trees. Behind the great house, in the distance loomed what looked like to Jayson an enchanted forest. No stranger to the most beautiful and expensive luxury homes all over the world, Jayson was awed simply because there was an aesthetic, nontinsel quality about the estate that stopped one in their tracks. The Range Rover was parked in the driveway but Aaryn was no longer in it.

A poignant desire within strongly urged him to go up and knock on the door. He almost did it too before he stopped himself and turned around to head back to the limo. Jayson didn't know who owned the home at 1800 Buena Vista Lane, but he knew how to find out.

He climbed into the limo and said to George, "Any idea who owns these properties, George?"

Shaking his head, George replied, "I don't know, but I reckon it's folks with a lotta money. These parts don't come cheap."

"Take me back to the hospital, George. I have a dinner date waiting for me." Jayson's cell phone rang. It was Wendy.

"Jay, you're in luck. I wheedled and whined and threw your name around and then paid top dollar for four courtside seats. Enjoy."

"Four? I only needed two. Hang on a sec." Jayson said to George, "Hey George, how would you like to see the Jazz play tonight? I've got two extra courtside tickets. Wanna come? You could bring the wife along if you like."

"Land sakes! Instead of the Old Ball and Chain, how 'bout my grandson? He'd love to come. That sure is right kind of ya, Fella."

"Jay, who's this George character? The Ghost of Barney Fife? That's some accent he's got. Are you in Mayberry by any chance?"

"Hush, Wendy. Look, I've got something else I need you to do for me. But I need to make another call to get more info."

"Okay. But you'd better call PT back." "PT" was Jayson's PR consultant. "It seems you've been up to your usual escapades. The rag mags have run a story that you dumped Rita Danza because she's pregnant. And guess who's the baby's daddy."

Jayson sucked his teeth in exasperation. The rumors the gossip magazines circulated were downright unbelievable. It never failed to amaze him that people believed whatever they read. It amazed him even more that people actually shelled out money to purchase the nutty rag mags.

"Look, Rita is a master thespian. She likely planted the story herself. Let PT handle it. I've got more important things on my list. I'll get back to you in a moment."

Jayson called Scott back and set up the meeting time for the game. He dialed another number and a voice answered saying, "J-money! What up, dawg? You don't love a brotha no mo? Naw, you don't love me. Why you don't love me, J? Huh? I heard you sprang inta Chi-town two weeks ago, dropped a coupla G's at Jordan's and was like 'poof-be-gone'. Couldn't even stop and wave at a playa. I thought I was yo' boy, J. But I guess my street cred ain't good enuf wit' chu no mo. Wut's up wit dat, J?"

Shaking his head, Jayson closed the glass partition. "Tyrone, are you finished? Can I get a word in this conversation?" Tyrone, a selfconfessed computer geek, was an ex-spammer now turned security consultant to several software firms in Chicago. The "ex" preceded his title because Tyrone was a former junk emailing king who, when nabbed by the FBI, agreed to cease and desist sending unsolicited junk email. On any given day, Tyrone had sent an estimated thirty million unsolicited emails from phony addresses that made them appear as though they were coming from legitimate mortgage brokers and lenders.

Before the FBI sprang its net, Tyrone was rolling in the dough. Even after paying a hefty fine, he still wasn't hurting too bad. Every time someone had clicked on one of his emails it had generated a seventy-five cent profit, earning him a sizeable bank account. He owned a stylish three-flat brownstone in Chicago's regentrified Lake Park community, a Hummer SUV and a Jaguar XJ8 parked along side it in his garage. Whoever said crime didn't pay never met Tyrone.

The spoofed emails and his fraudulent network of companies was enough ammunition for the FBI to reel him in. After painting a doomsday picture of him starring in a permanent "bridesmaid" role to his future cellmate, Tyrone suddenly became a changed man. He saw the light of God's restorative hand in the form of prison bars and quickly decided to set about helping to cork the flow of spam. Fast forward and suddenly Tyrone was a professional spam-fighter who helped internet companies fight spam.

But in addition to his past nefarious emailing operation, Tyrone was also an undercover expert computer hacker who could obtain information about anybody. His office in his three-flat boasted a state-of-the-art, complex web of computer and electronic devices that were way beyond Jayson's grasp. Whenever he needed personal and private information about someone that couldn't be found on Google, Tyrone was the man to call—for an astronomical fee. It hadn't occurred to Jayson before, but suddenly he wanted to know all there was to know about Dr. Aaryn Jamison. But first, it appeared he had to smooth some ruffled feathers.

"Tyrone, Jordan created the guest list. I had no control over who got invited. Listen, I'll send you a case of Opus One, how about that?"

"That's more like it, dawg. That's showin' me some love." Though Tyrone could well afford to buy his own champagne, Jayson figured it was just the idea of getting it free that appeased him.

"I need to know who lives at 1800 Buena Vista Lane. And I need to know fairly quickly."

"Hold on, Bro. Let me see. What city and state?" With business at hand, all traces of urban street vernacular dropped from Tyrone's vocabulary as he instantly traversed the social linguistic scale, dropping his street persona to become the Howard University Computer Science graduate that he was.

"Can't find the listing in Salt Lake City, J. Could you be in a suburb of Salt Lake?"

Jayson parted the partition to ask George where they'd been moments earlier and found out it was the city of Holladay.

"Bingo," Tyrone said. "The title deed is listed jointly to Dorothy Jamison and Aaryn Jamison. What else do you need to know?"

"A full report. Let me know everything you find on Dr. Aaryn Jamison."

"For you, Jay, it'll only cost you ten talents." In street terms, a talent was a hundred bucks.

"I'm good for it. Ring me back at this number when you're done. I'll tell you where to send it to." Jayson hung up and called Wendy. He asked her to do him a special favor. And being Wendy, of course no questions were asked.

Chapter Nine

Aaryn sat in her favorite recliner, an orange leather Human Touch massage chair. The chair yielded a full body robotic massage and a stimulating foot and calf massage that was the next best thing to live hands on her body. In each hand she twirled two chrome Chinese hand massage balls. Off to the side in the spacious wide-open livingroom sat a bigscreen television. The volume was midrange as the home-town crowd gave thunderous applause to each of the starting Jazz players being introduced. As she sat reclined in the chair, she stared upward, her gaze fixed on the log ceiling far above, her thoughts forming no particular pattern. Lying at her feet were two huge Great Danes, Baron and Max. Baron was pure steel blue while his counterpart, Max, was a deep yellow gold color. Both dogs were very smart creatures, weighed nearly 200 pounds and stood over three feet tall on all fours.

"Sweetie, you've been quiet since you arrived home today. And you hardly touched any of your dinner. Is something troubling you about work?" Dot came into the room and sat on a sofa. She placed her quilting material on the floor at her feet and slid on her thumb thimble. Dot loved making elaborate, colorful quilts that bespoke her history and heritage.

Aaryn had a special and unique relationship with Dot. Mother and daughter could openly discuss any topic and over the years had morphed into friends as well. But Aaryn wasn't sure she wanted to discuss Jayson Denali only because she couldn't quite analyze what had happened to cause her intensely negative feelings toward him.

"We had several new patients admitted today and there was one in particular..." Aaryn was interrupted by the chiming of the doorbell and Baron and Max's barking as they ran to greet whoever was there.

Neither she nor Dot was expecting anyone, but it was Dot who said, "I'll get it."

She came back a moment later saying, "Look at what I have for you, Aaryn." Dot carried the decorative, 4' x 4' box to the marble livingroom table and set it down. When Aaryn remained seated, Dot looked at her expectantly. "Well, aren't you going to open it?" she asked.

Aaryn sat up. She finally rose and hesitantly approached the box. She examined it, looking for a card. Finding none, she removed the box's handle. Slowly, she unfolded its decorative edges to reveal a stunning and elegant arrangement of thirty-

nine longstemmed bright yellow roses. Each rose was strategically placed between a mountain of baby's breath. The elaborate floral display was housed inside a gorgeous crystal Evasion vase that was shaped like an upside down pyramid. From every angle, the luxurious vase sparkled with a spectrum of dynamic colors.

So exquisite was the bouquet of flowers that it could have been designed by an artist. Add to it the dazzling vase and it made quite a statement. She and Dot stared at it in wonder.

"How beautiful," Dot murmured while feeling the velvety petals. "Yellow roses to signify friendship. Who do you think sent them?" She stared at Aaryn with open curiosity.

"I have no idea. I would guess one of the patients from the hospital. But they wouldn't have sent it here. I don't give out our home address."

"Surely there must be a card. The vase alone cost a fortune." Dot lifted the vase to remove it from atop the cardboard box. Underneath was a small yellow envelope.

Though Aaryn stared at the card as if she wanted no part of it, curiosity was driving Dot up a wall.

"Aaryn, the suspense is gnawing at me. If you don't open the card, I will."

Aaryn looked up at her mother and surprised her by saying, "Okay, then go ahead and open it."

With no hesitation, Dot grabbed the card and tore open the envelope.

"A field of roses for someone I hope to someday befriend." Dot stared at Aaryn. "It's signed…"

At that precise moment, the telecaster for the Utah Jazz announced, "Folks, it looks like we've got a game. And there's no doubt who Jayson Denali is rooting for." The television panned in for a closeup of the celebrated star.

"…Jayson Denali." Dot glanced from the television back to the note and back again before staring up at Aaryn.

With a smile, Dot put the note down and returned to her seat on the sofa. She resumed her quilting.

Aaryn picked up the cardboard wrapping and took it to the kitchen to throw it away. She came back and sat upright in her recliner. Leaning forward with her elbows on her knees, she cupped her chin in both hands. Dot made no further comments about the flowers or about Jayson Denali. In fact, she was humming to herself and Aaryn found her stoic silence annoying. "Well? Aren't you going to ask me anything?"

"You were about to tell me how your day went," Dot said without looking up.

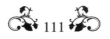

Now that she had a listening ear, Aaryn suddenly wanted her mother's take on the situation. "The best part of my day was running into James at the Front Club. We won fifty bucks from a rock climbing bet. Before then, things appeared to be going along swell. Until he showed up." Aaryn pointed her chin in the direction of the television.

"He doesn't look sickly to me." Dot stopped midway through one of her loops in the quilt to look at Aaryn.

"He came with his mother. Sylvia Denali. She's paralyzed on her right side." Aaryn sighed and sat back with her hands behind her head. She crossed her ankles. "I don't like him one bit. He's conceited, snobbish, totally selfabsorbed, and a womanizer who acts like the sun and the moon revolve completely around him."

"But who are you treating, sweetie? Him or his mother?" Dot resumed her quilting.

Impatiently, Aaryn said, "His mother, of course. But you know it's highly probable that I'd have to interact with the family members and since that appears to be him, I just decided it would be better if someone other than myself treated Mrs. Denali."

"I see," Dot said even though it was obvious from her tone of voice that she didn't see. "And that's why he sent you flowers? Because you made the decision to *not* treat his mother? The flowers are a token of his appreciation then, hmmm?"

"I don't know what the flowers represent. I just know I didn't get a good feeling about him. The man has a salacious reputation for unbridled vice. And for him to send me flowers, why that's just the kind of sneaky thing a snake like him would do." Aaryn stared at the floral arrangement, finding no pleasure in their esthetic beauty. "Someone else would send flowers as a sincere gesture. But not him, Mom. He's a cavalier slime-sucking cad. You should have seen the way he waltzed into Shriners, like he owned the place. I tell you, he came in as if we were his servants and he was welcoming us into the Kingdom of Jayson Denali. And then on top of everything else, he treated me like I was the cleaning lady. Like, *'surely she can't be the doctor?'* "

"He said those exact words?" Dot watched Aaryn closely.

"Well no, but it was written all over his face. He didn't have to say it. Mom, I'm telling you, he…" As Aaryn continued her diatribe against the many faults of Jayson Denali, she wasn't aware of how Dot stopped her quilting to study her. She was midway through another litany of his obvious character flaws when she noticed how intensely Dot was watching her.

"What?" Aaryn asked suspiciously.

"I'm just surprised, that's all. I've never known you to be so arrogant."

"Arrogant? How can you say that? I'm not arrogant at all."

"Hmmm. Then how about judgmental? Does that fit better?"

"But you weren't there. Had you seen him or met him for yourself, you'd understand." Aaryn stared petulantly at the television, her eyes narrowed into tiny slits.

"Well then, dear, I guess I'll just have to meet him for myself, then won't I?" Dot stared at the television as the cameras zoomed in again on Jayson. "He certainly is easy on the eyes, isn't he?"

In reply, Aaryn stood and left the room, unable to mask her irritation. Dot and both dogs stared after her curiously.

By 7:00 AM the next morning, Aaryn was inside the Kundalini Room seated on top of her patient as he lay on his stomach. She sat astride him straddling his thighs. The pressure of her full body weight flowed into her hands as she pressed her palms against his lower back just above his buttocks. Shifting her body side to side, she slid her calves under his thighs and crossed her ankles. He was completely naked except for the sheet wrapped around his lower body. When Aaryn took his arms and pulled them gently behind his back, locking him in a firm grip, Kenny Lewis smiled because he imagined he looked like a hog being tied and readied for the spit. Aaryn pinned his hands behind his back and placed her right hand around the back of his neck. He could feel the pressure being applied slowly at first and then a deep kneading of his neck muscles. When he felt her thumb press into his back just below the nape of his neck, the smile quickly left his face as he yelped in surprise at the pain. When her fingers applied more force to his upper back, it felt like little electric jolts passed through his body. "Agh!" he cried out loudly. But instead of easing up, Aaryn pressed down harder with all of her body weight, applying full pressure. As a rush of burning sensations shot through his upper body, Kenny thought the doctor had taken a white hot knife and plunged it between his shoulder blades. An agonized scream tore through his throat.

So sharp and intense was the pain, that before he was aware of his actions, Kenny Lewis found himself crying as he begged for mercy. Blubbering from excruciating agony, he could suddenly feel the aching pain spread to both his arms and lower back. He pleaded with Aaryn to stop torturing him. When the sharp pains increased, invading his thighs and calves, he gagged and emptied his bladder. But instead of releasing him, Aaryn held fast, her face turned upward to allow her own tears to run down the sides of her face. Yet she showed him no mercy. She lowered her face down to his and whispered angrily to him, "Fight!"

At her command, Mr. Lewis began to flop like a fish. He would do anything to bring an end to his unbearable pain and to unseat this mad woman who rode him into the ground like a beast. His arms jerked, his legs jerked and he even lifted his buttocks. But like a wild horse finally broken, his bucking motions suddenly stopped and he fell back onto the table limp like a wrung rag. Aaryn laid his arms back at his side and climbed off of him. Though she reeked from his urine, she sat on a small stool facing his head and gently began to massage his temples. His crying ceased as her fingers passed gently behind his ears and down to the nape of his neck and back again. Her touch was as light as a feather and Mr. Lewis felt as though he was lifted from the pit of hell and transported straight to heaven.

His facial expression bore traces of ecstasy when he heard her whisper softly in his ear, "Lift your hands, Mr. Lewis. Can you do that for me?"

Without giving it a second thought, Kenny Lewis slowly and gingerly wiggled the fingers on both his hands. Amazed, he lifted his arms ignoring the sharp, stinging needles of pain and brought them over the sides of the table. As he stared into Dr. Jamison's eyes he would swear it was the face of an angel, for her eyes bore straight through his and seemed to hold untold mysteries. He saw the tender smile on her face and his own shocked expression gave way to another multitude of tears. Exhausted, Mr. Lewis cried like a baby. He found himself murmuring thanks to his God for healing him and allowing him to feel his members once again. Mr. Lewis could feel every part of his body where only hours before he'd felt absolutely nothing. Paralysis from the neck down had left his members useless for the last seven years. His face pressed into the hole of the pillowed headrest as he wept in gratitude.

Aaryn embraced his shoulders and allowed him to release his tears. *That's the way it sometimes was,* she thought to herself. Sometimes, we have to endure tremendous pain just to get to the joyous part of anything. Despite the enormous pain that Mr. Lewis had just endured, five months of rehabilitation culminated in his moment of monumental healing. She ventured to guess that Mr. Lewis would say his pain had been worth it. From this point onward, it would be smooth sailing for him. As he shook with emotion, his body and spirit conveyed his gratitude in ways that words would never be able to communicate. Aaryn beckoned to Kyoko, who sat in the corner watching the entire sequence of events with awe, indicating that she should go get additional nurses to assist Mr. Lewis.

Aaryn stepped into the ladies room and showered because she was badly soiled from her patient's bodily waste. Kyoko returned and handed her a fresh towel and a change of garments.

Seeing the happy and smiling expression on Kyoko's face, Aaryn assumed she was elated about Mr. Lewis' healing transformation. She'd no idea Kyoko was smiling for a totally different reason. Aaryn was too thrilled to pay attention to her assistant's mysterious looks. She murmured silent prayers of thanksgiving as she buttoned her top. She would stop in and check on her patient after he was bathed and fed. Her next appointment was in another thirty minutes.

As Aaryn walked down the hall toward the elevator banks, passersby smiled at her with knowing eyes. She figured news must have spread about Mr. Lewis' healing. She smiled back at them because she had a warm feeling within herself as well.

"How beautiful and thoughtful, Dr. Jamison. You must be so pleased." More well wishers passed her by.

The doors opened and as she was about to step onto the elevator, three nurses got off saying, "There you are! You must be thrilled. You're just the most fortunate person I know, Dr. Jamison."

Aaryn smiled with one eyebrow lifted curiously and said, "Well, to God be the glory, then." The three women even waved as they continued to stare at her starry eyed as the elevator doors closed.

She still had a smile on her face when the doors opened to let her off. She'd been staring at the floor lost in thought, but as she stepped out into the hall her eyes lifted to stare straight ahead at the receptionist's area. The warm feelings immediately left Aaryn's face and body as she stared at six floral arrangements similar to the one she'd received at home the night before. Each bouquet consisted of three dozen roses and was housed in a stunning crystal vase. And each vase was shaped differently than the next. One floral arrangement contained light pink roses and bore a decorative tag that read, "Joy." Another arrangement was dark pink. It's engraved card read, "Thankfulness." But the ones that really stood out were the lavender and orange displays. Lavender read "Enchantment" and orange read "Fascination." The final floral arrangement held a mix of roses in all five colors, yellow, light pink, dark pink, lavender and orange. They were beautiful. Two hundred and sixteen roses. No wonder all the staff was agog with gossip and probable illicit thoughts.

"I've never seen anything like it in all my life."

"Honey, I wish I could find a man as gorgeous and thoughtful as him."

"Clearly he must be smitten with her."

"Can you imagine the expense and exquisite detail he must have gone through to send all of this?"

"And they all bear the same signature: With gratitude, Jayson Denali." All five women behind the nurses' station stared at Aaryn as though they had died and gone to heaven.

Aaryn knew she had to tread carefully. She was well aware of her image around the hospital and she freely admitted she wasn't the friendliest or easiest person to get to know. She wasn't thought of as mean, just someone who kept her distance from others. She didn't hang out or do the girlfriend thing with the nurses or other doctors on staff. She was, by all accounts, strictly professional.

How she handled their la-la land, starstruck reactions would forever solidify her reputation with the staff. She stepped forward trying as much as humanly possible to stamp out the blaze of anger that rested within her belly. "They're beautiful aren't they?" Aaryn made a point of smelling the roses. "It's such a thoughtful gesture. And so very magnanimous of Mr. Denali. But, ladies, here's what you don't know. When Mr. Denali realized that he couldn't sign autographs, he still wanted to express his gratitude for the way his mother has been cared for. He didn't know your names so he sent them all in care of me." Aaryn heard the elevators doors open and close behind her, but she was caught up in her story. What amazed her was the ease at which she was spinning her white lies.

"Had he known your names, Mr. Denali would surely have sent each of the floral arrangements to your attention. But this last bouquet, he wanted delivered straight to his mother." Aaryn should have known by their breathless silence that someone stood behind her. She didn't figure it out until she stopped smelling the fragrant roses long enough to follow their gaze. When she did, she turned to find Jayson Denali standing directly behind her.

Startled, at first Aaryn looked like a little kid caught with her hand in the cookie jar. Or, like Pinocchio caught in the act of telling the biggest lie of his life. Embarrassed, Aaryn refused to look him in the eye. She turned to the women behind the nurses' station and said, "Ladies, you should really thank Mr. Denali for his thoughtfulness. All of this generosity was his idea and his way of saying thank you."

Ignoring their open looks of disbelief, Aaryn picked up the multicolored floral arrangement and held it out to Jayson. "Here, Mr. Denali. I'll let you deliver these to your mother yourself."

This close to him, his stark beauty and animal magnetism caused her fingers to tremble and her body to quake. She was ill-prepared for the rush of heated adrenaline that shot through her because of his nearness. A quickening, an awakening coursed through her senses. Without even looking into his face, Aaryn knew this man was startlingly male. *Perfection made flesh...*

As she offered him the arrangement, taking care to avoid touching him, Aaryn dared not meet his eyes. Instead, she allowed her glance to start at his black Dolce & Gabbana calfskin leather loafers to his classy, beautifully tailored dark gray wool Gucci suit, up to his light blue Armani custom dress shirt and finally to the top of his matching silk Prada necktie. Refusing to make eye contact with him, she sidestepped him and quickly headed to the safety of her office. Even as she rushed away, Aaryn could hear the ladies gushing at him as they clasped his hand in gratitude of his generosity, their skepticism over his floral donation short lived.

Aaryn leaned against her door. A sigh of relief escaped her as her back slid down the door until her buttocks rested on the floor. She wrapped her arms around her knees and rested her chin on top of them. Feeling completely bewildered, she closed her eyes and whispered, "Father? Help me. All my inadequacies lay before me and right now all I know is that I'm utterly confused. I do not like this man and yet, something about him draws me. Help me, Father. Preserve me. Keep me. Show me how to deal with him and not make a fool out of myself. Please, Lord. Amen."

As Aaryn sat there, she lifted her head and rested it against the door. A distant memory from her childhood growing up in Kenilworth came to her. She was ten years old and her best friend at the time was a boy in her classroom named Peter Freeman. She and Peter had climbed trees together, caught frogs and competed to see who could throw rocks the furthest. Their friendship was innocent and sprang from the basis that they were both misfits. Their racial differences was never an issue. That is, until Peter's older brother and his friends started teasing him mercilessly about his girlfriend. They teased him so until Peter started avoiding Aaryn. After school, he would race home without acknowledging her and because she didn't understand his rejection, Aaryn had followed him home one day to ask him what she'd done to offend him. When she arrived at his house, Peter was sitting on his front porch looking gloomy while his brother and his brother's friends played catch in the yard. As soon as they saw Aaryn, they started teasing Peter by singing, *"Peter and Aaryn sittin' in a tree, k-i-s-s-i-n-g."*

Over and over, they sang the song tossing their baseball from one to another. As Aaryn looked at each of the boys, their silly song meant nothing to her. Her gaze finally stopped at Peter. His face was scrunched and he looked as though he was about to cry. Finally, he picked up a rock and threw it at his brother screaming the words, "She's not my girlfriend. How could I like her when she's a *nigger*." When Peter saw the look of devastation on Aaryn's face, he turned and ran inside his house leaving his brother and the other boys laughing in the yard.

As Aaryn walked home that day, she would never forget the dagger of betrayal that pierced her heart. She'd never thought of Peter as a boyfriend. She just enjoyed being in his company because they liked the same things. But on that day as she trudged home, she felt dirty, ashamed and lower than low. She knew what the "N" word meant. She also knew people only used it to wound someone deeply. She and Peter had played together since the third grade and she never knew he felt that way about her. She wasn't aware that embarrassment and the overwhelming need for his brother's approval had caused Peter to act out of character. All she knew was that she'd thought they were friends and yet, he'd hidden hatred for her in his heart. At that moment, Aaryn decided, *boys can't be trusted.* As she walked home, she repeated it over and over until the mantra was finely engraved in her psyche. She didn't know it at the time, but her first lesson in betrayal from someone of the opposite sex would go a long way toward how she viewed men and conducted her future dealings with them.

Aaryn's eyes opened and the Wasatch mountains came into her view. Remembering that incident brought back all feelings she associated with rejection. Aaryn realized that the one childhood incident, though it had happened over twenty-five years ago, colored all her dealings with men. As she'd grown older, her distrust of the opposite sex never waned. Boys became men and her mantra shifted to reflect the changing times. Instead of *boys* couldn't be trusted, it was now *men* couldn't be trusted. Like a broken wing that never properly healed, Aaryn allowed one childhood incident to fester until it overshadowed her ability to put the past in proper perspective. And so, at 39 years of age, Aaryn knew she'd built a fortress around herself so she would never have to risk being rejected by someone of the opposite sex. She assured herself that her singleness was the result of never having met a man whom she considered trustworthy enough to let her guard down for. Since this could only lead to betrayal and unhappiness, Aaryn's life revolved around her work, her patients, her mother, her outlet of physical activities, and of course her belief in her God. It was a rich and full life, and yet, missing was one element that she was loath to name.

All Aaryn knew was that Jayson Denali reminded her of that missing element. The thought of him made her aloneness glaringly obvious. She wasn't lonely, she was alone. There was a huge and distinct difference between the two. Aaryn told herself she remained unattached because she was unique and unwilling to lower her standards just to have a man at her side. She doubted she would ever have a relationship representative of the way her father had loved her mother. But whenever Aaryn thought of love, that's what came to mind. Jayson Denali made her think about relationships, or in her case, the lack thereof. Why he, of all men, would have that effect on her, she hadn't a clue. His beauty made him untrustworthy in her eyes and she would never fall for him or anyone like him. She could read his spirit well enough to know that too many women had tried unsuccessfully to gain his affections. She would neither fall prey to any of his tricks or wiles, not that he needed to employ them. Through no fault of his own, women would forever be drawn by his animal magnetism like moths to a flame. Each woman would willingly sacrifice herself just to have a small token of his affection. She would not be swayed by his insincere gifts of flattery and she would not be made a fool of by him at any cost. Aaryn decided her best course of action was to avoid him and to ignore the yearnings he evoked within her.

She got up and pulled from the miniature refrigerator in the corner of her office a small glass jar. It contained a rich blend of organic olive oil, pure lavender and pure jasmine essential oils which she'd blended herself. She poured several drops of the blend onto a towelette and dragged it over her face until she felt refreshed. As she headed to her next appointment, Aaryn told herself everything was going to work out fine.

Chapter Ten

By noon that same day, Aaryn was famished and thoughts of food were her most pressing concern. Shriners' offered a healthy smorgasbord of food choices where she could always find something good to eat. She hurried to the lunchroom to grab a sandwich and salad and took her goodies up to the rooftop of the building. Aaryn loved sitting there because the view reminded her of a lake's promontory point. A huge cascading waterfall was built there at her insistence. The granite rocks and colorful water sprays combined for a serene effect.

She waved her key card over the reader and the automatic doors parted for her. Aaryn stepped out onto the roof deck and had only taken several steps before she heard her name called.

"Aaryn, there you are. Why don't you join us for lunch?"

She swiveled around and stopped in her tracks at the sight of Kyle, Jayson and Sylvia Denali sitting off to the side at a table laden with a white linen cloth and a feast set for a king.

"I see you've already brought your lunch. Please eat with us. We have room for one more and there's plenty."

Aaryn approached the table reluctantly. One hundred percent of the time when she came to the rooftop to enjoy her lunch, she was able to do so in solitude. However, to refuse and turn around when everyone was staring at her would be overtly rude on her part. She stared at Kyle, the traitor, as if to say, *et tu, Brutus?* Realizing there was no way out, she decided to hurriedly eat her lunch and escape. Aaryn ignored the fact that Jayson was watching her closely and spoke to his mother as she sat down beside her.

"How are you feeling, Mrs. Denali?"

"I'm a little tired in my body today. But that can be attributed to old age. Other than that I am well."

Something in her voice caused Aaryn to stare at her intently. A tinge of weariness had laced her words. But to the untrained ear, it went unnoticed. "Have you eaten today, Mrs. Denali?"

Sylvia stared at the young woman. "I managed some toast earlier."

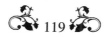

Aaryn scooted her chair back and stood behind Sylvia's wheelchair. She stepped close to her and said, "I'm going to put my hands on your shoulders, just like this, okay?" As Aaryn stood over her, Sylvia nodded.

"I'm just going to use my fingers to stimulate your nerves, so don't be alarmed. I want you to relax." Again, Aaryn felt her nod.

Jayson and Kyle watched transfixed as she began to softly knead Sylvia's shoulders. Light pressure was applied as her fingers slowly eased their way to her neck area. Aaryn gently cupped Sylvia's chin and lifted her head so that it rested against her lower abdomen. Turning Sylvia's head to the side, she allowed her fingertips to trail down her neck, stroking its base.

As Jayson watched Aaryn, each touch seemed like a warm caress and he was intrigued by the tender care that was invested in every gentle stroke. Slowly, she turned Sylvia's head this way and that before tilting it forward to softly squeeze her neck. Her thumbtips pressed to the corners of Sylvia's eyes, temples, the corners of her mouth, the bridge of her nose all the way up to her forehead. It was just a series of light touches and yet, Jayson couldn't help but be intrigued by this woman's latent sensuality. There was nothing erotic about the way she soothed his mother, and yet, Jayson couldn't help but envision her touching him in the same manner. He realized that outwardly, she came across as brusque with her straight forward approach. It could be she lacked appropriate people and social skills, but the gentleness within her surfaced when she was touching people, helping to heal their infirmities.

Aaryn lifted Sylvia's head and brought her hands back down to her shoulders. She patted them before taking her seat beside her.

"Can I be next?" Jayson asked. When Aaryn looked up at him in surprise, he thought "Gotcha." She hadn't met his eyes since she'd stared through him the day before. He'd finally forced her to look at him. He even imagined he saw a hint of a smile on her face.

Kyle handed Aaryn a hot cloth and as she cleansed her hands he asked, "How do you feel now, Sylvia?"

"I feel like I've been renewed underneath a healing waterfall." She said to Aaryn, "Thank you very much, dear. That felt magical. I think I'll have a bite of salmon now. My appetite seems to have returned."

She took a bite of her salad as Jayson said, "Tell us about your patient today, Dr. Jamison. Kyle says the man can walk again after seven years of being paralyzed."

Aaryn noticed that everyone seemed to be on a first name basis at the table. "Well, Mr. Lewis is far from walking. But he'll get there soon. He's no longer afflicted with paralysis, so the worst is over for him."

"You must be thrilled." Jayson willed her to look at him again but she continued eating.

"I'm very pleased for him. It's been a rough five months of rehabilitation. But once you see someone walk who everyone else has said will never walk again, you realize miracles are around us everywhere and that we exist in the midst of them. Only, we don't know it because we're too busy to notice. It's the little things, Mr. Denali, that people become grateful for when they've been healed or given a new lease on life. A beating heart, a healed body, another breath taken—when it all boils down to it, it's the priceless things that we assign so little value to, that ignite sparks of joy within us. No one who comes here ever leaves without reassessing their lives and reprioritizing the things they esteem."

"...*In the midst of miracles.* My grandmother once said that to me when I was a little girl."

Aaryn smiled at her and asked, "Did you know your grandmother well?"

Before Sylvia could answer, Jayson interrupted her, "How about a few of these string beans, Ma? They're delicious. Here, let me cut them for you." Jayson did not want his mother discussing the weird story she'd told him earlier. The good doctor already thought him a decadent reprobate. He didn't want her adding the term loony to whatever image she held of his mother. He turned to Kyle and asked, "Kyle, who designed the waterfall? It's stunning and definitely unique."

Kyle spoke proudly. "That's Aaryn's doing. There are only a few staff members who come up here for the mountain view. It seems Aaryn is fascinated with mountains. She's also an excellent climber, is our Dr. Jamison. Last year she even climbed Mount Everest."

Closing her eyes so she wouldn't roll them in annoyance at blabber-mouth Kyle, Aaryn wondered what on earth had gotten into him?

"Attempted is the better word, Kyle. I didn't reach the top. My group halted our climb in order to save the life of another climber. We stopped about three hours short of reaching the summit. It still bothers me that out of a group of ten people, only two of us wanted to help the man who had fallen into a crevasse. Turns out, he would have died had we not stopped when we did. You see, near the summit of Everest, is what we call the 'dead zone.' It's called that because the amount of oxygen in the air is about a third of what people are used to breathing at sea level. You risk your own life to save someone else's. And that's the moral dilemma. Do you continue climbing when you see someone fall, or do you stop to lend assistance? I guess the answer depends on how much value you attach to someone's life." Aaryn glanced at her watch. "Look at the time. I'd better be getting back." She turned to Sylvia and said, "I'll see you soon, Mrs. Denali."

Both men stood as she rose to leave the table. Jayson knew better than to offer her his hand.

When she passed through the automatic doors, Sylvia said, "See there. I told you that you could accomplish more with honey than you could with vinegar. She'll treat me now that she knows you can be well behaved, Jayson. I had a dream last night that Dr. Jamison was massaging me in a pool of water and I realize now that it must have been the water fountain over there that I saw in my dream." With a smile on her face, she said, "Thank you as well, Kyle. I don't know what you both said to change her mind, but I'm grateful. When do my treatments begin? I can't wait." Sylvia's smile was like that of a child's as she stared complacently into the waterfall with its changing rays of colors.

Jayson didn't have the heart to tell his mother that nothing had changed since he'd last spoken with Dr. Jamison.

It was Kyle who got them into even deeper hot waters. "We won't know until later this week, Sylvia. But as soon as we create the schedule, I'll let you and Jayson know." Kyle stared at Jayson as he spoke, the two of them seeming to share a common goal. How that goal would be accomplished, neither of them knew.

After lunch, Jayson sat with Sylvia in Shriners' rose garden. His mother was happy as she regaled him with stories from her childhood. Her memories from yesteryear seemed to press upon her and she told him all about them. She spoke of her mother and even his father. Jayson was simply content to listen to her. It had been a long time since he'd sat in his mother's presence just enjoying her. But he noticed she didn't speak of Carmin.

Jayson had worked it out with Kyle to meet with Aaryn as soon as she finished making her daily rounds. They wanted to try once more to persuade her to add Sylvia to her patient list. When Kyle sent an assistant to collect him from the rose garden, as he entered Kyle's office, his disappointment showed when he didn't see Dr. Jamison.

Kyle looked stumped. "I believe Aaryn is gone for the day and I didn't have an opportunity to speak with her before she left. She normally spends time in her office after she finishes up. It's most unusual of her to leave so suddenly."

A determination that wouldn't be denied came over Jayson. "She's avoiding me. That much I know. But I also know I can't stay here another day waiting and hoping to speak with her. I think I know where to find her."

"You do?" surprise laced Kyle's voice.

"Yes, and I'll have an answer either way before I leave Utah." With a look on his face that bode ill to anyone who crossed him, Jayson walked from Kyle's office and headed to his waiting limousine.

"George, take me to the climbing club we visited yesterday. I want to see if the Range Rover is there." But as they pulled into the lot thirty minutes later, Aaryn's SUV was not there. Without giving it a second thought, Jayson said, "Let's visit the Buena Vista address. She might be headed home."

When George arrived at the home, Jayson had him stop just before the entrance to the driveway. He got out and walked up the red brick road. He had nearly reached the house when he drew to an abrupt halt. Two dogs as huge as horses galloped toward him. Jayson had always heard that one should stand still to avoid being attacked by a dog. But he stood stock still not from instruction but out of fear. What scared him further was that although the dogs weren't barking or growling, they looked menacing to him. He wondered if silently frightening people to death was their normal routine before they ate their victims. Just as Jayson took a small step to slowly backpedal, the tan horse-sized animal crept behind him and pressed his wet nose to Jayson's butt. Trying not to panic, he turned slowly only to have the dark gray monster close in to sniff his groin area. Self preservation made him squeeze his legs together tighter.

Damned freaky dogs, he muttered to himself. With tails wagging wildly, the two horses circled Jayson smelling him in the oddest of places, nudging him with their wet noses as if to bait and mock him. When the tan giant suddenly jumped up on Jayson resting his paws on his shoulders, the animal stood at least seven feet tall. "Agh, God!" Jayson groaned as the canine sloppily licked his face, the excess drool sliding down onto Jayson's neck. Meanwhile, the gray ogre sat looking on as if daring Jayson to bust a move or try to get away. Resting his hands on both sides of the dog's head, Jayson held him firmly to stop the unwelcome licking.

"Max, get down. Come here, both of you." As if sensing they were in serious trouble, the two horses turned to slink to the front door where an impressive woman stood inside the doorway. As she stared at them sternly, both dogs dropped their heads toward the ground.

"Max, you should be ashamed of yourself." She spoke in an austere tone.

With his face still scrunched in disgust, Jayson couldn't help but think, "Damned straight they aught to be ashamed! Perverted mutts."

"Believe me, their size is purely deceptive. These two phonies really wouldn't hurt a fly. I assure you they were only being friendly."

Friendly? Jeez, Jayson thought. He wondered if she realized how unbelievably naive those words sounded coming out of her mouth. The way he saw it, if she hadn't happened along when she did, the twisted beasts probably would have raped him. Besides, all pet owners claimed their animals were lovable, saintly beings—especially the ones who owned vicious-looking monsters like these two.

"Well, don't just stand there, young man. Come, let me have a look at you."

Since the dogs had gotten chewed out, Jayson figured it was his turn on the chopping block. With the dog's spittle drying on his face, Jayson approached her. There was no doubt she was Dr. Jamison's mother. Not so much in terms of looks but the regal way she carried herself. As he stood before her, she studied him so intently that he half expected her to tilt his chin and turn his head this way and that. Her look reminded him of the way the creature in the movie *Predator* studied Arnold Schwarzenegger prior to serving him a royal beat down.

"You'll have to excuse Baron and Max. We don't get visitors very often."

Gee, I wonder why, Jayson thought. Aloud, he managed, "You don't say."

"Best come in so I can get you a towel to clean your face." She opened the door wide and stepped aside to allow Jayson entrance. As if waiting for permission, the dogs stared at her expectantly until she said, "Yes, you too. Come on." She patted their massive heads and all seemed to be forgiven as the horse-sized devils marched proudly inside throwing Jayson a look that he swore was one of smirking mockery.

"This way, Jayson." Surprised that she knew his name, Jayson assumed Aaryn must have discussed him with her. If so, he was sure she hadn't said anything good.

Jayson stared around him as she led him to a bathroom on the first floor of the home. It was just as striking on the inside as it was on the outside. Everything was colorful and exuded warmth and hominess. He quickly washed his face and hands and rejoined her in the livingroom where she sat waiting for him. He took a seat across from her, unbuttoning his jacket as he settled into the recliner. He had no clue he'd just sat in Aaryn's favorite chair.

"You must be Dr. Jamison's mother." Jayson leaned forward with his elbows on his knees. An excitement was building in him, as if he was presented with the key to cracking a secure code, he wanted to pull every bit of information he could from this woman. Her countenance was beautiful and Jayson knew she'd aged well. Her skin was clear and her face was lined with very few wrinkles.

Her silver gray hair hung loosely about shoulders which were erect. "Sit next to me so I can examine you for myself."

With a conciliatory smile, Jayson rose to sit beside her. When she reached out her hand to him with her palm facing upward, it felt natural for him to take it. At least *she* had no qualms about touching people. Even her smile was welcoming as she said to him, "Tell me, who is Jayson Denali? Speak to me your truth."

Immediately, Jayson found himself immersed in a twoway conversation as he spoke of his childhood, his modeling career and how it led to acting with him being cast as America's newest superstar. He didn't just converse about himself. He was deeply curious about her family and how they had come to live in Utah. Dot, as she insisted he call her, filled him in on their beginnings but told him that the other things he yearned to know, he would have to ask Aaryn directly.

At the mention of her name, Jayson grew guarded and told Dot that he didn't see that ever happening. Dot, however, knew otherwise but didn't correct him. She stood and said, "Come with me." With the dogs trailing alongside, she led him out into her garden watching with pleasure the awestruck expressions that crossed his face. Dot gave him a tour of her "enchanted forest" as he called it, explaining to him how she cared for it.

"Every living thing, Jayson, even the trees, possess a spirit. And it is that spirit that we either nurture, feed, starve, abuse, mistreat or heal. I believe that when we're born, we all know this. But as we grow, we become desensitized to listening to and hearing from our spirit—God's spirit that indwells within us." Sensing that he was receptive to the things she revealed to him, she stopped and knelt before a ten-foot high fig tree and feeling its bark, began to tell him about her ability to heal plants and trees. It wasn't something I went to school for, but it is a gift from God. Take this fig tree for example. Its roots were spreading unnaturally and had begun to strangle two of its nearby neighbors. I pruned it and clipped its roots to restrain it. Days later, I noticed the leaves began to marble with yellow spots and its veins turned a light color. At first, I thought it was a potassium deficiency, or the result of a mosaic virus. But when that turned out not to be the case, I began to listen, commanding the tree to speak its truth. What I found Jayson, was that this fig tree felt abandoned, cut off from its lost members. And so I began to speak life to it, commanding it to live and not die."

Seeing the disbelieving look on Jayson's face, Dot smiled and said, "Oh yes, I earn my living by talking to trees, Jayson. I travel this entire state healing people's plants and trees. Laugh if you must, but people pay well to preserve their trees and plants. I've even received travel requests from people as far away as upstate New York, but nowadays I limit my traveling to Utah. I'm not the spring chicken I once used to be, you know." Dot smiled as she stroked the fig tree's bark lovingly. "Gardens are the center of my joy. At least they're one of the centers, that is. I believe that if we listen, every living thing will scan us for ours and consequently will speak its own truth." Before Jayson could move to assist her, Dot jumped to her feet and dusted the dirt from her smock.

"It is why Max felt the need to give you a tongue bath. He wanted to know your spirit, whether you were friend or foe." At the mention of his name, the dog's ears pricked and he looked as if he was waiting for instruction. Dot patted his head absentmindedly and then had to pat the other dog's head as well since he would not be ignored or left out. "Though the human spirit can lie, there's no guile in plants and animals, Jayson, only truth."

"Are you saying then that we should only communicate and surround ourselves with plants and animals? No one's perfect, Dot. We all have our faults."

"Yes, we all have character flaws. Plants, trees and animals are simply the element in which I'm comfortable. Take me away from that and I'll find a way to incorporate these things back into my life, wherever I am. Take Aaryn for example. God has gifted her and graced her with the ability to heal people. She's not *the* healer, but she's a vehicle God *uses* to heal because of her receptivity. Healing is her element. Take her out of it and she, too, will find a way to integrate it once again." Dot stopped walking and turned to stare at Jayson.

"What is it for you, Jayson Denali? What is your truth? What is it that you refuse to live without? What is so precious to you that if stripped from you, you'll find a way to return it to your life?" Dot extended her hand to him and Jayson stepped closer to grasp it. His hand was sandwiched between hers when she said, "When you discover the answer, Jayson, happiness will never elude you."

As they walked further, Dot began to regale him with stories about the healing journeys of trees and plants which she'd witnessed. Jayson didn't disbelieve her, he just figured it wasn't his calling so he didn't have to understand the ins and outs of what she described. He said to Dot, "It sounds fulfilling for you, but what about other people? Don't you miss them? All this, it's beautiful and remote, but it seems so…" He searched for the right word, "lonely."

"It's never lonely, Jayson, because we're never alone. We only think we are. There's much to be learned within the quiet stillness of solitude. That's when God begins to speak to us. But we can't hear Him because we've become accustomed to surrounding ourselves with noise. I'm not advocating a life of solitude. I'm just saying that all of us need time by ourselves to fully develop that inner voice that lies within."

Dot turned and they began to walk back toward the house. Jayson looked into the distance and the house seemed so far away. He had no idea they had walked so far. He'd gotten caught up in their conversation.

"Your mother is finding this out as well, Jayson. There's a peacefulness that's settling within her spirit as she comes to grip with certain tragedies she's experienced. Tragedies either weaken or strengthen us. Sometimes, they accomplish both. That's the state that your mother was in, weakened at first, but now she's healing emotionally. I sense that your mother grieves deeply over the loss of loved ones. One of them was a child, another was a long-lost love. And yet, just as it was for the biblical Shunamite woman, it shall be well with her."

With a puzzled expression, he said, "But how do you know these things, Dot? Did Aaryn let you read her medical files?" The look on Jayson's face demanded to know the truth.

"No, Jayson. No one has mentioned these things to me. I doubt you'll even find them in her files anywhere. That leaves only one source from where I could have

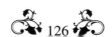

gleaned this information. So let me ask you something. When did you start believing there is no God?" A sternness entered Dot's voice.

"That's not true, Dot. I do believe in God. I just believe..." Jayson's voice trailed off because he didn't know what he believed anymore. It had been a long time since he'd even thought about the subject.

"I see. And then do you believe you've gotten where you are all on your own? Look at you. Strong, tall, astronomically successful. Blessed with a beauty so profound that at times it has been a curse. Out of all the stars around today, you Jayson, have emerged as one of the most electrifying actors in the world. You believe all that is your own doing? Look around you. This very garden that has captivated your attention, do you think I can take credit for it all by myself? I've played a huge part, yes. But to say I caused it on my own would be to ignore the grace that God equips me with to accomplish those things most precious to me." As they reached the house, Dot said, "Just think about the things we've discussed, dear. Only you know the answer to them. Only you can speak your own truth."

They entered the huge kitchen, replete with exotic smells when Dot asked, "Now, how about a slice of pecan pie?"

"I'd love it," Jayson replied. He washed his hands after Dot.

As they were seated at the marbled island in the middle of the kitchen enjoying the pie, Jayson had Dot squealing with laughter. "...and then the little boy turned to the minister and said, 'If God is so powerful, how come he doesn't have a cell phone? Everybody has one of those.' You see, the boy thought that if he couldn't reach God by phone then how could He be omnipotent like the minister claimed?"

Jayson took another bite of the scrumptious pie as Dot smiled at him fondly. Her fork was lifted mid air as she continued to laugh and it was that scene that Aaryn walked into as she entered the kitchen carrying grocery bags in both hands. When she saw Jayson seated eating a slice of pie, her mouth dropped open in surprise.

Taking advantage of her shock, Jayson eased off the stool and took the bags from her hand, setting them onto the counter.

Dot said, "Tonight is Aaryn's night to cook, Jayson. Would you like to stay for dinner?"

"Of course, Dot. I'd love to join you."

"No, Mom, Mr. Denali would not like to stay for dinner."

Both Jayson and Aaryn spoke rapidly at the same time.

"Well, I'll let you two work it out. Baron, Max, come." Dot walked from the kitchen with a smile on her face.

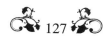

Aaryn wasted no time letting loose her vitriol. Her voice was low and held a husky dose of anger. "How dare you come here! You have no right, Jayson Denali. What *is* it with you?"

"Listen, I'm sorry I trespassed, okay? I wanted to speak to you before you left the hospital but you left abruptly and none of the staff could find you. So I came to where I thought you might be."

"I left early because I had an outside consultation that I was running late for. And since when do I owe you an explanation of my comings and goings?"

"You don't. You don't owe me anything." Jayson was trying to stamp out the annoyance beginning to swell inside him. It seemed that every time he came into this woman's presence, an argument ensued. This was not good. "I just wanted to know if there was anything I could say or do to change your mind about treating my mother. She says that if you're not going to be her attending physician, then she won't stay." Jayson walked to the island that separated them. "Look, I know we didn't get off on the right foot with each other. But my mother likes you. You seem to like her. Tell me what you need me to do and I'll do it. Just please, please don't allow your dislike of me to interfere with treating my mother. I'm begging you."

Aaryn sighed with disgust. She rued the day Kyle ever mentioned the Denalis to her. *Would there be no end to this? The man was standing in her home for God's sake!* Aaryn closed her eyes for a full minute to calm her volcanic nerves. When she opened them, she spoke through clenched teeth. "Alright. Listen to me and hear me well, Jayson Denali. I'll treat your mother. But with a few conditions that you either agree to right now or you walk out of here and never, ever return."

Relieved, Jayson said, "Sure. What are they?"

"First, they'll be no contact between you and I. So when you visit your mother, I want to know about it a day in advance. Second, tell your driver to stop following me. And third, do not ever send me flowers again. Agreed?" Aaryn's arms were wrapped around herself to contain her anger.

Jayson nodded slowly. "Thank you." He turned and walked toward the entrance to the kitchen. He stopped and asked her, "Have we met before? Did I offend you and just don't remember it?"

Aaryn squeezed her eyes shut and shook her head. If this man did not leave her house she was going to scream!

Seeing the look of consternation on her face, instead of pushing her for more information, Jayson turned and continued through the house, closing the front door behind him. He had accomplished what he'd come there for, so by all accounts he should have been elated. But far from feeling like he had something to celebrate, Jayson had a hollow emptiness inside him.

Part III

*"Love does not begin and end the way we seem to think it does.
Love is a battle. Love is a war. Love is…growing up."*

~ James A. Baldwin

Chapter Eleven

"Why was all hell breaking loose in *her* life," Erika wondered. Virtual tidal waves dense with potential calamity swirled threateningly about her. It seemed to Erika that in the midst of all the chaos, she was barely remaining afloat. To add to her mounting woes, here she sat in the principal's office of the International School of Indiana (ISI) dusting off her conflict resolution skills as she waited to speak with the principal and two egregiously offended parents.

Granted, her six year old daughter, Mia, was a peculiar and oft difficult to understand child. However, she certainly was not the menacing firebrand the accusing parents were making her out to be. It was times like this when Mia hummed quietly to herself that she appeared angelic. The meeting called by Principal Gomes was delayed 15 minutes to accommodate Michael Slaughter, who was the real crux of Erika's problems, and who currently was stuck in traffic. *How fitting,* she thought with an illconcealed scowl. Increasingly, his "day late 'n a dollah shawt" treatise was becoming the story of Michael's life—always tardy or unavailable whenever the circumstances involved his wife and children.

ISI was one of the finest, premier educational institutions in the world. Tuition did not come cheap. With fees starting at $15k per year for preschoolers, tuition skyrocketed even higher for grades K through 12. Only a limited number of highly sought-after slots were issued each year. Parents vied for their children's admittance to ISI much like lion prides battled over the remains of a meager carcass. Only the brightest and most affluent students were enrolled. To assume that wealth and status was a requirement was not a non sequitur.

ISI students were taught in a multilingual and multicultural environment. In the first, second and third grades, the children's bilingual education was accomplished by immersing them in French, Italian and Spanish. Only twenty percent of their overall curriculum was taught in English. ISI was proud of its diverse multiculturalism and took great strides to promote unity within a student body that put the rainbow coalition to shame. Ergo, fisticuffs of any kind were not tolerated.

That little six-year old Mia Slaughter was all but being branded a terrorist should have been an insult. But righteous indignation was a luxury Erika was willing to forfeit to the offended parents. What Erika had in lieu of it was a dull but persistent throbbing headache. At issue was a homely, battle-scarred Carebear nicknamed "Hully" and a receding egg-sized lump on the forehead of one Richard Brent Cunningham, III.

In addition to little Richard's bruised forehead, it appeared he was having psychological nightmares after his schoolmate, one Mia Slaughter, accused him of being a "file" demon from the pit of hell. Though she'd mispronounced the word

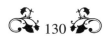

"foul," Mia's point was well made and as a result, little Richard now feared he was destined to "burn in hell, chained to a bottomless pit" just the way his merry little class chum, Mia, had foretold. Each night for the past week the poor boy had awakened screaming and crying from terrifyingly realistic dreams. When he refused to return to school, his parents quickly turned to therapy and out poured Richard's version of events.

Thus, the Cunninghams sat before the principal, Dr. Ronald J. Gomes, filled with moral outrage. Short of demanding a pound of flesh, they wanted assurance that Mia Slaughter would be kept far away from their precious child. Dr. Gomes had called the meeting so the parents and both children could interact with each other, exchange dialogue and resolve this unfortunate incident. Of course, it didn't help matters that little Richard sat glued to his mother's lap, refusing to look in Mia's direction.

Precisely fifteen minutes later, Principal Gomes' assistant opened the door to admit Michael and the meeting officially got underway.

Erika watched her husband take over by putting the Cunninghams at ease and asking to hear their side of the story. Afterwards, without bothering to hear Mia's version, he apologized for his daughter's illogical behavior and would have disciplined her on the spot had not Erika intervened.

She viewed Michael's apology as an indictment against her own maternal skills. She knew her child was not an unprincipled roughneck and found it odd that she would attack the Cunningham boy without provocation. It was Erika's experience that once parents got involved, they tended to muddy the waters by intervening in simple matters that most children would work out on their own, if left to their own devices. She was more interested in hearing the children explain in their own words what had happened.

When Richard refused to speak and barely glanced up from his mother's chest, the way he latched on to Mrs. Cunningham told Erika that he was far more sheltered than any of her children had ever been. While he sat on his mother's lap, Mia sat in a chair between her and Michael. Erika asked her daughter to explain what happened.

Not surprisingly, "Hully" was interspersed throughout Mia's story. From what she described, Richard was goaded by his friends into sneaking the Carebear from Mia's backpack. When she discovered it missing, Richard claimed he'd hidden the ugly bear so she would never find it. Distressed, Mia had kicked the boy in both shins, unintentionally knocking him to the ground. With her anger on full blast, another child realized things were getting out of hand so he quickly retrieved the bear and handed it to Mia. By this time, Richard, who was taller and bigger than Mia, had struggled to his feet with tears in his eyes. But when Mia discovered one of Hully's eyes was missing she went ballistic and "attacked" Richard by kicking him in the forehead. Thus, knocking him back to the ground, this time screaming in terror. Everything happened so quickly the teachers never had a chance to intervene.

Taken at face value, Erika admitted that her daughter's actions probably *did* appear over the top. But she also knew how attached Mia was to Hully and how much the Carebear meant to her. The bear was a gift her aunt Aaryn had given her four years earlier and it was the favorite of all Mia's toys. For some strange reason, Mia did not like dolls, but instead loved stuffed animals. She'd given each of her stuffed toys a unique name and when she turned three, she began calling the Carebear "Hully."

Time had not been kind to Hully. So it came as no surprise to Erika that the other children would refer to him as a "scaredy" bear. With his once-upon-a-time curly main, he certainly was not the most attractive toy in Mia's possession. Nevertheless, he maintained his status as her favorite toy. Her attachment to the bear was odd to Erika but even when Mia began to sleep with it and carry it with her everywhere she went, Erika still didn't question it. When she refused to leave home without it, Erika relented and bought Mia a tiny backpack that would hold the Carebear. It wasn't until a year later when Mia turned four that the bear finally became a source of irritation for Erika.

Increasingly, Mia would say things like, "Hully said this," or "Hully says that," until one day Erika was compelled to ask her daughter why she'd chosen to name the bear Hully.

Erika would never forget Mia's response. "I didn't name him, Momma. Hully told me his name. He said his name is Hully Speeret. But, Momma, Hully says I can just call him Hully because it's easier."

A chill went straight through Erika. She'd been dicing green peppers and carrots when Mia's words registered. She stopped chopping and turned to Mia who sat sprawled on the ceramic floor in an awkward position that only the limberness of childhood would allow. She was drawing with crayons while the Carebear sat looking on from his usual position beside her. Momentarily, Erika glanced at the bear and then felt foolishly relieved to find its blank expression devoid of intelligent life.

Did she say, "Holy Spirit?" Erika wondered. She knelt down beside Mia. "What did you call the bear, Darling?"

Purposely intent on her drawing, Mia looked up with an exasperated expression on her face and spoke as though Erika was the three-year old and she, the adult. "His name is Hully Speeret, Momma. And Hully says I'm destined to be great."

Watching her carefully, Erika said, "That's wonderful, Pooh." And then as if testing her, Erika asked, "Can I be great too?"

Without hesitation, Mia looked at Hully as if for confirmation. She then spoke as if one needed to belong to a secret sect in order to achieve greatness. "No Momma, you can't be great. I have to wait for Hully to say if you can be great." Mia turned to the Carebear and proceeded to consult with him as if he was the sovereign king of all the land.

Moments later, she looked up at Erika and said with happiness, "Hully says it's okay for you to be great, too, Momma. Just you, not Daddy. Hully doesn't like Daddy, Momma. Hully says Daddy is mean to him. But Hully says when my little brother gets here, he can be great too. Are you gonna bring him home soon, Momma?"

"Pooh, you must mean your older brother Josh. You don't have a little brother."

"I'm not talking about Josh, Momma. Hully says we're gonna have a little baby boy. Are we gonna get him from the hapspittle soon? I know how to hold him, Momma."

Erika suddenly stood up and took a seat at the kitchen table to stare at Mia eerily. Early that morning as soon as Michael had left the house, Erika had used the First Response pregnancy test kit she'd purchased from the local pharmacy. She'd nearly swooned when the color on the stick returned a positive result. Her relationship with Michael was already turning sour. And the last thing she needed was another pregnancy.

Everything they did of late seemed to stem from anger. Things had even been strained that night two months ago when they had coupled after arguing. Erika hadn't wanted to believe she was pregnant and was hoping the test kit was inaccurate. But here her daughter was talking about a little brother. If she really was pregnant, Erika wasn't even sure she wanted to have it.

She reached down and lifted Mia onto her lap. "Darling, I don't want you to speak anymore about having a little brother, okay? It has to be our secret."

"Okay, Momma. I won't. Daddy doesn't want us to have a little brother, does he? Is Daddy gonna leave us, Momma?"

In response, Erika closed her eyes and hugged Mia to her bosom. *Out of the mouths of babes.* Children sometimes said the darndest things. And many times, truth was laced within their innocent words.

Indeed, Michael hadn't been at all happy to learn of her pregnancy. Where before Erika had been weighing her options, when Michael told her point blank to abort it, at that moment she decided to have the child. She was galled by his callousness and remembered asking him if he was having an affair. He refused to answer, but his cynical sneer gave him away.

Now that Marcus was two years old, her marriage to Michael seemed beyond repair. It was more a psychological war that they were waging on one another. But it was their children who were the casualties. Why they remained married when clearly neither of them was happy was an unsolved puzzle to Erika. Only now could she admit that keeping up appearances was one of the main reasons.

Michael's career in corporate finance had taken him to amazing heights. He'd risen through the ranks to become Senior Vice President of Corporate Development and Strategic Planning at Haliburton Holdings. He was their chief financial expert in acquisition targets, investment options, and licensing deals. He traveled internationally to assess the best firms to buy or invest in that would either extend the company's product line or mitigate its competition. Businesswise, Michael had the midas touch and the fact that he'd grown quite comfortable with ambiguity and lax with his integrity, ensured he represented the company well in its dealings with senators and lobbyists on Capitol Hill.

He'd become quite the man, Erika thought. The proverbial H-N-I-C! *Head-Nincompoop-In-Charge!* was a more accurate way to put it. She marveled at her disdain for him and knew it was only because the feeling was reciprocated. The spark of friendship and affection they had once held for one another, had long since slipped away. She remembered how she'd run after Michael and once she'd gotten him, had pushed him to pursue a career path that at first he hadn't wanted. It was her idea to move to Indianapolis. She'd wanted him removed from his mother's tentacles. She'd pushed him to work harder and to network within his company. She socialized with other company wives and quickly learned who was who.

Before long, in her mind, Erika had Michael's career all mapped out and she spurred him to make it happen. She was determined to be a stay-at-home-mom so the moment she became pregnant, she quit her high-paying job and forced Michael to work even longer hours to compensate for her missing salary.

In her quest for the "All-American Dream," Erika realized she'd created a monster. Her pursuit of a place called "there" had led to her current state of unhappiness. Now that Erika had "arrived" she recognized that there was no "there." She had money, prestige, a successful husband, a fabulous home and all the material things she'd ever longed for. And yet, happiness eluded her.

"...I don't understand how you can condone your child calling another child a demon from the pit of hell. We would never..."

Erika had drifted away but she managed to catch the last part of Mrs. Cunningham's sentence. Erika interrupted her. "We're not here to debate what is or what isn't appropriate, Mrs. Cunningham. But since you brought up the subject, was it appropriate for your son to steal my daughter's toy and deface it? Did you teach him to do that?"

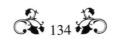

Erika had become irritated with the direction of the meeting. In her opinion, it had gone on much too long. When Michael moved to speak, Erika silenced him with a "talk to the hand" gesture. His placating the Cunninghams was a major reason the meeting had lasted as long as it had.

"If nothing else, I believe we can all agree that children will be children. As for my child, we will not run to therapy over a small matter such as this. If she can't hold her own amongst her fellow six-year old peers, how on earth can she be expected to succeed in the real world?"

Mrs. Cunningham gasped and appeared flummoxed. She took Erika's statement as a suggestion that *her* son was weak and mollycoddled. "How incredibly insensitive…"

Even Michael, who sat seething over the way that Erika had just cut him off midspeech, looked appalled. *It was so typical of her,* he thought angrily. Always needing to have the upper hand along with the last word. It was the primary reason he could no longer stomach being in her presence. In his opinion, Erika had bungled this meeting from the beginning. He loved his child, but even he was tired of hearing her churn out such foolishness as "Hully this" and "Hully that."

It was always some nonsensical dribble the bear had supposedly told her when he knew good and damn well that Mia had heard the words she repeated straight from her mother's lips. Michael still burned with indignant anger whenever he thought about the time Mia had come to him saying, "Hully said your girlfriend is a very, very wicked woman" before scampering from his presence. The shocked expression left on Michael's face had indicated he could have been bought for free. He was too outdone to even chase after the child to question her. The fact that his wife would reveal to their children her suspicions about his affairs was dastardly. How else could his six-year old daughter know to call someone a foul demon from the pit of hell unless her mother *had* taught her? Michael refused to sit quietly while she caused him further humiliation.

Before he could speak, it was Mr. Cunningham who brought focus and harmony back to the group. "Why don't we all start over by having the children apologize to each other. They are the ones who will interact with one another long after the four of us are gone. Richard, come here." Reluctantly, little Richard climbed down from his mother's lap and approached his father.

"Finally, a voice of reason," Erika thought. She completely agreed with Mr. Cunningham. She leaned down and whispered into Mia's ear. Mia then walked over to Richard who stood with his back against his father's knees. She hugged him and said, "I'm sorry, Richy, for hurting you. Please don't ever touch Hully again or the curse will return."

Richard mumbled a quick, "I'm sorry" and looked up at his mother for approval.

Before anyone could comment on Mia's "curse will return" prediction, Dr. Gomes injected a "can't-we-all-just-get-along" speech that lasted several minutes. Afterwards, the parents shook hands and the meeting ended. But it seemed to Erika that she and Mr. Cunningham were the only ones relieved that it was over. It was obvious that Mrs. Cunningham and Michael felt the matter had not been completely resolved.

Erika lingered to thank Principal Gomes and by the time she turned to take Mia to her classroom, Michael had vanished. On her way home, she stopped at the sitter's to pick up Marcus and it was while she was driving that she realized she no longer wanted to remain married to Michael Slaughter.

"Stayed just a little too long...now it's time for me to move on...they say I'm hopeless..." went the lyrics of the song Erika heard playing on the car's radio. After seventeen years of marriage, it was finally time to call it quits. Unconsciously, her shoulders slumped as she stared straight ahead, her hands gripping the steering wheel. She made no attempt to stop the tears from falling from her eyes. *What a waste,* she thought.

The blaring horns from cars behind her caused Erika to jump. The light had turned green and she was holding up traffic.

Seventeen years. Where had the time gone? How had her marriage become so bleak? Erika could not honestly recall when she and Michael had last said a kind word to each other. It was likely they were staying together for the children. But if that was their only reason for remaining locked in a miserable marriage, they were doing their three children a disservice. What good did it do them to see their parents constantly bickering with one another or ignoring each other completely? Was that the image she wanted her children to remember when they grew up?

Marcus coughed in his sleep and Erika looked at him through the rear view mirror. She was parked in her own driveway, but for the life of her, she had no recollection of how she'd arrived at her home. How long she'd been sitting there she couldn't even say. All she knew was at this moment in time, her life was a complete mess. And she was the only one to whom she could assign blame. She could no longer point to Michael and say he was the reason for all of her problems. If truth was being told, she'd lost interest in her husband from the time she became pregnant with their first child.

As she walked through her front door, it hit Erika like a ton of bricks that she'd treated Michael like her personal meal ticket and little else. Erika laid the baby down in his bed and turned to walk throughout her home. And a beautiful home it was. Big and fashionably decorated. She and Michael had carved out a good life. They attended A-list functions, their children went to the best school, they both drove luxury cars. And yet, she hadn't slept with her husband in over a year and a half. They barely saw each other anymore and when they did, neither could hide their contempt for the other.

For the first eight years of their marriage, Michael was the center of her life. Everything revolved around him, whether it was pushing him to work harder, steering his career in the right direction, picking out a designer tie for him or surprising him in her black or red Victoria's Secret. But all of that came to an abrupt end as soon as she became pregnant with Josh. Preoccupied with his care, she barely had time for Michael anymore. Their weekly date nights gradually dwindled to none at all. How fair had that been to him? For the first time, as much as she hated to admit it, Erika could imagine what it must have been like for him (from being the center of her universe) to suddenly be relegated to the status of an orbit given only a passing thought. Yet, in her own defense, there were only so many hours in a day and with three children clamoring for her attention, exhaustion knew no limits. Michael was the one left holding the short end of the stick.

One of the many things Erika had enjoyed doing for Michael was preparing his meals. Cooking was just another way for her to express her love. Once the children were born, she still cooked, but gone were the elaborate candlelight meals for two. She and the children ate out only on rare occasions. Certainly, not because they couldn't afford it, but because it was still her pleasure to put a hot meal on their table. These days, she enjoyed cooking for the children only. Michael was not even an afterthought. Cooking was a trait Erika had picked up from her mother. It was one of the few characteristics she'd inherited from Dot that she'd not taken great pains to stamp out.

And speaking of Dot, Erika had especially blown things in that area. She'd chosen Indianapolis because it was a distance away from Nashville, but also because it was nearly 1,600 miles away from Utah. Her children had only visited their grandmother once when Josh was five and Mia two. She was pregnant with Marcus at the time. She knew Dot was hurt over the way she kept the children from her. But Erika freely admitted that she was ashamed of growing up in "Hicksville, USA." She hadn't wanted that lifestyle for her children. She certainly hadn't wanted them growing up hearing "spirit" voices in their heads.

Still, Erika managed to take the children to church every now and then. But it was a Catholic church and the service was over in forty-five minutes. Her children didn't know anything about spending hours in a single service the way she had when she was growing up. She knew Michael thought she'd taught Mia about demons and devils. But that had not been her doing. Even she was sometimes amazed by the things Mia attributed to the bear, Hully.

These days, Mia avoided her father because she was angry at him. Hully had apparently told her that, "Daddy was leaving to be with his evil girlfriend."

God as her witness, Erika had never even uttered such words. As for Josh, her son was hurting because Michael rarely spent time with him. Erika was the one who showed up for all his little league games. Erika knew Josh would do anything to earn his father's approval. But Michael's time seemed to be spent elsewhere away from his family. While she believed he was seeing another woman, she would never reveal that to the children.

Erika believed that the Holy Spirit did speak to Mia. The things that were revealed to her child were just easier for her to say them as long as she could blame Hully for having told her. One thing was certain, Erika no longer dismissed the things Mia said as mere foolishness. Yes, her child was only six years old, but it was clear that she knew the voice of God. As much as she hated to admit it, Erika saw the similarities between Mia and Aaryn. She remembered how, as a little girl, Aaryn had disliked dolls, shunned ribbons and lace, and was a complete tomboy with a penchant for fighting. Mia was more a replica of Aaryn than she was of Erika.

As for her, Erika felt like her house of cards was crumbling. She knew things with Michael were going to have to change. But she hadn't worked a normal 9-to-5 job in over eight years. She had a degree in Chemical Engineering but the position she'd held as an Applications Engineer, responsible for marketing product lines in industry trade shows, may as well have been in a past lifetime. She'd grown accustomed to structuring her days around her children. She was more comfortable with Sesame Street, Blue's Clues, Barney and Arthur than she was with maximizing some company's bottom line. The thought of having to reenter Corporate America and become another rat on a wheel was too intimidating. She'd do it if she had to, but she'd much rather rob a bank.

What was even more frightening was the thought of actually getting divorced. *Divorced.* The word carried a stigma that almost sounded shameful. Divorce was something Erika had never imagined would be a part of her life. It was what happened to *other* people. Not to her. She acknowledged she and Michael were no longer happy with each other. But she guessed in the back of her mind, she thought they would work out their differences with time.

In all honesty, Erika knew there was another woman. Michael was too lustful a man to remain celibate. She remembered how he used to want her every night. Thank God those days were over! Did she even care about the other woman? No, not really. Not as long as Michael didn't flaunt her in her face. And certainly not as long as he didn't expect to come home and have intimate relations with her.

Nights of passion. The thought floated across Erika's mind. As far as she was concerned, the concept was something other women fantasized about or either read about in a book. It certainly wasn't her reality. Nor was it her fantasy. At least not anymore. Before the kids, it was something spontaneous that they engaged in many

times a week. After the children's birth, she just wasn't up for it anymore. Though Michael complained that she was no longer meeting his needs, Erika felt as if her sex drive had simply abandoned her. These days, it was something she rarely even thought about. If they ever developed Viagra for women, she might try it.

In another year, Erika would turn forty years old. The Big Four-O! It hadn't even registered until that moment. Forty? Erika plopped down on the sofa feeling as if her life was already over. Yes, she was married and had three children to show for it. But her sister, Aaryn, was a big time doctor with all manner of accolades to her name. And what had Erika accomplished? Outside of Michael and the children, nothing. Suddenly, the thought of being 40 years old and divorced didn't seem so appealing. As soon as the doubts hit her, Erika questioned whether she could even make it on her own. There had always been someone taking care of her, whether it was her father, her mother or Michael. If she left Michael, how would she make it? She was accustomed to her current lifestyle. She had no savings of her own. Even if they split everything down the middle, she still might not be able to maintain her current standard of living.

In light of the alternatives, were things really all that bad between her and Michael? Surely, they could work out their differences? If they had to, they might even go to counseling. Erika may not have carved out a niche in the corporate world, but she'd worked too hard to build her family just to throw it all away. She would talk to Michael as soon as he came home. For the children's sake, something had to give.

Chapter Twelve

Jamarra Sanders was proud to be the other woman in Michael Slaughter's life. Giddy and ecstatic were better descriptions because in her young and impressionable mind, things couldn't have been better had she'd outright won the lottery. She may not have been one of the lucky people who got their picture taken while holding a blown up, mammoth-sized check and flashing a crooked grill of less than pearly whites. But being Michael's girlfriend was the next best thing. His Boo, his Groove, his Main Squeeze, his Mistress—however anybody chose to label their relationship, Jamarra was okay with it. Michael was her personal jackpot. He was handsome, successful, generous, and above all, he treated her like she was special. In her eyes, which were blinded by hero worship, he could do no wrong.

They'd been together for over two years and the fact that he was married was never an issue. Jamarra knew all about his wife—how she'd tricked him into marrying her, how she quit her job as soon as she got pregnant. And when Michael

had wanted a divorce, how she'd trapped him by deliberately getting pregnant with their third child. From listening to Michael rant and rave about her, Jamarra knew Erika Slaughter to be the kind of woman who only cared about herself and the things Michael could provide. In every picture Jamarra had seen of her, she looked like a beauty queen, always beautifully dressed with not a hair out of place, as if she'd just stepped right out of the pages of a magazine.

Once, shortly after Jamarra had moved to Indianapolis, Michael had taken her to his home when his wife was away visiting her mother. He had needed to retrieve some business papers so he let Jamarra come inside instead of having her wait in the car.

She remembered feeling like Alice in Wonderland as she entered the beautiful home. Although Michael told her she could make herself comfortable, Jamarra knew she didn't belong there. So she walked around in awe, touching nothing but observing everything. She went from room to room memorizing every detail. The neatness, the orderliness, the charm of everything in the home that she knew was taken for granted by its occupants because they were accustomed to such affluence. Framed pictures of the wife and children were everywhere as were the ones of Michael and Erika standing side by side always looking as if they belonged on Hollywood's red carpet. Jamarra wandered through one room after the next, studying the contents intently, trying to imagine what it must feel like to live in such surroundings.

She slowly made her way up the winding staircase and walked down the plush carpeted hallway carrying her heels in her hands. She stood in the doorway examining each bedroom. But when she reached the little girl's room, a sense of wonder enveloped her. The huge room was painted a bright pinkish-lavender color and its walls were dotted with lovable cartoon and animated characters. The pink carpet and white bedroom furniture was a perfect match for a room that somehow seemed lifted from the pages of a fairy tale book.

Jamarra closed her eyes and envisioned the little girl playing with all the stuffed animals that lined the room, some of which were larger than life. The pink lace-covered canopy bed held even more of the stuffed toys. Jamarra stepped further into the bedroom and in her mind's ear, she could hear the tinkling laughter of a small child, one who knew only happiness and endless love.

When she was a child, Jamarra had never known the kind of love like the child did who inhabited this room. Growing up in one foster home after another in Washington, D.C., her own childhood had been less than stellar. Jamarra was two years old when DCFS workers had first taken her into custody. She was found in an abandoned boarded-up row house on a stretch of 19th Street that was littered with dreary-looking liquor stores and weary, rundown woodsided fast-food chicken and rib shacks with names like Ribz-Be-Us and Wangz 'N Thangz. The section of northeast Washington, D.C. where Jamarra was found was certainly a roughneck, hype-infested neighborhood. No aerial postcard photos of D.C.'s tourist attractions had ever been taken from this particular district.

Jamarra's mother had died promptly from a drug overdose of tainted Magic. The powerful and highly sought-after drug was a mix of heroin and fentanyl, which by itself was a legally produced prescription painkiller eighty times stronger than morphine and commonly used by cancer patients. The lethal drug, Magic, was blamed for hundreds of deaths in the D.C. area alone. When free samples of the drug had first been introduced into the community, scores of customers were found dead on broken sidewalks and in the middle of side streets riddled with potholes.

The FDA had quickly issued a televised warning to people about the dangers of taking the drug, Magic. But money couldn't have bought a more effective PR marketing campaign for the illegal narcotic. Rather than be deterred by its high fatality rates, people wanted the powerful drug all the more. Even customers from the more opulent and wealthy predominantly white suburbs came in droves, eager to experience for themselves the drug's "pure quality" effect.

A recipient of a free sample, rigamortis had already set in Jamarra's mother's limbs when area cops, trailed closely by DCFS, had come to check out an anonymous tip of an abandoned baby. Police and DCFS workers alike knew within moments of entering the rat-infested tenement that other dwellers inhabited the address. But long before police could even announce their presence, everyone had cleared out like roaches fleeing the glare of sudden light. More than likely, another squatter fed up with all the crying had placed the anonymous call to inform police of the whereabouts of the child.

By the time Jamarra was five, she was on her fourth foster home, having been shuffled through the system time again after suffering broken bones and physical abuse by foster parents intent on collecting the money caring for her would bring from the state. Because she hardly ever spoke, both DCFS workers and foster parents assumed she was either mute or suffered from ADHD (attention-deficit hyperactivity disorder). Nobody bothered to take the time to find out if either was the case. Had they done so, what they would have found was that Jamarra was an exceptionally bright child who had learned to suffer quietly the afflictions doled out to her by inattentive, sadistic adults. But no matter how many times she was returned to one of the state's foster care homes, because she was a pretty child, she was routinely chosen over others like an adorable puppy in a pound.

Inevitably, Jamarra was always sent back after it was discovered that she was not socialized enough around other children her age. She was fine as long as she was left to play by herself, but woe unto the person or child (especially the *defenseless* child) who inhabited her space and took what she thought of as her own. Jamarra gained a reputation for her violent explosions.

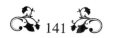

By the time she was eight years old, Jamarra had been raped repeatedly by male employees of the staterun foster facility where she lived. There were no guardians to whom she could turn for help. Trust was something she had no experience with. And she wasn't the only child who suffered such abuses. Employees either knew and didn't care about what was happening or they chose to look the other way. Her attention span in school was minimal and she eventually was placed in a school for special-needs kids. By the time she was ten, no longer did foster parents make a pretense of wanting to adopt her. Her reputation for violent outbursts preceded her. One look into her eyes that were menacing and dead, told potential foster parents that this one was unreachable—this one fought back.

It was out of self preservation that Jamarra became adept at using the SLB hunting knife that she'd lifted off one of the facility workers. The 4½-inch knife had a highly unique blade design that was perfect for skinning animals. Its short, stout blade was built like a tank and was ready for use at a moment's notice.

One night when one of the male facility workers tried to force himself upon her, Jamarra stabbed him clean through the gut. As he screamed and writhed on the floor in pain, a male and female employee rushed into the room. While the man quickly knelt to press a pillow to his dying co-worker's gaping, blood-soaked wound, it was the woman who looked on in amazement at the cold, remorseless expression on Jamarra's face. Her smug look hinted that she'd *enjoyed* stabbing her would-be attacker. In the rush to get medical assistance for their co-worker, nobody thought to retrieve the weapon from Jamarra. Afterwards, the knife was nowhere to be found.

Within days, the case made national headlines as the courts battled over what to do with an eight-year old child guilty of murder. It prompted all manner of investigations into dealings at the state-run facility. After a thorough review, it was determined that the young girl had only been protecting herself against further sexual abuse. No charges were formally filed against Jamarra and the state home itself was targeted for closure. But workers there knew that once Jamarra's case fell from the front pages of the newspapers, things would go back to business as usual. There were too many children being passed through the system, too many kids that nobody wanted, for the government to close the gates of the desperately needed, understaffed and overcrowded foster care facility.

And so it was that when Jamarra was sent to a different state-run home in Anacostia, a hard-luck neighborhood just a few blocks from Capitol Hill, the small hunting knife that she'd hidden away, the same one that she'd become quite adept at using, became her best friend in an unfriendly environment. She tried hard to concentrate in school, hoping that it would provide an outlet of escape. But she found that showing signs of intelligence caused the other students to target her maliciously. It was safer to appear uninterested.

Each year a group of do-gooders would pay an annual visit to the area schools. Jamarra desperately wanted to believe them every time they came singing the praises of a program called *No Child Left Behind*. But in her world, what the program really stood for was, *"Every" Child Left Behind*. Once a year, the do-gooders would pop in with their obligatory "I Have A Dream" speech or the "Mind Is A Terrible Thing To Waste" speech or the "Stop The Violence" speech. Whatever the topic, their words were intended to lull the students into a false belief that they could be, do or have anything they wanted in life. The do-gooders sincerely wanted the students to believe everything they said. They wanted them to believe everything except…the truth. And unfortunately, the ugly truth was that on the mean streets of Anacostia—a neighborhood of broken dreams—daily survival was what really mattered most and becoming the local drug king or one of his many minions or women was about the highest aspirations any of its young residents had.

Still, Jamarra remembered always holding onto a hidden belief that there had to be something better in life. Even as she fought her way through her sophomore year of high school, she kept feeling as if she didn't belong there in that neighborhood or in that city. She remembered the many times when depression would settle on her young shoulders like a heavy anvil. She'd think to herself, "if this is all there is to life, why bother?" And yet, selfpreservation, the will to survive, made her press on.

Located in a southeast section of Washington, D.C., Anacostia was a scant distance from the nation's capitol. But the sorely neglected area, known as one of the worst neighborhoods in the country, may as well have been in another state. Anacostia stood at the juncture of Poverty and Obscurity and was polluted by drugs and violent crime. Hope had no audacity in an environment where the murder rate for African-American men was so high that many saw themselves as endangered species. Unemployment was epidemic and two-thirds of its residents lived below the poverty line. If ever there was a haven for a nation to dump its poorest souls, its dregs and damaged vessels, whom society had chosen to throw upon a garbage heap, Anacostia was surely the poster city for such a blighted urban area.

Much of the landscape was crowded with projects and boarded-up shells of row houses with gardens of discarded tires, broken liquor bottles and trash-filled vacant lots. Competing with the trash in many of the vacant lots were rusty, broken down jalopies that were left to die a slow-roasting death. Each rust-covered automobile emitted the pungent perfume of urine and came garnished with all manner of drug paraphernalia, cigarette butts, burger wrappers and fastfood drink cups piled atop their hoods like ugly decorations left on a pitiful-looking Christmas tree.

The neighborhood was a national disaster that was a haven for drugs, gangs, jails, prostitutes, incinerators and power plants. War zones being equal, Iraq had nothing on Anacostia. Here, weapons of mass destruction were prominently positioned just inside the doorways of nearly every abandoned building in the form of a young person equipped to shoot first without bothering to ask questions later.

Thus, it was into this avenue of hopelessness that Jamarra was thrust and forced to develop and fine tune her individual survival skills. She knew her neighborhood as a place where accidentally stepping on someone's shoe or looking at someone too long or the wrong way could mean the difference between life and getting one's head blown off. Gunfights and acts of vandalism were common in a place where people were suffering and the value of life was little to nothing. Because police cars rarely frequented the area, many residents no longer bothered to dial 911 whenever a crime was in motion. Sadly, 411 was a better option. The Anacostia motto was "do unto others *before* they do unto you."

Yet, there was something cruelly familiar about the misery of her neighborhood. It was a way of life bound by unspoken dog-eat-dog survival codes. So Jamarra became just another irascible loner with cynical, all-seeing eyes skilled in the art of prowling faded streets. Shortly after turning sixteen, the state home where Jamarra lived became too dangerous for her to continue residing there. Gang activity was at an all-time high and for anyone who chose not to align themselves with either of the rival gangs, meant to mark one's self as an automatic, unprotected target. Even continuing on in school required a chosen gang affiliation.

Fence dwellers were not allowed. Although Jamarra refused to join a gang and become a soldier for the drug cause, she was her own brand of soldier. She had neither the stomach nor the inclination to suffer through the mandatory ritual required of females to join gangs: first, submitting sexually to legions of men through the right of initiation and secondly, killing a person to "make grade" or be accepted into the fold.

Experience had taught her that she could and would kill if her survival was threatened. She discovered this one night when two men attempted to accost her inside an abandoned building that she frequented. They came at her so fast she didn't see them until it was too late. She recognized them as gangbangers even as one of the men swung his fist to clock her in the face. She ducked but not before his fist connected with the top of her head. She crumpled to the ground, but maintained consciousness. Both men were bigger and much stronger than she was, but her fearlessness gave her an advantage. The second man quickly tied her hands loosely behind her back and forced her to her knees as his friend unzipped his pants, intent on humiliating her. Her head was forced backward, held in a tight grip that threatened to snap her neck.

Gagging as the man slapped his member against her face, Jamarra used her bound hands to retrieve one of the knives strapped to her back. With her hands now unbound, she had the element of surprise as the man penetrated her mouth. An uncanny speed enabled her to swing the blade in an upward arc that castrated her assailant in one clean swoop. The man holding her head was fondling himself with his free hand, and it turned out to be to his detriment. Jamarra twisted out of his grip

and swung the knife at his jaw cutting clear to the bone. He stumbled backward clutching his throat.

Quickly, before their moans reached a loud pitch that would be heard by others, she stepped to the first man and quietly slit his throat. In shock from the loss of blood, the second man was unable to mount an attack as her knife hurriedly sent him to his death. Jamarra dragged the bodies of both men to a covered spot that hid a well rumored to be a hundred feet deep and threw them both down the hole. Using the tip of her blade, she retrieved the man's still-erect member from the spot where it lay and tossed it down as well. Momentarily, Jamarra stood there marveling at how easy it was for her to take both men's lives. Yes, she'd killed in selfdefense, but there was more to it than that. In the place of remorse, she felt a strange satisfaction—as if she had the potential to kill someone else. Did that make her a serial killer in the making? She smiled thinking, only time would tell. Already she could feel a formidable knot growing on her head from where the first man had socked her, but at least *she* was still among the living.

Though she'd recognized the men, she'd no explanation for why they attacked her. But she knew their brothers-in-arms would note their disappearance. What if they had mentioned to others their plans to attack her? What if they had meant to force her into a life of prostitution? Or, they might have intended to make her a bender in one of their "sister" gangs. Jamarra knew the life of a bender was hard. Being a bender was to become a willing or unwilling prostitute for gang members. It had aged most of the girls she saw on the street. The lifestyle had stripped them of their livelihoods, leaving them helpless on side streets looking broken and dried up like autumn leaves.

She would not join anybody's gang and she would not risk doing hard time for anyone to whom she owed no allegiance. No one had been there for her when she was growing up. No one. Feeling as if her days were numbered, she dropped out of high school and took to living on the streets. Her mantra was *trust no one* because enemies were all around her in the form of men who, if given half the chance, would rape her and toss her body aside like a wrung rag without a second thought. And female gang members her own age who, without provocation, would beat her senseless simply because she was without protection.

Scraping together a living by doing odd jobs was not easy. Hunger was her constant companion. Most people thought they knew what hunger was. But Jamarra knew that *real* hunger was going to sleep not having eaten and not knowing where your next bite was going to come from. Real hunger meant digging through garbage cans and hanging around alleys where restaurants were located in hopes of getting first dibs on the scraps. Real hunger was knowing what time the local halfway houses served each of their meals if she wanted to survive. Hunger was poverty; and poverty was the sting of rejection knowing that you couldn't step inside most businesses or churches because they didn't want or accept your kind. Homelessness carried with it its own detectable stench.

Safety dictated that Jamarra take to dressing and looking like a boy. She dressed in loose, oversized clothing and wore her long hair in cornrow braids underneath a baseball cap with the bill facing backwards. Makeup was spurned and baths were a quick wash from a bucket of suspect water. For the next year, she barely scraped by until she finally decided to try it "the man's way" by going to places outside her neighborhood to look for a job. She went from one business after another only to be laughed at when she answered truthfully that she had no high school diploma. She kept searching until she got lucky and managed to get hired on at minimum wage at a KFC restaurant within the Capitol Hill area. For the next three years she worked at the restaurant by day and by evening she'd wander around the city, always avoiding Anacostia, and late at night she would check into a local shelter, sleeping with one eye open.

The night Jamarra met Michael Slaughter, the evening was filled with a series of unfortunate events. She'd been asked to work a double shift at KFC and because she left work after ten o'clock that night, she missed the cut off time to check into any of the local shelters. With no destination in mind, she walked north towards Capitol Street. She reached Union Station and just as she crossed the street, Jamarra spotted three thugs sticking up a man in a three-piece business suit. The street was deserted of all traffic and she knew better than to become embroiled in the robbery.

Just as she was about to cross the street to avoid the scene of the crime, one of the assailants punched the man in the chest and when he tried to fight back, the three hoodlums jumped him, knocking him to the ground and kicking him about his body. Before Jamarra was aware of her actions, she crossed the street and stood about two feet from the action when one of the punks pulled out a gun and pointed it at the man on the ground.

"Don't do it," she heard herself say. Her voice was neither cocky nor did it hold any traces of fear.

Suddenly, the gun swiveled in her direction and the boy moved in front of Jamarra pointing the nozzle right between her eyes.

"Who's gon' stop me? You? I oughta blow yo' damn head off. You don't even know me." All this while his two buddies were rifling through the man's briefcase and wallet.

Jamarra had her hands spread out at her side. "I aint even seent you, blood. All I'm sayin' is, don't cap the brutha. Take his money 'n go. You kill em, five-o gon' be breathin' hard all ovah this mutha. You can bet they prolly even got them seein'-eye-dog cameras everywhere. Just take his money and go, man. I don't know you and I aint seent chu. No harm, no foul."

The thug who was checking the wallet let out a shout as he swiped the cash and threw the wallet in the man's face. "Dawg, this nigga got three birds 'n a fitty on 'em. Let's roll." A bird was street slang for a hundred dollar bill. The thug stuffed the money in a pocket of his jeans that hung dangerously low and threatened to fall from his rear end. "We straight 'n all good, dawg. Come on, let's roll!"

The boy pointing the pistol in Jamarra's face twisted the 9mm Glock to the side. With his free hand he made a gang signal and pounded his closed fist against his chest. "I see yo' face again, chickenhead, you's one dead mutha. You got dat?"

Jamarra nodded. She'd make sure she never saw any of them again.

The three teens ran like bats out of hell, highfiving each other along the way using a quick succession of rapid hand movements that appeared ritualistic of a highly choreographed dance sequence. Jamarra walked to the man who had struggled to his knees and asked, "You okay, Mister?"

Stressed to find his breath, Michael could only nod his head. At the moment he was seeing two of everything and his body felt as though it had been mistaken for a punching bag in a gym.

Jamarra picked up his wallet and the papers that had scattered over the ground from his briefcase. She stepped directly in front of him and peered at him closely. "At least you're not bleedin' or seriously hurt. And at least you're alive."

"Good point," Michael said as he attempted to rise from the ground. His legs were still too shaky to hold him and if Jamarra hadn't rushed to assist him, he would have sunk back to the concrete.

"What are you doin' out here this time of night, Mister? Don't chu know better than to get caught out like that?"

"Young man, had I known…" Michael's words were cut off when the person he mistakenly thought a boy pressed her chest into his side to bear him up. The young man had breasts.

"You're a girl?" Michael asked incredulously.

"Yeah, I'mma girl. The same girl who just saved yo' black ass. You alive ain't chu?"

Suddenly, Michael found the situation hilarious. But his shout of laughter quickly cut off as pain shot through his right side. "I didn't mean any harm, Sister. It's just crazy, that's all. If anything, I should be the one protecting you. Not the other way around."

"I doubt it, Blood. I been takin' care of myself since I was a little girl. At least I'm not the one who just got his head busted. At least I'm not the one who's stoop. That's short for 'stupid' by the way. Maybe you should hire me as yo' bodyguard."

Wondering what the world was coming to, Michael said, "You just might be right."

"Where you headed?" Still holding onto him, Jamarra bent down and swooped up his briefcase which now held his wallet.

"I'm staying at the Phoenix Park Hotel on North Capitol Street. It's on the next block."

Jamarra whistled through her teeth. "You livin' large like all that, huh? Well, you won't get no cab this time o'night. You'll have to walk it. Think you can make it?"

"Will you be my bodyguard?"

"Oh yeah, for a slight fee. Come on, let's get outta here before you get robbed again. Or get us both kilt." Jamarra helped Michael limp to the hotel where they took the elevator up to one of the penthouse suites.

All that was two and a half years ago. Since then, Michael had been nothing but generous to Jamarra. Because of him, she'd gotten a mailroom job at the D.C. branch of Haliburton, a small apartment on 17th Street close to Penn Avenue (which he helped pay the rent) and she'd gone back to school and gotten her GED. Jamarra didn't know what love was, but she knew what loyalty meant. And she was loyal to Michael Slaughter. He didn't try to sleep with her, but seemed to genuinely care about her well being. It was new for her because she didn't trust people, especially men. She figured that sooner or later he would want to get in her pants, but he never even spoke to her out of the way, always addressing her as "young lady."

She knew he lived out of town but whenever he visited D.C., he always stopped in to visit her. After a time, Jamarra found she looked forward to his visits. One night he visited her apartment and they ordered takeout and talked to the wee hours of the morning. Jamarra told him all about her life on the street and what it was like to be homeless. He told her about his wife and children. When he fell asleep on her sofa, Jamarra got a blanket and covered him. She lay down on the floor not far from him and stared up at him. Unable to sleep, she recognized that for the first time in her life she wanted to be intimate with a man. She wanted him to touch her, to recognize her as a woman and to speak about her with the same fondness that he talked about his family.

Her newfound stirrings were foreign to her, but Jamarra rose from the floor and went inside her bedroom to take down her cornrows. She washed and blow dried her long hair and pressed it out. She didn't own any sexy lingerie, but her Hanes underwear was skimpy enough. A pair of earrings, a dash of lipstick and a splash of after-bath cologne and Jamarra felt transformed. She was an attractive, striking looking girl. That much she knew from her days on the street when people called her Pretty Boy Floyd. Even women had tried to hit on her, but Jamarra hadn't been interested in the opposite sex or in members of her own. She'd always thought of sex as something people took from one another and she associated it with heaving, heavy grunts. Whether it was pleasurable or not, she hadn't wanted to indulge. For some strange reason, Michael made her feel differently. Yet, he'd never looked down on her or treated her with anything except kindness.

Michael woke the next morning to the tantalizing smell of biscuits, bacon and eggs. He was shocked when he stepped into the kitchen and found the person he used to think of as a hood urchin, was indeed a fullbodied woman. As he took in the fullness of her body, he wondered how on earth she'd managed to disguise herself as a boy.

Jamarra turned away from him to hide the triumphant look on her face. She set two plates on the table and sat Michael down. Seeing his look of desire, she sat directly in his lap and wrapped her arms around his neck. Before she knew it, they were falling down onto her bed. What she lacked in experience, she made up for in enthusiasm and hours later when breakfast had long grown cold, they continued to warm each other with the throes of their passion.

He refused to leave her apartment that day so she called in sick to work. The next day he took her shopping for clothes and then took her out to dinner that same night, marveling that it was her first time having ever dined inside a restaurant. When he left her apartment to fly back to Indianapolis, Jamarra nearly cried at how bereft she felt without him. Michael promised to return soon.

Soon became every other week. But after her phone got disconnected and he was unable to reach her for ten whole days, he chided her for not asking him for the money to pay her phone bill. He then began to visit every week. Jealousy over the way other men looked at her and the thought of what she might be doing in her spare time, prompted Michael to move her to Indianapolis to be closer to him. He set her up in an apartment and encouraged her to enroll in college. And whenever he traveled, he wanted her by his side.

Jamarra just enjoyed being in Michael's presence. She never considered that he was using her selfishly to satisfy an urge that wasn't being met within the confines of his marriage. All she knew was that for the first time in her life, she understood what it meant to care about someone and all she wanted to do was please him. When he talked about his wife, it was always with anger at how she was turning his children against him. Because Michael hated his wife, so did Jamarra. Years later, when Michael let it slip that he was so angry at his wife that he could kill her, little did he know that Jamarra took his words to heart. If Michael suffered, then so did she and anybody who was a threat to Michael was a threat to her. She would not let anything steal away their happiness. Out of loyalty to him, Jamarra knew she would kill anyone who stood in the way of their being together.

If that person happened to be his wife, then so be it.

Chapter Thirteen

Three weeks later at the Universal Pictures' premiere of Jayson's film *The Mission,* downtown Chicago (the city best known for its graft, political corruption and well-fed patronage troughs) was transformed into Tinseltown, complete with A-list actors and actresses, red carpets, paparazzi, and screaming fans all jostling for a closer view of legitimate, bona fide celebrities. The moment Jayson exited his chauffeur-driven limousine, throngs of fans pressed up against barricades waving their movie placards while straining to get a closer look or perhaps a memorable photo. They pointed at him frantically and screamed his name with delight.

Bumping his Swarovski-studded Cartier glasses up the bridge of his nose, Jayson leaned down to offer his hand to his escort. A pair of well-heeled shapely legs extended toward the ground followed by a sensational bombshell who looked as though she'd been poured into her Chanel evening gown.

Jayson smiled down at his companion before whispering in her ear, "Same madness, different movie. Shall we?"

No man deserved to possess such breathtaking beauty, Lisa Tennamen thought to herself as she stared up at Jayson, her eyes lingering on the deep grooves on either side of his smile. It was that captivating smile which could light up a room that had captured her heart (and many others) years ago. As she tucked her arm possessively through his, her own triumphant smile plainly told the world that tonight the hot man beside her who possessed so much potent, masculine virility was hers alone. As a long-standing top model in the fashion industry, Lisa was wildly flamboyant and known as much for her temperamental tantrums as she was for her exotic looks. She'd known Jayson ever since his modeling days when Porsha Bertini had monopolized all his time. When he and Porsha had finally parted ways, Lisa had quickly flown to California to rush in and make her move. To this day, a cruel smile curled Lisa's lips whenever she thought of how haggard and aged poor Porsha had appeared in the days and weeks following her breakup with Jayson. In her bid to keep him under lock and key, and away from all the women who longed for just a smidgeon of his attention, Porsha had become a laughingstock whom no one had felt any sympathy for when Jayson had finally come to his senses and escaped her grasp.

Lisa was only too willing to help Jayson assuage the other woman's memory. Now, every time she appeared with him in public, it was her name that was linked romantically with his. According to the rag mags, Lisa's on-again-off-again relationship with Jayson was rumored to be the result of a secret marriage between the two. It was a rumor Lisa never denied (especially since it was she, herself, who had secretly planted it with *People* magazine). They were, in actuality, occasional lovers who had managed to remain friends over the years.

Because Lisa knew to shelve her dramatic nature when in Jayson's presence, she was one of the few women he remained in contact with. *Friends with benefits* was how Lisa described their precarious relationship. But she wanted more. She would gladly have married Jayson in a heartbeat. In fact, she'd married several years ago only after Jayson plainly stated he wasn't ready for marriage. Constantly comparing her new husband to Jayson hadn't helped and less than a year later, her marriage had gone kaput. Although she hid her emotions well, she was crystal clear about who and what she wanted. She was still in love with Jayson and was merely waiting for him to recognize what a gem she was.

With his date firmly at his side, much as he'd done hundreds of times before, Jayson strolled the red carpet with the same confident stride pausing intermittently to accommodate the flashing bulbs of the paparazzi's cameras. As his eyes flitted over the people in front of them leading to the entrance, he spotted Rita Danza with her newest beau on her arm. She glowered at Jayson when his gaze met hers. "What's she doing here?" Jayson wondered to himself.

As if reading his mind, Lisa said grimly, "Had I known I was going to have to fight off all your exlovers, I would have packed a knife." Her words were matter-of-fact and tinged with jealousy.

"Not all of them, sweetheart. Just one. But since Rita's been known to pack a knife of her own, don't worry, I'll protect you. And no, I did not invite her. I had no idea she would be here, so just ignore her. Now be a good girl and smile for all your adoring fans."

Lisa flashed her megawatt smile at the crowd. Even as she did so she said to Jayson, "I think it's rather obvious that you're the one these fickle fans adore. I swear, the crowds of people seem to grow larger with every movie you make. And by the way, I'll be good alright. But I'm warning you, Jay, if that witch, Rita, comes in my direction, the westside of Chicago girl that's deeply embedded in me will show her how we roll. Right here on national TV."

"God, Lisa, will you please sheath your claws? The night hasn't even begun yet and I'm beginning to regret asking you here." Jayson shook his head barely managing to mask his look of irritation. Everybody knew that women from the west side of Chicago had a wild, combative streak, but one would think that since Lisa had risen to the level of international stardom on the catwalk, she would have put her ghetto-girl mentality behind her. *You can take the girl out of the hood, but you couldn't take the girl out of the hood,* Jayson thought.

"Did you catch the scowl Rita Danza threw Denali's way?" The Entertainment Tonight co-host whispered to her cameraman amidst the gaggle of celebrities. They were awaiting their turn to interview Jayson.

"Sure did. I got a good close up of it along with the look of daggers Lisa Tennamen threw back at her." Years of quickly angling his camera at in-demand stars had given the cameraman an acute sensitivity to the nuances of facial expressions and body language. His swift ability to catch people off guard with his camera had brought him good fortune over the years. He hoped tonight would be no different.

"I want you to stay as close to Denali as you can. I have a feeling fireworks might explode this evening."

"Yup. With Lisa Tennamen in tow anything can happen. Denali sure does draw a crowd, doesn't he? I mean, the cult following he's amassed is incredible. Look at all these people." For a quick moment he angled his camera at the crowds and back again to the stars. "You know, all one has to do is log onto MySpace or any website that keeps up with the celebs to see how many people just love the man."

"I agree. It's totally insane." With what sounded to the cameraman like a note of longing in her voice, the co-host added, "But you have to admit, you'd be hard pressed to find a more masculine, unconscionably gorgeous man. And wherever he goes, money follows. So be sure to keep your camera on him. Oh look, there's Harrison Ford! Let's get a quickie with him before our interview with Denali."

"So much for keeping his camera trained on Jayson," the cameraman thought as he hurriedly followed the flighty co-host. But then he was used to the capricious vagaries of those in the entertainment world. It was his experience that the ones who sat behind the showbiz desks were sometimes more megalomaniacal than the stars he covered.

Inside the theatre, Jayson met up with all four members of his personal entourage and they mingled with other stars doing the Hollywood facial smooch thing while never managing to actually touch each other. Appearances were everything, so a happy gaiety threaded the event as all the stars wore their game face for the adoring public. It was a look and façade that screamed, "Don't you wish you were as happy, beautiful and famous as me?"

Jayson watched with a smooth detachment as all the A-listers preened for the glare of the cameras. Even people that he personally knew who couldn't stand each other, were willing to put their personal differences aside under the hot glare of the camera's lenses. Of late, he noticed he'd become much more cynical since his return from Utah and his tolerance level for tinsel moments such as these had diminished severely. A quick glance at his Swiss Tourbillon watch indicated he had another forty minutes to go before everyone filed into the theatre to view the film. For a fleeting moment, Jayson wondered how badly would it piss off his studio execs if he skipped the previewing all together.

Two of his co-stars approached him. The three of them were posing for more photos when the Entertainment Tonight co-host snagged them for another interview. But it became evident after only a few questions who her real target was. She peppered Jayson with personal questions about his love life under the guise of it being his doting fans who wanted to know. "Was there really truth to the long-standing rumor that he and Lisa Tennamen were secretly wedded?" Despite her questioning, the invitation in her eyes and body language signaled to Jayson that the ET co-host was clearly flirting with him. With a subtle nudge of her hip, she shooed her cameraman away. Her pursuit of him became even more blatant and Jayson's firm denials quickly evolved into jocular demurrals and artful deflections. As attractive and available as she was, Jayson marveled at his own restraint at not taking her up on her offer to visit her hotel room later that night.

As Jayson was attempting to extricate himself from the demanding television co-host, his posse was busy blocking Rita Danza's path. She was making a beeline toward Jayson so two of his crew members stopped her. When Lisa Tennamen walked by the two unaccosted, throwing Rita a dirty look, things rose to an unexpected level.

"Take your hands off me! How dare you touch me!" With a few drinks in her belly and one in her hand, Rita's ire was inflamed. "If anything, you should be watching that puta there!" With her accent, Rita's words sounded like "eef enyting" but Lisa Tennamen had no problem discerning the word "puta," its meaning, or that it was aimed at her.

Having had a few drinks of her own, before anyone could stop her, Lisa pivoted and backhanded Rita across the face causing her drink to crash to the carpeted floor and nearly sending Rita to the floor along with it. In a fury, Rita regained her balance and with a stream of illreputed Latin words flowing from her tongue, launched herself at the scowling Lisa Tennamen.

As the two women rolled on the carpeted floor slapping and pulling each other's hair amidst a tangle of priceless silken garments, a crowd quickly formed. The bystanders stood watching the melee in shock, their morbid delight mingled with curious fascination. But when one of Rita's plump melon-sized breasts broke free of her gown, their shock quickly gave way to pure tabloid voyeurism.

Minutes after the fight started, Jayson became aware of all the commotion. When someone hollered, "A fight is on!" some arcane instinct told him who the contestants were. He dashed forward toward the scene and pushed his way to the front before stepping between the two women. With one arm around Rita's waist, Jayson was extremely thankful that Harrison Ford had quickly stepped forward and grappled Lisa before she could dropkick Rita while Jayson was holding her.

With their hair splayed all over their heads and their beautiful designer gowns in shreds, the entire scene was captured live and upclose. It was that wild, scandalous image of the four of them (Jayson, Rita, Harrison and Lisa) that would appear on all the newsstands and airwaves the very next morning.

That very next morning, Aaryn was finishing up her healing session with Sylvia Denali in the Rophe Room. During the previous weeks, as much as she'd tried to separate herself and maintain a certain amount of professional distance from Sylvia, in spite of herself, Aaryn was drawn to Sylvia. She had a need to ferret out Sylvia's life story. Not via words, however. Aaryn desired to know what secrets Sylvia's body would reveal. After the first week, she found herself sitting with the older woman during meal breaks and stopping in to check on her many times during the day. Sometimes she'd find Sylvia sitting by the window, lost in memories that took her far beyond the glass panes which she stared out of.

Whenever Sylvia's gaze was locked on thoughts and visions that lay somewhere between the window and her eyes, Aaryn sensed a deep melancholy within her. An emotional tsunami that remained untouched to the degree that even her blood cells and tissues were unwilling to yield its truths. Aaryn knew that whatever it was that Sylvia refused to speak about, it was a key to the woman's healing. Still, some progress was being made. A trust was established between them and even Sylvia recognized her body was beginning to respond to the Quantum-Touch treatments.

Feeling extremely relaxed and in need of a short nap after the therapeutic massage, Sylvia nearly forgot that Aaryn hadn't answered the question she had put to her at the start of their session. "So what of it, Doctor? Did your mother happen to send any goodies for me today?" Sylvia's expression was expectant.

Aaryn was walking alongside Sylvia as she was being wheeled back to her room by one of the nurses' aides. They were entering the room when Aaryn replied with a smile, "It's barely eight o'clock in the morning, young lady. What kind of goodies might you be referring to?" Aaryn had taken to periodically addressing Sylvia as "young lady." Her doing so always brought a huge smile to the older woman's lips and the smile seemed to soften her entire face. Sylvia was smiling now as the nurses' aide helped her onto her bed.

"All I know is that I expect a nice sized slice of homemade pecan pie with my lunch meal. Will you join me?"

"I think I..." Aaryn's words were cut off as the commotion on the overhead television caught her attention and interrupted her midstream.

Both she and Sylvia stared at the television screen in wide-eyed amazement as two beautifully dressed women rolled on a red-carpeted floor in a fierce battle while reigning blows on each other's head. Suddenly, a small blurry image appeared on screen blocking out what must have been one of the women's breasts. It seemed every word grunted by them was bleeped out by the show's broadcasters when from out of nowhere, Jayson Denali dashed forward to separate the entangled women. As he swooped one of them up, on his heels was Harrison Ford who hurriedly grabbed the waist of the second woman to pull them apart. There were more bleeps as the women hurled vicious threats at one another as they clawed at the hands of the men who restrained them. The camera panned out to take in the elaborately decorated surroundings, along with the appalled (yet excited) looks on the faces of those gathered nearby. The scene could have been a snapshot from a Jerry Springer show. Only these players were wellknown celebrities bedecked with expensive jewels and haute couture clothing. Seconds later, the morning news reporters were back on screen.

Laughing at the breast-baring clip just aired, one of the morning show hosts said, "Talk about the catfight of the century! This actual footage of actress, Rita Danza and top model, Lisa Tennamen fighting over Jayson Denali is creating a bigger stir than the heavyweight battle between Joe Frazier and Muhammad Ali!"

More laughter as the co-host added with glee, "Could either Jayson Denali or Harrison Ford have looked more stunned? Of course publicists for both women are claiming the fight was staged to promote the movie, but if that's the case, it sure looks as if only the two women were in on the secret. Everyone else appeared completely flummoxed. Comments from several guests attending the movie premiere suggest a longstanding feud between the two women for the affections of that famous, wealthy avatar better known as Jayson Denali." With that, the newscasters were already segueing to the next story.

Flabbergasted and at a loss for words herself, Aaryn looked at Sylvia who still had her right hand pressed against the "O" of her lips.

Sally, the nurses' aide, penetrated their silence. Said the short, buxom redhead, "Hmph. I don't know what an avatar is, but even a blind man could see those two women couldn't have picked a better specimen to fight over." She continued to fluff Sylvia's pillow and tuck her in as if nothing out of the ordinary had happened. Seeing the strained look on Sylvia's face, she added, "Mrs. Denali, you just let what you saw on that television pass through one eye and out the other. Why, back in my day the women were even worse. When we saw a man we wanted, we just hogtied 'em and carried him straight to the altar. End of story. Men weren't scarce back then like they are today and women didn't have to fight over 'em. Men fought over us!" She stood back with her hands on her hips and stared from Sylvia to Aaryn as if waiting for them to nod or give credence to her version of the way things used to be back in the day.

Aaryn was exceedingly fond of Sally and admired the woman's work ethic. However, she did not want to engage her in a discussion of men's behavior, past or present. She said, "Sally, I think you have a point. At least, Sylvia, the women were fighting each other and not your son. But if either of them had a smidgeon of common sense they would have turned all that wrathful vengeance on him and saved themselves from looking like immoral clowns." She stepped to the bed and ran her hand across Sylvia's hair in a gesture meant to soothe. "You get some rest, okay? We'll have lunch in the Lemon Garden and I'll see that you're served that slice of my mom's pecan pie."

Sylvia smiled absentmindedly, already retreating into herself as she turned her head into her pillow.

Her brief gesture spoke volumes to Aaryn. As she left the room, she couldn't help but feel another spark of anger towards Jayson Denali. In the weeks since she'd discovered him inside her kitchen infecting Dot with his copious charm, she'd thought about him more than she cared to admit. It never failed that just when she'd effectively put him out of her mind, Sylvia would mention him or she'd pass a group of nurses in the corridor reminiscing about his visit or discussing how great his films were. Even as she passed the nurses' station enroute to her office, several of the ladies were surreptitiously reading copies of *The National Enquirer, Star, Globe* and *Us* magazines trying to get the latest tidbit on what people were calling the catfight of the century.

"Morning, Dr. Jamison," one of the nurses said cheerfully, loudly alerting her peers to the fact that Aaryn was approaching.

She noticed as she passed that two of the women closed their magazines and busied themselves with nearby patients' charts.

"Good morning, ladies." Aaryn kept walking toward her office. She figured that as soon as she reached a safe enough distance they would continue reading their gossip sheets with relish. Aaryn made a mental note to avoid the lunchroom where she was sure the staff would be watching the catfight replayed on the overhead screens. It wasn't as though Jayson Denali's dustup affected her personally, she just preferred not to engage in conversations about it or anything else that concerned him.

She stooped to retrieve the copy of the Salt Lake Tribune newspaper that was left just inside her office. She had thirty minutes until her next appointment. Tossing the paper onto her desk, she pulled Sylvia's file preparing to record notes about her progress when a photo on the front page of the Tribune caught her eye. A closeup of four faces from Jayson's premiere stared back at her.

Picking up the paper, she stared intently at each face in the picture. The photographer had captured the naked intensity of each of their facial expressions. Pure hatred shown on the faces of the two women who sought to break from their captors to re-engage their bid to tear one another to pieces. Harrison Ford looked surprised, yet the smirk on his face made him appear thrilled. With his arms locked around the model, his pose reminded Aaryn of a throwback to his film, *Raiders of the Lost Ark*. And then there was Jayson, looking for all the world—not smug as Aaryn had initially thought—but disgusted and angry.

Suddenly, Aaryn stared hard at the photo trying to discern what there was, if anything, within the picture that she was missing. She had no doubt that the fight between the women had not been staged. But could it be that Jayson Denali looked displeased to have the two women vying for his affections? And why should it matter to her either way, Aaryn found herself wondering. It was just another confirmation that he was invading too much of her thoughts. Still, she couldn't put the paper aside. She found herself examining the photo more closely.

Even with the glaring frown on his face, Jayson was beautiful and overtly masculine. Aaryn shook her head recognizing that women must fight over him all the time. He was probably used to it by now. She was sure that women gravitated to him like a flock of fluttering, hungry birds. A man didn't gain a reputation such as the one he had—one of unbridled vice—for naught. In all honesty, Aaryn couldn't even blame the women for pursuing him. Like bees drawn to honey, she knew he would attract a swarm of women wherever he went. Woe unto the woman unwise enough to allow herself to become caught in his captivating web.

Nevertheless, any woman could be forgiven for thinking or dreaming about him. The photo before her was just a base reminder of the fallout of what could happen if one allowed themselves to fall prey to the likes of a Jayson Denali. Suddenly, Aaryn felt the urge and need to climb. Not the passive rock at The Front, but something much more fierce and challenging. She needed that adrenaline flow that came from battling the solid rock. Nothing man made. She needed to feel the wind at her back, muscles straining while her hands clung desperately to the smooth cracks. Just herself. No one else. Just her against the cursed elements fighting for survival. With her eyes closed, Aaryn pictured herself on "Moral Dilemma" or "Flying Off The Handle." Both rocks were steep climbs that would give her the challenge she craved at the moment. So real was her visual of herself climbing in her mind that her phone rang twice before she was aware of it.

"Dr. Jamison speaking."

"Dr. Jamison, this is Jayson Denali. How are you today?" His voice was deep, rich, powerful—a delight to the senses.

Shock widened Aaryn's eyes. "Fine, thank you." So surprised was she that she didn't think to ask what he wanted.

"As agreed, I'm calling to let you know I intend to visit my mother early next week."

"Thank you for informing me. Does Sylvia know of your impending visit?" Now that her nerves were back under subjection she could focus with clarity.

Jayson noted her first name familiarity with his mother. "Not yet. I'll call her after I finish speaking with you."

"I see." Her voice was noncommittal as she prepared to end the conversation.

For a moment Jayson wondered exactly what she did see. Her tone was one of guarded neutrality. He sensed she was about to cut the conversation short so he said, "I spoke with her several days ago and she's really excited about her treatments. She sounded…happy. How's she doing in your opinion?"

Careful Aaryn, she thought to herself. How do I respond to that without opening a hornet's nest? "She was doing quite well this morning, Mr. Denali, up until after her scheduled treatment. But then, unfortunately, she saw the video clip of your sparring match." There was silence until Aaryn heard him sigh.

"You mean the debacle at the movie premiere," Jayson corrected her.

"A movie premiere?" Mock surprise laced Aaryn's voice. "Huh. Somehow, I thought it was a taping of a Jerry Springer show."

"Funny." But not really. Not when hot anger still ran through him at the thought of being dragged into a fiasco that pitched him as the butt of all jokes. Jay Leno had already roasted him in the opening shot of his nightly monologue on *The Tonight Show* mere hours after the fight occurred. And to add insult to injury, Jon Stewart of *The Daily Show* aired an impromptu spoof of Jon jumping over his news desk in the middle of his broadcast to break up a mock fight in his audience between two women who were supposedly fighting over him! Jayson had also been told that the fight clip was causing a major stir all over the web and that it had garnered more hits on YouTube and other videosharing websites than any other clip ever— including the Janet Jackson breast fiasco.

Hours after the fight occurred, media outlets were blowing up his office phone to either invite him onto their shows or to get his take on the matter. When his publicist declined their invitations, unable to get to him, they hunted down Harrison. Jayson was more than willing to cede the glare of the spotlight to the others involved. Despite what anybody thought, these days he didn't relish the kind of notoriety that was being imposed upon him because of angry, selfabsorbed women who were hungry for his time and attention.

He didn't owe the good doctor any explanations. Yet, curiously, he found himself wanting to do just that: explain.

"Look, it's none of my business…" Aaryn began.

"I never meant for what transpired to…" Jayson started.

With Aaryn suddenly not wanting to engage in a volatile debate and Jayson overcome by a need to have her understand that encouraging women to fight over him was not something he perpetuated—both of them spoke at the same time.

For his part, Jayson didn't want to give her reason to add anymore black marks against his name—given the depths of villainy she already thought him capable of. "Why am I even having this conversation with her?" Jayson wondered to himself. "And why does her opinion of me matter at all?"

As for Aaryn, she just wanted to bring an end to their conversation. "Mr. Denali, your mom will be fine. My request is that when you speak with her, that you explain to her all about what happened at your premiere. I'm sure smoothing things over with her won't be a problem for someone like yourself who's used to charming his way out of a paperbag. Plus, once you let her know you're planning to visit her, I'm certain she'll be ecstatic. But to your question, yes, she's making progress. Right now, however, it's more mental than physical. I can have Dr. Baldwin fill you in on all the specifics when you arrive."

"Ahhh, I see. Dr. Baldwin will speak to me. And not you. Why not admit, Dr. Jamison, that you'd rather not converse with me at all? Could it be that you're avoiding me for some unspoken reason?"

Incensed by the tone of his voice, Aaryn snapped, "I'm certain this is the part, Mr. Denali, where some women would bat their eyelashes and pretend not to have a clue as to what you're talking about. But thank God I'm clueless about the semantics or protocol for using feminine wiles. Since you went there, let me give it to you straight, no chaser. No, I *don't* prefer to converse with you—for reasons which I've already divulged. And yes, if possible, I *do* prefer to avoid you, so Dr. Baldwin gives me the perfect opportunity to do just that." Despite every intention she had not to spar with him, she found herself doing so as she strove to keep her blood pressure from rising.

"Are we arguing?" His voice was quiet, silky and filled with a curious wonder.

"Excuse me?" Aaryn was warming up to gut him verbally when his question threw her off kilter. Was the man obtuse?

"I'm just wondering if your animosity is about what happened at the premiere. Or are we really circling around the question of why I'm drawn to you? Could it be that you're drawn to me too, Dr. Jamison?"

Aaryn's mouth hung open in speechless outrage. "Of all the unmitigated gall…" Her voice was a whisper as a tick pulsed in her jaw.

Heedless to the seething anger in her voice, Jayson added, "You see, I'm sitting here wondering, 'why am I explaining myself to this woman' when suddenly it hits me. I'm doing it because I want you to understand me, Dr. Aaryn Jamison. Because I need for you to know that I'm not the illiterate, crass womanizer you've created me to be. And, yes, because you intrigue me with your brutal honesty and your no-holds-barred demeanor. On top of all that, Dr. Jamison, I'm explaining myself to you because I find you attractive." *Wow,* Jayson thought with a smile. He didn't know where all of that came from, but suddenly, it was as if a heavy cloud was lifted from him. He felt…wonderful. And free.

Aaryn on the other hand felt as though that same thick cloud had descended upon her. "You're completely insane," was all she could muster as she shook her head in astonishment.

"About thirty minutes ago, I probably would have agreed with you. But right now I'm clear as a bell. Why don't you have dinner with me one day next week so we can discuss my theory further?"

Ignoring his ridiculous dinner question, Aaryn replied hotly, "What you are, Mr. Jayson Denali, is thoroughly deluded. Only a narcissistic idiot would think every woman he meets is attracted to him. You are without question, the most…"

Jayson's smug laughter interrupted her. "Dr. Jamison, I hate to disrupt your diatribe but, can I call you back? My assistant is about to have a stroke because I've kept Stevie holding for several minutes when everyone knows Spielberg hates to hold for anyone. I'll call you back as soon as I'm done with him. I promise to even let you finish telling me what an egotistical cad you think I am." Seconds later, the line went dead.

As the tick continued to pulse wildly in her jaw, Aaryn sat staring hypnotically at the phone in her hand as if it had just sprouted wings.

"Dr. Jamison, you seem distracted. Is everything okay?" Sylvia had eaten only half her slice of pecan pie as they sat in one of the three gardens that Shriners boasted. This one was redolent with the smell of lemon trees, orange blossoms and honey suckle shrubs. Its design was another of Aaryn's insisted upon creations.

With a faint sigh, she said, "All is well, Sylvia. I'm fine. Really." Aaryn turned her head to look at her. She recognized she hadn't been much of a lunch date. Too many unanalyzed thoughts were roiling through her brain. "How are you feeling?"

"I feel much better now that I've spoken to my son. It seems that whole brawling mixup was all a misunderstanding."

"Sure it was," Aaryn thought sarcastically. "And pigs fly while purple cows jump over the moon." She merely nodded and turned her head away rather than force a smile to her face that she didn't feel. Just as she suspected, Jayson had wormed his way back into his mother's good graces. Who knew what kind of story he'd concocted for her benefit? Conniving, ungodly cur that he was. Aaryn was certain Jayson existed in a neverland where the normal rules of etiquette and honesty did not apply. "The man could probably wiggle and charm his way out of the mouth of a lion," she thought. All the more reason for her to maintain her vigilant guard against him. Unconsciously, she crossed her arms over her chest. Whenever she replayed their recent conversation in her mind (which was often) it made her want to throw up.

"I've got some good news." Sylvia said as she watched Aaryn closely.

Aaryn turned to look at her once more. "And what might that be?" she asked, trying to be more sociable.

"My son's coming to see me next week."

Aaryn closed her eyes and turned her head away. But not before Sylvia caught her unmasked expression.

"You don't like my son, do you Dr. Jamison?" The question was asked with a knowing smile.

Shrugging, Aaryn replied sourly, "What's not to like, Sylvia? He's rich, he's famous, and seemingly he has the world at his feet."

"And yet, you still don't like him. Please, tell me why."

Aaryn sighed. "Sylvia, I hardly think it's appropriate for me to discuss your son with you. I'm not a psychologist—not that he couldn't benefit from one. Plus, whether I like him or not is irrelevant. All that matters is that you like him. What's more important to me is that you become whole and complete again. I couldn't care less about your son and I'd really rather not discuss him at all going forward."

"How refreshing." Sylvia was actually smiling.

"I'm almost afraid to ask you to expound on that comment. In fact, I forbid you to." Feeling suddenly restless, Aaryn said, "Let's change the subject."

"Well, dear, since it appears that you find the topic of my son so distasteful, what would you like to talk about?"

Aaryn surprised Sylvia by rising and coming over to her side of the table. She knelt before her and sat with her legs and feet tucked beneath her. Pulling off

Sylvia's slippers, she took hold of her feet and rested them on top of her thighs, stroking the tops of her feet.

With her hands now around Sylvia's ankles, Aaryn took one foot and began to knead it lightly, massaging it from the tips of her toes down to the ball of her foot. She said conversationally, "In all the years that I've been an attending physician, I've never allowed myself to become attached to any of my patients the way I've become attached to you, Sylvia. I've asked myself why that is. Why you, of all people? I'd like to believe my attachment to you is because of a divine connection and that it has nothing to do with any member of your family. I believe, Sylvia Denali, that you are a strong woman, a woman who's had to be strong for herself and for her family. But I also believe that you've been severely wounded and that those wounds have caused you to retreat inside yourself. You've forgotten the inner strength you possess.

"You remind me at times of my own mother. You see, she too, was wounded once. And she turned away from the One who heals all wounds. I believe that illness sometimes comes to shackle our bodies just to remind us of our inner strength and to draw us closer to the One who heals. Some hurts and pains cannot be avoided, they can only be endured. So, when illness comes, the challenge is to derive what the message is behind it. We should always ask ourselves, 'What is my lesson in my time of illness? What will I have to release in order to obtain my healing? What have I lost that I'll be grateful for when my healing returns?' And above all, we should ask ourselves, 'What will I do differently when I heal?' You see, Sylvia, I don't think you came here by chance. I believe you were sent here to be reminded of your first love. Only you know who your first love is. Only you can reclaim the love you once knew."

Aaryn switched feet and began to massage the other one. "When I was a child, a great tragedy befell our family. But my mother was wounded more than any of us. She was sick for a time. That's when, as children, my sister and I discovered that an "incurable" disease simply means curable from within. As time passed, Dot too had to recall who her first love was. After searching her heart, she remembered and from that day forward, my mother was made whole." Aaryn glanced down at Sylvia's foot in her hand. "You'll meet Dot someday. I'd like that because it would please me."

With her eyes closed and her head lifted toward the sky, tears ran down the sides of Sylvia's face. So many emotions were flowing through her body that she couldn't identify the predominant one. She just knew that filtering through her mind were fleeting images of her deceased daughter, Carmin. Sylvia thought, "If only I could have a second chance. If only I could have told my baby that I loved her. That I was wrong to never take the time to listen to her and help build her dreams. If only I'd been a better mother to her. If only…If only…"

Minutes later, Aaryn slid the slippers back onto Sylvia's feet. Thank God it was Friday. After her next appointment, she was free to head out to the mountains. She had her own demons that she needed to release. She needed to empty herself out emotionally so that she could be refilled again, cleansed in a sense. She needed some quiet time to herself because without that, she couldn't give another person something that she, herself, did not possess.

After Sylvia had dried her eyes, Aaryn wheeled her back to her room. Both of them were silent, lost to their own thoughts. Since it was time for Sylvia's healing bath, the nurses were already waiting at the door to her room.

True to his word, Jayson called Aaryn back—and promptly got her voicemail. He knew she would not return his call but he left a voice message anyway. Lounging in his leather chair with his hands cupped behind his head, uncharacteristically, Jayson felt like whistling. Before he could even think about it, he found himself whistling Etta James' lyrics, *"At last, my love has come along...my lonely days are over...and life is like a song. At last...the skies above are blue...my heart was wrapped up in clover...the night I looked at you..."*

With a huge grin on his face, it gratified Jayson to know that he'd found a way to disarm the venerable Dr. Aaryn Jamison. By turning the tables on her and putting the romance ball in play he'd taken the tiger by the tail and stripped her of her barbs. Not that he expected the good doctor to be an easy conquest. But now that he recognized what he felt toward her as attraction, he could begin to lay the groundwork for getting to know her better. That's likely what he needed, a change of venue and a shifting of his focus. He could not honestly recall a time when any woman was so vehement in her reaction toward him. It would be good for a change to pursue a woman instead of always being the one pursued. Because he was a betting man, it never occurred to Jayson that he wouldn't be able to persuade Aaryn over to his way of thinking. *It may take some time,* he thought. Plus, a little more persuasion than the norm, but ultimately he figured he'd win her over.

Jayson was inside his home gym pumping iron when his phone rang. He answered it on the fourth ring. "Denali."

"JD, I've been fending off calls all morning and afternoon long. Quite frankly, I'm sick of it. I'm sick to hell of having to defend you because of that bonehead, Lisa Tennamen. How many times do I have to tell you, that tramp is bad news? You tell me you'll handle it and the next thing I know, there she is again hanging on your freaking arm at some movie premiere. And always saying something so stupid that I have to clean up after her just so she won't make you look like a dunce for being with her. I tell you, every time she gets you into hot water, all the woman has to do is bat her eyes, promise she'll never do it again and, wa-lah, she's back in your bed.

I don't get it, JD. And I'm done trying. I'd do anything for you. You know that, JD. But no more. Not after today. I'm drawing the line right here, right now. Not another second will I defend that harebrained bee-yatch! It's either her or me…"

Resisting the urge to laugh at her impenetrable ravings, Jayson smiled as he listened to his whirlwind of a publicist, PT. When she got on her hump, the best thing to do was ride it out and just listen—especially since she was rarely off target. And given he was in such a magnanimous mood, Jayson was content to yield her the floor. PT was also a heck of an attorney. She'd saved his behind and gotten him out of more scrapes with the media than he cared to admit. Regardless of how many times he'd put his foot in his mouth, PT was always there to save the day. The woman was graced with a silver tongue and could sell snow to an Eskimo.

To his advantage, when PT spoke, the media listened. Normally, she was even keeled—except when Lisa Tennamen's name came up. That's when PT flew off the handle. On more than one occasion, she'd threatened to dump him from her clientele because of Lisa. Plus, it didn't help matters that PT had it on good authority that it was Lisa, herself, who was keeping alive the rumors of their supposed "secret" marriage. Jayson realized that this time, Lisa had gone too far. Even he was tired of her antics and if only one good thing came out of the entire fight episode, it was that he intended to put her out of his life for good.

Putting PT on speakerphone to return to his bench pressing, Jayson said, "I agree with you one hundred percent, PT. Lisa's history. You have my word on it."

But PT was so caught up in grumbling about Lisa that she apparently didn't hear him. "…What's with you men that you can't see past the stick between your legs? Along comes a loose, no account woman like Lisa Tennamen and…"

"Uh, you-whooo…PT? Did you hear what he just said? You won the bet, honey." Wendy, Jayson's assistant, broke into the conversation.

"Well, well, well. What is this? A conversational gang-bang?" Jayson sat up again. "What are you doing on the line, Wendy? With you and PT plotting my demise, no wonder my ears were burning. What bet did PT just win?"

"Don't tell him, Wendy. Let him rot." PT was still put out over the fight affair and having to defend him over someone who in her opinion was "trailerpark trash." Any minute Jayson expected her to break out with her famous reminder that she didn't do the "chitlin' circuit" because her clientele included top corporations, influential politicians and an assortment of A-list actors and actresses.

Wendy said, "Suffice it to say it had something to do with your compulsive skirt-chasing ways."

"Why do women assume that all I do in life is chase skirts? Don't any of my other good deeds come into play? I've done more philanthropic deeds in the last few years than many other actors in their entire careers. And all people remember about me is the number of women I've had on my arm? What about the homes I've built for Katrina victims? Or the rehabilitation center I funded for Iraqi war vets? Or the countless number of scholarships the Bestow Foundation has given out over the years? Our private school for boys in Detroit has graduated more than 500 underprivileged, at-risk boys, 90% of whom go on to college with full scholarships. Yet, I have to fight to get news coverage about it. Not to mention other things that I've done anonymously. So why is it that as soon as a fight breaks out between two vampish women, it gets plastered all over the news in a matter of minutes?"

Undeterred PT said, "I know for a fact chasing women is not all that you do. It's what you do with them after you catch them that I'm talking about."

"See? That's exactly my point. My charitable contributions don't warrant mentioning while my alleged philandering gets top billing."

"At least, PT, he gives his women highend jewelry as a thankyou send off. Nobody will ever accuse you of being cheap, Jayson. Certainly not Rita Danza. The diamond you gave her as a 'please go-away' gift was as big as the soccer ball-sized jugs she's got surgically affixed to her chest."

"I hate to be the bearer of good news, girls, but Rita's soccer balls happen to be The Real McCoy. They're part of her allure, you know."

"There he goes. See what I mean, Wendy?" PT sighed heavily.

"Well, real or not, it doesn't change the fact that she's gonna sue you if you drop her from your next film," Wendy said.

"We'll just have to deal with that when it comes. Plus, I've already spoken to Spielberg about it this morning, so it's already done. Let his people deal with the fall out. I have no intention of ever working with her again. Now, what exactly did you two ladies call me for? Obviously it wasn't to discuss my better qualities."

"PT called to inform you she was quitting. But me, being the loyal assistant that I am, I persuaded her to at least speak with you before she dropped you like a hot potato."

"Which means, Wendy, that you probably were the one who encouraged PT to cut me in the first place. You women are so cutthroat, it scares me. Whoever made up that foolish nonsense about 'sugar and spice and everything nice' to describe women and girls, clearly got it wrong. I've yet to meet one of you who wasn't secretly a black widow spider just waiting to move in for the kill."

"See how jaded the bastard is, PT? And after all we've done for him. By the way, does that lovely description of us women include your mother?"

"It includes all you women except my sainted mother. Listen, Wendy, I have a change of venue for you. I'll be on the east coast tomorrow through Tuesday. I've got the Obama fundraiser to attend, Oprah's blacktie gala and then the Wall Street

Roundtable where I'm the keynote speaker on film investments. I'll wrap things up in Detroit with the dedication of our new youth facility. After that, I'm taking off to Utah for three weeks."

"Three weeks! In Utah?" Both Wendy and PT interjected simultaneously.

"Yes, and if possible, I'd prefer not to be disturbed."

"But shooting of the Ridley Scott film starts in three weeks! And what about all the Hollywood events you've got lined up before then? If you cancel now, you won't have a friend left in town." All Wendy saw ahead of her were scheduling headaches and nightmares if she was forced to juggle Jayson's itinerary.

"I'm confident, Wendy love, that you can clear my calendar. So, just make it happen. Besides, if I ever need a friend here in Hollywood, I'll get a dog. Oh, and PT? From now on, I'll be showing up solo at events. You can hold me to it."

A little over an hour later, Jayson was the topic of another chatfest that consisted of the four members of his posse.

"Utah for three weeks? Ugh! It's not even ski season. Okay, who's going? And let's not all volunteer to go at once." Tara, the lone female amongst the group, piped her displeasure. She typically coordinated their travel schedules.

"Get this: according to Wendy, none of us are invited. He's going out there to spend time with his mother." Steve served as the go-between for Wendy and the rest of the posse.

"That's a relief. We've got a lot of loose ends to tie up in New York and Milwaukee before the school semester starts. Jayson wants this year's basketball tournament to be even more of a success than last year's." Marshon tended to handle the administrative details while Teferro, the remaining member, was the numbers cruncher who managed the budget.

"Still, I don't envy his jaguar. He's going to be bored as hell." A "jaguar" was street terminology for a bodyguard. Jayson's jaguar was Cedric.

"I doubt it," Steve said. "Even Cedric's not invited. Again, according to Wendy, our boy doesn't see the need for a bodyguard while in Utah."

"Okay, hold up. Does anybody else see anything odd about this picture? Am I the only one who's noticed that Jayson's been acting outside the norm the last couple of weeks? Surely you guys have peeped it too?" Tara asked the questions.

"No. I've definitely noticed," said Steve. "A couple of weeks ago, we were hanging out at the club, Privilege, in West Hollywood when two sitcom beauties joined us and started putting a heavy mack on Jayson and me." For all his bluster, Steve fully recognized the good thing about going out for a night on the town with one of the most talented actors to ever grace the silver screen, was that all the ladies flocked to them. "Anyway, by the time we decide to roll, one of them agrees to come back to my hotel room and the other one goes home with Jayson. The next morning when I asked him about it, he said nothing happened. Said he dropped her off at her apartment, saw her to her door and kept rolling. Definitely not like Jayson. She was a looker too."

Teferro nodded his head. "Remember the Weather Girl from that New York station? The one Jayson asked me to get a number for? She texted me for weeks saying how game she was to go out with him. But when I gave Jayson her number, he never called. She started hassling me even harder. So the weekend he's finally in town, I set up a meet. She tells me she's bringing one of her chick friends, so now it's a foursome. We meet at Daniel's on East 65th Street, so I figure the ladies'll be impressed right off the bat. Afterwards, we were gonna have a nightcap at the 40/40 Club. Weather Girl shows up with her friend, who I take one look at and I'm like 'Jayson, my brother, don't fail me now.'

"Chick was stacked in all the right places! She knew I was checking her so she gave me this look like she's game for whatever I have in mind. Fifteen minutes later, we're all seated with drinks hitting it off and having a ball. Except, no Jayson. Meanwhile, the chemistry between the friend and me is so off the chain, I'm like forget the nightcap cause as soon as dinner's over we're parting ways and heading straight back to my hotel room. Man, that chick was hot! She was all over me, too. So there we were, laughing and eyeing one another and playing footsie while Weather Girl is growing angrier by the minute. I could tell she was about to put a real cramp in my game, so I try calling Jayson on his cell, but no answer.

"We order our meals and when the food finally arrives some thirty minutes later, still no Jayson. So now Weather Girl is ready to explode. She's pissed off and makes it clear she wants her friend to be angry too. But I'm not about to let her rain on my parade, so I start apologizing and making excuses for Jayson like I'm his babysitter or something. Weather Girl starts telling her friend they should book. Because she's pissed, she's like 'Aint no fun if I can't have none.' So I say, 'What is this, grade school? Your friend can't stay because you got stood up?' As soon as I say those words I became public enemy number one. The friend feels obligated to take Weather Girl's side. They get up and leave and I'm stuck sitting there with a rock in my pants."

They all snickered at him. Tara said, "Teferro, you are such a jerk. Serves you right." She added seriously, "After the fight broke out at the premiere, I've never seen Jayson so angry. He didn't even want to be in the same hotel with Lisa, let alone adjoining rooms. While everyone was watching the film, he had me go back to his hotel suite at The Peninsula, pack up all his stuff and move him to a different hotel. Personally, I was thrilled to do it. That no-good Lisa Tenna-monster is nothing but a loser. Hopefully this time, he'll dump her for good."

Marshon said, "I guess I would say he's been more distant than anything. It's like he's pulling away. Not just from us, but in general. A couple of months ago, don't you think Jayson would have called and asked us to draw straws to see who would go with him to Utah? And he definitely would have taken his jaguar, Cedric." As an afterthought, he added, "I'll check in with Dez to get his take on things."

"It's possible he's going to Utah to get some R & R" Tara said. "Or, there might be a woman he's going to see out there."

"Psst," Teferro sucked his teeth. "In Utah? Hell, ain't no women in Utah. If you're heading out west, you've got to make it to Las Vegas or California before you even catch a glimpse of a woman. Once you hit any of them mountain states, you might as well forget about the ladies. It's all about the cowboys."

"Man, shut up," Steve said. "What do you know anyway? I say we give a brother some space for a minute. Marshon, go ahead and check with Dez to get his take. Tara, let's send his mom some flowers while we're at it. In a couple of weeks when Jayson comes back, he'll be as good as new and everything will be copasetic again. Just like old times."

"Let's hope so," they all agreed. As concerned as they were about Jayson, in the back of each of their minds also laid a measure of concern for their own livelihoods.

Chapter Fourteen

Jayson was flown into Evanston, a private airstrip about sixty miles outside of Salt Lake City. After a whirlwind weekend filled with public appearances and speeches on his part, as soon as they landed, he intended his first stop to be his hotel in Park City where a grand suite awaited him at the Stein Eriksen Lodge. From his view, 16,000 feet in the air, Salt Lake City was a green and vibrant metropolis bounded by the stunning Wasatch Mountains. He combed the mountain foothills with his eyes, their natural majestic beauty coming alive before him, making him wonder how he'd overlooked such splendor the few times he'd visited.

He was looking forward to seeing his Sylvia. He could share things with her without embarrassment because he knew she'd be completely honest in her assessment. And there was something he wanted to talk to her about. He didn't know if he would remain in Utah the entire three weeks as originally planned. Certainly, Dez was among the skeptics who doubted he'd survive without all the fanfare. According to Dez, Jayson would be back in LA or somewhere on the East Coast before the first week was out. He thought about that particular conversation.

Jayson's limo driver had pulled up to Dez's Carriage House while he sat inside reviewing his speech for the Wall Street Roundtable. Seconds later, the driver opened the rear door to help Dez's date inside.

She was striking and unfamiliar, her form lushly opulent in a classic Oscar de la Renta evening gown. Ever the gracious host, he ignored Dez as he extended his hand. "Jayson Denali. Pleased to meet you."

A surprised smile appeared on her face. Before she could reach her hand all the way out, Dez slid inside and threw his arm around her, saying, "Hands off, Jay. This one's mine exclusively. Besides, she's not in your league." Dez knew from experience that women often were more than willing to switch loyalties after meeting Jayson so he was establishing boundaries up front. "Dionne Stalling, my kid brother, Jayson Denali."

"Your kid brother? Desmond Lloyd, you told me you were an only child." Dionne turned to search Dez's face, as if looking for hidden truth.

Jayson got the territorial memo Dez was sending loud and clear. He said, "Don't pay him any mind, Dionne. We've been friends for so long, it's just that we feel like brothers. Did he tell you how we met?"

Dez groaned and tried to refute the story before Jayson could even begin telling it. "Dee, don't believe a word this miscreant says. He's been a serial liar ever since kindergarten."

"Actually, Dee," Jayson said, smiling as he poured on the charm. "May I call you Dee?"

Sitting back against the softest leather in the most luxurious limo she'd ever had the good fortune to ride in, Dionne rested against Dez and said, "Please, I'm curious to know how you met."

Sitting across from them, Jayson put aside the pages of his financial speech and stretched his legs, crossing them at the ankles. "Well, like I was saying before Junior here interrupted me, it all started way back in kindergarten. I, of course, being the gifted and brilliant thespian that I was destined to be even at the ripe old age of five…" He shrugged his shoulders and spread his big hands as if his fate had already been sealed long ago and there was nothing he could have done about it. "Well, let's just say I had more than my share of all the ladies." Jayson had a captive audience of one as Dez was already rolling his eyes and loudly sucking his teeth. Not to be deterred, Jayson continued. "Did I mention that I was brilliant?" Seeing the indulgent smile on Dionne's face, he shrugged again and said, "Yes, it's true. You see, at five years old, I was a child prodigy who could read at the high school level. But math, or anything having to do with numbers, was where I really excelled."

"Man, you lying dog!" Dez threw up his hands unable to stand anymore of this fictitious tale. The fact that Jayson had swiped the numbers portion of the story when it was really Dez who'd been the brainiac was even more of an insult.

"Dee, I'm telling you, you can't believe this brother. Hollywood has tainted him. He's become a legend in his own mind. He's incapable of getting his facts straight. When we met, we were actually in the first grade—not kindergarten. And by that time, he'd already flunked—twice! So it was *me* who took *him* under my wing and tutored him in the finer points of life. I knew that if I didn't step in, he was on his way to becoming a firstclass dropout. So I taught him how to read, how to spell and how to count. I mean, had it not been for me, he would never have made it past the second grade."

Laughing, Dionne pulled away from Dez to watch the two of them in action. It was clear from their jesting that they were going nuclear on each other and no sane person would believe a word either of them said. Yet, she was enjoying them because beneath all the teasing verbal jabs, one thing was clear: these two loved one another as brothers.

"Nope. Not true at all, Dee. You have to understand that as Dez ages, his memory becomes more and more foggy. Now, what *is* true is that because I was smart and gifted beyond words, I agreed to mentor him. So I took him with me wherever I went and taught him everything I knew."

"Which wasn't much, I assure you." Dez added, while impatiently drumming his fingers on the seat.

"Whatever. Well, as I was saying, Dee, being the prodigy that I was and all, I started teaching Knucklehead here the three Rs: reading, writing, and 'rithmatic."

"See what I'm talkin' about, Dee? After all these years, Simple Sam still can't spell worth a damn!" Dez complained.

Jayson sighed, "It was rough at first. I kept thinking, 'this is a hopeless cause.' But I stuck with it. I made him repeat everything over and over. Until one day it all started to sink in for him and, lo and behold, turns out he loved numbers as much as I did. Fast forward to today and you find that managing millions of dollars for himself and others is something he has a natural talent for. But, if I may add," Jayson facetiously adjusted his tie. "His talent never would have flourished had I not invested countless hours by hanging with him when all the teachers and other students gave up hope on him." Shaking his head, he flicked imaginary dirt from his fingernails. "But this is the thanks I get, Dee. You see how ungrateful he is?" Jayson stared directly at Dez and said, "As much as I've done for you, son, you've never once thanked me. Now why is that?"

"Thank you? Dawg, you're lucky I don't have a gun right now. Since you dissed me in front of my lady friend with that crazy story, now I have to tell her about how I rescued you from prison and saved you from a life of rectal servitude."

"Rectal servitude?" Dionne made the "T" hand sign to bring an end to their good natured bantering. "Hold up. You two are nuts!" She affectionately grabbed Dez's hand. "And you. You led me to believe that Jayson Denali was someone you took a picture with because you just happened to be attending the same event. Turns out you've known him since childhood. You could have told me the truth, Dez. I may not move in the same circles as you do, but I assure you, I'm not star struck. But I'm really curious, why the subterfuge? Was there a past incident where your buddy ran off with your girl? If that's the case, then there's something I should warn you about. You're the one I have a crush on, Dez. That means I'm not interested in dumping you for your best friend." Dionne turned to look at Jayson. "You're a gorgeous man, Jayson Denali, but I think I'll stick with Knucklehead here."

Silence. Not uncomfortable, but each seemed to be waiting for someone else to speak. Jayson wondered how long these two had known each other, since Dez had kept her under wraps and because she seemed so comfortable in laying claim to him.

Marveling at the smooth way she'd brought him to heel with her casual remark about her crush on him, Dez couldn't even take offense at how she reprimanded him for not telling her more about Jayson. She was correct in that they didn't travel in the same circles, still Dez was finding he liked her more and more. There was an air of simplistic honesty about her that he enjoyed.

Into the silence, Dionne said, "I'd love something to drink." When Jayson reached for a bottle of champagne, she shook her head and said, "Just water, please. But I'll have it in one of your fancy flute glasses, that way I can pretend it's something alcoholic."

Jayson handed Dez the bottle of tonic water and let him pour it for her. "I take it you don't drink?"

She shook her head and after taking a sip asked, "So, is there a Mrs. Denali?" Seeing Jayson's arched eyebrow and his cautious expression, she laughed. "Forgive me, I tend to be blunt. I promise, I have no match-making designs. I just find it strange that there's no one on your arm."

Dez said, "Actually, it is a pretty good question. Why no date tonight, bro? This is a change of pace for you, isn't it? You should have called me. I would have brought someone along just for you."

Dionne looked at him and said, "Oh, would you now? Tell me more about this extra someone you would have pulled out of your hat."

"Yeah, Dez, don't go silent on us now. Enlighten us." Jayson had no qualms throwing Dez in the line of fire. "That's quite generous of you to offer me someone from your little black book. Especially since I've never had a problem securing a date on my own. So, who would you have recommended?"

Dionne released Dez's hand. "I'd certainly love to hear all about your little black book. Not that I intend in any way to compete with all the women you probably have in it. I'd just like to know how many 'extra someones' you have lying around."

Feeling defensive, Dez asked, "How did I wind up under the bus? If I recall correctly, you asked about Jayson's marital status. So how did this become a referendum about my life?"

"It's no referendum. I'm just displaying a natural curiosity about your dating habits. Every woman desires to know who the competition is when she meets someone she's attracted to. No need to feel trapped, Dez. I'm not a desperate woman and you're not my meal ticket."

"I wasn't implying that you were."

Watching them, Jayson couldn't contain his smile. *Well, well, well,* he thought. *Look at Dez eating crow.* He said, "You definitely don't look desperate to me, Dee. A $15,000 Oscar de la Renta gown tends to eliminate the look of desperation by screaming class every inch of the way."

Dionne's mouth hung open. "Fifteen thousand dollars? You're mistaken. This dress didn't cost anywhere near that amount of money. Right Dez?"

Something in the tone of her voice indicated that a lot rode on his response. Dez said, "Jayson's just throwing out numbers. The dress is a gift, Dionne. How much it cost is not important."

But in Dionne's mind, how much the dress cost was suddenly very important and she regretted accepting it. No matter its price, she felt as if she'd just been bought. Perhaps in Dez's world it was commonplace for women to ask for and expect things from him. But it wasn't her policy. She knew gifts often came with strings attached and couldn't help but wonder what Dez expected from her in return for his $15,000 "gift." Then again, the women in his circle probably had tons of dresses like the one she was wearing. Dez could have given it to her because he didn't want to be embarrassed by anything she might have worn from her own wardrobe. Either way, she felt belittled.

Recognizing he'd made a major gaffe, Jayson changed the subject. "By the way, I'm traveling to Salt Lake City, later this week. I've decided to go hang out with Syl for the next three weeks."

"Woah. You're going to Utah for three weeks? It's not even ski season. What will you do for recreation when you're not with Syl?" Dez explained to the suddenly distant Dionne who Sylvia was.

"Ever heard of rest and relaxation? That's how I intend to entertain myself. Just me. No crew, no posse, no jaguars and no clinging women. Present company excluded of course." Jayson stared at Dionne who he could tell was troubled at the thought of Dez spending fifteen grand on a dress. It was noble of her, but he knew Dez blew that and more some days when he was out on the greens.

"Who's idea was the Utah trip? Yours or Syl's? I hope it was your's because you'll never last three weeks alone in Utah."

Smiling confidently, Jayson said, "We'll see, won't we?" The limo came to a halt in front of The Carlyle Hotel on East 76th Street. When the driver opened their door, Jayson wondered how long it would take Dez to erase her pensive look and bring the smile back to his date's face.

"Mr. Lewis, I can't accept this." Aaryn glanced down at the check in her hand. "Please, don't misunderstand me. Believe me, it's a wonderful gesture, Sir. But it's so not necessary." The check she was holding was for half a million dollars—a small token of appreciation from a Texas oil tycoon who had more money than he could spend in a lifetime.

"Shucks, Gal. Don't you go givin' ole Kenny a hard time bout nothin'. Why, that's just a drop in the bucket compared to what you done gave me. My Pearl an I talked it ovah and what's done is done. We won't have it any other way, right Pearl?" Pearl, Kenny Lewis' third wife, was gripped along the right side of his shoulder while Aaryn was bear hugged tightly against his left.

Kenny Lewis may have once been paralyzed from the neck down, but his booming voice gave no indication. Now that he again had full use of his limbs, today was his big day. Kenny was being released from Shriners and would walk out the doors unassisted—a complete turn of events given that he was wheeled through the same doors as a paraplegic some nine months earlier. His exuberant countenance bore no resemblance to the broken man he'd once been.

Neither did his wife, Pearl, have any qualms agreeing to the liberal sum he insisted upon donating to Dr. Jamison. Pearl felt strongly that Aaryn deserved the money since she'd witnessed firsthand how patient she was with Kenny even while he constantly mumbled and later screamed obscenities at her. Whereas Pearl would have strangled him and left him to rot in his own stool, Aaryn had withstood his verbal attacks and patiently encouraged him to heal.

Numerous doctors had asserted their professional authority by proclaiming her husband would never again have full use of his extremities, but Pearl remembered how Dr. Jamison had stepped in a short time ago as a replacement for Dr. Naoto, who had departed for Japan. She'd made no assertions that Kenny would walk again. Instead, she'd said only that whether he healed or not depended solely on him. And damned if Kenny hadn't proven everybody wrong. Just when certain members of their family were desperate to get their hands on his last will and testament, Kenny sprang back to life like a phoenix rising. Pearl had brought with her about fifty of the Lewis clan to witness her husband walk out the hospital on his own accord.

Earlier, when Aaryn came to his room to say her goodbyes, Kenny had insisted she be present when his family arrived. Now, his loud baritone voice boomed with a Texas accent as he said, "Kyle, you convince this lil' lady that she's doin' the right thing to accept my gift. Left the check blank so she can do whatevah she wants with the money." A man used to having his every command obeyed, he took the check from Aaryn's hand and stuffed it inside her coat pocket. For him, the matter was settled. He beckoned to his family and said, "Y'all gather round so we can take some more of them pictures." Beaming for the camera, Kenny looked like a man who'd just been given a new lease on life. And now that he was once again the center of his family's attention, he wasted no time letting every one of them see that the big dog was back on the block.

As soon as was permissible, Aaryn hugged him one last time and excused herself. As for the check in her pocket, she knew of several charities she'd share it with.

She was returning to her office when a voice said, "Hold the elevator Aaryn, I'll ride up with you." Kyle briskly strode the distance and as the doors closed he said, "That went well, don't you think?"

With a fond smile Aaryn replied, "I do. Now that he's back in rare form, that man is about to terrorize the state of Texas. Did you know he was planning to write this check?"

Kyle nodded. "I explained to him the hospital's policy but he didn't want to hear about Sarbanes-Oxley or any other tax implications. He insisted you could do anything you wanted with the money. Speaking of which…"

Aaryn interrupted him. "It was very charitable of him, I know of several organizations that will be delighted to receive donations. Also, some of it should be gifted to the members of the staff who assisted Mr. Lewis's healing. Admit it, Kyle, it's unfortunate that we doctors tend to get all the glory."

They were stepping off the elevator as Kyle said, "Aaryn, if more people had your level of integrity, the world would be a better place."

"Don't patronize me, Kyle. This check is not going towards a single doctor's annual bonus. I'm choosing to disburse this money for purely personal reasons. I'm not some great Samaritan and I'm certainly no angel."

A familiar voice from behind said, "I couldn't agree more. How are you, Dr. Jamison? Kyle."

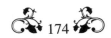

Aaryn turned to find Jayson behind her. He reached to shake hands with Kyle. "I was referring to your level of integrity, that is," he said to her.

His sheer magnetism and the unexpectedness of him standing so close made her feel like her space was being invaded. But that's what Jayson Denali did to her, scrambled her senses and caused her emotions to dovetail. Aaryn doubted she was alone in feeling this way. With her hands in her pockets, she nodded her head in his direction and said, "Mr. Denali."

With what seemed like great familiarity to Aaryn, Kyle said, "I wasn't expecting you until after lunch, Jayson. How was your trip?"

"Great. I got in a couple of hours ago. I thought I'd come early to escort Sylvia to lunch. Have you two eaten already? Would you like to join us?" Jayson's gaze hardly left Aaryn's face. She was staring somewhere between him and Kyle and he found himself willing her to look at him. When her eyes finally met his, he wondered about the measured look in them.

Kyle replied, "Unfortunately, I'm scheduled to meet with someone else, so I'll have to take a raincheck. By the way, I did some comparisons on the Shannon and the Sunreef sailboats. I just might take you up on that offer you were telling me about."

More than the usual number of nurses and attendants were passing by them and it became obvious that they wanted to greet Jayson or get a closer look at him. Aaryn wondered if he was so used to drawing crowds that he was oblivious to them. Taking advantage of the attention he was giving Kyle, Aaryn backed away saying, "I have an appointment myself, so I'd better get going."

Jayson was about to respond to Kyle but he turned to Aaryn and asked, "Can I walk you to your appointment?" Before he could finish the sentence, in a flash, she was gone. Staring after her, he was surprised that she could move so fast. One moment he saw her and the next she'd vanished through a side door.

Kyle was smiling when Jayson turned back to him. "Boats are strange creatures, aren't they?" he asked.

"They are very peculiar creatures indeed. Just when you think you understand them, they shift on you." Neither of them was thinking about boats.

Outside Sylvia's room, Jayson waited for the attendants to finish helping her dress. Since she insisted upon dressing up for their lunch date, he'd made arrangements for them to dine in the Green Room. It was a small upscale restaurant within Shriners that catered to those patients who wanted fine dining in a white tablecloth atmosphere. The Green Room had a delightful ambiance with chandeliers that illuminated its marble pillars and velvet drapes. The service was attentive and the chef-made cuisines were exceptional. Special emphasis was placed on the

beautiful presentation of the food. Men were required to wear jackets and if a nurses' attendant was needed to escort a patient to dinner, they too were required to wear a dinner jacket. Most of the clientele could feed themselves, but for those who couldn't, the attentive service of a nearby nurse justified the dinner indulgence.

For the two of them, Jayson ordered the baked lobster and crab with fresh ginger.

"Ma, you look ten years younger." The smile Sylvia threw at him softened his heart.

"You, on the other hand, don't look any worse for the wear. Considering you were nearly clawed to death by your two ladyloves."

"I object to your description of them. However, you'll be pleased to know that both are out of my life for good."

"Let me see, where have I heard that before?"

"Not from me you haven't."

"So, who are you seeing now then? Tell me about this new woman."

"There is no 'new' woman. I'm swearing off. I even promised PT that I'd show up solo at events from now on. Taking a break from the dating scene is probably just what I need anyway."

"Sweetie, you could be looking in the wrong places. Or perhaps you're looking for someone to fit a mode that's not realistic. You know, what you seek might even be right underneath your nose."

"I doubt it. Don't act as if I'm the only man in the world who's unlucky in love, Ma." Turning the tables, Jayson asked, "What about you? Do you still miss Mr. Lloyd?"

Sylvia stared at him thoughtfully. "Yes, I do miss him, Jayson. I had two loves in my life. Your father and then James. He loved me, too, you know. As much as I loved him. Before he died, he even wanted to marry me, but I couldn't stand the thought of being known as a home wrecker. So you see, I know a thing or two about being in love and having that special someone who feels the same way about you as you do about them. It's why I happen to believe that the person you're seeking might not fit inside the special box that you've created."

"It's not as if I'm asking for the impossible, Ma. I just want someone who loves me for me. I'm not interested in a woman who wants a career in Hollywood. I want someone who'll be devoted to me and not to an image they think they know from the silver screen. Someone who I can be devoted to and someone who shares the same interests that I do."

"Someone beautiful?" Sylvia asked slyly.

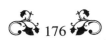

"Yes, that's a part of it, certainly."

Their meal arrived and Jayson began cutting up Sylvia's food into small pieces. His gesture was unconsciously tender and Sylvia loved him all the more for it. It was the little things about her son that she loved. Qualities that got lost under the glare of the cameras and were never mentioned by the stalking paparazzi. When he finished, she took a bite of the succulent seafood and watched as he did the same.

"What about someone like Dr. Jamison?"

Jayson nearly choked on his crab. "What? Where did that idea come from?"

Calmly, Sylvia replied, "Nowhere. I'm just asking. Would you ever consider dating someone like her?"

"Ma, surely you've noticed the woman avoids me like the plague? I come within ten feet of her and she flees like I'm Jason from *Friday the 13th*. Plus, she's got a tongue like a viper. I say one thing and she's off to the races. I'm telling you, Ma, that woman says the darndest things. On top of all that, she seems to think I'm some gross womanizer. Some 'anything goes' libertine who encourages women to commit suicide when they can't have me."

Sylvia marveled that just mentioning Aaryn's name could evoke such a strong response. "That's stretching it a bit, isn't it, dear? And you have to admit that seeing those women fighting over you on national television certainly didn't help your cause any."

"No Ma, I'm not stretching it. Those were some of her exact words. When I spoke to her on the phone, she chewed me out about the catfight incident and was ready to tell me about the dark, fiery place I could retire to, but our conversation was interrupted—in the nick of time, I might add."

"So you've spoken to her by phone, have you?" Sylvia was smiling.

"Yes. I didn't tell you this before, but part of our agreement for her taking you on as one of her patients was that I contact her in advance every time I intend to visit you." Jayson laughed at Sylvia's surprised expression. "Of course I agreed to it, especially after you started raving about some dream you'd had that she was already your doctor. By then I was so desperate for her to be your attending physician that I would have agreed to anything. Talk about pressure." Jayson was only partly teasing.

"Why do you think she wants to be informed in advance of your visits?"

"So she'll have enough time to avoid me. I'm telling you, Ma, the woman is strange."

"And yet, you like her." Sylvia watched him closely.

"I…" Jayson put his fork down. "She's different, that's all. I wouldn't go so far as to say that I like her."

"Okay, then fascinated by her. Is it because she doesn't fawn over you like all the other women you meet?" Sylvia leaned forward with anticipation as though she was watching a riveting movie on TV.

"No, Ma. That's not it." Jayson was becoming irritated and didn't want to discuss Aaryn anymore. "Let's not even talk about her, okay?"

"But I want to, dear. I mention her name to you and you go off on a tangent. I mention you to her and she clams up like a shell."

"You mentioned me to her?" Jayson looked disgusted.

"Of course. She's quickly become one of my favorite people and since you're already my favorite person, who else am I going to talk about the two of you to, except each other?"

Curious despite himself, Jayson asked, "What did she say about me?"

"Well, for starters, not much. She told me not to bring up your name anymore."

Jayson laughed. "See, didn't I tell you? The woman hates my guts." He picked up his fork again, relieved that Aaryn hadn't blasted him to his own mother.

"I wouldn't go that far. She hasn't said so, but I think she finds the whole concept of you dating a slew of women distasteful."

"Ma, we're not living in the dark ages. It *is* okay for men and women to date before they decide to get married. Besides, how else can I be sure that I want to be with a person unless I spend time in their company?"

"That's true, dear, but do you have to sleep with every one of them as you're deciding whether or not you want to continue the friendship? That's why those women were fighting on national TV. No woman wants to be used and cast aside." Sylvia shook her head. "Back in my day, women weren't nearly as loose as they are now. Back then, we knew how to make men salivate for us without bearing every asset we owned. Nowadays, women walk around practically naked and jump in and out of a man's bed at the snap of a finger. And you men are no better."

Jayson threw Sylvia an exasperated look.

"Don't give me that look. You know it's true. Thank goodness Dr. Jamison is not the loose kind of woman that you're used to. She's too private though. She won't even tell me if she's dating anyone." Sylvia sounded frustrated.

"I seriously doubt that Dr. Jamison would even allow me within arm's length of her. So that's one worry you need not concern yourself about. What are you doing asking her about her personal affairs anyway?"

Sylvia shrugged. "She does have a way of seeing through you, doesn't she? It's almost as if she can read your thoughts. Which reminds me, one morning the strangest thing happened. I'd been having a nightmare. I dreamt that death angels were fighting over my body. But then suddenly another angel swooped in to battle them. It overtook them and chased them away. I woke up with a start to find Dr. Jamison sitting on the edge of my bed, Indian style, with her legs crossed in front of her. She was smiling at me and it was like she was saying, 'It's okay now. Everything is going to be okay.' And I felt completely safe. It was the strangest thing, yet it felt completely natural to find her sitting on the edge of my bed—as if she was the angel from my dream come to protect me. The next thing I knew she was holding me in her arms like I was a child. I don't think I'll ever forget that."

A few short weeks ago, it would have seemed strange to Jayson too. But now it didn't. Not after meeting and being in her mother, Dot's, presence. "What's with her, Ma? I don't get her. Yes, she is different from other women. She's not…" Jayson paused trying to think of the right description. "I can't explain it, except to say there's not much subtlety or phoniness about her. Being in her presence makes me feel different from all the other women I've ever been with. The few times I've spoken to her, despite being angry at her, I was aware of a quiet clarity. When I first met her, I couldn't stand her. But after meeting her mother…"

"You met her mother?" Sylvia was surprised and a little miffed that he'd been holding out on her.

Jayson smiled. "Yes and because of it, I think I understand her just a tiny bit better." He began to tell Sylvia all about his visit to the Jamison home beginning with the two humongous dogs. When he finished, they both sat with the silence, lost to their own thoughts.

"Sometimes, Ma, when I think back on that visit with Dot, you know what I remember most about her garden?" Jayson stared at his mother intently because of what he was about to say.

Shaking her head, Dot said, "Tell me."

"I remember the trees. The way they swayed, the sounds they made, it was magical. When I think back on it, in hindsight, I'd swear those trees were whispering. And something else. I'm no animal lover, but every male dog I've ever seen loves to hike his leg on a tree to mark his territory. But not once did either dog piss on any of those trees. It was as though they had as much respect for them as Dot did."

"Will you visit her again?" Sylvia was eager to meet Dot and find out more about her.

"Yes, I think so. In fact, I'm really looking forward to seeing her."

"Then why not ask Dr. Jamison how she feels about it? You realize you're invading her home."

"If I ask her, knowing her, she'll probably just say no."

"Then tell her you intend to ask her mother's opinion on the subject. But don't make it seem like you're sneaking behind her back to communicate with her mother."

"Okay, Ma. I will. But I'm telling you, the woman's going to say no." The waiter came to remove their plates and they sat talking a while longer before Jayson escorted Sylvia back to her room.

Jayson met with Kyle as scheduled and learned from him what the rest of Aaryn's day would be like. But catching up with her proved tricky. He figured his best chance of running into her would be when she made her final checks on some of her patients. Because her routine was so random, he didn't know which rooms she would visit. He approached the nurses' station to see if any of them could shed some light.

"Dr. Jamison?" A nurse to his right was distributing three large cups of Starbucks coffee from a styrofoam tray. "I just passed her downstairs. She was on her way to get coffee as I was getting on the elevator." Her pose became provocative and she was about to say more but Jayson had already turned to take the stairs to the lower level.

Aaryn was in line buying a latte when they spotted each other. Ignoring everyone else in the line, Jayson came and stood within inches of her. "Look who it is. Just the person I've been searching for." His eyes flitted over her face to the tendrils of wavy hair that escaped the bushy ponytail at the back of her head. He had the alarming urge to pull it, but common sense or self preservation warned him not to press his luck.

Although there was no outward change in her facial expression as she returned his gaze, Jayson could tell she'd already begun to bristle inwardly at the way he was staring at her. She reminded him of a porcupine puffed up with all its spikes on full display. As he stared at her, Jayson wondered when and if she ever smiled. Each time he'd seen her, she looked so severe. Was she always this serious? Did anything cause her to become animated and let her guard down? She just seemed so tense and uptight. As he continued to stare, Jayson acknowledged that while she wasn't the most attractive woman he'd ever met, there was something unique about her that drew him and all he knew was that he wanted to discover just what that something was.

Ignoring him, Aaryn turned away to reach for her latte when the woman behind her said with breathless excitement, "You're Jayson Denali, aren't you? I'm Katie Adams. I just love your movies." She stretched out her hand and Jayson was forced to take it, politely telling her it was a pleasure to meet her. When he tried to release her, she held on tightly attempting to engage him in conversation before he interrupted her. "Excuse me, but I have to catch Dr. Jamison. It was good to meet you, Katie."

With a smile on her parted lips, Katie and all the other women behind her stepped out of line to watch Jayson stride away. Had he looked back, he would have seen a chorus of women with their necks craned in unison trying to catch a better glimpse of him.

Aaryn was already a good distance away from him so he jogged to catch up with her. She didn't acknowledge him when he settled at her side. They were nearing the elevator as the doors opened and out stepped a couple who, judging from their wide-eyed expressions, recognized Jayson. The woman, whom Aaryn guessed to be in her mid sixties, was all aflutter while her husband stood nearby smiling indulgently.

Even seasoned women fall prey to the man's charm, Aaryn thought dourly. Taking advantage of the woman's excited prattling, Aaryn slipped into the elevator and pressed the seventh floor button. Before the doors could close completely Jayson's arm slid inside and the doors opened to allow him entrance.

He stepped in and leaned against the opposite wall. Undeterred by her silence he said, "It's a good thing these elevator doors have motion sensors or I might be missing a limb. Thanks to you, of course."

Keeping her eyes straight ahead of her, Aaryn took a sip of her coffee. "Why do I have the sense, Mr. Denali, that unless I address you, you're not going to go away? Am I being stalked? I thought you were here to visit your mother."

"Since you're her attending physician, I was hoping to have a moment of your time."

Aaryn glanced at him sharply. "Kyle has already filled you in."

Jayson smiled. "Kyle relented after I told him I preferred to hear about my mother's progress from her doctor. So we discussed the finer details of a yacht he's purchasing from me."

The elevator doors opened to the seventh floor and Jayson held them for her exit.

With a sigh, Aaryn stepped off and said to him, "Sylvia's doing great. She's a real trooper." She was about to say something else but she glanced in the direction of the nurses' station. All four of the nurses were staring straight at them. None of them attempted to disguise their interest in anything else but the conversation she was having with Jayson Denali. "I could say more, but I really don't have the time. I have an outside appointment." Aaryn walked in the direction of her office hoping he'd take the hint and leave her in peace.

Jayson continued in step with her. "May I join you? There's got to be a way I could be of use to you. Surely you could use a good man?" His tone was jovial, not intending to cause offense. Yet that's exactly what it did.

Aaryn stopped abruptly. Her professional patience had reached its limit. What was it with him? Why did he feel he had the liberty to speak to her like she was another of the flighty women in constant pursuit of him? She was certain she'd done nothing to give him the impression that she was attracted to him. And yet, he seemed to think that very thing. She gave him a look that spoke volumes.

Recognizing the glare, Jayson glanced at the ladies at the nurses' station and found them all still staring as if he and Aaryn were fish in a glass bowl on display. Time to avert a scene. Without giving it a thought, he lightly put the flat of his hand to the small of her back pushing her in the direction of her office. Unprepared for the jolt that went through him when he touched her, Jayson finally said, "Can we please discuss this in private? I'd really rather not have you ream me out in front of the entire hospital staff."

Aaryn had felt it too. A simple touch. It was just a light touch and yet…She quickened her step forcing Jayson to drop his hand away from her.

Inside her office, she leaned against her desk with her arms folded over her chest. It had been her hope that in the weeks since she'd last seen him, that her animosity towards him would fade, leaving indifference in its place. Not so. Despite the frustration she currently felt, Aaryn was determined not to blow her spout. All she wanted was to calm her screaming nerves and quietly express the level of anger she felt toward him for barging uninvited into her world. Shaking her head, she took a deep breath and when she finally spoke, her voice was so soft that Jayson had to step closer to hear her words.

"I don't know how to say this any plainer than I already have. Obviously, some wires got crossed and you're picking up on something I'm not aware of. Whatever it is, I assure you, this is not normal. I'm not an unpleasant person, Mr. Denali, but you are treading on my very last nerve. So I'm going to say this once more…"

"Wait." Jayson interrupted her before she could finish. "Are you still angry about our telephone conversation? Is that what has you so wound up? If that's why you're steamed, forget about it. It was just a conversation. Look, why don't we start over? I don't believe we got off to a good start anyway. My offer of dinner still stands. No strings attached. Just dinner so we can have a pleasant conversation. You do eat, right?"

Am I talking to a five year old in an adult's body? Is he crazy? Aaryn began to consider that he might actually be missing a lube or two. She spoke slowly because she didn't want him to miss what she was about to say. "Mr. Denali, help me, help you, help me."

Using her name with great familiarity, Jayson spoke patiently, "Aaryn, let me interject something. I'm not a kid and I'm not retarded. So stop addressing me like I'm some three-year old who doesn't know what time it is. Obviously, that's just how you treat the men who you lump into the 'all dogs go to hell' category. It would certainly explain the rough treatment you've given me. But I'm trying to tell you I'm not like that. I promise you, once you get to know me, I'm really not a bad person."

Get to know him? What on God's earth would make him think she wanted to get to know him? Aaryn could feel a small throb developing in her temple. Unconsciously, she closed her eyes and touched two of her fingers to the side of her forehead. When Jayson stepped closer to her, she threw him a look that stopped him short about a foot in front of her. Her expression was malevolent.

Jayson had to admit that her narrowed gaze was unnerving because she possessed eyes that seemed to look right through him. Add to it the fact that she rarely blinked and never cracked even a hint of a smile, for a woman of average stature, she was quite intimidating. Maybe he *was* a little crazy for deliberately pushing her buttons.

Though she stared at him sternly, Aaryn noted for the first time the color of his eyes, a very warm light brown. *Eyes are the windows to the soul.* His were eyes that she could get lost in—if she allowed herself to. And that was something she'd no intention of doing. As she struggled to find the right words that would resonate with him, without warning, Aaryn was catapulted back to a time in Jayson's childhood. She saw a small boy holding tightly to a woman who was clearly angry about something. Aaryn recognized Sylvia. She was ranting as she shoved pots and pans inside a cabinet. The weight on her leg made her look down at the little boy clinging to her.

"Not now, Jayson. I'm busy," Sylvia said angrily. But Jayson continued to hold onto her and minutes later she stared down at him again, preparing to lash out at him just as she had the young girl who'd fled the kitchen moments earlier. Instead of hitting him, she got down on her knees and clasped Jayson to her. Aaryn saw him throw his arms around his mother's neck and hold her until her anger subsided. He pressed his forehead against hers and kept whispering over and over, "I love you, Mama." Before long a sigh escaped his mother and as she released her penned up emotions, all anger seemed to leave her body.

But what the occupants of the home didn't know was that, as Sylvia relinquished her anger, a torrential swirl of dark, violent spirits departed the house leaving in their wake an eerie quietness and a sense of peacefulness.

The vision faded as Aaryn came back to the present to find Jayson watching her curiously. She suddenly realized he was adept at diffusing anger because he'd dealt with it so much as a child. Anger was the one emotion he could not be with and when faced with it, he tended to go into mediator mode. From that one childhood scene, Aaryn recognized that Jayson was especially used to handling argumentative women because he'd experienced it up close and personal with Sylvia and his sister.

Aaryn found her own anger towards him subsiding. When she spoke there was no apparent ill will in her voice. Instead, she sounded resigned—as if she hoped he'd take what she had to say and go away, but somehow knew he wouldn't.

"I'm not attracted to you, Jayson Denali. If I've done anything to give you that impression, I apologize. Unlike other women, I'm not happy about your presence here, so don't expect me to fawn over you. I am not one who cares about what others think of me, but I will not have my name linked in any way with yours. I will not be fodder for gossip because of silly preconceived notions people may have. So, I don't want or need you to buy me dinner. As far as your mother is concerned, I meant it when I said she's doing great. My professional opinion is that she will walk again. But only Sylvia can say when that will be."

Jayson didn't know what had caused her to shift from being so angry, but he was glad that her rage was gone. Instead of addressing any of her remarks, he asked, "How's your head?" Though he wanted to, he knew better than to touch her. Given how intense her anger had ran just moments earlier, he was lucky she hadn't slapped him in her fit of anger. Then again, she might be the lucky one, because he didn't know how he would have reacted had she done so.

"I'm fine," Aaryn replied. She was suddenly conscious of how close he was standing to her and she became aware of him in ways that her anger had prevented moments ago. His height, how broad his shoulders were, the rich smoothness of his skin, even the muted scent of his cologne was causing her senses to go haywire. Afraid that her turmoil would show, Aaryn directed her gaze away from him.

Sensing her discomfort, Jayson wondered if she was feeling what he was. He was intensely aware of her as a woman and he was again conscious of that certain something that drew him to her. This was the closest he'd ever been to her and he refused to step away. When her eyes left his, for the life of him, he wanted to touch her face and bring that penetrating gaze of hers back to his. He decided to level with her.

"I won't apologize for being attracted to you, Aaryn. While I don't know what it is, there's something about you that draws me to you. Trust me, you haven't done anything to give the impression that you like me in the least. In fact, you've gone out of your way to show quite the opposite. Still, I find that you intrigue me. I can't promise to keep my distance from you, however, I will promise not to do anything that besmirches your character. But I'm giving you fair warning that I intend to pursue this until I know exactly what it is that has me drawn to you." Jayson's eyes flitted over her face. Any other woman would have been in his arms by now. But not her. He saw her lips tighten and knew she was not pleased by his remarks. "I

have one more request. I intend to visit Dot while I'm here and I'd like to do that with your permission."

Aaryn was shaking her head before he even finished. "Why are you doing this, Mr. Denali? I get the fact that your mother is here for treatment, so you have to visit her. But why are you straying into people's lives that you really don't give a darn about? I'm trying to discern what's motivating you. What spirit is this? Do you even know?"

No he didn't and because he didn't know anything about spirits, Jayson wasn't about to touch the subject. "Nothing's motivating me. I think you're selling yourself and your mother short. Why can't you accept the fact that I'd like to know the two of you better?"

"Because I'm trying to determine if this is some game with you. You're right, Jayson Denali, there is something to this. But it's not what you think. You may define it as a physical attraction, but that's not what it is for me. There's something happening in the unseen realm that I don't quite understand right now. But I'll figure it out—and the sooner, the better. I've never allowed anyone to waltz into my world and cause turmoil within me the way you have. And I don't like it, either. It may not appear so to you, but my life is happy and full. So the last thing I need is for someone, whimsical like you, who's guided only by his physical urges, to direct that type of energy my way. Apparently that's why you lay with so many different women. You meet them and because of what you feel, you end up between the sheets. That's not going to happen with me.

"You may think you're physically attracted to me, but I'm examining your spirit, Mr. Denali. I'm more interested in that part of you that you've shut off from the rest of the world. If you ever stopped to think about it, you'd recognize that your lower anatomy is a small substitute for what you really have to offer. Until you come to grips with that, Jayson Denali, you'll continue to hop from bed to bed in a meaningless quest for temporary satisfaction. Many of the women you've been with, you don't even remember their names. How pointless when all that energy could be directed in ways that fulfill you so much more."

Aaryn was staring into his eyes again. This was comfortable territory for her. She could deal with him on these terms. Judging matters from a spiritual context was much more familiar to her than trying to deal with him on his worldly terms. As long as she waded in these waters, she was in charted territory. It was that same comfort level that caused her to become overconfident. Despite her better judgment, Aaryn gave in to an impulse she would later regret.

"Give me your hand," she said to Jayson matter-of-factly. She held her right hand out with the palm facing upward and waited for him to place his on top of hers.

Still smarting from the words she'd stung him with, Jayson asked, "What's this? The hand of truth? Okay, why not?" He slid his hand onto hers. As his gaze met hers, the first thing he noticed was the warm smoothness of her skin and then he noted how his hand dwarfed hers. The smile left his face as small shivers began to course up and down his spine. Shivers that felt intensely pleasurable. When she moved to snatch her hand from his, Jayson found himself gripping hers more tightly.

The same pleasing sensations continued as their gaze locked on one another. Their present surroundings faded as Jayson found himself magically transported to an exotic room filled with white scented burning candles. All around them, white diaphanous curtains fluttered under a gentle breeze. Sheer white netting surrounded a huge bed replete with white silken sheets. The couple occupying it was lost to everything except the wonders of each other. Pleasurable, heated sensations traveled along Jayson's spine as his bare skin brushed against her bare skin. His light, creamy skin blended tantalizingly with that of rich, smooth dark chocolate-toned skin.

Muted sounds of whispered pleasure escaped those same parted lips as his fingertips lovingly traced them. His other hand cupped thick, wavy hair pulling her head backward, exposing her neck invitingly. As his body slid possessively over hers, his mouth clung greedily to hers as he savored her essence. Tasting her, sampling her, teasing her, loving her. His hand lowered to tenderly search her body as his kiss deepened into a scintillating exploration. His soul sent his brain irrevocable messages that loving this woman was what he'd spent a lifetime searching for. Until this very moment, he'd traveled the world over in search of the exact person he held captive beneath him. His mouth moved to nibble an accessible ear and he couldn't resist the temptation to throatily whisper her name, "Aaryn."

Jayson's eyes widened as he stared into Aaryn's stricken face. Seeing her confused, almost frightened expression, he knew at that moment that she was feeling, sensing and seeing the same incredible vision. And all the while, he continued to grip her hand unrelentingly.

Aaryn's own breathing had quickened and her lips were parted as shock waves traveled through her being. Awe gave way to fear as she recognized her own body laying beneath that of Jayson's amidst the twisted sheets. There was no denying that it was her head which was thrown back in unbridled pleasure. *It couldn't be! What madness was this?* Again she struggled to untangle her hand from his, but he wouldn't release her.

In the vision, hot molten lava coursed through her veins as Jayson reigned kisses over her face, her lips, her chin, her neck, the top of her torso. His tongue trailed a wet line of fire along her every nerve and then back up to her lips which parted invitingly as her head twisted to one side in indescribable pleasure. He bit softly into the arch of her neck while his hand gently squeezed her waist. His teeth and

tongue savored with pleasure the roundness of her shoulder. And as his mouth lowered unhurriedly to take in one of her cresting peaks, Aaryn found the will to shout "No!"

Unable to wrest her grip from his, she slapped Jayson soundly with her left hand causing him to finally release her. The connection was broken.

Feeling as though he'd just been plummeted back to earth after dwelling on a galaxy of euphoria, Jayson mechanically rubbed his smarting jaw. Somewhat dazed from the life-like dream, he watched Aaryn wipe her lips with the back of her hand. Her lips looked swollen and ripe to him, as if he'd actually been kissing them. As she moved to cover her mouth with the front of her hand, her breathing came in rapid bursts. Her gaze was fixed upon the floor and her left hand was pressed tightly to her stomach.

For a man who had just experienced something he didn't know how to explain, Jayson was utterly calm. "Talk to me, Aaryn. Tell me how something so strange could happen. You felt the same emotions that I did, didn't you? You had to, because you were right there with me. How was that possible? Do *you* even know?"

But Aaryn refused to answer him. She kept staring at the floor shaking her head as if to deny what had taken place.

When he saw tears sliding down her face, instinctively, he moved to embrace her but she turned away from him saying, "Please Jayson, I really need for you to leave right now. I just need to be alone."

Feeling protective of her and somehow responsible for what had just happened, he said, "I'm sorry, I can't do that. Alright, I won't touch you, but I need to know for my own peace of mind how what transpired was possible." The vision, if that's what he could call it, now seemed fleeting as if he might have imagined it. But he knew he hadn't. He had kissed her passionately amidst images simmering with sensuality. Images that were now seared onto his brain and were still impacting him in his lower region.

Seeing that he remained close and was not about to leave, Aaryn completely turned her back to him as she wiped the tears from her face. Her knees felt weak as she moved away to step closer to the floor-to-ceiling windows and stood staring at the mountains looming in the distance. The last thing she wanted was to face Jayson Denali and try to answer questions for which she didn't have any answers.

Jayson watched her direct her gaze toward the mountains and sensed that she'd purposefully withdrawn from him. It bothered him that she could detach so easily, as if he was no longer in the room. Seeing her drift away so intentionally reminded him of how Sylvia sometimes retreated to some internal, yet distant world within herself. As he moved closer to her, he saw Aaryn's lips move silently and he wondered if she was practicing some yoga technique to deliberately tune him out.

So intense was her gaze that for a moment he thought she was looking at something in particular. But when he stared out the window all Jayson saw was mountain vistas. Squelching the frustration that roiled within him, he turned from the view and sat on the sofa at the other end of her office. He removed his suit jacket and threw it down beside him. With his elbows on his thighs, he stared around him, taking in the chic décor of her office and all the certificates and plaques she had hanging on the walls. None of it gave him a deeper clue as to who the woman was standing in front of the window.

He stared at her hoping to find answers to his every question. His own mind couldn't come up with any plausible explanation for what occurred between them except that he might have imagined it. Had he? No, it was why he was sitting on her sofa looking puzzled and why she remained in a trance-like state in front of her own office window effectively tuning him out. It wasn't like he could ask anyone else either. What would he say? "Hey, can you explain this vision that Dr. Jamison and I had at the same time? We were in bed together, pleasing each other thoroughly. I was having the time of my life. And then I woke up." *That's the story of my life,* Jayson thought wryly. He always woke up because nothing was ever as good as it seemed.

A knock sounded at the door and the simultaneous ringing of the phone startled him out of his reverie. Momentarily, Jayson felt like a kid with his hand caught in the cookie jar. When the phone rang again he rose to his feet unsure if he should answer her door or her phone, but given that Aaryn was still lost in space, he felt he had to do something.

"Aaryn, will you snap out of it?"

Just as Jayson opened her office door, Aaryn turned to snatch up the telephone.

Kyle stepped inside looking curiously from Jayson to Aaryn. "I brought the contracts for your signature, Aaryn."

Aaryn's back was to him as she signaled with her finger that she'd be right with him. Her caller provided an effective cover allowing her to collect her thoughts.

"Dr. Jamison was giving me an update on Sylvia's progress," Jayson said to Kyle.

"Good, I'm sure that takes a load off your mind." Kyle was surprised to discover Jayson in Aaryn's office given how determined she'd been to avoid him. Was there tension between them or was he imagining it? Kyle had the sense that he'd interrupted an argument but he couldn't be sure.

Feeling like a third wheel, Jayson picked up his jacket and was preparing to leave when Aaryn said, "Mr. Denali, someone would like to speak with you." She handed him the phone.

With raised eyebrows, Jayson took it noting that she made sure their hands did not touch. As he pressed the phone to his ear he heard her say, "I would have come and gotten these, Kyle. You didn't have to make a special trip. Are they ready for our signatures?"

"Hello." Jayson's voice was thick with curiosity.

"I was hoping I would warrant a visit, young man. Will I have to wait until the end of the month before I see you?"

A smile broke out on Jayson's face when he recognized Dot's voice. "Never. You have one coming soon. In fact, I was just getting clearance from your daughter to pay my regards. How did you know I was in town?" Jayson walked to the window, genuinely pleased to be talking to her.

"Ahhh, if I told you, I doubt you'd believe me."

"Try me. Anything you say to me, Dot, I know I can take directly to the bank."

Aaryn was engaged with Kyle over the papers she was signing but still marveled at the ease with which Jayson conversed with Dot.

"Can you come for dinner tonight?" Dot asked.

Jayson's eyes swiveled to Aaryn who was seated with her head bent over the contracts in front of her. *She seemed back to her normal self,* he thought, once again in control of all things. He said to Dot, "I'd love to, but I'm not sure tonight would be good. How about lunch tomorrow at noon?"

"I accept. Until tomorrow then."

Jayson replaced the phone in its cradle and slid his jacket on. "I'll see you two later," he said heading for the door.

"If you wait a second, Jayson, I'll walk out with you." Kyle glanced at his watch before gathering up the signed contracts.

Holding the door as Kyle walked through it, Jayson glanced back at Aaryn. She was sliding files into her briefcase and refused to look at him. He closed the door behind him responding to Kyle's question about sailboats.

The moment the door closed, Aaryn sighed heavily. If ever there was a time she regretted her ability to "see" or glimpse into a person's future, it was now. She'd known since her early teenage years, that both she and her sister, Erika, were endowed with prophetic tendencies. While Erika had blocked her precognitive abilities, Aaryn remained open to hers. If eyes really were the windows to the soul, then the hands were the gateway to a person's spirit. Aaryn was intrigued by her ability. She noticed a quickening within herself whenever she touched another person's palms. She touched people at whim and immediately felt as though she was swept through a rabbit's hole—one that afforded her a view of the person's past and immediate future. Several years later, what once fascinated her slowly began to repulse her as she witnessed the horror of people dying in the immediate or not too distant future.

Where before she shook hands with people as a matter of intrigue, the need *not* to know a person's end prompted her to begin nodding her head as a form of greeting. If someone was fated to die a sudden or violent death, she didn't want to know about it. It was during this chaotic phase of her teenage years that Dot began to show her how to channel her gift so that it didn't overwhelm or destroy her. Dot taught Aaryn that instead of denying her gift, as Erika had chosen to do, she could use it to heal others. Already deeply disappointed in Erika because she'd chosen to disavow herself of something that Dot perceived as a gift from God, she was thoroughly supportive of Aaryn's desire to use her gift to benefit others.

Now that she was a mature woman, Aaryn had long since mastered the ability to control images she derived from touching people's hands. It depended largely on how attracted or repulsed she was by a person's energy field. Something about an individual drew her, repelled her or, most preferably, sparked neutrality within her. If her sensory antennae spiked in response to a person, she either engaged them without touching them or avoided them all together. When she was drawn to a person, she could hardly wait to discover their hidden mysteries. Thankfully, most of the people she encountered were neutral, which meant that she would have to forcibly connect with them in order to envisage their lives.

Where Jayson Denali was concerned, the man was making her apoplectic. From the day she'd first met him, she was both drawn to and repulsed by him. Everything within her screamed that she touch him not. She'd gone out of her way ever since to avoid him. And when she found herself thinking about him more than she should, she consumed herself with physical activities just to evade the thought of him. Why she gave in to the sudden desire to touch him, the desire to *know* what it was about him that drew her, she could only surmise.

As disheartened and demoralized as she was, she consoled herself with the knowledge that she had the power to mold and shape her own destiny. She didn't have to take what she'd seen in the vision as immutable law. She could choose not to become involved with Jayson Denali. She would mentally block out the vision she'd had of being in Jayson's arms.

There was really no other choice. To pursue such a hopeless path would lead only to a cruel twist of fate.

Part IV

"The art of love is largely the art of persistence."

~ Albert Ellis

"Love is an irresistible desire to be irresistibly desired."

~ Robert Frost

"Love conquers all."

~ Virgil

Chapter Fifteen

Jayson glanced down at the landmark he'd circled on his tour map. Following the directions displayed on the SUV's navigational system, he angled the Lincoln Navigator onto I-15 toward Highway 92. According to the mapquest display, it would take him slightly less than an hour to reach his destination, the Mt. Timpanogos wilderness area near Provo, Utah. After his peculiar encounter with Aaryn, he wasn't quite ready to go back to his hotel suite. There were still too many unanswered questions he was wrestling with. He thought about calling Dez, but quickly decided against it because he wouldn't know where to begin and would probably end up sounding idiotic.

The concierge at Stein Eriksen had recommended he visit Mt. Timp, as it was commonly called, referring to it as a place of great beauty. Jayson had learned to be a little skeptical when people promoted certain "must see" destinations. A beautiful tourist attraction to one person often appeared little more than a dump to the next. In the course of his travels, he'd seen much of the world and remembered many places and sights because of their rare beauty. Like the unforgettably radiant sunsets he'd witnessed in South Africa's, Cape Town; the unspoiled beauty of the blue lagoons of Bora Bora, Tahiti; the sublime Mayan Ruins of Belize; and the rich architectural heritage of the Greek Islands with their golden stretches of sands. He even thought of his own villa in the south of France. Somehow, vast mountain peaks had never quite made it onto his list.

Songbirds Rachelle Ferrell and Will Downing harmonized the blissfulness of finding that perfect significant other as *Nothing Has Ever Felt Like This* crooned through the Navigator's sound system. Jayson tried to recall the last time he'd taken a drive just to enjoy the surrounding scenery. In the midst of his moviemaking bouts, the times were few and far between when he'd traveled leisurely to exotic locales just to explore the wonders of nature's creations. He was hard pressed to remember when last he wasn't running somewhere in response to an invitation he'd felt obliged to accept. What did come to mind, were his visits to Shriners. Despite what others thought, his trips here were never dull. Not knowing what to expect, he naturally assumed something out of the ordinary would happen.

The landscape changed as he approached Mt. Timp. For much of the drive, he was surrounded by an endless terrain of reddish-orange sand with occasional patches of brown shrubbery and cacti that created a desert wonderland. Suddenly, lush greenery became the backdrop for sweeping meadows of knee-deep alpine wildflowers in an amazing blaze of colors. Jayson slowed as the road began to narrow just before he reached the mountain's entrance. Ahead, the twisting roads resembled well-paved arteries that climbed to over 8,000 feet. With its narrow curves and steep grades, the Alpine Loop was a 24-mile-long stretch that provided an intimate view of the towering granite monoliths that dominated Utah's eastern skyline.

Ten minutes on the driven path and Jayson understood why the brochure described the climb to the summit of Mt. Timp as "climbing a stairway to the sky." He climbed past camp grounds that housed visiting RVs, still somewhat taken aback that he could scale a mountain from the comfort of his own vehicle. Jayson was sure he'd meant to remain cynical about his excursion. But somewhere between the colorful tapestry of autumn leaves from maple trees, babbling brooks, small lake reservoirs and brief wildlife sightings, he lost his cynicism. Ironically, he kept hearing in his mind something Dot had said to him during his last visit: "It's the little things that bring contentment."

A few miles down the road, Jayson began to hear the collective sound of a mighty rushing river. At least that's what he thought it was until into his view appeared the unexpected spectacular vision of one of the most magnificent waterfalls he'd ever seen. Before he knew it, he'd pulled over, grabbed his binoculars and exited the Navigator to stare in inspired awe at the cascading wonder. As the sun beat down with high-ultraviolet intensity, a huge rainbow as tall and splendid as any he'd ever seen surrounded the falls. The scene before him was breathtaking, the kind of panorama that would make anyone stop to marvel at one of nature's imposing creations. Oddly, Jayson felt humbled in the face of such grandness and it seemed to him that all of life's challenges became infinitesimal, paling significantly beneath the aura of mountains that had withstood the test of time, enduring throughout centuries.

As Jayson looked across the great divide, far below him he saw hikers on trails that crisscrossed through the solid rock of the mountains. He had the sudden urge to join them. Glancing down at his Timberland shoes, he was confident that he could climb for hours in them. He angled his binoculars to get one last close up of the waterfall when an idea hit him.

Shooting of his next film, *A Season to Hunt*, in which he played a rogue cop matching wits against a psychopathic serial killer, was scheduled to begin in just over three weeks.

The film location was set for Toronto, Canada. But as Jayson stared at the landscape around him, he thought it would be perfect for the part of the script that required a woody, forest-like area. His only question was how much hell would he have to go through to make it happen? Already, he could hear the director, Ridley Scott, screaming about the change since Canada had already been nailed down as the film site.

The film location manager won't be too happy either, Jayson thought. With shooting to begin in a matter of weeks, Paramount Studios was contractually obligated to film in Toronto. But Jayson was almost certain the contract didn't call for a hundred percent of the film to be shot there. Besides, once the production team saw what he was seeing, he had no doubt they would see things his way and agree that a portion of the movie could be filmed here. He might ruffle some feathers, but that was not a concern. His track record and box office clout entitled him to make unexpected demands.

"Mr. Denali, may we have your autograph?"

Wrapped in his own thoughts with the roar of the waterfall in the background, Jayson hadn't heard the trio approach him until they were several feet away. He turned to find two eager teenagers with a woman he presumed to be their mother. All of them were clearly excited.

"I told you it was him!" the male amongst the trio exclaimed triumphantly.

"Ohmygaw, we just saw *The Mission* last night. You were awesome!" said the girl, ignoring her brother's "I-told-you-so" look.

Jayson extended his hand to the woman who'd initially asked for the autograph. "Glad you enjoyed the movie. You must be their sister."

The mother gushed at the obvious compliment. She hadn't known what to expect as they approached the popular star. Her son had spotted him first and she and her daughter had insisted on coming along to meet him. She'd been prepared to find him haughty and standoffish, but standing face to face with the handsome superstar was something out of the ordinary. He'd only spoken a few words, yet his warmth and magnetic appeal was overwhelming. *The charming Jayson Denali could count her as a fan for life,* she thought.

"Oh no, she's our mom," the daughter interjected almost disparagingly. She was all animation compared to her sibling and mother who'd suddenly grown silent in the presence of a larger-than-life movie icon.

"Would you take a picture with us, Mr. Denali? Our friends back home in Kansas will die when they see it." But as the daughter pressed the camera into her brother's hand, it was clear she wanted no one else in the picture except herself and the hot actor.

Jayson had heard the "friends-back-home-won't-believe-it" line a million times or more. As the brother hoisted the camera looking for the best angle, Jayson was standing side by side with the girl. Suddenly, he was thrown off balance when she threw both her arms around his neck and pressed her ample chest into the sides of his arms pulling his face down to hers.

Jayson couldn't believe the suggestive words she whispered hurriedly into his ear. Her open-mouth gum chewing reminded him of a young Britney Spears. But there was nothing childlike about the salacious act she was offering to perform for free. Jayson frowned in disapproval as he firmly disentangled himself from her. Meanwhile, the camera never stopped clicking, leaving Jayson to wonder if the trio was in bed with The National Enquirer or some other magazine that paid handsomely for unusual photos.

After the first flurry of flashbulbs, Jayson knew he'd made a mistake when he saw a crowd of people quickly heading in their direction. Within moments, he was surrounded by about twenty people all wanting autographs and photos. Several were hell bent on introductions as they, themselves, were trying to break into acting, while others reacted as if they were in the presence of royalty. When people responded to him as though they just wanted to touch the hem of his garment, it was the aspect of stardom that irritated Jayson the most. Few seemed to grasp the reality that no matter who a person was or how much money they had, celebrities still struggled with the same fears and insecurities as the next person. Most just had a larger safety net from which they indulged their hang-ups. He'd come to believe that people put others on pedestals because of their own personal need to cling to fantasies of the grass being greener on the other side.

It took him nearly thirty minutes to extricate himself from the crowd by edging closer to his vehicle. Instead of the crowd getting smaller, more and more people gathered as news of him being in their midst spread like wildfire. Cell phones captured his image as people downloaded it to YouTube, GawkerStalker and other Celebrity Sighting websites. Not wanting to cause a stampede or take the chance of someone getting hurt and himself getting sued, Jayson said, "Sorry, folks, I'm out of time. If you haven't seen it already, please check out my latest film, *The Mission*." Flashbulbs were still going off as he closed the door of the SUV and drove away. Though he didn't get to see all of Mt. Timp, Jayson had seen enough to know he wanted it as a secondary location in *A Season to Hunt*.

He hit a button on his cell phone and dialed his agent's number.

The Children's Research Hospital of Salt Lake City was dedicated to treating children with catastrophic diseases. It was a place where doctors from across the world sent their toughest cases and their most traumatic patients. But more importantly, it was a place where no one paid for treatment beyond what was covered by insurance and where even those without insurance were never asked to pay. Aaryn was among a host of gifted doctors who donated their time towards the children's treatment and who gave of their fortune to enable researchers to do more scientific studies.

Hours after her ordeal with Jayson, Aaryn left the Children's Research Hospital drained from working with a pair of three year-old twins diagnosed with spina bifida. As groundbreaking as her work was with adults, her Quantum-Touch studies were proving even more effective on children. The demand for her time and services far outweighed her availability on any given day.

As she climbed into her Range Rover to head for home, her own internal scan revealed that she was more dejected than tired. Battling the range of emotions that Jayson evoked within her was far more draining than a full day's work. Thoughts of him were becoming increasingly harder to resist. Much as she was trying to avoid him, the man kept turning up like a bad penny that just couldn't be gotten rid of. By the time she stuck her key in her front door, Aaryn remembered an anecdote from her childhood. She would ask Dot about it, because it might prove a preventative measure she could use against Jayson.

Baron and Max greeted her with wagging tails as she headed upstairs to her room. The smell of Italian seasonings and fresh baked bread wafted throughout the house by the time she'd showered and changed into shorts and a tee shirt.

"How was your day?" Dot asked as Aaryn took a seat on a stool at the ceramic tiled island in the middle of the huge kitchen.

A long sigh escaped her as she lowered her head into the cup of her hands.

"That good, hmmm?" Dot removed the pan of breadsticks from the oven.

"Mom, remember Mrs. Hendersen?" Aaryn asked.

Dot paused as she placed the pan on top of the stove. She noted that Aaryn had called her "Mom." Not that Dot minded, but when Aaryn had turned thirty, she was the one who had requested permission to call her "Dot." That Aaryn reverted now to calling her "Mom" told Dot that she had a lot on her mind.

"From our days in Kenilworth?" Dot asked as she removed the tossed salad from the fridge and began setting the table.

"Yes. Remember how she used to complain all the time about her husband?"

Dot came to the island where Aaryn sat. "What made you think of her?" she asked curiously. Somehow, Dot was afraid she already knew the answer.

"Her husband used to beat her badly, remember? People would whisper about how Mr. Hendersen would fight her every day and twice on Sundays. I guess I've never understood how people can call it a "fight" whenever a woman gets beat up by her husband. How is it a fight if the victim never has a chance to defend herself? Anyway, whenever she came to visit you, all Mrs. Hendersen would talk about was how much she wished her husband would go away. One day, she came to the house with her eye as big and purple as a plum from where Mr. Hendersen had socked her. She cried in your arms like a baby. Don't you remember?" She threw Dot a look that questioned how she could forget.

"Vaguely," Dot said as she sat on a stool across from Aaryn. "That must have been more than thirty years ago."

"True. But I still remember it like it was yesterday. You cleaned Mrs. Hendersen's eye and hugged her, telling her that if she started crying she was going

to mess up your apron and her one good eye. Then you got up and pulled a bag of something white from deep inside the cabinet. I distinctly remember you telling Mrs. Hendersen to sprinkle the entire contents in front of her door step and that in seven days her problem would be gone. The next week, Mrs. Hendersen returned rejoicing that Mr. Hendersen had left her for another woman and had moved to another city. Remember?"

"How do you know this?" Dot watched Aaryn closely. By now she should be used to her daughter's near photographic memory, but still she never ceased to be amazed at the things Aaryn retained from her childhood. Incidents which Dot never gave a second thought, Aaryn recalled with deadly accuracy. Dot marveled that she knew about the one involving Mrs. Hendersen.

"I hid in the kitchen closet and listened to the entire conversation. What was the white stuff in the bag, Mom? Surely you remember."

"Why would you want to know?" Dot avoided answering her question directly.

"Because, if whatever you gave Mrs. Hendersen worked for her, I'm hoping it will also work for me." Aaryn stared down at the counter instead of looking Dot in the eye.

Her fears realized, Dot said, "It wouldn't. For a variety of reasons. First of all, you're not married, and as far as I know, neither do you have anybody harassing you. Who would you want to use a parlor trick like that on anyway?"

Aaryn looked up and smiled triumphantly. "So you do remember! Well, you didn't think it was a parlor trick when you carefully instructed Mrs. Hendersen all those years ago. And *she* certainly didn't seem to regard it as a parlor trick after it worked. Plus, you know good and well Jayson Denali is who I have in mind."

"How could I know that, dear? You've never talked to me about the fellow."

"That's because he vexes me so. Besides, I wouldn't know where to begin."

Dot's shrug was noncommittal. She rose to finish placing the food on the table. "The beginning is always a good starting point."

With a sigh, Aaryn got up to help and then took a seat at the kitchen table. "What did you say to him earlier when I handed him the phone?"

"I invited him to dinner."

"Without consulting me first?" Aaryn looked and sounded taken aback.

"Since when do I need your approval to invite someone to dinner?" Dot unfolded her napkin, ignoring the open-mouthed expression on her daughter's face.

"That's not what I meant." Aaryn shook her head. "Why him of all people? You don't know him like I do."

"Ahhh, I see. And you know everything there is to know about Jayson Denali?"

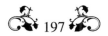

"Of course I don't. I just know what I've picked up on. I know enough about him to avoid him."

Dot placed some of the spinach lasagna onto her plate and passed the dish to Aaryn. "And how's that working for you? Avoiding him, that is."

Aaryn took the dish and set it down in front of her. With her chin once again cupped in her hands, she admitted, "Not too well, I'm afraid. That's probably what made me remember Mrs. Hendersen."

"Aaryn Jamison, I've never known you to be a coward. What are you running from?"

"I'm not running from anything, Dot. The man simply vexes me, that's all."

"I see. And since when do you resort to parlor tricks to get rid of someone who 'simply vexes' you? If we all stooped to that level, I'm afraid there wouldn't be anyone left in the world. I'd venture to say, we all vex someone at some time or another."

Aaryn placed her forehead in the palm of her left hand. "Mom, you're twisting my words and you know it."

"How can I twist your words when you haven't given me anything to twist? What is it about this particular fellow that vexes you so? You still have yet to answer me that."

"Okay, okay…" Aaryn started placing food on her plate as she struggled for words. Finally, she said, "He makes me uncomfortable. And I don't trust him, Mom. He's hurt too many women as it is. I just don't want to be one of the many casualties left on the Jayson Denali battlefield. Not that I would ever fall for him," she added hurriedly before lapsing into silence.

Dot wasn't about to let Aaryn clam up on her. "Go on, speak more about the uncomfortable part."

"Well, there's not much more to say. I try to avoid him, but it's just not working. Instead, I'm so aware of him that I know when the man is inside the hospital. That's how attuned to him I am. And the more I avoid him, it seems the more he follows me. I hoped that by making him inform me in advance of his visits, I'd have an opportunity to skedaddle and get lost whenever he's in town. But then, here he comes again. The man is like a bad nightmare. I can't figure this thing out, Dot. It's a game to him, I know it is. He's finally met someone who doesn't kneel at his feet and worship at the altar of his good looks, so he thinks he's got to conquer me because I'm not interested in him the way every other woman is. I don't know how any woman could trust him. But then, you should see the women, how they fawn over him. I don't get it. Really, I don't. Yes, he's handsome. But then so are tons of other men." Nonplussed, Aaryn shook her head.

"I ask him to stay away from me, he sends me flowers. I tell him what a jerk I think he is, he invites me to dinner. Mom, I don't kid myself about my looks. I never have. You of all people know that. I'm not one of the gorgeous-looking starlets that run in his circles and I never will be. In every picture I've ever seen of him on some magazine cover, he's always with a beautiful bombshell of a woman. I'll never fit that bill. Nor am I trying to. He and I have nothing in common besides the welfare of his mother. On top of all that, after one minute in his presence, he irritates the heck out of me. It almost pleases me to say that I've never ever seen one of his movies. And from what I hear, he's made tons of them. I guess I'm just frustrated, Dot, because I don't know what to do about him. And to make matters worse, you seem to like him more than I do. I mean, you've had more conversations with him than I have and you definitely seem to get along with him better than I do. It's too bad he's not older and that you're not younger. The two of you could have dated!"

Dot had set her silverware down in the midst of Aaryn's tirade. She said in jest, "Well, daughter, that was quite a mouthful. Why don't you just say how you really feel?"

Aaryn rolled her eyes at Dot's wisecrack. "The thing is, Mom, my life was going along so smoothly before he appeared. I didn't think I wanted for anything. And then he parachutes in like an unwelcome guest and disrupts every part of my daily routine. Now, I'm thinking about him when I shouldn't be and even when I don't want to. I swear I was content. Suddenly I'm reminded that there's this mountain-sized void in my life. Instead of seeing my accomplishments, all I see is what's missing. I don't have any children. I don't have any romantic prospects. And it doesn't look like I'll ever have either.

"Until he showed up, I didn't even realize how badly I wanted to have children. I thought I had come to terms with it. Years ago, I wanted nothing more than to have a relationship like the one you and Dad had. Honestly, I did. But I never found anybody. Over the years I've come to rule out that possibility and I've replaced that desire with my work and with other things and people. I wasn't attractive like Erika, so I've always tried to compensate for what I lacked in the beauty department with brains and brawn. I wrapped myself in my life with you, my patients, the children who I've helped to heal and my research. I never complained because I knew the purpose and plan for my life and I became content with that. But suddenly, along comes Jayson Denali to throw a monkey wrench in every one of my goals, my dreams, hopes and visions. Here he comes to remind me of all that I *don't* have."

At some point tears had begun to roll down Aaryn's face and for a moment she made no attempt to wipe them away. Finally, she sighed and wiped her face. Blowing out a deep breath, she said, "It doesn't help that he also makes me think about Erika. How we used to be so close until she just threw me away like yesterday's newspaper. I call her and she acts as though she doesn't even know me, much less want to be bothered. Erika ripped out both our hearts, Mom, when she made it clear that she didn't want to have much to do with us anymore. As hard and as long as I've prayed about it, I still don't know what we did to cause her not to love us anymore.

"Erika may have abandoned us but there's not a day that goes by that I don't think of her and pray for her and send loving thoughts her way. Even when I sense she's in distress, I'll reach out to her in the spirit *and there's nothing there*. I don't want to love somebody the way I loved her only to have my heart torn to shreds. And that's exactly what Jayson Denali would do if I ever gave him half the opportunity. He doesn't know how to love someone unconditionally. He's too used to people wanting something from him, so his idea of love is warped and totally different from anything I've ever known. It may not seem like it to him, but my life is full and rich. I have you, Mom. I have my faith. I have my work and that's enough for me. I don't want anything to change within my world, right now or ever. I'm perfectly happy and content for things to stay exactly as they are."

As she wiped away the tears streaming down her face, Aaryn gave a short, humorless laugh. "I don't even know where all these tears are coming from."

Dot's heart melted with a mother's love. "Aaryn, there's nothing wrong with wanting to be loved. The need and the desire to love and be loved unconditionally, why that's just humanity. But how can you ever experience it if you block it every time it shows up? Even with the unique gifts that God has blessed us with, when we're allowed glimpses into the future, the wonderful thing is knowing that we have choices. And because of the choices we make, we create our destiny as we go along. You created yours masterfully when you chose not to let people's hurtful comments about your skin color get to you. I've watched you from a small child deflect people's negative remarks and use whatever energy it generated to become a better person. I've told you time and time again that you are beautiful because beauty comes from the inside. Yes, the world is drawn to outward physical beauty, yet those rare people who look beyond it are the real gems in life. But you made the decision to push your suitors away, Aaryn. Even Dr. Kyle."

Dot saw Aaryn's eyes widen in surprise. She continued anyway. "After Dr. Kyle's wife died, I knew he'd fallen in love with you. You never talked about it, but I've known since the night of that charity function you made me attend. I knew it simply because of the way he watched you when he thought no one was looking. I just wasn't sure how you felt about him, so I kept telling you, Aaryn, that I didn't want you feeling like you were obligated to stay in this house because of me. You have your own life to live. My life is full, too. I've lived it and I've done the things I've wanted to do. Right now, I'm still doing the things I want to do. The demand for the Nature's Brew line of teas has expanded supernaturally so I'll always be okay financially. But then finances aren't a concern for either of us. If you were to marry and leave here tonight, Aaryn, I'd miss you terribly. But I'd still be whole and complete.

"Now you listen to me where Erika's concerned. I love her and hurt for her as much as you do, even more so because she's from my own womb and has prevented me from knowing my own grandchildren. I, too, have prayed about what I may have done to contribute to the situation. But all I hear is silence. You see, Erika has to learn for herself, that no matter how far she travels, she can't escape her past. If there's one thing I've learned over the years, it's that when you're given a gift by the Creator and you refuse to use and honor that gift, you'll be stripped of it and it'll be passed on to someone else who'll use it. Like it or not. No one can change that because that's the way the world's designed." Dot paused to swipe at her own tears. She had her own unhealed wounds regarding her lost sheep of a daughter.

"We can't help what Erika chose. Her turning her back on us was her decision alone. And yet, we love her no less. You can't make someone love you, Aaryn. Never forget that. The hardest lesson I was forced to learn as a mother was that I had to let my daughter go. But as surely as there is a God, know that the Creator has her in the palm of His hand. Soon, she's going to have to weather life's storms on her own. Because she's made things and people her God, Erika will be brought low. Those very things that she's put her trust in are going to be stripped away from her. Believe me, I've seen her future and it is not a pleasant sight. But I'll tell you this much, it's because of our effective and fervent prayers that no harm will come to her. She will lose everything she's got and after what she's about to endure, her pride will be but a remembrance."

A shudder went through Aaryn at the harshness in Dot's voice. She could feel a sudden coldness enter the room.

"But enough about Erika," Dot continued. "Let us speak of you. I don't know why things didn't work out between you and Dr. Kyle. He has his flaws I'm sure, but he's a good man. I didn't think race had anything to do with it, but again, I didn't know. When I stared into the open doors in the spirit realm, I didn't see his face alongside yours. I saw someone else's."

Dot held up her hand. "No, don't ask me who it was because I won't reveal that. Besides, we have choices, remember? Aaryn, as sure as there is a living God, you will marry and bear a child. Yes, you're right, I don't know Jayson Denali. I just know what I, myself, have gleaned of his spirit. I don't want you to prejudge him as you've done. How do you know things wouldn't work out between you? Especially if you keep spurning him at every turn? The poor man doesn't know whether he's coming or going when he's around you. Try looking at things from his perspective. He didn't ask to be born with his good looks. Because everyone has a hidden agenda when it comes to him and his money, he's not a person who trusts easily. He's learned to thrive by his own established set of rules. Just be yourself when you're around him. Stop fighting and allow the universe to unfold before you. If he's to be a part of your future, you'll know it. And if he isn't meant to be, your spirit will let you know that as well."

Dot shook her head. "Change is inevitable, Aaryn. Nothing remains the same forever. If we're fortunate, the winds of change blow favor in our direction. And sometimes, the winds of change just blow. We may not grasp the significance of it at the time, but everything we've undergone prepares us for what's to come. You're a strong woman, Aaryn. I'm proud that I've raised a daughter who doesn't take any wooden nickels. But all of us are vulnerable in some area of life. It's God's way of making us remember that we need Him. Every one of your accomplishments aside, dear, no mother could ask for a better daughter than that which you've been to me. I love you and I'd give my own life just to see you happy."

"I love you, too, Mom. More than you'll ever know." Aaryn stared at Dot with pride. "I'm the blessed one in this relationship. Without your guidance, I wouldn't be who I am and I certainly wouldn't be where I am. I don't know what I did to deserve you for a mother, but if I could choose of my own free will, I would choose you all over again."

As Aaryn reached her hand across the table to grab hold of Dot's, something clicked inside her. Some inner awareness shifted and in the place of anger, discomfort, fear and rejection, a gentle peace entered that passed all her understanding. Suddenly, it didn't matter what the future held because she knew Who held the future and she realized she'd show up to face it come what may. She wouldn't fear Jayson Denali or the emotions he sparked within her. Neither would she reject him. She was not about to encourage him. She would face him head on.

Chapter Sixteen

The balcony of Jayson's grand suite was a rich blend of European elegance and rustic mountain architecture that offered a breathtaking view of Rocky Mountain peaks. Dressed in a simple pair of D&G Dolce & Gabbana pajamas, his shirt was open and the string of his pants drawn tight. The cool breeze blew against the expensive fabric outlining the six pack of his abs and the tautness of his thighs. He leaned over the thick log rail holding a tall glass of OJ in one hand while clasping his cell phone to his ear with the other.

Engaged in conversation as he was, he was unaware of being under intense scrutiny and the subject of much ribald conversation from a trio of women over 1,500 feet away. They were taking turns looking at him through a pair of high-powered Leica binoculars. From their balcony within the main lodge, each deep groove of Jayson's smile was categorized with breathless delight and the bronze of his chest ogled with singular joy as the women gave voice to heated versions of what a fantasyfilled night with the handsome superstar would entail. As they worked themselves into an early morning lather, they began eagerly placing bets as to which of them would be the first to "bump" into him.

"Tell you what," Jayson said, "let me do some leg work before we get anybody else stirred up. I'll set up an exploratory meeting with the film commission. Since I'm already out here, I can easily meet with their Board of Directors. Plus, it'll give me an opportunity to find out how the numbers look. Let me get back to you before you book your flights. No, it's no problem but I'll keep it in mind."

Jayson's conference call with the film's Producer, Production Manager and Location Manager had taken more time than expected. He'd spent much of the morning discussing potential script changes and detailing his quest to add Mt. Timp as a secondary film location for the project. Because it was so last minute, his recommendations were met with hesitancy. But because of his experience and box-office appeal, Jayson didn't doubt he would make it happen. When he finally ended the call he chugged down the last of his OJ before stepping back inside his suite to shower and change. He had things to do before his noon lunch date with Sylvia.

Aaryn was in high spirits as she made her round of appointments and consultations. Before she knew it, the morning had flown by and noon was fast approaching. Tuesdays and Thursdays were days she wasn't scheduled to work with Sylvia, but on this particular Thursday Aaryn figured she'd have time to stop by to say hello before Jayson arrived to take Syl for their regularly scheduled lunch date in the Green Room. Glancing at her watch she noted she had thirty minutes until he was due. That was plenty of time to have a quick chat and be on her way. Not that she was deliberately avoiding him, she merely saw no harm in disappearing before his arrival.

Aaryn knocked softly on Sylvia's door before poking her head inside. Her expression froze.

Jayson was at the foot of Syl's bed, his bodyweight resting on his fists which were making indentations in the styrofoam mattress. The recipient of his reproach was sitting up in bed still dressed in her night gown. Instead of her hair combed into her usual coiffed twist, Sylvia's single braid lay in disarray. The creases in her forehead and her look of consternation indicated she, too, was spoiling for a fight.

"Sorry, I'll stop by later," Aaryn said as she tried to ease the door closed. It didn't take a genius to recognize they were quarreling.

"Please, come in Dr. Jamison. I wonder if you can put an end to the nonsense my mother is spewing." Jayson walked to the door and held it open for Aaryn to enter. There was a determination about him that told her he would drag her inside if he had to.

Sensing the undercurrents between them, Aaryn stepped inside looking from one to the other,

"My mother is under the impression that I accosted you yesterday. According to her, I manhandled you by roughly pushing you down the hall. She claims to have a firsthand account, but I don't recall seeing her there. Unless she was hiding behind a plant or something, her 'firsthand' account as she calls it can only be secondhand gossip. Yet, she won't say how she came by this misinformation." Jayson stared at Aaryn challengingly. His expression questioned whether *she* was the deliverer of said mistruths.

"Sylvia, there's no truth to such rumors. Is that what you two are bickering about? I'm the one who should be offended." Aaryn stepped away from Jayson's close proximity and moved closer to the bed. "I may be smaller than your son, but I can take him easily. I'm a fifth level black belt in Tae Kwon Do." In response to the dubious looks on both mother and son's faces, Aaryn turned to Jayson and said, "It's true. And I've taken down men much larger than you. Anyway Sylvia, who would tell you such a thing? You know your son better than anybody, so why would you believe the gossipmongers around here? Or perhaps you have reason to be concerned. Mr. Denali, you don't have a history of violence towards women, do you?"

"If that were the case, Dr. Jamison, I'm sure you and the entire world would have heard and read about it by now."

There he was, staring at her with such intensity that Aaryn felt everything around her fade away except him. Jarring herself before she succumbed to his enthralling spell, she turned to Sylvia and said, "Well, there you have it. I promise that your son has never accosted me. Had he done so, he would not be standing before you whole and in one piece." Aaryn surprised both of them with a rare smile. "Although, I must thank you for coming to my defense. That's sweet of you. Now, are you going to reveal how you came by this preposterous notion?"

Holding her head in the air, a mollified Sylvia said, "A woman never reveals her sources. Besides, I had it on good authority that the two of you were seen fraternizing combatively."

"And you were willing to believe what someone told you about me just like that? If anyone should know me better, I thought it would be you, Ma." Jayson wasn't ready to let go of the matter. Behind his fading anger, he was irritated that his mother would take a stranger's word about his alleged behavior.

"Well, in this instance, it appears that my informant was misinformed so, dear, I apologize."

"Your informant?" Jayson and Aaryn chimed in unison.

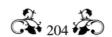

"Why yes. How else am I to keep abreast of all the goings on in this hospital? My sources tell me the two of you can't be in each other's presence without nearly coming to blows. They also tell me, Aaryn, that you are so tight-lipped that they know nothing of your personal life. In fact, the only thing they could tell me was of your mountain-climbing expeditions."

A gleam coated Sylvia's eyes and her voice hushed conspiratorially. "But they sure know everything about everyone else. For instance, did you know that Mr. Fitzgerald down the hall is a U.S. Senator? I'm told the night of his accident he was caught with his pants down, literally, after his car crashed into oncoming traffic. They say an intern was servicing him at the time. And that Mrs. Winifred two doors down? Well, she's had seven husbands. Can you believe it? One would think the woman would know when to throw in the towel and leave well enough alone. They say she's already grown sweet on one of the male nurses here and that Dr. Kyle has threatened to fire the young man if he goes anywhere near her again. The dear woman obviously needs a chastity belt. And then there's that Mrs. Betty Billenjer right across the hall. She's really a handful. Why, I'm told she deliberately bares her breasts to the male nurses just for the extra attention and the commotion it causes. Imagine, at her age." Sylvia sounded offended as if she were the one forced view Betty's mountain of a chest.

Jayson and Aaryn weren't imagining anything. They stared at Sylvia as if she'd suddenly grown two heads.

"I'm going to pretend that everything you just said was a joke." Jayson looked as if his mother had just eaten a worm.

Alarm bells had gone off for Aaryn. She only hoped the gossip wasn't a symptom of a deeper problem. "Unfortunately, I don't think she's joking at all. You've got far too much time on your hands, Sylvia. And that tells me it's time to step up your program."

"I agree, Dr. Jamison. Could you start right now? I wouldn't be surprised to find a stack of National Enquirers underneath her pillow. I can't believe this, Ma. When did you become such a gossip magnet?"

Uncomfortable with their disapproving looks and recognizing she may have let too much of the cat out of the bag, Sylvia grew defensive. She said snippily, "Oh, for goodness sakes. It's just a little harmless gossip. You two are acting as if I bombed Pearl Harbor!"

Aaryn sat at the foot of the kingsized bed. "Let me explain to you, Sylvia, why it's not as harmless as you think. The person that you're gossiping with may appear to be passing on innocent tidbits about other patients in this facility, but I assure you it's not innocent at all. What you don't know is that every now and again we're forced to fire someone after it's uncovered that the person violated our privacy policy. People who'll gossip *with* you will gossip *about* you.

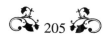

"So, imagine discovering that all the juicy little tidbits you shared with your source in private are now on the front covers of the latest gossip magazines. That's how it's done, you know. Your source, the one you're protecting right now, cozies up to you and gains your confidence by telling you everything they can about the lives of the other people around here. Before you know it, they're slyly pumping you for information about your own personal life, or more to the point, about Jayson's personal life. What was he like as a child? Is he dating anyone? Where's Mr. Denali, Sr.? All are relatively benign questions wrapped, I'm sure, in a tone meant to falsely convey caring and concern. Next thing you know, you're revealing information that you shouldn't be telling anyone."

Jayson nodded his head in agreement. "That's exactly how it's done. Whoever the person is, and I'll bet top dollar it's a woman, they're playing you like a piano, Ma."

"This is the part, Sylvia, where I could say that you should know better. However, what you fail to realize is that you're vulnerable right now. You're away from your normal surroundings, away from your loved ones. It's not uncommon to find yourself bored or lonely. I'm not telling you anything you don't already know. If you weren't out of your element, you'd have no problem recognizing this same situation for what it really is, a buddy trap. The next time you're in the mood to play Chatty Cathy, just remember that it's not illegal to record someone without their knowledge in the state of Utah. As unethical as it may be, it's not against the law if someone secretly tapes you. All they have to do is claim that you gave prior consent."

The smug look was completely gone from Sylvia's face. It was replaced by one that hinted she may *have* eaten a worm.

"Because of the intense screening we do here at Shriners, it doesn't happen very often. But every now and again, the lure of quick money is too much for a person to resist. It's amazing the length reporters and magazines will go to and what they'll pay to gain information about the lives of some of the guests in this hospital. The bigger the fish, the bigger the reward. Would you still think it harmless if your picture wound up alongside Jayson's with a caption labeling you as the mother he abandoned or as the mother who's strung out and addicted to drugs? Though most of its not true, you see the strangest things on the magazine racks. But the truth is not what's cared about, unless it's salacious or titillating. I've seen it done before—ordinary pictures altered, innocent remarks made to a supposed 'close insider' stretched out of context. It never fails to amaze me the things the tabloids make up just to create gossip so they can sell more papers. Meanwhile, you're left feeling used and betrayed. When you look at the picture from that perspective, suddenly it's not so innocent anymore, is it?"

Jayson stood looking on sternly as Sylvia's shoulders sagged with each point made. Unlike the last time when he'd jumped to his mother's defense, he was content to let Aaryn handle Syl's dressing down in her own way.

"Based on the things you've told us, whoever your source is, I can almost guarantee they're out to make a quick buck. They may already have done so. But your source is lying about Mrs. Bellinjer. Betty has been my patient since the day she arrived and I know her intimately. I can promise you, she would no more bare her breasts to any of the male nurses here than you would. I wonder what else they're lying about just to get you comfortable with revealing information about your own family's background. Some things appear harmless on the surface, Sylvia, but when you peel back a layer or two, you begin to see what's really hidden underneath."

Aaryn glanced at her watch as she stood to her feet. "Well, my time is up. I was only stopping by for a quick chat. Better hurry to get dressed if you're going to make it to the Green Room by noon."

"I couldn't eat anything right now. Jayson, why don't you go without me?"

His stance softened at the dejected look on Syl's face. Jayson said, "We can order something and have them deliver it here."

But Sylvia only shook her head. "I'm afraid I'm no longer hungry. How foolish I've been."

Aaryn stared at Sylvia. "Is there something you'd like to tell us?"

With her eyes closed, Sylvia sighed heavily, "I think I've already said more than I should have. What was I thinking?"

Aaryn and Jayson's eyes met in a moment of shared understanding.

"Who is the person you've been speaking with?" Jayson asked.

When Sylvia admitted who the person was, disappointment filtered through Aaryn.

"It may be that there's no cause for concern. Still, to be on the safe side I'll need to inform Kyle." She walked to the door and said to Jayson over her shoulder, "You should have some hot soup brought up to her."

Pausing at the door, she turned to face him. Jayson was laying Sylvia on her side. Aaryn started to say something but changed her mind as she glanced at Sylvia's back. Suddenly, he was striding toward her. As her eyes locked with his, it felt as if a million steps separated them.

"What is it?" Jayson's voice was low, concerned.

"I..." With him standing so close in front of her, Aaryn lost her train of thought.

Jayson softly grasped her elbows and bent to hear her more clearly.

With his ear near her mouth and the faint pleasant smell of his cologne filling her nose, clarity was slow to return. Aaryn quietly took a deep breath and whispered, "I think you should ask her what she may have revealed during their conversations." At least that's what she hoped she said.

Her lips inadvertently grazed his ear causing shimmers to travel the length of her body. Jayson was staring at her so intently she couldn't be sure exactly what she'd whispered. All she knew was that he hadn't yet released her and the slight touch of both his hands on her gave the impression that she was in his arms.

She saw his eyes flutter over her face. Flashes of the vision they'd shared once before passed through her mind. She met Jayson's gaze and something told her he was remembering the encounter as well. "I should leave," Aaryn thought but found herself rooted to the spot. What she saw in his eyes, the intent to possess, made her knees grow weak. She hurriedly shifted her gaze to his adam's apple. Unable to move but knowing she needed to collect herself, she finally was able to whisper softly, "Release me...please."

Jayson's hands slid from her elbows to her back. It was as though he sensed she needed help gathering her thoughts. He moved his hands to her shoulders and gently turned her toward the door. "I'll do all that you suggested starting with the soup. Before you leave today I'd like a word with you. Will that be okay?"

Aaryn nodded as Jayson quickly opened and closed the door behind her. She was still trying to snap out of the blanket of fog that had descended upon her as she walked down the hall.

Two hours later, Jayson and a recomposed Aaryn were seated at the conference table in Kyle's office.

"I met with Sally Fielders. You were right to be concerned, Aaryn. I reminded her of our company guidelines when she broke down crying from guilt and shame. She confessed that Star Magazine paid her $20,000 for the information she collected on Jayson and Sylvia. She says the money and information have already exchanged hands so I don't know if anything can be done to stop them from publishing it."

Aaryn shook her head disbelievingly. She liked Sally a lot and would never have suspected her of becoming involved in such a deceitful scheme. The way she duped Sylvia made her seem like Linda Tripp without a phone.

"She's been with us for fifteen years. Why would she stoop to something like this?"

"Gambling. She's amassed huge gambling debts and was on the verge of losing her home. She swears the magazine approached her first. I don't disbelieve her, not

208

that it makes a difference. Somehow they found out she was Sylvia's nurse and sifted her until they found a weakness. As difficult as it was, we've terminated her. It would have been impossible to keep her on after such a breech of trust."

Jayson was shaking his head. "It doesn't add up," he said. "Sylvia said most of what they discussed was my childhood. I can't see the Star shelling out twenty grand for information that anybody can easily find on the web. That's not their usual M.O. They don't pay that kind of cheddar unless there are photos involved."

Kyle sighed. "I see you've dealt with them before. That brings me to my next point. Sally also confessed to stealing photos of your sister from among your mother's things. It seems Sylvia talked a lot more about your sister and her death than she did about you. From what I gather, the Star may be preparing to run a story about Carmin Denali."

"I'll be damned!" Snatching his cell phone from inside his suit pocket, Jayson jumped to his feet. "I'll sue the bastards. And I'll sue this Sally Fielders woman right along with them." Jayson hit a button as he stalked purposefully toward Kyle's floor-to-ceiling windows. "PT, I need you to have Bloom get an injunction against the Star."

Aaryn and Kyle watched Jayson pace back and forth as he spoke in rapid fire succession to whoever was on the other end of his phone. Though his voice was low, his anger was palpable. Neither Aaryn nor Kyle had seen him in this mode before, viciously dolling out instructions. Gone was the jovial, easy-going, peace-making actor whom they'd witnessed patiently feeding spoonfuls of food to his mother. The man standing before them had morphed into a barracuda, albeit one clothed in an expensive creation by New York's master suit maker, William Fioravanti.

"If the story was about me, I could live with whatever they print, but I will not allow them to sully and malign my sister's memory." Jayson stopped pacing to listen intently. "Now that's what I'm talking about, PT." His voice held a note of satisfaction as he clicked a button to put the caller on speaker phone.

"Damned straight we'll sue the 'effers'..." Jayson's publicist was wearing her legal hat as she foamed at the mouth. In the string of curse word sentences she quickly let loose with, everything was "F" this and "F" that. And of course, everyone involved *except* Jayson was referred to as an "effer." The more she talked, the more riled up she became. And the more "F" bombs she dropped.

Apparently, PT was in her glory. "Let the 'effing' bastards bring it on! We'll go after the Star with every big gun we've got. I'm telling you, JD, we'll own that 'effing' magazine before this thing is over. And believe me, I can't wait to put my foot up the assess of those incompetent 'effers' at that hospital. It's their 'effing' fault to begin with! First, we'll target the sh!tbird CEO. Whoever the sumb!tch is, we'll sue the pants right off the 'effer.' By the time we finish dragging those rotten assholes through the courts, they're going to wish they'd never met Ms. Sally Sleazebag, let alone hired the c..."

Nodding his head in fierce agreement, Jayson stared into his cell phone. It wasn't until he heard Aaryn's gasp after PT referred to Sally as the four-letter "c" word that rhymed with hunt, that he remembered his audience. Jayson looked over to find Aaryn with her hand clasped over her open mouth, a wide-eyed appalled expression on her face, while Kyle was as white as a sheet.

All Aaryn could envision was a woman sitting behind a motley desk wearing a gallon-sized wig, sipping from a gallon-sized jug of rot-gut alcohol and smoking a fat cigar. Aaryn couldn't recall ever hearing one person spew such foul language in her entire life. She was finding it incredibly hard to believe that Jayson would associate with someone of such obvious low morals, manners and character.

As for Kyle, his heart had dropped into his scrotum. All the good doctor saw was wing-tipped hundred dollar bills flying out of his bank account in slow motion while a pack of vicious hyenas (Jayson's lawyers) ripped gaping holes into a helpless animal (his hospital). The menacing tone of the woman's voice had struck immediate fear in his heart. So intimidating was she that Kyle completely forgot Shriners had a stunning legal team of its own. "Whoever this PT person is," Kyle thought, "she's *not* a publicist or an attorney. No sir. This woman's obviously an assassin!"

Jayson took one look at Kyle's white-as-a-sheet face and said, "Whoa, PT. Hold up a sec. We're not suing the hospital. They're on our side. But you just gave me an idea. We'll have this Sally woman sign an affidavit stating the Star put her up to it. When Bloom puts the fear of God into 'em, we might be able to squash this thing before they print it."

Jake Bloom was Jayson's high-powered entertainment attorney. He was known for his tough negotiating tactics whenever he hammered out contracts. His attention to detail had earned his clients millions of dollars.

But Bloom's real value came in the form of the "personal services" his operation provided. From tax advice to real estate purchases and audits, Jake's outfit handled all aspects of its client's *specialized* needs. Where his team of lawyers excelled was in their ability to litigate against the rag mags and nefarious people who sought to slander or take advantage of those on Bloom's glitzy list of clients. Since celebrities were made to seem as if they occupied a different world than the rest of society, there was no limit to the depths the paparazzi would sink in order to obtain the next photo worth thousands or hundreds of thousands of dollars. The media's glorification of celebrities and their fan's never-ending lust for more details about their lives, made for strange bedfellows. Given this was unlikely to change, Bloom advised his client base on how to cope with the stalkerazzi.

He'd earned Jayson's respect when paparazzi violated the actor's privacy by breaking into his Beverly Hills home to snap a single nude photo of him. Bloom had initiated a lawsuit and won unspecified damages from the rag responsible for orchestrating the mission. Another time, Jayson was ambushed by a bunch of celebrity photographers when two cars trapped him in his Bugatti Veyron forcing him off the road. The cars piloted by stalkerazzi had left two pedestrians in critical condition. Using footage confiscated from their own cameras, Bloom cleaned house to the tune of millions.

As rich and high-profile as Bloom was, he managed to remain in the background by doing a lot of his work anonymously. The real players in Hollywood, those with backend participation and clout such as Jayson's, knew they couldn't operate without someone like Jake, who possessed a broad range of experience, acting as their counselor.

"PT, get with Bloom and holler back at me this evening. Yes, I will. I'll keep it turned on just for you. Until later." Jayson cast looks at Aaryn and Kyle and said, "That went well. Sorry about the colorful language. Believe me, if you met her in person you'd really be impressed by her proper diction." In the face of their dubious expressions, he said, "It's true. I've never met anyone who had a better command of the King's English than PT."

"I was impressed," Kyle said. He was also relieved that his golden egg was not about to be party to a mudslinging lawsuit. He asked, "Weren't you impressed, Aaryn?"

"Royally." Aaryn shrugged. "But what do I know? Just another typical day at the office for you, Jayson, I'm sure."

Jayson smiled. "You have no idea. I wish I had the liberty to work in an environment like this where everybody walks around loving everyone they come in contact with. I haven't seen so many people hugging each other by way of greeting since my last movie premier. What can I say? My world is a jungle of people who are more verbally graphic, while out here, people are more polite."

"At least, Kyle, we now know who to call should we ever find ourselves painted in a false light by the tabloids," Aaryn said.

"I agree. Anyone dreaming of becoming a famous actor really should shadow you for a day, Jayson. I think they would be disavowed of their celebrity aspirations. There's something to be said for being a simple country doctor."

Aaryn smirked. "Simple country doctor? Kyle, you wouldn't know such an animal if it examined you on the side of the road! You're the biggest media hound within fifty miles of here."

Jayson was noticing the easy camaraderie between Aaryn and Kyle when a disagreeable thought snaked through his mind. His nostrils flared and jealousy burned through him as he suspiciously observed their ease of communication. A sharp edge hardened his view and his look became probing as he listened to Kyle deny Aaryn's charge.

"Spare me, Kyle. Every time I turn around you're posing for the latest cover of some medical magazine. If there's a megastar of this field, it's got to be you." Aaryn rose from the table. "Jayson, does this mean the good people here at Shriners won't have to worry about eating soup for the rest of our lives because of your fancy-speaking lawyers?"

This was twice she'd called him by his first name. Jayson didn't want his misgivings to spoil whatever goodwill that had caused her to do that. "Something tells me it would take more than a slew of lawyers and one humble actor such as me to accomplish that feat."

"All this masculine humility coming from the two of you is making me nauseous. It also has me doubting my sanity." She threw Jayson a look. "Did you still wish to speak with me before I leave?"

Jayson nodded, still watching her closely. He questioned the sharp twinges of jealousy that still lurked within his members. He hadn't felt such emotions since his modeling days. It felt odd and he wasn't sure he liked it.

"I'm headed to my office now if this is good timing for you."

Jayson held the door for her and as they walked down the hall he said to her, "Will you come somewhere with me?"

"Excuse me?" Aaryn stopped in her tracks.

"I'm asking you to take a ride with me." Jayson stared at her challengingly.

"I...Where to?" Thrown off guard, Aaryn's heart started beating rapidly. She caught herself just before she nervously clasped her hand to her throat.

"To someone's office. Yes or no?" He stood there quietly putting a demand on her, mindless of the people who walked by them with curious looks.

"Well, I'm not sure. I have somewhere to be in a few hours. I can't just take off without..."

"Yes or no, Aaryn. Make a decision." Jayson walked back the few steps to stand in front of her. The way he stared down at her made it seem as if they were the only two people in the world.

Jesus! Flustered, Aaryn couldn't prevent the gesture of touching her hand to her throat. Not only was her heart racing but her breathing was accelerating. "For heaven's sake," she thought. "All I have to do is say no."

Jayson saw the panic-stricken look on her face as she struggled to make up her mind. He had the sense that he was forcing her out of her elemental comfort zone but he stood mercilessly waiting for her answer. Who would have thought he'd have to help the good doctor make a decision? Jayson said patiently, "You'll need to lose the white coat. But other than that, you're fine." He assumed part of her concern was whether she was wearing appropriate clothing.

Her apparel was the furthest thing from her mind. What was front and center for Aaryn were the many trust issues she had with men. Jayson may have been asking her to take a short ride somewhere, but in her mind the question she was asking him was, *"Can I trust you?"*

Surely she couldn't seriously be thinking about going any where with him, could she? Why would he ask her in the first place? Was it a joke? And what ulterior motive did he have?

Taking a deep breath, she said, "Okay. But can I trail you in my own car? I really do have an appointment in a few hours."

Jayson grinned because he'd managed a small concession from her. "Sure, you can. But it would be a lot easier if you rode with me so you could give me directions on how to get there."

Fidgeting, Aaryn recognized she was feeling trapped.

"I promise to have you back within two and a half hours." Jayson recognized her indecision. But helping women make up their minds was well within his comfort zone. He knew how to powerfully persuade them. Except with Aaryn, he found himself thinking, "Easy does it, man. One step at a time."

Aaryn's eyes lingered on that unforgettable pearly white smile of his. When he smiled she could believe that the whole world was smiling with him. An unwelcome tiny fission of pleasure sparked within her core and she deliberately kept herself from smiling in return. Instead, she stepped around him and spoke sternly. "This better be on the up and up, Jayson Denali."

The grin didn't leave his face. As he walked alongside her, incredibly Jayson found himself thinking, "There are so many layers to this woman. And I'm going to uncover them all."

Chapter Seventeen

Aaryn stopped at the door to her office. She turned to Jayson and asked, "Where are you parked?'

"Near the front of the building." The way she stood there reminded him of a sentinel guarding its station. "Why?"

"Let me change jackets and I'll meet you downstairs. Five minutes is all I need."

"Okay, I'll wait for you." Not budging from his spot.

"That's not necessary. I'll see you downstairs." With her back against her office door, Aaryn eased inside.

Jayson was dimwitted by no means, but it wasn't until she closed the door softly in his face that it clicked for him that he wasn't invited inside. With a raised eyebrow he headed downstairs to the parking lot.

Inside her office, Aaryn leaned against her door kicking herself for not declining his invitation. All she had to do was just say no. What the heck was wrong with her?

"Okay, pull yourself together," she whispered. In her office closet were several suits she kept for unexpected events. She selected a tan pinstriped pantsuit with a champagne colored silk blouse. Slipping into a pair of tan pumps, she grabbed her briefcase and was ready to go.

Jayson was standing near the hospital entrance surrounded by a number of people. "Darn," Aaryn thought. She certainly had no desire for others to see her secreting away with Jayson Denali. Before she could leave via another exit, Jayson spotted her and waved.

She walked toward him saying, "Mr. Denali, I'd be happy to direct you to your destination. Why don't you trail me in your own vehicle?" A path was cleared for Aaryn as she approached.

Jayson was signing an autograph for a visitor when he looked up to stare at her curiously.

Before he could respond, Aaryn dashed out the door heading briskly toward her Range Rover.

Several paces behind her, Jayson said, "Slow down, will you? What happened? I thought we agreed to ride together?"

Aaryn didn't slow her pace, if anything she walked faster. "I changed my mind. I think it best that we take separate cars."

A "lightbulb" thought moment hit Jayson that stopped him on a dime. He asked incredulously, "You don't want to be seen with me, do you?"

Aaryn halted abruptly. She didn't turn around to face him until she heard loud guffaws of manly laughter coming from behind her.

She turned to find Jayson with his hands on his knees, bent over wracked with laughter.

"What's so funny?" Aaryn didn't know what he was laughing about, but she suspected the joke was on her. Her sudden fear was that TV cameramen would jump

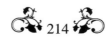

from behind cars while others came out of hiding only to laugh about how gullible she'd been to believe that someone like Jayson Denali actually wanted to be seen with her. Suspecting that she'd been punked, Aaryn wasn't laughing at all. If anything, she was quickly becoming enraged.

"Stop it!" She spoke sharply as she walked to stand in front of him.

Jayson laughed so hard until tears were in the corners of his eyes. "You just don't get the irony of it, do you?'

"No, I'm clueless. Perhaps you'd be kind enough to enlighten me."

Jayson sensed her anger, but he was caught up in the hilarity of the situation.

"Aaryn, listen to me. Whether you know it or not, people pay through their noses to have a photo taken with me. Sometimes, when it's in my interest to do so, I'll pose with fans. Otherwise, believe me when I tell you that I'm paid handsomely for a few minutes of my time to show up at parties and social functions. In other words, people pay dearly *to be seen with me*. Some people even consider it an honor. But not you, my tightly-wound, independent, hard-to-please sister. You couldn't care less about a photo op with me. In fact, you're probably wondering how I managed to convince you to join me in the first place. I'll bet you, Dr. Jamison, would pay *not* to be seen with me. Wouldn't you?"

Nailed to the wall, Aaryn sighed loudly. "Yes, Mr. Denali. As much as I *don't* hate to admit it, you're absolutely correct."

Still smiling, Jayson said, "This is priceless."

"No, that's where you're wrong, Jayson Denali. It's not priceless. What this is, is my life." Aaryn stepped closer to him. "Long after you've left these parts, I'll still be here with my good name intact. In order for that to happen, I will *not* have it associated with yours as though I'm another floozy vying to be added to your cotillion of mistresses. My soul is not a game. My spirit is not a plaything. And my emotions are not for sale. Why I'm even standing in this parking lot talking to you while only God knows how many people are watching us from the windows of this building, I have no clue. If you but speak the word, I'd be more than happy to compensate you for your time and we can go our separate ways right now."

Shaking his head, Jayson replied, "I have no interest in your money, Aaryn. What I would like is a little of your time. I want you to come with me. If I didn't, I wouldn't have asked. It's not a date and it's not a pick up. We'll be in an office filled with people. You won't even have to speak. All I need is for you to listen." He was trying to be serious but God help him he still found her aversion to his company humorous—especially since all the women he knew clamored for his attention.

"I wasn't laughing at you, Aaryn."

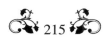

In the face of his dominant grin, Aaryn was only slightly appeased. "Yes, you were laughing at me. And don't deny it."

"Okay, I was. But just a little. You do have to admit, it's funny." When she still refused to smile, he asked her, "When was the last time you ducked and dodged because you didn't want to be seen with someone? See? You can't even remember. As edgy as you're acting, I'm surprised you didn't wear sunglasses and a mask."

Grudgingly, she said, "Okay, I admit it. What do you want, a cookie? Can we go now? Don't you have to arrive at your destination by a certain time, Mr. Denali?"

"Yes, we do. But first, how about a truce, Dr. Jamison? No more 'Mr. Denali.' From here on out, I'm Jayson to you."

"A truce." Aaryn sampled the word. "Yes, I'd like that very much. A truce that stipulates we coalesce around Sylvia's health. A truce that dictates you put your male pheromones in check. A truce that specifies you and I have a 'working' relationship centered on Sylvia's healing. Thank you, Jayson. I like the sound of that a whole lot."

Jayson stared down at her, his face devoid of expression, his eyes liquid pools of contemplation. In that moment something passed between them—some arcane alchemy that he couldn't quite define, promised him they were on the verge of entering a new level in their dealings with one another.

"I like the sound of it too, Doctor. But I've got stipulations of my own. First, you sheave your claws when you're in my presence. Second, you stop running and putting up walls the moment I walk into a room. And my final stipulation? That you shelve your anger over the fact that I find you attractive."

Aaryn's brows furrowed together but Jayson kept right on speaking. "If you can agree to mine, I can certainly agree to all your stipulations. Just tell me where to sign. But make it quick because we're running late. Let's take your SUV, I'm sure you'll be more comfortable in the drivers' seat anyway." Jayson stepped around Aaryn and started walking towards her vehicle.

Aaryn clicked her remote control to unlock and start her Range Rover. "You, Jayson Denali, are the most vexing man I've ever had the misfortune to meet. And I won't bother asking how you knew which car was mine."

"Good girl," Jayson said as the automatic seat belts fastened him in. "If it's any consolation, I feel the same way about you."

"If I had a magic wand, I'd wave it and Syl would be up and running by the time we returned from wherever it is you're dragging me. That way, you'd be out of my hair."

When his eyes strayed to her bushy tendrils, she said, "Don't even think about touching it, Mister. It's unpermed barb wire. Where are we going anyway?"

Jayson gave her the address as he fumbled with the dials to push his seat back to accommodate his long legs.

"If I had a magic wand..." he began.

Aaryn interrupted him, "You already do. That's your problem as it is. You live in a world whose principles are alien to the rest of us normal civilized folks. You're so used to people kowtowing to you, that you expect everybody around you to jump at your every command."

"I wonder if you would react the same if I was Bill Gates, Michael Jordan, or Tom Cruise? Or would you have no problem, as you say, kowtowing to them?"

"Bill Gates, even with all his money, is one of the most down-to-earth people I've ever met. Anyone who donates their time and treasure to helping children without the benefit of the glare of cameras earns a special place in my esteem. As for Jordan and Cruise, if they're as egotistical as you are, no, I wouldn't kowtow to them. I'd treat them the same as the next person."

Jayson believed her. "What makes you think I'm egotistical? I'm not. You, on the other hand, you could benefit from some specialized people-skills training. It's not as if you're the friendliest bulb in the bunch."

"Who cares? At least I call a spade a spade when I have to. I shoot straight from the hip and you'll always know where you stand with me. If you want it straight, no chaser, I'm your girl. If not, find someone else to mince words for you. I know you think I'm a b!tch. But I'm not. I'm very tactful. You, on the other hand, don't know anything about tact. You burst in a place and simply take it over." Aaryn couldn't help glancing at him in her passenger seat. The image of his length and manliness was emblazoned in her mind and she knew her vehicle would never be the same.

"Would I ever describe you in such harshly fitting terms?" Jayson threw her an innocent glance. "You have no idea what it's like to walk in my shoes. When you look at something from one side only, you don't get the benefit of seeing the whole picture. To you it seems as though I take everything for granted. My lifestyle may appear easy, but trust me, it's not." Jayson thought of all the demands that came with stardom—the fact that he had few trusted friends, yet hoards of hero worshipers—and grew silent. He thought of how cutthroat the film industry was and how one could go from being "wonder boy" to "I wonder who that boy is" in a nanosecond. At this point in his career, he had star power to burn, although success had been a strange struggle for him. Sure, he was demanding. But it was a small consolation considering everything he had to put up with. Normal society, as Aaryn called it, really had no clue as to how cumbersome and annoying stardom could be at times.

Jayson looked around noting how neat her SUV was and that it smelled faintly of vanilla. He noticed how confidently she handled the road and he also noticed she let other women drivers pull in front of her with no questions asked. He bet she'd probably ignore them if they were men. "You know, someone once told me that people who drive aggressively are constipated. They say most road-rage drivers are so full of fecal crap that's what causes them to explode. Here they are on the verge of killing someone, when all they really need is a good colonic. Not that a person of my humble stature would ever tell a doctor as exalted as yourself to get a colon cleanse."

"I'm a bad driver so that means I'm full of crap?" A small laugh escaped Aaryn. "You are stupid, Jayson Denali."

Somehow she made it seem like a twisted compliment. "Then we're reflections of each other." Just to be sure, he asked, "Stupid's good, right?"

Throwing him an exasperated look, Aaryn said, "Of course it is. It's impossible for anyone to stay angry with you, isn't it?"

"What can I say? Life's too short to walk around angry all the time."

They lapsed into a comfortable silence. They were driving for nearly forty minutes when Jayson noticed the silence in the car. No radio, no music, no talk show hosts, just silence. He marveled that he hadn't noticed it sooner. Jayson didn't think he'd ever ridden in any of his vehicles in total silence. If he didn't have his television, radio or CD player going, it was because he was on the phone. Speaking of phones, he'd turned his cell off again when he'd told PT that he'd leave it on. Dez, Wendy, his crew and all manner of people were probably blowing up his phone and going ballistic because they couldn't reach him. It wasn't as if any of them needed anything urgent. But those who had his cell phone number were unaccustomed to not being able to reach him. He was amazed that he could turn it off for so long a time and not miss talking to any of them. Utah was opening his eyes to a number of things about himself.

Jayson was about to ask Aaryn if she always rode in silence and what kind of music she liked when he noticed their destination not far off: the offices of the Provo, Utah, Chamber of Commerce.

Pointing, he said, "There's the Chamber of Commerce up ahead. Pull into that spot closest to the building."

"Jeez, Mr. Front-Seat Driver, what if I don't want to park up front but over there?" Aaryn pointed in the opposite direction.

"Contrary as you are, it wouldn't surprise me at all. Park in front in case we need a quick getaway." After she'd parked, Jayson said to her, "When we get inside, I'm going to introduce you as my lawyer."

"It may not work. What if someone recognizes me from the medical field? If you'd told me this back at the hospital, I could have saved you some time."

"Then I'll introduce you as my counselor. Is that ambiguous enough for you? You could be my advisor or either an investor in one of my film projects."

"Jayson, do you always get your way?"

"What's wrong with winning? And no, Aaryn, I do not always get my way. Since I've met you, I can't begin to count the number of times I've been denied the simplest of things."

As they mounted the concrete steps, people were exiting through a pair of revolving doors. They gawked at the sight of Jayson who nodded but didn't stop for autographs.

Once inside the lobby area, they went straight to the information desk.

A light flow of traffic streamed back and forth as people passed by them. Some did double takes, some pointed in Jayson's direction, and others glanced over their shoulders as they exited the building. Aaryn caught one woman staring so hard as she entered the revolving doors, that the doors spun 360 degrees before the woman realized she was going in circles.

"Good afternoon. Can you direct us to the Office of the Commissioner?"

The lady manning the information desk was buried in the pages of People Magazine. She glanced up, prepared to give them directions. Startled, her mouth fell open and remained fixed until Jayson smiled at her.

"You..." She hurriedly raised her spectacles to stare at Jayson closely. "You're that Denzel Washington fellow, aren't you?"

"No Mam, I'm not." Jayson waited patiently for her to answer his question.

"But..." Her fingers quickly flipped the pages of her magazine and pointed to a picture perfect photo of Jayson. In the midst of her "ah-ha" moment, she looked down at the magazine photo and back up at Jayson. "I'm sorry. I meant you're Jayson Denali. Hot diggity-dog!" She smiled as if she'd just discovered King Tut's Tomb.

"You were about to tell us what floor the Commissioner's Office is on." Aaryn reminded her, albeit gently, as if she was talking to someone with a winding staircase for a memory.

"My goodness! Yes, it's on Lower Level 4. Take the last bank of elevators to the bottom floor."

"Thank you," Jayson said courteously.

"My pleasure, Mr. Denali."

As they walked away, Aaryn shook her head in near disgust. "Shameless. Even elderly women go atwitter in your presence. That woman's got to be in her late sixties."

"There's nothing wrong with seasoned women. You could learn a thing or two from her. Did you notice how deferential she was? You should try it sometime."

"Yeah, right. You need me as another of your 'yes-sir' groupies and followers like I need a hole in the head."

"I'm beginning to think you do have a hole in your head, as crabby as you are."

Aaryn laughed as they approached the elevators. She said mockingly, "Mr. Denali, may I have your autograph? Please, Sir, may I carry your bags? May I shine your shoes? May I wash your feet with my hair? Can I please be your servant?" Aaryn's voice took on a wheedling quality as she spoke mockingly.

"That's more like it. I'm glad to see you catch on fast." Jayson held the elevator door for her.

"And you, Sir, really are stupid."

Jayson shrugged dismissively. "Stupid's good, remember?"

The doors had nearly closed when a woman yelled, "Hold the elevator, please!" She ran toward them with shopping bags in both hands.

Aaryn quickly stepped forward to press the "open" button. Instead, she managed to hit the button that read "close."

The doors closed just as the woman reached them. Pressing the button repeatedly, Aaryn looked down and noticed her mistake. "Oops."

"I won't even ask if you did that deliberately."

"Of course not. I wouldn't do that to anyone—not even to a scandal-plagued rogue who happens to be egotistical and selfcentered."

Jayson shrugged skeptically.

"Don't pretend you've never hit the wrong button before, Jayson. I didn't see you dashing to hold the door for her."

"I didn't have to. That's why you're here." When the smile left Aaryn's face, Jayson couldn't help laughing at her. "You've got temper issues, Lady. Didn't you just volunteer to be my maid servant a second ago? Shape up, Doc. Your attitude's unacceptable."

Aaryn was still pursing her lips as the elevator doors opened on LL4.

Jayson said, "Remind me to find you some good anger-management and social-skills classes after we leave this place. Don't worry about the cost. It's on me."

Chapter Eighteen

The first thing they noticed when they stepped off the elevator was how quiet everything was compared to the bustling of the upper floors. The hallway stretching before them had a museum-like quality, as if people rarely frequented the area. At the end of the long corridor, the words "Office of the Commissioner" were inscribed in big bold block letters on the wall above a set of deeply-tinted double doors.

They walked down the long hallway whose walls were lined with thick, silver framed, four-by-four photos and paintings. On one wall were portraits of people who had helped build Provo, Utah, back when the town was first settled by Mormons in 1849. On the opposite wall, the paintings of everyday people dated all the way back to the mid 1700's, when Utah Valley had become the traditional home of the Ute Indians. Fur trappers and traders exchanged wares from wagons during a time when Provo served as the focal point of Utah Valley's industry, commerce, and government. In most of the paintings, Mt. Timpanogos loomed in the background.

Jayson tried to remember at least one of the tall tales he'd heard in childhood about Buffalo Bill and the Davy Crocketts of that era. But he couldn't. Studying the pictures, he wondered if there weren't any black settlers during that time. He didn't see any in the photos.

"Have you been here before?" Jayson glanced at the black carpeting that looked as if it belonged outdoors.

"Yes, but only to the upper levels. I've never had cause to come down here. It's so hushed, it's sort of creepy." Aaryn felt like Dorothy walking the corridor to see the great Wizard of Oz.

Peering through the black glass double doors was impossible. It was like looking into a oneway mirror. Jayson pulled the handle almost expecting the doors to be locked. They were.

Irritation laced his voice. "What kind of Chamber of Commerce is this?"

Aaryn didn't have an answer, but ominous warning signals started radiating in her spirit telling her to be on guard. Purely by chance she spotted the nearly undetectable doorbell on the wall adjacent to the double doors.

Jayson examined the tiny button camouflaged on the wall. "I would never have seen that."

"I don't think we weren't meant to. Something tells me walkin visitors are not encouraged. I don't suppose now would be a good time to ask why we're here?"

A buzzer sounded and Jayson snatched open the door. Instead of allowing Aaryn to enter in front of him, he stepped inside first as if to assess any potential threat.

Not knowing what to expect, once inside they were unprepared for the lavish state-of-the-art office décor. The space was brightly lit compared to the dim starkness of the long hallway. No standard government furnishings or Paul Bunyan-type pictures here. Everything was silver, grey or black in leather, granite or lacquer. All that lined the sleek walls were expensively framed photos of past Republican Presidents, Utah Senators and Provo Commissioners.

They were confronted by a smallish woman manning a large, halfmoon desk.

"May I help you?" She spoke brusquely as if taking them to task for staring around. If she recognized Jayson, she gave no sign of it as she waited impatiently for a response. She didn't bother looking in Aaryn's direction.

"Jim Oden." Jayson walked to the desk and stared at her.

"Do you have an appointment to see the Commissioner?" Her voice was sharp and stern as if Jayson was a vagrant fresh off the streets asking to meet with the President of the United States.

"I wouldn't be here if I didn't." Jayson spoke slowly as if to someone trying his patience. Over the years, he'd encountered faces such as hers all over the world—people who took pleasure in trying to make others feel small. Sensing cordiality would be a waste of time, he stood staring at her without blinking.

As if against her better judgment, the woman picked up the receiver and dialed a number. She glanced at Jayson and spoke dismissively. "Your name?"

"Denali." If the gatekeeper's personality was indicative of the others she worked with, specifically those he was about to meet, Jayson felt he was in for an unpleasant meeting. He found it curious that the battle ax of a receptionist would be allowed to be so rude since she was likely the one giving any firsttime visitors their initial impression of the department. He doubted he was the first person she'd treated in such a crude fashion. It was likely she was kept out front purposefully to ward off anyone unwise enough to show up without an appointment. If so, hers was an easy assignment given that she had the temperament of a dragon.

As the woman waited for someone to pick up on the other end of the line, her sighs gave the impression that Jayson was imposing upon her time—that if it weren't for him, she could at this very second be saving the world. She acknowledged Aaryn for the first time by frowning at her. "And you are?"

"My consigliere." Jayson interjected before Aaryn could speak. He saw the woman's puzzled look. She was so busy peering at them over her hornrimmed glasses that Jayson knew she wouldn't ask for clarification. To the elite players in Hollywood, consiglieres were indispensable counselors.

He cast a look at Aaryn and caught an odd expression on her face. So intently was she watching the gatekeeper that he thought she was going to address her. Without waiting to find out, he took Aaryn by the arm and steered her toward an area where leather sofas and chairs formed a square around a table covered with an array of hunting and outdoor magazines.

They were sitting side by side when Aaryn said softly, "I'm not a loose cannon, Jayson. You don't have to be concerned that I'll embarrass you. But there's something about this place that's not quite right."

"In what way?" Because her voice was low, Jayson matched hers in volume. He figured she was referring to the receptionist, who he knew wasn't capable of making anyone feel warm and fuzzy. He asked, "Are you concerned because of the way she treated us?"

Aaryn shook her head as she watched the gatekeeper who, from across the room, was staring at them closely. "No, her actions don't mean anything. She's responding from a place of deep woundedness because of her own hurts and insecurities." Aaryn paused as if choosing her words carefully. "She was raped as a teenager and misused as an adult and she's never fully healed from it. Now, all these many years later, she rejects people before they have a chance to reject her."

Jayson peered at Aaryn with narrowed eyes. "Do you know the woman?"

Aaryn shook her head as she continued to stare straight in front of her with pursed lips.

Jayson released a sigh of exasperation. "Then how the hell could you know anything about her personal life? You can't just look at somebody and make snap judgments about them. What sense does that make? The woman might just be having a bad day." Jayson found himself becoming irritated with Aaryn. What he didn't say was, "Of course there's something wrong with this place. It's you." He should never have invited her.

Aaryn just shook her head. Gone was the playful woman in the elevator Jayson had glimpsed earlier, replaced now by the quiet, serious, take-no-prisoners Aaryn he'd first met. She didn't know Jayson well enough to tell him of the things she was picking up in the unseen spirit realm. He wouldn't believe her even if she tried. All she said was, "Just be watchful of the people here, Jayson. I know it sounds farfetched, but there are forces at play here that you know nothing about."

To distract himself, Jayson picked up a copy of a *Fur-Fish-Game* magazine and flipped through it. The caption read *"For the serious pursuer of nature's wild bounty."* The cover bore a photo of a gigantic Elk with mammoth-sized antlers. Somehow, Jayson couldn't get with the idea of hiding behind bushes for hours or days waiting for Rudolph-the-Reindeer to waltz by just so one could blow him away with a bazooka. "It'd be more impressive," Jayson thought, "to hear about how a man knifed another man in the gut. Or at least kicked another man's ass in mano-mano combat. Killing a helpless animal to brag about how it was the 'greatest kill of the century,' that didn't take any balls. Cowards." Jayson tossed the magazine back onto the table. At least he'd effectively blocked out whatever it was Aaryn was talking about. He had no clue what she meant and he, again, chided himself for inviting her.

Ten minutes later a second gatekeeper, one much younger than the one sitting behind the desk, came to greet them.

"Mr. Denali, I'm Commissioner Oden's assistant. He'll see you now. Can you come with me?"

Aaryn trailed them. On a whim she turned to glance back at the crackpot receptionist and was not surprised when the woman flipped her the bird.

They were lead past a string of offices with closed doors until they reached a large conference room. The room was equipped with cherry oak furniture and chairs along with all the latest gadgetry. A plasma TV, videoconferencing equipment, star conference phones, laptop connections and of course a lifesized portrait of Commissioner Jim Oden.

Four people were already seated around the large conference table when they entered. A tall, wide, heavy-jowled man with white hair and a bulbous nose rose from the table to greet them. From the pictures on the walls, Jayson easily pegged him as the Commissioner. He wore a pair of suspenders that strained to keep his pants over his beachball belly.

"I'm Jim Oden. Pleased to make your acquaintance." He extended his hand to Jayson.

"Jayson Denali. Thanks for agreeing to meet on such short notice." Oden's pudgy hand felt so soft and moist that Jayson had the urge to wipe his on his pant leg.

"We try to accommodate everyone around these parts."

Jayson doubted that very seriously. Not with a miniature Russian Gulag guard for a receptionist.

Oden pointed around the table. "This here's Stanley Prisom, Mayor of Provo. George Pinkerton is head of Business Development and Mitch Myers is our Corporate Counsel. You already know Shelly, my secretary."

While each of the men stood to shake hands with Jayson, Oden was staring at Aaryn as if he recognized her from somewhere but couldn't quite place her.

Now that the round of handshaking was over for the men, they were all staring at Aaryn who stood near Jayson without offering to shake hands with anyone. Knowing that wasn't going to happen even if they made the first gesture, Jayson quickly moved behind the seat next to him and pulled it out so Aaryn could be seated.

He said, "Gentlemen, this is my counselor, Dr. Jamison. Again, I want to thank you for seeing me on such short notice. You received the contract from New York?" More looks from around the table as they took their seats. "Are there questions or can we proceed to the next phase?"

As if on cue, Shelly rose from the end of the table to pass everyone a copy of the contract that was faxed earlier to their office.

Oden leaned back in his executive leather chair and spread his hands behind his head. He was so laid back, Jayson half expected the man to kick his feet up on the conference table. "Tell us why you big time folks want to use lil ol'Mt. Timp in your film."

"For no other reason than what's proposed in the contract. It's a beautiful site. And, it's the perfect backdrop for a particular scene we're filming. Your office will be listed in the credits. More importantly, and probably to your concern, a production like ours leaves money behind with other people and businesses in the area. If you've reviewed the contract, I'm sure you'll agree it's a generous opportunity for the entire community. The benefits of us using your site far outweigh any negatives. The only question I have is whether or not we can reach an agreement in terms of cost."

Oden pulled a pipe from his pocket and fiddled with its contents before lighting up. "Tell me more about these monetary benefits." He lounged back in his chair again all ears.

"Money spent on wages, products and services. You can count on the production company spending significant dollars with your local businesses on lodging, clothing, groceries, restaurants, fabrics, lumber, hardware, electrical and office supplies, laundry services, you name it. That's money funneled directly into Provo. Also, cast and crew members spend money on leisure activities and entertainment, books, magazines, souvenirs—the list, gentlemen, goes on and on. Not to mention that even the curious visitors from the neighboring areas will leave additional dollars within the community. That's not a bad deal for merely hosting a production company."

"Then we're talking really big bucks." This matter-of-fact statement came from Stanley Prisom, the Mayor, who was already thinking of ways to fatten his re-election coffers.

"To the tune of millions." Pinkerton, the Business Developer, responded.

"That depends on how long the shooting lasts and whether we're able to negotiate a reasonable usage fee for the site." Jayson already had a dollar figure in mind that he would not go beyond.

Oden took a few puffs and threw his head back to blow a plume of smoke in the air. Obviously, the no-smoking signs posted everywhere in the building didn't apply to him. Oden shot a glance down the table.

"You had a question about the contract, right Myers?" Mitch Myers was a mousy-looking man. Bald on the top, fuzzy tendrils on the sides and a bow tie at the nape of his neck. As he buried himself in the contract to search for a question to ask, it became clear that he took his orders directly from Oden.

Pinkerton imposed. "It's too short a notice. You're talking weeks from now when we'll enter the busiest part of our tourist season. What you're proposing for Mt. Timp would require us to shut it down to visitors. You can't expect us to do that. That's money lost, son."

Anticipating where the conversation was headed, Jayson ignored Pinkerton's "son" quip. Money was now the bottom line. He doubted Mt. Timp had ever so much as been featured in a commercial. Now that they'd received an offer from the "big time Hollywood folks" they were salivating at the prospect of lacing their individual pockets with a cut of the revenues. How much the players at the table would walk away with in their personal bank accounts was what was at stake. They didn't mind him using Mt. Timp as long as they got a significant piece of the pie.

Jayson addressed Oden. "We're not asking you to close all of Mt. Timp. Just the surrounding area where the filming takes place will be closed off to tourists and the general public. That's non-negotiable because our production company is liable in the event anyone gets hurt. Also, the loss of any tourist income is already built into the contract. I'll also point out that more tourists will be drawn to the area just on the basis of our name recognition alone. There are several heavy hitters in this film, including myself. You might have heard of Al Pacino, Matt Damon or Angela Bassett? Throw in the fact that Ridley Scott is directing, plus Universal Pictures is the production company, well gentlemen, that's major star power.

"Don't forget, it's a pretty darn good highlight to put in your future tourist brochures. It immediately propels you out of the nickel and dime arena and plunges you into the world of A-list players. Not that you haven't done well reaping from tourist revenues. But having the site featured in a major film like this one, adds new meaning to the term tourist attraction."

Mitch, the lawyer, had highlighted several passages in the contract and made notes on the pages. He slid them to Oden, who glanced down at them.

With his political cronies used to being wellfed from a patronage trough, it was clear Oden was used to conducting business to his advantage. Blowing smoke out one side of his mouth, he said, "It all sounds really great, Denali. But I'm still not seeing the big picture."

Oden chewed on his pipe. He spread his hands to indicate the people sitting at the table. "What's in it for us?"

Chapter Nineteen

As the hardball negotiations got underway, Aaryn sat silently observing Oden, Pinkerton and Prisom. These three were the ones wielding the power, they were the ones to watch. Especially Jim Oden. While they were talking, she'd read over the location contract. Interesting stuff, she thought. But as she allowed herself to just be in tune with the people in the room, her eyes poured over each of them. The three men were hiding something and Aaryn felt urgently compelled to discover what it was.

In order to read the men's spirits, Aaryn permitted herself to do something rare—she allowed herself to have an out-of-body experience. It was accessing the unseen spiritual dimension to get a "behind-the-scenes" view of why people operated the way they did. It was like climbing onto a higher plane of existence and observing the different pockets in people's lives. The caveat was knowing how far to traverse in the spirit realm without trespassing—without violating those spiritual laws set into existence long before the foundation of the world. There was something sinister in the room that Aaryn couldn't quite define. Hence, the crucial need to have a clearer picture of the kind of people Jayson was dealing with. Because her sensory preceptors were flashing bright neon signals, she expected to find something out of the ordinary. Just not to the degree that she did.

Aaryn started with Mitch Myers. Of all the men seated at the table, he was the weakest vessel. Using a form of spiritual telepathy, she gently probed around the edges of his spiritman. She felt strong waves of intimidation and fear emanating from within his spirit. Something was going on with Mitch that had him constantly feeling threatened, as if he was being held under lock and key. His spirit sent indicators that his fleshly body was being subverted. Mitch had not always been so fearful. Aaryn saw dim pockets of contentment in his spirit which she instantly zeroed in on. She entered deeper into that same doorway in the spirit realm and saw Mitch in a state of relaxation. He was seated comfortably in a well-lit room filled with books. Chaucer, Thoreau, Shakespeare, Hemingway, he was surrounded by all the great classics which he derived so much pleasure from reading.

Mitch Myers was a lover of words. A man who took pleasure in the solitude his world provided him. Yet, somehow he'd gotten himself entangled with these nefarious men. How? Aaryn departed from that particular spiritual door and entered another one still within the realm of Mitch's life. She began to see that he was a very detailed man. An attorney by trade, his area of focus was reviewing business contracts from which he earned a decent living. She saw him happy until the time he stumbled over a passage in several City of Provo contracts he was reviewing. In a matter of a few sentences, Mitch connected dots he was never intended to see. He uncovered a fraudulent patronage scheme of kickbacks that amounted to millions of dollars and involved nearly every major business in the City of Provo. The money, Mitch discovered, was being funneled back to the group Oden was a part of.

"What kind of group is Oden part of?" Aaryn inquired. But instead of receiving a response, she hit a brick wall—a thick barricade in the form of a hedge which would take time to penetrate. Time she didn't have. Mitch's spiritman shied away from her and was refusing further communication.

Unwilling to give up, Aaryn tried to flit through another door in the spiritual dimension of Mitch's life, but it was as if all windows had come hurtling down in response to the one threatening question she'd asked, *"What kind of group is Oden a part of?"*

Traveling at the speed of light, Aaryn's spirit attempted to mine each layer of Mitch's spirit. In the various dimensions of the spirit realm, everything moves at warp speed. But in real time, it's like a butterfly fluttering against a window pane, unable to pass through the daunting glass. Now more curious than ever, Aaryn again tried communicating with Mitch via her spiritman. *"Is all well, Mitch Myers? Why are you stuck here when it's apparent you don't want to be connected to this circle? Why are you allowing your soul to whither? Don't you realize the longer you stay, the more toxic your spirit is becoming?"* Aaryn pounded these questions into the ether of Mitch's spirit.

Sitting across from her at the cherry oak table, suddenly Mitch jerked and raised his head to fix Aaryn with a piercing glance. Where before he'd been doodling aimlessly on the tablet in front of him, he looked up because he had the sense that something invasive had just brushed the back of his neck.

Mitch continued to stare at her until a slightly confused look appeared on his face. Slowly, his eyes traveled over Aaryn as a dawning recognition transformed his awareness. As if she was whispering directly into his ear, he heard an unfamiliar voice inside his head ask, *"Is all well, Mitch Myers? Why are you here? What kind of group does Oden belong to?"*

Mitch's mouth dropped open. And just as quickly, he closed it and focused his eyes on his notepad. "Careful," Aaryn heard his spirit whisper warningly. "Be very careful."

A beep sounded in the room causing Mitch to nearly jump out of his skin. When all eyes turned in his direction, he stood hastily and pulled a Treo smartphone from his pocket. Staring down at it, he said, "Excuse me, gentlemen. I have to take this call." Without looking at Oden or the others, Mitch Myers escaped the room.

After he left, Aaryn stared at the closed door. She had probed through the viscidness of Mitch's spirit, treading carefully while trying to uncover why he was so afraid. But the image she saw of him being held over a barrel told her that someone was holding his spirit hostage. And what that translated to in the earth realm where people could hear, smell, taste, feel and see was that someone was forcing Mitch to do immoral things against his will.

Aaryn felt someone staring at her and her eyes immediately swiveled in the direction from where the intensity came. Shelly, the second gatekeeper was watching her closely. Fearlessly, Aaryn stared at her until the woman grew uncomfortable and looked away.

The secretary didn't know exactly what had taken place between Aaryn and Mitch, but she was perceptive enough to know that something out of the ordinary had transpired.

Aaryn sensed that Shelly, like the receptionist manning the outer desk, was part of whatever group was assembled at the table. She picked up the contract and pretended to read through it. Mentally, Aaryn started probing Shelly's spirit. The woman was a blocked force field and would not permit herself to be scanned. But in this arena, the unseen spiritual realm, Aaryn was the stronger, more dominant vessel. And since Shelly was so close to her in proximity, Aaryn was able to break through her shields undetected. What she saw repelled her.

When Shelly later recounted her version of events to Oden, she told him of the penetrating look that had passed between her and Jayson Denali's socalled "counselor." From that one look, Shelly identified the counselor as what the "enforcers" in her assembly labeled an "enemy combatant." Shelly was not a high-ranking member of the cult's inner circle and yet, because spirits recognize each other, and because there exists a hierarchy in the spirit realm, Shelly distinguished Aaryn as a strong spiritual warrior.

In the spirit, Aaryn plumbed the embers of Shelly's spiritman to glean information. She saw her kneeling in a chamber filled with men that included Oden, Prisom and Pinkerton. Some kind of initiation ritual was being enacted to induct Shelly into their demonic fold. She was on all fours before the men—servicing them one by one. Each man waited his turn to use her as their human receptacle. Repulsed, Aaryn quickly slammed the door to that depraved realm of Shelly's life and entered another doorway. This door opened to a time when Shelly was a teenager. She saw Shelly being struck by her father, while her mother watched television oblivious to the drama playing out right in the next room. Aaryn closed that doorway as well and crossed through several more in search of one that would enlighten her to the current events.

Bingo! She found a doorway where Shelly was in her early thirties. Through this door, Aaryn saw that for over thirteen years, Shelly had worked for Oden. She'd

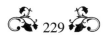

been a part of his sect for the same length of time and was now a replacement for the woman manning the outside desk. The older assistant had once been young, vibrant and fertile. Now that her body was used and sucked dry, she'd been replaced by a younger model. Though Shelly couldn't see it, the older woman knew the younger one was destined to share the same twisted fate. There was, however, one level where the two women were equal. Both knew where all the bodies were buried.

Sticking with the vein she'd tapped into, Aaryn peered through another spiritual doorway and saw five people seated at the very table she and Jayson occupied. They were counting money collected from several of the local business owners. Each owner feared Oden and was indebted to him. There were many others involved who weren't at the table and they, too, all feared Oden, who had a hand in every profitable pot within the City of Provo.

Aaryn exited all doorways to Shelly's life and focused on the three remaining men. Cautiously, she pried around the perimeter of each of their spirits until she recognized that there was no separation between them. Their spirits were entwined. Because of all the evil they practiced together, in the spirit, the three men were as one.

After what seemed a very long time, it wasn't a doorway that Aaryn finally found that allowed her access, but a slither of an opening in the spirit realm—a tear in the fluidic fabric, the ectoplasm that housed their spirits. She squeezed inside and abruptly recoiled at what she saw. Greed, lust, murder, mayhem, initiation sacrifices. And the worst kind of evil of all—*devil worshiping*.

The Cognisetti.

When Aaryn heard the words, self preservation made her want to flee. But she steeled herself against slamming the accessway shut. She forced herself to remain still in order to view what few others were ever allowed to see.

She found herself inside another chamber, this one filled with men and women, but mostly men. Everyone was dressed in long, hooded red garb. All sat in chairs placed in circles that fanned outward until the one circle was comprised of many inner circles. Each member held a small, round red candle. Starting with the outer circle, a single candle was lit and its flame was used to light the next candle. The flame passed from person to person within each circle.

In the center of the inner circle, lay a young white ewe that bleated and struggled helplessly, its neck gripped tightly by a wire tethered to a stake in the ground.

As the lighting of the candles made its progression to the innermost part of the circle, Aaryn heard a low chanting that increased in volume as each circle of candles was completely lit. And when the final candle was set ablaze within the innermost circle, the man holding the last lit candle stood and removed a long hunting knife from his garment. He stepped to the frightened animal, and kneeling, grabbed its head and plunged the knife into its heart.

The animal's cries were drowned out by the loud volume of chanting in the room. As blood drained from the animal, it was collected in vials, which they began passing to each member within the circles. Each one dipped their forefinger inside the vial to mark their foreheads with the animal's blood. The remaining residue on their fingertip, they swiped across their lips.

The Cognisetti.

Aaryn knew of it. A secret society—it was an army of darkness consisting of high priests and lesser vessels who were used to disseminate misinformation about Christianity. Many of its members were affluent, powerful and well educated. And because of it, they could fool the very elect. Theirs was a sect manned by new age, fundamentalist-type adherents.

In times past, Aaryn had even encountered spirits who were deep into its wayward practices. They were people who did all manner of things to gain riches and power—from selling their souls to enrich themselves, to enticing others to do the very same. All their rules and doctrines were formulated by the highest-ranking members and funneled down through the lower ranks to be practiced and deployed.

While in the spirit realm, Aaryn saw cult-like figures recruiting from a pool of select people by tempting them with promises of riches, fame and glory. Once blinded, these poor souls were lead to take a form of oath and were then slowly indoctrinated deeper into the deceptive cult. Only by then, it was too late to have second thoughts. For most, the only way out was death.

Aaryn exited the spirit realm by closing all doorways leading to it. Her spirit was then jolted back into her body. Presently, her eyes were still cast downward as if focused on the contract in front of her. To the more observant person, it may have even appeared that she'd fallen asleep. But her out-of-body experience had lasted no more than ten minutes.

She looked up to find the four men locked in a fierce numbers debate. Testosterone surged as each of them stuck rigidly to their own guns about how much the contract on the table was worth. Oden's pipe lay abandoned in an ashtray as he thumped his fat fingers on the table emphasizing why the dollar amount Jayson proposed was insufficient. With her bearings fully gathered, Aaryn focused her attention on Oden.

"...you'll have carte blanche to everything in the City of Provo. Hell, you can have the keys to the city if you start talking with a bit more sense." Oden was about to say more, but he noticed the intense way Aaryn was staring at him. Not used to being challenged by a woman, he stopped and directed a glare her way. Everyone else turned to look at her as well.

Aaryn's eyes locked with Oden's and she sensed a changing undercurrent in the room. A subtle awareness on both of their parts weaved itself through the look which passed between them. A look that said, *"I know who you are."*

On a mental level, she and Oden engaged in a silent battle of wills where neither of them was willing to be the first to drop their gaze. She'd tapped uninvited into their world—a world where power, lust and evil principalities ruled the day. Aaryn sensed that what was at stake was not the contract lying on the table—that was the decoy. *Jayson's soul was what Oden really wanted.* He wanted Jayson as an inroad to even greater riches and wealth. Spirits like the ones Oden possessed were attracted to power, fame and money. And Oden wanted the power that rested within Jayson. Even the others at the table were attracted by Jayson's fame, his money, his looks and even his ethnicity. Everything about him drew them and it was their intent to lure him into their sect.

That was why, unbeknownst to himself, Jayson had invited Aaryn to join him in this meeting. Jayson Denali, the man, the myth, the eponymous star, had no clue as to the plans of those amidst the present demonic realm. But because the Spirit of God knew all things, Aaryn was brought to this meeting to intercede for Jayson's soul. Aaryn was, in effect, his warrior angel on this occasion and he, Jayson, was none the wiser for it.

The message Aaryn sent to Oden and his imps was clear: *"This one you cannot have. Touch not the anointed one—or face direct consequences."*

"Who are you?" Oden harshly addressed his question to Aaryn. The bidding war was momentarily forgotten as he focused on the woman on the opposite side of the table.

Ignoring his question, she said to him, "You know who I am. You've known since the beginning. As of right now, this meeting is over. The final offer is on the table. If you want the deal, sign the contract in our presence—now—before we leave. Otherwise, once we exit this office, the deal's off the table." Aaryn placed her hand on Jayson's arm. "Mr. Denali has been more than fair. Therefore, either reject the offer or accept it." Aaryn did not release Jayson's arm and neither did her eyes leave Oden's face.

Oden picked up his pipe and clamped it in his mouth. Angrily, he reached for a copy of the contract and ripped it in two.

Aaryn turned and smiled at Jayson. "I believe we have our answer. Shall we?"

Jayson rose to pull out Aaryn's chair. They had nearly reached the door when Oden said gruffly, "Alright. You got yourself a deal. But only because I like you, Jayson Denali."

Oden signed two copies of the faxed contract and handed his ink pen to Jayson who returned to the table to sign as well. Afterwards, the two men shook hands.

Oden rose and approached Aaryn to stare down at her. His eyes narrowed as if he was attempting to see inside her soul. "You got balls, Counselor. But we'll meet again." Oden made his statement sound like a promise. And a threat.

Aaryn tilted her head to stare back at him. "If that time should ever come, believe me, we'll be ready." The "we" Aaryn was referring to was the host of angels in the spirit realm who work unseen in the life of every person. Those who knew their authority in the spirit arena, could command legions of angels to war on their behalf. Aaryn was such a one. So she'd no reason to fear Oden or any of his people. She knew it. And so did he. As she stood at the door waiting for Jayson she said, "We'll see ourselves out."

As soon as the door closed behind them, she and Jayson started walking toward the exit. Aaryn's eyes closed momentarily as a sudden fatigue swept over her. She put her hand to her forehead.

"What is it?" Jayson stopped and touched Aaryn's shoulder.

"Nothing. I just felt a wave of dizziness. I'll be fine." Aaryn was about to continue walking when suddenly, to her complete dismay, she was swept off her feet. Jayson was carrying her in his arms.

"Cat's got your tongue, doesn't he?" Jayson grinned at the shocked, speechless expression on Aaryn's face.

"What in God's name are you doing? Jayson, put me down!" But Aaryn latched her arms around his neck.

"No way, Lady. You just saved me a million dollars. I'll carry you all the way to the moon if you but speak the words." Jayson was striding fast as they approached the area where the mean and nasty receptionist awaited them.

"Jayson Denali, have you lost your mind? If you don't put me down right this second, so help me, I'll…"

"You'll what? Don't worry, I'll tell anyone who dares to ask that you tripped and sprained your ankle. And then I'll tell them that you always do this when you're in my presence so that I have no choice but to carry you to your destinations."

Aaryn couldn't stop the laughter that spilled from her mouth. "Good Lord, Jayson, you really *are* insane! No one's going to believe such hogwash!"

"They will after I put you down and they see you walk without a limp. Hush now, we're about to meet the big bad wolf of a receptionist. She won't be impressed at all. I should throw you over my shoulder and smack your rump. Bet that'll impress her and make her a loyal fan of mine for life."

"If you dare do such a thing, Jayson, I promise I'll shoot you the moment we reach my car."

"You keep a gun in your car?"

"I'm not telling. You'll find out soon enough if you don't put me down."

Jayson swept past the receptionist. "Can you buzz us out, please? My consigliere seems to have fallen ill." The doors buzzed and Jayson waltzed through them still carrying Aaryn in his arms.

"Stop. Please. Stop, Jayson. Put me down so I can laugh." Her hand was pressed against the flat of her belly which quaked with laughter.

He finally stopped as requested and set her on her feet. "You, Counselor, are my good luck charm and you've made me a very happy man. You were brilliant, Aaryn! It was like something just grabbed me and told me to follow your lead. I'm telling you, it was perfect! I couldn't have planned it better had I written you a script. How did you know to intervene by threatening to walk out? I should introduce you to my agent. He could learn a thing or two from you. Do you play hardball like that often? Scratch that. Of course you do! You're just like your Mom—you're one of those precognitive people. Well, thank the stars I brought you with me. Even though you're a royal pain in the ass, Doc, you're worth it. Now, how shall we celebrate? I know, let's go dancing. You do dance, don't you?" He had one hand on her shoulder and the other on her waist.

In that moment, Aaryn understood why all women loved him. Yes, Jayson Denali was a beautiful man. But he was also a giving, generous man with a heart of gold that was wider than the Amazon River and deeper than the Artic Ocean. In his mind, he thought she was negotiating to save him money on a contract when, in actuality, she'd been fighting to save his very soul. Anyone capable of out-of-body experiences knew that it was a rewarding and fulfilling phenomenon. But afterwards, it left one completely drained. Add to it the fact that she'd had to engage in spiritual warfare with the occupants of the office, and it was no wonder that a wave of dizziness had tried to envelop her.

But at least one question was answered for Aaryn as far as Jayson Denali was concerned. And even as the answer filtered through her mind, she masked the swell of disappointment that threatened to overtake her. She now knew why Jayson had been thrown so haphazardly into her life—assigned to her, so to speak. As successful, rich and famous as he was—physically, he wanted for nothing—spiritually, he was bankrupt. There were so many forces seeking to pull this man in their direction that he'd been sent to her just so she could steer him the right way. He didn't even know it, but he was lost and Aaryn was his guardian angel for this season of his life.

The disappointment came in knowing that that was all there was. The attraction she'd allowed herself to admit she felt toward him, was never meant for her to act upon. It was only meant for her to lead and guide him in a certain direction. If she allowed their paths to intersect physically, woe would be unto her. For a moment, a sense of great loss threatened to overwhelm her. But out of nowhere a graceful peace covered, enveloped her and allowed her to compose herself once more.

Aaryn turned from him and walked toward the elevator. "No, Jayson Denali, I do not dance."

"Oh, come on, Woman. Everybody dances."

She shook her head. "Not me. I'm the most uncoordinated black person you're ever likely to meet."

For some reason, Jayson wanted to pick her up and carry her again. It was a spontaneous, spur-of-the-moment thing. But he'd enjoyed having her helpless in his arms. They reached the elevators and he pressed the button.

"I could teach you, you know." Jayson mockingly teased the knot in his tie for an exaggerated effect. He raised his eyebrows up and down and lowered his voice. "I have skills."

Aaryn stared at him, a half smile on her face. In spite of herself, she reached up and straightened his tie. "I'm sure you do. But, as much as it pains me to admit it, this dog don't hunt. Besides, need I remind you that less than fifty minutes ago, you were ready to curse me out and throw me from the train? Now all of a sudden, I'm your best friend."

"Aw, woman, that was because you were busy trippin' over that lousy receptionist. I kept telling you she was probably going through PMS or something. You know, her wig could have been on too tight. Her shoes could have been too tight. Her girdle could have been too tight. With all that going on, it's a wonder she didn't try to kill us."

Aaryn stepped into the elevator shaking her head. "You are truly dense, Jayson. Men. I swear, you all can't see the forest for the trees. Without us women, God only knows where you would be."

"I'm not even going to touch that statement. I've found no good ever comes of debating the man vs. woman issue. You women simply can't take hearing about the supremacy of us men."

As she leaned against the wall of the elevator, Aaryn tilted her head back and closed her eyes. She still had a small smirk on her face even as she shook her head at his comment. She felt him move closer to her and when she opened her eyes, Jayson was standing over her with a look of concern on his face.

"Are you okay?" Even knowing she wouldn't want him to, he smoothed back the wild tendrils that had escaped her pony tail. It was a simple touch of concern, but for him it sent smoldering heat through his body. He couldn't say how it affected her because the elevator doors opened and she ducked under his arm to walk through them, leaving him behind. Jayson shook off the longing that he felt.

As soon as they turned the corner and hit the lobby area, they were met by a gaggle of photographers and cameramen.

"Jayson, is it true you're changing the film location of *A Season to Hunt* to the City of Provo?"

"Has your mother's health improved since she's been in Utah?"

"Mr. Denali, do you have any comment about the sexual harassment charges filed against you by Rita Danza?"

"Who's the new woman on your arm, Jayson?"

As flashbulbs went off around them, instinct made Jayson throw his arm around Aaryn's waist to usher her forward. She may have been surprised by and unprepared for the wave of reporters, but for him it was an everyday occurrence.

"Give me your keys." His steely tone brook no argument.

Aaryn fished in her jacket pocket and handed them to him.

Outside, Jayson opened the passenger door and helped Aaryn inside the vehicle. He entered the driver's side and adjusted the seat of her car. Outside the SUV, six reporters continued to aim their cameras at the vehicle even as he pulled away.

"Well, that was lovely." Aaryn released a deep breath that she didn't even know she'd been holding.

"Welcome to my world." He threw her a glance. "Imagine having to deal with that every day—many times a day. Still think my life's a cakewalk?"

"Better you than me, Sir." Aaryn turned to look at him in her seat. Now she knew her car would never be the same.

"Where to?" Jayson glanced at her. She still seemed a little tired to him. "Have you eaten anything today?"

Aaryn smiled. "I had something earlier. I'm not hungry though. I can wait until I get home. Dot's cooking something scrumptious. By the way, are you really coming for dinner tonight?"

"I plan to. Unless you're uninviting me."

"I'd get creamed and banned from my own house if I even tried. What did you do to my Mom? Secretly send her some diamonds or something? She's no better than all the other women you've got wrapped around your finger."

"How do I wrap you?"

"You don't. What you have in me, Mr. Jayson Denali, is a bona fide friend. Nothing more. Nothing less. That's a new novelty for you, isn't it?"

Jayson didn't want to admit that she was right. But she was. It would definitely be an anomaly for him.

"You were about to tell me where we were headed."

"Changing the subject already? Okay. You're going somewhere with me for a change. And I'm not telling you where until we get there. That way you can't change your mind. Stay on I-15 until you get back to Salt Lake City. When you pass an exit called Sheridan Road, wake me." Aaryn let her seat all the way down and curled up to take a nap.

"You're just going to fall asleep on me?" Jayson glanced at her disbelievingly.

But Aaryn didn't answer. She turned her back to him and dozed off.

Jayson drove in silence. No satellite radio. No music. No laughter from wisecracking DJs. No lovelorn callers dialing in to bemoan the fact that their cheating girlfriends were worse than their nagging wives. No ringing cell phones. No pages or text messages to answer. And no paparazzi. Just the serene sound of silence and the peacefulness of his thoughts. It was a new paradigm shift for Jayson—one he almost couldn't believe was happening.

As he adjusted his legs and settled deeper into the seat, a rare contentedness settled over him. He recognized that for once, he felt no need to distract himself in order to avoid the calamitous chatter in the back of his mind that never seemed to cease. He felt no need to check his voicemail or to be in communication with anyone else in the world. It was as if Jayson had everything he needed right there in the tranquility of the SUV—right there beside him.

Chapter Twenty

Forget the war of the Roses. This was the war of the Slaughters. And Erika was wound tighter than a clock spring.

Standing in the checkout line at Neiman Marcus, she visibly took a deep breath. "Can you please try running the card again? There must be some mistake."

With a thinly veiled sigh, the sales clerk took the card she'd just handed back to Erika to swipe it through the credit card machine for the third time. After a few seconds, just as it had previously, the card reader displayed the message, "Card Declined."

Erika swept her hair away from her face, embarrassed by the thought that the sales clerk, along with the other people in line, probably saw her as some vagrant who couldn't pay her bills. Or worse, as a credit card thief. "Here, use this one."

"I'm afraid this one isn't working either, Mam. Would you like to pay cash? Or would you prefer to talk to a supervisor?" The sales clerk tried to keep her tone from sounding patronizing even as she hoped the woman opted for a supervisor so someone else could deal with her high and mighty attitude. *Sheese, these snooty-snobbish ones were the worst to deal with!*

Erika stuffed her credit cards back into her wallet. "Can you put my things to the side, please? I'll come back later and pay cash." She looked up in time to catch the "sure-you-will" smirk on the sales clerk's face.

Erika stalked off. She wasn't sure who she was madder at—herself for not checking the balance on her credit cards or the sales clerk for making her feel humiliated. Still, Erika couldn't wait to get home to call the credit card companies to find out what was going on with her accounts. Since both were no-limit credit cards, they were supposed to have unlimited balances. She wondered what was behind the snafu.

The problem with that line of thinking was that Erika feared she already knew the answer. It was more like *who* was behind the snafu than anything else.

Two weeks had passed since Michael had moved out of the house. Fourteen days since their marriage had ruptured, shattering even the tiniest hope of any reconciliation.

In the days leading up to the walkout, tensions between them had swelled as some unseen force propelled them toward a fullblown confrontation. Though they managed to avoid speaking to one another, it hadn't been enough to prevent the build-up of hostilities. Yet, right up to the night before the split, Erika still had hopes of salvaging the union.

One night, she was sitting up in bed waiting for Michael to return home. It was after 1 AM when he finally arrived. She knew he would be up again by five the next morning. So, if she intended to speak with him, the time was now. It wasn't the first time he'd arrived home in the wee hours of the morning. His routine was set. It was as though they'd adopted a "don't ask, don't tell" policy in response to his comings and goings. A part of her hadn't cared why he came home so late and the other part didn't really want to know—at least not until recently. Despite the hard evidence of their marriage tearing apart at the seams, Erika figured marriage counseling could be the needle that repaired the torn and gaping gashes.

"Things have changed between us, Michael." Erika hit him with her words as soon as he walked through the bedroom door. "I think we should see a marriage counselor. We're not a couple anymore and I think counseling would help us to be happy again."

Michael removed his tie from his pocket and tossed it on the dresser. He shrugged out of his suit jacket and laid it across a nearby chair. "I think it's a great idea. For you. You certainly could benefit from all the counseling you can get. At least you finally noticed our marriage is abnormal. What took you so long?" He stripped down to his underwear and slid beneath the covers of the kingsized bed. He turned his back to Erika and for him the conversation was over.

Erika stared at his form almost wanting to hit him. "The whole idea of marriage counseling, Michael, is for *both* parties to attend. It's nice to know you feel so strongly that I could benefit from counseling. However, you need to take a good, long look in the mirror. You might be surprised by what you find—a wife who you barely see and communicate with, two sons who don't even recognize you as their father and a daughter who's terrified of your presence. I think that makes *you* the ideal candidate for counseling. God, you're disgusting. At least have the decency to shower before you climb into our bed. You reek of the other woman you've been with."

"Whatever." Throwing off the covers, Michael rose from the bed and walked to the closet to grab his robe. "Isn't it amazing that you're not jealous about me sleeping with another woman? Any other wife would be enraged to discover that her husband was screwing around. But not you, Erika. You're more concerned that I don't sully your precious designer sheets."

Erika got up and grabbed a bottle of Chanel perfume from the dresser to spray his side of the bed.

As he threw on his robe, Michael returned to find her fumigating the spot where he'd lain. He looked at her with loathing. "What a total shrew you've turned out to be. There ought to be a surefire way for a man to tell if the woman he's marrying will turn out to be a hag. For someone who's so disgusted by the thought of having sex with her husband, you sure didn't act like it when we were dating. That whole sexy-siren thing you had going back then was nothing but smoke and mirrors. You wouldn't know how to please a man if he gave you step-by-step instructions. Be sure to explain that to the marriage counselor when you make your appointment." Michael stalked out to go sleep in one of the guest bedrooms, leaving Erika with her mouth hung open and her hands on her hips.

Shortly after five the next morning, Michael was standing at the kitchen counter reading the New York Times and sipping a cup of hot coffee. From the corner of his eye, he caught a movement and turned to find little Mia standing just inside the entrance to the kitchen. She was dressed in her nightgown, clutching that stupid, tattered Carebear. Something about the way she stood watching him with narrowed eyes and a cautious, mistrustful look made Michael give her his full attention. Instinct urged him to go to her and pick her up to reassure her that everything in her tiny world would be okay.

But before he took the first step, Mia gripped the bear tighter and said to him, "Hully says you and your girlfriend are wicked fools. He said you're both going to burn in hell!"

Chills crawled up Michael's spine even as the cup he was holding crashed to the floor. Coffee splattered everywhere. As weird and surreal as the moment was, Michael's mind flashed back to the time in D.C. when thugs had robbed him. The sensation he felt now was the same spark of fear that had come upon him when one of the thugs had pulled out a gun. But this was his daughter speaking to him *as if she was an adult*—as if she was God administering judgment on Judgment Day.

Michael snapped.

"That's it goddammit! I've had enough of this crap! It's high time I beat the hell out of you, you little twerp! I'm your father. You don't talk to me that way!"

Michael charged towards Mia who turned and ran as if the devil himself was on her heels. Her earsplitting screams resounded throughout the whole house.

"Mommy!" Screaming at the top of her lungs, Mia scampered like a bat out of hell with Hully gripped tightly to her side. She reached the staircase and was climbing as fast as her short little legs could take her when Michael grabbed her around her waist.

He picked her up and spun her around to face him. He was enraged as he tore the bear out of her arms intent on destroying it. "Shut up!" he shouted at Mia who was crying as though he was already torturing her. When she continued to struggle in his grip he began to shake her like a ragdoll.

"Michael, what are you doing? Put her down!" Erika came running down the upstairs hallway with Josh on her heels. She shouted at him from the top of the stairs. "Are you out of your mind? You don't shake a child like that! What's wrong with you?" Erika bounded down the stairs to wrestle Mia from his grip. "Let her go, I said. Can't you see she's terrified of you?"

When Michael roughly shoved Erika out of the way to drag Mia back into the kitchen, Erika stumbled but quickly regained her balance. Rage made her fly at him in fury.

Michael released Mia and turned to backhand Erika with a vicious blow that knocked her to the floor. Blood splattered from her split lip. He came and stood over her. His voice filled with disgust. "The sight of you sickens me!"

Dazed, Erika struggled to her feet with Mia and Josh both crying at her side. She wiped the blood from her lip with the back of her hand. Her jaw was already beginning to swell. "Get out! I want you out of this house right now! And don't even think about returning. I'm glad the sight of me sickens you. How do you think I feel having to look at your warped face night after night? This marriage is over—I want a divorce. By the time I'm finished with you, Buster, you'll be lucky if you have two nickels to rub together. Try paying your ghetto whore's rent with that!"

Michael's head jerked as if she'd slapped him.

"Oh, I know all about your other woman. You think I'm stupid? You ought to be ashamed of yourself, Michael. She's almost a child. What are you, some sick, twisted, perverted pedophile?"

Michael looked as if he'd been cut all kinds of ways. "I always knew it was you poisoning my own children against me. Look at them. They're frightened of their own father. I've never hit them. It's been all your doing. You're damned right I've got someone else. At least she knows how to appreciate a man. Something you've never known how to do. She may be younger, but she's ten times the woman you'll ever be. Look at how you've let yourself go, Erika. You look pathetic. You *are* pathetic. I don't know what I ever saw in you in the first place. I should have listened to my mother and never married you. She used to say I was blinded by your looks and that you were using witchcraft to get me to marry you. My mother swore you would ruin my life. Damned if she didn't turn out to be prophetic! I hate you, Erika. You're nothing but a cold, selfish pile of bones. To think I passed up my childhood sweetheart to marry you—I had to be high on dope. *You,* divorce *me?*"

Michael laughed a cruel laugh. "You're so stupid you can't even see the writing on the wall. You? Divorce me? You dunce, I've already got the paperwork ready and waiting. You better lawyer up as soon as possible. Because those same two nickels you think I'll be rubbing together, you're going to be begging for them by the time I'm through with you. I'm leaving alright. But take a good look around the house this morning, Erika, because you won't be here for much longer. I'll personally see to it that you're out of this house within the next thirty days. After I kick you out, you'll be grateful just to find space in a shelter. Without me, you're nothing but a great big zero, because we both know you can't survive on your own." Michael turned away to storm up the steps. He paused at the top.

"Not only were you a poor excuse for a wife, but you're an unfit mother, Erika. I intend to seek custody of the children. By the time I get finished proving just how unfit you are, if you're lucky, you might be able to see them once a year."

As Michael stalked off down the hall to pack his clothes, his threatening words hung in the air like an ominous dark cloud.

That was two weeks ago. Since then Erika's world had morphed into total chaos. She and all three of the children had come down with severe cases of the flu.

Marcus, the baby, had gotten so sick Erika had rushed him to the emergency room. His breathing so deeply labored that for a moment, she'd feared she might lose him. She hadn't bothered contacting Michael. He would only have accused her of being a neglectful mother. Her own sickness, Erika had fought with everything within her because she knew she had no one to care for her children for days at a time. Not even Michael, who had expressed his hatred of her in no uncertain terms. Though Michael had directed his acrimony toward her, Erika took it to include the children as well.

Unfortunately, with so much going on, she hadn't had time to retain a divorce attorney.

As she held the line for an American Express representative, Erika had pressed what seemed to her a thousand buttons just to be connected with an agent. After an eternity, she finally got a live voice on the other end but struggled to understand the rep because of his thick foreign accent. Neither was she pleased when he asked her to recite her 15-digit credit card number after she'd already punched in the number twice. Why'd she bother keying in all that information if they were just going to ask her for it when she finally got someone on the line?

"Mam, thank you for your patience. I am Sharif and I am happy to be your American Express account representative. Just a few questions, Mam…"

Erika rolled her eyes at the rep's attempt to sound like a genie about to fulfill her every desire. She was doing her best to understand him but the strain of listening to him intently served only to heighten her irritation. She interrupted his spiel about who he was and how it was his pleasure to service her. She didn't have time for inane niceties—not when her world was falling apart.

"I'd like to know why my accounts are being declined since I have unlimited balances."

"Yes, Mam, I am happy to assist you. If I understand you correctly…"

"Blah, blah, blah," Erika thought. *You've blown enough smoke up my behind so just get to the point and answer my question, will you?* Tired of straining to understand him, she interrupted him. "Sir, I can barely understand you. Can you please transfer me to someone who speaks English with less of an accent?" It didn't occur to Erika that the rep couldn't understand her either.

When he fell silent, Erika waited impatiently. Because of the quietness on his end of the line, she assumed he'd placed her on hold to transfer her to another agent. During the silence, Erika's mind began to wander. Somewhere in the distance she thought she heard the doorbell chime but figured she must have imagined it.

A full minute passed when a voice spoke haltingly. "Mam, I can understand your frustration…"

Erika couldn't believe she was hearing Sharif's voice again. She barked at him out of irritation. "Mister, I doubt very seriously that you even have a clue about my frustration. Don't take it personally, but I simply can't understand you. Now please, I need you to transfer me to a supervisor who I don't have to be multilingual in order to comprehend." Erika's patience was stretched paper thin. "Look, Sharif, you've been great. But I need to talk to a supervisor immediately."

When an American-sounding supervisor finally came on the line, Erika muttered, "Thank goodness!" She quickly explained her dilemma.

"Mrs. Slaughter, I apologize for your inconvenience, but you no longer have unlimited accounts. According to our records, ten days ago you phoned in to terminate both of your no-limit accounts and requested they be switched over to our standard individual account. We issued you new cards that were activated from your home phone. Since the time of activation, both your credit cards have been maxed out. You received the 'Card Declined' message because the cards you attempted to use are no longer valid. Is there anything else I can help you with?"

Erika felt as if the rug was pulled from underneath her feet. A hollow knot formed in her belly as she grasped the significance of what he'd just said. The two Amex cards in her possession were the only credit cards she owned and she used them to make most, if not all, of her purchases. Her mind reeled as she tried to think of what other resources she had.

"You're mistaken, Sir. I never called your company. Neither did I receive any credit cards. And I certainly didn't activate them from my home phone. How could something like this happen?"

"I'm reading the notes on your account, Mrs. Slaughter. It says that one of our reps spoke with you about converting both your no-limit credit cards to accounts with $15,000 limits. In fact, both of these cards are over their limit right now and we'd need to receive a payment from you before you could use either card again."

Erika stood clutching the kitchen counter. This was Michael's doing, she knew it. "Sir, I'm telling you I did not call your company. I'm sure my husband is behind this. We just separated. This is a case of credit card fraud if ever there was one. I don't have more than a $3,500 balance on both my cards combined. How could you allow this without calling to verify that it was actually me you were talking to?"

"Mrs. Slaughter, are you denying that you recently made a vehicle purchase from the Tom Wood Jaguar dealership in Indianapolis, Indiana?"

"What?"

"Mam, this was a $30,000 purchase. Fifteen thousand dollars was charged to each card."

"Look, this is becoming more and more ridiculous. It's very obvious this is fraud since I never called your company, never received new credit cards from you

243

and I certainly did not just purchase a brand new car. The BMW I have works perfectly fine."

"Mam, I have no reason to disbelieve you. I'll need to transfer you to our fraud department. Please hold while I connect you."

Full of anger and nervous energy, Erika began pacing back and forth. Before she knew it, she found herself biting her nails to the quick—an old habit she hadn't resorted to since high school. Several minutes passed as she waited for a fraud specialist. As she listened to the generic hold music, she had the impression that her call was taking on the legs of a PBS telethon.

She paced the length of the huge kitchen, which was large enough to comfortably accommodate more than one cook at a time. She was staring into the adjoining breakfast alcove wondering why Michael would do something so underhanded when she thought she heard muffled voices coming from the dining room area.

"What the...?" Startled, Erika spun toward the kitchen entrance. The voices were clearer now and she distinguished at least two of them. "Who the hell is in my home?" was Erika's first rankled thought as she moved to investigate. Her second thought made her stop to snatch a titanium chef knife with a 10-inch blade from the cutlery block. The thought that Michael might have sent people into her home to frighten her sent Erika into a black rage.

She strode purposefully into the adjoining dining room and came to an abrupt halt at the sight of a man and woman standing with their backs to her as they openly admired the dinnerware inside her Bonaparte buffet and hutch. The classic Royal Doulton tableware was perhaps the best bone china crockery in the world and it was among Erika's most prized possessions. Oblivious to the fact that they were trespassing, the pair stood ogling the elaborately designed tea set, plates, cups, saucers and service bowls all richly displayed. While the dinnerware created a lasting impression, it was the glittering Bohemian crystalware that sparkled richly and added exclusive beauty to the entire dining room. Bathed in soft glows from the lighting inside the hutch, the grandiose dinnerware and stemware became pieces of art that Napoleon himself would have died to have as art in the Louvre. If nothing else, the intruders reminded Erika that she had at least $25,000 worth of tableware in her possession.

"What the hell are you doing in my home?" Erika had crept into the room so subtly that neither the man nor the woman had heard her enter.

Both of them whipped around at the sound of her voice and took a step backward at the sight of the crazed look on her face as she held what appeared to them to be a large hunting knife. The woman, who was small in stature, eased behind the man who was burly by anyone's standards.

Fearlessly, Erika advanced upon them. Had the knife she was holding been a gun, she knew she would already have pulled the trigger. "I asked you a question. If I don't get an answer, one of you is about to be pinned to the wall." Erika stood patting the knife against her jean-clad leg.

"We…" The man stuttered as he eyed Erika's twitchy fingers. He spoke in a rush of words. "We're here to appraise the home. We weren't expecting anybody to be here. We were told the house would be empty. We rang the bell, but used our key after no one answered."

Erika could feel her head beginning to throb at the expanse of anger inside her. She clicked a button on the cordless phone she was holding and dialed 911. "This is Erika Slaughter of 848 Holcome Lane in Timberview Estates. Two thieves have just broken into my home. Can you send a patrol car immediately?"

"We didn't break into your house, Mam." The man's face reddened in indignation.

The 911 operator asked calmly, "Miss, are you in any danger? Are they threatening you?"

"I'm not in danger, Operator. But they are. If the police don't arrive soon, somebody might just have to die." Erika clicked off the phone. She stared malevolently at the pair.

"Mam, if you'll just put down the knife, we can explain everything."

"I'll bet you can. You're working for my husband, aren't you? How much is he paying you?"

"We're Real Estate agents. I can show you my identification…" He moved to reach into his jacket.

"Don't move," Erika spoke harshly as she lifted the knife threateningly. She heard police sirens and seconds later there was pounding on her front door. She jet past the couple, who was staring at each other as if they'd just stepped into the Twilight Zone. Erika flew into the foyer to yank open her door.

"Are you Erika Slaughter?" Two policemen stood just outside the entrance staring past her but taking note of the knife in her hand and the fading bruises on her jaw.

"Yes. Two robbers broke into my home claiming to be Real Estate agents. But they're lying because my home is not for sale."

The alleged robbers stood transfixed as the police walked into the dining room.

"Do you want to explain what you're doing inside this residence?"

Both of them spoke over each other in their haste to explain the situation. Finally, the man said, "We're not thieves. We're Real Estate agents and we came to view the home in order to put it on the market. We were told the house would be empty. The owner even gave us a copy of the key." He held up the key as proof. "That's how we were able to enter the home. We did not break in."

"Can we see some identification? Both of you."

Erika said, "They're in collusion with my husband. We separated two weeks ago. My credit cards have been stolen. A car from a Jaguar dealership has been purchased fraudulently without my knowledge and now my husband's trying to sell the house right from under me. Well, he won't be able to, because both our names are on the deed."

The policemen examined the couple's IDs before returning them.

"The lady says you're trespassing on her property. She's the owner so I'm afraid you'll have to leave."

"We would have left a long time ago but she started brandishing that hunting knife."

The woman finally spoke up. "Officer, we ran a title search on the home before we came here today. We can assure you that the home is registered only to a Michael Slaughter. His is the only name that appears on the title deed. Since this seems to be a marital dispute, we're more than willing to let them settle things before we get involved." Comfortable now that policemen were on the scene, the woman eased her way from behind her partner. To her, Erika appeared slightly unbalanced.

"If it's okay with you officers, we're leaving now." The couple wanted only to escape.

"Give me the key to my home." Erika moved to block their paths, the knife still in hand.

"Put the knife down, Mrs. Slaughter." The policeman spoke sternly.

As the man tossed the key to one of the officers and ushered his partner towards the door, Erika placed the threatening-looking knife on the table.

"Mommy!" Marcus called from the upstairs landing.

"Officers, can you excuse me one second? I need to see to my child." She hurried to check on Marcus. When she came back into the room she was carrying him on her hip.

"Can I get either of you something to drink?"

"No, we're good. But we have some questions for you."

"Please, come into the livingroom, will you?"

The officers trailed Erika, admiring the handsomely decorated home. It was obvious that its occupants were well off. But then, all the homes in the Timberview subdivision were priced at a million dollars and up. So, the luxury didn't come as a surprise.

"You said earlier that you believed your husband was responsible for the intruders. Tell us why you suspect him."

Erika sighed. She knew the police could probably care less about her dilemma but it still felt good to unburden. She told them everything. How Michael had hit her in the jaw and how, when she'd taken the children to the hospital, the nurse had taken pictures of her face because of the bruises and discolorations. Even now the scars hadn't fully faded.

As the policemen listened to Erika's story, they took note of her appearance. They saw a woman dressed in designer clothes who was beautiful, even though she wore no makeup. Her long hair was piled on top of her head, but some of it had escaped the holding pin which served to give her a wild, unkempt look. The nails on her left hand were immaculate and polished but the nails on the right hand looked as though they had fought a losing battle.

"Mrs. Slaughter, from what you've described, the first thing I'd advise you to do is file a restraining order against your husband. And you definitely need to get yourself a divorce attorney. I'd also recommend changing the locks on all the doors. You should think about changing your security code as well."

There were more recommendations before Erika saw them to the door. With Marcus peering shyly at the officers from behind her leg, she said, "I can't thank you gentlemen enough. Thank you for coming so quickly and I definitely appreciate all the advice you've given me."

"No problem, Mam. I'd get started as soon as possible if I were you."

"I will, Officers. Believe me, I will." Erika had no intentions of delaying another moment. As soon as they drove off, she would follow up with Amex, change the security code on her alarm system and call a locksmith. She intended to find the best divorce attorney in the United States. As soon as she set up an appointment, she'd head down to the police station to file a restraining order against Michael. She may have been late out of the gate, but now that she had a plan of action, she felt less like her life was spiraling out of control.

As the policemen closed the doors of their patrol car, one of them remarked, "It took her two weeks to think about getting a lawyer? Not the sharpest pencil in the box, is she?"

"She's screwed is what she is. You heard her say her husband's one of those lawyers at Haliburton. Everybody knows how cutthroat those bastards are. She might as well kiss the house goodbye. By the time he's finished with her, she'll be lucky to receive food stamps."

Chapter Twenty-One

The following day a chain of events was put into play that escalated the Slaughter's divorce proceedings and sealed their hatred for one another.

Erika was sitting in the law offices of Dowder & Associates talking to the famed divorce attorney, Sheila Dowder. The attorney came highly recommended—as evidenced by the slew of magazine and newspaper articles and the promotional commercials playing nonstop on the plasma TV in the waiting area. The commercials featured testimonials from ecstatic women clasping fistfulls of money in hands adorned with diamonds. Each woman's testimony (and the men's too) seemed to scream, *"Sheila Dowder helped show me the money!"*

Along with all the media attention the attorney garnered because of her successful, if somewhat cutthroat tactics, she'd earned the moniker *Snow White* since she inevitably took her client's spouses to the cleaners. If there was a clandestine lover in the background or bundles of cash secretly stashed away, the clever attorney could ferret it out like a bloodhound hot on the trail of an escaped convict. When the formidable lawyer showed up for client representation, she rarely came empty handed.

Salacious evidence such as indecent photos, incriminating text messages and audio tapes of illicit conversations typically induced vindictive husbands (or wives) to bring a swift end to proceedings. Her modis operandi was that everybody had something to hide, one just needed to know where to find it. It was debatable whether the lengths to which her investigators went to obtain their information stopped short of breaking the law. While her techniques may have been questionable, her results were not.

The attorney was painted as a vicious media hound because of her endless appearances on cable news networks such as Nancy Grace, Gretta Van Sustran and Hannity & Combs where she railed against perceived injustices suffered by divorced women. Wherever she went, there was always a reporter lurking in hopes of capturing a newsworthy or inflammatory sound bite. Camera shy, the attorney was not. In fact, it was said that she'd never met a camera she didn't like. She caught more face time on television than some of the showbiz clients she represented.

Though reviled by lawyers, husbands and wives who she'd raked over the coals, she was adored by feminists and women's organizations who labeled her a champion of women's causes. Scores of women within these groups proclaimed that without Attorney Dowder's legal representation, their husbands would have left them destitute, vying for admission to Skid Row.

Licensed to practice in all fifty states, Dowder & Associates had offices in ten cities. Adversarial divorces were the attorney's specialty. Her golden goose was the wealthy husband hell bent on dumping his middle-aged wife for a much younger woman. *Cha-ching!* Or the loyal wife who discovers that her husband's nightly decrees of "I have a headache" don't extend to his gay lover. *Cha-ching! Cha-ching!* Or the case that required setting aside a so-called iron-clad prenup. In Attorney Dowder's world, the only iron-clad prenup was one she'd drawn up herself. If it wasn't the legendary Dowder Prenup, *cha-ching, cha-ching, cha-ching!*

The old saying "it's cheaper to keep her" was never more fitting than when Attorney Dowder settled a case. When she delivered the goods, counsel for the opposing side often advised their clients to settle out of court as quickly as possible. Better to part with money than to lose pride, their reputations *and* their ducats.

Those who misjudged her got sucker punched and paid dearly through their wallets. About five feet tall, rail thin with reddish-gold hair, the ballsy attorney crackled with energy and vitality. It was difficult to guess her actual age because her zeal and passion for her work made her appear younger than what she was. Only the wrinkles and deep blue veins in her hands gave away the fact that she was a woman past her prime. Erika put her somewhere in her early sixties.

Attorney Dowder silently drummed her fingers against the arm of her chair and took occasional sips from a Starbucks container as Erika spoke softly in response to her questions. Her assistant sat nearby furiously taking notes.

"Tell me when you first suspected Michael was cheating on you. And I want to know precisely what he said to you before and after he hit you."

As she described that fateful morning, Erika was relieved to finally be able to talk to someone about what was going on in her life. While she found the attorney easy to talk to, she couldn't tell if that was because the woman was genuinely interested in her story or if it was because of the astronomical hourly rate she was charging. What struck Erika most about Attorney Dowder was her penetrating gaze. Her startling green eyes stared unblinkingly until you were made to feel uncomfortable.

It reminded Erika of Aaryn, who habitually did the same thing. It was the type of stare that signaled the recipient's facial expression and body language was being examined as if to divine truth. She could understand why some would be hesitant to face the attorney in court.

Erika's vivid description of the altercation caused her emotions to well. Noting her client was on the verge of tears, Attorney Dowder shifted the conversation away from that particular emotional sandtrap to the couple's finances. She started with general softball questions, to which Erika knew the answers such as, where they banked, their account balances and their annual income.

When the questions became more in depth, Erika realized she didn't know as much about her and Michael's finances as she'd thought. Faced with a series of questions to which she had no answers, it pained Erika to realize that when it came to managing their overall financial holdings, she had been content to leave it up to Michael. Sure, she paid the household and her credit card bills. But stocks and bonds and their investment portfolio? She handled none of that. Sadly, neither did she have an account of her own. All their checking and savings accounts were held jointly. Erika had trusted her husband so completely that it had never occurred to her to open a separate account. Suddenly, she became frightened as the realization hit her that after all these years she had nothing of her own. She felt like an even bigger dunce for not thinking of protecting herself in the simplest of ways.

Attorney Dowder came around her desk to lay her hand on Erika's shoulder. She recognized the mingled expressions of shock, shame and fear on her client's face. It was time to demonstrate why she was paid $400 an hour.

"Mrs. Slaughter, you're not the first wife who naively trusted her husband to do the right thing. You probably were raised in a good Christian home where they taught you that the man is the head of the household and you're the lowly subject born to do his bidding. I'm not speaking against your religion. I'm just here to point out that concepts like the one I just mentioned are antiquated. Any woman still adhering to the Adam and Eve premise, as I call it, well, she's bound to get nailed to the wall sooner or later. The perfect marriage with the white picket fence is nothing more than a costly illusion. I've always hated fairy tales. In real life, Cinderella turns into a hag left homeless by a prince charming who's little more than a sadistic pedophile with two beer guts who practices bestiality." Attorney Dowder caught the look of revulsion on Erika's face and knew she needed to take a different tact. Apparently Mrs. Slaughter wasn't out for her husband's blood. The attorney intended to change that.

"What I'm saying to you, Mrs. Slaughter, is don't be too hard on yourself. While I don't want to alarm you, neither do I intend to deceive you about the divorce process. It's brutal and painful. It doesn't have to be. But with men like Michael, it's best to count on it. Your husband may be a big shot lawyer from Haliburton, but he's already made a major blunder. His first mistake was that you hired me. He thinks because he's entitled to free legal representation from his firm, he's in line for a free ride. Believe me, I see his kind every day. Men who, forgetting that children are involved, lash out any way they can to maintain a hold over their spouse. Men who use all manner of scare tactics to torment their wives mentally and physically. Men who would rather see their wives dead before they parted with a single dollar.

"By now, your husband's hired the toughest, meanest, most expensive lawyer at his firm. Meanwhile, you're sitting in that chair looking like Alice in Wonderland trying to figure out why it had to be you who fell down the rabbit hole. Believe me, stealing your credit cards and trying to sell the house right from under your feet is the least of the stunts he's likely to pull. Look for him to try to gain custody of the children by accusing you of being an unfit mother. You, who's done your best all these years to be the perfect wife and mother. You're the one who's remained faithful and true. And look where it's gotten you. No matter how hard you search your brain to gain an understanding, you may never know what caused your husband to start behaving so irrationally."

Her client was staring at the carpeted floor with a pained expression. She could tell Erika was caught up in past memories of a once-upon-a-time sweet and wonderful and rosy marriage. She figured that probably flashing through her client's brain were snapshots of memorable occasions that in reality were little more than a flight of her imagination. What reasonable person *would* want to remember being socked in the jaw or kicked in the gut when they could fantasize about the rose handed to them just before the beat down? The mind rarely wanted to hang onto such rough and tumble images anyway. Attorney Dowder knew her client was in that predivorce state where she was still questioning what she could have done differently. It was typical of wives who never dreamt they'd be left staring at the short end of the stick, while "Mr. Used-to-be-Right" was off, busy impressing the new soon-to-be, "Mrs. Right."

Attorney Dowder sighed inwardly as she glanced at her watch. She would give Erika sixty seconds to get over it. Later, in the privacy of her own home, her client could take all the time she needed to pretend she could still smell the roses. While they were on the attorney's clock, Dowder needed her focused, able to move on to weightier matters. Given she'd little patience for wimpy weeping willows, the initial client meeting was always the most trying for the attorney. The thrill of the battle was what engaged Dowder. The quicker she brought Erika up to snuff, the better. She needed her prepared for conflict—not stuck in a "woe-is-me" corner stewing in a valley of tears. *"Don't cry. Get revenge!"* was the attorney's motto.

Pop. Pop. Pop. Dowder impatiently snapped her fingers to get Erika's attention. When Erika looked up with a sad face, the attorney jolted her out of the doldrums.

"Listen to me, Erika. From this point forward, you must think of yourself and your children. The personal protection order you've obtained is a good start. However, there are other matters which you must consider—such as your current and future financial straits. Since your husband controls the purse strings and has already proven himself untrustworthy, we'll freeze all assets immediately to ensure he doesn't drain your accounts."

Pacing back and forth, her voice and hand motions became animated as she reeled off a series of "next steps."

"We'll begin discovery proceedings today to gather facts in preparation for your divorce. We'll request financial documents and depositions. But we won't wait for the information to strike. We've got enough to bury Michael right now. Adultery, domestic battery, child abuse, neglect, identity theft and outright fraud. The son-of-a-bum'll be lucky if we leave him with a nail on which to hang his hat."

Seeing the glazed-over look on Erika's face, Attorney Dowder stood right in front of her and fixed her with a hard stare. "We're going to hit Michael with a double whammy. Not only will we freeze all of his assets, we'll have the court award you temporary custody of the children. We'll simply tell the judge that he abused Mia, battered you and terrorized the two other children. Toughen up, Erika, because as we paint your husband as a "Dead Beat Dad," he isn't going to take it lying down. Deny him access to the children. And if he tries to come back into your home, call the police.

"This may seem harsh, but it's time to face up to the fact that your soon-to-be ex-husband is quite capable of snatching your babies just to get back at you. You've heard the expression, 'hell hath no fury like a woman scorned.' Well, fearsome and terrifying is the vindictive man who holds the power to his wife's physical, mental and financial well being. Thinking he holds all the high cards, your husband will be quite anxious to display them."

I can't do this, Erika thought. *I can't accuse Michael of these things.* "Attorney Dowder, I realize this is your profession and that you're very good at it. But isn't there some other way? I mean, this whole process already feels slimy and grotesque."

"Look, Kid, I know this is all new to you. I promise you, I'm just looking out for your welfare. You may not see it now, but you'll thank me long before this process is over. My methods may seem cruel, but I've learned from experience that strength respects strength. Your husband is counting on you to be a doormat, Erika. If you honestly believe a man who'd sell your home without caring whether you and the children he fathered have a place to lay your heads is worth all the tears you've shed, then you might as well leave right now because I can't help you. I don't sell Brooklyn Bridges, but I can guarantee you'll have a roof over your head when it's all said and done.

"You're not the only wife who's been forced to face these facts. Most times, when a divorcee such as yourself wants to quietly go about the painful business of ending a miserable, cruddy marriage, it's always the controlling spouse who won't let that happen. Even though all you want, is to peacefully get on with your life.

You have to look to the future, Erika. Ask yourself, 'How are you and your children going to survive?' The last thing you want to believe right now is that your husband of seventeen years would kick you and your children out on the street without a penny to your name. Yet, it happens every day. Here, don't take my word for it, take theirs."

As if on cue, the lights lowered and a pair of cabinet doors opened to reveal a 27-inch plasma screen TV. A rolling slideshow opened with images of a happy family frolicking in a huge backyard filled with children's toys. A man wrestled in the grass with five children and the family dog all scrambling on top of him. A woman flashing a huge grin stood nearby cooking hot dogs and hamburgers on a grill. In the next set of pictures, the season changed as the children were sitting around a Christmas tree happily unwrapping gifts. The husband and wife snuggled near a fireplace sharing a light kiss.

The next photo, however, was disturbing. It was the same house, but where before it was beautifully decorated with love and expensive furnishings, it was now barren. The front of the home flashed on screen with a "For Sale" sign in the front yard. The house that seemed so vibrant, now had a depressed quality about it. The children who once were happy, now appeared destitute as they stood with their mother just outside a homeless shelter. The slideshow continued with more images of other happy families that ended grimly with the mother and children standing in front of shelters or YWCAs. The last slides were of abused women with bruises on their faces and bodies.

It was a riveting slideshow. From lavish million dollar homes to the degradation of homeless shelters, obviously none of the women pictured envisioned the outcome they were faced with. The images left only one thought emblazoned on the viewer's mind. "If this happened to them, it could happen to me."

Imagining herself in similar circumstances, Erika slowly inhaled a strong dose of reality. Though her mind was telling her it could never happen to her, she remembered every one of Michael's dire threats. She couldn't risk ending up like the women in the photos, finding her bank accounts emptied, facing financial ruin, losing her home and not receiving a dime in support.

Convinced that Michael was fueled by anger and greed along with a vindictive desire to punish her, she now believed him capable of anything. Erika made her decision and relinquished control of her divorce to Attorney Dowder. By the time she signed all the papers, Erika left the attorney's office thinking she'd need a gun to protect herself from Michael.

As she walked to her car, Erika glanced at the stack of materials she'd been given to read. On top was a copy of the New York Times Bestseller, *"How To Conduct A Dirty Divorce Without Losing Your Sanity Or Your Finances!"* Erika took note of the author's name. She wasn't the least surprised to discover that Attorney Sheila Dowder had written the book.

Chapter Twenty-Two

"I could kill her. I swear to God, I could strangle her with my bare hands!" Michael banged his fist on the waisthigh counter.

"Mike, as your attorney, I'm advising you not to say another word." Keith Olbermann glanced around the inventory room to see if those standing nearby were listening to his not-so-wise client. Luckily, the workers behind the counter were busy filling out paperwork or retrieving property. The patrons standing in line on either side of them were engrossed in conversation, or too impatient themselves to leave the Marion County Jail, to pay attention to Michael's tirade. Although, a few of them did cast admiring glances his way.

Michael bared his teeth as he seethed. His blood was boiling as he lowered his voice to speak through clenched teeth. "Filthy animals took my goddamned clothes, Keith. In case you hadn't noticed, I'm standing in my briefs. Thieving bastards even stole my shoes. What kind of popsicle joint are the police running here?"

Keith nodded sympathetically, thankful not to be in his friend's shoes. Or lack thereof given that he'd just been stripped of everything except his birthday suit and a pair of drawers. "Your anger is understandable, Mike. Just let me do the talking, okay? We need to worry about getting you out of here with clothes on. The last thing you can afford is for a photographer to snap your picture leaving a jail house. I don't have to remind you how well that would go over back at the firm."

Michael groaned at the thought of the senior partners at Haliburton seeing his picture in the paper labeled as a common criminal. All the many times he'd been featured in the Wall Street Journal and the New York Times wouldn't even be remembered. He had fought too hard to carve out his corporate image to have it go up in flames over rap charges he wasn't even guilty of.

Earlier, Michael had been inside one of the Marion County Jail's holding cells sitting on the floor with his back against the wall like the other prisoners. The holding cells were built to accommodate a maximum of six people. Overcrowded and short on space, he'd been forced to share a cell with a host of notable pillars of the community—local drug dealers, gangbangers, rapists and pimps. Dressed as he was in his designer suit, he stood out from the hoodlums with their lowhanging jeans, wife-beater teeshirts, FUBU jackets and Timberland boots, like a three-legged wildebeest among wolves. Seconds after the guards pushed him inside the cell and

vanished from the scene, Michael was surrounded by a pack of ten street pharmacists all admiring his "slammin' rags."

"Deezam! Lookit dis old-skool ballah! He be dippin' in da bling-bling!" one of them shouted in admiration.

"Whutup dough, Playah-Pimp?" asked another punk as he eagerly hopped off the top bunk to go inspect the newbie.

"Pimp-Daddy mus' got sum ser'ous cheddah! Whut chu in fo, nig?" Without waiting for a response, he said quickly, "I got dibs on nem kicks. Hand em ova."

For the life of him, Michael couldn't understand a word the thugs were saying, but it didn't take a genius to figure out they wanted his clothes and shoes.

"Yo man, you don' need to be all up in ma grill, lessin you wont me ta put dat smack-a-lackin on ya! Gif up da kicks, mithi-ficki, else I gotta can of whoop-ass rite here wit cho name on it!"

At least that's what it sounded like he'd said to Michael, given that the boy-punk had a mouthfull of silver hardware where his every tooth was capped with some kind of faux diamond design. One by one, each of the twenty-something year olds surrounding him demanded an item from his person. With no guard anywhere in sight, Michael figured it in his best interest to donate his $3,500 Versace suit and his $1K Mezlan Brando shoes, than to be killed or beaten to a pulp. As he stripped and tossed them his clothing, it was his ears that felt assaulted. The ghetto slang they were using was so offensive and foreign to him that Michael gave up trying to comprehend what they were talking about. He couldn't help but think, *"A half a century spent fighting for civil rights and this is the end result? Where was Bill Cosby when you needed him?"*

Hours earlier on that same Friday evening, Michael had been enjoying dinner with Jamarra at an upscale eatery in Beech Grove, IN. As they exited the restaurant and handed their parking ticket to the valet, three Marion County Police Officers appeared out of nowhere and ordered him to hit the ground. At first, Michael had looked around, sure that the officers were out to apprehend someone standing behind him. By the time he figured out they were talking to him, guns were drawn and he was forced to the ground with a pistol pointed to the back of his head.

Michael was handcuffed, read his rights and roughly jerked to his feet. Though he kept proclaiming to the officers that they had the wrong man, he was thrown into the back seat of the police cruiser. Just before they slammed the car door, he managed to call out to Jamarra, who was being held at bay by a fourth officer, "Get a hold of my attorney, Keith Olbermann!"

They drove Michael straight to the Marion County Jail where he was booked at the police station. He was taken to a search area where he was subjected to a rough-rub search before all his property was seized, inventoried, and sealed in a bag. They fingerprinted him and snapped his picture all while ignoring his requests to call his lawyer. The only thing they would tell him was that there was a warrant for his arrest and that he was being held on domestic battery charges. Michael was informed that because it was a Friday night, he would have to remain in police custody 48 hours pending a court hearing the following Monday morning.

Thus, he'd spent a harrowing two days in the filthy foulsmelling, urine-reeking cell. No way would he touch the garbage they served as food. When Monday finally arrived, Michael never even went before the judge. Keith Olbermann went on his behalf and paid the bail which was set at $150,000.

As he stood in line with Keith, the embarrassing events replayed through Michael's mind over and over in an endless loop.

"In over forty years, Keith, I've never been arrested. Never even been pulled over for DWB and now, all because of one woman, I find myself incarcerated and falsely accused of every imaginable crime." Michael shook his head. Nearly every black man he knew had a horror story of being pulled over by the cops for "Driving While Black." That he'd managed to avoid that trap and still found himself in jail on trumped-up charges, filled him with rage.

"At first I couldn't understand why, since you were arrested in Beech Grove, they didn't take you to the local Police Department, as opposed to bringing you back here to Marion County. However, after I looked over your arrest warrant, Mike, I realized this was done to send a message. Have you ever heard of Attorney Sheila Dowder?"

In no mood to play guessing games, Michael said grimly, "No. I haven't."

"The woman is bad news. She's an adversarial divorce attorney and she's worse than any ambulance chaser you've ever dreamed of. Unfortunately for you, she's representing your wife. Before your divorce is over, I guarantee you're going to know far more about her than you bargained for. She had a private investigator trailing you. That's how she knew when and where to have you busted. It's her doing that reporters are suddenly hanging out in front of the station."

Bitterness laced Michael's voice. "Then I should just kill her *and* my wife. That would solve all my problems right there."

Keith started to warn him again about voicing idle threats but it was Michael's turn to claim his items. Instead, he said to the worker, "My client's wardrobe was confiscated by his cellmates, can you issue him something to wear?"

She looked Michael over saying, "Happens all the time. Let me see if we have some greens in stock." She returned minutes later carrying a mint green jumpsuit that looked like the previous owner had dragged it through the mud.

Keith spotted a man in line behind them who was near Michael's height and build. He said, "I have a plan to avoid the media."

Before Michael could turned the key in the lock, the door to the townhouse was snatched open. Jamarra stood just behind it with her head poking out waiting for him to step inside. The moment he cleared the entrance, she threw her arms around his neck. Standing on her tiptoes, she planted a solid kiss on Michael's lips.

Behind them, Keith closed the front door and cleared his throat.

With a wry grin on his face, Michael made introductions. "Keith, this is Mara. And this, babe, is my attorney who sprung me from jail, Keith Olbermann."

Oblivious to the fact that she was nearly naked, Jamarra stepped to Keith and extended her hand.

Keith must have shaken it. He couldn't remember. Caught up as he was in the vision that stood before him. Keith knew he should look away. Tried to do so, in fact. But his eyes were glued to the girl in front of him. Her caramel-colored body was scantily covered in a pair of pink lace boy shorts that rivaled a bikini. She was about 5'9" and looked to be all curves and legs. Unable to stop his eyes from pouring over her lithe body, he noted the narrowness of her waist and the perfect-sized breasts that strained against the see-through pink lace material like ripe melons.

Michael must have whispered for her to go put some clothes on because she turned and drifted up the stairs. The lower half of her wellrounded behind was bare for all to see and Keith found himself watching her cheeks sway with fascination, until she disappeared from his view. *Talk about junk in the trunk.*

"Mara has that effect on men."

Keith's face reddened as he cleared his throat, "I'm sorry about that. You should have warned me." The girl had a face like Toni Braxton (or was it Pam Grier?) and definitely had a body like Beyonce. *This girl spells trouble,* he thought to himself. It would be weeks before Keith would be able to purge her image from his memory.

"Apology accepted. Let's go into the dining room." Michael led the way.

Keith followed him, taking note of how sparsely furnished the place was, as if the occupants had recently moved in. It wasn't that the house didn't look lived in, it just didn't have that "woman's touch." There was not a single knick knack and no pictures adorned the walls.

"Whose place is this, Mike?"

"It belongs to Mara. I picked it up eighteen months ago for a steal."

Keith took a seat at the dining room table. "How long have we been friends, Mike?"

"Uh oh. I can tell by the look on your face, this can't be good."

"I cut my vacation in the Galápagos Islands short to fly back here. That's what took me so long to get you out of that place. I didn't get your friend's messages until yesterday. You're not going to like what I have to say, Mike."

"Fair enough. First, give me ten minutes. I'm dirty and I smell foul. Ten minutes in the shower will change all of that."

Keith suspected showering wasn't all Michael was anxious to go upstairs to do. Knowing he wouldn't be disturbed, as soon as Michael departed, Keith gave himself an uninvited tour of the first floor of the townhouse. True to his earlier impression, the house was furnished sparingly as if the livingroom and dining room sets were ordered as an afterthought. The kitchen was the exception. It was the only room he saw that had a lived-in feel. There were plenty of pots and pans and the fridge and cabinets were stocked with food. He helped himself to the hot pot of coffee on the counter.

Exactly twelve minutes later, Michael came down the stairs dressed in a casual shirt and pants looking refreshed in more ways than one. They took seats at the dining room table and Keith removed a packet from his briefcase.

"I'll spare you the mano-a-mano talk. I have the sense I would only be wasting my breath. I hope you know what you're getting yourself into, Mike. How old is she?"

There was no need to ask who "she" was. "Twenty."

"At least she's over the legal age limit. But that doesn't stop me from pointing out, Mike, that your decisionmaking of late has been considerably short of shrewd."

"Sixteen years is how long we've known each other, Keith. We've always been straight shooters since we watched each other's back at the old firm."

"True. We've been brothers in many ways, Mike. You being black, me being Jewish, racial differences never made a dent in our friendship." Keith opened the packet and removed the contents and spread them before Michael. "So who better than me to give you, as they say, the straight dope?"

"Son of a b!tch!" Michael glared at the incriminating photos. "She's gone too far, Keith."

Keith rubbed his forehead. He'd been astonished when he first saw the photos himself. "Mike, as far as I know, every accusation in these documents is a lie. The picture of Erika with the split lip and swollen jaw, for all I know it could be the work of a makeup artist. As your attorney, if you tell me that's what it is, we can fight on those grounds. Credit card fraud, child endangerment, abuse, neglect, the charges are pretty damning. But what really has me worried, Mike, are the photos of you and your friend upstairs. You've been followed, Mike, so add philandering to the ever-growing list."

Several of the pictures of him and Jamarra were taken in different cities he'd traveled to on business.

"When Tiffany and I went through our marital woes, who more than anyone else, talked us into staying together? In case you can't recall, it was you, Mike. I didn't even know you and Erika were separated." Keith was waiting for Michael to defend himself but his client remained silent.

"You've been married longer than I have, Mike. You're just going to throw all that away? What about your children? You're throwing them away too? For what, Mike? A girl who's half your age? You really think five years from now she'll still want you hanging around her?" Keith shook his head, unable to comprehend his friend's astounding lack of judgment.

He picked up the photo of Erika. "I can't even wrap my mind around the thought of you hitting Erika. And what gives with the credit card fraud? What the hell were you thinking, Mike? Yes, the girl upstairs is a beauty, but it doesn't change the fact that she's twenty years old. You're willing to throw away your marriage for a May-December piece of tail?"

"I didn't mean to hit her, Keith. It just happened. The credit card charges are lies. I have no clue what she's talking about." But he said nothing of his intentions toward his lover.

"Mike, even if I wanted to, I don't have the time to take on a divorce case. I'm up to my ears in litigation. I don't think I'd be the best person to represent you anyway. This Dowder woman, she's going to ruin you, Mike. It's not just about money with her. She genuinely hates men who cheat on their wives. Right now, with all that she's got on you, I'd advise you to settle the case out of court so none of this dirt makes it into the papers. Get them to agree to have the details of the divorce sealed. If it leaks, don't think Haliburton won't cut its losses, Mike. You could steal a half a billion dollars from someone and nobody at Haliburton would bat an eye. Become known as someone who beats his wife and you're a pariah, a public relations nightmare."

Keith picked up one of the photos of Michael and Jamarra leaving the Omni Hotel in Manhattan.

"But I can tell you'd rather fight the charges because you're tuning me out. Fine, as long as you recognize the risks involved. If you can't give this girl up, which is my recommendation, then give Erika half your net worth and move on with your life. What's your portfolio worth? Roughly $50 to $100 million? Settle this thing now, Mike, before it blows up in your face. If she takes you to court, you run the risk of losing much more than that. Unless you can buy yourself a male judge, it's unlikely you'll find sympathy in court. That's all I have to say, Mike. You've got until Friday to decide what to do. Don't bother getting up. I can show myself out."

"Nonsense." Michael saw Keith to the door.

They shook hands before Keith walked down the steps to his car. "What the..." His mouth dropped open as he stood staring in dismay. All four of his tires were slashed.

Michael ran down the steps and walked around the car. "It's that goddamned Erika. I'm telling you, Keith, she's not the angel you think she is."

Something made Keith glance up at the second floor window of the townhouse. Jamarra was staring down at him with a look that he couldn't decipher. Hatred? Malice? The look she threw him fell somewhere in between. At that moment, Keith knew what it was about the girl that disturbed him. As physically pleasing as she was to look at, genuine warmth was missing from her eyes. She had a coldness about her that hinted she viewed people with the same displeasure that some might view a bug. Something about her indicated that to her, people *were* bugs.

Michael may have been convinced that it was Erika who had put his car on all flats, but Keith didn't believe it for a second.

Jamarra stared down at Keith Olbermann with a cold glint in her eye. He really didn't realize how lucky he was that it was just his tires that got cut. Anybody who tried to separate her from Michael was in for a deadly surprise. Clearly, Keith was an enemy.

And speaking of enemies, Jamarra couldn't wait to spring the trap she had carefully laid for Erika.

But a new person was now added to her hit list. Tomorrow, she'd find out just who this Sheila Dowder woman was. She, too, might have to be eliminated.

Part V

"It is difficult to know at what moment love begins;
It is less difficult to know that it has begun."

~ Henry Wadsworth Longfellow

"For it was not into my ear you whispered, but into my heart.
It was not my lips you kissed, but my soul."

~ Judy Garland

Chapter Twenty-Three

"How is it changing my mind if I didn't know about it? I'm only saying you should have told me in advance."

"I see. Like the advance notice you gave me about your crooked friends back in Provo? What gives, Jayson? Is it because they can't pay through their noses to have their photos taken with you? I never figured you for a snob."

"That's not it at all. This is different, Aaryn."

"Fine." Aaryn knew when to back off. "At least tell me why you're so adverse to it."

They were parked in a reserved spot on the first floor of an indoor parking garage. Through the tinted windows of Aaryn's SUV, Jayson stared at the words flashing on the overhead LED sign: Welcome to The Children's Research Hospital.

His profile was turned away from her as she waited for his response. When his fist clenched on top of his thigh, she knew he was reliving some distant memory from his past. Though the silence remained unbroken, she sensed waves of anger emanating from him. Moments later, the waves were followed closely by pockets of grief and pain. Curious as to what was causing the groundswell of emotions, Aaryn leaned over and slid her hand on top of his. Her fingers curled over his knuckles and her entire demeanor softened.

"Forget it, Jayson. You're right. I should have told you what I had in mind. Why don't we…" A flash flood of images from Jayson's past assaulted Aaryn's senses. A young Jayson trustingly held the hand of a girl slightly older than him as she led him across a wide street. Him, hiding behind a bush waiting to ping the same girl with a huge snowball. Him, older now, standing in a kitchen watching his sister hastily eat the remains of a chicken drumstick. Him, filled with agony at the realization that drugs were slowly draining the life from her emaciated figure.

"I'm so sorry, Jayson." Aaryn whispered the words because she could feel the vale of pain buried inside him. Painful memories of his sister that he'd kept hidden away from the world were fighting to surface. Asking him to visit the children's hospital had somehow triggered memories of his loss. He'd never spoken to anyone about how deeply Carmin's death had affected him. Whereas the hurtful memories should have healed and faded with time, they had stockpiled into a huge ball of anguish and sorrow.

Something in her voice caused Jayson to look at her. A tender quality stemming from empathy or some recognition of his loss told him she knew of his pain. The moment his eye met hers, something passed between them. *Trust me. Your secret's safe with me.* She hadn't spoken the words aloud but Jayson heard them in his mind

as clear as a cricket on a midsummer's eve. His fist unballed and she slid her fingers between his. Without hesitation, his hand closed to squeeze her fingers. From nowhere, a blinding flash of pain hit Jayson in the frontal lobe of his brain. It felt like someone had smashed a bottle against his head.

Jayson's hand grabbed the side of his head and Aaryn quickly leaned her body into his. She slid her palm around the nape of his neck and pulled his head toward hers. Their foreheads rested against each other as she gripped him tightly. Over and over she whispered softly, "It's okay."

With his emotions threatening to erupt, Aaryn knew he wanted to bolt, so she gripped him tighter. Her words came in a whispered rush. "Your sister loved you so very much, Jayson. Her death was not your fault. She was battling forces much too strong for her. The advanced stages of her illness coupled with all the drugs she was using…" Aaryn struggled to find a better way to articulate that Carmin had battled a host of demonic spirits. Finding none, she simply said, "She was out of her league and fighting a losing battle."

His eyes were closed as he shook his head. "I don't want to hurt you, Aaryn. Let me go."

When she felt him pulling away she said, "Shhhh. Just listen to me, please? Give me thirty seconds." Aaryn pulled Jayson's head down to the crook of her shoulder. She wrapped her arms around his shoulders and clasped her hands together.

"You meant more to Carmin than life itself, Jayson. She knew how much you loved her and that love was the most precious gift she had. It hurt her to come around you because she couldn't stand seeing the wounded look in your eyes. She knew she was dying of AIDS. Your mother knew it, too, but they chose not to tell you." Aaryn felt his body jerk.

"In the end, Carmin didn't want you to see her as she was. She wanted you to remember her as a beautiful girl. Even in death, she never stopped loving you. There was nothing you could have done to save her, because she didn't want to be saved. Toward the end, all Carmin wanted was to slip unnoticed from this world. That was her choice, Jayson. It's time to stop berating yourself for her death. It's time to forgive yourself. It's time to release the guilt so you can heal."

Aaryn heard Jayson's low, muffled groan. She could feel his head turning from side to side against her shoulder and she could feel moistness seeping into her jacket. Aaryn knew the release of his tears was a hard thing for him. Even when she felt some of the tension go out of his body, she continued to hold him, rocking gently, whispering softly and stroking her right hand down his back. Minutes passed before he moved to pull away. This time, Aaryn released him.

Jayson leaned back against his seat with his eyes closed. He felt drained, as if surge of energy had left his body. "How do you know these things about Carmin Did my Mom tell you? Why didn't she tell me?" Jayson turned to stare at her. "An how can you break a person down like that? Tell me the truth. Do you practic sorcery?"

"Your mother hasn't spoken to me about your sister. I'm waiting, thoug because I believe it to be a key to her healing. And no, I do not practice witchcra The very term offends me. Do you know so little about the spirit world, Jayson? (do you only believe in things that you can see, touch, taste and feel?" Aaryn shoc her head at his skeptical look. "Let me ask you something. Have you ever seen yo thoughts? No? Then how do you know that you can think?"

Jayson threw her a look that said, "Oh, come on!"

"You just know it, right? You don't question it. Well, that's how the spir world works, Jayson. You can't see it with your natural eyes. You can't touch with your fingers. But you can sense it. You can intuit it. And you can feel it *wi* your senses.

"Ever since I was a little girl, I've seen things about people that I never asked see. How, I couldn't begin to explain. I touch someone and I see their pa experiences. If they're ill, I can see when death is coming. And somehow, I kno when people are lying, Jayson. The only way I can describe it is to say we all hav an energy field. It doesn't matter how clear or toxic a person's spirit is, I can rea them like a map. If someone's lying or if they're sick, their energy emits a certa color and I can pick up on it like you could snatch a lightning bug out of the air.

"My twin sister, Erika, she could peer into the future. She hated being able to (that, so she shut down her gift and turned away from everything—even her famil And Dot? She can see past *and* future. We're a weird bunch, Jayson. The thing th keeps us sane is that we've channeled our abilities into healing. We don't (psychic hotlines. Although, Dot used to occasionally work with a special unit of tl FBI when they needed help tracking a particularly heinous killer. But she doesn't (that anymore because it takes too much out of her. She might tell you about it if yc ask her. Now, she focuses on plants. Me? I've chosen to heal people.

"Since I'm batting a thousand here, I'll tell you something else you're not goir to believe. Those men back in Provo were evil people, Jayson. Don't becom involved with them. Make your film, but severely limit your contact with them. It not just your money they're after. They want your soul. And that's a whole oth discussion unto itself. I won't even touch it because if I shared some of the thin, I've seen in the spirit realm, you'd really think I was off my rocker."

Aaryn saw the thoughtful expression on his face. She looked at hi challengingly. "That's it. That's who I am. Still attracted to me after learning a that? I doubt it."

Jayson stared straight ahead. It was a lot to take in. He was weighing what he knew of her against all that she'd revealed.

"Why don't I call a cab so you can ride back to your car? I'd drop you off myself but I have to be back here in fifteen minutes." Aaryn reached in the back seat for her purse. Her cell phone was in it.

Jayson grabbed hold of her hand. "So, you just drop all that on me and I'm supposed to do what? Run? Forget I ever met you? I don't scare that easily, Doc." Jayson looked at her hand which was engulfed in his. "I believe you, Aaryn, even though I don't understand it. I don't believe in things like UFOs but I'm broad minded enough to know that there are things that exist that no one has a valid explanation for. When I was a kid, I remember reading a section of the bible that said God created the worlds. Worlds. Not singular, but plural. So I used to wonder whether this was the only world God had made. But as I grew older, I stopped thinking about things like that. I prefer things that I can see, touch, taste and feel. I prefer to have my feet on solid ground. Life's much simpler that way. And no, what you shared with me doesn't change the way I feel. I still want to get to know you. What's wrong with that?" He tightened his grip on her hand when she moved to pull it from his. There was the slightest pause in his voice as he added, "I want to know everything there is about you."

Jayson shifted his body so that he was facing her. His eyes bored into hers. As he devoured her, it wasn't great beauty that he saw. He saw a woman full of compassion. He saw a complex woman who was busy keeping the world around her at bay. He saw a woman who he'd fight tooth and nail to get closer to. He saw a woman who made his loneliness disappear. Surprisingly, he saw someone to whom he wanted to be more than just a friend. Jayson saw a woman he could care deeply about—someone that he could grow to love.

Love? Jayson had no clue where that thought came from. He only knew it must have been there in the back of his mind.

Aaryn made a mistake by looking into his eyes. There was no deception there. Only naked intent. An intent to own, an intent to possess. And being possessed by Jayson would mean...An image of him slowly loving her as she lay on a bed of white silken sheets glided through her mind. Hastily, she squashed the tantalizing vision. Still, Aaryn's heart raced almost as fast as her temperature was rising.

At the intentional look on his face, she turned away. "There's nothing more to learn, Jayson. Let me go."

"What are you afraid of?" He refused to release her.

"I'm not afraid of anything. I'm not." Aaryn spoke the last words as if to convince herself.

"Okay. You want me to play hero to the kids in the hospital? I'll make a deal with you. I'll come inside with you, if you do one thing for me." His thumb started drawing lazy circles on the back of her hand. An innocent move that unexpectedly sent heated tremors through both of them.

Though her concentration was deserting her, she snapped around to look at him. "What?" Her tone was cautious and mistrustful. She became even more wary when she saw the smile on his face.

"Kiss me."

Her eyes were drawn to his lips even as she shook her head. "You're crazy."

"But you know that already." Jayson edged toward her, his smile broadening.

Aaryn inched backwards toward the door.

"No. That would be bribery. Besides, I…" If she moved any closer to the door, she'd be out of the car.

"Just one kiss."

"You're insane." Aaryn fumbled to unlock her door. All she knew was that she had to escape.

Jayson reached for her so swiftly that she felt like a cornered rabbit. His one hand pulled her toward him as his other hand gently wrapped around her neck.

"One kiss," he whispered as his thumb pushed her chin upward.

Time stood still as his body hovered over her. Unhurriedly, his lips drifted downward to meet hers. At their touch, he slowly explored their softness, parting them gently with his tongue. Tenderly, like velvet whispering across silken skin, his tongue tasted her, savored her, pressured her. She tasted like honey and lemons as he leisurely enjoyed the feel of her mouth. One kiss. A slow, tender heated kiss. A kiss that pulsed with passion. As tingling sensations filtered through his every nerve ending, he could feel himself melting into her. With one kiss, he had the sense he was embarking on a new journey. A journey that went beyond the usual temporary burst of satisfaction—a journey that promised him a deeper, more fulfilling level of satiated pleasure. One kiss. A kiss like no other, Jayson found himself basking in the moment even as he forced her tongue to accept and mate with his. A kiss that left him content, yet yearning to experience her even more.

Aaryn felt like she was immersed in a liquid pool of shimmering magic. Tingling sensations shivered through her veins. This was much more than one kiss. It was an exploration of her soul. It was a kiss that burned a trail of molten lava down to the tips of her toes. Never had she been kissed like this—until she felt lost, robbed of strength and filled with a deep euphoria. Never had she given in to such deep abandonment. The willingness to trust, the need to let herself go completely and the desire to be owned by this man, was intense. *Leap and the net will appear.*

As she reveled underneath his strength and tenderness, the world around her became one muted sound. The wet feel of him, the unexpected gentleness that hinted of a restrained wildness and the overwhelming feeling of being carried away to a place where nothing else other than him mattered—it was all there as his lips engulfed hers. It was there as a naked hunger enflamed her and demanded satisfaction.

It was still there even as Jayson reminded them both that a world existed beyond the shelter of the SUV. He raised his head from hers.

"Wow." The breathless wonder that filled her voice seeped into her facial expression.

"Wow, indeed." Heated sensations still pulsed within his members.

Needing just a bit more of her, his lips lowered again to nibble gently at hers, pulling them, suckling them, commanding them to yield.

The kiss had left Aaryn with little strength to resist the onslaught of gentle bites to her lips and corners of her mouth. She managed to raise her fingertips to rest upon his lips. In a faint voice, she reminded him, "You said one kiss."

"So I did. What was I thinking?"

"You're really a very sweet man, Jayson."

He groaned at the regretful note he heard in her voice. "Woman, no man wants to be told that he's sweet. It's the kiss of death."

"Really?" Aaryn was simply trying to gather her faculties. It *had* only been a kiss, right?

"Yes, really. Come on, let me get you inside. You're late as it is."

Late by fifteen minutes to be exact. She glanced at the dashboard but made no move to exit the SUV.

Jayson stared at her enervated figure. "Am I going to have to carry you again?"

"Absolutely not." She tried to stir herself.

Jayson got out and came around to her side of the vehicle. He opened the door and a look of concern dotted his face.

"Are you sure you're up to this? We could come back another time. I won't renege on you."

"No, I'm fine. I just feel like my breath was taken away. Do *you* practice sorcery?"

He laughed heartily. It was a rich sound that she liked. "I'm afraid I'm forbidden to. It's part of my acting contract. Ever since the time I…"

Aaryn's mouth opened wide to emit a great big, unladylike yawn.

"Jeez, Lady. You're really great for my ego, you know that?"

She laughed at him. Waving her hand, she said, "Forgive me. Go ahead with your story."

"Forget it. I'll find a more appreciative audience inside the hospital." With a mock scowl, he reached inside to help her from the vehicle.

❖

The mixed aroma of lemons, lobster sauce and freshly baked bread assailed Aaryn's nose as soon as she opened the front door of her home. Baron and Max greeted her with forlorn looks as she set her briefcase on the table in the foyer. The Great Danes were banned from the kitchen while Dot was cooking. They knew the routine and they had the look of a pair of outcasts.

"I'm home, Dot!" Aaryn called out as she headed upstairs. After the day's ordeal, she wanted a long bath.

Afterwards, she forced a comb through her hair and pulled it back into a gigantic ponytail that Diana Ross would have envied. She threw on a pair of mauve slacks with a matching sweater, added a pair of pink pearl earrings and a coat of lip gloss and headed downstairs. A whistle escaped her lips as she paused to admire the dining room table. Dot had brought out her best tableware on account of Jayson joining them for dinner. The floral centerpiece arrangement and the place settings were so elaborate it looked like they were dining at an upscale restaurant.

"Smells delicious, Dot. I hope I'm invited. What's on the menu?" Aaryn straddled one of the backless wooden stools under the marble kitchen island. She grabbed an apple from the oak fruit platter and bit into it as Dot flitted around the kitchen putting the finishing touches on her meal. "Roasted crab cakes in lobster sauce. It was a special request from Jayson."

"My, my. So you're taking special requests now, are you? I recall asking you to make crab cakes about two weeks ago and you nearly bit my head off. Said you weren't a maid and that you didn't have time to be slaving away in the kitchen. What has *he* done to receive such preferential treatment?"

"Daughter of mine, don't exaggerate and stop putting words in my mouth. I'm sure I said no such thing." Dot leaned over the sink to strain her pasta.

"I'm pretty sure those were your exact words. But I'll let it go since you seem to have conveniently forgotten. You look really nice, Dot. Who's the fourth table setting for?" *To be 78, she did look good,* Aaryn thought. Dot wore a burgundy dress that showed off her trim figure and highlighted her still beautiful legs. Her long silver hair was pinned elegantly atop her head. It was obvious who had taken greater pains with their appearance. Aaryn's bouffant ponytail looked like a lion's mane held in place by the strongest of rubber bands.

Dot came and stood across the island from Aaryn. "Ray will be joining us. When I mentioned I was baking crab cakes, he couldn't resist."

Aaryn smiled, "I'm sure the crab cakes aren't the only thing Ray can't resist. That man's smitten with you."

"Child, please. Ray Burns has his pick of houses he can go to for a home-cooked meal. Believe me, it's the food that he's coming for."

"Anything you say, Ma. But we both know he's sweet on you." Ray had been a good friend of the family for many years. He was the one who encouraged Aaryn to take up rock climbing as a young teen. Ray used to climb professionally but these days he owned and worked at The Front Climbing Club. Regardless of what was said, Aaryn knew he had a crush on Dot and she suspected it was mutual.

"Tell me what happened today. Something was going on with you around 3:30 this afternoon because I picked you up in the spirit. I was in the garden when I stopped planting and started interceding for you. I was going to call you, but after about thirty minutes or so, the feeling passed and I knew that all was well."

The two of them were so closely connected that it was common for them to sense when the other needed a lift in the spirit. Aaryn said, "Thank you, Ma. I needed it because today was really strange." She described all that had taken place in Provo.

"As we were leaving the Chamber of Commerce, that's when it hit me. I'm a guardian for him. Jayson's rich in so many ways, but in the spirit realm, he's vulnerable. He's literally a principality magnet." Aaryn set the apple on the counter. "I won't lie and say I wasn't disappointed to learn the true reason for our connection. I don't know why he affects me the way he does, but at least now I know why our paths have crossed." Aaryn sat up straight. "What do you see, Dot? I can tell from your facial expression that you've seen something. What is it?"

"Do you find him attractive?"

"What woman doesn't find him attractive?"

"Don't disseminate, Aaryn. You know I'm not referring to his physical looks. Do you find him attractive spiritually?" Dot would not allow her to skirt the question.

Aaryn stared at the ceiling fan. "I didn't at first, but he's grown on me. Somewhere between wanting to give him a good dressing down and wanting to smack him senseless, I find myself drawn to him. So, yes. As flawed a person as he is, I'm beginning to like him."

"Then don't close the door on that possibility. You protected him today. Continue to intercede for him. But, Aaryn, intercession may not be all there is to this budding relationship the two of you have."

269

"You aren't going to tell me, are you?" Aaryn was slightly piqued.

"Time itself will tell you, Love. Quit sulking and give me a hand here."

"Ma, I dreamed about Erika again last night. She's going through something, isn't she?"

"Yes. But it's of her own doing. When you've been given an assignment, you can't turn your back on it without facing the consequences. My prayers for her lately have been that, as the enemy tampers with everything around her, that he not be allowed to harm her or the children. Come, let's speak no more of Erika tonight."

Chapter Twenty-Four

Jayson followed the directions Aaryn had given him to her home. It was refreshing to have spent this much time without an entourage and the paparazzi in tow. But after this day, it seemed as if that was destined to change. His visit to the Children's Hospital would ensure that. It had gone better than he'd imagined. He'd thought the place would be gloomy and full of sickness but it had proven to be just the opposite. Because they were children, and didn't know any better, the only sadness he experienced came from the adults. The children themselves were full of laughter and play even in the distressed state that many of them were in.

It was upon his return to his hotel suite that things had taken a turn. He had stopped at Shriners to check on Syl before heading back to the Stein Eriksen Lodge. The light on his phone blinked ominously and he almost decided to wait before retrieving his messages. Twelve in total. There were threatening messages from PT, his PR guru. Pleading messages from members of his posse. And whining messages from Wendy, his assistant. All were threatening to descend upon Salt Lake City if he didn't return their phone calls. About the only person he hadn't heard from was Dez. But after checking the voicemail on his cell phone, he found that even Dez had called him three times. It seemed everyone was wondering if he was on crack cocaine or if he was being held hostage in what they labeled as that "Godforsaken wasteland." Jayson vowed to return their calls the next day. The thought of the entire gang intruding on his rare interlude was not a good one.

The other messages he ignored completely. Mostly, a bevy of invitations from women—many of them his peers—inviting him to brunch, lunch, dinner and breakfast in bed. The things some of the women offered to do to him left little doubt that they had no shame. Obviously, they didn't think he had any either. And if truth were being told, there were far too many times when he hadn't had any shame. But of late, his amoral nature seemed to have shifted.

The only call Jayson returned that evening was to the home of *A Season To Hunt's* Director. He wanted to give Ridley Scott the good news about the negotiated usage fee for Mt. Timpanogos.

As he showered and dressed, he thought back on his earlier visit with Syl. She'd wanted him to stay for dinner but he'd declined. He told her he'd made other dinner plans but didn't say with whom. Neither had he brought up the issue of Carmin's death. It angered him that he hadn't been told of her illness. Not that there was anything he could have done at the time, but he still would've liked to have known. At some point, he and Syl would have that discussion.

Jayson shifted his focus to the evening ahead, admitting to himself that he was more excited about Dot's dinner invitation than he was about several of his own movie premiers. And then there was Aaryn. The turn of events with her was completely unexpected. He'd known he was physically attracted to her but he hadn't thought there would be anything beyond that. When he was with her, something *felt* different. Unlike with other women, there was no pretense and no subterfuge. He knew he hadn't felt that raw, naked comfortableness with another woman since his days with Porsha. There! He'd said it. Now that it was out in the open, maybe he could admit that that was what troubled him. Too many of his interactions with Aaryn reminded him of his time spent with Porsha—times when he'd cared for another unguardedly. He'd loved Porsha in a way that he had vowed never to love another woman again—wholly, unconditionally and without thought for his own protection. Something about Aaryn challenged that vow which he'd made. She was simply an unusual woman. She didn't want anything from him. She didn't care about his stardom. Didn't care about his money. And she certainly wasn't into stroking his ego. No one could ever accuse her of that!

It wasn't even that she was among the most attractive women he knew. Still, there was a uniqueness about her that he couldn't define. She was the total opposite of the "typical" woman he tended to date. She wasn't Hollywood beautiful, didn't dress to the nines, and while most women he knew went out of their way to show off their "assets" she seemed to do otherwise. Was she a prude, he wondered? She didn't kiss like one. Jayson hoped she wasn't because he was a legs and a breast man. The good doctor did, however, seem to go to great lengths to draw people's attention away from her most flattering parts.

She intrigued him, is what she did. Despite her acid tongue and her less than sugar and spice demeanor, he was drawn to her like a bear to a pot of honey. The way she'd broken him down in the car and then comforted him was something he'd never before experienced. But did he really believe all that stuff about prophesy and what not? How else could he account for her knowing so much about Carmin? Hadn't he also questioned how Dot had known so many details about Syl?

Unbidden, Jayson recalled a time many years ago when he and Porsha had visited a tiny village in Romania about fifty miles from the city of Bucharest where their Vogue fashion shoot was set to occur. A fair was in progress on the grounds of the village, which was populated with gypsies. The two of them had squeezed through the crowd and landed in front of a fortune teller's booth. Once inside, Sylvia had looked at the woman and turned away. But Jayson had already taken a seat, so he pulled her down onto his lap. Laughing, he threw a hundred dollar bill on the old woman's rickety table and challenged her to tell their fortunes. Jayson kissed Porsha roughly and said, "I predict we'll be together forever. What say you?"

The old woman had scooped up the money and seemed to hesitate before speaking. Finally, she said in a thickly accented voice, "You will only share two more fortnights together." To Jayson, she said, "Your future is in the stars." She looked at Porsha and muttered the words, "*femeie nesăbuită,*" which meant "foolish woman" in Romanian. She tilted her head and said, "You already know the future, no?" At her illboding words, Porsha looked nauseated.

Her words held such finality that they sent chills up Jayson's spine and cast a pall over the remainder of their evening. Jayson stood abruptly, forcing Porsha to her feet. That evening, they made love with the fierce passion of lovers staving off the ending of an affair.

Less than two months later, the old gypsy woman's words had come to pass. Porsha had indeed left him and he went on to star in his first major film. Like the old woman had said, his future was in the stars. Coincidence or accurate prophesy?

As he shook off the old memories, Jayson wondered if that was the kind of ability that the Jamison women had. On face value, it felt eerie. But as long as he viewed them as regular people and not as anomalies, he continued to be intrigued.

❖

"Aaryn, can you get the door please. It's Jayson." Laughter drifted from the kitchen where Dot and Ray were talking as Aaryn went to answer the door.

He stood there dressed in his custom-made suit with his $1K tie looking for all the world like the handsome, well-sought-after movie star that he was. "A human weapon of mass destruction," Aaryn thought. "His picture should be featured alongside the words to define them. Surely, it was because of men like him that women fought their own private wars."

Aloud, she said, "Well, well, well. Look who's come for dinner. If it isn't Mr. Preferential Treatment, himself. Come to mingle with the local hillbillies, have you?" She stood inside the doorway with hands on hips. No offer was made for him to come inside.

"Puh-lease, Doctor. You wouldn't know a hillbilly if one dunked you in a pool of mud. Am I invited inside? Or will I be forced to dine on the front steps?"

"Depends. How much money have you got? We slaved for hours cooking your 'special request' of a meal. You can't just show up and expect to dine for free. Admission will cost you something."

"Hmmm. I wonder who the 'we' is that allegedly put forth so much effort. I've got about two bucks on me, Mam. If that's not enough I'll just have to give my good friend, Dot, a call and tell her I'm being squeezed out by a pintsized mobster claiming to have done all the cooking. You didn't know I was in tight with the owner of this establishment, did you? I'll also be sure to tell her how you gave me crooked directions in hopes that I wouldn't make it."

"I did no such thing!"

"Well then, it's your word against mine. Since I'm in such good graces with the owner, I'll take my chances."

A slight smile curved her lips. "And I wouldn't bet against you either. Being the rogue charmer that you are. I'm supposed to be her daughter, yet I've never received the royal treatment she's afforded you."

"I see. And because of this special treatment, I'm expected to pay up?" Jayson inched closer into the doorway. His voice lowered to a whisper as he said, "How about I pay you with a kiss?" He leaned toward her, an eager smile of anticipation on his lips.

Tiny spheres of pleasure slithered along Aaryn's nerve endings. She quickly stepped back and opened the door wide for his entrance. "Blackmail, bribery, enticement, why there's no end to your talents, is there, Sir?"

"Sure there is." Jayson advanced on her.

"Behave yourself, Denali," she hissed at him. But she was unable to contain her laughter at the sight of his leering grin.

"Shouldn't you close your front door?" She walked backwards as he walked forward.

"And be caught in your clutches? I think not. You close the door."

He shrugged. "I guess I'll have to go find the owner on my own then." She stood just beyond the entrance to the foyer.

Rolling her eyes, Aaryn returned to close the door. A mistake. Because as soon as she turned around Jayson was standing in front of her, forcing her back against the door.

"Just one kiss." The indelible imprint of sensual memories had caused him to thirst for her, creating in him an intense hunger.

She shook her head. "No way. That's what you said the last time." She put he
hand on his chest to keep distance between them. "You nearly sucked all the oxyge
from my body. I could barely think straight afterwards."

His body was inches from hers as Jayson pinned her against the door. "I lik
you when you're barely thinking. Saves me from that acerbic tongue of yours." Sh
smelled faintly of vanilla as he lifted her wrist to his mouth. Turning it slightly, h
began to plant tiny kisses on her skin.

At the series of light touches, Aaryn's knees grew weak. How was it possibl
that he affected her as he did? That one person could cause such havoc to he
orderly world wasn't fair.

Jayson held her knuckles tenderly to his lips. "I would have driven a thousan
miles to see you tonight."

"Help! I'm drowning," she screamed inwardly. Somehow, Aaryn tore herse
away from him. "Luckily for you," she said breathlessly, "you only had to drive
few miles. We both know you came for the food."

"Yes, the food of the gods. I thought I had to pay to join you tonight. Change
your mind so soon?" She certainly was skittish.

"Let's consider your presence as payment enough, shall we?"

"I was hoping for something more."

"Behave yourself tonight, Denali. I expect you to be a gentleman."

"Ah, if you expect me to wear my gentleman's hat tonight, you'll have to brib
me." He approached her and encircled her neck with his big, thick long fingers.

Her neck craned on its own as he caressed her throat. When his head lowered t
bite gently into the side of her neck, she melted against his chest. There was n
mistaking her reaction to him. Aaryn felt her nipples harden to the size of cherries.

Jayson felt them through his suit jacket. And as his gaze held hers, she kne
from the look of arousal that swept across his face, he was enjoying the feel of her.

The beast in him made him push her away just enough for him to stare down a
her luscious breasts. The needful way he stared at her made her nipples harden an
expand even more.

Feeling naked though she was fully clothed, Aaryn crossed her arms over he
chest. Embarrassed to the core, she could have sunk through the floor. Jayson ha
no way of knowing that for her, the largeness of her nipples had been a
embarrassment to her all her life. Generally, she wore extra thick gauze pads in he
bras to avoid the telling problem. She just hadn't worn them tonight.

Far from it being a problem for him, all Jayson wanted was to carry her off back to his suit at the Stein Eriksen and hopefully stay there forever. Sensing her embarrassment (she refused to look at him) he released her to get himself together.

"Did I ever tell you the story about the three-legged giraffe who got lost in the big city?"

Aaryn's eyes remained closed but a smile lifted her lips.

"Well, did I?" Unfortunately for him, her arms remained crossed over that beautiful chest of hers.

Aaryn looked up at him. "You are stupid, Denali."

"I doubt it. At least you're smiling again, aren't you?"

Dot's voice carried from deep inside the house.

"My goodness, I thought you two had been whisked away by the wind. What's taking you so long?"

Jayson stepped into the impressive, oversized room. The house was ablaze with light. "Dot, you look lovelier than ever." He walked toward her and embraced her heartily. "I would have been here sooner, but someone gave me bogus driving directions."

"That's absolutely untrue, Dot. My instructions were quite clear. The real problem is that your favorite actor can't read."

"That's good, Doctor. But I think it's really that chicken scratch of yours that you call writing. Your daughter flunked penmanship, Dot."

Looking from one to the other, Dot said, "I'm pleased to see the two of you finally getting along so well. Thank you again, Jayson, for the beautiful floral centerpiece. Of all the flowers I've *not* planted, only a very observant man would notice the lilies missing from my collection."

Jayson grinned and shrugged as if to say, "Shucks, Dot."

Standing behind and slightly to the side of Dot, Aaryn rolled her eyes. She should have guessed he'd bribed Dot in some form or fashion.

Dot couldn't see Aaryn, but Jayson could. The moment she uncrossed her arms to point inside her mouth as if she was gagging, his smile deepened as he allowed his eyes to feast on her breasts.

Shaking her head in exasperation, Aaryn said, "Excuse me, Dot. I'm going upstairs for a second."

"Sure, dear. But don't be long. We're eating as soon as I introduce Jayson to Ray."

"Don't change on my account, Aaryn. That color suits you well."

Aaryn kept walking toward the stairs. *Rotten goat,* she thought. As if he cared about what color she was wearing. Men! Can't live with them, debatable as to whether she could live without them. But even as the thought crossed her mind, Aaryn glanced down at her traitorous chest. She figured the excited state she found herself in answered the age old question of whether the male species was a necessity.

Chapter Twenty-Five

"It's good to meet you, Ray." Jayson recognized the tall, reddish haired man from the climbing club where he'd trailed Aaryn to some time ago. Ruggedly built, he appeared in excellent shape in his jeans and stark white shirt. His grip was solid.

"Same here. I've heard a lot about you."

"It's only true if you heard it from Dot. Discount whatever you hear from anyone else in this household. Do you climb, Ray?"

Those were magic words to Ray, who immediately engaged Jayson in conversation.

Everyone was seated when Aaryn returned. She took the empty seat on Jayson's right.

"Jayson's not a creeper, Ray. I'm sure he has no interest whatsoever in rock climbing."

Jayson examined her as he said, "I've done some indoor rock climbing. Nothing on the scale of anything you and Ray have accomplished."

"You have to be a little nutty to do the kind of climbing that they do, Jayson. I've never understood the attraction." Dot held out her hand to Ray and the other to Jayson, who was seated on her right. They all held hands when she said, "Will you bless the food, Ray?"

After the prayer, Jayson was curious about the nature of Dot and Ray's friendship. There was an ease between them that hinted they'd known each other for a long while. He wondered if they were more than friends. If so, he wondered how the good people of Utah felt about interracial dating.

When they removed the silver warming tops from their plates, Jayson was impressed.

"This looks scrumptious, Dot!" he said.

The oversized, oven-roasted crab cakes were served in a delicate lobster sauce made with cream and sweet red peppers. The cakes were accompanied by a bed of spinach fettuccine with asparagus spears cooked with olive oil. Two bottles of crisp white wine complimented the meal.

Ray said, "I've been trying to steal Dot's crab cake recipe for years. Haven't been able to wrestle it from her yet."

"Hmph. As if you're going to cook anything, Ray. I don't believe you know your way around the kitchen."

Aaryn said, "He knows, Dot. He just pretends not to so you'll take pity on him."

Dot waved away Aaryn's remark. "They say presentation is everything, Jayson. Aaryn tells me even the worst of meals can appear palatable if I present it lavishly. I've learned to cook well in order to get a certain finicky person to eat." But their compliments pleased her.

"Don't blame it on me. You've always enjoyed cooking, Dot."

"It was more of a necessity than anything else. Tell us about the hospital visit, Jayson. I hear you made quite a few new fans."

"Ma, it was hysterical! You should have seen the looks on everyone's faces."

"Excuse me? Is your name Jayson? I believe Dot was speaking to me." Jayson sipped from his wine glass.

Aaryn swatted the air beside her. "No, Denali. You have to let me tell this. The kids went crazy, Ray. When I brought him into the play area, they all started screaming, 'Mr. Incredible!' They gathered around him like he was their personal Christmas gift. Touching him, hugging his leg, pulling on his arm, it was so funny to see how they perked up at the sight of him. It was as if we'd given them a shot of adrenaline. When we visited some of the individual rooms, even the ones who were sleeping, their heads popped up prairie dog style. I've never seen any of those children smile and laugh as much as they did today. You know, Denali, that's when it hit me that you really *are* a superstar. I've become used to the adults fawning over you. But to see the children go ballistic? That's what did it for me. I left there vowing to buy one of your movies just to see you in it."

Jayson put down his fork. "You've never seen any of my movies?" His tone was incredulous. "Come on, Aaryn, you're kidding me, right?"

"Well no, but at least I'd heard of you. Don't stare at me like that. So, I don't watch a lot of television. Shoot me." It seemed to Aaryn that everyone at the table was glaring at her as if she'd made a major faux pas. "Ray, don't you even try it. How many Jayson Denali films have you seen?"

"Uh-uh. Don't shift the blame. I don't expect Ray or Dot to have seen any of my films. But you? Have you been living under a rock? In a cave somewhere? You've not seen even one of my films? That hurts, Doc."

"I said I'm going to buy one of your movies, didn't I? I'll do it this weekend, I promise. Now, back to my story. The best part came toward the end of Jayson's visit."

"It wasn't the best part for me," Jayson said glumly.

"A family was having their child baptized at the hospital. When they saw Jayson, the parents pleaded with him to attend the ceremony. And being the generous man that he is, Jayson said, "Yes." Everything went smooth right up to the part where the minister dipped the baby in the water and lifted him out. But without his diaper on, he started spraying everyone in the vicinity. Poor Jayson caught the brunt of it. We couldn't believe it." Aaryn held one hand to her neck as she shook with laughter.

"You have an A-list celebrity attending your baptismal, and the baby pees all over his shirt? At first we were stunned but then the minister started laughing and we all burst out laughing. It was hilarious."

"Hilarious because it wasn't you who got the golden shower. Look for the video to be all over the internet in no time." Jayson shook his head. "She set me up, Ray. I'll bet she knew from the start the little tyke was going to pull a squirtgun move. No wonder she stayed in the background after leading me up front and center."

"That's not true. The parents wanted you in their keepsake video. They didn't care anything about my presence. It was the star, Mr. Incredible, they wanted to film holding their baby."

After dinner, they moved outside to the huge balcony where Dot served a light dessert of fresh strawberry almond tarts. There was a lot of laughter, camaraderie and good natured ribbing as everybody shared a story or two. Even the dogs were permitted to join them.

Jayson realized that he felt welcomed, as if he was a part of the family. He recognized with pleasure that not once during the evening had he felt like a specimen under a magnifying glass. It was unfortunate, but that was how he was sometimes treated because of his celebrity status. People acted as if they expected him to roll over and perform special tricks for their viewing pleasure.

Feeling as if he belonged in their circle, he watched Aaryn tease Ray and Dot. She even poked fun at him. Jayson didn't know if it was the glass of wine she'd had with dinner, but she was much more relaxed in his presence.

It wasn't until Ray said, "Dot, let me help you with the dishes" that Jayson realized nearly four hours had passed.

After they left he said to Aaryn, "Don't clam up now. You were on a roll."

"The evening went by so swiftly, didn't it?"

"It does that when you're enjoying yourself. Tell me about the man or the men in your life, Aaryn."

She shrugged. "There's nothing to tell."

"Nothing to tell or nothing you *want* to tell?"

She smiled at him. "I mean there's nothing to tell, Denali. We can't all be world class libertines who perform wonders in the bedroom."

"I suppose not. But then, I've never met such a wonder myself, so I wouldn't know."

"Fibber." She sat across from him in one of the comfortably padded deck chairs. "You're forgetting that I, along with the rest of the world, watched two women fight over you shamelessly."

"That could happen to anyone. I'm just the unfortunate lout who got caught up in the mix." As comfortable as she was with him, he sensed she would bolt if he decided to share her seat, though it was big enough for two.

"The hefty price of stardom."

"Are you artfully avoiding talking about the men in your life?"

Her smile broadened. "I'll tell you about all the men in my life if you'll tell me about the one woman who you loved so deeply. I keep hearing the name Porsh."

Jayson wondered who she kept hearing the name from. He guessed Syl must have told her. "Porsh" was his personal nickname for his old flame. Jayson corrected her. "Her name was Porsha."

"Yes, that's it. Will you talk to me about her?"

"I should ask you to tell me." Jayson was goading her, as if to see if all the things she'd said to him earlier were true.

"I can tell you what I've picked up in the spirit."

Here we go, Jayson thought. "Whatever works," he said.

"She was beautiful. She was older. And she was your first love."

He nodded.

"You were together for a number of years. I see you laughing and holding hands with her. You traveled to many cities together. You were happy with each other and you thought that that happiness would last forever. Except, you weren't the only one who loved her. So did her husband."

"Bravo. You should think about playing the lottery." Jayson still wasn't convinced of her socalled prophetic prowess. She could have gotten that information anywhere. It was yesterday's news.

Aaryn shrugged. "Why? So I can have a shot at having as much money as you? What do I need with half a billion dollars?" At least that's what she'd overheard the women at the nurses' station say. According to them, that was the figure the magazines reported he was worth.

"You could own part of the world."

She shook her head. "Haven't you read about all the woes of the people who hit it big? Many of them wind up worse off than they were before they came into the money. Besides, I earn a good enough living. I have money to travel and to buy the things I desire. I've got very little debt. I'm content, Denali, with such as I have."

"And yet there's no Mr. Jamison."

"I don't see a Mrs. Denali."

"You see her every day. You're her doctor."

"Funny. I meant a Mrs. Jayson Denali."

"Tell me about the men." His tone grew insistent. He needed to know.

She shook her head. "The bargain was that you'd share about your first love. You didn't do that. Instead, you tested me to see if I could tell you about her. I did, so that's that."

"Porsha's old news anyhow. I would have told you anything you wanted to know. But it seems you already knew everything. So talk to me now."

"There are no men to tell you about, Denali." She sounded matter of fact and not at all regretful.

"Everyone has someone they can talk about. A secret lover, someone they keep hidden away for special moments."

"In your world, I'm sure. Not in mine."

Jayson was intrigued. "Never?"

"Not even once, Denali."

Was she telling him she was a virgin? Jayson's mouth dropped open.

Aaryn took a swig of her bottle of Perrier water. "Stupefying isn't it? In this day and age, to find a woman of my advanced years who's never had sex. Takes the word celibate to a whole new level, doesn't it?"

Jayson was speechless. He managed, "Why?"

Again, she shrugged. "I never met a man I wanted to lay with." She smiled at the puzzled expression on his face. "Not even you, Denali. As talented as you are and all. I'm just not into one night stands."

Jayson shrugged. "That's a noble concept," he thought. It was one he could even understand, risks being what they were. Still. A thought crossed his mind. "Are you waiting for marriage?" he asked. But when she shook her head, Jayson was stumped.

He had this overwhelming need to comprehend why she'd held herself back for so long. *What a waste,* he thought. The fact that she'd never shared herself with another person in all this time, for some reason her sacrifice repulsed him. He questioned what possessed her to throw her life away like that? It reminded him of how the JWs had pumped him full of all that religious dogma about sex being something dirty that should only be done in secret and in shame.

"Are you a Jehovah Witness?" He felt relief when she shook her head. "Mormon?"

Now she was smiling at him as she shook her head.

"Hard to wrap your head around, isn't it Denali? I'm a 39-year old virgin. Don't worry. It's not some disease you need fear catching."

Jayson would never have guessed she was 39, three years his senior. Based on her physical appearance, he'd figured she was 29. He reached for his wine glass but he'd already emptied it. He wondered if they had anything stronger.

"If it's any consolation, I've never shared that with another person. I guess I've come to like you, Denali. You've grown on me. You remind me of something that's hard on the outside and soft on the inside. I think you used all those women in your past because you needed to prove to yourself that you weren't as gullible as your sister and this Porsha woman said you were. It's strange, isn't it, that no matter how badly you treated some of them, they still kept coming back for more. The women in your life have always returned, haven't they?" She thought of Porsha and said, "Most of them anyway."

Jayson didn't answer. He was staring into the distance looking off in the direction of Dot's garden.

"Now I've gone and put a morbid twist on the evening, haven't I?" When he still didn't answer her, she said, "Jayson, why don't we bring the evening to an end?" She set her bottled water down on a nearby table.

He stood to his feet. "Yes, let's do that."

Aaryn noticed he made no move in her direction. The predinner Jayson Denali would have tried to paw her. But now, with his hands in his pockets, he acted as if

she was fragile glass that could only be looked at from a distance. When she stood to her feet, the slight smile she gave him held a tinge of disappointment.

"Thanks for coming to the hospital with me. You made a lot of people happy today—both children and adults." She knew because she was one of them.

"It was my pleasure." Was this goodbye? "Thanks for coming to Provo with me. You saved me a lot of money."

"You're welcome. I guess that makes us even then." A note of sadness tinged her voice. It felt like a goodbye.

"I should say good night to Ray and Dot."

"I could say it for you to save you some time."

"That would be great." It was a goodbye after all.

Aaryn led him to the front door. After he left, she didn't want to join Ray and Dot in the kitchen where she knew they'd be laughing, chatting and drying dishes like forbidden but irresistible lovers. Who cared about race anymore anyway? But Aaryn knew that in Utah, plenty of people cared about race and still frowned upon interracial dating. She headed up to her room, unwilling to dwell upon anything that required her to think too deeply.

Jayson drove back to his hotel lost in thought. The stereo poured out his favorite songs by Kem, Jill Scott and Brian McKnight, but his mind was stuck on a balcony back in Holladay, Utah. He was sure he'd somehow bungled the situation. But how was he supposed to have responded? These days, nobody was a virgin. Except for kids, and small ones, at that, given the loose nature of society. And yet, she was one. In a way, Jayson felt sorry for her. Hell. Maybe it was himself he felt sorry for because of the lost opportunity. He just knew he couldn't shake the feeling of aloneness that had come over him. It wasn't loneliness. It was a feeling of separation. He wondered if it was how Aaryn felt.

After she'd told him her big revelatory news, he'd felt the need to get away from her, to get from out of her presence. Admittedly, he *had* reacted as if she'd contracted some disease. He hadn't meant to, it just happened. He'd had the feeling he was being led into a trap of some kind when it definitely wasn't his intention to be trapped into marriage. Not that the good doctor had ever hinted of such. But if marriage was what she was holding out for, even though she claimed it wasn't, good luck. As much as he was attracted to her, he was still in a dating frame of mind. Marriage, not that she'd given off any signals, was the furthest thing from his mind.

❖

The next morning, Jayson awoke to a firestorm. The phone by his bedside was ringing. It took him a moment to focus but when he did, he realized someone was knocking urgently at his door. He glanced at the near empty bottle of Courvoisier

Erte #5 and swung his feet off the huge bed. The phone stopped ringing as he struggled to the door.

Jayson wore a puzzled look as he stared at the blonde in the shiny red raincoat standing at his door. She was holding a breakfast tray filled with food in her hands.

"Aren't you going to invite me inside?"

Jayson shook his head as if to clear the cobwebs. "I'm sorry. You must have the wrong room." He was hung over but he knew he didn't recognize the woman, looker though she was.

"Oh, I've got the right room alright. Didn't you get my note yesterday evening?"

When Jayson had returned to the lodge late last night he'd gone into the bar and had a few drinks. He wound up buying the $1,000 bottle of Courvoisier and returning to his room after a number of women had crowded around him. He bought them a round of drinks and headed back to his suite. Alone. A note had been slid underneath his door. But he'd tossed it, thinking the author had the wrong room. The invitation was for breakfast in bed.

"That was me," she said sheepishly.

"Look, I'm sorry. I'm not in the mood…"

Blondie set the tray down and unwrapped her raincoat.

Jayson stared at her naked flesh and despite himself, he hardened at the sight of her. She served to remind him how long he'd been without a woman. Months. What the hell was wrong with him anyway?

"Oh my gosh!" Blondie gushed. "It's true!" The sight of the huge imprint of Jayson's maleness drove her into a frenzy. The woman started licking her lips like she had the residue of a lollipop on her mouth. In her haste to step forward, she knocked over the breakfast tray spilling food everywhere.

Her franticness was exactly what Jayson needed to snap himself out of the mental miasma he'd fallen into. He glanced behind him and eased the door slightly closed.

"Look, I've got someone inside already. Can I call you in a couple of days?"

"Days?" The woman gulped as if her fire needed putting out immediately. "Please, Mr. Denali, let me come in. I can't wait days. I've got to have you now. I'm leaving Utah tonight." Blondie was no longer looking Jayson in the eye. Her attention was riveted on another part of his anatomy, clothed in his pajamas though he was.

"I'll call you." Jayson closed the door and locked it. He had no intention of calling her. Neither did he have anybody in his bed. Not that he wouldn't have liked to. In fact, one certain doctor would fit the bill nicely. He felt himself stir again as he headed for the shower.

"Do not disturb? Do not disturb?" PT's voice climbed several octaves.

"Listen to me you dumb asshole. I'm his publicist slash agent slash attorney slash any friggin' title you want to give me. You wake him up, you hear me? You wake him up, goddammit or I'll come down there and shoot up your entire facility until it looks like Rambo or the Terminator got ahold to it. Call the police, call the FBI, call Homeland Security or whoever the hell you need to contact. But if You. Do. Not. Get. Jayson. Denali. on this phone within the next five minutes, I'll hire Osama bin Laden and all his terrorist minions to blow that friggin' place to shreds!"

Foam was coming out of PT's mouth as she screamed into the phone. When she heard a loud click just before the phone was disconnected, steam could have streamed from her ears.

Jayson was toweling himself dry as he reached for his cell.

"Denali"

PT fumed, "Where the hell have you been, JD? The world is blowing up in friggin' flames and you're out there in some Godforsaken wasted town jerking on your chain. How the hell am I supposed to represent you if I can't even find you? The hell is wrong is with you, JD? You don't answer your phone. You don't check your messages. And you don't return calls. Are you smokin' crack? You downin vicadens or somthin'? What the hell is really goin' on?"

Jayson's second line beeped as another call came through. Instead of responding to PT, he simply said, "Hold on, PT."

"Denali."

"What an incredible bastard you are Jayson."

"Wendy."

"Don't 'Wendy' me. I quit."

"Why is everybody threatening to quit? You can't quit, Wen. You're the best Personal Assistant I've ever had. Plus, I haven't been gone long enough for you to quit. I thought you said you couldn't wait to get me out of your hair."

"What hair, Jayson? What hair do I have left after being plagued with you? You don't need me. You don't answer the phone when I call. You don't return my calls. What am I? Here people are calling me, ringing my phone off the hook with questions that need answering yesterday and I can't even get a hold of you. What

good is an assistant who can't reach out to the person she assists? You tell me that, Jayson." Wendy's voice escalated to the point of screaming with each point made.

Jayson's head hurt like a mother. Surely he hadn't drank *that* much? Still, he knew an ego when it needed soothing. He wrapped a dry towel around himself and pulled a bottled of OJ from the stocked fridge. In the livingroom he took a seat on the plush sofa. "Wendy, love, I'm all yours. Tell me what you need."

"It's about good and damn time. Why don't you start by telling me who the hell this Dr. Aaryn Jamison is? And why the hell do I have to find out about her from Liz Smith of Page Six of the New York Post? I should have guessed something was up in the first place. Visiting your mother for a few days is one thing. But who the hell stays in Utah when it's not even ski season? But nooooo! My dumb butt defends you to everybody who points this out—only to get blown away like this. By the way, PT quits too."

Jayson sat straight up. "What are you talking about?"

"This is a betrayal, Jayson. You lied to me." Her voice rose several octaves. "You found a new set location for *A Season to Hunt* and didn't tell anybody?"

Wendy sounded so near to tears that Jayson thought she deserved an Oscar.

"I've tried for years to get you to visit the Children's Hospital here in New York. But would you go? Absolutely not. And what do I find on the front page of the Globe this morning but a big photo of you getting pissed on by a three-month old baby. I don't know you anymore, Jayson. You used to call me every damn day to keep me in the loop. And now…Pft!" Wendy made a spitting sound. "Nothing. Nada. No calls, no messages, nothing. There was a time when I could reach you even if no one else in the world could. But now if I want to know where you are or what you're up to, I have to go out and buy a gossip magazine. So who the heck is this Aaryn Jamison?"

Jayson spoke slowly. "Wendy, please slow down and tell me what you're talking about."

"You're drunk aren't you? I can't even let you out of my sight without you turning into an alcoholic. You never used to drink."

"Wendy." His patience was running out.

"Don't they sell newspapers down in that backwater town? It's all over the news, Jayson. Even the baby video has been aired on Entertainment Tonight. Poor PT. She's being harpooned because Michael Sneed of the Chicago Sun-Times feels like she's been scooped."

"Wendy, I'm hanging up if you don't start making some sense."

"I thought I was making perfect sense, Jay."

"I've not seen Liz Smith's or Michael Sneed's gossip columns so I can't comment. Since when did you start believing everything you read?"

Wendy grew quiet. "We've got our tickets, you know. Every one of the crew has a oneway ticket to Salt Lake City. Even Dez says he plans to come. Me and PT are coming, too. We all plan to be there by tomorrow."

"Wendy, I'm returning everybody's call later today. In the interim, I want you to let everyone know that no one will be coming to Utah. Anybody who shows up here without my invitation is fired. There'll be no need to quit."

Now Wendy's silence was deafening. *Oh my god! Is he serious?* she wondered. After awhile she voiced her thoughts.

"I'm very serious. I'm enjoying my space and I don't want any intrusions on my world." Jayson's voice was hard and adamant.

"What's going on, Jay? Are you alright?" All kidding was cast aside as a new level of unease crept into her voice.

"Nothing is going on, Wendy. And all is right in my world. I've tapped into something that I'm enjoying and I'm not ready for it to end. All of you coming here would be nothing more than a major distraction."

"If all is right with the world, Jay, how come you've got a hangover?"

"Nothing more than a misunderstanding."

"I see." She didn't really, but she was trying to. "And does this Dr. Aaryn Jamison have anything to do with everything being right with your world?"

"Possibly. I haven't quite figured that out yet. But I'm working on it."

Wendy felt like she was probing her way gingerly around a mine field. "I'm staring at a slew of invitations on my desk, Jay. Invitations from Senators, Ambassadors, International Emissaries and corporate sponsors, some of which you've already committed to. I hope you're not planning on staying in Utah beyond your original three-week timeframe. There are several major charity balls lined up that you've already given your word to attend. One of which is Oprah's. I'm not calling her to cancel, Jay. If you plan on reneging on Oprah, you'll have to make that phone call yourself."

"I wouldn't dream of missing her gala. I hadn't forgotten about it; it's not until two weeks from now anyway. But everything else in the month of July, cancel it. My not showing up for some dinner ball is hardly the end of the world. There'll be so many people at these affairs that my presence will certainly not be missed."

Jayson no longer thought the world revolved around him? Something was definitely amiss. "Should I be worried about you, Jay?"

"Not at all. You should take a vacation next week, Wendy. That's what you should do. Go somewhere special, just you and your husband, Vince. My treat. Forget well-worn seduction trails like Venice or Paris. Take Vince somewhere less traveled. Go to Seville, or Portofino, or Monte Carlo. Anywhere where the two of you can get lost in each other. If he refuses to go, strap him to a bed and threaten him with a cattle prod or something. Go have yourself a ball, Wendy. Go create some memories to last you a lifetime."

"Now I'm really worried about you, Jay."

"Don't be. As soon as I get my head on straight, I'm going to work out and return some of the calls I've told you about. It's all good, Wendy. I'm dead serious about you guys not coming down here and I'm serious about your vacation with Vince. Let me know when you've booked the flights. And don't give me any of that crap about 'now not being a good time.' I've heard it all before. Anything else before I hang up?"

Wendy was speechless. "I don't think so, Jay. Nothing that I can't handle with a phone call or two. I guess I'll see you when I see you."

Forgetting PT was still holding on the other line, Jayson shut down his phone and looked at the time. He couldn't believe it was barely 6 o'clock in the morning. After making himself an ice bag for his head, he laid back against the sofa. Before he knew it, he was out like a light.

Chapter Twenty-Six

Aaryn stood at the rooftop railing lost in thought as the sun rose over the city. As the cool breeze brushed over her, she found herself thinking, "Thank God it's Friday."

She knew what her weekend plans were. She was taking a four-hour drive to Zion National Park to go hiking and climbing. Getting away for the weekend was just what she needed. Time spent to herself so she could regroup. No patients, no consultations, no outside engagements—and no Jayson. A wry smile crossed her lips. From the way he'd left her home the night before, Aaryn figured her association with Mr. Denali had run its course. She could finally put it in proper context: a professional relationship. Up close and personal? Well, there would be no more of that. She would continue to intercede for him, but she'd keep her distance while doing so.

Did she regret revealing that private detail of her life? Not really. She just hadn't anticipated his reaction. She hadn't figured he would be repulsed. But the way he'd rejected her and back pedaled his way out the door was surprising. At least now that he was out of her hair, she could finally put him out of her mind. As she made her way toward the rooftop exit, Aaryn hoped that would be all it took to release him from her heart.

"You're quiet this morning, Syl. Is everything okay?" The nurses had wheeled Sylvia into the Yahweh Room for her early morning treatment. Usually, Sylvia was a chatterbox whenever the nurses brought her into the room and lifted her onto the massage table. This morning, however, she appeared preoccupied.

"I'm worried about Jayson." Sylvia lay on her stomach with her arms by her sides. Her head was turned so that her cheek rested against a pillow. She was naked under the sheet that covered her.

Aaryn came and stood at the head of the treatment table. "Why?"

"He hasn't been his usual self with me."

Aaryn waited for Syl to elaborate.

"The last couple of times he visited, he was curt toward me. As if he was irritated about something. He hasn't stayed to have dinner with me so I haven't had a chance to unmask what's bothering him. It's just that I thought we had grown closer. But these last several days seem to dispel that."

"Hmmm," was all Aaryn offered. She wasn't going to discuss Jayson with Sylvia. Instead, she checked the temperature of the black basalt massage stones. "Syl, these heated stones are going to help remove toxins and increase the flow of your blood circulation. Your body won't feel them, but your mind will know they're there."

As if she hadn't heard a word Aaryn had said, Sylvia continued. "I've been having dreams about my daughter lately."

Aaryn's pause was slight. She'd been waiting for the subject of Carmin to come up. Eight weeks into Sylvia's treatment, here it was. As she went to work on the left side of Syl's body she asked, "Why can't you say her name? You sound like you're speaking of someone you barely know."

"I didn't mean it like that." Sylvia's voice was just above a whisper. "It's just that I wasn't the best mother to Carmin. I wasn't able to give her the love she needed. It wasn't as though I awoke one morning and decided I didn't love my child. As hard as I tried, I just couldn't stop myself from being the kind of mother to her that my mother was to me. What's cruel about it is that I swore I would never treat my children the way Mama treated me: as if I was invisible. But Carmin was so

288

clingy I couldn't stand it. Between working two jobs and taking care of a husband, at the end of the day I didn't have much left to give her.

"I'm not making excuses for the way I ignored her as a child. I'm just conceding I wasn't there for her. I consoled myself with the knowledge that her father took time with her. The man loved Carmin. The more time and attention he gave her, the more I permitted myself to withdraw. And then Jayson was born."

Aaryn kneaded Sylvia's flesh keeping her strokes light because she didn't want to distract her from her story. Aaryn sensed a breakthrough on the horizon. She heard every word Sylvia said about centering her affections on Jayson. But it was her body that Aaryn listened to attentively as she let it guide her hands to the appropriate spots. The heated stones formed a wide "W" across Sylvia's back and it was the areas in between that Aaryn targeted.

"...after his dad died, I loved Jayson to the exclusion of everything else. But Carmin felt the loss as deeply as I did. For five years she'd been a daddy's girl and in the blink of an eye, that all changed."

Aaryn could feel a steady stream of emotions begin to seep through the pours of Sylvia's skin. An energy that had lain dormant had awakened and was manifesting itself by spreading to different parts of her body. Aaryn's task was to quickly "capture" the potentially harmful energy and release it through the pours of the skin. She rearranged the stones to form a "T" across Syl's shoulders. More pressure was applied as she started kneading her body's right side. Sylvia's words became muted to Aaryn's ears as she tuned in to the signals her body was delivering.

"...to high school, I couldn't do anything with her. She was out of control. Once she started having sex, my house became a battleground. Everyday was an argument waiting to happen. It was dèjávu all over again for me. In my mind, I was my mother and Carmin was me. We just seemed to fight all the time. When she stopped going to school to hang out with boys, that was the last straw. I put her out. I had no idea..." Sylvia's voice cracked.

Aaryn detected Sylvia's emotional pain as she kneaded the throbbing flesh beneath her fingers. Quickly, she removed the heated basalt stones and replaced them with chilled white marble ones to spur the dramatic movement of fluids through her body. She also poured a generous amount of heated almond and coconut oil onto the outer areas of Syl's bare back. Straddling her lower half, Aaryn leaned forward and applied the full pressure of her weight to the paralyzed region.

Sylvia was crying now. Through her sobs she managed, "I thought in time she would quit the drugs and get herself together. But one day Carmin came to me with the horrible news that she had AIDS. Instead of embracing her, I rejected her. I didn't know enough about AIDS and HIV back then. I thought it was something you could spread to others by touching them. I don't know, I guess there were too many unsubstantiated rumors going around. All I could think of was protecting Jayson."

Aaryn's thumbs were pressed deep against the muscles of Syl's back. She eased up to give the area a series of lightning fast chops as if she was tenderizing a steak. She brought her hands back to rework her upper back area tapping hard on the trapezius muscles and out to the deltoids. Aaryn's movements had become furious.

"Carmin was losing so much weight I couldn't stand to look at her. When I did, it only reminded me of my failures as a mother and as a woman. Then came the night I was leaving a hotel with a friend. I saw Carmin going into one of the rooms with two men. She had this dazed look on her face, like she was high on drugs. I don't know if she recognized me because she looked right through me. When the men slammed that hotel door, I jumped because it sounded like the doors of a tomb had slammed shut.

"At first, I was so humiliated to be seen in the same hotel as my daughter that I just got in the car and allowed James to drive me onto work. But I was numb with worry thinking about the things those men might be doing to my daughter. An hour into my shift, I couldn't stand it any longer. I left and caught a taxi back to the hotel.

"I banged on the door until they opened it. There Carmin was, tied naked to the bed. And instead of two men, there were four of them. Those beasts had inserted objects…" Sylvia's sobs grew louder as her body shook with painful emotions.

Aaryn could feel ripples in the flesh beneath her hands. Pockets of skin had risen to form lumps that pulsed and throbbed. The lumps resembled the pale disc-like suckers found on the tentacles of an octopus. They covered Sylvia's right side. She put pressure on the marbles so they would push the fluid and waste out of her inflamed tissues. Aaryn knew what was coming next. She hunkered down in preparation.

"…the cab driver helped me take her to a hospital. All she had covering her body was a bed sheet. By the time we made it into the emergency room, it was covered in blood and vomit. She was so out of it, I didn't realize she'd OD'd while I was holding her in my lap. I waited hours after they wheeled her away. When the doctor finally came and told me there was nothing they could do to save her, that she was dead…" Her voice broke.

Between gulps for breath, Sylvia managed, "…all I felt was…*relief!* Not sorrow…but relief that it was finally over. No more worrying about where she was sleeping, was she warm, was she safe…was she…But then came the guilt. Guilt at not being a good enough person to care that my own child had died."

When the furor hit, Aaryn was prepared, but at that moment, she wished she had Dot in the room with her.

Unprepared for the waves of pain that rushed over her, a horse scream tore from the back of Sylvia's throat as sensations flooded back to her formally numb body. She'd never felt such excruciating pain. Giving birth to two children had not been as

harrowing as the pain she felt ripping through her as sensitivity returned to her entire right side. It felt as though someone had doused her skin with lighter fluid and set her on fire. Sylvia tried to claw her way free from the weight that was holding her down, but her arms were trapped at her side. Forced to endure the onslaught, all she could do was cry and plead for the pain to stop.

Aaryn was not immune to Sylvia's painfilled experience. Her own face and body was covered in sweat at the strain of holding Sylvia's twitching form to the table. Ignoring her cries, she held Syl down and applied pressure to the back of her neck until the last of the lumps on her body had released its puss and faded away leaving only the tiniest of marks on her skin.

Aaryn had taken a quick shower after her encounter with Sylvia. The nurses had given Syl pain meds and she was resting comfortably in her room.

All eyes followed her as she took a seat in one of the available chairs in Shriners' conference center. Kyle had met with the support staff earlier and this impromptu meeting with the doctors was to discuss tightened security measures at the hospital. The meeting was near to wrapping up when Aaryn entered, which was good because she had only thirty minutes before her next appointment.

"Aaryn, with all the media exposure we've been getting in the last few weeks and days," he added, "we've beefed up security to prevent photographers from breaching any of our floors. It seems we can't underestimate the gossip mags. We've seen how even the most trusted staff members can be tempted by them."

Aaryn nodded. She assumed Kyle was bringing her up to speed on things he'd already discussed prior to her arrival. One of the doctors sitting at the opposite end of the table slid a copy of the Salt Lake Tribune her way. It hurtled down the table like a fast ball. As she brought the paper to an abrupt halt, it seemed everyone was staring at her as she lifted her hand to glance down at the front page. On the right half of the page was a photo of her and Jayson leaving the Provo Chamber of Commerce. The caption read, "Star Power Comes to Utah." Further down was another photo of her and Jayson inside her Jeep surrounded by media just before they drove off. The article went on to name the other A-list stars slated to join Jayson in Provo for the filming of A Season to Hunt.

Aaryn suddenly understood why her peers were staring at her as if she had the inside scoop. She looked up to find everyone watching in hopes that she might provide an explanation for the photos. She pushed the paper away without finishing the article.

"You've been in treatment with Mrs. Denali, so you're probably unaware of the media crews lurking outside. It seems news of Mrs. Denali's recovery has been

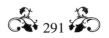

leaked. Two photographers managed to gain access to restricted areas. We think they were hoping to snap a picture of her or possibly some of our others guests. Fortunately, we spotted them before any damage was done. The crews waiting outside are probably hoping to photograph Jayson arriving at the hospital."

Aaryn was taken aback. Her session with Sylvia had ended a little over an hour ago. Despite how media thirsty Kyle was, she doubted even he would have leaked such news. Given the front page coverage of Jayson and the hospital, any of the staff personnel could have made the call.

Still, Aaryn was annoyed. "Kyle, you well know that Mrs. Denali hasn't fully healed. She's barely in the initial stages of her recovery process. Reports of any type of physical improvement are precipitous at best." She viewed the leak as an intrusion on her patient's privacy. "I'm glad you've increased security, Kyle. This could easily turn into a circus now that rumors of her being here and Jayson's film shoot have made the news."

The other doctors waited for Aaryn to continue but she only glanced at her watch.

Knowing her as he did, Kyle knew Aaryn would add nothing more. He stood to indicate the meeting was over. Yet, it seemed as though everyone was reluctant to leave. They were hoping Aaryn would shed more light on developments surrounding the film and her photo session with Jayson.

Aaryn rose to leave when Kyle put his hand on her arm to detain her. The others filed out and when they were the last ones remaining he said, "You've been busy. There's quite a buzz around here."

"Anytime someone's healing manifests, it should generate a buzz, Kyle. Internally, that is."

"I wasn't referring to Mrs. Denali. I meant you're causing a stir with Jayson. Are the two of you an item?"

Aaryn assessed him. "That's hardly any of your business, Kyle. But for the record, no we're not. Not now, nor in the future."

Oddly, Kyle found himself relieved to hear it. He said to her, "I ask only because I wouldn't want to see you hurt."

"That's kind of you, but I'm a big girl, Kyle. There's no need to offer a shoulder for me to cry on."

"I don't mean to sound patronizing or over protective, Aaryn. It's just that I care about you."

She did know that. Her voice held a gentle rebuke. "Kyle, we've been over this before."

Frustrated, Kyle ran his fingers through his thick head of salt and pepper hair. He'd simply wanted her to treat Sylvia Denali. He hadn't anticipated anything developing between her and the son. He'd assumed she would continue to rebuff Jayson as she'd rebuffed him. With time, Kyle had even managed to suppress his feelings for her. But seeing the photo of her with Jayson had sparked a flame of jealousy within him.

Aaryn had no desire to continue the thread of conversation. She said, "I must be going, Kyle. I have an appointment with Betty Bellinjer."

Kyle watched her retreating figure. Of all the women he could have fallen for, what was it about her that captivated his attention?

Providing leading edge creature comforts and accommodating the unique demands of their high networth guests was The Stein Eriksen's specialty. So, true to his word, Jayson worked out on the state-of-the-art Bowflex Home Gym they'd set up for him in his suite of rooms. Working out in The Lodge's private facilities would have caused mayhem with everyone wanting either a photo or his autograph. Although The Lodge's guest list consisted of the ultra rich, even they tended to go ga-ga over A-list celebrities.

Jayson was in the middle of a bench press when his cell rang. The call was on its way to voicemail when he snatched up his phone.

"Denali."

"What's the dilleo, JD?"

"Can't call it, Dez. What's up, Bro?"

"Ordinarily I'd say same ol' same ol'. But with the way everybody's cracking about you around these parts, apparently it's your world."

Jayson sat back down on the bench. "Man, not you too? Wendy called me early this morning trippin' over some Page Six article. You folks read one news clipping and all of a sudden everybody's got the urge to visit Utah. You can't be serious."

"Back this up a couple of paces. It wasn't just the Liz Smith article, JD. From the way I hear things, you were weirding out before you left for Utah, which seems about right to me because you did show up dateless for the Wall Street Roundtable here in New York. That was the first red flag. Add to that the fact that you hightailed it to Utah and went all double-o-seven on a brotha, stopped answering your cell phone, didn't respond to voicemails or text messages, blew off your security detail *and* your entire crew, plus Wendy *and* me. I don't think one article can top any of that. Not to mention that I have to find out by chance that you changed part of a scene in *A Season to Hunt* just so you can film in Utah. If you were ten years older I could blame it on midlife crisis. But, man, you're just bogus."

Dez made a loud sucking noise with his teeth. "With all this madness from a formerly somewhat sane brother, I say a woman's got to be somewhere in the background orchestrating the show. I've known you for a gazillion years, JD, and have never known you to give ultimatums like what I'm hearing. Since I *used* to be your best friend, I used to have the inside track. But ever since you've hit Utah, I can't even get a return phone call."

"Are you trying to guilt me, Dez? Won't work, Bro. And what makes you think a woman is involved? A better explanation is that I got tired and needed a break from you chickenheads. You mugs definitely drive a brotha crazy. Coming out here, I never had so much peacefulness in all my life. Should have found my way here a long time ago."

Dez was puzzled. "Peacefulness? Man, you don't even know how to spell the word. Since when did you become thirsty for *peacefulness*? Am I talking to the man who normally has two phones to his ears at one time? The one who juggles multiple scripts simultaneously? The one who handles four women at a time complete with all the mad drama each one brings, plus keeps several others waiting in the wings? That's you, right? Or am I missing something?"

It was him alright, Jayson thought. But Dez's description of him didn't sound pleasant. If anything, it made him feel like a hamster spinning feverishly on a wheel going nowhere. That's the very lifestyle he was trying to get away from.

"Yeah, well that's why I'm here. So I could take a break from all that. It's called burn out."

"Uh-huh. Who's the newbie?" Dez called all of JD's women "newbies" since they tended to come and go so frequently. If they lasted longer than a week or two, only then would he bother to learn their name.

"That's what I've been telling you. There is no newbie. Dr. Jamison happens to be Syl's physician. Once you meet her, you'll understand what I mean."

"Cool. So when do I get the pleasure of meeting her?"

"You don't. I just told you it's not what you think. How's Dionne by the way?"

"Dionne's great. I'm great. Everybody's great. You would know that if you returned a brotha's phone call every now and then. So everything's hush hush with you and this Dr. Jamison, huh? Anything I should know about that wasn't in the Page Six article?"

"Not that I know of. Then again, I didn't read it, so all I can tell you is, if anything develops you'll be the first to know."

"Like I was the first to know about everything else that's been going on? No problem. When are you blowing back this way again?"

"I'll be back to New York in a couple of weeks. I'll pass through on my way to Toronto for filming."

"How's Syl? She getting any better?"

"Yep, improving daily. Aaryn's doing phenomenal work with her. She's definitely making progress."

Dez caught the use of the doctor's first name, but he let it go. He said, "Check in with me in a day or so, JD. I've got good news pending on the investment network for your next indie film."

"I'll hollah." Jayson clicked off his cell and got ready to go meet Syl for lunch.

When he arrived at Shriners he was surprised to find the grounds staked out with news crews, even though they were far enough from the entrance to the facility so as not to violate privacy laws. A flood of flashes went off as he exited his vehicle.

Inside, everyone was all smiles as he approached the visitor's station. As he signed in, one of the receptionists said to him, "I'm so happy to hear about your mother's recovery, Mr. Denali. You must be ecstatic."

"Her recovery? What do you mean?"

Recognizing she may have made a verbal snafu, the woman buttoned downed. The second receptionist threw the woman a meaningful look and said, "You'll want to speak with Dr. Jamison, Sir."

"Thank you. I'll do just that." Jayson went in search of Aaryn.

Chapter Twenty-Seven

With the divorce looking like everything was shaping up in her favor, there was only one way Erika wanted to celebrate Michael's departure from her life. She planned for him a royal send off. A homegoing, if you will. One not quite fit for a king. Albeit, the funeral director thought it a little strange to have a special homegoing funeral service for someone who was still alive and well. And never in the history of his 45 years as a funeral practitioner had he ever had someone request the 60's hit song by Ray Charles, "Hit The Road Jack" as the funeral service theme song. But who the heck was he to tell a cash-paying patron what they should or shouldn't do with their money? People were entitled to celebrate the dead, or in this case, the nondead, any way they saw fit. Different strokes and all that being the case. Capitalizing on the unique occasion, he recommended the most expensive amenities they had to offer.

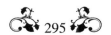

Erika wanted only the best for her dearly departed husband, especially since American Express was generous enough to send her a platinum card in Michael's name. Why shouldn't he foot the bill given that the service was in his honor?

Everything inside the chapel area designated for Michael was decorated in bright reds—from the closed marble casket, to the silk draperies adorning the walls, to the nylon slip covers on the pews, to the shiny mylar balloons which floated from the ceiling with their colorful curly strings dangling from each swaying balloon.

The only other color that graced the chapel was black. All the floral arrangements were the blackest of hues. Right down to the humongous plastic rose wreath strategically placed on top of Michael's closed casket. A four-foot framed picture of Michael rested on a black easel just behind the casket. And right behind that, a banner hung from wall to wall in the pulpit area with the words emblazoned on it: "The wealth of the wicked is laid up for the just..."

To inform the world of her soon-to-be-ex's departure from her life, Erika had posted Michael's death notice in the Indianapolis Star. She scripted it as a special celebratory invitation to all "friends and enemies of that rotten bastard Michael A. Slaughter." Anyone who knew the deceased was invited to attend his homegoing service.

Of course, Erika hadn't come up with the notion all on her own. No, she had her prescient daughter, Mia, to thank for that. With Hully tucked tightly under her arm, little Mia had marched into the bathroom while Erika was bathing and announced, "Hully said you need to dig a grave and give Daddy a funeral." With two missing front teeth, Mia pronounced "funeral" as "few-nal."

Erika knew her daughter said the darndest things. She swore, but sometimes she could only stare at her child in amazement. Like the times when Mia would stand in front of the TV and accurately predict the winning lottery numbers before they were even announced. Or, how she could predict when someone would call minutes before the phone would ring. But as for the whole funeral business, the more Erika thought about it, the more the concept grew on her, until she had it all mapped out in her head.

When she ran the idea by Sheila Dowder, the attorney deemed the affair a fitting denouement that would liberate Michael from Erika's life. Given that he'd tried unsuccessfully to gain custody of the children by branding Erika an unfit mother, the attorney certainly hadn't needed much persuasion to encourage Erika to move forward with the homegoing service. So the event was set in motion.

Just as Attorney Dowder had calculated at the onset of the divorce proceedings, any timidness or reservations Erika once held were erased. Now, she was just as the attorney had assured her she would be: a vindictive barracuda swimming comfortably in her element.

And so, to the funeral, the people came. Most came with sorrowful expressions that quickly morphed into befuddlement upon entering the oddly decorated chapel. They couldn't decide if they were attending a funeral to honor a man whom they knew as a wealthy, successful business tycoon, or if they were at a party to pay their last respects to an unrepentant, reprobate sinner who had lived a life filled with debauchery and excesses of the worst kind. The scandal-laden narrative of Michael's obituary clearly indicated the latter.

None, however, doubted the sincerity of the nongrieving widow-in-red, who was obviously celebrating her husband's demise with transparent glee.

Many of Michael's co-workers who came were struck by the suddenness of his passing since they had either dined with him a few short days before or had just spoken to him by phone. One man was particularly moved because he'd bumped into Michael at a private airport mere days ago, where the man could have sworn Michael had told him he was traveling out of the country to the Middle East.

Although it was customary to say a few words of encouragement to the grieving widow, it just didn't seem as though condolences were needed. If anything, congratulations seemed more the order of the day. With the casket closed, it wasn't as though people could walk up and view the body. So they sat nervously in the pews, a quiet anxiety pervading the air while the minutes ticked by. Ray Charles' song playing in an endless loop added to the uncertainty of the event.

"It is a funeral, right?" were the whispers.

"Sure. There's his casket."

"Yes, but are they certain he's dead? What if they have the wrong Michael Slaughter?"

"Has to be him. That's his picture. Plus, why else would they have his funeral if he wasn't dead?"

"But I overheard the lady over there say she heard that someone spoke to him just this morning."

"Well, I don't know how that could be true. The obit says he died from a festering illness. Why I'll be! Is that champagne they're passing out?"

"Looks like it. Waiters dressed in red with black velvet gloves at a funeral? Never seen anything like it in all my years!"

As the waiters distributed champagne in flute-shaped glasses, some of the people appeared reluctant to accept the bubbly drink, but the waiters insisted. With her own glass in hand, Erika stepped to the podium. She tapped the mike and the music lowered, as if on cue.

"Let me start by saying thank you for coming today. Contrary to what many of you may be thinking, this is not an occasion for sadness. As you can look around and tell, this funeral was designed to be a joyous celebration in honor of a man who lived a double life.

"Some of you may have known Michael Slaughter as a man expert at constructing and deconstructing contracts worth billions of dollars. But very few of you knew that this same man possessed a dark side. It was this man that I, as his wife, lived with for 20 years. The Michael Slaughter I knew was…" Erica paused for effect. "…a wife beater, a serial adulterer, a neglecter of his own children. And worst of all, he was an amoral, sanctimonious man who abandoned his wife and children without a second thought just to take up with a teenager—a young girl more than half his age." Erika paused as her guests gasped appropriately. She held up her hand as if to dissuade them from stoning Michael's casket.

"Yet, it's fitting that we honor his memory. Today's funeral is meant to liberate me from this blackhearted bastard of a husband."

More gasps came from the pews as some looked on aghast. Others nodded at Erika approvingly.

"Good people, please join me in a toast celebrating the death of Michael Slaughter!" Erika lifted her glass high, tilted it and poured a few drops onto the casket before bringing the glass back to her lips.

Despite the macabre tone of the event, not knowing what else to do, most of the guests joined Erika in the toast.

From her spot at the back of the church, Jamarra Sanders seethed with anger. She'd sat through the proceedings with clenched fists fighting to keep the bile from rising in her throat. Pure discipline kept her from dashing up front and butchering the woman on the spot. Jamarra couldn't bring herself to even utter the woman's name. That she would hold a funeral for Michael when he was alive and well, made Jamarra want to slice her up from head to toe. Bleed her good with a thousand cuts. Watch the life force drain from her eyes. All in good time, Jamarra promised herself. She would make the woman pay for humiliating Michael.

Jamarra could count on several fingers the number of funerals she'd attended in her lifetime, despite all the violence she'd encountered growing up. Still, she knew enough about them to know that the woman was making a total mockery of Michael. It was bad enough that she faked Michael's death. But nobody tricked out a place with red get-up and called it a celebration of someone's death. *Even drug kingpins possessed more class than this woman*, Jamarra thought. A drug dealer might pimp out a casket to look like a car, but this woman had gone too far. Nevertheless, red was the perfect color, because Jamarra intended to make sure the woman paid in blood.

To reign in her fury, she focused her animus on the attorney seated in the front pew. She, too, would pay for the heartache she'd caused Michael. Every lie that she'd told or written about him, she would pay for it dearly. All the embarrassment she'd caused Michael on his job after mailing filthy photos and lies to all the company's VIPs and Board Directors, oh yes, she would pay. After this day, the only threat she'd be to anybody else would be to the adulterers in hell. If even the place existed, which Jamarra tended to doubt anyway. To her, if there was such a thing as a heaven or a hell, earth had to be the hell part. Besides, folks that kept it real knew heaven was just a hyped-up fantasy place for losers.

Dressed in oldfashioned clothes and with her face shielded from view by the netted veil of her widebrimmed hat, Jamarra knew no one would recognize her. The guise of the funeral provided her the perfect opportunity to settle some scores, first with the attorney and next with that other woman.

Jamarra had done her homework. She knew just what to say to the attorney to reel her in. She had a plan.

As the guests began to mill around and gather together in pockets, Jamarra hung back. She loosely joined a group who turned out to be Michael's co-workers. They were all murmuring about the appalling nature of the funeral services. Jamarra stood with them until the attorney finally broke away from that woman to head for the exit.

The corridor was empty but for the two of them as Jamarra hurried to catch up with Dowder before she could leave the building.

"Mrs. Dowder?"

Hearing a voice soft and low, Attorney Dowder turned toward the sound. A woman, seemingly timid and unimposing stood about ten feet from her nervously clutching the arm of her purse. The woman hesitated as if ready to flee should she so much as raise her voice.

"Yes?" Dowder couldn't make out the woman's age or identity. Her appearance screamed middle aged and, well, dowdy. She wore an old fashioned dark blue pleated skirt suit with the skirt hanging low to her ankles. A widebrimmed hat with dark blue netting prevented Dowder from seeing her face. She wasn't a big woman, but she was extra thick around the waistline. She could have been a genteel woman anywhere from age 50 to 60.

"May I help you?"

"Yes. I desperately need your help." She stepped just a bit closer. "I've been following Michael Slaughter's case very closely and I needed to talk with you. I know he's not dead. You see, I have a five-year old son by Michael and I'd like to know if you'd represent me in a paternity suit against him. Ever since he took up with that young woman of his, he's stopped paying me child support."

Dowder couldn't put her finger on it, but something fleeting about the woman seemed youthful, except that her demeanor and clothing and lowheeled, granny-like shoes fostered an oldfashioned, matronly look. Dowder brushed the notion aside, unaware that by ignoring her instincts, she was making a fatal mistake that would cost her her life.

"A third woman?" she wondered. This Slaughter case just kept getting better and better. Dowder's eyebrows raised as her interest was piqued.

"I was hoping you could spare just a few minutes to hear my story."

The woman could have passed for someone's grandmother. She looked too senior to have borne a five-year old child. Something didn't add up and it made Dowder look to the woman's hands to determine her true age, but she was wearing white gloves. "I'd love to talk to you but I can't at this moment. I have a press conference in less than twenty minutes and my driver is waiting. Why don't you call my office and set an appointment? I'm very interested in hearing your story. Here, I'll give you my business card." Dowder reached into her purse for her wallet.

The moment her head was lowered, Jamarra moved in swiftly. A stun gun suddenly appeared in her hand and she lunged forward to wield it relentlessly. Up to fifty thousand volts jolted Dowder's body, overriding her central nervous system. Jamarra caught her before she hit the floor. Throwing the attorney's arm over her shoulder, she wrapped her own arm around Dowder's waist and carried her toward the rear exit. Anyone watching from behind saw one woman helping another distraught woman from the building.

With Dowder completely immobilized, Jamarra forced her into the back seat of her rental car. She laid her out flat, cuffed her hands behind her back and threw a heavy blanket on top of her.

Though the strength of her limbs had deserted her, Dowder's mind remained alert and her eyes were wide with alarm. When her abductor hastily covered her with the blanket, she drew close enough for Dowder to finally peer through the veil on her face. She recognized the facial features! This was no middle aged woman. This was the young girl Michael Slaughter had taken up with! Raw fear coursed through Dowder's body. What frightened her most was what she saw in the girl's eyes—an absence of all emotion. As the girl handcuffed her, there was no hesitation, no sense of wrong doing. She could have been completing one more item from a laundry list of tasks.

Wasting no time with small talk, Jamarra jumped into the driver's seat and drove away from the funeral chapel.

Three hours later, they were still driving as the numbness began to recede from Dowder's limbs. She thought she might have passed out because she found herself fighting fatigue and struggling to regain her mental alertness. She gingerly wiggled

fingers and toes before drawing the conclusion that even her ankles were cuffed. Spittle had dribbled down the side of her mouth.

"Where are you taking me?" Dowder struggled to sit up but with low energy levels, she flopped like a fish out of water. "Why are you doing this?"

No answer.

Trying to speak with authority, Dowder said, "I know who you are. I don't know what you think you're doing, but you're in big trouble."

Still no answer from the front seat.

"You'll never get away with this. My driver is searching for me. If you turn around and take me back right now, I won't press charges. I'll help you explain to the authorities that Michael Slaughter put you up to this." Dowder paused. "You're doing this for him, aren't you?"

When there was still no answer from her captor, Dowder said angrily, "Young woman, I demand that you turn this vehicle around this very moment!"

Still no response.

Twisting to get a better look at her surroundings, Dowder suddenly became aware of all the plastic that covered the floor and the seats. She recognized the vehicle as a Lincoln Town Car, a model similar to the one her chauffeur owned. The interior was the same, as were the deeply tinted windows. With her movement restricted, she couldn't make out where they were or in what direction they were traveling.

A short while later, the car abruptly pulled to a stop.

Jamarra killed the ignition and removed her veiled hat. In slow motion, she pulled the short, graystreaked wig from her head and the pillow from her midsection. She turned so Dowder could get a good look at her. A cruel smirk crossed her lips at the look of puzzlement on Dowder's face. Jamarra savored the moment.

She reached for the glove compartment. "Do you know why you're about to die?"

It was Dowder's turn to be struck silent. The bug-like quality of her widened eyes were riveted on the stainless steel ten-inch hunting knife Jamarra suddenly held in her hand.

"What? Nothing from the famous attorney who's never at a loss for slick, lying words? Let me see if I can help you. I believe you called me a 'ghetto skank.' No use denying it. I might have the exact wording wrong, but that's what I got from reading that nasty letter you sent to Michael's job. According to you, I'm nothing but a young, gullible 'ghetto-fabulous' retard whose only accomplishment in life is my good fortune to be dumber than a pile of rocks."

Jamarra rotated the knife in her hand, expertly cradling its carved base. "Remember that investigator you paid to follow Michael and me? The one who took all those pornographic pictures of us? He doesn't think I'm dumber than a pile of rocks. At least not anymore. Then again, I guess when you're missing your head, you don't really think at all, do you?"

"Nonsense. You don't even know what you're talking about." A look of impatient disbelief was reflected on Dowder's face.

Jamarra smiled. "He didn't believe me either when I told him *he* was going to die. Not at first. But after I cut off his ear and jammed it inside his mouth, he suddenly became a believer. Wanna know the best part about slicing him up? He never saw it coming. With each cut, it was like he couldn't believe he'd been duped by a 'silly young thing' like me. All I had to do to lure him, was hold a towel over my eye and pretend like I was crying. You know, now that I think about it, it was way too easy to get him into my car. He probably thought I was gonna give him a blow job or something." Jamarra shook her head, rather pleased with herself.

"When I asked him how long he'd been spying on people for you, he said ever since you hired him away from your husband by paying him double. He was a big man, Attorney Dowder. Still, I rather enjoyed carving him up like a Christmas turkey. You believe me now, don't you? You should. The cut of this knife feels the same whether it's a seven year old or someone seventy doing the cutting. Don't worry, they'll never find all the pieces of his body. Compared to you, he was very easy to get to. He didn't have a constant shadow like you. I'll say this for you, old woman, you're not an easy target. That's for sure. But then, when you tell as many lies and ruin as many lives as you've done, I guess you need a jaguar. If I were going to let you live, I'd give you a piece of advice and tell you to make sure your body guard never left your side. Not even at a bogus funeral."

Jamarra shifted in her seat. "But enough about me. Let's focus on you." She reached into the back and jerked Dowder upward until she was sitting up straight. "Now then. Is there anything you'd like to say before we begin?"

Suddenly, the reason for all the plastic in the vehicle made sense to Dowder. Though her heart rate was accelerated, her fear had receded and in its place was a new calm. "Before we begin what? I see you've stolen my jewelry. Is that what this is about? They're traceable heirlooms that date back to the early 1900's. The moment you attempt to sell them, you'll be caught. I'm not afraid of you, young lady."

"Oh, so I'm a 'lady' now? I guess it's better than being a skank. As for getting caught, I doubt it. We're in a slum on the South Side of Chicago. You know why the cops haven't bothered to investigate what a fancy car like this is doing in the neighborhood? They probably think I'm a big shot politician getting a blow job from one of the local prostees." Jamarra lifted one of the diamond rings to admire it.

"Don't worry about your jewelry. Where you're going, you won't need it anymore. Your diamonds and rubies will be a reminder to me of how you suffered before you died." Jamarra tossed the ring in the air and caught it on the way down.

"No, I don't think I'll get caught. You're about to be my fifth kill, Attorney Dowder. That's five people I've cut up into tiny pieces without getting caught. Stop looking at me like that. They all deserved to die. And so do you, for how you've ruined Michael's life."

Dowder's entire body stiffened and her head turned to the side when Jamarra suddenly rested the knife along her jawline.

"Why are you doing this?" she whispered.

Jamarra trailed the tip of the knife down Dowder's throat and chest. "One of my teachers once said that we should find something to be passionate about. He said to ask yourself, 'what would you do for free?' For the longest time I couldn't think of anything. And then one day, I was driving on Indy's low end when I saw a guy deck this woman. One hit laid her out cold. I figured him for a pimp so I followed him until he parked in front of a liquor store. I wormed my way into his car and convinced him that I'd been watchin' him and wanted to join up. Can you believe that bastard wanted me to blow him to prove that I was serious? Dumb fud. What is it with men and stupid blow jobs? Just when he thought I was gonna do it, I surprised him and gutted him like a fish. Every time I stabbed him, I was answering my own question. I knew what I would do for free."

Jamarra stared at Dowder with a pleased grin on her face. "I guess you could call me sort of an avenging angel. A real live superhero. *Ridding the world of scum, one person at a time.* That's my new motto."

"You're crazy."

"Because I enjoy killing people? I don't think so. People do it every day. No one's going to miss you either, Attorney Dowder. Not even that selfish witch who's paid you to hurt Michael. But not to worry, she's going down next."

"What do you hope to gain by doing this?" Dowder stared at Jamarra with loathing.

Jamarra looked at her pityingly. "For someone who gets paid tall cash, you really are clueless, aren't you?"

"What happened to you? You're too young to be a maniacal sociopath. Clearly, all the time you spent in those many foster homes has ruined you. You're the one who's clueless, honey. You're a motherless loser and you don't even realize it."

In the blink of an eye, Jamarra lashed out and sliced Dowder across her jaw. Blood spurted everywhere even as Dowder screamed.

Jamarra jumped into the back of the car. Grabbing a fistful of Dowder's hair, she held her head against the seat. "What the hell do you know about living in a foster home, old lady? You think I had a choice? You think everybody should grow up in a fine mansion like the one you live in and wear diamonds and fancy clothes?" Jamarra railed into Dowder's face while holding the knife against her throat. With the blackness of her rage in full throttle, she spat into the attorney's face.

"Why am I wasting time talking to you? This is for what you've done to Michael!"

As Jamarra let loose with a flurry of stabbing blows, blood splattered everywhere. When she finished, when Jamarra's rage was finally spent, the car looked like someone had defaced the interior with buckets of red paint.

"Mommy, Hully doesn't feel good. Can we sleep with you?"

The words registered somewhere in the back of Erika's champagne-soaked brain. It took her a moment to reply. "Sure, baby. But tell Hully he has to be very quiet, okay? No questions tonight because Mommy can't take a lot of noise right now." Although her head felt like someone was beating a drum inside her skull, Erika honestly couldn't remember the last time her body had felt so good.

She smiled when she felt three little bodies gingerly crawl into bed beside her. If she could have laughed without it causing her pain, she would have. It meant that her children had made a pact and once again assigned the final and most important step to Mia: Asking permission. At this moment, however, Erika needed them quiet because her temples were pounding.

The funeral was a raving success. At least by her standards. The guests were frosty towards her at first with the worst (or most offended) of them leaving as soon as she'd delivered the eulogy.

But for those who remained, after a couple of flutes of champagne, nobody seemed to care that they were imbibing bubbly inside a funeral chapel. Loosened up from the flowing drink, everybody acted as though they were one big happy family toasting Michael's departure as if he'd merely gone away to college. Even the funeral director, who was initially askance, had unwound to the point where he was circulating with a bottle of champagne in one hand and a halfempty flute in his other. He toasted Erika several times from across the room thanking her for buying the "good stuff."

By the time the last guest departed, every hors d'oeuvres had been eaten and every bottle of champagne emptied. Nobody left without embracing her and wishing her the brightest of futures.

Somewhere on the evening drive home, Erika found her mood of elation deflating to one of gloominess. She wasn't quite ready to return home. It was only 6:30 and the baby sitter she'd hired would remain with the children until she returned. She found herself pulling into the W Hotel, a place where she and Michael had come often during the early days of their marriage. Before she could talk herself out of it, she entered the lobby and headed straight for the bar area.

All eyes were riveted to the striking figure that she was. But Erika was impervious. She would have been more apt to believe that she was the ugliest woman in the building, as opposed to the beautiful one in red whom the hotel guests saw gliding through the lobby. She had come to believe Michael's nasty barbs about her own attractiveness.

The moment she took a seat at the bar, the bar tender was on top of her.

"What'll you have, Princess?"

It had been so long since Erika had gone out to drink socially that she couldn't think of anything. "What's popular with a kick that won't kill me?"

He smiled. "In that case, I wouldn't recommend the Jon Stewart Kamikaze. How about an apple martini?"

"Sounds delightful." He disappeared as Erika removed the pin from her hat and unraveled the bun at the back of her head. Her hair fell well past her shoulders as she ran her fingers through it.

"May I buy you a drink?"

Pleasantly surprised, Erika turned to survey the man offering to pick up her tab. "I just ordered one. But then it's early, so why don't you join me?" At first glance, it wasn't that she found him attractive. It was the way he carried himself. He was a manly man. But the more she stared at him, the more attractive he became. He was fair-skinned, fit and thick with big, long hands and fingers. These were a definite plus on any male. Besides, they were just going to talk and have a drink, so what difference did it make anyway?

The bartender brought her drink and placed it in front of her. Her newfound buddy ordered a Pearl Harbor.

He extended his hand in greeting. "Dexter Greenley."

"And here I was about to ask if you were…" Erika searched for some athlete's name.

"A football player?" He smiled. "No, but I get that a lot."

"I'll bet you do," Erika thought to herself. Her initial impressions aside, her apple martini was making him look more and more attractive with each sip. She took a gulp and lifted her empty glass to the bartender.

"Are you from around here?" he asked.

Erika even liked the deep tone of his voice. But she liked the firm, gentle grip of his hand even more so. Another sip of her second martini and any reservations were gone.

"I've been living here for about fifteen years. I'm Erika." She saw his eyes flit to her wedding ring. Erika twisted it on her finger. "Are you married, Dexter?" Truth-telling time.

"Yes, Erika. I'm married with three children."

Erika's smile broadened. At least he was honest. Besides, technically, so was she.

"I just came from my husband's funeral."

Dexter's hand soothingly covered hers. "I'm sorry to hear that. You must be devastated."

"Do I look devastated, Dexter?" Erika held her head to the side challengingly as she stared into his eyes.

He swallowed. Instinct warned him to tread carefully less he blew it with her. She was beautiful and sophisticated and it had taken all of his courage just to approach her. "Not at all. What you look like, Erika, is a beautiful woman in need of solid consolation. You look like a woman who could use a good man."

The way his voice lowered and the way his eyes drifted over her body from top to bottom, Erika's nipples hardened in spite of herself. The look Dexter bore into her, left little doubt about the type of *solid* consolation he was offering.

Erika looped her hair behind her ear. "Are you willing to console me, Dexter?"

"A beautiful, sexy woman like you? At this moment, I would enjoy nothing more. I have a room inside the hotel. We could finish our drinks in private." He wanted the decision to be hers.

Erika took another sip of her martini. "I think I'd like that."

Dexter signaled the bar tender. He put the bill on his hotel tab and ordered a bottle of champagne sent up to his room. They headed upstairs for an encounter neither of them would forget.

Three hours later, Erika felt like an out of shape contortionist whose body had been put through the ringer in the most delicious of fashions. Dexter had awakened her from a deep sleep and taken her through one more mindbending round, which left her grasping for her own name and sapped of all strength. He nearly had to carry her to her car.

Recognizing Erika was in no shape to drive home, he hailed a taxi and had the driver trail them as he drove Erika's car to her residence.

Now, hours later, the children were all asleep as Erika clutched her head and eased her way from the bed. If she took five or six aspirin, her hangover might go away. She'd had way too much to drink in one night. Nor was her body accustomed to the likes of a Dexter Greenley. What a lucky woman his wife was. *Strike that,* Erika thought. If he made love like that all the time, then his wife wasn't so lucky after all. With her own muscles tender in every place, Erika knew she didn't have the physical stamina to maintain an acrobatic bout with Dexter on a daily basis. Her own marriage was living proof of that.

Erika found herself staring into the bathroom mirror. She hadn't looked at herself in a fond manner in a very long time. But tonight, one man had made her feel womanly, attractive, desirable and even beautiful. The words whispered into her ear would remain with her for a very long while. Something told Erika that Sir Dexter had been sincere.

She was about to swallow three Advil pills when her hand paused halfway to her mouth. A feeling came over her so intense that it immediately catapulted her back to her teenage days in Kennilworth. As her skin crawled, every vestige of her hangover vanished as the years fell away. Without questioning it, or second guessing herself, Erika knew immediately that an evil spirit had entered her home.

She spun toward the bathroom door only to find Mia standing there clutching Hully tightly. Erika swept her up and carried her into the bedroom. "Stay here," she whispered to Mia, putting her finger to her lips.

Erika crept down the stairs. The house was cast in shadows, the darkness made less dim from the night lights that glowed throughout the house. Inside the livingroom, Erika pulled a poker from near the fireplace. The alarm hadn't sounded, but someone or some *thing* was definitely inside her home. Wielding the iron in her hand, she crept softly toward the kitchen.

She was almost inside when a movement to her left caught her off guard. Swinging the iron in a wide arc, Erika hit nothing but air. But immediately the advancing figure lunged head first into her chest, tackling her to the floor. Erika fought as if her life depended on it, wrestling with the blackened figure until something crashed into her skull, knocking her senseless.

She felt duct tape being applied to her mouth. Her body was flipped so her hands could be taped behind her back. Next, her ankles were taped together and she was dragged by the collar of her gown into the livingroom. Near the fireplace, Erika was roughly turned onto her back before the intruder straddled her.

Through the fogginess of her haze, Erika knew it wasn't Michael. Whoever it was, they were dressed in black from head to toe. Even the mask with slits for the eyes, nose and lips was black. Something told Erika that her attacker was female. It took all her strength to focus on the knife that glinted in front of her face.

Erika stiffened and went perfectly still as the blade trailed down her face and then along her throat. She heard a voice whisper, "You are going to die." Erika didn't doubt it. She twisted her head and stopped cold at the sight of Mia standing just inside the livingroom, no more than fifteen feet away.

Mia had crept down the stairs so quietly that not even the intruder had heard her. But at Erika's riveted gaze, Jamarra turned to see what Erika was staring at. Renewed strength flowed into Erika's body at the sight of her child. She bucked and went wild.

Jamarra grabbed a handful of Erika's hair. "Stop or I'll kill her, you hear me?"

Jamarra turned her glare upon the child. This was the one whose room was done up in fantasy pink. The one who was showered with love. Through the blackened haze of her rage, something registered that struck Jamarra as intensely odd: there was no fear on the child's face. Instead of running away, she seemed to be advancing closer.

Jamarra's eyes were riveted. She sensed there was something about the little girl even as her ears picked up a mumbling that the child was making. A low rumbling came from the girl, as if she were speaking in another language. Something old. Something guttural. Something that sounded like it wasn't from this world.

Jamarra was wondering if the child was retarded when the sounds she was making began to give her the creeps.

"Shut up!" Jamarra yelled at her. But little girl's voice grew louder.

Suddenly, the child stared at the ceiling, still speaking in her unknown language, when to Jamarra's amazement, the room came aglow with a strange light. Underneath her, Erika's body had grown completely still. She, too, was witnessing the strange occurrence.

Jamarra could not take her eyes off the child. When Mia pointed toward the ceiling again, Jamarra's eyes swiveled in that direction. She gasped when she saw a small pinpoint of a light glow and grow larger and brighter until a ten-foot *something* emerged to form some kind of luminous shape. The child pointed in another direction and the same thing happened again. Another ten-foot shape emerged from a tiny sparkle of light.

Soon six, ten-foot shapes filled the room. They bathed the entire room with a bright, ethereal, neonish glow. As the child advanced toward Jamarra, so too did the floating figures. Jamarra eased off of Erika and scooted backwards toward the fireplace.

"What the...?" Jamarra's head swiveled in one direction to another as she found herself at a lost for words. She couldn't even begin to comprehend what she was seeing. Were these things angels? Were they ghosts? Were they beings from another planet? What were they? They appeared barely there. And yet, they floated in air and hovered protectively over and around the little girl.

Standing over her mother, Mia pointed her little finger at Jamarra and screamed, "Get out!"

Unable to move on her own accord, Jamarra could suddenly feel herself being lifted to her feet and carried toward the front entrance. The door opened on its own accord and she was forcibly thrown outside, landing on her knees.

Jamarra sat there momentarily stunned, her hands gripping the graveled pavement. She was literally unable to move. Moments later, she stumbled to her feet and ran the distance to her car. Jamarra ran as if bats from hell were on her very heels.

Reaching the safety of her car, for the first time in her life, Jamarra didn't want to be alone. She actually wanted the company of other people. Since Michael was in Dubai, she drove to a nightclub where she knew other students hung out. She bought a drink which she intended to nurse and took a seat in a corner. The music was blaring at earsplitting decibels but Jamarra didn't hear a note. When another student from one of her classes came and took a seat at her table, Jamarra didn't notice him either. Her thoughts were riveted elsewhere.

Some sixteen hundred miles away, at approximately 12 AM Mountain Time, Dot sat straight up in her bed. She looked at her clock, realized it was 2 AM in Indianapolis, but still reached for the phone. When Erika's phone rang without answer, Dot dialed a number to a friend who worked for the FBI. He was one of the only people Dot could call and say, "I need you to send a police car to such and such an address" and it would be done without fail. Their relationship was forged after the Kennilworth slayings were solved. And it was with Patrick Gatlin that Dot had worked with to solve other cases. He trusted her instincts.

Patrick answered his cell phone in Virginia and when Dot explained the circumstances, he hung up and immediately called the Indianapolis Police Department. Minutes later, a squad car was dispatched to the Slaughter address.

Like sand cascading downward in an hourglass, time slipped quietly away as the weary traveler found herself plunged into another abyss-like valley. Would she never find her way out of this dry, forsaken place? Each time she thought she'd found an exit, it turned into another dead end, another road to perdition, another vale of wasted dreams and empty promises. When would it all end? If only there

was hope. If only there was someone or some thing to help her find her way. To help her win this war of attrition. Beat down from all of life's battles and travails, the traveler didn't think she had strength to keep going, nor the will to carry on. No hope. No more dreams. No more goals. And no future. Each turn presented another fight that left wounds with little time to heal. But, if she could try just one more door, just one more time, she might find her answers. Perhaps then she could make sense of the devastation that lay waste around her. One last try and if that didn't succeed, then she could give in, give up and surrender to this "thing" that was pursuing her. Her will to survive had once been strong. If she could just make it to the next destination, maybe hope would be waiting behind the next door...

Chapter Twenty-Eight

Jayson stood over Syl's bed watching her sleeping form. She looked at least twenty years younger, like her old self in the days before Carmin had died. Childhood images of his sister flooded his memory as he stared at the peaceful expression on Syl's face. The two of them were splitting images of one another; so much so, that Jayson felt as though he was peering into a looking glass that revealed the woman Carmin would have become had she lived to reach her potential. He smiled at the sudden recognition that his thoughts of Carmin were no longer accompanied by the usual feelings of guilt and shame.

Jayson readily acknowledged that in the last few weeks, much had changed for him. His whole outlook on life seemed to have altered in that brief window of time. All that he once held sacred, Jayson found himself re-evaluating. The myriad jetsetting with his skirtchasing, scandal-tinged posse had caused him to be branded as just another corrupt rogue with hunger in his heart and little mercy in his soul. His world of rich friends, adoring fans, private jets and countless women whose faces all blurred into one, no longer held sway for him.

Mercurial as his lifestyle was, it all seemed so pointless to him now. Like cottoncandy clouds of confusion, his life flashed before him as a series of melodramas with glamorous settings, vivid characters and topshelf production values. Was it all vain and shallow? Yes, a good deal of it had been. Nevertheless, it was how he'd conducted his days. Could he truly pivot on a dime and give it all up?

As soon as he set foot in New York, LA or on his next movie production, he knew automatically what people would say: "It's so nice, Jayson, to have you back where you belong." And where did he belong in their eyes? At the center of a worldclass, spare-no-expense, fuel-the-helicopters media-type frenzy. Was that how he really wanted to spend the rest of his life?

Maybe he was getting older. Or, it might be something else entirely. Whatever "it" was, all he knew was that it had silenced the noise, all the background chatter that constantly ran in an endless loop inside his head, that same noise which kept him jumping from one thrillseeking moment to the next, had given way to silence.

He took a seat in a nearby chair and was soon overcome with a deep reflective sense of gratitude. In no way would Jayson describe himself as a praying man, but he was suddenly profoundly grateful for Syl, for her recovery, and even for where his own life's journey had brought him thus far. He accepted the good with the bad. And the good included Aaryn. In such a short time, she'd made him believe that there was something more. Something better and deeply fulfilling than what had come before. Aaryn made him believe that there was still good in the world, that there was good within him, and that there was time to add purposefulness to his life beyond all his cinematic achievements.

When Syl's eyes opened, she saw her son in deep repose with his chin resting on steepled fingers. He looked thoughtful and full of concern.

"What's wrong?" Her voice was soft, but it came out like a croak.

A smile lit Jayson's face as his eyes latched onto Syl.

"Absolutely nothing. How are you feeling?"

"Thirsty. Hungry. Drained. And a little scared." Syl gingerly flexed her muscles and winced slightly.

Jayson came to her bedside with a glass of water, sat, and rested his hand on her shoulder. It drifted down the side of her body that once was paralyzed.

"Can you feel that, Ma?" A note of curious awe tinged his voice.

"Yes." Syl's smile was like that of a giddy kid. "I think I feel like a new person."

"It's incredible. What happened, Ma? I mean…How did..?" His sentence trailed off as he shook his head in wonder.

"Speechless. Yes, I believe I know how you feel. There's this sense of 'Is it true? Did it really happen? Can I really move again?'" As if to answer her own question, Syl gingerly swung her feet over the side of the bed. She brushed Jayson's hands aside when he moved as if to stop her from falling.

"I have feelings again, Jayson, in parts of my body that were dead. But you want to know the strangest thing? It's my mind more so than my body that feels renewed. I know this may sound crazy. But when I think back to the exact instant when I was healed, there was this moment, in the midst of all the pain when I felt feelings rushing back to my body, that the pain just fell away. In that moment, I could see, Jayson." Syl's voice was hushed as her arm stretched out as if to touch her own thoughts.

"I saw something. I mean, it wasn't my imagination. I really saw it. It wasn't like the yellow light that many people say they see right before death. But it was similar. Whatever it was, it wasn't of this world. I can't explain it, but I've never encountered anything like it before. Not even in my dreams. 'Another dimension' is how Aaryn defined it when I tried to describe it to her. She said it wasn't even something that she, herself, could explain. She just knew that all her patients experience it the moment healing comes."

Syl's mouth opened and then closed again just as quickly. "I know I'm not making sense. But I know what I saw. I honestly want to tell you about them, but I'm just not sure how it'll come out. So I…"

"Them? Who're 'them?' Tell me, Ma. What did you see?" Jayson leaned forward hanging onto Syl's every word.

She shook her head in wonder. "You wouldn't believe me. *I* wouldn't believe me." She held up her hand as if to stay his barrage of questions.

"I asked Aaryn that if I didn't imagine it, that if I really saw and experienced what I did, then why is it that no one talks about it? Talks about *them*?" Syl stared into the distance.

"Aaryn said to me, 'Ask yourself, Syl, why are you having such a hard time believing what you witnessed. You experienced another dimension. You observed firsthand the spirit beings who are forever among us. For one tiny moment in time, the eyes of your understanding were opened and you glimpsed what very few people ever get to see in a lifetime. People don't talk about it because no one would believe them. There are many, many dimensions in the universe, Syl. And if they're able to tap into any of them, some people don't come back to themselves. Especially, if they reach the dimension that you did. Something happens to your mind because once you experience it, once you have had such an encounter, you don't want to come back. It's like experiencing nirvana. There's so much goodness and purity in the dimension that you tapped into, that you don't want to come back to this earthly realm. That's where I came in for you, Syl. I was there to help guide you safely back to the here and now.

'If not, you would have snapped. You'd be surprised to know that the bulk of individuals in psychiatric wards and those walking the streets across this country are where they are because they've tapped into another dimension, another realm in the spirit that they couldn't traverse. You've seen them plodding along, eyes dull and vacant, talking to themselves, or ranting at the world around them. They were trespassers in an unknown time zone and they couldn't handle it. Their minds couldn't coalesce around the gravity of what they encountered. The world calls these people crazy. But I don't. I say they're mentally brittle because they're stuck between worlds, they're trapped in another dimension. But enough of this. No more of these kinds of questions, Syl. No more talk about asylums. The key for you is to focus on the present. You've got to continue your healing. So bring your mind and your thoughts back to this realm. To the here and now, Syl. Any and all questions you may have, I promise you, someday they will be answered. All in good time.'"

Syl stared at the bewildered expression on Jayson's face.

"You don't believe me, do you? I told you it would sound crazy."

"No, it's not that, Ma." Jayson could only shake his head. "I guess I don't know *what* to believe. After what you've told me, I should run as far away from Aaryn as I can. But instead I'm drawn to her even more. I want to get to know her, intimately."

When Syl's brow furrowed together in a frown, Jayson explained.

"No. I don't mean physically, I mean, yes, there is that. But deeply as in what makes her tick? Why does she think the way she does? What makes her have these experiences that the rest of us are immune to because it's not even on our radar screens? I want to befriend her. I can't even believe I'm saying this, but I think I feel something for her beyond a curious fascination."

Jayson stared at the floor. "There's been only one other time in my life that I've wanted someone like this."

"Porsha." Syl uttered the name that used to fill her with animosity because of the heavy sense of betrayal she'd felt.

"Yes. Aaryn makes me believe I can have that again."

"Nothing would make me happier, son, than knowing that you're happy and content. But…" Syl frowned as she hesitated. "Does Aaryn even *like* you?"

As soon as she said it, they both burst out laughing and whatever heaviness that was in the room evaporated.

"That's a valid point. But I was hoping to change that."

"Well, you didn't hear it from me, but you've got your work cut out for you."

"I know, Ma. I know. Any tips for me?"

"As a woman, I could tell you any number of things. But in Aaryn's case, I wouldn't even know where to begin."

"That bad, huh?"

"Well…They do say nothing is impossible, don't they? I thought all the papers and pundits said you were supposed to be the supreme charmer. Are you losing your touch? You should find a good time to have an honest heart-to-heart with her about what's the best way forward. You might try convincing her that you finally got religion and decided to radically change your ways. You could start by telling her you're the leopard who's changed his spots."

"I don't know, Ma. From what I hear about religion, it's like soap: it only works if you use it. So the last thing I'm going to do is pretend I'm now religious. Anyway, I can't believe you. You're enjoying this, aren't you? What's that about?"

Syl shrugged her shoulders, pleasantly surprised that she could now move them both. "Son, you know how much I love you. But you've had your way with women for far too long. They drool over you, they fight over you, and they rush to do your bidding. It's sickening how they debase themselves just to be seen with you. It's absolutely ridiculous. Over the years, I've watched you go through some of the most classiest to the most sleaziest females in the world. I don't care how rich they were, how famous they were, or how outwardly beautiful they were: none of them could hold a candle to Aaryn. And that, dear son, includes Porsha."

A note of pride crept into Syl's voice. "Dr. Aaryn Jamison is different. She's a lady. And she's no push over. Your money, your status and even your looks don't mean anything to her, Jayson. I'm just not sure you're in her league."

Sylvia picked at her gown. "I did ask her about you a couple of days ago. You want to know what she said?"

"Of course I do."

"It's not pretty."

"Somehow I didn't think it would be."

"Well, she said you suffer from 'celebrity-itis.' According to Aaryn, that's when you're insulated with an unrealistic view of how you're perceived in the world. She said you surround yourself with staffers and acolytes who act like you walk on water, and that when the bravest of them venture forth to suggest that you're doing something that isn't playing well, you typically don't pay them any mind. She said that in the rapturous eyes of those who flock around you, you can do no wrong. After all, you're the celebrity, not them. Although, she did say that you're not unusual in this behavior. Aaryn thinks that because Hollywood is such an ego-soaked enterprise, it's set up to elevate all celebrities like they're minipotentates."

"How the hell would she know that? Of course you came to my defense, right?"

Syl shook her head. "One more thing. She ended by saying that because most celebrities tend to play in the same sandbox, they have weak, dependent egos that constantly need propping up like the loose signposts you see in the desert." At the look on Jayson's face, Syl added, "But I'm sure she wasn't referring to you, dear."

"You certainly know how to hit below the belt. Where did the woman go who used to be my mother? Remember her? The one who thought I could do no wrong? The one who used to be my staunch defender? I'd like to have her back."

"I'm still here. I'm just not enamored to the point where I don't see your flaws. I love you no less, Jayson. You'll never have to doubt that. I just want what's best for

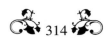

you. Personally, I think it would be wonderful to have Aaryn as a daughter-in-law. But I don't know how she'd feel about that. I can tell you one thing. If you're not ready to settle down, go find yourself some other female to toy with. Aaryn's not the kind of woman you're used to."

"Are you saying I don't deserve her?"

Syl lifted her chin defiantly. "I'm just saying she's not to be toyed with. She's a lady."

Jayson laughed. "Any minute when you're ready to climb down off your high horse, let me know. I believe I can change her mind is all I'm saying. Maybe it is time for me to get married. I thought you wanted grandchildren and all that good stuff anyway. We'll just have to see what Aaryn says about it."

"Hmph. Yes, we shall see, won't we?"

"I think I'll go find your doctor right now." Jayson left to go in search of Aaryn.

"What do you mean she's on leave of absence?" Jayson stood inside Kyle's office pacing in front of his desk.

"She had an emergency, so she's taken a brief leave of absence."

"What kind of emergency? Is she sick?"

"Jayson, I'm not allowed to release further information. I can't tell you anything more." It was, in fact, all the information that Kyle had himself. But he wasn't about to let Jayson know that.

Jayson headed for the door. "Never mind, I'll find her."

As he stared at the retreating figure, Kyle didn't doubt that he would.

"Dot, where's Aaryn?" Jayson strode briskly down the corridor, his phone to his ear.

"Hello Jayson. I'm fine. Thank you ever so much for asking."

"Sorry, Dot. How are you?" Before Dot could respond, he asked, "What's this I hear about an emergency? Is everything okay?"

"All will be well."

"I'm sure it will, but where is Aaryn? Why did she take a leave of absence? What's going on?"

Silence.

"Come on, Dot. You're killing me. This can't be that difficult. You know where she is, so tell me. Is she standing next to you?"

"No, Jayson. She's en route to the airport."

"The airport? Which one, Dot? Where's she traveling to? And why all the secrecy? Why can't you just tell me what's going on?"

"There's no secrecy, Jayson. We happen to be private individuals. Why are you asking these questions anyway?"

"Because I need to talk to her, Dot."

"I don't know that she wants to talk to you though, Jayson. She needs to be focused on the tasks ahead of her and she may not want to deal with you on top of everything else."

"I'll take that risk. Now, which airport?"

Dot sighed. "Salt Lake City."

"A commercial airline?"

Dot laughed. "Yes, Jayson. I realize you rich celebrity-types occupy a different world than the rest of us, but here's a newsflash: Not everybody owns a private jet like you do. For those of us who don't happen to have a plane in our backyard, commercial airlines are the way to go."

Frustration was in Jayson's voice. "She could have told me and I would have taken her any where she needed to go. And we would have gotten there a lot faster. Where's she going? Come on, Dot. I need to know. I thought you were on my side?"

Jayson pushed through the revolving doors of the hospital to head for his vehicle. He walked about fifteen feet when he stopped abruptly. "Oh, hell no!"

Approximately thirteen photographers, reporters and television crews had staked out their positions at the entrance to Shriners Hospital. Unbeknownst to Jayson, the paparazzi siege had thickened during the time he'd spent inside Syl's room as photogs staked their claim outside the hospital.

Blinded by flash bulbs, a visibly annoyed Jayson Denali was nearly mobbed by the paparazzi before he spun around and rushed to re-enter the hospital.

"I take it your adoring fan club is not about to let you play the part of Romeo in peace, hmmm?"

"Doesn't look like it. Okay, Dot. Fess up. How long ago did Aaryn leave for the airport?"

"Hmmm. I'd say if you can manage to evade your media mob, you just might be able to catch up to her on I-80."

"Piece of cake. You're talking to a man who's become expert at avoiding the media wolf packs."

"I guess this is the kind of society we've become—one that feeds on celebrities like locusts feed on crops. Unfortunately, we've created stars out of nothing but bright lights and mere hype."

"Are you calling me a piece of fluff, Dot?"

"Not at all, you're the rare star, Jayson, who happens to have earned your stripes the hard way. You're different from the Hollywood train wrecks, those other poor pretty people who seem eternally plagued with problems which constantly get splayed across the pages of magazines for the viewing public's voyeuristic pleasure. I think you might be the last person in tinsel town to develop a conscious, Jayson. Even though it is late in the game."

Jayson shook his head as he impatiently waited for the elevator. "Dot, I'll never have to wonder from where Aaryn got her sharp, straight-shooting tongue. Apples apparently don't fall far from the tree. But just so I don't leave you with any illusions, know this: If you want a piece of this business, you have to be able to deal with it. You can't complain about the press, the pressures, the stalkerazzi, or the madness that comes with it because it's all part of the job. While it's unfortunate that the press has become all about tabloids and the next 'gotcha' photograph, that too is part of the job. It just so happens that I'm also very private about my personal life and I don't like talking to them about aspects of my love life."

"I didn't realize 'love' had anything to do with your life, Jayson."

"Well, it does now. And as much as I'd love to continue this enlightening, yet selfconflagrating conversation, I have to go. There's a very elusive woman who I have to catch up with."

Aaryn was lost in thoughts that were consumed with images of Erika. Just hours ago, she was basking in the glow of Sylvia's recovery. A short time later, she'd received a call from Dot about Erika having been hospitalized. The facts were sketchy as the police were reluctant to release the full spectrum of details over the phone. The bottom line was that Dot was the one they contacted and asked to come take the children into her custody. As far as Aaryn knew, Erika's husband had not been informed about the attempt on Erika's life. From what Dot had said, they considered him a suspect in a murder-for-hire plot.

"It's crazy," was all Aaryn repeated over and over as she drove toward SLC International. If there was an upside to the whole tawdry Erika affair, it was the fact that it had driven all thoughts of Jayson from the front pages of her mind. Her thoughts were focused purely on Erika and the children.

In her rearview mirror, Aaryn suddenly saw flashing lights, so she reduced her speed and steered into the righthand lane. Two police vehicles were hurtling forward at breakneck speed, lights flashing wildly. Aaryn assumed an ambulance

had to be pulling up the rear. But as they rapidly approached, she didn't see one. She noticed also that they weren't using their sirens. Just minutes ago, Aaryn recalled seeing a helicopter overhead and had thought at the time that they were airlifting a patient for emergency surgery. It was likely that the state troopers pulling alongside her now had something to do with the helicopter.

To Aaryn's dismay, the second police cruiser pulled directly behind her as the first one pulled dangerously close along side her.

"Pull over!" were the words she heard loud and clear.

"What the...?"

Aaryn was thrown for a loop. Why would state troopers be pulling her over like some common criminal? She hadn't been speeding. Her tags were in order. What gave? Not knowing what to expect, she complied quickly and pulled the SUV over to the far side of the road.

Instead of reaching for her license and insurance card, Aaryn rolled down her window, curiously irate at the interruption. But even more so irate at the fact that they had chased her down like she'd just robbed a bank. And speaking of robbing banks, the police obviously had themselves a case of mistaken identity.

"Are you Aaryn Jamison?" the officer asked upon exiting his vehicle.

"Yes, I am."

Aaryn released her seat belt.

"Mam, we'll need you to step outside the vehicle."

"What is this about, Officer? I'm sure there must be some kind of mistake. I've got a flight to catch and I don't care to miss it. Can you tell me what this is regarding?"

"Mam, we just need you to come with us."

Aaryn stepped out of the vehicle and was lead to the second police cruiser.

A black unmarked squad car with windows so deeply tinted that she could not peer inside.

The rear passenger door was opened by one of the officers who waited for Aaryn, clearly expecting her to climb inside.

Aaryn stopped just short of the opened door. "Look, this has gone far enough. I'm not going another step and I'm certainly not getting into that car until somebody tells me what's going on. Who's in charge here?" She looked around, her irritation no longer thinly veiled.

"Come on, Gentlemen. We're wasting each other's time."

"Aaryn." Jayson alighted from the back of the squad car.

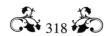

"Jayson?" Now Aaryn was truly alarmed.

"Come. I can explain everything." He waited for her to approach and gestured for her to climb inside. He should have known she, of all women, would not just go peacefully into the night without asking a million and one questions.

The door closed behind them.

"What's going on, Jayson?"

So this is what it's like to grab a tiger by its tail, Jayson thought. "I needed to find you. Dot told me you had an emergency and I wanted to offer my services."

Out of nowhere, Aaryn could feel a distant not-so-gentle drumming in her left temple just as she had in the beginning days of meeting Jayson. She thought they had at least gotten beyond this, but apparently she'd imagined that they'd reached the nadir of their relationship.

"Jayson." Aaryn stopped to rub her temple. When she spoke again, her words were slow to mask her anger. "I smell the aroma of rat. So please tell me that this patently grandiose scheme of yours was not orchestrated simply because you 'needed to find me.' That can't be the case, am I right? Please tell me that I'm not about to miss my flight all because you needed to prove some point that escapes both of us."

Jayson could feel her anger and he knew the best thing he could do to tame this tiger was to get out in front of it and ward off the tsunami that he knew was about to erupt. And as much as he wanted to, he realized the last thing to do was to touch her.

"Aaryn, look at me." He waited for her to do so. "I don't know all that's going on here since nobody seems to think they can trust me with the inside scoop. But I do know there's some kind of trouble brewing. And I simply want to help. That's all. Dot told me you were flying to Indiana. She didn't say why or what for. Now I don't know how long it's going to take you to get there on your commercial flight, but I can have you there in a jiffy. And whatever it is that you're about to head into, I want to be there with you. I want to help you face it."

Aaryn shook her head sorrowfully. "I don't have time for this, Jayson. I really don't." For some odd reason, she felt tears welling up. They might have been caused by her intense concern for her twin, wondering about her welfare and her state of being. Try as she might to get a feel for Erika in the spirit, she couldn't. Aaryn couldn't sense her, couldn't pick her up in the spirit and that frightened her more than anything else. All Aaryn could ascertain was that her sister hadn't left this earthly realm. Even Dot refused to discuss it with her. Thus, sick with fear, Aaryn had been in an almost numb state right up until the state troopers had pulled her over.

She pressed the base of both hands to her temples. The last thing in the world she wanted was to break down crying in front of this man who had the uncanny ability to hold her emotions hostage.

"Give me your hand, Jayson." With her eyes closed, Aaryn reached out her right hand and waited for him to slide his into hers. Truth-telling time.

Jayson seemed to sense the weight of the moment himself, because he almost hesitated to put his hand in hers. But then he did so with a quickness.

Aaryn's hand fastened onto his as she leaned back against the seat. As she scanned his body, it was as though her inner eyes took over. She could "see" or feel his heart beating. Using her innervision, she quickly scanned his organs. If nothing else, the man was in great physical shape. *Apparently his degenerate lifestyle had not yet caught up with him,* she thought. Probing further, Aaryn reached the recesses of Jayson's thoughts, that place where he harbored the will of his intentions.

Truth-telling time, indeed. She could feel Jayson jerk imperceptibly, but then he relaxed and soon a warmth began to emanate from him.

Aaryn "saw" a man determined. A man who wanted something. A man bent on pursuing until he conquered. Was he telling the truth? You bet he was. This man wanted *her.*

Instinctively, impulsively, she shied away from him and tried to grab her hand back. Aaryn wanted to sever the connection, to break the thread of thought, but this time Jayson was the one who wouldn't release her.

"No." Neither of them knew who uttered the word.

Suddenly, Aaryn found herself embraced inside arms that were strong and welcoming, protective, shielding, and even...loving.

Jayson didn't quite know what had just transpired. But it was similar to the last time when they'd shared their heated moment. All he knew was that once again, he'd felt this seismic desire, this subterranean pull, this deep need and intense hunger for her. He pulled her to him and began to stroke the back of her head.

"It's okay." He found himself whispering. "I'm for real. I won't hurt you. Please trust me. Let me help you. Please, just let me help you."

Aaryn buried her face into his chest. For just once she wanted to forego being the decision maker. She only knew how good it felt to rest in someone else's arms, to share the burdens of life. To not have to think about the consequences of reveling in the feel of this man. This man who the spirits were telling her wanted so much simply to be with her that she almost couldn't fathom it.

After waiting for so long that it had felt like a lifetime. After waiting so long that it had felt like her sell-by date had come and gone. After never thinking that love would or could ever come her way, it was now presented to her on a platter. All she had to do was reach out and grab it. Reach out and trust.

The first tear slid unbidden down her check and then was followed by the next and then the next after it until she tasted their saltiness. Lulled by the gentle stroking of his hand on her head, her avalanche poured forth. A groundswell of torrential tears which she neither had the willpower, nor the desire to staunch.

And yet, Jayson's embrace of her only tightened. His only thought was to help ease the loneliness he'd sensed locked inside her. That part of her that she kept locked away from the world. He now knew what Syl meant when she said she "saw something."

As she'd grasped his hand, he too, could "see." He empathized because he knew well what it was like to experience a dearth of loneliness so deeply intense that he couldn't even whisper it aloud. He knew what it was like to stand in the center of a room with massive crowds around him and yet be disconnected and unrelated to every soul within it. He knew what it felt like to wish for that one person to whom he could relate to when the world felt like it was closing in upon him.

Moments later her tears ceased and Jayson lifted her from his chest. "I'm coming with you." When she nodded, he tapped lightly on the window and the rear door on the driver's side was opened. He stepped out to give instructions.

The police cruiser pulled off the moment he climbed back inside.

"They're going to drive your car and trail us to the private airport where my plane is waiting. Where are we going, Aaryn? My captain will need to know that." Jayson's voice was tender as he watched her collect her thoughts. He was aware that the time to touch her had passed.

Aaryn took a deep breath. "It looks like we're going to Indianapolis."

Part VI

"You don't love a woman because she is beautiful,
but she is beautiful because you love her.

~ Anonymous

"If you press me to say why I loved him,
I can say no more than because he was he, and I was I."

~ Michel de Montaigne

"I love you not only for what you are,
but for what I am when I am with you.
I love you not only for what you have made of yourself,
but for what you are making of me."

~ Larry S. Chengges

Chapter Twenty-Nine

Awe obliterated indifference. Having floated up the stairs of Jayson's Gulfsteam 650, Aaryn was beyond all pretensions, royally impressed as she was.

"You know that saying? That friends don't let friends drive drunk? I guess in your case Jayse, friends don't let friends fly commercial. This is pure, unadulterated opulence."

Jayson smiled. He liked how she'd shortened his name. His top-of-the-line plane always had that affect on first timers. He'd spared no expense to make his private jet every bit as luxurious as the homes and hotels he'd grown accustomed to. Since money wasn't an issue, he could indulge himself by reinventing what it meant to fly private.

To Aaryn, the aircraft made one statement: *Welcome to the true mile-high club where only the ultra high-networth individual can afford the cover charge.* It was the classiest, most comfortable cabin she'd ever been inside. This is what it meant to truly fly first class.

Plush seats and carpets, rare woods, intricate state-of-the-art satellite entertainment systems, and a palatial bedroom and bathroom with gold-plated plumbing and light fixtures, combined to sate the desire for luxury private air travel. The plane's interior design could have been ripped from the pages of a luxury homes and gardens magazine. This was a private jet turned into a palace.

To top it off, the aircraft was staffed with a personal assistant, a chef and a regular flight crew.

After traveling in such extravagance, Aaryn thought, "Who *would* want to waste time in a crowded airport when they could get away from all the hustle and bustle inside a lavish, state of the art, flying machine such as this?"

After her tour, when Aaryn was finally shown to her seat, it was clear the panoramic windows would offer a magical glance of the world from the sky.

She was curled up with a pillow, lost in thought, when Jayson returned to take a seat in front of her. She turned her gaze from the window and locked it upon him.

"Tell me you're not going to fall asleep on me." With her bushy eyebrows and untamable bouffant ponytail, Jayson thought she looked adorable.

Aaryn shook her head. "It's been a particularly eventful day. I'm more accustomed to teaching people how to walk again than I am to being chased down by law enforcement. I was sure those officers had the wrong person. How on earth did you arrange that?"

He shrugged. "I know people who know other people. People who owe me favors." His was a give and take world where everything was based on reciprocity. In this case, Jayson was the one who now owed the Utah Police Commissioner a favor or two. But the end result was worth it.

"Thank you." Aaryn meant it as she took in the sight of him. His legs were stretched before him as he lounged in a plush seat clearly designed with him in mind. Even in a pair of jeans with a stark white cotton dress shirt, he was every bit as handsome as the world lauded him to be. Aaryn glanced away from him. She didn't want to get lost in his magnetic pull. Despite her gratitude, she needed her wits about her.

"Tell me why we're going to Indiana."

"My sister."

"Your twin. The one who it's so hard to get either you or Dot to talk about."

Aaryn nodded grudgingly. "Yes. She needs us now. Someone tried to take her life the other night. I don't know all the details because the police wouldn't say much over the phone. But she's in the hospital and my nephews and niece need us even more."

"Someone tried to kill her?"

Aaryn nodded. "She was assaulted with a knife in her own home."

"How bad are her injuries?"

"I'm not sure. The police won't say. The strangest thing is that I can't feel her anymore." At his curious look, she said, "Imagine feeling someone's pulse. Well, my sister and I have this connection where we can sense one another across time and space. Though she pulled away from Dot and I many years ago, we were still able to connect with each other. Even if it was just to check in mentally and say, 'I have no desire to talk to you. Just give me my space.' But right now, I can't get anything from her. There's no pulse in the spirit. Nothing. That's what most alarms me."

"You think she's dead?"

"No, her lifeline is still present. I just don't know how badly she's been wounded. Or if that's why she's not responding."

To this, Jayson had too many questions. He didn't want to open a can of worms but neither did he want to pretend like he wasn't fascinated by what she'd just told him.

"What do you mean 'her lifeline is still present?' Are you saying you'd know it if she were dead?"

"Yes, Jayson, I would know. I'm sure it sounds crazy, but imagine that you and I have an invisible thread tied around our wrists. That thread connects us no matter how far apart we are. Because the thread is invisible, it's there but just not discernable by the naked eye. And yet, the moment you pulled on your end of the thread, wherever I am, I'd know that my wrist was being tugged. Well, right now, I'm tugging on that thread, but my sister is not responding."

"How do you know or sense these things, Aaryn? Why is it that normal people don't have the slightest fathom of what you're experiencing? Why couldn't I sense my own sister, Carmin, the way you sense yours?"

"Jayse, I don't have a clear answer for you. When scientists say that we use only about five percent of our brain power, they're on to something. There's so much more to this cosmic universe that we don't know about. As humans, we can't possibly know everything there is to know. So we tend to confine people and things to a box so we can label them and feel comfortable about it. It's like having a powerful computer at your disposal but because all that you know about it, is that it can type words on a screen, that's all you ever use it for. Therefore, its vast capabilities go unknown to you. Meanwhile, someone else is using the same computer but maxing out its capabilities.

"When we were much younger, my sister and I would dream things that would come to pass within days or weeks. And then one day, Erika dreamt that my father was killed in an explosion. Two weeks to the day of her dream, the mineshaft my father was working in exploded. He died that day. But Erika never recovered. Something shifted for her. The 'gifts' that we've been graced with, for her, they became a curse.

"So, to answer your question: I'm not sure why 'normal' people aren't tapped in. But there are more people like Dot and I than you could imagine, Jayson. We're not witches and neither do we adhere to any of those kinds of precepts. We believe in Jesus Christ. We've simply been gifted with the gifts of prophesy and the discernment of spirits. Because we can see and detect spirits, we know that there are unseen forces that battle for the souls of human kind. And because our family can see things others cannot, we've learned to adapt. We've learned not to draw attention to ourselves, Jayse. It's why I could peer straight through Commissioner Jim Oden and his kind to divine that his motives were not pure."

Aaryn looked down at her hands. "God has placed an incredible gift in my hands, Jayson. So I use that gift to honor Him through helping others to heal. That is my mission in life. It's a mission which I've chosen to accept. That is who I am."

He had to ask, Jayson thought as he marveled. He took a sip of his drink. "Your sister, is she married?"

"Yes, for nearly twenty years. But now they're going through a brutal divorce. Isn't it amazing how a relationship can turn from the bloom of love to twisted hate on the drop of a dime?"

"There's nothing amazing about that, Aaryn. It happens every day. Welcome to a little thing called life."

"You might be right. But then it seems so much wiser to make decisions about love and relationships in the cold light of day as opposed to when your emotions are scattered and fragile. There's something to be said about not having any illusions."

Their drinks were brought in on a gold platter by his flight assistant, Kim, a young Asian woman. "Even the stemware is of Baccarat crystal and screams first class," Aaryn thought.

Jayson didn't want to lose the thread of their conversation and he didn't want her to draw back into herself. "I guess that's why they say that love is blind."

"It doesn't have to be, Jayson. Love doesn't have to mean you're oblivious to someone's flaws. Love should be open and accepting. That's the power of love. Loving someone *despite* their flaws, that's the greater premise. Love is trusting. Love is give and take. Love is daring to believe that someone cares as crazily about you as you do for them. The dilemma is that it's just not always reciprocated. Love is so much more than climbing in and out of someone's bed, having traded a piece of your soul for a temporary piece of satisfaction."

Jayson lifted his glass and saluted her. "And of course, you're the expert in all things involving love and romance."

Aaryn brushed aside his sarcasm. "I don't have to have slept with a thousand men, Jayson, to know what love is. Equally as important is knowing what love is not. It goes back to the 'cold light of day' phrase I mentioned a moment ago. There's something to be said for that. It may not put a romantic spin on things, but it does paint a more honest and accurate picture."

"But you've never been in love, Aaryn. So again, how would you know? Anybody can be a Monday morning quarterback. Meanwhile, the real players are out there on the field risking it all. I'd rather play the game, Aaryn, than sit on the sidelines and judge from afar. I'm not saying what you've got going for yourself isn't noble. But the bottom line is that you've created no memories. Isn't that what life is all about? Creating memories, making inroads, carving new paths for yourself? That's what this whole search for happiness is about."

Jayson saw her shrug. "No, I'm not saying I haven't made mistakes. But at least I'm in the game. So don't judge me."

"I'm not judging you, Jayson. And I have created memories. Just not in the same areas that you may have."

"Okay, I'll give you that. Your judgment of me may be in check right now, but you've judged me in past times. I'll never forget some of the things you've said to me. But everybody's entitled to their own opinion so I just 'man up' and take in what you've got to say. Doesn't mean I agree with it, but what the heck?"

"Okay, you're right, Jayson. I have judged you. I apologize for that. I'm not perfect either, okay? Take my temper, for instance. As you've noticed, I have issues there."

"What a shocker."

Aaryn flicked her hand at him. "But, I'd like to say in my defense that I've never been this way with anyone else."

"So I'm supposed to feel honored to be on the receiving end of your temper tantrums?"

Aaryn turned to stare out the window as the plane took off. It was safer for her to not get drawn in to a tit-for-tat vein with him. That was a surefire way to arouse her temper.

"Look, this is new for me. You're new for me, Jayson. My life was going along smoothly with no glitches until you dropped into it. I'd honestly resigned myself to the fact that my shelf life, my sell-by date, had expired. And then you're dropped into my world like a whirl-wind tornado bent upon uprooting everything in its path. Because of you, I've been forced to confront so many aspects of my life that I'd become content with. Areas that had lain dormant, all because of you, are suddenly alive and demanding answers that I don't have."

"Are you complaining?"

Aaryn sighed grudgingly. "Not so much anymore. I think I'm in the 'acceptance' phase now."

Jayson drained the last of his cocktail. He needed another one. Definitely something stronger than the water Aaryn was drinking.

"If it's any consolation, Doctor, it's been no picnic in the park for me either. I'm not used to this…" Jayson trailed off. He wanted to say, "this forced celibacy." But he didn't because she hadn't asked it of him. It was something that had happened miraculously. It certainly wasn't something he'd been wishing for. Jayson wasn't even sure he appreciated it. The problem he had was that, of all the women available to him, he found himself fixated on this particular one in front of him.

"This is different for me, is all I'm saying. I'm not much for talking about feelings, but this is new to me. So where do we go from here? Or, is there a 'next' for us? What about you, Aaryn? How do you feel about me? Am I spinning my wheels? If so, just tell me. I'm not the kind to waste my time where I'm not wanted.

I'd say to anybody, 'reject me' if you don't want to be bothered. That way I can move on with my life."

"Honestly, Jayson, I don't know where we go from here. As for how I feel about you? I…" She found herself at a loss for words. She offered tentatively, "Can we be friends?"

Jayson laughed. "I don't think anyone's said that to me since grammar school."

"That's unfortunate. You should hear it much more often." Aaryn paused. "You've got a good heart, Jayson."

"Lady, pul-lease. Spare me the 'Dear John' crap."

"No, I mean it. When I push past all the blockages you've erected to keep people from getting to know the real you, there's so much more to you than these outward trappings." Aaryn spread her hands to indicate their surroundings.

"It's great to have money, Jayse. Let's face it, some things in life are just plain easier to deal with when you have the financial wherewithal than when you don't. But all this? This is living on another level. So, as you continue to fly to greater heights, don't forget the little people, okay? You know, us peons?"

"Ha! Peons? You? Dot? You've got to be kidding me. Dot's tea business took in six million dollars in profits last year. You, yourself, have made $1.7 million this year alone, and the year ain't over yet, Lady. So how does that qualify you as a peon? Don't try to sell yourself as something you're not."

"Spying, Jayson? Why am I not surprised?"

"In my world it pays to vet the people you're interested in. You'd be surprised what a good due diligence report can unearth."

Aaryn shook her head. She wasn't shocked at his speculation and need for information about her and her family. Surprisingly, neither was she angry.

"Tell me more about this 'friendship' thing. Does this friendship of ours include benefits?"

"What kind of benefits, Jayson? What do you mean?"

"You've never heard the expression, 'friends with benefits' before? You're pulling my leg, right?"

"No, Jayson, I'm not pulling your leg. And you know what? Based on how excited you're becoming, I don't think I even want to know what the phrase means. The answer is already, NO."

"Wait. You can't say 'no' without letting me explain."

Aaryn threw him a "don't even try it" look.

"Seriously, we can create our own version of what 'benefits' our friendship should include. Why don't we do that right now? Set the parameters, if you will."

"Jayson, you are forever trying to seal a deal, aren't you? If it's not negotiating some oil windfall profits contract, it's another movie deal where you're trying to carve out another piece of the pie."

"Babe, life is all about the art of negotiation. It's getting the jump on others before they get the jump on you. Now, back to establishing our benefits package."

"Jayson, for all your business savvy and acumen, and your very high boardroom IQ, you are to me...simply...stoo-ped." Aaryn stretched out the word's pronunciation.

"You're the one who told me way back when that in some cases, stupid is good, remember?"

"I'm speechless."

"I doubt it. That would be a first for you."

Jayson's flight assistant came and whispered to him in a hushed voice that someone "important" was urgently trying to reach him. He whipped out his blackberry and thumbed through his messages. He found what he wanted and pressed a button.

"Excuse me a second, Aaryn."

Aaryn figured he would leave for privacy reasons but she heard him say, "Ridley? What can I do for you? Yes, I know you revised the schedule. Don't worry, I'll be there. Then let's plan to shoot the explosion scene in a week's time. I'm glad they were cooperative. Tell them there's no reason for alarm. If we're one second behind schedule, it won't be because of me. I'll see you in seven days."

Jayson released the call.

"Seven days? So that's all the time I have left with you? Just when I was starting to like you." This to hide the swell of disappointment which she felt.

Jayson felt the pull of the world and all the obligations which he'd adroitly managed to hold at bay imploding upon him. Contractual commitments were tugging at him, demanding that he answer the call.

"Seven days is a lifetime, Aaryn. The world's an oyster."

Aaryn threw him a glowing smile. With a few words, he'd orbited her world and put things back into proper alignment. "Enjoy the remaining moments for what they were," she thought.

"Have you really been here for five weeks? It doesn't seem that long. It feels like yesterday when you landed on Shriners' doorsteps." Aaryn had no way of knowing that bets had been lost because of his additional two-week stay.

Jayson held up his blackberry. "Trust me, it's been that long. Do you know that I was supposed to be here for only three weeks? Everybody around me said I'd be climbing the walls within days of arriving and that I'd come crawling back to LA begging them to take me in." Jayson laughed. "Boy, were they mistaken. Not only did I cross the three-week threshold, but then I had to go and extend the timeline. As we speak, I'm supposed to be filming in Canada. I asked Ridley Scott to delay shooting my scenes and to proceed without me. Since I'm not there, people think I've snapped out or something because they know I'm like clockwork when it comes to a production."

"Your people didn't think Utah was big enough to hold you, did they?"

"What they thought was that I'd be bored to tears. Hell, to be honest, *I* thought I'd be bored to tears. I wondered, 'what the heck do people do for entertainment in Utah?' Other than climb mountains and attend basketball games, that is."

"Jayson, if you love the outdoors, there's a lot to do here. You can't always lump everyone in the same basket. I'm non-Republican, non-Mormon, and yet I've existed here happily all my life. If I chose to look at my situation the way you do, I would feel pretty isolated here. But I don't. I'm content. I really, really love the outdoors, and I especially feel connected to the Utah mountains. And speaking of mountains, I've had this desire to visit the Denali National Park in Alaska ever since I've met you. We should go one day."

"Let's do that. You know, Aaryn, I didn't see it at first, but I'm beginning to understand how easy it is to relate to this place. There's a sereneness that I can't explain. I've been content during my time here. It's unusual that I haven't reached out to anyone, yet my phone hasn't stopped ringing since the day my plane touched the ground weeks ago. I got to the point where I just shut it off. Something I've rarely done in the past. That's definitely not the norm. You see? All these 'firsts' for me. It's driving people around me crazy because they're used to getting me live whenever they call. The only things I've checked daily since I've been here are my investment portfolios, my online accounting systems and my film scripts. Everything else has gone bust."

"Wow. I didn't realize that. You seemed to be busily enjoying yourself so I figured…" Aaryn shrugged. It had crossed her mind that he'd been occupying himself with other women. "I guess I don't know what I thought."

"Several times, my posse has threatened to converge upon Utah. But I told them if they showed up, they'd be canned. They think you've kidnapped me, you know."

"No they don't. They don't even know of me."

Jayson laughed at her unawareness. "Oh yes, Lady. Believe me, they know about you. We've been photographed twice and even appeared in a New York article. Some people are speculating about my intentions towards you."

"You've got to be kidding me." Aaryn looked askance.

"All jokes aside, babe, it's true. I'm shocked that we've outwitted the media bloodhounds for as long as we have."

"What do you mean, 'we'?"

"I say 'we' because it's already been whispered that I've got a new lady love hidden away here in Utah. However, the stalkerazzi don't know for sure your identity, but that hasn't stopped them from speculating or snooping to ferret you out."

Aaryn groaned. She surely didn't need additional headaches of these kinds.

Jayson leaned forward with excitement. "So tell me, how do we celebrate this next week?"

When Aaryn patted the plush leather seat beside her, Jayson flew next to her in a flash. A boyish grin dotted his face. "You're enjoying this aren't you?" she asked. But even she was smiling. "Come." She patted her thighs and motioned for him to curl up with his head in her lap.

Jayson stretched himself out like he'd done this very move with her a thousand times before. That's how natural it felt to him. Her thighs were the only pillow that he needed. The first touch of her fingers on his head sent tantalizing shivers down his spine. The light persistent kneading of her fingers on his scalp and Jayson couldn't suppress the sigh of pleasure that escaped him. His temples, his chin, his neck. One set of fingers massaged his shoulders, the other, everywhere above. *This was heaven,* Jayson thought. Or surely the closest thing to it.

With twelve pairs of cranial nerve endings set aflame, Jayson figured he was experiencing the lap of nirvana. The steady drumbeat of her massage produced such a soothing, tender effect on his sensory preceptors that his entire body felt as though it was immersed in a warm jar of wax. Jayson savored each second. He couldn't recall the last time he'd felt so relaxed and comforted. His mind drifted. The cares of the world fell away. And before he knew it, he was out like a light. The huge grin painted on his face, fixed in place.

The Gulfstream landed a scant few hours after take off. It was early evening and a far cry from the seven hours it would have taken Aaryn had she flown commercially via connecting flights. As the plane taxied to a stop, Aaryn looked out the window and saw a Hummer stretch limo idling on the tarmac.

She shook her head. "Please tell me that's not for us."

"It was. But since I already know what you're going to say, the word I'm stressing is past tense. Whatever happened to spreading your wings and trying something new? Have you ever been inside a Hummer limo? Then how do you

know you wouldn't like it? You and your preconceived notions." Jayson mimicked her in a mocking voice. "I don't wanna ride in that thing! It's too flashy!"

"Umm…may I have a turn to say something?"

He let out a loud sigh while throwing her an exasperated look.

"Jayson Denali, that thing is nothing but a showboat. Just look at it. It's a monstrosity. It screams, 'look at me, everybody!' Believe me, I have no desire to see the inside of it. And since you're able to read minds now, do you think we could ride in something considerably less ostentatious? Something subtle like a Lincoln Town Car, perhaps?"

"I'm already on it. But you're cramping my style, Lady." He beckoned Kim and told her of their change in plans.

"You have no style, Jayse. That vulgar display of tastelessness right there on the tarmac proves it. No wonder the media hounds can spot you a million miles away. Hey? You know what? That's how we can use the next seven days. I'll teach you the art of discretion."

"No thanks. I'm already well-versed on the topic. I'm sure I could teach you a thing or two."

"We have seven whole days to find out, don't we?"

"That may be your seven-day game plan. But I've got an entirely different agenda."

Jayson took her arm and helped her down the steps of the plane.

"As long as your plan includes three small children and at least one adult, we're on. I'm the one adult, by the way."

"In your dreams." Their ride arrived and the driver got out to open the doors for them.

"This is no Town Car, Jayson."

"Quit your whining. It's half the size of the Hummer Stretch SUV you just rejected. Besides, by the time we load the kids inside, you'll be thanking me for having the foresight to hire a limo."

"I hadn't thought of that. You may be right after all. So, good job."

"You're welcome."

Inside the much smaller limo, Jayson stretched out his hand to Aaryn, who had taken a seat away from him on the U-style leatherette sofa. Although half the size of the 140-inch stretch Hummer, it was still spacious.

When she hesitated, he said, "You should know by now that I don't bite."

"Says you." But Aaryn slowly sidled closer to him.

Jayson clasped her hand. "What did you do to me back there on the plane? Did you slip me a mickey, Doctor Jamison?"

"Of course not. Maybe you were just tired and your body wiped out."

"All I know is that I slept like a rock. Why not let me return the favor? Come closer. I know how to give a good massage, too."

"Your fingers on my body? I don't trust you that much, Jayson Denali."

"I'm wounded. Did I say such a thing to you? Absolutely not. I trusted you blindly. Gave you permission to have free will with my body. Now, that's what we can do in these next seven days. I'm going to teach you to trust me. How's that?"

Aaryn slipped her hand from his and removed her jogging jacket. After folding it neatly and placing it in Jayson's lap, she edged closer and rested her head there, stretching out much like he had on his plane.

"Are there any rules to these trust lessons of yours?" she inquired.

"Sure there are. First, rule number one is that you must do everything I tell you. No questions asked. Second, no whining. The third and final rule will be most important for you." Jayson paused to let what he was about to say sink in. "And this will also be the difficult part given that you have a limited amount of home training. Of course, that's Dot's fault for overpampering you by allowing you to have your…"

Aaryn interrupted him. "Umm…Jayse? Will you just get to the point and tell me what rule number three is? I'm growing all grey just laying here waiting."

"See this sarcasm of yours? This is exactly what I'm talking about. Which leads me directly to rule number three: you must learn to obey me."

"You're kray-zie." Aaryn stretched every syllable between yawns. "Straight crazy."

"Whatever. You have forty-five minutes, Doctor, before we reach your sister's house. Get some rest."

Aaryn snuggled closer, sleep overcoming her. Only this time, it was her turn to smile broadly.

As Aaryn drifted off to sleep, Jayson couldn't resist running his hand over her hair. Contrary to her claims, it wasn't barb wire. She had natural hair. Curly, wavy and unpermed. His hand drifted tenderly over her pony tail where he softly tugged the ends of it just to see how long it was. Her hair extended well down her back. Jayson knew women all over the globe who would kill to have the length and grade of hair Aaryn possessed. He found himself running his hand repeatedly over her head. He hadn't had the desire to play in a woman's hair like this since the time he'd dated Tracy Ross, whose hair Aaryn's reminded him of. And speaking of

Tracy, he hadn't called the sexy, sinewy movie star back as he'd promised he would.

He'd had every intention of reaching out. He'd just gotten busy with other things. Then Aaryn fell into his life. And now it was too late to think about ever calling Tracy. Not when he felt so strongly about the woman in his lap. With Aaryn, Jayson felt he had everything he needed.

As he soothingly rubbed the hair on her head, his mind drifted. He thought of his script, the lines he wanted to embellish; his oil stocks, where much of his wealth had come from. He thought of Syl and her incredible healing. Dot, and what she might be doing back in Utah. He thought of the three children who were waiting for Aaryn. To Jayson, it was such a rare moment of serendipity that all he could do was smile. For in that moment, it felt like everything was right with the world around him.

Lost in the throes of idealistic possibilities, little did Jayson suspect that worldly winds of *mis*fortune were gathering, swirling at the edges of his newfound happiness, and promising to wreck havoc upon his impending blissfulness.

Chapter Thirty

"Why are you so nervous?" Jayson asked. She'd been fidgeting for the past few minutes as they approached her sister's home. "Talk to me."

"Well, because I haven't seen the children in years. What if they don't recognize me? What if they don't even like me?"

Jayson squeezed her hand. "Like you? They're going to love you. What's not to love?"

Erika threw him an exasperated look.

"I'm serious. Have you forgotten I've seen you in action? You're much more charming around children than adults. Trust me, they're going to adore you."

Aaryn took a deep breath. "I hope you're right." She titled her head back against the seat, surprised by her own nervousness.

Without asking permission, Jayson leaned over and kissed her. Unable to resist, he'd meant to lightly peck her on her lips. But the moment his lips met hers, he felt her body melt. As their kiss deepened, pulling her on top of him so that she straddled him felt like the most natural move in the world. His hands spanned her waist, pressing her down upon him.

Aaryn could literally feel him stretching underneath her. Her nerves spiked and she didn't know whether to bolt or to submit. But the choice was stripped from her

when his tongue penetrated her mouth. When he pressed her down against his full length, she collapsed onto his chest. A contented sigh escaped her.

"Jayson Denali." His name was a soft whisper upon her lips. "I think," she paused to burrow her face into his chest. The faint smell of his cologne was divine. "I think I'm going to keep you."

She felt his chest rumble with laughter. "That so? I should get it in writing. By this time tomorrow you'll have changed your mind. Wasn't it just yesterday that you accused me of being a hypocritical rogue who also happened to be shallower than a reflection in a puddle?" Jayson's own emotions were going haywire, less tempered by the knowledge that he'd been without a woman for months now. It took all his willpower to prevent him from just taking what he wanted, what he needed.

"No. I don't think so, Jayse. You're in my system now." Aaryn eased upward to a less dangerous spot on top of him. She stroked both hands over his forehead to the back of his head. "As much as I fear I might regret saying this, I've come to rely on you. I'm getting used to having you around, Jayse, and it's going to be very difficult to see you leave me."

"I'm not leaving you, Aaryn. Come with me."

When she shook her head at him, he said, "Then I'll come back for you. As soon as I'm done filming, I'll fly back to Utah. How's that?"

"Promise?"

"Yes, babe. I promise. I'm hooked too, you know. You've spoiled me for other women."

"No!"

"It's true. My only thoughts are of one Dr. Aaryn Jamison. I fear I'm whipped."

Aaryn slid off of him and onto the seat beside him. She leaned forward with her elbows on her knees, her chin cupped in her hands. "Jayson?"

"Mmmm?" His look was one of fondness.

"I think I'm falling in love with you. I've never been here before. It feels like I'm on top of the tallest mountain and I'm being asked to take a leap of faith and just…jump."

Jayson smiled as he tugged at her ponytail. "Are you wearing a parachute?"

She shook her head. "I don't think so. That's what makes it so scary. I've never been in love before."

The way she whispered it caused Jayson's hand to cup the back of her neck even as he hardened the more. Possession was the word that whipped through his brain as his imagination catapulted him back to a scene in his mind where they lay

entwined, loving one another. Such memories were not serving him at the moment. He had to pull himself together for his own sanity's sake.

"What's love to you, Jayse?" She glanced at him sideways.

Thoughtfully, he said, "It's beauty, it's joy, it's pain." With that, he suddenly wanted to change the topic of conversation.

"Looks like we're here."

"And not a moment too soon, eh?" Aaryn smiled at him as though she knew his secret.

The door was pulled open as Jayson said, "Let's go charm some children."

The first place the man looked to assess capability was the eyes. They told it all. Did they waver, did they flinch, did they lie? This one's didn't. Not a scent of hesitation. That they came from all over the country no longer surprised him. Some had even come from overseas. And all it took to sum them up was one long glance. They either had it or they didn't.

This one did. She had the eyes of a killer. Minutes after she'd stepped from her Hummer SUV and knocked on his door, he'd known it. He didn't advertise, but she'd managed to find him anyway. She'd found him buried in the Black Hills of South Dakota.

"When they want it bad enough, they turn up" the man thought. This one wanted desperately what he had to offer. She wanted to learn to shoot. Not just any gun, she wanted to master everything there was to know about high-powered firearms. Pistols and revolvers like the Glock, the Steyer GB and the Colt/Browning for starters. Every other assault and sniper rifle the man had in his collection would be frosting. All in a week's time.

"Can't be done," he'd told her. He meant it, too, because the kind of training he offered took more than a week. He would know. He'd spent thirty years in the US Special Operations Force training in counter terrorism. Weaponry had been his specialty. Retired, these days he ran his own elite survivalist boot camp that wasn't for the faint at heart. But then she'd plopped down cold hard cash on his counter and the man had given her a second look. It wasn't at all the money that impressed him. At his ripe age, he had more than his fair share. It was the girl's silent, no nonsense composure and her flat steady gaze. She wanted to shoot, so he would teach her. But only if she agreed to be stretched to the limits of her physical capacity.

Three days into the initial combat training, he marveled that the girl hadn't uttered one complaint. Extreme obstacle and circuit courses seemed to bring out the best in her. To see if she could detect cues that barely stood out from the background around her and still hit her mark, he designed a series of target courses that challenged her perceptions. Turned out she had excellent vision and motor skills. The girl also had serious fast reaction times. In short, she was one of the sharpest two-eyed shooters he'd ever schooled, Marines and Navy Seals included. "Too bad she was a girl," he thought. Women couldn't join Delta Force. She would have made one hell of an assassin.

Meanwhile, Jamarra knew the man was trying to break her. Grind her down and make her quit. She wasn't about to. He was right about one thing, though. She was created for this. The cruel, urban streets of Anacostia had been her training ground and this preparation was her missing link.

Finding him was the easy part. After her mysterious encounter at the Slaughter's home, Jamarra had sought refuge in a night club. She hadn't been there long before someone she recognized from around campus took a seat at her table. He had ash-blond hair and blue eyes. With his looks and physique he could have been a jock, but like her, he seemed just another loner. They nursed their drinks, lost in their own thoughts despite the spinning strobe lights, the loud thumping music and the gyrating bodies on the dance floor. Two beers later, he shouted over the music, inviting her to his place. Not wanting to be alone, Jamarra trailed him to his off-campus apartment.

Inside, there was one moment of awkwardness when he gave Jamarra a "what now?" look that lingered on her breasts and left little doubt what he wanted next. But that wasn't why Jamarra had come, so she strolled further into his pad and that's when she spotted his gun case. She grew excited at the different models and sizes. "Tell me about your guns," she whispered.

Her excitement fed his as he told everything he knew about weapons. And he knew a lot. His every other sentence referenced his dad who, according to him, was the best marksman in the world. Jamarra soaked up everything he said about his gun collection as well as about the father who had trained with Special Ops and now ran his own training camp back in South Dakota.

Having sex with him was the furthest thing from her mind. That is, until he let her handle one of his guns. Holding the Glock in her hand, she felt a stirring in her lower body. And when he stood behind her to clasp his hands around hers as she gripped the 9mm, she didn't complain when one of his hands moved to squeeze her breasts before drifting down her stomach and reaching deep into her jeans.

Jamarra stayed the night and when she left late the next morning, she knew South Dakota was her destination.

But that was before two plainclothes detectives greeted her at her doorstep.

"Are you Jamarra Sanders?"

"Who's asking?" she slid her key in the lock.

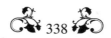

The officers flashed their badges at her. "We are. Let's see some ID."

Jamarra slipped her Drivers License from her money belt and handed it over.

"We'd like to ask you a few questions. May we come inside?"

"I'd rather you didn't. I wasn't expecting visitors. What is it you'd like to know?"

Neither appreciated her tone of voice which stopped just short of indicating that she didn't hold police in high esteem. "Where were you last night around midnight?"

"That's easy. At a club with a friend. Afterwards, I spent the night at his place. And now here I am being grilled by you."

They didn't like her attitude either. But she appeared to have an alibi for the previous night's assault and attempted murder on a Mrs. Erika Slaughter. They would see if her story checked out.

"What's the name of the club and this friend of yours?"

Only then did Jamarra realize that she didn't know the name of the man she'd spent the night with. She only knew his surname, which he'd used to reference his father. "He goes by the name of Bartlett. How about I give you his address and you speak to him yourself." The way she said it, it wasn't a question.

"Is that all?" she asked.

"For the moment." Both detectives noted that she never asked them why they were questioning her. It was the first thing most people would want to know. It made them wonder if she already knew why they were asking her whereabouts. "We'll circle back if we have more."

Hours later, Jamarra had showered and withdrawn a sizable chunk of the money Michael had deposited into her savings account. The note she left him was cryptic at best. She'd return in a week or two.

Her mind had effectively shelved her brutal slaying of Attorney Dowder. But as much as she wanted to, she couldn't stop thinking about the strange sequence of events with Michael's little girl. She didn't know exactly what had transpired. She might have imagined it. What she did know was that she hadn't finished the job. Hungry for revenge against perceived injustices, Jamarra vowed to finish what she'd started. This was now her personal war. The next time she went after the woman and the little girl, she'd be better prepared.

"Oh. My. Golly. God! You're Jayson Denali!" The babysitter cupped her hand over her open mouth, disbelief riveting her gaze.

"Auntie Aaryn!"

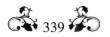

"It's Mr. Incredible!"

Three children, plus one starstruck, twenty-something year old adult, stood poised inside the door.

Nine-year old Joshua wore an open expression of hero worship. Six-year old Mia stood clutching the scuffed bear, Hully, that Aaryn had given her years ago. Her other hand held fast to the hand of her two-year old brother, Marcus. She had eyes only for Aaryn.

"Do we get to come inside?" Jayson smiled at them and Aaryn thought the babysitter was going to faint as she backed into the house, her hand still clasped over her mouth.

Aaryn took Mia's hand while Jayson had no choice but to reach down and pick up Marcus, who with arms outstretched, clearly wanted to be held.

After all the warm greetings, hugs and kisses, Aaryn had the children show her to the kitchen where she threw together a quick, light dinner which they ate inside the den. Though it was connected to the livingroom, Aaryn noted that the children avoided the area. She assumed it was because that was where the attack on Erika had taken place.

Joshua and Marcus were connected to Jayson at the hip and they begged him to watch with them their favorite movie starring Jayson, himself, as Mr. Incredible.

Aaryn rose and beckoned the babysitter to follow her into the kitchen where she could speak with her privately. However, Mia refused to be left with the others. So, as soon as Aaryn stood up, so too did she.

But the babysitter didn't really know anything other than there had been a break in and an attack on Erika.

"All I know is that Erika was rushed to the hospital. The doctors said she didn't have any knife wounds but she's comatose." When the babysitter kept staring at Mia, Aaryn was finally able to pin down what nagged her about the young woman's relationship to the children. She was fine with the boys, but she seemed distant toward Mia. At least, she hadn't made any attempt to go near her since Aaryn and Jayson had arrived.

"You should hear the story that Mia told to the police. It doesn't make any sense. But then she's six-years old and she's probably traumatized by what she witnessed." The babysitter added the last part as an afterthought in case her words sounded too harsh.

"I did tell the truth, Auntie Aaryn!" Mia had turned from the kitchen table toward the island counter where Aaryn and the babysitter sat. She spoke as though she was tired of people calling her a liar.

Aaryn glanced at Mia who sat running her fingers over Hully's tangled hair. "Why don't you let me talk to Mia alone?" Aaryn indicated that she wanted privacy with her niece.

She pulled a chair close to Mia at the table. "Mia? Tell me what happened to your mother."

When Mia looked up from Hully to stare at Aaryn intently, Aaryn marveled because she could sense that her niece was assessing her spiritually. She was scanning her as if to see if she, Aaryn, could be trusted with the truth. Aaryn hid her surprise. She'd long known that there was something special about Mia. Now she was learning firsthand.

"Hully stopped the bad woman from hurting Mommy."

"How, baby? How did Hully do that?"

"He called the angels from heaven to help save Mommy."

"Did you see the angels, Mia?"

Mia nodded. "The bad lady was going to hurt Mommy, so Hully told me to call the angels before it was too late." She stared again at Aaryn. "Nobody believes me."

"I believe you, Mia. I know you're telling the truth. Hully's a really good friend to have, isn't he?"

"Yep. You gave him to me, remember Auntie Aaryn?"

"Yes, I remember. I told you he would be your friend as long as you wanted him and took good care of him."

"It was me who named him Hully."

"And that was a wonderful choice. Tell me about the bad lady who tried to hurt Erika. Why are you sure it was a woman?"

"'Cause it was Daddy's girlfriend. She's evil. Hully says she and Daddy are going to hell. Daddy doesn't want us anymore. Did you know that?"

"I don't think that's true, honey."

"It is true. I heard him say it to Mommy." Suddenly, Mia looked like she was carrying the weight of the world on her tiny shoulders. "I'm scared for Mommy, Auntie Aaryn. Hully doesn't know if she's going to be okay. What do you think?"

"I'm certain your Mommy's going to be just fine. You watch and see." Aaryn placed Hully on top of the table and lightly grasped Mia to pull her onto her lap.

"Darling, Mia, you're a very special little girl. Do you realize that?"

Mia shook her head. She didn't feel special at all.

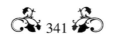

"It's true. You are. When your mother and I were your age, we didn't get to see the angels. We didn't see them until we were much older. But you, Mia, you've seen them already. Look at me, I want to tell you something." Aaryn lifted her on top of the table and grasped both her hands.

"You know why you saw the angel spirits, Mia?"

She shook her head.

"Because you believe in them, Mia. The angels used your belief to work a miracle for your Mommy. Not everybody believes as strongly in angels like we do. They may believe a little bit. But they don't believe people can see spirits. That's why they don't believe you. But you and I know the truth."

"And Mommy, too?"

"Yes, your Mommy too."

"Mommy fainted when she saw the angels. She hasn't woken up yet. I think she was scared of them. But they weren't going to hurt her. I don't think she knew that."

"It's possible that she did become frightened. But she's going to get better. You'll see. Now, listen to me. I don't want you to tell anyone else about the angel spirits, okay? You know why?"

When Mia shook her head, Aaryn said, "Because people won't understand, baby. It's *because* they don't understand that they don't believe you. They've never seen angels the way you and I, Erika and Grandma Dot have. You can't tell everybody what you saw that night because people will think it's strange."

"But who can I tell then? I want to talk about it but no one believes me."

"I believe you. Grandma Dot will believe you. And when your mother gets well, she's going to believe you, too. And what about Hully?" Aaryn smiled at her. "He believes you." She reached over and picked up the bear.

"I can tell that you're very fond of Hully. Except Hully's just a teddy bear, Mia. But still, you've given him a really great name. Do you remember telling me what his name meant? You told me Hully was short for 'Hully Speeret.' But it's really called 'Holy Spirit' and now you're old enough to know that when you hear things, when you see things that other people can't hear or see, now you know it's Holy Spirit that's speaking to you. It's not Hully. It comes from inside here and here." Aaryn pointed to Mia's heart and her head. "Do you understand me?"

Mia nodded.

"As you grow older, Mia, you're going to see things and go places that no one else has. Not even Grandma Dot or me. But starting now, it's important that you recognize that most people aren't going to understand you. Like the babysitter, she doesn't understand you. You know that, don't you?"

"She doesn't like me."

"She doesn't *understand* you, Mia. It's not that she doesn't like you. When people don't understand things, sometimes they don't know how to react to them. She's not quite sure how to react to you. That's why I'm taking this time to explain to you why you can't talk about the angels and the other things you've seen with just anybody."

"Can I talk to you?"

"Always. And as soon as we get to Utah, I'm going to teach you how you can talk to me no matter where you are."

"I already know how. That's how I talk to Grandma Dot. We talk all the time. Just not on the phone."

"Oh my." Aaryn's mouth was open. Dot had never even mentioned it. This child *was* something else.

"Can we go see Mommy tomorrow?"

"I'm going to call the hospital first thing in the morning to see what time visiting hours are. Do you want to go back and finish watching the movie with your brothers?"

"Mr. Denali likes you, Auntie Aaryn. He keeps staring at you when you don't know he's watching you."

Aaryn had grasped Mia's hand. But she stopped to stare down at her.

"Mr. Denali's going to ask you to marry him." Mia said it so matter-of-factly that Aaryn kneeled down at her side.

"No, I don't know that. And you don't know that either."

Mia looked at Aaryn with such a deadpanned gaze that Aaryn took a deep breath and said, "Okay. Maybe you do know it. But you can't say that around him, okay? Trust me, he won't understand."

"Okay."

As they left the kitchen, Aaryn asked teasingly, "And what about you? Do you have a boyfriend at school?"

Offended, Mia replied, "Of course not! Boys are icky. Besides, everyone knows girls are smarter than boys are. We're tougher, too."

Aaryn rolled her eyes. Mia was Erika and Aaryn wrapped up into one. "She was going to have her hands full teaching this one," Aaryn thought.

The next morning, Jayson was pouring himself a cup of coffee when Mia strolled into the kitchen with her bear, Hully. She sat at the table watching him pour his coffee.

"Hello, Little Lady. How are you?" Jayson asked in an attempt to put her at ease. Unlike her brothers, she hadn't been overly friendly towards him. And with her hand on her head, she looked like she was contemplating something.

"I'm fine. Mr. Denali?"

"Yes?"

"Do you believe in God?"

Jayson looked as surprised as he felt. With eyebrows lifted, he murmured, "Sure I do."

Mia actually looked relieved. "Good, cause I wouldn't want you to burn in hell."

Jayson's mouth dropped open. He didn't know whether to laugh or be offended. But the child looked so earnest, he decided against laughter. "How old are you again?"

"I'm six now. Next year I'll be seven."

"Well alrighty then." Special emphasis was put on the word "alrighty."

Aaryn walked into the kitchen and spotted the nonplussed look on Jayson's face.

"Good morning."

Jayson lifted his coffee cup to Aaryn. "Top of the morning to you, too, Mam."

"Mia, go get your brothers and tell them to come down for breakfast."

She scampered off.

"Okay, tell me. What'd she say to you?"

Jayson spread his hands. "Just asked me if I believed in God. If I didn't, she wanted me to know I was destined to burn in hell."

"Oh, Lord. No she didn't say that."

"Yeah. She did. Should I be concerned?"

Aaryn smiled. "No. She's just a tad precocious. That's all."

"Like her Aunt, I'd say." Jayson placed his cup on the counter and approached her.

"Good morning." His voice grew slightly husky as he bent towards her.

She didn't shy away from him as she lifted her face to his. When his lips slowly met hers, it was such a tender kiss. Full of promise and passionate possibilities.

Tearing herself away before she drowned, Aaryn said breathlessly, "Behave yourself, Denali. We'll have G-rated company in just a second." She moved toward the fridge to get breakfast started and to put distance between them. "How did you sleep?"

Knowing she was sleeping just a few doors away from him, all things considered, he'd slept relatively well. "I made it through the night."

"I've got quite a lot to accomplish today, Jayse. First, the hospital to check on Erika, next the children's school and then I have to talk to the police. I was thinking."

"Uh oh. That can't be good."

"Whatever. I was thinking that you might want to stay here."

"Trying to get rid of me?"

"Never. It's just that it would be less of a distraction and I might be able to wrap things up quicker if it's just me as opposed to everybody wanting your autograph, your time and your attention."

"So it's like that now?" But Jayson wasn't in the least disappointed. Relieved actually.

"Did you notice we had to practically push the babysitter into the taxi cab last night? She didn't want to leave, Jayson. And as much as I'd like to attribute it to my charming personality, I can't. You heard Joshua. She never watches movies with them. Now that you're here, suddenly she can't get enough of Mr. Incredible, the animated movie. And don't bother denying it. She stared at you more than she watched the movie. Anyway, that's my point. With you by my side, a 15-minute stop will turn into an hour-long journey. Without you, I can wrap this up in one day and we can head back to Utah first thing in the morning. How do you like your eggs?"

Jayson couldn't argue with her logic. "Over easy. Actually, it works because I've got calls to make. Plus, I need to go over my script."

"Have I told you lately that you're the best?"

Jayson fanned his ear. "I'm waiting."

"Hmph. It was just a figure of speech, Mister."

"Obedience training school, here you come. They're holding your spot, by the way."

"In your dreams, Buster."

"After they get finished choking all the sarcasm out of you, you're going to wish it was a dream. Hello boys." As they came into the kitchen, Jayson hoisted Marcus into the air.

By the time was breakfast ready, the children were seated and the noise level had climbed several decibels as they all talked over themselves to get Jayson's attention.

Afterwards, Aaryn insisted on taking her sister's car. Armed with Google Map directions, she and the children were off.

Rather than hang out at the house, Jayson had his driver take him back to the private airport where he could conduct business on his plane.

Chapter Thirty-One

"JD. You're killing me, Man. Straight killing me." Dez didn't know whether to be angry or relieved that his friend had finally made live contact.

"What's up, Partner?"

Dez gave a sigh of frustration. "I don't know anymore, Jay. I'm doing my part to keep the ship afloat. But I'm not feeling you on your end."

"We trade emails. I hit you up with a phone call every now and again. What else is there? Since when did you start needing to hear from me on a daily basis?"

"Ever since we started getting pushback from Ariel Capital. Remember them? Hedge Funders with $10 billion AUM? Assets Under Management? In case it's slipped your memory, they were hot to sign on to finance your film, *Hyperion Fields*. Ring a bell? "

"So what's changed?" Jayson was scrolling through emails on his laptop, eyeballing the relevant ones he hadn't yet read on his handheld.

"Not 'what' has changed. It's more like 'who' that's changed. You've changed, JD. Ariel needs a face-to-face, Jay, to gauge your commitment. They don't just want it in writing, their BOD wants to physically press the flesh."

"Understandable. Anytime $250 million is put on the table, any Board of Directors has a shareholder responsibility to ensure ROI."

"Exactly. Glad to know Return on Investment still matters to you, Jay. It means we're almost on the same page. The meeting with Ariel takes place this week. Thursday at 10 AM. Today's Monday. Will you make it? I hope to high hell you do, Jay. Because I've got money riding on this thing, too." Dez paused.

"What the frick is up, JD? You blew off Oprah's gala. You no-showed at Obama's *Night With The Stars* fundraiser. You played ghost at Bloomberg's Times Square dinner. The Mayor of New York, himself, approached me to ask where you were. No more BS, Jay. I need to know where your head is at. Because from my vantage point, things aren't the way they used to be. All jokes aside. Straight-talk express."

Jayson could hear the disappointment and confusion in Dez's voice. As much as he wanted to empathize, he couldn't explain what he didn't quite understand himself.

"I'm supposed to be your best friend, Bro, yet I have to call the hospital to find out that Syl's up and walking again? I'm forced to read about you on the internet and in the papers just to know what's going on in your life? That hurts, Jay. That hurts." Dez shook his head as he stared out of his office window.

"All I can say is that she'd better be damned well worth it. Because this is some crazy stuff. In all the years we've known each other, I've seen you hold it down time after time. But I've never known you to blow a deal because you didn't have it together."

"Dez, everything's okay. Ariel's headquartered in Chicago, right? I'll be there with bells on."

"No bells required, Man. I just need you to show up and be on time." Dez stared down at the picture he held in his hand of Jayson and Aaryn leaving some government building in Provo, Utah. "Who *is* this Dr. Aaryn Jamison? Whoever she is, she's got your nose wide open."

Jayson smiled wryly. "You could say that. Listen, Dez. I know I've been out of pocket lately. If I could explain it, if I had an answer, believe me I'd give it to you. But I don't. All I can tell you is…" Jayson paused. What *could* he tell him?

"If you said anything after 'all I can tell you,' then I must have missed it. Either the phone went dead or you dropped it. Maybe you lost your train of thought. I have no idea. But here's a clue for you, Jay. Try this one on. Are you in love with this Dr. Jamison?"

"You speak like you know all about her."

"I know as much about her as the information Tyrone could provide."

"Whoah! You went there?" Jayson was taken aback that his friend had ordered a dossier on Aaryn.

"Hey, I'm looking out for a Brother. I'm also looking out for me. Certainly wouldn't want you to get caught up in something you couldn't get yourself out of."

"Have I ever?"

"You really want me to answer that?"

"Yes, I do. If my memory serves me right, all the escapades I've ever gotten 'caught up' in were because of you."

"This is different," Dez replied.

"Yes, D. This is different. I don't want the world intruding on whatever happiness I've found."

"Wow. You really are serious about her then, huh? When do I get to meet her, Jay?" When he got no response, Dez asked, "Does *anybody* get to meet her? Or do you intend to try to keep her a secret? I hope that's not the game plan because if I could find out about her, you'd better know the rag mags are already prepping their pages for the next salacious Jayson Denali story."

"I don't want her tarnished by all the fake Hollywood glitz, that's all. Not that she could be. You'll see that right away when you do meet her. I warn you, though. She's not what you'd expect. She's been totally disabused of fandom."

Dez stared at the photo of Aaryn. She definitely wasn't the beauty that Jayson typically fell for. It had to be something else. "I believe I'll pay a visit to Utah."

"I wouldn't advise it unless you have a legitimate reason for coming."

"Visiting my best friend and his Mom isn't reason enough for a visit?"

"Not this time. You'll meet Aaryn soon enough. Until then, I guess I'll see you in Chicago on Thursday morning. How's Dionne, by the way?"

"She dumped me. Said I was too conflicted for her. She wanted marriage. I wanted something else. To add insult to injury, she returned every gift I gave her. Women. Can't live with 'em. Can't live without 'em."

"You're preachin' to the choir, son."

"Whatever, Junior. I'm thinking of taking a hiatus from women. When I climb back on the wagon, who knows? I could get lucky and hit the jackpot like you." Dez said it sarcastically.

"*Maybe* it's time for you to tie the knot and settle down. Dionne seemed pretty cool to me. A heck of a lot better than those other money-grubbing skeezers you've dated. How many women do you know that return gifts when they walk?"

"Jayson was recommending marriage? Hell must have frozen over," Dez thought.

"For you to even jokingly mention marriage, dawg, you must be delusional or either strung out on drugs."

"Could be I'm turning a new leaf. Anyway, if I don't speak to you before Thursday, I'll see you in Chicago. Later, D."

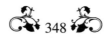

Wendy, his assistant was up next. "Wendy, do you realize you're the only person who hasn't been blowing up my phone lately. How are you?"

"Who is this?" Wendy's voice was mock angry, as if she was addressing an harassing bill collector.

"Very funny."

"Excuse me? Should I know you? I think you dialed the wrong number."

"Whenever you're ready to talk business, just let me know."

"Given that I haven't spoken to you in a couple of weeks, suddenly you want to talk business? What happened to cause you to come up for air? Did Dr. Jamison dump you like your best friend's girl dumped him?"

"I didn't realize my personal life was of such interest to the world."

"Then you really are clueless. Your personal life, Jayson Denali, is my personal business. What do you want anyway? Why are you bugging me? Do you have any idea of how much work I have to do? By the way, my hubby thanks you for the trip to Puerto Vallarta, Mexico. It was two of the most relaxing weeks I've had since I've known you."

"Glad that I could be of service. So, what have I missed?

Wendy proceeded to demonstrate why Jayson paid her the big bucks to juggle multiple balls and handle the many moving parts of his life. She rattled off an extensive list of open items, urgent requests for his time, a number of matters she'd put on hold that now demanded his attention, calls that had to be returned only by him, plus the litany of checks that required his signature since Jayson believed in signing his own checks.

When he wrapped things up with Wendy, he spent time talking to his agent and to his crew who ran his Milwaukee and New York-based not-for-profit foundation. More time was spent reassuring his old posse that he'd not abandoned them despite his threat to fire them if they showed up in Utah.

His last call was to his jaguar, Cedric, the body guard he'd ditched since his arrival in Utah. Jayson would need him again as soon as his plane took off for nether parts of the world. It was that world which now beckoned him as he had to hit a number of cities in a limited amount of time. And yet, leaving Aaryn and Utah was feeling like one of the hardest decisions Jayson was forced to make.

"Mommy's sleeping so we have to be quiet." Mia.

"Can she hear us?" Joshua asked.

"Yes, she can hear us." They were inside Erika's hospital room. Although she was hooked up to breathing tubes, she did look peaceful, as if she was merely sleeping, which she was.

"When is she going to wake up?"

"I don't know, baby. We'll have to ask her doctor."

"Is Mommy coming with us to Utah?" Mia again.

"Yes, she's coming too."

"What about our Daddy? Why isn't he coming?" Joshua had anger in his voice.

Aaryn understood that he missed his father. "We're still waiting to hear from your Dad, Josh. As soon as he contacts us, we'll let him know where you are."

Josh wasn't finished. "I heard our sitter talking on the phone. She said Daddy paid someone to try to kill Mom so he wouldn't have to give her any of his money."

Aaryn shook her head. "That wasn't a nice thing for her to say. She shouldn't have said it at all because it's not true."

"Then where is he? Why hasn't he at least called us to check up on Mom?"

"Josh, we've been over this. I don't know where your Dad is. I'm sure if he knew about your Mom, he'd be here with us."

"No he wouldn't," Mia said. She had Hully packed just inside the pocket of her bookbag on wheels. "Why doesn't anybody want us, Auntie Aaryn? What did we do that was so bad?"

"Stop it, Mia. Don't say untrue things like that." *Good grief!* Aaryn thought. No wonder she didn't have kids. This was like being on Jeopardy, 24-7. Always a question to be answered. Hard, highstakes questions at that.

It took Aaryn hours to complete all her stops. After she'd spoken to Erika's doctor and made provisions for her travel, she headed to the children's school and finally, to meet with the detective assigned to Erika's case.

By the time she called Jayson, she was longing to hear his voice. "Jayson."

"Hey, babe. Where are you?" Hers was a welcome number programmed into his phone.

"On our way back to Erika's. I take it you're no longer there?"

"I'm at the airport getting some work done. Are you hungry? Let's go grab lunch. You can update me on your sister's progress."

"Okay. But I have no idea where we could go to eat."

"I'll find a place. I'll meet you back at your sister's so we can ride in one vehicle."

The Eagle's Nest Restaurant on Capitol Avenue was known for its fine dining. It was Indianapolis' only revolving rooftop restaurant where one could take in the stunning high altitude view. Its décor was elegant, complementing an upscale, romantic atmosphere. Live music was part of the dining experience. It was perfect because it provided them a modicum of privacy and yet catered to the children. The owners were ecstatic that Jayson was patronizing their place of business. In anticipation, the proverbial red carpet was rolled out and Jayson and his guests were treated like royalty.

They were seated in a secluded area of the restaurant, but Aaryn noticed that didn't stop the rest of the patrons from preening as they tried to get a glimpse of the in-house celebrity whose name automatically guaranteed box-office success. And when Jayson insisted on taking the boys to the restroom himself, Aaryn saw a number of cell phones discretely capture his image.

When he returned to their table carrying Marcus in his arms, Aaryn indulged herself by watching him approach. "Such tantalizingly male animal beauty," she thought. Surely it was too much for one person. What must God have been thinking to pour so much physical beauty into one human being? Lost in her thoughts, Aaryn didn't hear Mia call her name.

As Jayson slid into his seat, his hand covered Aaryn's to lift her knuckles to his lips. "Miss me?"

Before Aaryn could respond, Mia said innocently, "Yes, she missed you. She was watching for you since you left the table. Auntie Aaryn, I called you three times but you didn't hear me cause you were staring at Mr. Denali."

"Oh Lord...Child, what are we going to do with you?"

"Thank you, Mia. What else did your Auntie do while I was gone?"

Aaryn chimed in. "Nothing. Right, Mia? If you expect ice cream with your meal, you'll say nothing more."

Mia motioned her fingers over her lips to indicate she was zipping them. Obviously a gesture she was well familiar with.

Jayson was enjoying the children far more than he thought he would. He asked Aaryn, "Do you think we can return to Utah tonight?"

"Tonight? But we haven't packed. We haven't..." Aaryn halted in the middle of her excuses. The quick, wry smile on Jayson's face spoke volumes. There was so much in the look he'd given her. With one glance, she knew he was leaving before the week was over. She'd known he was departing and had slowly been preparing herself for it. But with one look, she knew he was leaving even sooner than planned.

She reached across the table for his hand. "Will you help me pack?" Already, she missed his touch.

"We're all going to help you pack. Aren't we, team?"

"Yes." They answered in unison and then Mia added, "Can we have ice cream now?"

It wasn't until they were on the plane returning to Utah that Jayson and Aaryn had their first moments alone with each other as the children slept, worn out from the day's events.

In a separate area of the plane, the two snuggled with his arm around her, her head resting on his shoulder.

"Will your sister be okay?" he asked.

"I pray so, Jayson. Her children need her. I didn't mean to sound harsh or defensive earlier when I stopped them from talking about demons and angel spirits. If they don't learn when and when not to have such discussions, they'll be ostracized because other people won't understand them. I know what that's like and I don't want it for them."

"No arguments from me." Jayson had been amazed when Mia and Josh had launched into a full description of demons and angels. He didn't quite believe Mia about the giant angels that supposedly saved her Mom. But he was willing to temporarily suspend disbelief. "They're gifted in the same way that you and Dot are, aren't they? How else would they know about these things?"

"Yes, they are uniquely gifted, each in their own way. I'm not sure it's something you can teach. It wasn't like Dot held a special class for Erika and me. We came into our own naturally. That's partly why we need Erika to come back to herself. These children need both their mother and their father. Which is also why it's so difficult to imagine that Michael would go to such lengths to try to harm Erika. Why not just agree to divorce and remain peaceable for the children's sake?"

"Money makes people do strange things, Aaryn."

"But to abandon your own children? To attempt to have someone murdered?"

"You don't know for a fact that he did those things."

"The police suspect he did. I didn't want to believe it myself at first. But when the detective told me that they identified *the head* of a body they believe to be Erika's lawyer and they think her death might be connected to Erika's case, I don't know what to believe anymore. Frankly, I find it very odd that we've had to leave messages at Michael's job to get in touch with him. What kind of man doesn't want his family to have a means of reaching him? Why wouldn't he at least provide them with his cell phone number? The people at his place of employment acted as though we wanted to serve him with a subpoena. It's very strange."

"What's strange is that they've questioned the girl he's been living with. But now she's disappeared." Jayson shook his head.

"When I held Erika's hand, I picked up that she knew about this girl that Michael's been living with. Erika and Michael were so angry with each other. There was so much bitterness between them. They weren't avid church goers, but I gleaned that Michael felt Erika was feeding the children religious fantasies. He never understood that Erika probably had very little to do with that aspect of the children's development. In fact, I'm willing to bet she hid that part of herself from her husband. She should have been more honest with him. But then, her unwillingness to own her gifts was why she withdrew from Dot and I, so I'm not surprised. All I know is that until she gets well, Dot and I will do everything we can to ensure the children are happy with us in Utah. It's going to be a big adjustment for all of us. And speaking of adjustments, what of you, Jayse? Tell me, when must you leave?"

He sighed. "Wednesday night. I have to be in Chicago for an early morning meeting on Thursday."

Aaryn remained quiet for a long while until he felt her head burrow deeper into his shoulder. He heard her whisper his name so faintly that he barely heard it.

"What is it?" Still, she didn't reply.

Jayson shifted to pull her face upward. "Hey? What's wrong?" She had tears on her face.

Aaryn shook her head. "Don't mind me. I'm just suddenly very emotional." She wiped her face. "Who knows? I might be crying for Erika and the children." Or it could be the sense of loss she was suddenly feeling. She said, "Jayson? No matter what happens, don't forget me, okay?"

Jayson's heart melted. He pulled her onto him, forcing her to straddle his thighs. His hands cupped the sides of her face. "Don't even think it, Lady. You're not getting rid of me. Come with me, Aaryn. Bring the children. I'll give all of you a crash course in how Hollywood makes a movie."

It was Aaryn who fastened her lips to his as she laced her hands around his neck. But her tongue was no match for his as he invaded her mouth, passionately returning her kiss. His hands pulled her silk blouse free of her slacks to rest against the bare skin of her waist, gripping her tightly.

She felt him trail his mouth along her jaw to her ear where he nibbled voraciously. Aaryn heard him softly whisper something unintelligible in her ear until she recognized he was speaking to her in Italian.

"Bella, l'amore della mia vita."

Aaryn had no way of knowing he was whispering to her that she was beautiful to him and that she was the love of his life. But the next words she understood clearly.

"Marry me."

Aaryn gasped as she stared down at him. A part of her was thinking of the words little Mia had uttered the day before. "You don't mean that, Jayson." The smile she gave him was tinged with momentary sadness.

Jayson had shocked even himself with his words, for they came forth unrehearsed. He stared at her somewhat bemusedly until finally, he said, "Yes, I do mean it."

Aaryn shook her head slowly. "What a lovable nut you are, Jayson Denali." She took his hand and placed it over her heart.

Jayson's hand drifted down to possessively cup her breast as he thumbed the nipple which neither her bra nor her blouse could hide the size of. His hand tightened on her breast until Aaryn winced.

"Jayse, you're hurting me."

He relaxed his grip but he didn't release her. Instead he cupped the back of her head forcing her mouth again to his. It felt like he was branding her, imprinting himself on her memory. Until finally he released her and buried his face in her neck.

"Think about it, Aaryn. You're perfect for me. Everything I own and know myself to be doesn't impress you. Not my money, the cars, the houses, not even my fame. You were never impressed with any of it. It's like you looked past all of that and saw me for who I really am." He stared into her eyes. "And for who I'm not. To be accepted unconditionally, that's something I'm not accustomed to. These past weeks have been the most fulfilling for me. I've discovered things about myself that I didn't know. When I'm with you, Aaryn, I'm not lonely anymore. I no longer have that emptiness that I used women to fill." Jayson paused to take a deep breath.

"The first time I visited your home, Dot asked me something. She asked me what is it that I refuse to live without. She asked what was so precious to me that if stripped away, I'd find a way to return it to my life. I couldn't answer her at the time even though I thought about money. But I know now what it is. It's love, Aaryn. Love is what I won't live without. Love is what I feel for you." Jayson didn't think he could articulate exactly what he was feeling. He only knew that what he felt was different from the numerous relationships and one night stands he'd had in the past. Maybe he was waxing naïve, but there seemed a purity and an honesty about his involvement with Aaryn that he'd not experienced before.

"Marry me, Aaryn. What do you want? A big, lavish wedding?"

"Jayson, stop. No lavish weddings for me. I wouldn't want the fanfare."

"Good, then let's fly to Vegas and just do it."

Aaryn laughed at him as she climbed off of him. "Jayson Denali. What am I going to do with you? We can't get married at the spur of the moment. You're not even sure. Let's wait awhile. Let's think this over. Let's talk this through. Let's give each other the time and chance to do a full inspection of one another."

"A 'look under the hood and kick the tires' kind of inspection, huh?"

Her hand was still draped around his neck. "Bay, I don't think marriage is as simple as checking out a car." Her look and tone was one of warm fondness.

Jayson leaned over to kiss her. "Mmmm. Say that again."

"Say what again?" He was nibbling her lips invoking in her body that wet noodle feeling.

"You called me 'Bay.' Say it again."

"I can't. You keep kissing me."

"Say you love me." Jayson pressed her.

"I do, Bay. I really do. I love you." When she heard his deep intake of breath, she was lost. "Jayson stop. Please. Don't do this to me. Right now, I'm not in a position to deny you anything. So I have to appeal to your better wisdom. I didn't abstain 39 years only to be stripped of my virginity on an airplane."

Jayson burst out laughing. "Okay. Good point." He released her. Stretching his legs out in front of him, he laced his hands behind his head.

Aaryn closed her eyes against the sight of the bulge in his pants. Her mind couldn't even wrap around the thought.

"Remember that speech I gave you about making decisions in the cold light of day?"

"Yes I do."

"Well, it's kind of cloudy to me, so could you refresh my memory? Tell me what was it I said?"

"It was some nonsense about…"

"Nonsense? No it wasn't!"

"Excuse me, Miss. But can you not interrupt me when I'm answering your question?"

She sighed loudly and rolled her eyes at him.

"Back to what I was saying before I was crudely interrupted. A short while ago, a certain person was mouthing off about how much wiser it was to make decisions regarding love and relationships in the cold light of day and about how important it is not to have any illusions."

"Jayse, you have to admit it sounded pretty good, wouldn't you say?"

"Sure. Except now it's a case of perception crashing into reality. The whole rubber meets the road thing."

"Are you hoping I'll say I was wrong?"

"You? Psst. Fat chance of that happening." Jayson shut his eyes.

"Ummm, excuse you?" Aaryn took mock umbrage at his comment.

"You heard me. I'm hoping that obedience school will choke that part out of you as well."

Aaryn snuggled up against him. "Know what I'm hoping for?" She traced her fingernail over his lips. She felt him smile.

"Tell me. Go ahead, talk dirty to me." Jayson's voice was gruff.

Aaryn laughed softly.

Despite her laughter, Jayson felt himself swelling again. "On second thought, don't start something you can't finish."

"I was going to say that I was hoping for sleep. But since you seem so fixated on this whole obedience school thing, I think I'm going to have to find one for you."

"Don't put yourself out. I've already enrolled you. By the time you check your mail tomorrow you should have received your registration. I expect no less than an A-plus."

Aaryn didn't know whether he was joking or serious. He sounded serious.

Aaryn stroked his head and temple. "I enjoy you Jayson Denali." She leaned over and whispered into his ear. "I know what you want. Believe me, I want it to, Bay. But not like this. Come, let me relax you like I did before. Let me stroke you until you fall into a deep sleep."

"I'll settle for whatever you give me."

Chapter Thirty-Two

Though it was after midnight, the driveway leading to Aaryn's home was lit up like a Christmas ornament. The entire house was brightly lit.

Where the children had been awed by Jayson's airplane, they were speechless at the sight of the two huge Great Danes, Baron and Max. The dogs sprang from the

doorway as soon as Jayson's limo came to a stop in the driveway. They circled the vehicle with tails wagging frantically.

"It's the dogs from the Harry Potter movie." Josh didn't sound eager to meet them.

"Horsies!" Marcus screamed with delight.

For once in her life, Mia was speechless as she stared out the window at the animals.

Other than Aaryn, no one wanted to exit the limo. Not even the driver.

"They're dogs, baby. Not horses. Baron and Max are their names. They don't bite, I promise. They're really gentle giants, aren't they, Jayson?"

Jayson reached up to massage the back of his neck. "More like slobbering giants."

"Come on Jayse, let's show the children they have nothing to be frightened of. Please?"

"What, woman? What do you want from me? How am I supposed to help? Other than carry everyone on my back?"

The driver was clearly staying put, so Aaryn opened the door and got out. "Come on Jayson, quit playing."

Jayson sighed. "How do I get dragged into these things?" As soon as he stepped out, Max, the tan Dane who had taken a fondness to Jayson (for some odd reason Jayson couldn't fathom) rushed to greet him. Like it or not, Jayson patted his chest and the dog happily raised up on his hind quarters to tower over Jayson, his front paws resting on Jayson's shoulders. To keep the seven-foot giant from slobbering all over his face, Jayson grabbed the dog's head and massaged behind his ears. "If it worked when Aaryn did it to him," he thought, "it was the least he could do to keep the dog from drooling all over him."

Marcus tumbled out of the limo. "I wanna ride the horsey!" Fearlessly, he approached Jayson and Max.

Jayson set the dog down and reached to pick up Marcus, the only one of the children eager to pet the dogs while Aaryn reached into the limo to take Josh's and Mia's hand to lead them inside the house.

The look of love on Dot's face as she knelt to embrace the three children was worth a thousands words. The love she exuded toward them humbled both Aaryn and Jayson.

Aaryn wrapped her arm around Jayson's waist. Her primary thought was how selfish it was of Erika to keep the children from Dot. "And wouldn't it be something," Aaryn thought, "if the winds of circumstance had been orchestrated just so the children could be brought into Dot's presence." Despite all of Erika's careful ministrations to keep her mother and sister from being part of her children's lives, her house of straw was now blown apart, buffeted by alternating gusts of infidelity and greed.

As tears of happiness and joy fell from Dot's eyes, Aaryn felt no sorrow for Erika. She wished her sister no ill, but in that moment she thought that, possibly, just desserts had been served. All the anguish Dot suffered over the years had just been erased as she embraced the children.

Dot took the children upstairs to show them to their room. Until they were comfortable in their new environment, she was having them share a room with three beds in it.

"It's late," Jayson said to Aaryn as they watched Dot mount the stairs carrying Marcus. "I should be on my way to my hotel."

"You're welcome to stay here, Jayse. We've got plenty of room."

"Or, you could come with me to my hotel suite. I've got plenty of room there too."

Aaryn cocked her eyebrow at him. "I don't have that much self restraint. And neither do you."

"Self restraint? I think I've demonstrated that I have plenty of it given all the torture you've subjected me to." Jayson turned her to face him. "Aaryn, let's do it, babe. I mean it. Let's get married. Let's fly to Vegas tonight." He glanced at his watch, saw that it was after 1 AM and said, "This morning, right now. Forget what time it is, let's just go."

He was holding her at the waist and as Aaryn stared at him, she was lost, caught up in the orbit that was Jayson Denali. For one moment, she was tempted to do as he suggested.

No stranger to a woman's sensate hesitations, Jayson pounced. He began a wicked assault, kissing her neck and whispering tantalizing secrets all the while.

Aaryn didn't stand a chance. "Jayse, wait. Wait. Please, just wait." She pulled his hands from around her waist and quickly stepped out of his embrace. Clasping her arms over her chest, she said haltingly, "Wait, Jayson, I just need to think for a moment."

"No thinking allowed." He stepped toward her even as she stepped back.

"Jayson, we have to be sensible about this. We can't do this without thinking about the consequences. I haven't signed a prenup agreement yet. You haven't even asked me to sign one. So I know you're not thinking straight. One of us has to have common sense in this process. Clearly, it's not you. It's probably not even me."

"Have I mentioned anything about a prenuptial agreement?" Jayson was shaking his head.

"No, Bay, you haven't. But you should be asking me that."

"You don't need to sign one."

"Yes, I do, Jayson. I don't want anyone thinking I rushed you into this or that I'm doing this because of the money you have."

This time, he grabbed hold of her. "Aaryn, I don't think that. I know it's not the case."

"Yes, but what about your friends? What will they think? Besides, I'd never want that to be an issue between us, so it's best to have such an agreement in place. You see, Jayse, there are many questions like these that we need to talk about first."

"Name them." He was persistent if nothing else.

"Children. Do you want them? If so, how many? Where will we live? I can't give up my work. You certainly can't give up yours. Besides, I don't want to leave Utah."

Jayson stared down at her with a victorious smile. She was acquiescing and didn't even realize it. They were sealing the deal and that was what, in his mind, this conversation was about. "Yes, I want children. As many as you'll give me. We'll live anywhere you like. I'll move right in here if you want. This place is a museum anyway. It's way too big for just you and Dot. It's high time there was a man heading this house. And when we're not living here, I'll toss you on my shoulder and we'll travel the world."

He lifted her chin up. "As for work? Only when you feel like it. I intend to make love to you ten times a day just to keep you barefoot and pregnant."

"Ha!" Aaryn gave a loud outburst of laughter. "Jayson, you're a terribly sick man. Do you realize that?"

"You've made me this way. I was perfectly sane before I met you. Now, I'm desperately chasing one hard-to-get strong willed, very opinionated woman."

"What? You mean, I don't have to go to obedience school as part of the prenup?"

"Thank you for reminding me. That *is* the prenup—all in a nutshell. Obedience school for you."

But Aaryn wasn't convinced. "Jayson, we need to think this through. What if we sleep on it and talk it over tomorrow?"

"Done. As a matter of fact, forget about Vegas. We can apply for a confidential license in California. Since neither of us wants a big wedding, we could have a secret marriage where there won't be any public record of the ceremony. We'll outsmart the stalkerazzi and the rag mags."

"You've got it all thought out, don't you, Buster? But it's not tomorrow yet and we're still talking about it."

"Look, Missy." Jayson threw his arm around her shoulders and walked with her to the door. "I know it's a woman's prerogative to change her mind, but when we men make a decision, we pretty much stick with it. This thing is a done deal."

"Isn't that why the Titanic sank? Because bullheaded men refused to consider other options?" ·

"No, baby. The Titantic sank because it hit an iceberg."

"My point, Jayson, is you're allowed to change your mind." She opened the door for him and stood with him inside the doorway. A thought occurred to her. "You know, Jayse. We really don't have to rush into this. When you return from Canada in a month, I'll still be here. It's not like I'm going to fall in love with someone else while you're gone."

Aaryn debated whether to say more. When he didn't jump in with a reply, she took the plunge. "It's not me you have to worry about, Jayson, it's you. Wherever you go, just trust your spirit. Let it guide you. All the women who throw themselves at you, just ask yourself what will it profit you to be with them? And possibly this is more for me than it is for you, but I'm mindful of that old axiom that says, 'If you love something, let it go. If it comes back to you, then you know it's really yours.' I'm not throwing you to the wolves, Bay. I'm just inviting you to try on the idea of waiting. Go to Canada. Make your movie. And then come back to me. If you still want to marry me when you return, I'm all yours. Deal?"

Jayson leaned down and kissed her on the forehead. "We'll talk about it tomorrow."

Aaryn shook her head as she watched him enter the limo. What *was* she going to do with him?

The next morning, Jayson awoke to a firestorm.

It was barely 7 AM when his cell phone started vibrating on the night stand as if it was possessed. He reached for it and saw that it was Wendy.

"Did somebody die?"

"Just your reputation. You'll never guess what's just hit the stands."

"Wendy, it's too early in the morning to play guessing games."

"It's almost 9 o'clock on the East Coast, JD. Plenty of time for all the rag mags to scoop one another. Guess which two have the biggest scoop of all?"

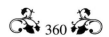

"I'm fresh out."

"You expect The National Enquirer to blow smoke up your nose. But when Liz Smith comes out the gate ripping you a new one, one has to wonder, JD, what the heck did you do to piss her off?"

"How about hearing the dial tone in 10 seconds? That wouldn't piss you off, would it?"

"Okay. Okay. Hold on to your hat!"

"Wendy? I'm not wearing a hat. Five seconds."

"You're not going to like this, so I might as well just give it to you with no grease on the pole." Wendy paused for dramatic emphasis. "Jayson Denali: Caught In Deadly Love Triangle."

Jayson was pretty much inured to the manmade fictitious tales the rag mags conjured up. Mostly, their stories were malicious cocktails of lies and fabrications. But this one caught his attention.

"Go on," he said cautiously, knowing he would regret it.

"Why don't I just read it?" To Jayson, she seemed thrilled to do so.

"Jayson Denali, king of big action fantasy commercial success, has caused his brilliant career to enter a sad twilight. Caught in a three-way love fest that has left the object of his obsessive desire, the beautiful Mrs. Erika Slaughter, in a deadly fight for her life. Married with three children, Erika Slaughter is in critical condition after nearly being knifed to death by an unknown assailant. Police suspect Slaughter's husband, international attorney Michael Slaughter of Haliburton Inc., discovered his wife's torrid affair with the hot and steamy actor. When Mrs. Slaughter filed for divorce, police suspect jealousy drove Mr. Slaughter to vengefully place a hit on his wife. Denali is said to be so heartbroken, he has been AWOL filming his latest blockbuster. His tragic denouement comes after quite a remarkable career..."

"Wendy, I've heard enough. Why would Liz print garbage like that? It's a bunch of BS."

"My, my..." Wendy continued reading the article to herself. "JD, it says someone in the Cabrini Green projects in Chicago found a severed head in a garbage bin that turned out to be Mrs. Slaughter's attorney."

"Fact is stranger than fiction, Wen."

"Goodness gracious! Apparently Mrs. Slaughter was on the verge of marrying you when she was violently struck down. JD? You couldn't make this stuff up if you tried."

"Someone did, since little of it is true."

"Little, huh? Does that mean *some* of it's true? One question for you?"

"Make it quick before the phone goes click."

"If you're as desolate and heartbroken over Erika Slaughter as Liz claims, how is it that you're in love with Dr. Aaryn Jamison? Her, I know about. But who's Erika Slaughter?"

"Who said I was in love?"

"JD, I know you better than anyone else. Therefore, I am an authority on all things pertaining to Jayson Denali. If I say you're in love, trust me, Duckie, you're in love. So who is Erika? Why have I never heard of her?"

"Wendy, how many times do I have to tell you that soap operas and gossip magazines are make believe? I could pick up the phone right now and tell Liz Smith you're an axe murderer who's just chopped up her husband's body and hidden all the pieces. And you know what? Liz would put a spin on it and run with it. No questions asked outside of making sure she's got the names spelled right. Certainly, that's what's happened here."

"Oh well, you must admit it makes for juicy, tongue wagging conversation."

"For people who have no life."

"That's your opinion, JD. Unfortunately for you, we happen to live in a world of demanding consumers, all of them attached to highspeed internet. Throw in YouTube and a billion or more blogs, why every misstep a celebrity makes is fodder for an information-crazed world. Since they don't pay deference to living monuments, JD, there's no such thing as a private life for you, my friend."

Wendy yawned as she tossed the papers on the corner of her desk. "But here's why I called. This can go either of two ways. The story dies down after a day's news cycle or either it blows up and the boys from Disney call you in to assess how likely this bit of news will damage the release of *Mr. Incredible II*. That one's a kiddie/family flick, remember?"

"You really know how to ruin a person's morning, don't you, Wen?"

"Thank you, dear. I do try my best."

"If we get blowback from this, have PT handle it. It's odd though that Liz didn't call me to get the 411 before running with this story."

"Ummm, JD? Liz did call you. She's the one on the list I sent you who has a '4' by her name. That's how many times she called. Could be this is her revenge for

you not returning her calls. I'll get on the horn now so PT can assess if there'll be any fallout over this."

While Jayson was ending his conversation with Wendy, Michael Slaughter was enroute to his home—the one he shared with Jamarra. After landing at a private airstrip, he needed to make a quick stop to spend some "quality" time with Jamarra. Michael couldn't care less about what his new attorney, Ann Freel, or anyone else said about his relationship with a woman half his age. His initial lawyer, Keith Olbermann, had dropped him like a rock and hauled tail to greener pastures the second MSNBC news came calling with an anchor position.

Screw Keith, Michael thought. Jamarra was the kind of woman he needed. A total tiger in the bedroom. He bore the bite and scratch marks to prove it. *Everybody* be damned, for that matter. He was never giving Jamarra up.

Less pressing for him was what to do about his current wife and children. In his mind, Erika was Jezebel incarnate. Hadn't his mother tried to warn him? His children, however, he would fight for. It was unfortunate that Erika had warped and twisted their minds so. If he could just get them away from her clutches, they would be fine. All three were extremely bright and intelligent kids. They just needed stricter adult supervision and a lot less religious brainwashing.

Michael had already instructed Freel (his own kickass "take no prisoners" high profile female attorney) to increase the settlement offer by $10 million if Erika would take the money and split—sans children. If she gave up custody of the children, he would bend over backwards to accommodate everything else she wanted, even permitting her to see the children from time to time under limited supervision. He was awaiting a response from her attorney prior to their upcoming court date.

Michael pulled into his cul de sac noticing the gaggle of news media in the area. He assumed they were in front of a home near his even as he wondered what was going on. As he drew closer, there was no doubt the reporters were camped out in front of his home.

"What the…" Michael let loose with a string of angry invectives as reporters ran to swarm his vehicle.

"Mr. Slaughter, is it true you tried to kill your wife?"

"Will you sue Jayson Denali for breaking up your marriage?"

"Are you still planning to go through with the divorce?"

"When did you discover your wife's affair with Denali?"

All at once the hungry media horde bombed him with questions.

Unable to get the remote control garage opener to work, Michael shouldered his way through the mob to his front door. "The crackhead bastards had probably jammed his garage door so he couldn't circumvent them," he thought. What the hell were they talking about anyway? He fumbled with his house keys before slamming the door in their faces.

"Jamarra! Where are you?" Frustrated, Michael's voice boomed throughout the house. But silence was the only echo returned. Several steps beyond the foyer, Michael paused. Something wasn't right. He may have been tone deaf at times but it became apparent even to him that an inescapable pall suffused the place. The furnishings were as he'd left them, yet the house seemed barren, as if no one lived there anymore. He dropped his luggage and moved further inside when he spotted the note Jamarra left.

"Mike, I need to get away. I'll be back in a week or so." The handwritten note was undated and signed J'Mar.

The initial frustration Michael hoped to relieve sexually now had no outlet and it quickly spiraled into anger. When did she leave? *Why* did she leave? Did Erika frighten her off? Did the reporters unnerve her? He reached for his cell phone and dialed hers. Michael walked toward the sound of muted ringing he heard in the distance. There, Jamarra's cell phone rested on its charger. She hadn't bothered taking it with her, so he had no way of knowing where she was. Or, who she was with. A torrent of jealousy swirled through his body at the thought of her sharing herself with anybody but him. Enraged, he picked up the phone and threw it against the wall, shattering it into pieces.

He wasted no time getting his attorney on the line.

"Freel? What the hell is going on? I've just arrived back from Dubai when I got mugged by a ton of media jackasses outside my home."

As Freel brought him up to speed and described what he was up against, Michael was stunned.

"I changed international cell phones, so no, you wouldn't have been able to reach me." Shocked to learn he was the prime suspect in the death of Attorney Dowder and the attempt on his wife's life, Michael took a seat on the nearby sofa. "I'm a person of interest? Why would they think me responsible? Of course, I'm innocent. Why should I *have* to give a statement?" No stranger to the law, Michael didn't recognize his own unreasonableness.

"Listen to me, Freel. People are plain jealous of Jamarra. How the hell should I know why? Maybe it's because of her looks or her body or her youth. I'm telling you, the girl is as harmless as a dove. I know her inside out. She wouldn't hurt a fly because that's just not the kind of person she is."

"What?" He jumped to his feet upon learning that police had produced a witness who swore he heard Michael Slaughter threaten to kill both his wife and her attorney. Said witness claimed to have shared a jail cell with Michael on the night he was released after Attorney Dowder had him imprisoned for a weekend.

"That's ridiculous! I wouldn't recognize this 'Fiddy P' character if he slapped me in the face. Of course it's a bunch of bull. Whoever Fiddy P is, he's lying, the lowlife dirtbag. I'll bet the bastard's trying to reduce a lifetime sentence so he's making this stuff up. Look Freel, it's no secret that I wasn't a fan of Dowder's, but I didn't kill her. Neither did I have anyone else knock her off for me. The woman had a ton of enemies. Hell, anybody could have done it. Of course I'm interested in how my wife is doing. What's her condition? The children are where? Freel, I'm their father, for God's sake. What do you mean I can't see them because of a restraining order? I'm no threat to them! I don't give a flying kite that the judge doesn't know that." Michael rubbed his neck in frustration.

He heaved a sigh. "I know you're on my side, Freel. But this is some major bull crap. And how the hell does Jayson Denali fit into the picture? I see. Evidently, they're lying about him too. What would a world class superstar of his stature want with a cold shrew like Erika? It's not as if they run in the same circles. It wouldn't surprise me if the man filed a defamation lawsuit."

Minutes later, a fuming Michael hung up the phone. Furiously outdone, he felt as though he could have been bought for free. Prohibited from seeing his children because his in-laws had filed another restraining order against him on Erika's behalf? Michael could only shake his head.

"Un-flipping-believable," he muttered. He was, however, addressing an empty home.

Chapter Thirty-Three

Having found what made her tick, Jamarra was in a zone. As she peered through the telescopic sight of her M40 sniper rifle, she was joyously having the time of her life. Though her target was some 1,320 feet (or two city blocks) away, she was unruffled. She was confident she would bag him because the one saint-like virtue in her possession was patience. She triple checked her adjustments for range, wind, and elevation so that the crosshairs of her scope would zero in on the target.

Because her intended victim was a moving object, she would lead him by pointing her aim in front of him. Her success or failure depended on her ability to accurately gauge the speed and angle of her target's movement. Estimating their behavior was critical to accurately nailing the shot. But Jamarra's confidence didn't rest so much in herself as it did her equipment. Bartlett had outfitted her with the best.

A fierce, unrepentant task master, Bartlett demanded and instilled a high element of proficiency in all things camouflage, concealment, stalking and observation related. He'd built her up by challenging her marksmanship under the severest of operational conditions.

Jamarra had quickly tired of blowing the head off squirrels and other vermin. Her training progressed rapidly and the better she got, the more she thirsted for greater competition. Jamarra wanted to kill something human. The highest compliment ever paid to her came the day Bartlett told her that she'd make an excellent soldier for hire and that with proper training, she could be an assassin after the true order. At this moment, Jamarra was putting his words to test amidst the dregs of society. She knew no one would miss the drug kingpins on her target practice list. As soon as she killed one, there were a dozen more waiting to fill their vacant shoes.

Her quarry moved into view, trotting along with his minions, unsuspecting that his life was about to be cut short. Jamarra tamped down the rush of excitement that coursed through her veins in anticipation of the perfect shot. When the moment finally arrived, she breathed deeply and then held her lungs empty while lining up her shot. Now! Pulling the trigger was the sweetest thing she'd ever felt.

Seconds after she got the shot off, the drug dealer crumpled to the ground like a dropped sack of potatoes. Blood from the gaping hole in his head, pooled around him.

"Gotcha, mother-dufus! Another one bites the dust," she whispered triumphantly. Lifting her forefinger to her mouth, she blew on it like she was blowing smoke out her nine. This was her only celebration as there was no time to stop to gloat or to admire her handy work. She quickly extracted the fired cartridge casing and chambered a new round. As pandemonium hell broke out around the felled gang leader, Jamarra packed up her equipment and walked away from the abandoned building as slowly as she'd entered. No one paid any attention to the deranged-looking homeless woman pushing her broken down shopping cart up the dirty streets of Anacostia.

Jayson knocked on the door to Syl's hospital room and entered without waiting for a response. Laughter greeted him. Aaryn and Syl sat atop the bed playing cards and whispering conspiratorially like two little kids.

"Uh oh. You two must be plotting something devious. This can't be good." He took a seat in a nearby chair and watched them.

"Us plotting? From what I've just heard, you're the one doing all the plotting."

"This *is* frightening. Do tell. What have you heard?" Jayson stared directly at Aaryn, who was intentionally studying her cards.

"I'm watching you, Sylvia Denali. I'm not about to let Jayson distract me just so you can take an extra card from the deck."

"Aaryn, I'm wounded. I would never do such a dastardly thing just to win at Gin Rummy."

"Sure, you wouldn't, Syl. I'm on to you."

"Ummm, Ladies? I'm waiting. One of you was about to tell me what it is you've heard?"

"Who needs to cheat when you're an expert such as myself?" Syl placed her winning hand face up on the bed.

"You bum! Jayse, did you see that? She cheated!"

"I did no such thing. I never figured you for a sore loser, Aaryn."

Aaryn threw up her hands in mock disgust.

Syl stood and stretched. "Jayson, dear heart, it's so good of you to join us. What do we owe to the pleasure of a visit from you?"

"Please. I've been sitting here twisting in the wind while you two ignored me."

"Come give an old woman a hug." Syl embraced him and then kissed him on the forehead for good measure. "Every now and again, you do something so thoughtful, Jayson, that it let's me know I've done a good job raising you."

"Now I'm really petrified. Aaryn, do you have any idea of what Syl is referring to?"

"I'm waiting to hear it myself."

"Oh how you two do go on. Jayson, it was most thoughtful of you to suggest to Aaryn that I come stay with her and Dot when I leave the hospital. However, you could have asked me first. And to insist that I come tonight? What if Aaryn and Dot considered it an inconvenience?"

At the blank look on Jayson's face, Aaryn spoke up. "Syl, we could never think of a visit from you as an inconvenience. Why, Dot's been raving about you ever since she visited you the other day. And with three children to care for unexpectedly, she'd truly be disappointed if you didn't come just to help out. When Jayson suggested it, both Dot and I leapt at the offer. If anyone is to be faulted, it's us for assuming you would accept. Please say you'll come stay with us. You're welcome to leave anytime you feel the pull of Wisconsin calling you."

Given that it was all news to him, Jayson saw no reason to reveal his ignorance on the subject by intervening. Especially since, according to Aaryn, it was his suggestion to begin with. Dot had come to the hospital to visit Syl? He'd loved to have been a fly on the wall during that conversation.

"Ma, since you'll be staying in Utah for the time being, do you think you can convince Aaryn that it's high time she got married?"

Aaryn threw him a "no, you didn't!" look of mortification.

"Well, as far as I can tell, any convincing will have to be done by you. I've already done my part. It is true, Aaryn, that I've never seen him as smitten with a woman as he is with you. At least not one who happens to be his own age."

Jayson rolled his eyes. "I knew it would only be seconds before you embarrassed me, Ma."

A knock on the door revealed that it was time for Syl's water therapy session, her last one prior to her release from the hospital.

Aaryn and Jayson left the room behind Syl and headed to Aaryn's office. As they strolled down the hall, they were impervious to the fact that all eyes were surreptitiously glued to them.

Inside, Jayson leaned against the closed door. "So Syl had a visitor while we were in Indiana and now she's coming tonight to temporarily live with you and Dot. And it was all my suggestion? Dr. Jamison, I didn't know you had it in you to tell such lies with a straight face."

Aaryn tossed several files onto her desk. "Jayson, I had to. If you could have seen her when I first entered her room, you'd know I didn't have any other choice. Her spirit was so despondent, it startled me. When I probed to get to the heart of the matter, she told me that she didn't know what she was going to do with herself now that she was well and wouldn't have anyone (namely you) to fuss over her anymore. Inviting her to stay with us seemed the perfect solution. You should have seen her face when I told her it was what you wanted. The fact that she and Dot hit it off so well the other day, practically assured her of her welcome. You don't mind, do you? You said yourself the place is too big for just Dot and I. Now that the children are there, Dot's going to need all the help she can get. Even without the children, we really would love to have her."

"No, I'm pleased. It's an excellent idea. I won't be worried about her now while I'm filming."

"There's one minor detail. Since I told her you were checking her out in time for her to have dinner with us at 8pm, you'll need to square her release with Kyle. She's preparing to pack her things right after her therapy session."

"Do you always invite your patients to move in with you after treatment?"

"Of course not. Syl's special."

"What about me? Aren't I special?"

Aaryn raised her thumb and forefinger together to indicate a wee tiny bit.

Jayson grinned at her. "I'll talk to Kyle. What did she and Dot talk about during their visit? Did she say?"

"I asked her but she wouldn't reveal a thing. She had the audacity to tell me to stay out of grown folk's business. The one thing she did share with me was that she's convinced you're sweet on me." She threw him a teasing yet challenging look. "Now what would make her think that?"

"I wonder myself." Jayson twisted the lock on her door before advancing on Aaryn.

Aaryn knew that look. She retreated with a smile on her face. "Jayson, stop."

"I haven't done anything to warrant you telling me to stop. Not yet." He leered at her.

Aaryn laughingly placed her hand over her mouth to keep herself from squealing. The staff was already agog at all the rumors about her and Jayson. If they heard weird noises coming from her office, there was no telling what they would think.

As she continued to back away from him, Jayson lunged and caught her by the waist. He swung her around and backed her up against her desk before his lips sought hers. Cupping her hips, he lifted her onto the desk and fit himself between her legs. His kiss deepened as his hands went about slowly exploring her body.

Once again, Aaryn found herself lost in the kingdom that was Jayson Denali. She was already weakened from his kiss but the moment his hands began touching her with light whispery strokes, she was wasted. Feathery touches here, there, everywhere, Aaryn was a ball of melted fusion. She heard him whispering in another language but her brain cells were too gooey to try to decipher it. She barely felt him unbuttoning her blouse, so lost was she. But the second one of his big hands cupped her breast, lightly palming the engorged nipple, his teeth nipped softly into her neck. Whatever selfcontrol Aaryn might have possessed up until that moment, evaporated like liquid under a hot blazing sun. She didn't remember him carrying her to her couch.

Jayson stretched alongside her, his leg sliding between hers. With her hands resting lightly on his chest, Aaryn closed her eyes to the intense look on his face. She saw gentleness there, possessiveness, ownership and love all in one glance. And then he was kissing her again. His mouth everywhere as his tongued trailed a wet blazing path along her throat down to the valley of her breasts.

A sweet whispered plea of pleasure escaped her the moment his mouth tenderly claimed her nipple. The already engorged knob expanded under his direct tutelage. Before Aaryn knew it, she was speaking in her own unidentifiable language.

When he finally lifted his head to stare down at her, Aaryn couldn't move. "Jayse, you promised," she whispered.

"What did I promise?" His voice was soft and low.

"That you'd be a gentleman and behave yourself."

"No. I never promised that." As his eyes feasted on her bountiful breasts, her hands moved to cover them. Jayson stopped her. "Marry me. Say it. Say you'll marry me."

"That's not fair, Bay. You're taking advantage of a disadvantaged woman. You know I can't think straight when you do these things to me. The second you kiss me, I'm like a ripe piece of lowhanging fruit."

"That belongs to me. Only to me." Jayson claimed her mouth again before disentangling himself and rising from the couch. Staring down at her, he began to slowly remove his tie.

"Jayse?" Aaryn sat up, not sure where this was going. And certainly not trusting the wicked grin on his face.

After the tie came his shoes, followed by his suit jacket. When he started unbuttoning his shirt, dunce that she was, Aaryn finally knew where this was headed. Her mouth dropped open.

"Jayson, stop," she whispered. "What are you doing?" Her tone marveled disbelievingly as the man standing before her began to sensuously disrobe.

His belt joined the clothing beginning to pile up next to her on the sofa. When he unbuttoned his pants, Aaryn gasped and covered her mouth. Jayson's pants fell to the floor at the same time did Aaryn's mouth.

A more beautiful and chiseled specimen had never graced the pages of any Chippendale magazine.

As her eyes feasted on every square inch of his body, Aaryn's breath caught in her throat. And when her eyes latched onto the thick maleness that protruded from his underwear, she clutched her heart in fear that she was having a panic attack. The second Jayson stripped his underwear away and palmed himself for her viewing pleasure, so heightened were Aaryn's senses and emotions, so intense was the pounding in her head, that when he took one step toward her, she fainted dead away.

When Aaryn came to, Jayson was wearing his pants with his shirt unbuttoned. He had taken water from her small fridge and poured it on the towel resting on her forehead. The look on his face was one of total concern.

"Are you okay? You scared the dickens out of me." He sat beside her stretched out form.

Aaryn touched the towel on her forehead before removing it. "I'm fine," she whispered. "I just had the most incredible dream."

"Tell me about it." Jayson leaned over her, checking the pillow under her head.

"I can't. It was too fantastical." Her hand raised to slide around his throat. "Something tells me it wasn't a dream though." She twisted her head to the side as a feeling of sad disappointment swept over her. "You must think me insane."

"No, babe. Don't say that. You were just overwhelmed, that's all. I shouldn't have come on so strong. It was all my fault."

She shook her head, still unable to look at him. "I'm not a prude, Jayson. I promise, I'm not."

"Awww honey, you don't have to tell me that. I know you're not. Look, from now on, I promise to be the perfect gentleman."

Aaryn smiled. "You're just saying that so I won't be embarrassed. I don't believe you. You aren't capable of being a gentleman." Her arms laced around his neck pulling him down to her. "Kiss me, Jayson."

He was only too happy to do so. "My, how he had grown to love this woman," he thought. She stirred within him a visceral hunger that was only replete with her in his life. This was happiness. This was joy. This was contentment. This was what it meant to feel fulfilled.

"I'm sorry, Bay. I didn't mean to pass out on you. It's just that I've never..." Aaryn felt his fingers cover her lips.

"No more apologies. When are you marrying me?" His hand drifted down to caress her stomach. "It has to be soon because you're going to be pregnant before you know it. I intend to make sure of it."

"Love me, Jayson. Tell me you love me, Bay."

Aaryn barely remembered getting through the rest of the day. Somehow, she must have pulled herself together because after her last appointment, she found herself back in her office staring out her window at the vast mountainous landscape.

She felt as though she had no control over anything within her midst. It was as if she was going through the motions, drifting on clouds. She searched inwardly for one small impulse to snap her out of the blind miasma she had fallen into.

Still dazed, she packed up her briefcase and made her way to the parking lot. To her, it felt like she was walking in slow motion. But to those she passed along the hall, she appeared intensely focused to the point that she didn't even acknowledge the few people who tried to stop her to engage her in conversation.

Aaryn traveled her normal route home. Still within a dazed-like sphere, she drove placidly along Main Street to the I-95 Expressway, doing what she thought was the speed limit. Before she knew it, her mind began to reflect on how manly and sensual Jayson was as he'd peeled away every layer of his clothing. She envisioned the golden pectorals of his chest, his biceps, his muscular thighs and calves. So real was her daydream, it was as if he were standing right in front of her. How beautifully masculine he was fashioned, perfect in every form. How big and thick and powerful his…

Suddenly, a loud scream tore through her trance-like daze!

Aaryn slammed on her brakes in the nick of time to avoid running down an elderly couple slowly crossing the street with the help of their wheeled walkers. Aaryn's hands were locked on the steering wheel as her breath caught in her throat. She literally had come a hair's breadth within blowing the stop sign and committing vehicular manslaughter.

A loud thumping on her drivers' side window caused her head to jerk in that direction.

"The hell is wrong with you, Lady? You almost killed them!"

Whatever fuzz had clouded Aaryn's mind was gone as she snapped back to reality. She wasn't the least bit concerned about the big burly man standing outside her door. Her concern was solely for the panic-stricken elderly couple frozen dead in their tracks in the middle of the street like helpless deer in headlights. She threw open her door forcing the irate man to jump out of the way lest he get pinged and walked hurriedly to the couple.

"My God, I am so sorry." Aaryn began to profusely apologize as she helped the two cross the street out of pure guilt. She noted the hearing aids in their ears and wondered if they even heard a word of what she was saying to them.

As she walked back to her car, which she'd left standing idle in the middle of the street, she figured she deserved the evil looks the passersby were throwing her way. As she approached her Jeep, the big burly man stepped forward to berate her further. Before he could open his mouth, Aaryn threw him an evil look of her own. "Put a sock in it, Mister."

At the violent look on her face, something told the guy to do just that.

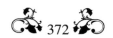

Chapter Thirty-Four

Just as Wendy predicted, there was fallout from the rumors surrounding Jayson's alleged love affair with Erika Slaughter as the news media wrongfully continued to blame him for the attack on her life. Tagged as an immoral home wrecker, Jayson was being publicly flogged for his selfish and reckless pursuit of a married woman. Why go after someone forbidden when there were so many unattached women available to him? Inquiring minds wanted to know. Since the only information coming out of Jayson's camp was "no comment," the lame stream media elected to piece together their own stories.

*Erika Slaughter was at death's door...Slaughter was beaten to a bloody pulp...Erika's eyes had been gauged out...She had nearly been decapitated...*Each news station seemed to offer a more grim and different version of his assumed lover's condition. Jayson realized the story was news *du jour* only because his name was associated with it. Remove him from the picture and the entire incident would have been as fresh as used tissue.

Though Jayson rarely ever watched TV, he followed websites such as The Financial Times, Huffington Post and MSNBC closely, so he knew that news of his "deadly love triangle" was the lead story on most television and cable news networks from East Coast to West Coast. Despite an ongoing war and starving children in Africa, the twisted Jayson Denali story was all anyone wanted to talk about. So it came as no surprise to him when the head Disney studio exec, John Benevides, tracked Jayson down with questions concerning the story since it continued to gain momentum at sensationalized speed.

"Denali, we've got to get a handle on this before *Mr. Incredible II* is released. Tomorrow, we want you to do a flurry of response television interviews denying the accusations. Plug the movie, while you're at it. Remind people that it's safe to take the family to see a Jayson Denali film. We've got *Good Morning America, The Today Show, Access Hollywood, Entertainment Tonight* and Jay Leno lined up. You can do them all in one day. No need to thank us. The PR chaps here at Disney were happy to set everything up."

"That's awfully generous of you to plan my life for me, JB. I'm sure I had no plans of my own. In fact, I was sitting here twiddling my thumbs just hoping you'd call." Jayson's sarcasm was not lost on JB, who laughed heartily.

"We're protecting our investment, Denali, and your contract stipulates you'll help us do that in any way you can. Don't tell me you'd forgotten this minor detail?"

Deliberately, he had. "Let's just get it done." Damn! Instead of leaving tomorrow night as planned, he would have to leave first thing tomorrow morning. Jayson sighed as he ended the call.

He was on the balcony of Aaryn and Dot's home when the call from Disney came through. Just earlier, he had carried all of Syl's bags up to her room so she could unpack and get settled in. Dot and Red (who Jayson teasingly referred to as her "beau" friend) were in the kitchen cooking, while the children were in the livingroom playing the Wii with Red's thirteen year old granddaughter, Sage. Jayson surfed the web as he worked on his laptop, but it was clear to him that he was marking time as he waited for Aaryn to arrive home.

He knew she had to stop at another hospital to make arrangements for her sister's transfer from Indiana. For obvious reasons, the two of them had agreed it would be better if Jayson did not accompany her. To do so would only give the already misleading story more legs than it currently had. With her and Dot the only approved visitors, Aaryn wanted to be certain a security detail was stationed at her sister's room at all times. The hospital was happily billing her for the extra security service.

When Jayson's phone vibrated he answered without looking at caller ID.

"Why haven't you called me back, Jayson? Didn't you get my urgent messages?" An irate Lisa Tennamen all but yelled into the phone.

Jayson regretted not screening the call. "You've got me now, so talk."

"Why haven't you returned my calls?" She couldn't keep her resentment and hostility from showing.

"What do you want, Lisa?" That she was someone he didn't want to hear from was unmistakable.

"What do 'we' want is a better question, Jayson. In case you haven't heard the news, I'm pregnant."

"Congratulations. To both you and the father. I'll have my staff send along a wedding gift."

"Not funny, Jayson. You *are* the father."

Jayson's heart plummeted in his chest. He'd been extra careful in his dealings with Lisa. Had he slipped up? As he wracked his brain to recall the last time they'd slept together, relief swept through him. He hadn't touched her the night of his movie premiere in Chicago. He'd had her things moved to another suite. Reassured, he said calmly, "I doubt that very seriously. It's been a good six or seven months since you and I did the do. I thought you'd gotten back together with your ex-husband."

"It's good to see you've kept up with my life, Jayson, but I'm hurt. Hurt that you would think me capable of stooping so low as to deliberately get pregnant by you. I know you think you're Jayson the Great, God's gift to womankind, but you're not that great. Your memory is faulty. We made love the night *before* the Chicago premier. On your plane, remember?"

What he and Lisa had done to one another could never be categorized as making love. "Lisa, you were drunk that night. I never touched you because you passed out. Thankfully, I spent the night going through scripts my agent sent me. What is it with you? How many times in the past have you told me you were pregnant with my child? Three, Lisa. In my book that's enough to make it a longstanding joke. The first time I believed you. I was even happy to hear it. But when I found out you were lying, well, let's just say you had your chance. If you really are having a baby, good luck. I mean it. The kid's going to need it. Since I've got you on the line, you might as well be the first to hear it: I'm getting married."

Jayson continued despite hearing her loud gasp. "You might want to spring a trap for someone else since timing precludes me from being the father of your child. Don't forget though, whoever you pick will want a DNA test."

"Well I'll be damned! So all those nasty rumors *are* true. I didn't want to believe it, but I should have known better. What a heartless bastard you are, Jayson. I hope you rot in hell for what you've put that poor woman through. *You're* getting married? Yeah, right! Tell me, how're you going to marry a corpse, Jayson? It would be better for her to die than to tie herself to a coldblooded jerk like you."

"I'm a jerk, yet you're willing to have a baby by me? What does that say about you? Face it, Lisa. You're like a revolving door. You couldn't keep your legs closed long enough to know *who* the father of your kid is. Good luck with rounding up the herd of Toms, Dicks and Harrys you've slept with over the past weeks and months."

"Oh, *hell* to the naw! No you didn't, you slimy black bastard! Like you can talk! You, the biggest male slut this side of the planet. I wouldn't have a child by you if you paid me all the money in the world." In her jealous rage, Lisa spat venom over the phone.

"God, you're ghetto." Disgusted, Jayson berated himself. What did it say about *him* given that he'd tolerated the Lisa Tennemans of the world?

Realizing the wheels had come off her train, Lisa quickly backtracked as if they hadn't just traded ugly barbs and accusations. "Jayson, you know I'm in love with you. How could you marry someone else? I thought what we had was special."

"What are you talking about, Lisa? All we had was sex. Love had nothing to do with it. We used each other to satisfy a purely physical urge. Look, we both know you aren't pregnant by me, but if you're going to claim you are, let's save time.

Have your lawyers get in touch with mine. Bottom line is I don't want to hear from you again."

"Don't you dare hang up this phone, Jayson Denali. I'm warning you. Nobody tosses me aside like a used tampon. Not even you, you asshole. You want ghetto? Just try denying you're the father of my child and see what happens. I'll sell stories to every gossip magazine in Hollywood. I'll bleed you good, Jayson. One way or another, I. will. make. you. pay!"

Jayson shook his head, immune to her threats. "Lisa, it should be a crime for someone to be as stupid as you are."

Something in Jayson's sharp rebuke, stunned Lisa into momentary silence. Did he just call her stupid? Outraged, Lisa launched into a profanity filled tirade.

Jayson had heard enough. He hung up on her and turned off his phone. Tomorrow, he would turn the page completely and get a new cell phone number. Still, the quirky call with Lisa left him with a poor disposition.

He heard the dogs barking as a car pulled into the driveway. Jayson walked to the end of the balcony and watched Aaryn get out of her Jeep. As much as he was looking forward to building a future with her, he was beginning to realize how difficult it was for him to divest himself of the tentacles from his colorful past. Utah had been like a haven of sorts for him, a respite from the normal craziness that was his life. But it was becoming increasingly harder to keep the two worlds from blurring. Jayson thought about his attention-starved posse and everyone else he'd kept at bay who were just waiting to pick up where they'd left off the moment he returned to their circle. He couldn't shield Aaryn forever. The fact remained that he would bring many of his past associations with him into any new relationship. Whatever else he was, perfect he was not.

Jayson paused in the doorway of the den to watch the children eagerly embrace Aaryn, who was on her knees. They were openly affectionate children who were clearly used to having their affections returned. Even the dogs seemed to want in on the hug fest.

Aaryn glanced up to find Jayson watching her. A strange look passed between them. When the children returned to their game, he made no move to approach her as she stood and walked toward him. It was more than just a look as both seemed to sense that something was in the space between them.

"Hello," her voice was not cold but neither was it inviting.

"To you," Jayson nodded. Warily, he wanted her to tell him what she was thinking without him having to pry it out of her. At the moment, he didn't feel like mining for emotional gold. Neither could he barter in an emotional currency that he did not possess.

The doorway was wide enough for her to pass through it without him having to step aside. She did so without looking him in the eye. "Excuse me," was all she said as she walked past him.

Jayson didn't follow her. As he continued to watch the children play, his face remained impassive.

In her room, Aaryn sat on the edge of her bed with her face in her hands. If ever there was a time when she needed guidance and direction, it was now. When Jayson knocked on her door twenty minutes later, she still hadn't moved.

"Rough day?" he asked as he leaned against the door. He'd thought long and hard before coming to find her. He was here only because he wanted to know where they stood with each other before he left Utah. Jayson was prepared to turn a new leaf with or without her.

Aaryn got up and came to stand in front of him. "I nearly killed an elderly couple today, Jayson. I came this close to running them down in the middle of the street." Anger laced her voice.

"Are you're blaming me?" At the moment, Jayson had his own anger issues.

"I can't do this, Jayson. I can't be this distracted. I want my old life back. The life I had before you invaded it and turned everything inside out."

Jayson shook his head. He wasn't willing to fight for a relationship that meant traveling solo down a oneway tunnel. He already knew firsthand how that disastrous journey ended. He bore the mental track marks as a reminder.

"Then don't let me stop you, Aaryn. Go back to your old way of being. Go back to being lonely, miserable and untrusting. That's a lot to look forward to, isn't it?" He would know, because he was referring more to himself than he was her. "Why do you keep thinking you're the only one who's making changes? You think this is easy for me?"

"Don't you see, Jayson? We're not even married and we argue and fuss like cats and dogs. That should be a hint to both of us. If we can't agree on the simplest of things, this can't possibly work."

"That's what people who love each other do, Aaryn. They fuss. They fight. They disagree. But in the end, they work it out. Who told you relationships were a walk in the park? We're totally different people, Aaryn. We're never going to agree on everything. We're both opinionated, we're set in our ways and we both have issues. So that means we take the good with the bad. I can't promise you that we'll know how every day will turn out, nor can I promise you that we'll never have trouble in our paradise."

A tomb of sadness suddenly enveloped her. "It's a fool's paradise, Jayson. That's what it is." Aaryn closed her eyes to try to stop the tears that desperately wanted to flow. "And I'm scared that I'll be the one who winds up being the fool."

Jayson clamped his teeth together. As much as he wanted to take her in his arms and reassure her, he refused. This had to be a decision she made on her own. Either she was in this thing or they were out.

Aaryn turned away from him as tears began to course down her face. She couldn't remember the last time her heart felt so heavy. She walked outside onto the balcony of her bedroom to stare at the mountains in the great distance. How could one person cause her to be so conflicted?

Jayson felt as though the chasm between them was as wide as the world. His heart was heavy, too. *Rocket Love,* he thought. He found himself thinking of a song Stevie sang years ago. *You took me riding in a rocket and gave me a star. About a half a mile from heaven, you dropped me back down to this cold, cold world.* Jayson had come so far, only to be turned away. He opened her door, prepared to walk through it when he heard her softly call his name.

Jayson's eyes closed to the pain he heard in her tentative whisper. They closed to the pain that was shattering his own heart into pieces.

"Wait, Jayson. Please don't go." Aaryn stood in the middle of the room, willing him to meet her halfway.

He quietly closed the door and came to her, but still he didn't touch her. He didn't trust his own emotions.

"However, I may want to, I can't go back to the way I was, Jayse. That person no longer is. Yes, I was able to map my day out from beginning to end knowing how most of it would turn out. But then I met you and everything changed. I don't want to be lonely again. You once told me that when you're with me, your loneliness disappears. The same thing happens for me when I'm with you, Jayse. I'm fulfilled when I'm with you. But the trusting part is going to take some time. I'm asking you to give me that. I don't know what it's like to be in love. I don't know what it's like to wear my heart on my sleeve. I just know it leaves me feeling vulnerable. My life isn't the flat line that it was before you stepped into it, and that petrifies me. Maybe love is what it means to lock your destiny in with someone else's. Maybe it's looking to the day unfolding because I know you're in it. Maybe love is me wanting you never to forget me."

She reached up and touched the side of his face. His beauty was so flagrant, so seductive that Aaryn realized in that moment, that that's what it was about him that made it hard for her to just let go and trust him. If he were a homely man, she could believe him more readily. That someone as beautiful as him could want her, of all the women in the world available to him, it was, in all honesty, overwhelming. What made her different from any of the legion of women who had come before her?

"You just are, Aaryn," Jayson said to her. "It has to be you." He didn't even question how he knew her thoughts. But the moment she touched his face, he felt her doubts about him and her doubts about herself. She'd touched him in a way that enabled him to glimpse just for a moment what it was that held her back.

"My looks don't change what I feel in my heart for you, Aaryn. I can't automatically make you trust me. All I can do is ask that you give me the chance to prove myself."

Aaryn stepped closer to him and wrapped her arms around his waist. She pressed her cheek into his chest where she could hear his heart beat.

When Jayson finally wrapped her in his arms, it felt like he was welcoming her home. And later that evening, when everyone was seated at the dinner table amidst all the food and laughter, Jayson posed the question to Aaryn, once more asking her to marry him.

In front of seven smiling, eager witnesses, Aaryn finally said, "Yes, Jayson. It would be my honor and privilege to be your wife."

It was after midnight when Jamarra returned to the place she shared with Michael. After four weeks away, somehow she no longer thought of it as home. Funny how she hadn't thought of Michael even once while she was gone. Consequently, it never occurred to her to speculate about what he would think of her absence. Her focus had been on surviving the next physically demanding litmus test Bartlett had thrown at her. If anything, Michael felt like a forgotten fixture from her past.

Just beyond the foyer, Jamarra flipped on the lights and paused as she lowered her army-colored duffle bag to the floor. The place was a mess. Beer bottles, pizza boxes and half empty takeout cartons littered the floor and livingroom tables. It looked as if homeless people had invaded it in her absence.

Jamarra looked beyond the filth and abject disarray to listen for any telltale warning signs of danger. Bartlett had taught her to trust her instincts and to always be observant of her surroundings. There was silence underneath the atmosphere. The house was completely quiet. Since nothing alarmed her, she advanced through it to the dining room and into the kitchen where dishes were piled high in the sink. Fruit flies circled lazily over rotting fruit left on the counter. She wondered if Michael had let the place become such a wreck thinking she would clean it upon her return. She hoped not, because disappointment awaited him if that was the case.

Jamarra opened the refrigerator and peered inside. No surprises there. He'd always waited for her to do the shopping, a much hated task she'd undertaken only

because he expected it of her. Wilted vegetables, rancid fruit and spoiled milk graced the fridge's shelves along with a bowl of molded egg salad that looked more like a science project. But stashed away at the bottom of the veggie bin was her quart of Fruitopia, a smoothie drink which she'd hidden from Michael because he liked it as much as she did. She tore off the top and drank straight from the carton. With the drink poised at her lips, Jamarra paused at hearing footsteps on the stairs.

When Michael came into view, it wasn't fear that caused her to take another gulp, but shock over his shameful state of dishabille. In all the time Jamarra had known him, his overall appearance was the main thing he took pride in. He was more painstaking about his looks than anyone she'd ever met. Clothes, shoes, and all the latest accessories, those were things Michael cared about. Left up to her, she would dress in a teeshirt and jeans 24/7. Only now, he looked as if he hadn't shaved in weeks. As he slowly walked towards her, he also smelled like he hadn't bathed in weeks. Her nose wrinkled in distaste.

He was wearing a long dirty robe loosely belted at the waist. She didn't think he wore anything underneath it. There was, however, something menacing about the expression on his face. Unshaved, unbathed with bloodshot eyes, he looked a little unhinged. Yet, Jamarra felt no fear.

"That's my drink you're drinking." His voice was raspy, as if he was in need of water. When she stared at him blankly, he said, "That's my refrigerator you're lookin' in. This is *my* goddamned house. You? You *used* to live here."

Was he drunk? Jamarra stared at Michael like he was some kind of rare bug she was seeing for the first time in her life. The look on her face was one of puzzlement.

In the wake of her silence, Michael said, "I wanna know where the hell you've been." There was no mistaking the threat in his voice.

With the Frutopia carton still raised to her lips, Jamarra cocked her head to the side as if she were studying him.

"I asked you a question, Dummy. Where the hell have you been?"

When she failed to answer, Michael stepped to her and slapped the drink out of her hand. With his other, he pimpslapped her across the face. So hard did he hit her with the back of his hand that Jamarra stumbled against the refrigerator door, nearly losing her balance when the door flew open wide.

She tasted blood. In slow motion, Jamarra lifted her hand to her mouth and looked at the blood on her fingertips. Curiously, she stared at Michael. She had no interest in fighting him. Her reluctance was partly because she held him in such high regard and also because his mean spiritedness had never been directed towards her. Up until now, he'd been good to her at all times.

Jamarra wiped her fingers on her army jacket. Her eyes were riveted to his. She made no move to run from him or to answer his question.

The way she stared at him inflamed Michael's rage. In the absence of any fear, what he saw was insolence. Roughly, he grabbed Jamarra by the sides of her jacket collar and lifted her off the floor. "You're gonna to tell me where you've been if I have to beat it out of you!" Spittle sprayed onto her face. "You thought I was gonna let you play me like some chump on the street, didn't you? Didn't you?" Michael shook her furiously with every word.

"You have no clue what I've been through since you've been gone. Did you know I lost my goddamn job? All because that stupid Attorney Dowder went and got herself killed. Good riddance if you ask me. But the asshole police think I had something to do it with. And then somebody tried to kill Erika. Whoever did it couldn't even get it right, the inept bastards."

Outraged women's groups, having already convicted Michael, had picketed Haliburton in protest of their harboring a corporate "wife-beating killer." Ensuing press coverage for Haliburton was not good. To avoid being the nightly media laughingstock, the company gave Michael a rich severance package.

"Where were you when all the madness broke loose, huh? Screwing somebody else, that's where you were. After all I've done for you, you go and give the goods to some other negro." Michael eyes traveled the length of her body. He hardened at the thought of violently taking what he wanted. He pressed himself against her and tried to kiss her, but Jamarra turned her head.

Roughly, Michael reached to undo her army fatigues, his motions frenzied. Not able to unfasten them, he tried yanking them open, but this allowed Jamarra to tug herself free of him and to skitter just beyond his reach. She just stood staring at him with that damned blank expression of hers that sometimes made him think she was mute and dumb. Yet, he saw something challenging in the look she threw him. To him, she mocked him, which only enraged him further.

A broom rested against the wall behind the refrigerator door. Michael grabbed it and broke it in half. He was going to teach Jamarra the lesson of her life. When he was finished with her, she'd think long and hard before two-timing him again. He told her so while moving in her direction. His robe came open to reveal naked flesh which he made no attempt to cover.

"I could kill you and no one would ever know it." He threatened her. "You're lucky I'm just gonna beat the crap outta you. Come here!" Michael lunged at her with the stick raised mid air.

Fast as lightening, Jamarra jetted away and jumped behind the sofa. The stick hit the wall where she'd been standing with such a loud impact that it broke in two.

Realizing she was much too quick for him to catch her, Michael picked up a marble obelisk statue and hoisted it through the air. She ducked just in time. The statue shattered and left a hole in the wall.

Jamarra knew that had the stone hit her in the head as Michael had intended, it would have killed her. Having proven his threats were real, Jamarra let her natural instincts take over. She lured him in. Slowly, she climbed over the couch and meekly shuffled toward him, her left hand reaching out to him plaintively.

Thinking he had frightened her into submission, Michael lunged the remaining distance to grab her.

Jamarra was ready. The moment he was within range, he crashed right into her fist which lodged against his Adam's apple with brutal force. Michael grabbed his throat in horrendous pain. Jamarra heightened that pain even more when she reared back and kicked him in the nuts with her hard-as-steel Corcoran desert combat boot. Michael dropped to the floor as if he had just been tasered.

As he writhed on the floor in unbearable pain, he reminded Jamarra of the cockroaches and waterbugs she used to torture as a kid. She would trap them with her bare hands before lighting a match to burn off each of their legs and then their antennas and heads. She would burn the creatures until she could no longer stand the stench of their smoldering limbs. She now thought of Michael as one of those bugs. She left him whimpering on the hardwood floor to retrieve a little gift from her SUV.

When Jamarra returned, Michael had crawled into a ball. He took one look at the crowbar in her now gloved hands and a yelp escaped him. She hadn't even yet touched him. But touch him she would.

Jamarra stooped down and tapped the tip of the crowbar on Michael's forehead. He flinched.

"Do you know why you're a lucky man, Michael Slaughter?" Jamarra didn't really expect an answer, so she continued. "Because unlike Attorney Dowder, you're going to live. I killed her, Michael. I sliced her up from head to toe. You should have been there, you would have been proud of me. Know why I'm telling you? Because if you tell the police, I'll just say you threatened to kill me if I didn't do it. I'll tell them you gave me step-by-step instructions on how you wanted me to carry out the deed. By the time I'm finished, I'll convince them that I'm all but innocent. Don't think I'm so dumb now do you, Michael?" The fact that he could run circles around her intellectually just didn't seem to matter at the moment.

"But you? Well, like I said before, you're a lucky man. When this is over, you will still have life in your body. But I have one question for you, Michael. Just one question. And if you lie to me, I promise on your own grave, you will never walk again. Understand? Nod your head, Michael. Let me know that you feel me." Jamarra tapped the crowbar none too lightly against his left knee.

When he nodded, she said, "Good. That was easy, wasn't it? Here's the $1.5 million dollar question." Jamarra spoke slowly. "What's the combination to the safe

upstairs?" When he stared at her like he was the deaf mute, she said, "I'm only going to ask once, Michael."

Through the haze of his pain, Michael was trying to keep up with her string of conversation. He heard her, but he was having trouble focusing beyond the white-hot ache in his loins. Combination? What the hell was she talking about? She might as well have asked him to name every planet in the galaxy. He literally could not think straight.

In the safe upstairs lay the key to Jamarra's future. All $1.5 mil. She knew Michael had it stashed there because he'd shown it to her and had told her it was bribe money he'd received from oil men during his trips to the United Arab Emirates. He'd told her he had many more millions hidden elsewhere in offshore accounts. She didn't doubt him.

It was a good thing that Michael closed his eyes in lieu of answering her. He didn't see the crowbar as it raised and lowered with quick silver speed to crash into his kneecap. Michael screamed.

The crunching sound of bone was music to Jamarra's ears. She took a seat on the floor Indian style just to watch him twist in agony. Gone was the brightness in his eyes and the sneering, swaggering smile. His face was now etched with the uncontrollable rigors of pain.

"How much is your leg worth to you, Michael? Do you care if you never walk again? How about if you never write with your left hand again, Michael? It should be easy for you to learn to write with your right hand, shouldn't it? Yeah, you'll figure it out. You're a smart man. At least that's what you told me every day as I recall. Let's see how many fingers I have to crush before you give up that combination. Man up now, Michael. Here goes."

"42-10-38-60." Michael frantically whispered the numbers through his cloud of pain.

Jamarra stood to her feet. "If you're lying to me, Michael Slaughter, you'll regret it." For good measure, she hefted the crowbar and broke his elbow before heading upstairs.

When Jamarra came back, she was whistling. The money was packed neatly in one of Michael's suitcases. She stood over him and peered down. He'd not only peed on himself, but he had lost control of his bowels. Not wanting to soil herself with his bodily fluids, she went and retrieved one of the knocked over chairs from the dining room. Jamarra sat in front of him with the halfempty carton of Fruitopia in one hand and the crowbar in her other.

"I was going to go back and kill your wife for you, Michael. But now I think I'll pass on it. Did you know your daughter can talk to spirits?"

In his state of tortured pain, Michael had nearly bitten through his tongue. Spirits? Clearly, Jamarra was deranged. A pure, stark-raving sadistic lunatic, is what she was. How she'd managed to hide this fact from him, he would never know.

"Your little girl, Mia? She talks to spirits. Yeah, it's true. I witnessed it for myself." She described for Michael what had happened the night she broke into Erika's home.

Jamarra didn't care about the pain Michael was in. Neither did she notice that he had stopped listening to her a long time ago. Instead, he was crying, caught up in his own misery.

"You know, I didn't understand it at first, until I searched the web and found people who claimed to have had similar experiences. Only, they called it 'supernatural phenomena' so I realized that's what it was. Your daughter saved your wife's life by commanding the spirits to do her bidding. Talk about power! What is she? Five? Six? Already she can do stuff like that? Now that's the kinda power I'm talkin' about! Imagine what's she's gonna be like when she gets older. You know, Mike, I think I'll keep an eye on her as she grows up. Purely out of curiosity, you know what I mean?"

As if she'd been talking to herself, Jamarra looked down at Michael as though she'd forgotten he was lying there. "How could you just dump your family like that? The wife, I can see. But the kids? What did they do to you? You know, now that I've had time to think about it, you don't deserve to walk again, Michael."

Jamarra stood up as a thought crossed her mind. "In case you're thinking of sending someone to look for me once I'm gone, let me give you a little reminder of why that's a bad idea." She removed her hunting blade from one of the pockets of her army pant leg and kneeled beside his head. Michael sobbed loudly as she touched the blade to his eye. And just as the knife tip began carving into his eyebrow, Michael passed out.

Jamarra sat back on her haunches to admire her handy work. She stared transfixed as small rivulets of blood trailed down Michael's cheek. She hadn't cut his eye out as he'd probably thought she would. "Just a little forget me not," she said aloud as she viewed the tattoo over his eye. She stood up to leave. Other than the money, there wasn't a single thing she wanted from the house. No clothes, no nick knacks, no keepsake reminders. Just the cash.

Jamarra looked around one final time. Suddenly, she remembered the naked pictures Michael had taken of her. She hadn't wanted to take those pictures, but he had insisted until she finally gave in. She went to retrieve them. As payback, before she left, she made sure many more of Michael's bones were broken.

"If the man ever walks again," Jamarra thought, "now that would be a miracle."

Epilogue
Two½ Years Later

In the aftermath of the awards ceremony, even before the cameras stopped rolling, everybody wanted a piece of Academy Award-winning Jayson Denali. Networks vied to interview the storied actor before he left the Kodak Theatre. Actors and actresses discretely loitered to have a word with Hollywood's most bankable star in order to whisper their congratulations. Others merely wanted to be photographed with the epochal superstar in hopes that a glimmer of his star power would shed itself on them.

The latest buzz from Hollywood's highest echelons hinted that Jayson was on the verge of forming his own production company. Having sold a billion dollars in ticket sales from his Academy Award-winning film, *Hyperion Fields*, many felt the timing was right.

Since he had married Aaryn, Jayson's life had changed remarkably. Marriage had settled him and cured him of his wanderlust. Even his films had taken a more dramatic turn as evidenced by the film, *Hyperion Fields*, which was set in wartorn Iraq.

As he was being photographed with several other Oscar winners, Jayson peered over the crowd, his gaze in search of his wife. He spotted Aaryn laughing with friends, Ashela Jordan and Sam Ross. Ashela had written the score for his Academy Award-winning film and he expected to work with her on many future projects. Jayson was a man content in all things.

Aaryn caught her hubby's eye across the crowed room. She knew he was in his element. It was, after all, the night when stars shined. Earlier, in their hotel room, Jayson had massaged her stomach with coconut oil and asked with concern in his voice, "Are you sure you're up to this?"

"And miss your big night? I wouldn't dream of it!" Especially after having spent hours being "made up" by one of Hollywood's best makeup artists, Aaryn had actually wanted to attend the allstar flagship event. Despite being three-months pregnant, she'd clamped down her sickness because she wouldn't have missed the occasion for all the world. She still wasn't fond of the Hollywood-style parties Jayson was often required to attend. Those that were important to him, she made time for. However, with work and a pair of one-year old twin boys at home, and another set of twin girls on the way, Aaryn was content to forgo the whole Hollywood scene. Surprisingly, so was Jayson. But on those occasions when she couldn't attend with him, Dez or other members of Jayson's posse, were always on standby.

Aaryn remembered how Jayson had once jokingly told her that he would keep her barefoot and pregnant. At least at the time, Aaryn had thought of it as a joke. But now, with numbers three and four on the way, it no longer seemed something to laugh about. Despite Jayson's wish for ten children, Aaryn was capping the count at four. Still, she too, was content in all things. Jayson was for her the best gift she had ever been given.

Dot and Syl watched the Oscars from the comfort of their home in Utah. Although the boys, Jade and Aaron, had fallen asleep by the time Jayson won for Best Actor in a Leading Role, Sylvia screamed when her son's name was announced. Meanwhile, Dot pretended to be surprised. She'd known all along Jayson would win the award, having dreamt it many months beforehand. With Syl now a permanent fixture in the home, and with a growing number of children to help care for, Dot's days were never boring. She, too, was a very happy woman.

Sitting on a sofa not too far from Dot and Sylvia, Erika and her three children were snuggled together. Two years had passed since Erika had awoken from her coma. It had taken her all that time to come back to herself. Her road to recovery had been slow. Doctors said she'd had a nervous breakdown which had caused her mind to regress. Now that she was near full recovery, it was ironic that Erika found the thought of leaving Utah, let alone Dot's house, terrifying. And yet, just the other day, she had surprised herself with the words she had spoken to Dot while they were gardening.

"I believed that if I married a good man, one who would keep a roof over my head and our children's heads, that if I was an obedient wife, I believed that everything would be alright. I never thought that one day, I'd find myself alone and starting over. Now, all I know is that when I look into the abyss of the future, despite being scared as hell, I feel I'm going to make it. Who knows? Maybe starting over is right where God wants me to be."

While everyone was basking in the joy of Uncle Jayson's Oscar award, eight-year old Mia got up from the couch to slip upstairs to the balcony of her bedroom. The Great Danes were right at her side. In fact, they followed her everywhere. And since Hully was now relegated to the bottom of her toy chest, Mia had come to view the dogs as her protectors. Mia peered out into the night. She couldn't see them, but she knew they were there. The spirits were all around her. They were always with her. Leading her, guiding her, protecting her. But, just as Aaryn had taught her, Mia never spoke of them to anyone outside the family.

On this night, the spirits whispered to her that danger lurked. Mia turned her face to the night sky. She lifted her arms wide and began to talk to her God. Soon,

386

she could feel her spirit floating in air like those of the angel spirits. As she floated, Mia was aware of a host of angels that traveled with her. Mia traveled until she found her spirit hovering over a building that was a great distance from her home. She no longer knew what city she was in, but she recognized the abandoned building from her dreams the night before. Fearlessly, Mia's spirit drifted up the broken stairs, past broken glass and drug paraphernalia, to the door that haunted her dreams.

She passed through it and spotted her classmate, the young girl who had been kidnapped two days ago. When Mia saw the kidnapper approach the young girl, it was his intentions that frightened Mia more than anything.

Suddenly, Mia's body jerked as she came back to herself on her balcony in Utah.

Mia had barely turned to run, when Dot seemed to appear out of nowhere to grab hold of her.

After Dot listened to Mia's story, she went downstairs to pick up the phone and call Patrick Gatlin, the FBI agent whom she had come to know so well.

While life was all good in the hood for everybody else, Michael Slaughter remained a man in peril. Up until about six months ago, Michael had looked like a cartoon character—given that he had been in a white cement body cast from neck to toe. While encased in the body cast, his left leg and right arm were raised midair by some contraption the hospital had created. But the constant itching had been the worst. Unable to relieve the uncomfortable sensation, many times Michael had wished for oblivion.

Now that the casts had finally been removed, he still had compound fractures requiring multiple surgeries to realign many of his bones in order for them to heal. Even with metal plates and screws, several of the bones had aligned improperly and the doctors were whispering that he may have deformity in some, while others, because of the way they'd been broken, might never fully heal. Already, doctors were promising more surgeries at a later date to re-break his bones just so they could reset them.

Michael had returned to Nashville to his own family. They were all the company he had these days. Despite Jamarra's warning to him not to search for her, Michael thirsted for revenge.

Because of all the pain he'd endured, he desperately wanted her dead. He already had a man on retainer whom he had guaranteed one million dollars if the man brought him Jamarra's head in a box. Michael couldn't understand why no one could find one slip of a girl. Even one who had managed to do him such bodily harm. Michael Slaughter was prepared to pay any amount to have the job properly completed.

❖

Unaware that there was literally a price on her head and that men were being paid to track her whereabouts, Jamarra Sanders was on an assignment of her own. Two years ago, Bartlett had sent her overseas to begin what he called "pure survivalist" training. Since then, she'd been all over Europe and the Middle East under many assumed identities. She may not have been able to join the US Special Ops because she was a woman, but Bartlett was sending her around the world to ensure that she learned from the best teams how to gather intelligence, destroy targets and get in and out of places quickly without being seen.

But Jamarra also knew that Bartlett had an ulterior motive. Something within had caused him to grow fond of her, as any teacher would a star pupil. But when his son, Keith, (Jamarra finally learned his name) discovered that she was under Bartlett's tutelage, he threatened to throw a monkey wrench in their entire plan. Keith swore he was in love with Jamarra and wanted to spend the rest of his life with her. Jamarra had stared at him as if he was speaking in a foreign language. Love? "Are you kidding me," she'd thought.

Jamarra remembered once reading a book for an English Literature class. Some old fart had said that religion was the opiate of the people. "Whoever the geezer was, he had it wrong," she thought. *Love* was the opiate of the people. To Jamarra, love was something people made up to pass the time to get themselves through life. Love was for chumps.

Keith couldn't seem to understand that just because the sex between them was good (it was certainly the best Jamarra had ever had), it didn't mean anything else. At least not to her. But her telling him this, didn't stop him from wanting to follow her everywhere. Bartlett had stepped in by sending Jamarra far away from South Dakota to places unknown to Keith.

Keith, and the Black Hills of South Dakota, seemed many lifetimes ago as Jamarra strolled through the Gendarmenmarkt in Berlin, Germany and into the German Cathedral. She was staring at her tourist map, looking every inch the part of a college student taking in the city's cerebral contemporary arts and diverse architecture. She could have been a young artist, herself, attracted by the city's liberal lifestyle.

Jamarra glanced up as her target walked by. So engrossed was he with the man at his side, that it never occurred to him that he was being trailed. The target, an older man, was obviously in love with the much younger man. It would be the death of him, which only further proved Jamarra's point. Love was for chumps.

Less than an hour later, Jamarra was safely aboard the U-Bahn railway heading far from central Berlin. The garrote she'd used to strangle the target, long since discarded. The next stop for Jamarra? Afghanistan, where she was joining Bartlett and the small team he had assembled.

Supermodel Lisa Tenneman was serving time at the Alderson Federal Corrections Facility in West Virginia. Better known as "Camp Cupcake," the minimum-risk facility for women looked more like a college campus than it did a prison. Known for her legendary temper tantrums, Lisa had gone a bit too far after clocking several members of the paperazzi with the fat end of a wine bottle. The first man was knocked out cold with a broken neck when Lisa laid into the second one. Unfortunately, for the supermodel, the bottle broke when she conked the second man upside the head, fracturing his skull, and nearly sending him to his death. Doubly unfortunate for Lisa, was the fact that it was all caught on tape. When the jury viewed the supermodel savagely beating the two men and slamming their cameras to the ground over and over, to them, Lisa looked like a madwoman on steroids—a definite threat to society. Because of previous public fisticuffs, the jury showed her no sympathy. She was sentenced to five years in prison where, for her, anger-management classes were mandatory. With good behavior, however, Lisa was due to be released after serving only two and a half. She remains childless.

❖

The dreamer stood before the entrance that preceded the crossway leading to the other side. She'd traveled a long way to find this place, the city of Perfect Peace. Having grown weary of wandering the earth realm, Carmin knew she was finally at the point where her spirit could claim its resting place. In spirit form, Carmin had hovered over Jayson and Sylvia, reluctant to leave them even though she could no longer be a part of their physical lives. But the little girl, Mia, had talked to her to let her know that everything was going to be okay.

Convinced that this once-weary traveler could now finally find her way home, Carmin's spirit no longer wanted to cling to the earth realm.

Carmin, the dreamer in spirit form, looked back one last time to see Jayson laughing and loving his wife, Aaryn and their children. With one last look, Carmin's spirit crossed into that other dimension. The place where righteous spirits go to be healed and made whole.

The End